STEPHEN JONES is the winner of two World Fantasy Awards and two Horror Writers of America Bram Stoker Awards, as well as being a nine-time recipient of the British Fantasy Award and a Hugo Award nominee. A full-time columnist, television producer/director and genre film publicist and consultant (the first three *Hellraiser* movies, *Night Life*, *Nightbreed*, *Split Second* etc.), he is the co-editor of *Horror: 100 Best Books*, *The Best Horror from Fantasy Tales*, *Gaslight & Ghosts*, *Now We Are Sick*, *The Giant Book of Best New Horror*, *H.P. Lovecraft's Book of Horror*, *The Anthology of Fantasy & the Supernatural*, and the *Best New Horror*, *Dark Voices* and *Fantasy Tales* series. He has also compiled *The Mammoth Book of Terror*, *The Mammoth Book of Vampires*, *The Mammoth Book of Zombies*, *The Mammoth Book of Werewolves*, *The Mammoth Book of Frankenstein*, *Shadows Over Innsmouth*, *Clive Barker's Shadows in Eden*, *James Herbert: By Horror Haunted*, *Clive Barker's The Nightbreed Chronicles*, *The Hellraiser Chronicles*, *The Illustrated Vampire Movie Guide*, *The Illustrated Dinosaur Movie Guide* and *The Illustrated Frankenstein Movie Guide*.

RAMSEY CAMPBELL is the most respected living British horror writer. He has received the Bram Stoker Award twice, the World Fantasy Award three times and the British Fantasy Award seven times – more awards for horror fiction than any other writer. After working in the civil service and public libraries, he became a full-time writer in 1973. He has written hundreds of short stories (most recently collected in *Alone With the Horrors* and *Strange Things and Stranger Places*) and the novels *The Doll Who Ate His Mother*, *The Face That Must Die*, *The Parasite*, *The Nameless*, *The Claw*, *Incarnate*, *Obsession*, *The Hungry Moon*, *The Influence*, *Ancient Images*, *Midnight Sun*, *The Count of Eleven*, *The Long Lost* and *The One Safe Place*. He has also edited a number of anthologies, reviews films for BBC Radio Merseyside, and is President of the British Fantasy Society. He is much in demand as a reader of his stories to audiences.

THE
BEST NEW
HORROR
VOLUME FIVE

Edited by
STEPHEN JONES
and
RAMSEY CAMPBELL

Carroll & Graf Publishers, Inc.,
New York

Carroll & Graf Publishers, Inc.
260 Fifth Avenue
New York
NY 10001
This collection published in the UK by Robinson Publishing
Ltd 1994. The Best New Horror Copyright © Robinson
Publishing Ltd

First Carroll & Graf edition 1994

ISBN 0-7867-0155-2

Printed and bound in the United Kingdom

10 9 8 7 6 5 4 3 2 1

CONTENTS

v

NOT Bad
sleeping bag
—

Great story
about a baby

ACKNOWLEDGEMENTS

We would like to thank Kim Newman, Jo Fletcher, Sara and Randy Broecker, Peter Coleborn, Chris Kenworthy, Steve Lockley, Michele Slung, Ellen Datlow, Stefan Dziemianowicz, John Maclay and Thomas F. Monteleone for their help and support. Special thanks are also due to *Locus*, *Science Fiction Chronicle*, *Necrofile*, *Variety* and *Screen International* which were used as reference sources in the Introduction and Necrology.

Royle. Originally published in *Interzone* No. 77, November 1993. Reprinted by permission of the author.

THE SIXTH SENTINEL Copyright © 1993 by Poppy Z. Brite. Originally published in *Swamp Foetus*. Reprinted by permission of the author.

THE BROTHERS Copyright © 1993 by Rick Cadger. Originally published in *Sugar Sleep*. Reprinted by permission of the author.

THE OWEN STREET MONSTER copyright © 1992 by J.L. Comeau. Originally published in *Borderlands 3*. Reprinted by permission of the author.

ONE SIZE EATS ALL copyright © 1993 by T.E.D. Klein. Originally published in *Outside/Kids*, Summer 1993. Reprinted by permission of the author.

MULLIGAN'S FENCE copyright © 1993 by Donald R. Burleson. Originally published in *Lemon Drops and other Horrors*. Reprinted by permission of the author.

HOW SHE DANCES Copyright © 1993 by Daniel Fox. Originally published in *Dark Voices 4: The Pan Book of Horror*. Reprinted by permission of the author.

PASSAGES copyright © 1993 by Karl Edward Wagner. Originally published in *Phobias*. Reprinted by permission of the author.

EASING THE SPRING Copyright © 1993 by Sally Roberts Jones. Originally published in *Cold Cuts*. Reprinted by permission of the author.

SAFE AT HOME Copyright © 1993 by Steve and Melanie Tem. Originally published in *Hottest Blood*. Reprinted by permission of the authors.

MOTHER OF THE CITY Copyright © 1993 by Christopher Fowler. Originally published in *The Time Out Book of London Short Stories*. Reprinted by permission of the author.

JUSTICE Copyright © by Elizabeth Hand. Originally published in *The Magazine of Fantasy & Science Fiction*, July 1993. Reprinted by permission of the author.

THE BIG FISH copyright © 1993 by Kim Newman. Originally published in *Interzone* No. 76, October 1993. Reprinted by permission of the author.

IN THE DESERT OF DESERTS Copyright © 1993 by Thomas Tessier. Originally published in *After the Darkness*. Reprinted by permission of the author.

For Dennis Etchison,
who introduced us both
to The Dark Country . . .

INTRODUCTION:

HORROR IN 1993

WE SAY IT EVERY YEAR, but in 1993 the much-heralded collapse of the horror market once again failed to materialize. In fact, the number of original horror books published on both sides of the Atlantic was slightly up on the previous two years.

There were no new novels from Big Names Stephen King or James Herbert, but Dean Koontz as usual top-and-tailed the year with a brace of better-than-usual books: *Dragon Tears* featured two cops being stalked by a superhuman killer, while *Mr Murder* dealt with a psychopathic clone.

Lasher was Anne Rice's sequel to *The Witching Hour*, about the titular demonic spirit, while *Darkest Hour* was the fifth in the Gothic "Cutler Family" series by Andrew Neiderman, writing as the trademarked V.C. Andrews.

Peter Straub's *The Throat* was a thriller sequel to both *Koko* and *Mystery*, Whitley Strieber's *The Forbidden Zone* concerned the reawakening of an ancient evil, and *The Last Aerie* marked the second volume in Brian Lumley's follow-up vampire series to his bestselling *Necroscope* volumes.

There were major new novels by such modern masters of the genre as Ramsey Campbell (*The Long Lost*), Dennis Etchison

1

(*Shadowman*), Charles L. Grant (*Raven*), Graham Masterton (*The Sleepless*), Kathe Koja (*Skin*), and Peter James (*Host*).

Richard Laymon kept himself busy with a pair of dark thrillers, *Alarms* (aka *Alarums*) and *Endless Night*, plus the unwieldily-titled *Savage: From Whitechapel to the Wild West on the Track of Jack the Ripper*. Meanwhile, Jack the Ripper's dog Snuff narrated Roger Zelazny's Hallowe'en fantasy *A Night in the Lonesome October*, illustrated with typical ghoulish glee by Gahan Wilson.

As usual, serial killers were popular as evidenced by *Facade* by Kristine Kathryn Rusch, *I'll Be Watching You* by Samuel M. Key (aka Charles de Lint), *Dark Visions* by T. Lucien Wright, *Bloody Valentine* by Stephen R. George, and *Flesh and Blood* by D.A. Fowler.

Garry Kilworth added the middle initial "D" to his byline for *Angel*, about a serial killer angel, which shared shelf-space with *Angels* by Steve Harris, *Angel Kiss* by Kelly Wilde and *Stone Angels* by Mike Jeffries.

There were also plenty of detectives around battling against the forces of evil, as detailed in Christopher Fowler's *Darkest Day*, a sequel-of-sorts to *Rune* which once again featured his characters Bryant and May; R. Chetwynd-Hayes' aptly-titled *The Psychic Detective*, and *Goodlow's Ghosts* by T.M. Wright, about another psychic investigator. *Sleepeasy*, from the same author, concerned the exploits of a dead detective; Shawn Ryan's *Brethren* featured a homicide detective who used the powers of his warlock ancestor to defeat a serial killer; while *The Thing That Darkness Hides* by Robert Morgan (aka C.J. Henderson) was the third in a series about private eye Teddy London, who had to buy a millionaire's soul back from Satan himself.

Michael Cadnum's *The Horses of the Night* was about another deal with the Devil, and demons and evil spirits turned up in *After Life* by Andrew Neiderman, *Panic* by Chris Curry, *Gideon* by Stephen Laws, *The Curse* by John Tigges, *The Living Evil* by Jean Ruby Jensen, *Playmates* by Abigail McDaniels, and *Harrowgate* by Daniel H. Gower.

Many of these manifestations were the result of witchcraft and voodoo, and the Black Arts were conjured up by Guy N. Smith in *Witch Spell*, Megan Marklin in *The Summoned*, Elisabeth Graves in *Black River*, Brian Hodge in *The Darker Saints*, and Ellen Jamison in *Stone Dead*.

The old-fashioned ghost story rematerialized in *Ghosts* by Noel Hynd, *Ghost Beyond Earth* by Australian author G.M. Hague, *Don't Take Away the Light* by J.N. Williamson, *And Then Put Out the Light* by Deborah Grabien, *Help Wanted* by Richie Tankersley Cusick, *Darkling* by Michael O'Rourke, and *The Possession* by Ronald Kelly.

It was no wonder that property prices were falling according to *Drawing Blood* by Poppy Z. Brite, *House of Lost Dreams* by Graham Joyce, *Cradlesong* by Jessica Palmer, and *The Voice in the Basement* by T. Chris Martindale (all featuring haunted houses); *Shattered Echoes* by Barbara A. Shapiro (a haunted apartment); *The Chosen* by Edward Lee (a haunted inn); or *Beloved* by Antoinette Stockenberg (a romance about a haunted cottage).

The family unit wasn't all that supportive either, with that old mid-list staple, the evil child, getting up to tricks in *Black Ice* by Pat Graversen, *Shadow Walkers* by Nina Romberg and *Animus* by Ed Kelleher and Harriet Vidal. In Stephen R. George's *Deadly Vengeance* a murdered child was reincarnated as the family dog, Shawn MacDonald's *The Darkness Within* featured a demonic grandmother, while Patricia Simpson's romance *The Haunting of Briar Rose* was about a family curse. Obviously hoping to appeal to all tastes, Rick Hautala's *Ghost Light* combined a ghost, a psychopathic father, and two abused children.

If you tried to escape into the country, then there were always the regional horrors to be found in the evil Scottish forest of Joe Donnelly's *Still Life*; Phil Rickman's *Crybbe* (aka *Curfew*), about a town on the Welsh borders where the dead don't stay dead, or the cursed mine of Mark Chadbourn's *Underground*. In *Bats* by William Johnstone vampire bats developed a taste for human blood, something nasty waited beneath the waves in both *The Lake* by R. Karl Largent and *Dark Tide* by Elizabeth Forrest, while hot-on-the-heels of Michael Crichton's *Jurassic Park* and Harry Adam Knight's *Carnosaur*, Penelope Banka Kreps decided that the idea of genetically-mutated prehistoric monsters was worth another shot in *Carnivores*.

The Book of the Damned by D.A. Fowler was a horror novel about people who read horror novels, *Pranks* by Dennis J. Higman featured a joker from beyond the grave, and *The Keeper* by Robert D. Lee (aka Mary Ann Donahue and Robert Derek Steeley) concerned a veritable circus of horrors. There were also new novels from Freda Warrington (*Sorrow's Light*), Shaun Hutson (*Deadhead* and *White Ghost*), Tanith Lee (*Elephantasm*), Graham Watkins (*Kaleidoscope Eyes*), and Ed Gorman (*Shadow Games* and, under his "Daniel Ransom" pseudonym, *The Long Midnight*). Veteran Richard Matheson also returned to the horror genre (almost) with an entertaining *Twilight Zone*-ish thriller, *7 Steps to Midnight*.

1992 proved to be a phenomenally successful year for vampires, thanks to the publicity surrounding Francis Ford Coppola's movie of *Bram Stoker's Dracula*. And proving that the old themes still remain popular, vampire fiction accounted for around 21 per cent of adult horror books published in 1993, an increase over even the previous year's rise.

The Golden by Lucius Shepard was a superior vampire murder mystery with more than a nod to Mervyn Peake's *Gormenghast* trilogy. Anne Billson's *Suckers* was satire about yuppie vampires in contemporary London, and there were more modern bloodsuckers in *The Book of Common Dread: A Novel of the Infernal* by Brent Monahan. Lois Tilton's *Darkness on the Ice* featured Nazi vampires in Greenland, a virus turned people into vampires in *Blood* by Ron Dee, and *Shadows After Dark* by Ouida Crozier was a lesbian novel about an alien vampire.

The undead overran Chicago in Yvonne Navarro's *AfterAge*, and they stalked the small town streets of Arizona and Oregon respectively in *The Summoning* by Bentley Little and *Golden Eyes* by John Gideon.

And still they kept bating away: *The Knighton Vampires* by Guy N. Smith, *The Night Inside* by Nancy Baker, *Night Blood* by Eric Flanders, *Blood Feud* by Sam Siciliano, *Blood and Roses* by Sharon Bainbridge, *Precious Blood* by Pat Graversen, *Blind Hunger* by David Darke (aka Ron Dee), *Insatiable* by David Dvorkin, and *Domination* by Michael Cecilione.

Steven Brust took time off from his successful heroic fantasy novels to produce *Agyar*, an acclaimed dark fantasy about a contemporary vampire's love affair. *Eternity* by Lori Herter was the fourth in her romance series about vampire David de Morrissey's search for an eternal companion, and other romance titles featuring the undead included *Forever and the Night* by Linda Lael Miller and *Twilight Phantasies* by Maggie Shayne.

The Phallus of Osiris by Valentina Cilescu was an erotic vampire novel and a sequel to her *Kiss of Death*, and *The*

Vampire Journals by Traci Briery was another sequel, this time to *The Vampire Memoirs*.

Chelsea Quinn Yarbro's *Darker Jewels* and *Better in the Dark* were both in her historical "Saint-Germain" series, set in the court of Ivan the Terrible and the Dark Ages respectively. Tanith Lee's *Personal Darkness* was the second volume in her "Blood Opera" sequence and a sequel to *Dark Dance*.

P.N. Elrod followed up her series *The Vampire Files* with *Red Death*, the first in a new series set during the American Revolution. In Laurell K. Hamilton's *Guilty Pleasures* vampire hunter Anita Blake, also known as The Executioner, was hired by the undead to hunt down a serial killer depleting their ranks in an alternate New Orleans.

Some Things Never Die by Robert Morgan was the second volume featuring private investigator Teddy London on the trail of killer vampires in New York City, while *Blood Pact* by Tanya Huff was the fourth book in her series featuring private investigator Vicky Nelson and her vampire partner Henry Fitzroy, this time involved with a Frankenstein-like mad scientist.

Making Love by Melanie Tem and Nancy Holder was an erotic reworking of the Frankenstein story, while Sophie Galleymore Bird explored a similar concept in *Maneater*, about the creation of a "perfect" woman. In another variation on the theme, Michael Blumlein's gender-swapping novel *X, Y*, concerned a man who found himself in a woman's body.

Another horror icon received the splatterpunk treatment in *Animals*, a novel about shapechangers and apparently the final collaboration between John Skipp and Craig Spector. *The Community* by Ben Leech (aka Stephen Bowkett) featured the inhuman Kin living among mankind, and there were more immortal shapeshifters in *The Others* by D.M. Wind.

Children of the End by Mark A. Clements was about a race of genetically-created lycanthropes, and *Moonrunner: Gathering Darkness* by Jane Toombs was the second book in a series about a family of shapeshifters. For a change there were also *Embrace of the Wolf* by Pat Franklin and *Wild Blood* by Nancy A. Collins, while *The Werewolf's Kiss* and *The Werewolf's Touch* by Cheri Scotch were both romances set in the Louisiana bayous.

Proving that horror was still not the moribund genre most people predicted, a wealth of debut novels appeared in 1993 by both newcomers and more experienced hands: Richard Christian Matheson's eagerly awaited first full-length work, *Created By*, skilfully blended the author's knowledge of Hollywood and the television industry with his proven skill as a horror writer. It also came with some of the most impressive quotes of the year (including Clive Barker, William Friedkin and NBC-TV's Brandon Tartikoff). Another book laden down with a remarkable number of quotes was *Wet Work* by Philip Nutman, however this expansion of an impressive short story about the walking dead didn't really live up to its hype.

Much more promising novel debuts were Nina Kiriki Hoffman's *The Thread That Binds the Bones*, about a family of witches, and Elisa DeCarlos *The Devil You Say*, an enjoyable P.G. Wodehousean-type spoof about psychic detective Aubrey Arbuthnot and his faithful manservant Hornchurch. An equally entertaining prequel, *Strong Spirits*, followed.

The first in a series, *Knights of the Blood* was an enjoyable romp mixing crusader vampires, undead Nazis and contemporary serial killings, created by Katherine Kurtz and written by her husband Scott MacMillan. Gail Petersen's *The Making of a Monster* featured a rock star vampire in modern Los Angeles, while *The Vampire Legacy: Blood Secrets* by Karen E. Taylor was the first book in new series about a vampire fashion designer.

Other first novels included *The Living One* by Lewis Gannett, *Rapid Growth* by Mary L. Hanner, *Night Sisters* by John Pritchard, *Imp* by Michael Scott, and John Boston's *Naked Came the Sasquatch* which was described as a cross between television's *Northern Exposure* and *Twin Peaks*.

The Unfinished by the late Jay B. Laws was a gay horror novel consisting of three stories and a framing device set in a haunted house in San Francisco. Another gay novel, John L. Myers' *Holy Family*, about demonic possession and ghosts, was the winner of the Lambda Rising First-Novel Contest. Robert Wise's *Midnight* was billed as a Christian horror novel.

In 1993, the burgeoning Young Adult horror fiction market almost doubled, accounting for nearly twice as many titles as the adult horror market. In turn, vampire novels apparently contributed to around 18 per cent of the YA total.

The undisputed stars of teenage horror remained Christopher Pike and R.L. Stine (with a reported 8 million and 7.5 million books in print, respectively). Amongst a slew of reprints, Pike's new novels included *Road to Nowhere*, *The Eternal Enemy*, *The Immortal*, and *The Wicked Heart*. Stine published *The Dead Girl Friend* and a new trilogy entitled *The Fear Street Saga* (1: *The Betrayal*; 2: *The Secret*; 3: *The Burning*) detailing the background to one of his most popular series.

Ghostly fiction was well represented with *A Ghost Waiting* and *A Box of Tricks* by Hugh Scott, *The Ghosts of Mercy Manor* by Betty Ren Wright, *The Summer of the Haunting* by William Corlett, *Summer Lightning* by Wendy Corsi Staub, *Acquainted With the Night* by Sollace Hotze, and *A Taste of Smoke* by Marion Dane Bauer.

Other teen terror titles included *The Wheatstone Pond* by the late Robert Westall, *Game Over* by Joseph Locke (aka Ray Garton), *Sweet Sixteen and Never Been Killed* by Richard Posner, *Somebody Help Me* by Beverly Hastings, *The Dead Hour* by Pete Johnson, *Call of the Deep* by Linda Piazza, *The Phantom* by Barbara Steiner, *The Initiation* by Dian Curtis Regan and *The Stranger* by Caroline B. Cooney.

Cooney also published *The Vampire's Promise*, while Angela Sommer-Bodenburg's *The Vampire in Love* was translated from the original German by Sarah Gibson. *Bad Blood* by Debra Doyle and James D. MacDonald concerned a werewolf on a camping trip, and *Children of the Night*: *Dark Dreams* by Ann Hodgman was the first book in a series about a young girl who turns into a lycanthrope.

Series fiction was the Big Thing in YA publishing, and there were plenty of examples to keep the voracious readership happy: eight volumes of *The Nightmare Club* appeared by such authors as Richard Lee Byers, Rick Baron, Vincent Courtney, and Bruce Richards. T.S. Rue contributed *Room 13*, *The Pool* and *The Attic* to the *Nightmare Inn* series, and Diane Hoh's new *Nightmare Hall* series included *The Silent Scream*, *Deadly Attraction*, *The Wish*, and *The Scream Team*.

Other new series included *Haunted*: *You Can Never Go Home Anymore* by Dyan Sheldon and three volumes of *Dark Moon Legacy* by romance writer Cynthia Blair. Charles L. Grant continued his *Midnight Place* series with two novels under the "Simon Lake" psuedonym (*Death Cycle* and *He Told Me To*), Michael August and Jo Gibson contributed to five more volumes in the loosely-connected *Scream* series, Jesse

Harris added volumes seven and eight to *The Power* series (*The Vampire's Kiss* and *The Obsession*), and *Terror Academy: Night School* by Nicholas Pine was the seventh book in that particular series.

Besides publishing a *Star Trek The Next Generation* novelization and two YA horror novels, *Talons* and *Shattered*, the prolific John Peel also launched another new series entitled *Shockers* featuring teens involved with aliens (*Alien Prey*), demonic killer wolves (*Blood Wolf*), a dream killer (*Grave Doubts*), and of course the ubiquitous vampire (*Night Wings*). Each volume had an initial print run of 50,000 copies.

Among those authors shying away from the genre appellation was Patrick McGrath, whose bizarre novel set in World War II Britain, *Dr Haggard's Disease*, was as usual classified under the evasive "New Gothic" nomenclature. Jonathan Carroll and his publishers also went out of their way to distance his latest novel *After Silence* from the genre, despite its theme of realistic horror.

Bradley Denton's acclaimed novel *Blackburn* was about the exploits of the titular psycho-killer in contemporary America, while *In the Electric Mist with Confederate Dead* by James Lee Burke featured the author's New Orleans detective Dave Robichaux solving a murder with help from a ghost.

Peter Ackroyd's latest, *The House of Doctor Dee*, was also a ghost story, as was *The Vanishment* by Jonathan Aycliffe (aka Denis MacEoin/"Daniel Easterman"), published as part of the boxed set *Here Lie Three Tales That Will Never Die*. A.S. Byatt's *Angels & Insects* was a collection of two novellas, one of which was a ghost story, and *The Oracle at Stoneleigh Court* by Peter Taylor contained eleven stories and three one-act plays, mostly about the supernatural.

Voodoo Dreams by Jewell Parker Rhodes was an historical novel about New Orleans voodoo queen Marie Laveau, John Whitbourn's episodic novel *Popes and Phantoms* was set in an alternate Renaissance Italy peopled by animated corpses, while *Mrs de Winter* was Susan Hill's belated sequel to Daphne du Maurier's classic *Rebecca*.

The List of 7 was a first novel by Mark Frost (co-creator of television's *Twin Peaks*) in which Sir Arthur Conan Doyle teamed up with the inspiration for his famous fictional detective to battle the Dark Brotherhood, a satanic secret society planning world domination. Screenwriter/director Nicholas Meyer used his third Sherlock Holmes pastiche, *The Canary Trainer*, to pit the great detective against the Phantom of the Paris Opera. As usual it featured cameos by historical figures, including Gaston Leroux, Degas and Sigmund Freud.

1993 was also a year to re-appraise some of the classics of the field: Leonard Wolf offered both *The Essential Dracula* and *The Essential Frankenstein*, two newly annotated editions of the novels by Bram Stoker and Mary W. Shelley.

Dracula: The Ultimate Illustrated Edition of the World Famous Vampire Play collected together the two stage versions of Stoker's novel – by Hamilton Deane, and Deane and John L. Balderston – edited and annotated by David J. Skal. Robert M. Philmus edited and introduced *The Island of Dr Moreau: A Variorum Text* by H.G. Wells, which included manuscript deviations and two essays by Wells.

Elaine Bergstrom and P.N. Elrod both contributed to the adventures of vampire Count Strahd Von Zarovich with *Ravenloft: Tapestry of Dark Souls* and *Ravenloft: I, Strahd* respectively, based on the dark fantasy game from TSR. And from Games Workshop came *Warhammer: Genevieve Undead* by Jack Yeovil (aka Kim Newman), which included three novellas featuring the vampire character first introduced in the same author's *Drachenfels*.

In the Fog edited by Charles L. Grant was subtitled *The Last Chronicle of Greystone Bay*, the fourth in the shared-world series, and Mary Gentle and Roz Kaveney edited *The Weerde: Book 2*, a shared-world anthology about a secret society of shapechangers.

The *Aliens* series of novelizations, based on the movie series from Twentieth Century Fox and the Dark Horse graphic novels, continued with *Nightmare Asylum* by Steve Perry, *The Female War* by Steve Perry and Stephani Perry, and *Genocide* by David Bischoff. Todd Strasser's *Addams Family Values* was another movie tie in.

The big Stephen King book of the year was *Nightmares & Dreamscapes*, with a first printing of 1.5 million copies. The 800-page volume collected together twenty stories and various associational material.

Lovedeath by Dan Simmons was subtitled *Five Tales of Love and Death*, only two of which were really horror. No such problem with *Alone With the Horrors*, an Arkham House retrospective of Ramsey Campbell's thirty year career, containing thirty-nine stories and beautifully illustrated by J.K. Potter. *Strange Things and Stranger Places* was another Campbell collection, containing ten stories and including the first US publication of his novella "Needing Ghosts".

Fruiting Bodies and Other Fungi by Brian Lumley collected thirteen tales of the macabre, while Thomas Ligotti's *Noctuary* contained seven stories, a new novella, an introductory essay, and nineteen vignettes.

Garry Kilworth published two collections, *In the Country of the Tattooed Men* and *Hogfoot Right and Bird-Hands*, both containing some horror material, the latter introduced by Robert Holdstock. Tanith Lee's *Nightshades* was subtitled *Thirteen Journeys Into Shadow*, while *Bestsellers Guaranteed* by Joe R. Lansdale was an omnibus volume of sixteen stories, revised from his 1991 Pulphouse collection *Stories By Mama Lansdale's Youngest Boy*.

In the Young Adult market, *Demons and Shadows*: *The Ghostly Best of Robert Westall* was the first of two very welcome volumes containing eleven tales. Joan Aiken's *A Creepy Company* collected the same number of stories, while *Night Terrors* by Jim Murphy contained twelve tales narrated by a sinister gravedigger. *Darkness Creeping* by Neal Shusterman consisted of eight stories and two poems, and *Bruce Coville's Book of Monsters*: *Tales to Give You the Creeps* offered a baker's dozen of YA shorts.

Martin H. Greenberg, the reigning king of the anthology market, was as prolific as ever during 1993. He solo edited *Frankenstein*: *The Monster Wakes* and teamed up with Ed Gorman for *Predators*, Carol Serling for *Journeys Into the Twilight Zone*, Mike Resnick for *Christmas Ghosts*, Charles G. Waugh for *Lighthouse Horrors*, Robert Weinberg and Stefan R. Dziemianowicz for *The Mists from Beyond*, and Richard Gilliam and Edward E. Kramer for *Confederacy of the Dead*. Although his name didn't appear on the covers, Greenberg was also involved with Robert Bloch's *Monsters In Our Midst*, a follow-up to the editors' earlier *Psycho-Paths*, and Ramsey Campbell's *Deathport*, the latest in a series of anthologies from the Horror Writers Association, featuring twenty-eight stories set in an airport built over a cursed Indian burial ground.

Veteran anthologist Peter Haining returned to the genre with *The Television Late Night Horror Omnibus* containing thirty-two stories used as the basis for late-night horror shows on television, while Richard Dalby's *Vampire Stories* included eighteen tales of the undead plus an introduction by Peter Cushing.

Pam Keesey edited *Daughters of Darkness: Lesbian Vampire Stories*, Michelle Slung followed up her bestselling 1991 anthology *I Shudder At Your Touch* with *Shudder Again*, and *Hottest Blood* edited by Jeff Gelb and Michael Garrett continued the series presenting "the ultimate in erotic horror". *Dark Seductions* edited by Alice Alfonsi and John Scognamiglio attempted to cover similar ground, and from the same publisher, Zebra, came *Spellbound Kisses*, an anonymous anthology of four romantic novellas.

The Mammoth Book of Zombies edited by Stephen Jones contained twenty-six stories of the walking dead but no mammoths, while *The Ultimate Zombie* and *The Ultimate Witch*, both edited by Byron Preiss and John Betancourt, failed to live up to their titles. *Phobias* was another theme anthology edited by Wendy Webb, Richard Gilliam and Edward Kramer, with an introduction by Robert Bloch, and Peter Crowther's *Touch Wood: Narrow Houses Volume Two* built upon the success of the first book.

Maria Lexton edited *The Time Out Book of London Short Stories* which included new fiction by Clive Barker, Anne Billson, Jonathan Carroll, Christopher Fowler, Neil Gaiman, Kim Newman and Lisa Tuttle, amongst others.

Despite Thomas F. Monteleone's claim that his much-delayed *Borderlands 3* was the only regular non-themed anthology in the field, *The Pan Book of Horror* reached its thirty-fourth year with *Dark Voices 5* edited by David Sutton and Stephen Jones.

Unfortunately, only members of the Science Fiction Book Club saw *Masterpieces of Terror & the Unknown*, containing fifty-eight stories and poems of the macabre, edited by the always-reliable Marvin Kaye. *The Oxford Book of Gothic Tales* edited by Chris Baldick included thirty-seven stories, while *4 Classic Ghostly Tales* edited by Anita Miller somewhat confusingly featured eight examples of Victorian horrors.

The expanding instant remainder/bargain book market was

ideal for value-for-money anthologies and, to be expected, Martin H. Greenberg was at the forefront of this growing outlet. Along with Stefan R. Dziemianowicz and Robert Weinberg he edited *To Sleep, Perchance to Dream . . . Nightmares, Nursery Crimes*, and *100 Ghastly Little Ghost Stories*, and teamed up with Al Sarrantonio for *100 Hair-Raising Little Horror Stories*. Cathleen Jordan edited *Alfred Hitchcock's Tales of the Supernatural and the Fantastic*, but nobody would own up to compiling *Horror By Lamplight*.

When it came to the Young Adult market, Greenberg was there again, editing *A Newberry Halloween* with Charles G. Waugh, containing thirteen ghost and horror stories by winners of the prestigious Newberry Award. There was also *All Hallow's Eve: Tales of Love and the Supernatural* edited by Mary Elizabeth Allen, *Don't Give Up the Ghost: The Delacorte Press Book of Original Ghost Stories* edited by David Gale, *Short Circuits: Thirteen Shocking Stories by Outstanding Writers for Young Adults* edited by Donald R. Gallo, *Please Do Not Touch* edited by Judith Gorog, and the anonymously-edited *Mysterious Christmas Tales: Horror Stories for the Festive Season*.

Sometimes it is easy to forget that America and Britain are not the only countries where horror fiction is published. As a timely reminder of this fact, Leigh Blackmore edited the first Australian mass-market horror anthology, *Terror Australis: The Best of Australian Horror*, while from Canada came *Northern Frights*, the first in a new series edited by Don Hutchison.

As always, *The Year's Best Fantasy and Horror: Sixth Annual Collection* edited by Ellen Datlow and Terri Windling contained a bumper selection of forty-nine stories and three poems. *The Year's Best Horror Stories* celebrated its twenty-first anniversary under the distinctive editorship of Karl Edward Wagner, and our own *Best New Horror 4* was once again the only annual showcase to appear on both sides of the Atlantic.

With most mainstream publishers already planning to cut back their output for the next couple of years, it has fallen to the small, independent imprints to pick up many worthwhile projects, publishing them in often beautifully designed, small press editions.

One of the fastest-growing of these young imprints is Minneapolis-based Fedogan & Bremer, which continued its policy of publishing the kind of books Arkham House used to with *House of the Toad*, a new Lovecraftian novel by Richard L. Tierney, and Basil Copper's *The Exploits of Solar Pons*, a collection of four novellas illustrated by Stefanie Hawks, based on the Holmes-like investigator created by August Derleth.

Another Minneapolis publisher, DreamHaven Books, issued Neil Gaiman's first collection, *Angels & Visitations: A Miscellany*, a very handsome collection which lived up to its subtitle with ten stories and various poems, articles and essays.

From publisher Mark V. Ziesing came Pat Cadigan's new collection *Dirty Work*, which pretty much covered all the genres, and a revised version of Harlan Ellison's impressive psycho novella *Mefisto in Onyx*.

Borderlands Press issued Poppy Z. Brite's first collection of Southern Gothic tales, *Swamp Foetus*, while from Deadline Press came Richard Laymon's collection of twenty stories, *A Good, Secret Place* with an introduction by Ed Gorman. Gorman's own collection, *Dark Whispers & Other Stories*, appeared from Pulphouse/Mystery Scene Press, and the long-delayed last volume of *Pulphouse The Hardback Magazine: Issue Twelve* finally appeared, edited by Kristine Kathryn Rusch.

Sinistre: An Anthology of Rituals edited by George Hatch was the seventh volume of *Noctulpa: Journal of Horror* from Horror's Head Press, illustrated with collages by t. Winter-Damon. It is perhaps easier to understand why no mainstream publisher would be interested in Spartacus Publications' *Blood-Lust of the Devil* by Desmond Edwards, an apparently self-published collection of nine horror stories.

Mindwarps was a self-published collection of twenty-two horror stories by John Maclay, and from the same publisher, Maclay & Associates, came one of the best anthologies of the year, *After the Darkness*, containing seventeen stories edited by Stanley Wiater. Claudia O'Keefe edited *Ghosttide* for Revenant Books, and from CD Publications came *Thrillers* edited by Richard T. Chizmar, the first in a new series, featuring an introduction by Joe R. Lansdale and new fiction by Rex Miller, Nancy A. Collins, Chet Williamson and Ardath Mayhar.

Cold Cuts was the first volume in another proposed series, edited by Paul Lewis and Steve Lockley, which included seventeen Welsh-based stories. Chris Kenworthy edited two anthologies for his own Barrington Books, *The Sun Rises Red* and *Sugar Sleep*, and also published Nicholas Royle's novel debut *Counterparts*.

A first novel about Native Indian magic, *The Charm* by Adam Niswander, was in danger of publicity overkill from Integra Press. Matthew J. Costello's novel *Garden* was a sequel to his 1991 book *Wurm*, introduced by F. Paul Wilson and published by Twilight Publishing Co., and Donald Tyson's occult novel *The Messenger* appeared from Llewellyn Press. Joe R. Lansdale's *Mister Weed-Eater* was a slim limited edition from Cahill Press.

As part of its "Creation Classics" line, Creation Press kicked off an H.P. Lovecraft reprint series with *Crawling Chaos: Selected Works 1920–1935*, edited by James Havoc and introduced by Colin Wilson. It was followed by a new edition of Arthur Machen's *The Great God Pan*. From Chaosium came Robert Bloch's collection of Lovecraftian stories, *Mysteries of the Worm*, and *The Hastur Cycle*, a collection of twelve Cthulhu Mythos tales and one poem edited by Robert M. Price.

The Gothic Society published a collection of eight supernatural stories, *Tales My Mother Never Told Me* by Jennie Gray. Richard Dalby's Ghost Story Press resurrected two welcome short story collections from obscurity, *Tedious Brief Tales of Granta and Gramarye* by "Ingulphus" (aka Arthur Gray) and *Flaxman Low, Psychic Detective* by Kate and Hesketh Prichard, and followed them up with *Two Ghost Stories: A Centenary* by M.R. James, edited by Barbara and Christopher Rhoden, and *Fear Walks the Night* by Frederick Cowles.

For those small publishers with slightly less resources, then regular journals or signed, numbered and illustrated chapbooks proved to be the best format for showcasing old masters, new authors, and important reprints.

Probably the most prolific publisher of these limited edition booklets was Necronomicon Press, who turned out a bewildering variety of titles on a regular basis: Ramsey Campbell's *Two Obscure Tales* would perhaps have been better titled *Too Obscure Tales*, while S.T. Joshi edited *The Count of Thirty: A Tribute to Ramsey Campbell* which contained fours essays, an interview and a working bibliography.

The Lodger by Fred Chappel was a Lovecraftian short story illustrated by Stephen Fabian, and William Hope Hodgson's *At Sea* included four previously uncollected non-fantasy stories, edited with an introduction by Sam Gafford. On the non-fiction front, there were various editions of *Crypt of Cthulhu* and

Lovecraft Studies, H.P. Lovecraft Letters to Robert Bloch edited by David E. Schultz and S.T. Joshi and its subsequent supplement, plus the first issue of *The New Lovecraft Collector*.

Necronomicon was also responsible for issues of *The Dark Man: The Journal of Robert E. Howard Studies* and *The Dark Eidolon: The Journal of Clark Ashton Smith Studies, Studies in Weird Fiction*, and the debut of *Other Dimensions: The Journal of Multimedia Horror*, which included an interview with Clive Barker. *Necrofile: The Review of Horror Fiction* clocked up four issues and is, quite simply, the best magazine devoted to the subject currently available.

From the World Fantasy Award-winning Roadkill Press came Edward Bryant's short collection *Darker Passions*, and a new author double featuring *Going Mobile* by Glen E. Cox back-to-back with *La Luz Canyon* by Royce H. Allen. Meanwhile, Del Stone Jr's *Roadkill*, from Caliber Press, was a post-holocaust zombie story illustrated by David Dorman.

Silver Salamander Press launched itself into the chapbook market with *Close to the Bone*, featuring ten erotic horror stories by Lucy Taylor, and followed it with Adam-Troy Castro's debut collection *Lost in Booth Nine* and a revised version of Michael Shea's novella *I, Said the Fly*. From Bump In the Night Books, another new imprint, *Voyages Into Darkness* contained stories by Stephen Laws and Mark Morris, illustrated by Frank X. Smith, and Jwindz Publishing collected six Brian Lumley stories in *The Last Rite*. *Lemon Drops and Other Horrors* was a debut collection by Donald R. Burleson from Hobgoblin Press, while *Southern Discomfort*, subtitled "The Selected Works", was a first story collection by Elizabeth Massie, published by Dark Regions Press.

From Rosemary Pardoe's Haunted Library came *Supernatural Pursuits*, three humorous ghost stories by William I.I. Read. Nigel Taylor's *Prodigies & Effigies* contained thirty-two short tales, and *Transients and Other Strange Travellers* by Darrell Schweitzer, published by W. Paul Ganley, contained fifteen stories illustrated by Stephen E. Fabian.

Crossroad Press tried to do something different with the chapbook format, producing Andrew Vachss' psycho story *A Flash of White* as a short story, a script adaptation by Rose Dawn Bradford, and a finished graphic sequence by David Lloyd. It was followed by Vachss' *Crossroads Drive*, which included the story, a treatment by Joe R. Lansdale, and the finished comics version illustrated by Gary Gianni.

Stanislaus Tal continued his bid for worldwide small press domination with his ubiquitous TAL Publications. Unfortunately, such releases as *Yellow Matter* by William Barton, *Bizarre Sex & Other Crimes of Passion II*, *Bizarre Bazzaar 93*, and *Deathrealm* only reflected the dearth of writing talent and editing skills, coupled with an adolescent treatment of sex and violence, which permeates far too much of the American small press. It was also hard to know what to make of Wayne Allen Sallee's episodic misery *Pain Grin*, t. Winter-Damon's non-fiction rant *Rex Miller: The Complete Revelation*, or even *The Best of D.F. Lewis*, although Ramsey Campbell made a brave effort with his introduction to the latter.

As usual, *Interzone* turned out some of the most eclectic and interesting fiction in the field on a monthly basis. Its companion publication, *Million: The Magazine About Popular Fiction*, included a Clive Barker interview, a look at Dracula movies by Kim Newman, and a controversial essay about Stephen King by S.T. Joshi. However, editor and publisher David Pringle admitted that it was impossible to keep *Million* afloat with a weak subscription base and poor bookstore sales and the two magazines combined with the August 1993 issue of *Interzone*.

The Magazine of Fantasy & Science Fiction continued to thrive under the editorship of Kristine Kathryn Rusch, but the enlarged-format *Weird Tales* only managed two issues, devoted to Nina Kiriki Hoffman and Ian Watson. *The Scream Factory* included stories and interviews with Brian Lumley and Andrew Vachss and also produced a special edition, *The Night of the Living Dead: A 25th Anniversary Tribute*, featuring (almost) everything you needed to know about zombies. The World Fantasy Award-winning *Cemetery Dance* included interviews with Clive Barker, Gahan Wilson and Poppy Z. Brite.

Dead of Night was resurrected with the seventh issue, after a three-year hiatus, and followed it up with a special holiday supplement in the eighth number showcasing a trio of Christmas tales by J.N. Williamson. Gordon Linzer's *Space & Time* was also revived under a new publisher with number 81. There were also various issues of *Aberrations: Adult Horror, Science Fiction and Dark Fantasy*, *Avallaunius: The Journal of the Arthur Machen*

Society, Chills, Dark Horizons, Eldritch Tales, The End, Grue Magazine, Peeping Tom, Pulphouse: A Fiction Magazine, The Silver Web, 2AM, The Urbanite, and *Weirdbook.*

The Australian magazine *Sirius* made its debut with an article on Dan Simmons and a checklist of Charles L. Grant's *Shadows* anthologies, and *The New York Review of Science Fiction* included David J. Skal's look at horror in the 1950s and '60s.

For news and reviews, Americans could choose between Hugo Award-winners *Locus* or *Science Fiction Chronicle,* while in Britain readers could pick from a revitalised *British Fantasy Newsletter* or the faltering *Critical Wave.* Looking like a poorly-produced copy of *Locus,* John Betancourt's *Horror: The News Magazine of the Horror & Dark Fantasy Field,* managed just one hard-to-find issue in 1993.

Probably the most entertaining non-fiction book of the year was *Once Around the Bloch: An Unauthorized Autobiography* by the always fascinating Robert Bloch. David J. Skal's *The Monster Show: A Cultural History of Horror* took an informed look at the role of horror in pop culture. Although many of the horror entries are missing from the updated edition, *The Encyclopedia of Science Fiction* edited by John Clute and Peter Nicholls still weighed in at a hefty 1400-plus indispensable pages.

Stephen King: Master of Horror by Anne Saidman was a biography aimed at children about the bestselling author. *On Poe: The Best from American Literature* edited by Louis J. Budd and Edwin H. Cady was an anthology of seventeen critical essays about Edgar Allan Poe published between 1934 and 1987. *Classic Horror Writers* edited by Harold Bloom looked at twelve nineteenth century authors of horror and Gothic fiction, while Clive Bloom edited the highly selective *Creepers: British Horror and Fantasy in the Twentieth Century. Wordsmiths of Wonder: Fifty Interviews with Writers of the Fantastic* by the reliable Stan Nicholls included chats with eleven horror writers, including Clive Barker, James Herbert, Ramsey Campbell, Kim Newman and Guy N. Smith. The British Library issued *Shadows in the Attic: A Comprehensive Guide to British Ghost and Supernatural Fiction 1820-1945,* compiled by Neil Wilson.

Katherine Ramsland's *The Vampire Companion: The Official Guide to Anne Rice's "The Vampire Chronicles"* was an encyclopedia for those devoted to the best selling series. *The*

Vampire Encyclopedia by Matthew Bunson was a coffee table volume aimed at fans of the undead, but didn't really live up to its title. Greg Cox's long-awaited *The Transylvanian Library: A Consumer's Guide to Vampire Fiction* might not have included every vampire story and novel, but it at least tried with the help of a bat rating system.

(Vampires) An Uneasy Essay on the Undead in Film by Jalal Toufic and *The Vampire Film: From Nosferatu to Bram Stoker's Dracula* by Alain Silver and James Ursini both looked at cinematic bloodsuckers, while *The Illustrated Vampire Movie Guide* by Stephen Jones reviewed more than 600 titles with bat ratings and included an introduction by Peter Cushing.

It was followed by the second volume in the series, *The Illustrated Dinosaur Movie Guide*, introduced by Ray Harryhausen, and dinosaurs proved to be big business in 1993 with *The Making of Jurassic Park* by Don Shay and Jody Duncan reaching the bestseller lists.

Brian Senn and John Johnson's *Fantastic Cinema Subject Guide: A Topical Index to 2500 Horror, Science Fiction and Fantasy Films* contained a fully annotated and cross-indexed filmography arranged in subject categories. With *Songs of Love and Death: The Classical American Horror Film of the 1930s*, Michael Sevastakis took a critical look at eleven horror movies, and Michael F. Blake's *Lon Chaney: The Man Behind the Mask* was generally regarded as the best biography yet of The Man of a Thousand Faces. Philip Riley continued his invaluable series of filmbooks reprinting the Classic Universal scripts with *The Wolf Man*.

Given all the fuss over its authenticity, perhaps *The Diary of Jack the Ripper* more properly belonged with the fiction titles . . .

Underwood-Miller continued its attractive series of art books with *Virgil Finlay's Strange Science* (with a foreward by Robert Bloch and an introduction by Harlan Ellison), *Virgil Finlay's Phantasms* (introduction by Stephen E. Fabian), *Ladies & Legends* by Stephen E. Fabian (introduction by the late Gerry de la Ree), and the very welcome *A Hannes Book Treasury* (with an introduction by Ray Bradbury).

Horripilations: The Art of J.K. Potter was another beautifully produced volume from Paper Tiger, with text by Nigel Suckling and an introduction by Stephen King. *The Art of Michael Whelan* was an equally impressive, if somewhat expensive, volume and included separate interviews with the artist by Anne McCaffrey, Terry Booth and David Cherry. Morpheus International's *Mind Fields* combined the distinctive art of Jacek Yerka with original short fiction by Harlan Ellison.

Danger is My Business: An Illustrated History of the Fabulous Pulp Magazines by Lee Server included chapters on the horror and science fiction titles, and *Playboy* fiction editor Alice K. Turner took her readers on an illustrated tour of *The History of Hell. James Herbert's Dark Places: Locations and Legends* was a collection of photographs by Paul Barkshire of locations which either inspired or featured in Herbert's novels, with accompanying text by the author himself.

Clive Barker created a variety of superheroes for Marvel/ Razorline's *Hyperkind, Hokum and Hex, Ecktokid* and *Saint Sinner* comics, and Eclipse continued its series of graphic adaptations of Barker's *Books of Blood* stories with *The Yattering and Jack* coupled with "How Spoilers Bleed" (illustrated by John Bolton and Hector Gomez), *Dread* with "Down Satan!" (illustrated by Dan Brereton and Tim Conrad), and *The Life of Death* with "New Murders in the Rue Morgue" (illustrated by Stewart Stanyard and Hector Gomez). Eclipse also used Ed Gorman to adapt Dean Koontz's *Trapped* into a graphic novel illustrated by Anthony Bilau.

Malibu continued its comic adaptations of Brian Lumley's *Necroscope* series with *Book II: Wamphyri*, illustrated by Dave Kendall. *The Ray Bradbury Chronicles* reached a fourth volume from NBM with original graphic adaptations of Bradbury's stories and a reprint from EC Comics' *Haunt of Fear*. New California publisher Tuscany Press released *System Shock 1*, featuring graphic adaptations of "Metastasis" by Dan Simmons, "Special" by Richard Laymon, and "Film at Eleven" by John Skipp.

Meanwhile Skipp and Craig Spector returned to one of their favourite themes – zombies – with a story called "Triumph of the Will" in DC Comics' *Green Lantern Corps Quarterly* No.7. Joe R. Lansdale scripted the five issue mini-series *Jonah Hex: Two-Gun Mojo*, illustrated by Tim Truman, and DC's new series *Anima* was a gritty combination of horror and magic dealing with, among other things, the AIDS crisis, written by Paul Witcover and Elizabeth Hand. Grant Morrison and Mark Millar took over the scripting chores on *Swamp Thing* from Nancy A. Collins, promising to expand the character in new directions. Morrison also published a new graphic novel, *The Mystery Play*.

DC collected Neil Gaiman's *The Books of Magic* into graphic novel format with a new introduction by Roger Zelazny. Gaiman's ongoing *Sandman* saga included such spin-offs as *Death: The High Cost of Living*, introduced by singer/songwriter Tori Amos, and *The Children's Crusade*, a crossover project involving characters from a number of different titles.

After 1992's sixteen year low, the boxoffice bounced back with the best year ever for movies. The estimated total American gross for 1993 was more than $5 billion. Despite Steven Spielberg's *Jurassic Park* becoming the highest-earning film of all time (almost $869 million worldwide and still climbing), it wasn't a particularly good year for genre movies. The only other title in *Variety*'s Top Ten was Disney's animated *Aladdin* at number six, which continued to add to its 1992 total, pushing past the $200 million mark.

The third most successful genre film of the year was the fantasy comedy sleeper *Groundhog Day* starring Bill Murray, followed by the science fiction adventure *Demolition Man*, which didn't do as well as *Cliffhanger* for revitalized star Sylvester Stallone. Arnold Schwarzenegger's *Last Action Hero* was not the hit everyone expected, and its domestic gross was little more than producer Tim Burton's delightfully bizarre *Nightmare Before Christmas* (which cost a great deal less to produce).

Among the rest of the top earners, the year's sequels included *Teenage Mutant Ninja Turtles III*, *Addams Family Values*, *Jason Goes to Hell*, *Army of Darkness (Evil Dead III)*, *RoboCop 3*, *Warlock: Armageddon* and *Witchboard 2*.

Stephen King had three movie adaptations of his work released, but *Sometimes They Come Back*, *The Dark Half*, and the unjustly ignored *Needful Things* all failed to work at the boxoffice. Films attempting to cash in on the success of *Jurassic Park* also never made much of an impact: *Super Mario Brothers*, Spielberg's animated *We're Back! A Dinosaur's Story* and *Carnosaur* did marginal business and only the latter, based on the novel by Harry Adam Knight, probably had a good gross-to-budget ratio.

Hocus Pocus presented a trio of comedic witches, *Man's Best*

Friend explored *Cujo* territory, and *Leprechaun* ("The Luck of the Irish Just Ran Out!") marked the start of another franchise series. Most of the following titles quickly found their way onto the video shelves: *Bloodstone: Subspecies II*, Abel Ferrara's powerful *Body Snatchers* (the third version of Jack Finney's novel), Jennifer Lynch's *Boxing Helena*, *Coneheads*, the underrated *Dust Devil*, Stuart Gordon's *Fortress*, *Freaked*, *Frogtown II*, *Maniac Cop 3*, *Puppet Master 4*, and *The Unnamable II*, which was supposedly based on H.P. Lovecraft's story.

One of the best new shows on television was *The X Files*, about two likeable FBI agents investigating the paranormal. *Highlander* badly needed the charm of Sean Connery, but at least *The Adventures of Briscoe County Jr* had Bruce Campbell. *Time Trax* concerned criminals from the future being hunted in the twentieth century, while *Babylon 5* suspiciously resembled *Star Trek Deep Space Nine*.

For superhero fans there was the wonderfully witty *Lois and Clark* (retitled *The New Adventures of Superman* in Britain for those who didn't get the joke), and *Batman* proved to be the most popular animated show in syndication, even spawning a theatrical feature, *Batman Mask of the Phantasm*.

ABC-TV's mini-series of Stephen King's *The Tommyknockers* may have been overlong but at least it was fun. Showtime's anthology movie *Body Bags* was not even up to the standard of HBO's variable *Tales from the Crypt* series, despite being directed by John Carpenter and Tobe Hooper. Home Box Office's remake of *Attack of the 50 ft Woman* starred Darryl Hannah and was just as cheesy as the 1958 original. The Spielberg-produced *SeaQuest DSV* was thankfully pulled from British screens after only a few weeks, and most people either loved or hated Oliver Stone's virtual reality (and virtually incomprehensible) *Wild Palms*.

In March, the third annual World Horror Convention moved to the snowbound climes of Stamford, Connecticut, where the guests of honour included authors Peter Straub and Les Daniels, artist Stephen Gervais, actor Paul Clemens, and Master of Ceremonies Stanley Wiater. The winner of the 1993 Grand Master Award was Richard Matheson.

The Horror Writers of America held their annual meeting and Bram Stoker Awards banquet in June in New York City. After speeches by HWA President Dennis Etchison, Whitley Strieber and movie director John Carpenter, the award for Novel went to Thomas F. Monteleone's *Blood of the Lamb*, Elizabeth Massie's *Sineater* picked up the First Novel award, and Novelette was a tie between Stephen Bissette's *Aliens: Tribes* from Dark Horse Comics, and "The Events Concerning a Nude Fold-Out Found in a Harlequin Romance" by Joe R. Lansdale (from *Dark at Heart*). Dan Simmons' "This Year's Class Picture" (from *Still Dead*) won in the Short Story category, Norman Partridge's *Mr Fox and Other Feral Tales* picked up Collection, and the Non-Fiction award was presented to *Cut!: Horror Writers on Horror Film* edited by Christopher Golden. The Life Achievement award went to Ray Russell. Because of complaints from international members, the HWA officially changed its name to The Horror Writers Association during the weekend's business meeting.

The eighteenth British Fantasy Convention was held in Birmingham in early October. Guests included Peter James, Tad Williams, artist Les Edwards, and master of ceremonies Dennis Etchison. The British Fantasy Award for Best Novel was presented to Graham Joyce's *Dark Sister*, while *Peeping Tom* was named Best Small Press for the second year running. Nicholas Royle collected both the Best Short Story award for "Night Shift Sister" and the Best Anthology Award for *Darklands 2*. Jim Pitts received the Best Artist award for the second consecutive year, Conrad Williams was voted Best Newcomer, and the Special Award went to Michael Moorcock.

Horror got a chilly reception at the 1993 World Fantasy Convention held in Minneapolis later the same month. Despite all-but-ignoring the field for their guests and programming, the organisers couldn't help but notice that the award winners continued to reflect the overall popularity of the genre: Tim Powers' occult fantasy *Last Call* won Best Novel, Best Novella went to "The Ghost Village" by Peter Straub (from *MetaHorror*), and Best Short Story was a tie between Joe Haldeman's "Graves" (from *The Magazine of Fantasy & Science Fiction*) and "This Year's Class Picture" by Dan Simmons. Jack Cady's *The Sons of Noah* was awarded Best Collection, while Best Anthology went to Dennis Etchison's *MetaHorror*. James Gurney was voted Best Artist, Dell/Abyss editor Jeanne Cavellos picked up the Professional Special Award, and the Non-Professional Special Award went to Doug and Tomi Lewis of Roadkill Press. Harlan Ellison received the Life Achievment Award.

When California dealer Barry R. Levin announced his 6th Annual Collectors Awards, Michael Crichton was voted Most Collectable Author of 1993, Mark V. Ziesing Books won the Most Collectable Book of the Year Award for the lettered state of *Mefisto in Onyx* by Harlan Ellison, and the Lifetime Collectors Award went to Arthur C. Clarke for "the creation of a body of classic works that ennoble the genre of science fiction". Unfortunately, the presentation ceremony had to be cancelled because of the Los Angeles earthquake.

To paraphrase an old saying, books and films don't kill people – *people* kill people. However, given the current moral climate on both sides of the Atlantic, it would appear that all society's ills can be neatly blamed on horror fiction, television violence or Britain's so-called Video Nasties (which have not legally existed since the Video Recordings Act of 1984). Obviously, this just ain't so.

More than two decades after its original release, Stanley Kubrick's *A Clockwork Orange* still remains banned in Britain, ever since the director withdrew the film from distribution in 1974 after a media outcry blaming it for outbreaks of senseless violence. In early 1993 the British courts upheld the ban in a lawsuit filed by Warner Bros., the movie's distributors, against a London cinema that screened the film – despite prints being freely accessible in almost every other country in the world.

At a TV Programme Executives meeting in January, Motion Pictures Association of America (MPAA) president Jack Valenti said he didn't "give a damn" about research which showed no correlation between television violence and the rising crime rate. He insisted that the entertainment industry should act as if television is a factor in anti-social behaviour and not leave to the government the role of "surrogate guardian of family value standards".

On April 2nd, author and bookseller David Britton was convicted under Britain's Obscene Publications Act, and ordered to serve a four-month jail sentence because of comics found in a 1991 raid on his bookstore. Manchester police had made numerous raids on the premises and in 1992 failed in their attempts to get Britton's satirical novel *Lord Horror* destroyed.

ELSPA, the UK trade association for computer and video game publishers, teamed up with the Video Standards Council to draft a self-regulating rating system for video games which are exempt from classification by the British Board of Film Classification. In 1992 the BBFC began to classify video games depicting human sexual activity or mutilation.

In February, two boys aged ten years old were charged with the abduction and horrific murder of James Bulger in the Merseyside area. At their trial in November, finding both boys guilty, the judge made spurious reference to a video – Universal's *Child's Play 3* – which one of the boy's fathers had rented prior to the killing. He inferred (without any proof) that the boy might have been exposed to the video and consequently influenced by it (a totally unsubstantiated conclusion).

This was quickly picked up by the UK tabloid press, which began a sensationalist witch-hunt, spurred on by Liberal Democrat MP David Alton (whose previous attempt at profile-raising was trying to repeal Britain's abortion law) and a moral minority who called for a ban on all films deemed "unsuitable for home viewing". All this despite the police stating that the video had absolutely no bearing on the case, James Ferman of The British Board of Film Classification denying any connection between screen violence and young offenders, and the British government describing the country's censorship laws as "Draconian" enough.

But in the end, it wasn't enough. The Newsom Report, a document claiming that a group of child psychologists had changed their minds about the effects of screen violence on children, was conveniently produced for Alton to cite, even though several of the signatories had not changed their minds at all. In April 1994 Home Secretary Michael Howard caved in to cross-party pressure and introduced new classification and censorship laws on films and video games. Films would be refused a release, or forced to carry a restricted classification, if the BBFC decided that a viewer could become a threat to society. Twentieth Century Fox succumbed to pressure to drop its UK theatrical release of *The Good Son*, in which Macaulay Culkin plays a child murderer. Vadim Jean's *Beyond Bedlam*, based on the horror novel by Harry Adam Knight, was initially denied a video certificate by the BBFC and condemned, like the acclaimed *Reservoir Dogs* and *Bad Lieutenant*, to languish in the UK video wasteland.

David Alton has said that he plans to target television and books next. British booksellers are already resisting horror titles and several films have been "voluntarily" withdrawn from video distribution or denied television screenings. So long as such controversy can be fanned by the cynical media, hypocritical politicians and misinformed public opinion, we should all be on our guard. It is all too easy to use horror fiction and films as a scapegoat for economic and social deprivation. As most intelligent people realise, fiction is only a reflection of life. The real problems exist elsewhere . . .

The Editors,
May, 1994

MICHAEL MARSHALL SMITH

Later

MICHAEL MARSHALL SMITH's first novel, *Only Forward*, was published to critical acclaim by HarperCollins in 1994. A freelance graphic designer and radio scriptwriter, over the past few years his short fiction has appeared in various anthologies, including several volumes of *Dark Voices*, *The Mammoth Books of Frankenstein*, *Werewolves* and *Zombies*, *Shadows Over Innsmouth*, *The Anthology of Fantasy & the Supernatural*, *Darklands* and *Darklands 2*, *Touch Wood*, *The Year's Best Fantasy and Horror* and two previous editions of *The Best New Horror*.

He has twice won the British Fantasy Award for Best Short Fiction and he was voted Best Newcomer in 1991.

I REMEMBER STANDING in the bedroom before we went out, fiddling with my tie and fretting mildly about the time. As yet we had plenty, but that was nothing to be complacent about. The minutes had a way of disappearing when Rachel was getting ready, early starts culminating in a breathless search for a taxi. It was a party we were going to, so it didn't really matter what time we left, but I tend to be a little dull about time. I used to, anyway.

When I had the tie as close to a tidy knot as I was going to be able to get it, I turned away from the mirror, and opened my mouth to call out to Rachel. But then I caught sight of what was on the bed, and closed it again. For a moment I just stood and looked, and then walked over towards the bed.

It wasn't anything very spectacular, just a dress made of sheeny white material. A few years ago, when we started going out together, Rachel used to make a lot of her clothes. She didn't do it because she had to, but because she enjoyed it. She used to trail me endlessly round dress-making shops, browsing patterns and asking my opinion on a million different fabrics, while I half-heartedly protested and moaned.

On impulse I leant down and felt the material, and found I could remember touching it for the first time in the shop on Mill Road, could remember surfacing up through contented boredom to say that yes, I liked this one. On that recommendation she'd bought it, and made this dress, and as a reward for traipsing around after her she'd bought me dinner too. We were poorer then, so the meal was cheap, but there was lots and it was good.

The strange thing was, I didn't even really mind the dress shops. You know how sometimes, when you're just walking around, living your life, you'll see someone on the street and fall hopelessly in love with them? How something in the way they look, the way they are, makes you stop dead in your tracks and stare? How for that instant you're convinced that if you could just meet them, you'd be able to love them for ever?

Wild schemes and unlikely meetings pass through your head, and yet as they stand on the other side of the street or the room, talking to someone else, they haven't the faintest idea of what's going through your mind. Something has clicked, but only inside your head. You know you'll never speak to them, that they'll never know what you're feeling, and that they'll never want to. But something about them forces you to keep looking, until you wish they'd leave so you could be free.

The first time I saw Rachel was like that, and now she was in my bath. I didn't call out to hurry her along. I decided it didn't really matter.

A few minutes later a protracted squawking noise announced the letting out of the bath water, and Rachel wafted into the bedroom swaddled in thick towels and glowing high spirits. Suddenly I lost all interest in going to the party, punctually or otherwise. She marched up to me, set her head at a silly angle to kiss me on the lips and jerked my tie vigorously in about three different directions. When I looked in the mirror I saw that somehow, as always, she'd turned it into a perfect knot.

Half an hour later we left the flat, still in plenty of time. If anything, I'd held her up.

"Later," she said, smiling in the way that showed she meant it, "Later, and for a long time, my man."

I remember turning from locking the door to see her standing on the pavement outside the house, looking perfect in her white dress, looking happy and looking at me. As I walked smiling down the steps towards her she skipped backwards into the road, laughing for no reason, laughing because she was with me.

"Come on," she said, holding out her hand like a dancer, and a yellow van came round the corner and smashed into her. She spun backwards as if tugged on a rope, rebounded off a parked car and toppled into the road. As I stood cold on the bottom step she half sat up and looked at me, an expression of wordless surprise on her face, and then she fell back again.

When I reached her blood was already pulsing up into the white of her dress and welling out of her mouth. It ran out over her makeup and I saw she'd been right: she hadn't quite blended the colours above her eyes. I'd told her it didn't matter, that she still looked beautiful. She had.

She tried to move her head again and there was a sticky sound as it almost left the tarmac and then slumped back. Her hair fell back from around her face, but not as it usually did. There was a faint flicker in her eyelids, and then she died.

I knelt there in the road beside her, holding her hand as the blood dried a little. It was as if everything had come to a halt, and hadn't started up again. I heard every word the small crowd muttered, but I didn't know what they were muttering about. All

I could think was that there wasn't going to be a later, not to kiss her some more, not for anything. Later was gone.

When I got back from the hospital I phoned her mother. I did it as soon as I got back, though I didn't want to. I didn't want to tell anyone, didn't want to make it official. It was a bad phone call, very, very bad. Then I sat in the flat, looking at the drawers she'd left open, at the towels on the floor, at the party invitation on the dressing table, feeling my stomach crawl. I was back at the flat, as if we'd come back home from the party. I should have been making coffee while Rachel had yet another bath, coffee we'd drink on the sofa in front of the fire. But the fire was off and the bath was empty. So what was I supposed to do?

I sat for an hour, feeling as if somehow I'd slipped too far forward in time and left Rachel behind, as if I could turn and see her desperately running to try to catch me up. When it felt as if my throat was going to burst I called my parents and they came and took me home. My mother gently made me change my clothes, but she didn't wash them. Not until I was asleep, anyway. When I came down and saw them clean I hated her, but I knew she was right and the hate went away. There wouldn't have been much point in just keeping them in a drawer.

The funeral was short. I guess they all are, really, but there's no point in them being any longer. Nothing more would be said. I was a little better by then, and not crying so much, though I did before we went to the church because I couldn't get my tie to sit right.

Rachel was buried near her grandparents, which she would have liked. Her parents gave me her dress afterwards, because I'd asked for it. It had been thoroughly cleaned and large patches had lost their sheen and died, looking as much unlike Rachel's dress as the cloth had on the roll. I'd almost have preferred the bloodstains still to have been there: at least that way I could have believed that the cloth still sparkled beneath them. But they were right in their way, as my mother was. Some people seem to have pragmatic, accepting souls, an ability to deal with death. I don't, I'm afraid. I don't understand it at all.

Afterwards I stood at the graveside for a while, but not for long because I knew that my parents were waiting at the car. As I stood by the mound of earth that lay on top of her I tried to concentrate, to send some final thought to her, some final love, but the world kept pressing in on me through the sound of cars on the road and some bird that was cawing in a tree. I couldn't shut it out. I couldn't believe that I was noticing how cold it was, that somewhere lives were being led and televisions being watched, that the inside of my parents' car would smell the same as it always had. I wanted to feel something, wanted to sense her presence, but I couldn't. All I could feel was the world round me, the same old world. But it wasn't a world that had been there a week ago, and I couldn't understand how it could look so much the same.

It was the same because nothing had changed, and I turned and walked to the car. The wake was worse than the funeral, much worse, and I stood with a sandwich feeling something very cold building up inside. Rachel's oldest friend Lisa held court with her old school friends, swiftly running the range of emotions from stoic resilience to trembling incoherence.

"I've just realized," she sobbed to me, "Rachel's not going to be at my wedding."

"Yes, well she's not going to be at mine either," I said numbly, and immediately hated myself for it. I went and stood by the window, out of harm's way. I couldn't react properly. I knew why everyone was standing here, that in some ways it was like a wedding. Instead of gathering together to bear witness to a bond, they were here to prove she was dead. In the weeks to come they'd know they'd stood together in a room, and would be able to accept she was gone. I couldn't.

I said goodbye to Rachel's parents before I left. We looked at each other oddly, and shook hands, as if we were just strangers again. Then I went back to the flat and changed into some old clothes. My "Someday" clothes, Rachel used to call them, as in "some day you must throw them away". Then I made a cup of tea and stared out of the window for a while. I knew damn well what I was going to do, and it was a relief to give in to it.

That night I went back to the cemetery and I dug her up. What can I say? It was hard work, and it took a lot longer than I expected, but in another way it was surprisingly easy. I mean yes, it was creepy, and yes, I felt like a lunatic, but after the shovel had gone in once the second time seemed less strange. It was like waking up in the mornings after the accident. The first time I clutched at myself and couldn't understand, but after that I knew what to expect. There were no cracks of thunder, there was no web of lightning and I actually felt very calm. There was just me and, beneath the earth, my friend. I just wanted to find her.

When I did I laid her down by the side of the grave and then filled it back up again, being careful to make it look undisturbed. Then I carried her to the car in my arms and brought her home.

The flat seemed very quiet as I sat her on the sofa, and the cushion rustled and creaked as it took her weight again. When she was settled I knelt and looked up at her face. It looked much the same as it always had, though the colour of the skin was different, didn't have the glow she always had. That's where life is, you know, not in the heart but in the little things, like the way hair falls around a face. Her nose looked the same and her forehead was smooth. It was the same face, exactly the same.

I knew the dress she was wearing was hiding a lot of things I would rather not see, but I took it off anyway. It was her going away dress, bought by her family specially for the occasion, and it didn't mean anything to me or to her. I knew what the damage would be and what it meant. As it turned out the patchers and menders had done a good job, not glossing because it wouldn't be seen. It wasn't so bad.

When she was sitting up again in her white dress I walked over and turned the light down, and I cried a little then, because she looked so much the same. She could have fallen asleep, warmed by the fire and dozy with wine, as if we'd just come back from the party.

I went and had a bath then. We both used to when we came back in from an evening, to feel clean and fresh for when we slipped between the sheets. It wouldn't be like that this evening, of course, but I had dirt all over me, and I wanted to feel normal. For one night at least I just wanted things to be as they had.

I sat in the bath for a while, knowing she was in the living room, and slowly washed myself clean. I really wasn't thinking much. It felt nice to know that I wouldn't be alone when I walked back in there. That was better than nothing, was part of what had made her alive. I dropped my Someday clothes in the bin and put on the ones from the evening of the accident. They didn't mean as much as her dress, but at least they were from before.

When I returned to the living room her head had lolled slightly, but it would have done if she'd been asleep. I made us both a cup of coffee. The only time she ever took sugar was in this cup, so I put one in. Then I sat down next to her on the sofa and I was glad that the cushions had her dent in them, that as always they drew me slightly towards her, didn't leave me perched there by myself.

The first time I saw Rachel was at a party. I saw her across the room and simply stared at her, but we didn't speak. We didn't meet properly for a month or two, and first kissed a few weeks after that. As I sat there on the sofa next to her body I reached out tentatively and took her hand, as I had done on that night. It was cooler than it should have been, but not too bad because of the fire, and I held it, feeling the lines on her palm, lines I knew better than my own.

I let myself feel calm and I held her hand in the half light, not looking at her, as also on that first night, when I'd been too happy to push my luck. She's letting you hold her hand, I'd thought, don't expect to be able to look at her too. Holding her hand is more than enough: don't look, you'll break the spell. My face creased then, not knowing whether to smile or cry, but it felt alright. It really did.

I sat there for a long time, watching the flames, still not thinking, just holding her hand and letting the minutes run. The longer I sat the more normal it felt, and finally I turned slowly to look at her. She looked tired and asleep, so deeply asleep, but still there with me and still mine.

When her eyelid first moved I thought it was a trick of the light, a flicker cast by the fire. But then it stirred again, and for the smallest of moments I thought I was going to die. The other eyelid moved and the feeling just disappeared, and that made the difference, I think. She had a long way to come, and if I'd felt frightened, or rejected her, I think that would have finished it then. I didn't question it. A few minutes later both her eyes were open, and it wasn't long before she was able to slowly turn her head.

I still go to work, and put in the occasional appearance at social events, but my tie never looks quite as it did. She can't move her fingers precisely enough to help me with that any more. She can't come with me, and nobody can come here, but that doesn't matter. We always spent a lot of time by ourselves. We wanted to.

I have to do a lot of things for her, but I can live with that. Lots of people have accidents, bad ones: if Rachel had survived she could have been disabled or brain-damaged so that her movements were as they are now, so slow and clumsy. I wish she could talk, but there's no air in her lungs, so I'm learning to read her lips. Her mouth moves slowly, but I know she's trying to speak, and I want to hear what she's saying.

But she gets round the flat, and she holds my hand, and she smiles as best she can. If she'd just been injured I would have loved her still. It's not so very different.

SARAH SMITH

When the Red Storm Comes

SARAH SMITH writes mystery, science fiction and hypertext (interactive computer-based fiction, including the dark fantasy *King of Space* for the Macintosh). Her novel *The Vanished Child* appeared from Ballantine in 1992 and was one of the *New York Times'* Notable Books of the Year, and she is co-author of the mosaic SF novel *Future Boston*, edited by David Alexander Smith. She has also had stories published in *Aboriginal*, *The Magazine of Fantasy & Science Fiction*, *Tomorrow* and *Shudder Again*, and she is working on a sequel to *The Vanished Child*, provisionally titled *The Knowledge of Water*.

Currently a full-time writer, she has designed and implemented tutorials and documentation systems for high-end computer products. She lives in Brookline, Massachusetts, with her husband, a varying population of neighbourhood children ("two of whom – on the average – are mine"), a 22-pound Maine Coon cat named Vicious, a very nervous parakeet, and four computers.

"I had read Michele Slung's *Crime on Her Mind* anthologies as they came out," recalls the author, "and when Michele asked me for a 'Victorian vampire', I wrote this story as a tribute to her delicious, half-criminal heroines. Like many resort towns, Portsmouth, New Hampshire, is more stridently Edwardian now than in 1905, but surprisingly little changed. I recommend the capuccino in Market Square where Miss Wentworth met her Carpathian count.

"Count Zohary may or may not be a vampire, but Susan Wentworth indubitably becomes one. Relationships are so often like that . . ."

"**D**O YOU BELIEVE in vampires?" he said.

I snapped *Dracula* closed and pushed it under the tapestry bag containing my neglected cutwork. "Mr Stoker writes amusingly," I said. "I believe I don't know you, sir."

"What a shame," he said, putting his hand on the café chair across from me. I looked up – and up; he was tall, blond; his uniform blazed crimson, a splash of blood against the green trees and decent New Hampshire brick of Market Square. The uniform was Austro-Hungarian; his rank I did not know, but clearly he was an officer.

"You should be better acquainted with vampires." He clicked heels and bowed. "Count Ferenc Zohary." Without invitation he sat down, smiling at me.

In this August 1905, in Portsmouth where I was spending the summer before my debutante year, negotiations were being held that might finish the long Russo-Japanese War. Aboard his yacht *Mayflower* at the naval yard, President Roosevelt had hosted the first meeting between the Russian and Japanese plenipotentiaries, Count Serge Witte and the Marquis Komura. Now the opponents met officially at the naval yard and schemed betweentimes at the Wentworth Hotel. My aunt Mildred did not encourage newspaper reading for unmarried women, so I was out-of-date, but knew the negotiations were supposed to be going badly. The town was crowded with foreign men; there was a storminess in the air, a feel of heavy male energy, of history and importance. Danger, blood, and cruelty, like Mr Stoker's book: it made my heart beat more strongly than any woman's should. *Don't talk to any of them*, Aunt Mildred had said. But for once my aunt was out of sight.

"You are part of the negotiations? Pray tell me how they proceed."

"I am an observer only."

"Will they make peace?"

"I hope not, for my country's sake." He looked amused at my surprise. "If they continue the war, Russia and Japan will bleed, Russia will lose, turn west; they will make a little war and probably lose. But if they sign their treaty, Russia will fight us five years from now, when they are stronger; and then the Germans will come in, and the French to fight the Germans, and the English with the French. Very amusing. My country cannot survive."

"Is it not wearying, to have such things decided and to be able to do nothing?"

"I am never wearied." My companion stretched out his hand, gathered together my half-finished cutwork linen, and waved it in the air for a moment like a handkerchief before dropping it unceremoniously on the ground. "Your mother makes you do this," he said, "but you prefer diplomacy. Or vampires. Which?"

I flushed. "My aunt controls my sewing," I said. Cutwork had been my task for this summer, sitting hour after hour on Aunt Mildred's verandah, sewing hundreds of tiny stitches on the edges of yards of linen, then clipping out patterns with my sharp-pointed scissors. Linen for my trousseau, said Aunt Mildred, who would not say the word "sheets." In the fall I would go to New York, planning my strategies for marriage like a powerless general. The battle was already hopeless; without greater wealth than I commanded, I could not hope to be in the center of events. I would become what I was fit for by looks but not by soul, the showy useless wife of some businessman, whose interest in war extended only to the army's need for boots or toothbrushes.

But now, because Admiral Togo had won at Tsushima, I had my taste of war, however faraway and tantalizing; I was sitting with a soldier, here in the hot thick sunlight and green leaves of Market Square.

"Do you like war," my companion asked, "or simply blood?"

An interesting question. "I think they both concern power."

"Precisely." He leafed through the book while I watched him secretly. In the exquisitely tailored crimson uniform, he had a look of coarseness combined with power. Above the stiff gold-braided collar, his neck was thick with muscle. His hands were short and broad-nailed, his fingertips square against the yellow-and-red binding of *Dracula*. Perhaps feeling my eyes on him, he looked up and smiled at me. He had assurance, a way of looking at me as though I were already attracted to him, though he was not handsome: a thick-lipped mouth, a scar on his jaw, and a nick out of his ear. And he had thrown my cutwork on the ground. "My name is Susan Wentworth," I said.

"Wentworth, like the hotel. That is easy to remember." No sweet words about my face being too beautiful for my name to be forgotten. "Do you stay at the hotel?" he asked.

A gentleman never asked directly where a lady lived, to save her the embarrassment of appearing to desire his company.

"My aunt has a cottage at Kittery Point."

"That is not far. Do you come to the tea dances at the hotel?"

"Seldom, Count Zohary. My aunt thinks the diplomatic guests are not suitable company."

"Very true. But exciting, no? Do you find soldiers exciting, Miss Wentworth?"

"Soldiering, yes, and diplomacy; I admit that I do."

"A certain amount of blood ... that is nice with the tea dances." With his thumbnail he marked a passage in the book and showed it to me. *As she arched her neck she actually licked her lips like an animal,* I read. "Do you find that exciting?"

"I am not a vampire, Count Zohary," I said, uneasily amused.

"I know that." My companion smiled at me, showing regular even teeth. "I, for instance, I am a vampire, and I can assure you that you are not one yet."

"You, Count Zohary?"

"Of course, not as this man Stoker describes. I walk in the sun, I see my face in my shaving mirror; I assure you I sleep in sheets, not dirt." He reached out and touched the thin gold cross I wore around my neck. "A pretty thing. It does not repel me." His fingers hovered very close to my neck and bosom. "The vampire is very sensual, Miss Wentworth, especially when he is also a soldier. Very attractive. You should try."

I had let him go too far. "I think you dare overmuch, Count Zohary."

"Ah, why I dare, that is the vampire in me. But you don't hold up your cross and say, 'Begone, *necuratul*!'" he said. "And that is the vampire in you. Do you like what you read, Miss Susan Wentworth? You look as though you would like it very much. Are you curious? If you will come to the tea dance at the hotel, I will show you the handsome hotel sheets, and teach you that vampires are – almost – as civilized as diplomats."

He looked at me, gauging my response: and for a moment, horrified, I felt I would respond. I wanted the brutal crude power of the man. "Count Zohary, you have mistaken me, I am respectable." I snatched the book away from him and stuffed it deep into my tapestry bag. "I have – *certainly* no desire to see your – " I would not give him the satisfaction of finishing the sentence. "You're making me talk nonsense."

He brushed his mustache with his finger, then lifted one corner of his lip. "What will convince you, dear respectable Miss Wentworth? My fangs? Shall I turn into a wolf for you? Come into your chamber like a red mist, or charge in like cavalry?" Over our heads the leaves rattled and wind soughed through the square. Count Zohary looked up. "Shall I tell you the future in your blood? Shall I control the sea for you, or call a storm? That is my best parlor trick. Let us have a thunderstorm, Miss Wentworth, you and I."

The tide controlled the sea, and the Piscatequa River called thunderstorms once or twice a week in August, without help from Hungarian counts. "If you can tell the future, Count Zohary, you know that everything you say is useless."

"It is not my most reliable gift, Miss Wentworth," he said. "Unfortunately, or I would not be here watching Witte and Komura, but back in New York drinking better coffee at the embassy. It works best after I have had a woman, or drunk blood. Shall we find out together what Witte and Komura will do? No? You do not wish to know?" On the café table there was a ring of condensation from my glass of ice water. With mock solemnity he shook salt from the table shaker over it and stared at the water as if into a crystal ball, making passes like a fortune-teller. "Seawater is better to look into; blood best. Ice water — *ach*, Miss Wentworth, you make me work. But I see you will come to the tea dance. Today, Wednesday, or Thursday you will come."

"I will not," I said. "Of course I will not."

"Tomorrow?"

"Certainly not."

"Thursday, then." From the direction of the ocean, thunder muttered above the white tower of First Church. Count Zohary made a gesture upward and smiled at me. I began to gather up my things, and he bent down, stretching out his long arm to pick up my fallen linen. "This is almost done; you must come Thursday."

"Why Thursday?" I asked unwillingly.

"Because I have made a bet with myself. Before you have finished this *Quatsch*," he said, "I will give you what you want. I shall have turned you into a vampire."

A sea-salt wave of breeze rolled over the square, hissing; the leaves were tossed pale side up like dead fish. I stared at him, the smell of the sea in my mouth, an acrid freshness. He smiled at me, slightly pursing his lips. Flushing, I pushed my chair away. Count Zohary rose, clicked his heels, raised my hand to his lips; and through the first drops of rain I saw him stride away, his uniform the color of fresh blood against the brick and white of the Athenaeum, darkening in the rain. A soldier, his aide-de-camp, came forward with a black cape for him. Unwillingly I thought of vampires.

That night the rain shook the little-paned windows of my white bedroom. *This monster has done much harm already*, I read. Moisture in the air made the book's binding sticky, so that both my palms were printed with fragments of the red name backward. *The howling of wolves*. There were no wolves around Portsmouth, nor vampires either. I could tell my own future without help from him: this fall in New York would decide it, whatever my strategies. Women of my sort all had the same future.

How much less alive could I be if I were a vampire's prey?

I pictured myself approaching young men of my acquaintance and sinking my teeth into their throat. This was fancy; I had no access even to the ordinary powers of men such as the count.

But he had told me one quite specific thing, and it intrigued me: he was with the embassy in New York.

The next day, though I was tired, I assiduously sewed at my cutwork and pricked at it with my scissors, and finishing this respectable task, I felt as though I were again in control of myself, triumphant over Count Zohary, and ready to face him.

At my instigation, Mrs Lathrop, my aunt's friend, proposed that we visit the Wentworth, and Aunt Mildred was persuaded to agree.

On Thursday, Elizabeth Lathrop and her daughter Lucilla, Aunt Mildred and I, all fit ourselves into the Lathrop barouche, and at a gentle pace we were driven through the curving streets of Kittery and past the Federal mansions of Portsmouth. It was a perfect day, the breeze from the sea just enough to refresh us, late day lilies and heliotrope blooming behind old-fashioned wooden trellis fences; a day for a pleasant, thoughtless excursion; yet as we passed through Market Square, I looked for his glittering red figure, and as we pulled into the handsome gravel driveway of the Wentworth, I found myself excited, as if I were going to a meeting of some consequence.

Aunt Mildred and Mrs Lathrop found us a table by the dance floor, which was not large but modern and well appointed. An orchestra was playing waltzes; a few couples practiced their steps on the floor, and many soldiers sat at tables under the potted palms, flirting with young women. Mrs Lathrop and Lucilla intended a sight of Count Witte, whose manners were reported to be so uncouth that he must eat behind a screen. I saw no sign of Count Zohary. At one table, surrounded by a retinue of men, the notorious Mme N. held court, a laughing, pretty woman who was rumored to have brought down three governments. While the orchestra played, Mrs Lathrop and my aunt Mildred gossiped about her. Lucilla Lathrop and I discovered nothing in common. From under my eyelashes I watched clever Mme N.

Three women from the Japanese legation entered the dining room, causing a sensation with their kimonos, wigs, and plastered faces. I wondered if there were Japanese vampires, and if the painted Japanese ladies felt the same male energy from all those soldiers. Were those Japanese women's lives as constrained as mine?

"The heat is making me uneasy, Aunt Mildred; I will go and stroll on the terrace." Under my parasol, I let the sea wind cool my cheeks; I stared over the sandy lawn, over the sea.

"Miss Wentworth. Have you come to see my sheets?"

"By no means, Count Zohary." He was sitting at one of the little café tables on the terrace. Today he was in undress uniform, a brownish-gray. In the sea light his blond hair had a foxy tint. Standing, he bowed elaborately, drawing out a chair. "I would not give you the satisfaction of refusing." I inclined my head and sat down.

"Then you will satisfy by accepting?"

"Indeed not. What satisfaction is that?" I looked out over the sea, the calm harbor. While yachts swayed at anchor, the Star Island ferry headed out toward the shoals, sun gleaming off its windows and rail. I had seen this view for years from Aunt Mildred's house; there was nothing new in it.

"Come now, turn your head, Miss Wentworth. You don't know what I offer. Look at me." On his table was a plate of peaches, ripe and soft; I smelled them on the warm air, looked at them but not at him. A fly buzzed over them; he waved it away, picked up a fruit, and took a bite out of it. I watched his heavy muscular hand. "You think you are weary of your life, but you have never tasted it. What is not tasted has no flavor. I offer everything you are missing – ah, now you look at me." His eyes were reddish-brown with flecks of light. He sucked at the juice, then offered the peach to me, the same he had tasted; he held it close to my lips. "Eat."

"I will have another, but not this."

"Eat with me; then you will have as many as you want." I took a tiny nip from the fruit's pink flesh. Soft, hairy skin; sweet flesh. He handed the plate of fruit to me; I took one and bit. My mouth was full of pulp and juice.

"I could have your body," he said in a soft voice. "By itself, like that peach; that is no trouble. But you can be one of us, I saw it in the square. I want to help you, to make you what you are."

"One of us? What do you mean?"

"One who wants power," he said with the same astonishing softness. "Who can have it. A vampire. Eat your peach, Miss Wentworth, and I will tell you about your Dracula. Vlad Draculesti, son of Vlad the Dragon. On Timpa Hill by Braşov, above the chapel of St Jacob, he had his enemies' limbs lopped and their bodies impaled; and as they screamed, he ate his meal beside them, dipping his bread into the blood of the victims, because the taste of human blood is the taste of power. The essence of the vampire is power." He reached out his booted foot and, under the table, touched mine. "Power is not money, or good looks, or rape or seduction. It is simple, life and death; to kill; to drink the blood of the dying; but oneself to survive, to beget, to make one's kind, to flourish. Komura and Witte have such power, they are making a great red storm, with many victims. I too have power, and I will have blood on my bread. Will you eat and drink with me?"

"Blood –?"

He looked at me with his light-flecked eyes. "Does blood frighten you, do you faint at the sight of blood, like a good little girl? I think not." He took a quick bite from his peach. "Have you ever seen someone die? Did they bleed? Did you look away? No, I see you did not; you were fascinated, more than a woman should be. You like the uniforms, the danger, the soldiers, but what you truly like, Miss Wentworth, is red. When you read about this war in the newspapers, will you pretend you are shocked and say *Oh, how dreadful*, while you look twice and then again at the pictures of blood, and hope you do not know why your heart beats so strong? Will you say, I can never be so much alive as to drink blood? Or will you know yourself, and be glad when the red storm comes?" He tapped my plate of peaches with his finger. "To become what you are is simpler than eating one of those, Miss Wentworth, and much more pleasant."

"I wish some degree of power – who does not – but to do this – " He was right; I had been fascinated. The next day I had come back to the scene, had been disappointed that the blood was washed away. "This is ridiculous, you must wish to make me laugh or to disgust me. You are making terrible fun of me."

"Drink my blood," he said. "Let me drink yours. I will not kill you. Have just a little courage, a little curiosity. Sleep with me; that last is not necessary, but is very amusing. Then – a wide field, and great power, Miss Wentworth."

I swallowed. "You simply mean to make me your victim."

"If it seems to you so, then you will be my victim. I want to give you life, because you might take it and amuse me. But you undervalue yourself. Are you my victim?" For a moment, across a wide oval in front of the hotel, wind flattened the water, and through some trick of light and wave, it gleamed red. "See, Miss Wentworth. My parlor trick again."

"No – I often see such light on the water."

"Not everyone does."

"Then I see nothing."

By his plate he had a little sharp fruit knife. He picked it up and drew a cut across his palm; as the blood began to well, he cupped his palm and offered it to me. "The blood is a little sea, a little red sea, the water I like best to control. I stir it up, Miss Wentworth; I drink it; I live." With one finger of his right hand he touched his blood, then the vein on my wrist. "I understand its taste; I can make it flow like tide, Miss Wentworth, I can make your heart beat, Miss Wentworth, until you would scream at me to stop. Do you want to understand blood, do you want to taste blood, do you want your mouth full of it, salty, sweet, foul blood? Do you want the power of the blood? Of course you do not, the respectable American girl. Of course you do; you do."

He took my hand, he pulled me close to him. He looked at me with his insistent animal eyes, waiting, his blood cupped in his hand. I knew that at that moment I could break away from his grip and return to Aunt Mildred and the Lathrops. They would not so much as notice I had gone or know what monstrous things had been said to me. I could sit down beside them, drink tea, and listen to the orchestra for the rest of my life. For me there would be no vampires.

The blood, crusted at the base of his fingers, still welled from the slit he had made in his palm. It was bright, bright red. I bent down and touched my tongue to the wound. The blood was salty, intimate, strong, the taste of my own desire.

The white yacht was luxuriously appointed, with several state-rooms. We sailed far out to sea. Count Zohary had invited the Lathrops and my aunt to chaperone me. On deck, Mr Lathrop, a freckled man in a white suit, trolled for bluefish and talked with Count Zohary. I heard the words *Witte, Sakhalin, reparations*; this evening there was to be an important meeting between the plenipotentiaries. Aunt Mildred and Mrs Lathrop talked and played whist, while Lucilla Lathrop's crocheting needle flashed through yards of cream-white tatting. I began still another piece of cutwork, but abandoned it and stood in the bow of the boat, feeling the sea waves in my body, long and slow. In part I was convinced Count Zohary merely would seduce me; I did not care. I had swallowed his blood and now he would drink mine.

Under an awning, sailors served luncheon from the hotel. Oysters Rockefeller, cream of mushroom soup with Parker House rolls, salmon steaks, mousse of hare, pepper dumplings, match-sticked sugared carrots, corn on the cob, a salad of cucumbers and Boston lettuce, summer squash. For dessert, almond biscuits, a praline and mocha-buttercream glazed cake, and ice cream in several flavors. With the food came wine, brandy with dessert, and a black bottle of champagne. I picked at the spinach on my oysters, but drank the wine thirstily. In the post-luncheon quiet, the boat idled on calm water; the sailors went below.

Mr Lathrop fell asleep first, a handkerchief spread over his red face; then Lucilla Lathrop began snoring gently in a deck chair under the awning, her tatting tangled in her lap. Mr Lathrop's fishing rod trailed from his nerveless hand; I reeled it in and laid it on the deck, and in the silent noon the thrum of fishing line was as loud as the engine had been. Aunt Mildred's cards sank into her lap. She did not close her eyes, but when I stood in front of her, she seemed not to see me. Alone, Mrs Lathrop continued to play her cards, slowly, one by one, onto the little baize-colored table between her and my aunt, as if she were telling fortunes.

"Mrs Lathrop?" She looked up briefly, her eyes dull as raisins in her white face, nodded at me, and went back to her cards.

"They have eaten and drunk," Count Zohary said, "and they are tired." A wave passed under the boat; Aunt Mildred's head jerked sideways and she fell across the arm of her chair, limply, rolling like a dead person. I almost cried out, almost fell; Count Zohary caught me and put his hand across my mouth.

"If you scream you will wake them."

Grasping my hand, he led me down the stairs, below decks, through a narrow corridor. On one side was the galley, and there, his head on his knees, sat the cook, asleep; near him a handsome sailor had fallen on the floor, sleeping too; I saw no others.

The principal stateroom was at the bow of the ship, white in the hot afternoon. The bed was opened, the sheets drawn back; the cabin had an odor of lemon oil, a faint musk of ocean. "Sheets," he said. "You see?" I sank down on the bed, my knees would not hold me. I had not known, at the last, how my body would fight me; I wanted to be not here, to know the future that was about to happen, to have had it happen, to have it happening now. I heard the snick of the bolt, and then he was beside me, unbuttoning the tiny buttons at my neck. So quiet it was, so quiet, I could not breathe. He bent down and touched the base of my neck with his tongue, and then I felt the tiny prick of his teeth, the lapping of his tongue and the sucking as he began to feed.

It was at first a horror to feel the blood drain, to sense my will struggle and fail; and then the pleasure rose, shudders and trembling so exquisite I could not bear them; the hot white cabin turned to shadows and cold and I fell across the bed. I am in my coffin, I thought, in my grave. He laid me back against the pillows, bent over me, pushed up my skirts and loosened the strings of my petticoats; I felt his hand on my skin. This was what I had feared, but now there was no retreat, I welcomed what was to come. I guided him forward; he lay full on me, his body was heavy on me, pressed against me, his uniform braid bruising my breasts. Our clothes were keeping us from each other. I slid the stiff fastenings open, fumbled out of my many-buttoned dress, struggled free of everything that kept me from him. *Now*, I whispered. *You must.*

We were skin to skin, and then, in one long agonizing push, he invaded me, he was *in me*, in my very body. Oh, the death pangs as I became a vampire, the convulsion of all my limbs! I gasped, bit his shoulder, made faces to keep from screaming. Yet still I moved with him, felt him moving inside me, and his power flowed into me. I laughed at the pain and pleasure unimaginable, as the sea waves pulsed through the cabin and pounded in my blood.

"Are you a vampire now, little respectable girl?" he gasped.

"Oh, yes, I have power, yes, I am a vampire."

He laughed.

When I dressed, I found blood on my bruised neck; my privates were bloody and sticky with juice, the signs of my change. I welcomed them. In the mirror, I had a fine color in my cheeks, and my white linen dress was certainly no more creased than might be justified by spending an afternoon on the water. My blood beat heavy and proud, a conquering drum.

I went on deck and ate a peach to still my thirst, but found it watery and insipid. It was late, toward sunset, the light failing, the sea red. In the shadows of the water I saw men silently screaming. I desired to drink the sea.

Mr Lathrop opened his eyes and asked me, "Did you have a pleasant afternoon, Miss Wentworth?" His eyes were fixed, his color faded next to mine. Lucilla's face, as she blinked and yawned, was like yellow wax under her blonde hair. Flies were buzzing around Mrs Lathrop's cards, and Mrs Lathrop gave off a scent of spoiled meat, feces, and blood. "Good afternoon, Aunt Mildred, how did you nap?" She did not answer me. Oh, they are weary, I thought, weary and dead.

Count Zohary came up the stairs, buttoning his uniform collar gingerly, as if his neck were bruised too. To amuse him, I pressed my sharp cutwork scissors against the vein of Aunt Mildred's neck, and held a Parker House roll underneath it; but he and I had no taste for such as Aunt Mildred. I threw my scissors into the blood-tinged sea: they fell, swallowed, corroded, gone.

Under a red and swollen sky, our ship sailed silent back to the white hotel. Count Zohary and I were the first to be rowed to shore. Across the red lawn, lights blazed, and outside the hotel a great crowd had assembled. "In a moment we will see the future," he said.

"I saw men dying in the ocean," I answered.

We walked across the lawn together, my arm in his; under my feet, sea sand hissed.

"Count Zohary, perhaps you have friends who share those interests that you have taught me to value? I would delight to be introduced to them. Though I know not what I can do, I wish for wide horizons."

"I have friends who will appreciate you. You will find a place in the world."

As we entered the even more crowded foyer, Count Sergei Witte and the Marquis Komura stood revealed, shaking hands. From a thousand throats a shout went up. "Peace! It is peace!"

"It is the great storm," said Count Zohary. For a moment he looked pensive, as though even vampires could regret.

He and I gained the vantage point of the stairs, and I looked down upon the crowd as if I were their general. Many of the young men were dead, the Americans as well as the foreign observers. I looked at the victims with interest. Some had been shot in the eye, forehead, cheekbone; some were torn apart as if by bombs. Their blood gleamed fresh and red. The flesh of some was gray and dirt-abraded, the features crushed, as if great weights had fallen on them. Next to me stood a woman in a nurse's uniform; as she cheered, she coughed gouts of blood and blinked blind eyes. Outside, Roman candles began to stutter, and yellow-green light fell over the yellow and gray faces of the dead.

But among them, bright as stars above a storm, I saw us, the living. How we had gathered for this! Soldiers and civilians; many on the Russian and Japanese staff, and not a few of the observers; the eminent Mme N., who bowed to me distantly but cordially across the room; by a window a nameless young man, still as obscure as I; and my bright, my blazing Count Zohary. The hotel staff moved among us gray-faced, passing us glasses of champagne; but my glass was hot and salty, filled with the sea of blood to come. For the first time, drinking deep, I was a living person with a future.

That autumn I was in New York, but soon traveled to Europe; and wherever I went, I helped to call up the storm.

MARTIN PLUMBRIDGE

The Exhibit

MARTIN PLUMBRIDGE was born in 1965 in Brentwood, Essex, and spent three years at Bangor University in North Wales doing his English Literature dissertation on Robert Aickman, Ramsey Campbell and Clive Barker. He describes himself as "the eternal student", and his interests include watching films and listening to the sort of music that is classified as "independent" – on vinyl.

He has worked as a bookseller, including a year's stint at Foyles in London, and his only other published story appeared in *Fear* just before the magazine ceased publication. "The cheque, sadly, bounced," laments the author. "I'd like to say that I'm working on a novel, but I'm not. Not yet, anyway."

He reveals that the story which follows ". . . came to me during a visit to Great Yarmouth. I'm not sure why. There's a waxworks there, but I didn't go in. A couple of my friends did, but I don't recall them saying much about the experience. And it isn't as if they've never been the same since. In fact, oddly enough, they've *always* been the same since . . ."

EVERYWHERE BRIGHT PAINTED letters shouted promises of FUN and PLEASURE, as though all you had to do to get them was queue up at a counter somewhere. FUN, Suzie imagined, would turn out to be pink and fluffy like candy floss, PLEASURE a cool, green syrup-like pine-scented bubble bath. Both would disappoint when taken home.

Her father was more easily pleased. She had already been obliged to accompany him in a game of crazy golf, wincing at his loud laughter and groans every time he missed a shot. She had won, not being fooled by the supposed craziness, the seeming obstacles – wooden rocket ship, windmill, water jump – which in fact were little more than cosmetic. Coolly, she negotiated each hole in no more than four putts. Her father, pretending dismay, was delighted, as though she had won for him. "Damn her! The new Arnold Palmer!" Now she stared out over the pier railings at the grey, troubled sea while her father shot at two-dimensional German tanks behind her. "Ohhh!" he exclaimed every time he missed, "Oh-Ahhhh!" He was the only holidaymaker to have responded to the blunt invitation of the gallery's sour looking proprietor, but it didn't faze him, nothing did. Not the atmosphere of desertion, not the determinedly grey sky, not even her.

She wished that she had gone shopping with Mum after all, instead of succumbing to the bittersweet pleasure of disappointing her expectations.

He appeared at her side, having finished empty handed. Following her gaze, he looked out to sea and said, as though speaking her thoughts, "The sea's so . . . *big*, isn't it?" "Mmm," she agreed. I'll jump into the waves, she thought, I'll jump. Just watch me.

"I dare say Suzie would prefer to go off with someone of her own age," her mother had suggested over dinner a couple of weeks ago, more to dampen her father's irritating enthusiasm for the holiday Suzie had felt, than for her sake. Instantly, it had in any case seemed to be the last thing she wanted. On her mother's lips "someone of her own age" sounded like a member of some despised, minority group; the phrase filled her with contempt. "I don't," she'd protested, with none of the violence that had risen up in her at the time. I won't, she'd thought. No one had asked her anyway.

"Having fun?"

"Yes," she said, looking up from the waves. Incredibly, this reply seemed to satisfy her father. Surely he could see that there was nothing for her here. Aside from a few gangs of pimply, paisley-clad youths, everyone here was either very old or mentally handicapped. It was worse than home. Couldn't he see that?

"The thing about the seaside − " her father began as they left the pier. She imagined that Paul Rees had ended up here on holiday too, that he would walk out of a shop now and see her, the incredible surprise forcing words from their mouths: "I can't believe it. I can't believe it . . .." "Paul! Fancy − " "Suzie. I can't − "

"Suzie!" She realised that her father had stopped, turning to look at something across the road.

It was a building that had caught her father's attention, and she wasn't surprised: painted scarlet and burnt orange, it glared even in the absence of sunshine. It was sandwiched between an arcade and a cafe. Gold pillars announced the entrance, supporting a tasselled canopy, along the front of which was written, yellow on black: WAX MUSEUM.

"Looks interesting, doesn't it?" Suzie didn't contradict her father; it seemed cruel to disappoint the childish excitement in his eyes. Not for the first time she had a dreamy sensation of unfamiliarity with this silly man. Why, out of all the possibilities, was *he* her father?

"Come on," he said, stepping out into the wide, quiet road, one of his hands moving to take hers, then falling back; some concessions, after all, had to be made to the fact that she was a growing girl. She followed him, but as the gaudy building approached so her resolve grew. She would not enter, even if it meant screaming, hurling obscenities or throwing up to indicate, finally, that she was sick of all this. Boards leaning against the flaking gold of the pillars displayed clumsy black-and-white caricatures of Rambo, Frankenstein's monster, and Kylie and Jason. "Your favourite," her father said, pointing at these last, "Eh?" Didn't he understand that they were a joke to her, and to anyone with a brain? Didn't he? "I don't want to go in," she said, having to rush the words in order to halt her father's quick progress.

He stopped dead, and in the moment before he turned to face her, she felt an icy dread. But his greying head turned to reveal a smiling mouth and eyes which held only faint concern, as at the amusing but obstructive antics of a family pet. "Come on, Suzie.

It'll be fun. Let your hair down a bit." Jesus, she hated him. With his wet brown eyes and large rounded nose, he looked just like some soppy animal, one of the "cute" figurines Mum bought for the mantelpiece. His smile held no fear of rejection or dislike. The upper teeth protruded from it, unafraid of exposure, stupidly trusting.

"I just need some air," she said, and was aware, even as she spoke, of how absurd it sounded. She'd already had plenty of air. It had been continually shoved in her face by the wind on the pier, more than enough of it. No wonder her father smiled. Surprisingly though, he didn't press the point and instead relented, looking regretful but oddly determined. "I won't be long," he promised, and she felt a quick stab of resentment at the ease with which he abandoned her. "I don't know, probably about . . . twenty minutes?"

"I'll hang around out here."

He went inside without further hesitation, and she heard him greeting whoever was on the door with conversation-inducing enthusiasm. She had to move. Already, a white-haired old lady was frowning at her as though she had no right to be there, and no right not to know what she wanted to do in a place where there was so much, and all of it so clearly signposted. So she walked, looking around for something to aim for.

The funfair's bright towers pointed to the clouds, where seagulls soared, shrieking. At the edge of an arcade a metal grab hovered over the soft bodies of expressionless teddy bears, caged in clear plastic. Next to them, a plastic chicken clucked mechanically over its collection of red and yellow eggs.

A shop displayed racks of postcards, beach balls, a flat metal ice cream cone. Behind the counter stood a bored young man whose tan had presumably come from somewhere else.

She could, she supposed, buy an ice cream. And she might tell the young man that he looked bored, and he would smile, his hard, cold expression softening instantly, – but did she want an ice cream? Not really.

She ended up in an arcade, where at least she was not required to feign enjoyment. The other clients – who were few, all male and all unhandsome – were notably undemonstrative, as though afraid of giving something away to the machines they faced. The room was full of bleeps and synthetic voices and silly loops and twiddles of noise. She won ten pence, won forty pence, lost it again, and saw, looking at her watch, that her twenty minutes were up.

He wasn't there.

A badly dressed, and in any case ugly, family stood looking at the boards leaning against the cracked-gold pillars, until the mother, giving a curious little moan of boredom and despair, walked off, the others following, leaving only an empty crisp packet on the pavement where her father should have been. She was annoyed with him, although he hadn't been definite about the time, could hardly have been expected to be, given that he didn't know what awaited him inside.

She went to wait by the entrance, but away from the gaze of whoever lurked inside. She stared at Kylie and Jason, their oversized heads pushed together, hearts and musical notes flying up from the collision, and felt, under the gaze of passers-by, as if she was pretending to wait for someone.

Five minutes passed and she crossed the road. White foam collapsed, hissing, against the stones. On the beach, a lone figure in an anorak was walking a dog called – as far as she could tell from the walker's muffled shouts – Walter. She stared out at a distant ship, but the real objects of her attention, frequently consulted, were her watch and the waxworks entrance, which remained deserted through ten minutes, fifteen.

She waited, as a Jason Donovan song played itself, annoyingly, over and over again in her head. Her father's promised twenty minutes grew even more distant, part of a cosy, predictable world where appointments were kept and things settled into place, the world seen through the bored eyes of passing holidaymakers, but lost to her now. Every tiny shift of the second hand on her watch moved her further into new, uncertain territory. There was nothing she could do to stop it. Twenty minutes passed.

Finally, something seemed to gather itself together inside her, bringing everything into focus; she saw what she had to do.

"Excuse me."

The booth looked too cramped for the tall, skinny body of the young man who looked up at her, eyes startled behind round glasses. His short hair, though fashionably cut, seemed, in exposing his large ears and the back of his neck, only to emphasise his vulnerability. *Student*, she thought with satisfaction.

"My Dad came in here three-quarters of an hour ago. He hasn't come out yet. I don't suppose you've seen him?"

He blushed immediately, pleasing her. "Three-quarters . . . yes I think I remember him," he said, as though the crowds had been too thick for him easily to recall individuals. "Well," he concluded tentatively, "I haven't *seen* him emerge, but when he does, he has to come out here."

"But he hasn't," she pointed out, with a smile.

"No." His gaze dropped to the paperback in his hands, darted to the curtains beyond the turnstile, whose folds concealed the interior.

"I mean, is there a lot to see in there?"

Staring into the purple folds, he considered. "Not really," he said, finally.

His utter uselessness and obvious discomfort struck her as something almost miraculous. At the same time, however, she found that she could be properly annoyed. She sighed loudly. "I mean," she said, her tone implying that she shouldn't be the one to suggest this, that it wasn't *his* place, "something might have happened, mightn't it?"

At least he didn't ask her to specify. He merely nodded, slowly, almost sadly, eyes still on the curtain.

"I could go and look, if you let me in."

"No." As if the suggestion had gone beyond the bounds of decency, he was suddenly, sharply certain. "No, I'll – I'll come with you. It's just that I'm the only one here at the moment." He looked around the lobby, confirming his own statement, seeing only her and a few movie posters and stills. She was beginning to wonder if his vagueness was not so much indecision as eccentricity, weirdness. "Oh well," he concluded with an abrupt, lopsided smile, "We weren't exactly throbbing with life anyway."

He locked the till and, opening a door at the side, emerged from the booth stiffly, awkward as something newborn. She thought momentarily of a baby giraffe in a wildlife programme, learning to stand on its long, spindly legs. But already he seemed to be growing in confidence, whistling with unashamed, even perverse, tunelessness as, with a drawn-out grating noise, he dragged the big, metal OPEN sign into the entranceway. Flipping it over to indicate closure, he turned to Suzie, who now recognised the song he was trying to whistle. It was "Too Many Broken Hearts", the same one that had been going through her own head out on the front: well no doubt an arcade or a car radio had been playing it, setting it off in both their minds. *There's too many broken hearts in the world*, sang her head once more as the student, silent now, came towards her.

A coin from the back pocket of his jeans let her through the turnstile and, retrieved, allowed him to follow. She pushed the curtain, whose rich plum colour belied the thinness of the material, aside.

MINGLE WITH THE STARS, advised a sign hanging from the ceiling. The stiff, smiling stars were set up as partygoers, holding glasses, dancing. The illusion was somewhat modified by the fact that they were arranged, facing outwards, along a central walkway and by the plaques at their feet which identified them. "Do you see him?" asked the concerned voice of the young man behind her. She said nothing. The walkway was clearly deserted.

Naturally, she found herself glancing at the figures as she passed them. They were a sorry bunch; it was hard to imagine mingling with any of them. An overdressed tailor's dummy named Joan Collins held a delicate champagne glass in one clumsy, congealed fist. A prominent page three girl grinned and thrust her scantily-clad breasts forward – a definite breach of etiquette at most parties, Suzie would have thought, particularly when the objects on display were so patently false. Jason too was there, limbs contorted in what was presumably intended to look like dancing, but where was Kylie? She'd always known that their romance was a fabrication.

Orange flesh was cracked and pockmarked; the whites of painted eyes had overflowed, drying on the lids. She doubted whether even her father would have been able to maintain his enthusiasm in the face of this. What could have kept him so long? Of course he must have left early, overlooked by the dick in the booth, buried in his book. He must have gone to look for her, got lost, waited for her now outside. Dull but true.

The student had overtaken her, walking briskly; anxious, no doubt that she not have time to get a good free eyeful. As if she wanted it! He had to duck his head in order to pass through the next doorway, which was flanked by self-explanatory double act Little and Large, their size exaggerated in both cases to the point of grotesquerie. Passing after him between the leering, bloated gargoyle and the starved, grimacing wretch Suzie ended up in a small room with metallic grey walls. THE TOUGH GUYS was written in huge black capitals on one wall. Beneath this a row of figures used guns and fists to maintain threatening postures, none of them convincing.

Her father was nowhere to be seen, but instead of moving quickly on to the next section the young man had stopped and was on his knees in front of Clint Eastwood, searching for something on the grubby floor. Stopping just inside the room, she saw him seize on what might have been a small, dead animal. Muttering, he stood, lifting whatever he'd found up to Eastwood's twisted mouth. It was, she realised as he attempted to stick it to the dummy's upper lip, a thin moustache which seemed to resist the young man's attempts to place it, wriggling out of his grasp to slip back onto the floor.

She sniggered as he bent down again to retrieve it, committed now to this absurd task simply because she was watching. His face reddened, at the mercy of her concentrated gaze. Satisfied, she smiled and turned her attention to the dummies. Sylvester Stallone's bulky torso was naked apart from a belt of cartridges, but the absence of nipples robbed it of conviction. Charles Bronson stared determinedly ahead, attempting to command respect despite his flaws, not the least of which was an incongruous nose, too large, too round.

"Found him?"

Startled, she turned to see the young man upright again, and wearing a smile which looked forced. "Who?" she asked, and at the same time the young man said: "You must have a nose for this kind of thing." For a moment she stared at him in complete confusion. Then she looked back at Bronson, at that ridiculous nose, and she saw that it was very like her father's. "Oh," she said. One brief syllable jumped from the young man's lips: laughter, she supposed. Just as abruptly, he turned and walked off.

If the nose was made of something soft like putty he might have shaped it into that likeness before she got into the room. Mightn't he? But he hadn't had time, it looked too solid . . . She had no desire to touch it, to find out. Coincidence, obviously.

But she was left with the uncomfortable feeling of having missed the joke.

She hurried after the student, suddenly afraid that Bronson's revolver would swing towards her, a hidden speaker blasting out the noise of gunshots. Cheap shocks wouldn't be outside the repertoire of a place like this. Above an arched doorway was written, in Gothic lettering, THE WORLD OF HISTORY.

She entered a long room, one of whose pale blue walls displayed a sketchy map of the world, or a pattern based on that general idea. The student stood in the middle of the deserted walkway. He shrugged, an insincere apology for her father's continued absence. "Popular place, this," she said, wanting to undermine him. Immediately, she wished that she hadn't spoken. The room seemed to magnify her words; distorting them, yet pinpointing the uncertainty that shivered behind them.

Nevertheless, they found their target. The young man blushed as though he had been personally insulted. "Well we're meant to be looking for your father," he said quickly, not looking at her. "I think."

The bemused pleasure of her unexpected success barely had time to register. The blush faded, the bespectacled eyes locked onto something, no longer simply avoiding her.

"Now where could he be?" the young man pondered, a frown troubling his pale forehead. He was looking at Hitler. "Maybe he knows."

Suzie was forced to recognise that his humour, if this was what it was, had merely gone underground, not disappeared. Hitler, for his part, played dumb: his expression suggested a simper, a parody of innocence. The young man compressed his lips in mimicry of this, then turned to the Queen Mother. He returned the smile that bared her plastic teeth and Suzie thought: perhaps the joke's on the dummies and not me.

In spite of herself, she was relieved. The young man smiled at her, winked, and strode onward. His gait was stiff, like a forced, jokey march. *Prick*, she mouthed at his back, but she followed, at ease. She'd be half-mad too if she was stuck here all day. The figures regarded them easily, as though finding themselves unworthy of this parade. Henry VIII looked like an insecure fat girl, cowering inside tinsel-edged robes. Gandhi was a skinny, wide-eyed child. Only the Queen Mother looked sure of herself, and that was down to her striking brown eyes.

Not that, in real life, she had brown eyes (did she?) so no wonder they were striking. Effortlessly defeating the pink she was wearing, they seized all the attention for themselves. They had depth, clarity, and a gleam; like oases in the desert of that stilted face, they alone managed to convince.

"Seen something you like?"

The student's voice made her immediately unable to understand why she had stopped to stare. She couldn't think of an excuse or a reply to his ironic question, she could only see herself from his mocking point of view: she was acting like a kid who thinks she's caught up in some thrilling mystery, set up just for her to unravel. All she could do was hurry over to him with a stupid smile, telling herself that the eyes were glass, that was all, just glass. That was why they had seemed so real in comparison to the others, mostly painted-on. If it hadn't been for that first, stupid coincidence she wouldn't have been taken in like that . . . The student raised his eyebrows, then turned and disappeared into the next room. The bright blue walls and the vague world map slid away as she followed, leaving her in darkness.

For a moment all she could see were those two brown eyes, superimposed on the blackness in front of her. They were lingering because they wanted her to recognise them but she couldn't, wouldn't. They were nothing but glass.

Seen something you like? Had the question been addressed to her or to the dummy, she wondered, trying to avoid the eyes, which were accusing, pleading. Fading . . . It became clear that she was in a corridor. Ahead of her the young man's pale shirt glided around a corner, drawing her on.

The corridor wound about in a deliberately baffling manner, occasionally shoving a smooth, clammy wall in front of her, thrusting her one way or the other; she saw herself trapped in a gloomy kind of pinball. Poorly lit tableaux were stationed at intervals on either side of the passage. A pirate clutched a cutlass, Shakespeare a quill pen – although the look of comic despair on the latter's face suggested that the feather might as well be all that he'd managed to retain of a fleeing pet, a budgerigar perhaps.

She saw that, like the young man, she could be amused by this place. In fact, her jokes were probably better than his. The corridor twisted again, confronting her, for some reason, with William Tell. He hadn't yet fired the arrow, and he seemed to be aiming at the white sky, as though the boy with the apple on his head was just incidental.

Strangely soothed, she followed her guide, whose faintly luminous shirt led her on, shorn of head, hands and legs.

They passed a semi-circle of old movie stars, grey and white. Suzie's glance was drawn to a movement among them.

One of the dummies was stretching out an arm.

It was Charlie Chaplin but her first thought was that this was her father, in disguise, that he was going to wink and step forward before collapsing, along with the student, into conspiratorial giggles at her fright. All a trick, a schoolboy jape: she wouldn't put it past him. However, the dummy's pale features remained immobile and its actions confined themselves to the repeated movement of that arm, backwards and forwards. The movement had no connection with Chaplin's neighbours (Al Jolson, Jean Harlow); it didn't seem to be greeting, or dancing, or even pushing away. Faintly, Suzie could hear the buzz of a motor.

"He used to have a stick," said the young man, who had stopped and now stood framed in an entrance full of reddish light. "But it went, I couldn't say where." Did that explain anything? Certainly the dummy's fingers were clenched, as though closed around something. There was an awkward silence in which they both stared at these fingers, as if in sad consideration of the loss. Suzie's eyes swivelled, following the hand's movement, and she thought, I'm being hypnotised! It was an absurd thought, a joke, except that now it seemed to her that the fingers were growing thicker, that there was hair on the back of the hand.

On its next journey forward the hand would spring open, a claw. She looked away to the young man's shadowy head, more embarrassed than scared.

"We've come to the end," he said in a hollow voice. "So soon? Yes. So soon. And of your father no sign."

He's trying to frighten me, she thought and was instantly afraid that she might shriek or giggle. "One possibility," the young man intoned, "remains."

"What's that?" The question emerged as tremulous, scared of what it might find. It wasn't what she'd intended.

The young man leaned closer to her. "My dear," he said in a doom laden, affrighted voice, "It's the Chamber of Horrors."

She couldn't help but smile: fear was laughable, in a place like this. The young man contorted his silhouette into a twisted, hunched shape and shuffled into the entrance, leading the way. She laughed. He was putting on a show for her, that was all, trying to please her in his own strange way. She had nothing to fear from this pathetic sideshow, except that he might want her to pay at the end.

She followed him into the Chamber of Horrors. ABANDON ALL HOPE, said a sign hanging on chains from the ceiling.

There were no customers, as she had expected, although in the thick, reddish dusk it was hard to be absolutely sure. Her father was outside, waiting. It was almost depressingly obvious, now that she came to think of it. The adventure was over.

A mummy, dressed in clean bandages, stared at her in stupid surprise, its eyes stuck to the surface of the bandage, not peering from within. To her right, Frankenstein's monster was frozen in the act of reaching up towards the spotlight above him with a conventional human hand which contrasted oddly with the boxy, greenish, bolted head. White-faced, red-lipped, Dracula resembled some weary old tart, long past it and trying to cover the fact with thick makeup. Over in the far corner, a dummy was caught helplessly in a ticking, creaking torture device.

Each exhibit stood in its own island of bloody light. Elsewhere was darkness.

In between Dracula and a ghoul there was a particularly murky area, as noticeable as a gap in a mouthful of white teeth. "Can't you put some proper light on?" Suzie asked, not believing that her father was lying in some dusty corner, simply feeling that the student still deserved having some trouble made for him: a balance needed to be redressed, she somehow felt.

"*Proper* light?" The student imitated her deliberately irritating whine. Features tinged with red, he turned to her. "Proper light? I'm afraid we don't run to that. However . . . I'll see what I can do."

Sniggering, he disappeared into the void between the two figures.

Not to be outdone, she sniggered too, although she no longer felt any amusement. *What was he up to*? She was uneasy again. Inside her there was only a nervous buzz of activity which wouldn't settle, and wouldn't clarify itself.

Should she move? Or speak? Images flickered and muttered in her head as around her the exhibits waited. The darkness yielded neither sound nor substance.

Then there was a rumble of thunder. She turned to the sound and saw Frankenstein again, as lifeless as any of the other dummies except, she now saw, for the reaching human hand, which really did look like it was stretching towards something. The taut fingers, the bulging veins, conveyed genuine tension. She could easily imagine that, if she concentrated for long enough, she would become aware of painfully gradual movement there . . .

And then she noticed that this hand certainly was backed with hair, and she thought she saw it tremble, as though on the verge of grasping what it was after.

She turned away. Of course it was her own trembling which had made the hand appear to shake.

The student was taking his time. Where was he? Vague shapes, black and red, swirled in front of her eyes as she tried to make out movement in the space he'd vanished into. Were she trying to escape, this would, she reflected, be the ideal opportunity. The exit sign glowed over by the torture victim, whose blood-spattered, serene face failed to register any reaction to his plight. Come on, she thought. Get on with it.

There was no sound from the darkness. There was only the slow, creaky rhythm of the torture device as it feigned the crushing or cutting or stretching of its contents.

She walked forward quickly, to mask her own indecision, and opened her mouth to speak. Then stopped. Someone stood just in front of her, making no movement or noise, unseen eyes looking into hers.

Shit, she thought. He wasn't harmless after all. A light clicked on and a black-clad figure seemed to leap up in front of her, knife raised.

It was Jack the Ripper.

His thin white face smiled, a warm and friendly grin from which the front teeth protruded slightly; as though, knife poised to stab you, he was about to do you a favour. The lips looked moist and flexible, not something that could be said of the rest of the face. Stubble had been applied to the chin, unless the wiry black hairs were growing there, pushing through the hard, chalk-white flesh like weeds through the pavement. She became aware of a strong, unpleasant smell, like disinfectant mingled with vinegar.

"Satisfied?"

The young man's head appeared over the Ripper's right shoulder.

"Nasty piece of work, isn't he? Yet he has his fascination. Clearly."

Suzie pulled her gaze away from the Ripper's face and its familiar smile. A dismal yellowish light now filled the room, revealing the dusty objects which lay behind the figures – stacked chairs, faceless heads, broken limbs, a ladder. A door had also appeared, just beside the exit. PRIVATE, said the letters on it, white on green.

"I wouldn't go in there," the young man told her, noting her interest in the door. "Not if I were you." His voice was calm, seeming to offer a neutral statement rather than a warning. He stepped out from behind the dummy. "Your father clearly isn't here. You may leave via the exit."

Suzie looked from the green door to the curtained exit.

She turned back to the Ripper's smiling mouth but, although it seemed suspended, frozen on the point of saying something, it told her nothing. She looked away, to the body parts scattered on the floor. All were smooth and bland, decidedly artificial. She made for the door marked PRIVATE.

"I wouldn't advise it. It's not for the young or the easily disturbed."

He might have been reading out an official health warning: his voice was toneless. Why wasn't he moving to stop her? Was he bluffing, pretending not to be concerned? Kicking an eyeless false head out of her way, she approached the door.

Her hand closed on the metal handle. She turned, briefly, back to the room. The student stood watching her, no longer animated, his mouth an expressionless line. "You won't like it," he said. The mouth seemed hardly to move as he said it. No emotion coloured the words, as if this was purely a statement of fact.

She opened the door.

Pushing the thin curtain aside, smelling that disinfectant smell again, she stepped into the lobby. The dull metal of the turnstile glimmered. The glass of the abandoned booth was clouded with vague, bright reflection.

Her father was resting his backside against the Open/Closed sign. He looked up at her and grinned.

"There you are!" he said.

She looked back, but saw only the purple folds of the curtain. This couldn't be right. She needed to think about this. (She remembered the winding corridor, pulling her round and dizzyingly round.)

"Come on Suzie. We're late!" That would be true, she realised: they were meant to be meeting Mum in town.

"What are you waiting for?"

The turnstile yielded to her hesitant push. Outside, the sun had finally emerged, bringing the front to life. Garish colours drew strength from the light. Cars, slipping past, threw it off in glinting shards. An old man, looking up at her as she stepped onto the pavement, seemed alarmed, as if one of the exhibits had tottered out into the sunlight right in front of his eyes. Did she look pale, sick?

Her father took her right hand in his left. He began to walk faster, pulling her along, laughing at his own exuberance. Taken by surprise, she was laughing too, but she wanted him to stop or slow down – this was too sudden, he was almost running now. She tried to free her hand but his grip was firm; tried to speak, to tell him to hold on a moment, but laughter and breathlessness got in the way. Obviously a part of her was having fun but she still wished that the flow of faces on either side of them, made liquid by their motion, would cease. She had the idea that, even when stilled, they would remain a blur, like things not properly finished.

KATHE KOJA

Leavings

KATHE KOJA lives in Berkley with her husband, artist Rick Lieder, and her son. She made her book debut in 1991 with *The Cipher*, which was the winner of the Bram Stoker Award and the Locus Award for Best First Novel, and a finalist for the Philip K. Dick Award. Since then she has published *Bad Brains*, *Skin*, *Strange Angels* and *Famished*.

Her short fiction has appeared in various magazines and anthologies, including *Isaac Asimov's Science Fiction Magazine*, *Pulphouse*, *The Magazine of Fantasy & Science Fiction*, *Omni*, *Best New Horror 3*, *The Year's Best Horror Stories*, *Dark Voices: The Pan Book of Horror*, *Universe 2*, *The Best of Pulphouse*, *Still Dead: Book of the Dead 2*, *A Whisper of Blood* and *Little Deaths*. She has also recently published a number of collaborative stories with Barry N. Malzberg, one of which appears elsewhere in this volume.

ANOTHER HAIR.
Stuck this time half-down his gagging throat; spit-clumsy fingers and Gordon reeled it out: long and dark and slick as surgical silk; unmistakably Sophy's.

And beside him Andra, roused by his movement, puffy blue eyes and last night's elaborate coif now gone to the dogs and beyond, "What's the matter?" and he reached beneath the pilling blanket to give her breast, big breast, a reassuring squeeze, tried to talk and coughed, gagged again, louder and wetter. On another hair. Wrapped around his tongue.

"What's the matter?" the balance between annoyance and concern, he shook his head, false cheer, tugged at the hair. It slipped through his fingers, savage tickle at the back of his throat, was he going to puke or what. Feel its curl, floss-like, between his front teeth.

"Gordon, are you all right?" Plop flop, somehow ludicrous in her concern, would she really give a shit if he choked to death? Of course. Grabbed for the hair again and missed, of course she would, he was projecting again, Sophy's leftover spite like a malignant fog, a big black fart; a long black hair.

Finally. Wiggling his tongue and grateful for the freedom, regarded the hair with a careful face, a neutral corner. As carefully put it in the wastebasket beside the bed, beside the others.

"Okay now?" Andra said, and he smiled, touched again those big breasts, self-reassurance this time.

"I'm fine," he said. "Just absolutely fine."

He drove her back to her car, brand-new Toyota, gutter's reflection on the spill of its insect hood. Carapace. She kissed him twice before she drove away; he managed to conceal the hair in his mouth until she was gone, retching silent the minute it was safe.

"Damn it," slimy in his touch, rubbing his fingers again and again down the seam of his jeans, new jeans. New jacket, too. New stereo, expensive prints, lots of nice new things. He owed it to himself. A bad time, a harrowing time, escalating carousels of pity and rage until the last one, oh yeah, some ride. And yes, Sophy had had a bad time too, Sophy's time had been so bad she died of it. Was it his fault?

Stop it, walking faster, get in the car. Drive. Stop for coffee, stop thinking about it, broken windows, the smell and shiver of the

room, how she looked when he found her. When she cut herself
with scissors. When she cut off all her hair. Stop it, Gordon, his
convulsive brushing, wiping at the blood, stop it, she said. You're
pulling my hair.

Finally, aloud, "Stop it!" to himself the only way to interrupt
the cycle, yes Sophy, wherever you are, it hurts me too but life
has to go on, that's what the shrink said, life's for the living and
none of it was my fault. Turning into a coffeeshop, the first place
he saw.

The thick black grind she taught him to favor, slow sip and
remembrance, coiled and futile, inescapable. Jealous Sophy and
her screech, how he had come to hate that special high-C rant,
to circumscribe his activities – innocent; or almost so, he was
in a relationship, not a grave – to go in fear, yes, in fear of that
sound, building like some diamondpoint tornado, pterodactyl
noise aimed straight at his head.

Such as: Near-morning, later than he planned but not as if he'd
stayed out all night. Dry eyes wide-awake, long white legs bare,
drawn up and oddly beautiful with tension, "Have a good time?"
Already, the sizzle, fingers nervous with rage twisting her hair.

Patiently, he always tried for patience, it was never his fault that
things always ended up so out of hand. "It was a meeting, Soph."
Or, "It kind of turned into a party, not really a party, but – "

"Forget how to use a telephone? Or were your hands full?"

Always, couched in those mocking questions, she could make
anything sound bad. He always came home to her, didn't he?
Even knowing she sat waiting, rehearsing herself flawless for the
screaming to come, giving herself all the best lines. Who wanted
to come home to that? He was pretty damned loyal, he thought.
Considering.

"If you keep patting yourself on the back," rising now, voice
and body scaling, girding, "you might knock yourself over," the
whip of her hair as, impatient with battle, she shook the touch of
it from her face, as she would shake away his touch, later, much
later, lying cold in the conciliatory bed. And in the morning,
always: the tears. Patting her back, now, petting her, bringing
her long scrolls of toilet paper to blow her nose.

"Shhhh. Sophy."

Not penitent, no; but entirely sorry. "I love you, Gordy."
Snuggling against him. Wet nose on his chest, for God's sake
Sophy, use the tissue. Red wet nose, red eyes, sore with a

long night's tantrum and still so hot, stroking the long scarf of hair, wrapping it around his fingers, his wrists, stray hairs gently scattering and her uncertain smile growing bolder as she slid lower, in the bed, all that hair drifting the tensing landscape of his thighs.

Smile, there in the coffeeshop, if you have to remember at all, remember her that way. Drinking the last of the coffee, slight cough on bitter grounds. He left a big tip.

Turning his key into the loft's artful disarray, smiling at the pleasing mess of the bed, last night's nest: on impulse he lay, shoes still on, lifting the pillow to track the warm primal scent of Andra's body, holding it against his face to catch instead the iron-dry smell of blood; the itch of hair.

"Shit," press and jerk of fright and on his feet, cat's cradle around his fingers just as it used to, she always did shed like a dog, petting her hair, tangles of hair like the grass underwater that reaches eyeless and warm, the grass you never see until it touches you.

The shrink kept saying he was projecting. The shrink knew Sophy only as montage, smiling snapshots, a morgue photograph.

Washing his hands, over and over, damp fingers on the phone book: Cleaning Services. How much to scour the place, just totally top-to-bottom; today? Fine. Leave the check on the counter. Gone for the day, and why hadn't he thought of this before. Grisly little souvenirs. I bet you think it's funny, Sophy, wherever the hell you are.

After the errands a movie, just to make sure, sitting through all the credits, deliberate amble to his car. Late, and even in the dark the loft was different, smelled disinfected. Cleansed.

Leisurely bedtime ritual, brush teeth, strip, set the clock. Clean sheets beneath him. He fell asleep right away.

all that blood

"Sophy?" his animal whimper

It's all over, all over her hair, all over his hands and smearing it back from her face, those are scissors, oh Jesus God what she did to herself

grinning at him

"I cut my hair, Gordy, like it?"

*   *   *

grabbing for the light, elbow to the clock so it fell, cracking sound and the light went on and he saw it, all of it, rich and matted at the foot of the bed, surreal pet awaiting his regard.

Bundling the blanket, hands shaking, call the fucking cleaning service first thing in the fucking morning, first thing and he did. With empty professional regret, No, of course not, of course if you're certain another crew can be dispatched, and residue of half-hysteria smothered by the light of day, the office sounds around him, coaled down like a fire but burning, still, beneath.

His hands, shaking on the phone, his first cup of coffee sitting too far to grab. "You can get the key from the building manager," he said. "I want that fucking place cleaned this time, all right?"

Hang up hard, whacked unwitting his elbow, swore and snatched the coffee. Lukewarm, he drank it anyway, up all night watching the blanket like a kid, certain it was moving, it was –

Moving like the hairs in the bottom of his coffee cup, slow swirl, unspeakable choreography, he flung the cup against the wall. Picked it up before the office door opened, made a gritty joke, a worse excuse, shut the damn door. Shut the damn door! Go away.

He bought two Pepsis from the machine in the cafeteria, drank them warm and suspicious. The cleaning service called around one to tell him that a crew had been out to his apartment, and in the future, please inform the service that there was a pet, there is an extra charge for pets.

He didn't want to go home, but he wasn't hungry, didn't want to sit through a movie, anyway he'd have to face it sometime, right? If there was anything concrete to face. Which there wasn't, don't be such an asshole, key in hand and pushing open the door. Are you going to get spooky about a bunch of hair?

Poised, he realized it, almost tiptoe with apprehension, but a walkthrough showed the apartment was clean. Clean and empty. He drank a glass of ice water (clear liquid, no darknesses to hide in), washed hard in the shower. Disconcerting erection. He called Andra from the bedroom: "How about I visit you this time?" and Andra thought that would be just fine.

Her apartment smelled like air freshener, room freshener, fake cinnamon in the kitchen and fake orchids in the john. The sheets of her bed were a raveling warm vermilion and he crawled between them like salvation, spread her slack honey thighs and felt beneath his fingers the sweet landscape of hairless skin, smooth and soft and safe.

hair on the blades of tile scissors
 her gummy touch, scrabbling for the scissors out of reach and her face, her face
 "Like it?"
 hair stuck to his fingers, bits of it under his nails

Hands on his shoulders, shouting and he struck at them, saw in the last confusing shreds of nightmare Andra's hands, coated with hair, swarming with hair and he pushed away, she started yelling but oh no, not again, not another screamer and he rolled out of bed and got gone, safe, leaning against the moving solidity of the elevator wall.

Called in sick. To hell with it. He washed his face in the bathroom at McDonald's, drank two cups of coffee, tried to eat the soggy muffin but found, nestled in its depths like a perfect pearl, a bloody hair.

Afraid to go home. Afraid to find out, to see. Just like old times, isn't it, Sophy, you cunt, you twat, you dead filthy hairy bitch, screaming in the car and get a grip on yourself! Get some kind of grip on yourself. Get some help. Go home. Call the shrink.

And tell him what?
And tell him nothing.

Clear things. Bouillon, and water and vodka, and weak tea, pale enough to see if anything waited inside, moving in the thin spoon-current. Sitting up in bed with an unread magazine, covers pushed a safe distance, the better to see you, my dear. Naked, to catch the drift and creep of hair, last night he had woken from the nightmare (again) to see a sly and messy braid halfway up his unsuspecting thigh, who knew what it was planning to do.

Hair in the shower, plugging the drain. Hair on doorknobs, the phone, coiled in cups and glasses, smoldering in the microwave. He had given up on restaurants, he had sent back enough food to fill a supermarket, a city of supermarkets, they all thought he was crazy. Hair up his nose, for God's sake, not many but enough, oh yeah, you didn't need many for what she had in mind. It took him long minutes, sweaty minutes, to blow it all the way out, and when he clenched it in the tissue it moved.

The bouillon was cold again. Tough shit. He put it aside, no hunger left, except of course a hunger for meaning, as in what is your problem, Sophy, smug and dead what is your trouble. No need to ask why me. Slivered ice in the vodka glass, clear glass, good going down because he was cold and it was warm, isn't that funny, iced vodka so warm, down his throat and tickling

like a hair

a lot of hair

and frightened fingers down his throat, jabbing hard for the gag reflex, come on, come on, reeling it up and the vodka bubbling back, swallow it

struggling into the bathroom, stop it, you're panicking, stop it! Trying for air. Trying for air as all the hair on his body stretched, curling undersea dance, slow and stately mimic as he saw, cloudy in the mirror, the empty bedroom reflected: and a figure, black like thready ropes, like slick necrotic veins, hair in the shape of a woman writhing sweet and ready on the bed.

EDWARD BRYANT

Human Remains

NEBULA AWARD-WINNING author Edward Bryant first met Harlan Ellison, who assisted his early career, at the Clarion Writer's Workshop in 1968 and 1969, and the following year he sold his first short story, "They Come Only in Dreams" to *Adam*.

Since then his short fiction has appeared in a wide variety of anthologies and magazines, and has been collected in *Among the Dead and Other Events Leading Up to the Apocalypse*, *Particle Theory*, one-third of *Night Visions 4*, and *Neon Twilight*. He has also collaborated with Ellison on the short novel *Phoenix Without Ashes* and has edited the original anthology, *2076: The American Tricentennial*.

More recently, his work has been showcased in various small press chapbooks such as *Save the Last Death for Me* and *Darker Passions* (both from Roadkill Press) – a growing publishing trend which he regularly champions in his monthly horror review column in *Locus*.

VICKY FIRST THOUGHT a little girl had lost the doll in the women's room just off the main lobby of the West Denver Inn. It was a Barbie, just like she remembered from years before. The doll was straight and pink and impossibly proportioned. It lay on the dull white tile beneath the tampon machine. Vicky had heard the clatter as she passed on her way to the sink. Perhaps she had brushed it off, somehow, with an unwary elbow.

Something wasn't right. The doll did *not* look at all as she remembered.

Vicky set her black patent-leather purse on the faux marble counter by the sinks, switched the soft leather briefcase to her left hand, and knelt. She saw that the doll was tightly bound with monofilament. Tough, nearly transparent fishing line wound around the doll, binding the ankles, the arms at the waist, the chest, the shoulders, the throat, even around the head, taut across the parted lips. The line wound so tight, plastic bulged slightly around the loops. The bindings actually cut into the doll's unreal skin.

She gingerly extended the fingers of her right hand and touched Barbie's shoulder. Cold. *Had* a little girl lost this here? Vicky forced herself to pick up the doll. Had one of the other women out in the restaurant bar left this? She brought the doll close to her face. Was that a glisten of something red at the corner of Barbie's lips? The fishing line caught and reflected the harsh overhead light. No, there was no blood. It was only a trick of the light.

Vicky wondered at the obvious strength of the line. If it could do this to the durable synthetics of the doll, what would it do to a caught fish? She had a feeling it would take superhuman – super . . . what *was* the word for fish? – strength to break these bonds.

Caught would be caught.

She saw no knots where the line ends connected. And maybe there was no need to find them. No point. Trapped. Caught for good. Vicky wound her fingers around the Barbie and turned toward the restroom door. Suddenly she wanted to leave the sharp light and the harsh, astringent odor of disinfectant.

She noticed nothing now save the doll's seeming to become warmer. Lose heat, gain heat. Barbie was taking heat from Vicky's grip, her skin, her body, her living, pumping, blood.

As she swung the door inward with her left hand, Vicky thrust the doll into her briefcase. Now she had a secret. It was a long time since she had had a *new* secret.

This weekend, she had a sudden feeling, it was important to keep a secret or two ready and waiting. Something chilling and exciting rippled through her.

When she'd left the table, her companions had been talking about politics local to Colorado, Utah, Oregon, Washington, presidential campaigns, ballot initiatives to alter the whole tone and conduct of capital punishment. Now the other four women were talking about shoes.

Vicky smiled and sat down. Her half-empty supper dishes had been removed. From her side of the table, she could look out the wide expanse of restaurant window, down across the Platte River valley, off to the east across the glittering October skyline of Denver. Above the lights, a nearly full moon had risen. It was another week until Halloween. Trails of fast-moving lights limned the freeway below.

Dixie, the Oregon blonde Vicky already thought of as the wannabe, was saying, "Listen, tomorrow's Saturday, there's gotta be a *lot* of fall shoe sales at the malls."

Sonya and Kate, the dark-haired sisters from Utah, looked at each other and laughed. Kate said, "Listen, we've got malls in Salt Lake."

"If we want to shop for pumps or ogle Birkenstocks, we'll just crank up the Shoe Channel on cable later tonight in the room." That was Sonya, the elder sister by maybe two years.

Vicky scooted her chair forward and took a sip of coffee. It had cooled to room temperature. Entropy. She remembered the word from a magazine article in her gynaecologist's waiting room. "Southwest Plaza has 27 different shoe stores," she said absently.

"You counted?" said Carol Anne. She was conspicuously younger than the other women at the table. Vicky wondered about that but had stopped short of asking directly. "I shop there too, but I never counted all the shoe stores."

Vicky shrugged. "Anyhow, you can't try them on on the Shoe Channel."

"I bet Mrs Marcos watches," said Dixie. "Is there really a Shoe Channel? We don't get that on cable in Eugene."

The supper crowd was beginning to thin out. Vicky realized

that most of the faces were women she had seen, and some she had talked to, earlier in the afternoon, when everyone had arrived at the hotel.

"Okay, I'm not going to argue," said Dixie, smiling. She, Vicky already had noted, laughed a lot. "Tomorrow's another day. How about tonight? Are we all going to go out somewhere? I know you two sisters have got a car. Is there a Chippendale's in Denver? Carol Anne? You look hip and you *live* here."

"Beats me," said Carol Anne. "I'm out west in Golden. That's the suburbs. No stud dancers out there." She seemed to be blushing a little.

Dixie looked at Vicky. Vicky realized she was hugging the soft briefcase with the bound Barbie doll. She could feel its hardness through the leather. "Don't look at me," Vicky said. "I haven't been to a place like that since –" A chill ran through her belly and up her spine. She felt her shoulders twitch involuntarily. *Since the ride.*

A man walked up to the table. Vicky at first thought it was the waiter, and then realized that he was another diner. She recognized him as the guy who had been sitting with a woman, probably his wife, at the next table. He was a florid man, perhaps in his fifties, in a dark gray suit. His blue eyes were small and piercing. He had a gray mustache.

He stared down at them. Vicky thought Dixie was going to say something.

"Listen," said the man, looking quickly from face to face. "I was talking to the manager. He's a friend of mine and he told me what you're all doing. I gotta tell you something. I think you're all a bunch of sick fucks." He turned on his heel and walked away. His wife quickly got up from their table and followed her husband toward the door. She had averted her eyes, Vicky noticed, from the whole exchange.

The five women at the table stared at each other. Sonya turned and looked after the retreating figures of the man and his wife. She looked angry enough to spit, but said nothing. Kate shook her head.

"Yeah," said Dixie, "me too. What a jerk."

Carol Anne looked as if she might cry.

Vicky hugged the doll in the briefcase even tighter, then took a few deep breaths and relaxed her grip. She reached over the tabletop and touched Carol Anne's hand, wanting to comfort her, reassure her.

The waiter picked that moment to return to ask if anyone wanted more coffee.

They tacitly agreed not to keep talking about the business-suited man with the silent wife. The enthusiasm for male dancers had dwindled. Dixie started talking about movies. Sonya mentioned that the front desk rented VCRs to guests. "Do any of you have the tape?" she said. "The Dobson tape? $29.95 before it got discounted at K-Mart?"

"I looked at it once," said Dixie. "All that bullshit about booze and porn."

"I —" Carol Anne started to say something but stopped. She looked to be in her early twenties. Very pretty, Vicky thought. Long brown hair styled back across her shoulders. Maybe like my daughter would have looked if I'd ever had one.

"You were saying?" Dixie said encouragingly.

An alarm sounded in Vicky's brain. Don't push her, she thought. Maybe she really doesn't want to talk.

Carol Anne said, "I watched it, oh, maybe a hundred times." The rest of the women stared.

"Why?" Vicky almost breathed rather than said the words aloud. Obsessed, she thought. And so, *so* young.

The younger woman looked down at her lap. "I thought maybe there would be . . . a clue. Something. Anything." She drifted off into silence.

Vicky knew the others wanted to ask, *what clue?* What are you looking for? No one said anything at all. But lord, they wanted to. *Obsessed.*

And then there was another new presence at the table. It was a young man in a busboy's jacket with brown corduroy trousers. "Bobby" was stitched over his heart. He looked from one face to the next. His eyes, Vicky thought, looked far older than his fresh face.

"'Scuse me, ladies," he said, "did one of you forget — "

Vicky's hand was already unconsciously reaching for the black purse. Which wasn't there on the corner of the table where it should have been.

" — your bag?" He raised his hand and there was Vicky's black purse.

"It's mine." She reached and took it from him.

"You left it in the ladies' room," said Bobby. "You gotta watch that around here. This is the city." He caught her eye. His gaze lingered. Boldly.

Vicky touched the leather with her fingertips. This was mildly disorienting. "Thanks," she said. "I appreciate it. Thank you very much."

"Don't think nothing of it," said Bobby. He made a vague waving gesture with his left hand. "No harm done." He bobbed his head as if embarrassed, caught Vicky's eye again for just a moment, then turned and walked back toward the kitchen.

Vicky stared. Had the young man smiled? She thought she'd seen a fleeting twist of his lips as he turned. Had he just flirted with her? Returning lost items would be a great way to meet women. *Flirt.* She hadn't thought about that word in a long time.

And then she thought of something else. Could lost items be used as bait? But who was fishing?

"Vicky?" Dixie was saying. "Hello, Earth to Vicky? You there, girl?"

Vicky started, realized she was shaking a little, tried to breathe regularly. "I'm here. I guess I was just thinking about how terrible it would have been to lose this," she said, cradling the purse in her hand.

"Cancelling the cards would be a royal pain," said Kate, the younger sister.

"Never mind the cards," said Dixie. "I'd be worried some wacko'd track me down from the driver's license and show up on my doorstep."

"Isn't that a little paranoid?" Kate said.

Her big sister smiled faintly. "Aren't we all probably just a little paranoid?"

As it turned out, no one went anywhere. The five of them stayed until first the restaurant kitchen, then the bar closed. They talked. Lord, how they talked, Vicky thought.

They talked about that fatal, climactic morning in January, those few years before. Sixteen minutes past seven, EDT.

It was like, where were you when President Kennedy was shot? When John Lennon died? When the Challenger exploded. What were you doing at 7:16 in the morning, January 24, 1989?

Listening to a radio. Watching television. Praying his appeals would be turned down.

"I slept through it," said Dixie. "I'd been watching on CNN most of the night. I went to sleep. I couldn't help it."

"Let me tell you something," said Kate. She glanced at Sonya. "My sister and me, we know a woman whose daughter was killed. But she was also against capital punishment. She wrote letters and made a thousand phone calls trying to stop the execution."

Sonya looked off toward the dark space above the bar. "What can you say? She was entitled. She was wrong, but she was entitled." Her voice dropped off. She said something else and Vicky thought it was something like, "Burn him. Burn them all."

There was muted laughter at the table behind them. But none at Vicky's. They talked more about the execution.

"I'll tell you something *really* interesting," said Dixie, "though the rest of you may already know this." She shrugged. "I didn't. I just found out. There was a guard who looked real close at the executioner. The guy with the hand on the switch was all covered up, with a black hood and all, you know, just like in a horror movie? Anyhow, the guard says the guy's eyelashes were incredible. Thick and long, he said. He thought maybe the executioner was a woman."

They all thought about that for a moment. "No reason why she couldn't have been," said Sonya. "Poetic justice."

"How would she get the assignment?" said Carol Anne.

No one had a good answer.

"Maybe it was just a job," said Kate. "They all drew cards, maybe. The officials, I mean. The queen of spades or something meant pull the switch. I would have done it."

"I would have too," said Sonya. "Under the hood, I think I'd have smiled." Her teeth clicked together. "I'd have laughed."

Dixie nodded. Vicky and Carol Anne said nothing.

The already low lights in the bar flickered momentarily and everyone jumped.

They had never met one another before today. Perhaps they would never meet again. But the five of them had, Vicky thought to herself, an incredibly strong bond tying them together. Or more precisely, maybe, they just had something lucky in common.

Sonya and Kate talked about living in Midvale, a little Utah community south of Salt Lake City. In 1974, in October, when

Sonya had been 19 and Kate 17, they had been driving home from an Osmonds concert in Salt Lake. One minute the Chevy had been running fine, the next, it was making grinding noises, and the next, it was coasting off on the shoulder on 1–15, just past the exit for Taylorsville.

"It was bizarre," said Sonya. "Here we were on an Interstate, and it was only about midnight, and nobody would stop. It was like we were invisible."

And that was when the handsome stranger wheeled his Volkswagen off the highway and pulled in behind them. It was too dark to tell what color the VW was, but the teenagers could see his face in the domelight. He offered to give Sonya a ride into Midvale, but suggested Kate stay with the Chevy to keep an eye on things.

"We said no deal," said Kate. "We both would go into Midvale, or none of us would."

The stranger put his fingers around Sonya's wrist as though to drag her into the Volkswagen. Kate held up a tire iron she had picked up from the Chevy's floor. And that was it. The stranger let go, apologized like a gentleman, spun out on the gravel and disappeared into the Utah night.

"He killed a girl from Midvale," said Sonya. "We knew her. We didn't know her well, but after they finally found her bones, we went to the funeral and cried."

Dixie's was a lower-key story, as Vicky had suspected.

"It was 1975," said Dixie. "I was a blonde then, just like now, and I know what you're thinking. Well, he killed two blondes. He wanted brunettes, but he'd settle. He wasn't that predictable."

Vicky was glad she hadn't said anything earlier. She'd known about the blonde victims. She simply, for whatever reason, had been suspicious of Dixie's attitude.

"I was picking up some stuff for my mom at Safeway," Dixie continued. "In Eugene. I remember coming up to my car with a bag of groceries in each arm, thinking about saying a dirty word because I couldn't reach the key in my jeans without either putting a bag down or else risking scattering apples and lima beans across half the lot. Anyhow, just as I got up to the car, there was this good-looking guy – I mean, he looked way out of place in the Safeway lot – with his arm in a sling. I was concentrating on getting hold of my key, so I didn't pay much attention to what he was saying at first, but like I said, he was pretty cute, so I didn't ignore him completely. He wanted help getting the tire changed on his Volks, he said. Not much help, just having me jump up and down on the spider to loosen the nuts." Dixie grinned. "I thought I'd be a Girl Scout, so I went over a few steps, still with the bags in my arms, and sure enough, there was the VW. It was a metallic brown Beetle, but I couldn't see any flat tire. It was about then I heard my mom's voice telling me about talking to strangers, so I said to him there was a Texaco station with a mechanic just about four blocks down Willamette, and he should get some help there."

"That was it?" said Sonya. "He didn't try to grab you?"

"He was a perfect gentleman," said Dixie drily. "Didn't say another word. Just thanked me, turned around and started walking down the street. I got in my mom's car and left. That was that."

Then they asked Carol Anne for her story, but the young woman demurred. "I'm really tired." They looked at her. "I mean, I don't want to talk about any of this right now," she said. "I guess I'm having a little trouble just listening to what all of you are saying."

"So why are you here?" said Dixie.

"Give her a break," said Vicky quickly. She's just a kid. That's what she didn't say. It would just have triggered more questions. She made a sudden decision to get Carol Anne off the hook. "Anyway, I'm all psyched to play confessional."

"Okay," said Kate.

Dixie glanced at Carol Anne, then looked back to Vicky and nodded. "Then it's your turn."

"I was hitchhiking," said Vicky. "It was April 1975 and the school year was winding down." I just flunked out, she thought, and then wondered why she just didn't admit it. Maybe she did have a little pride left. "I was in Grand Junction, over on the western slope. I had the cash, but decided to catch a ride back to Denver just for the hell of it." For the adventure, she thought. Right. The adventure. Hanging around the club where they'd let her dance topless for tips.

"I waited a while out on the east edge of town. It was morning and there seemed to be a lot more people driving west into the Junction. Finally I got a ride. I think you know who picked me up."

Slow, serious nods from Kate and Sonya. Dixie's mouth twitched. Carol Anne just looked back soberly.

"He was the most charming man I'd ever met," said Vicky. And still is, she thought. "We drove for almost an hour before anything happened." She fell silent.

"So?" Dixie prompted.

"He pulled off on a dirt road. He said there was something wrong with the engine. It sounded like something you'd hear from some highschool jock taking the good girl in class out to lover's lane."

"And?" said Kate.

Vicky took a long breath. "He tried to rape me. He had a knife and some handcuffs. When he tried to force the cuffs on my wrist nearest him, I bit him hard on his hand. I was able to get the door open, and then I was out of there." It wasn't rape, she thought. It was mutual seduction. She'd never seen the knife, though the cuffs were real enough. But her moment of panic had come at the point of orgasm when his strong fingers had tightened around her throat. At that moment, she had . . . flinched. Chickened out, she sometimes told herself in the blackest of moods. At any rate, she had kicked free of the stranger. "I ran into the scrub trees where I knew he couldn't drive a car, and then I hid. After dark, I still waited until the moon rose and set, and then I walked back to the highway. I was lucky. The first car that stopped was a state trooper. I don't think I would have gotten in a car with anyone else that night."

Sonya and Dixie and Kate all nodded. Wisely. Then Dixie started to turn toward Carol Anne again.

Vicky said, "Sorry to break this up, but it's getting late and I'm exhausted. We'll all have the chance to talk tomorrow." She glanced pointedly at Carol Anne. The younger woman got the hint.

"I'm going to call it a night too," she said. "Tomorrow," she said to Dixie. "I promise."

The sisters from Utah decided to stay a while longer and finish their soda waters, though the ice was long since melted. Dixie headed for the elevator.

Carol Anne said to Vicky, "I want to get some fresh air before bed. There's a kind of mezzanine outside, up over the parking lot and the valley. You want to come along?"

Vicky hesitated, then nodded.

"What time is it?" said Carol Anne. They passed through the bar exit. The bartender locked the door behind them.

"I don't have a watch on," said Vicky.

"It's two-thirty," said a voice in the dimly lit hallway.

Vicky recoiled, then peered forward. "You," she said. "The guy who brought back my purse. Bobby."

"Bobby Cowell," he said. "At your service, ma'am." There was something in his tone that was not deferential at all. "Always at your service."

"Thanks again, Bobby," Vicky said. She realized Carol Anne had retreated a step.

"Did you count the cash?" said Bobby, stepping closer. He had a musky scent.

"I trust you," said Vicky. And she did. Sometimes she surprised herself.

Bobby must have realized that. He nodded slowly. "If there's anything I can do for you while you're here, anything at all . . ." The man's voice was carefully modulated, sincere.

"Thanks again." Vicky led Carol Anne past Bobby Cowell.

The man faded into the hallway. "I'd like to get to know you," he called low after them.

Vicky walked faster.

"I think he likes you," said Carol Anne.

"He's more your age," said Vicky. But she knew she did not completely mean that with sincerity. "Attractive guy." She had seen his type before. Oh, yes.

Carol Anne laughed. Vicky couldn't recall having heard her laugh aloud. "He looks like a Young Republican." She paused.

"And he probably drives a bronze VW." Carol Anne laughed again, but this time the sound was hollow. The two women stood against the railing overlooking the Platte Valley. Traffic below them on I-25 was minimal. To the south they could see the bright arc lamps of some sort of highway maintenance. Vicky could feel heat radiating from Carol Anne's side.

"You know, I keep wondering about something," said Carol Anne.

"What's that?" Vicky found her eyes attracted to the red aircraft warning lights blinking on the skyscrapers less than a mile away.

"This is really petty and my soul'll probably burn in hell just for thinking it."

"Let's hear it." Vicky's attention snapped back to the woman next to her.

"My dad told me once that he figured maybe a million people went to Woodstock."

"That may be a little exaggerated," said Vicky.

"No, I mean, a lot of people were so in love with the idea of having been there, but even if they didn't go, they *said* they did. Maybe they even *thought* they did."

"So are you talking about this event here?" said Vicky. "I think everybody here believes she went through whatever she went through." She suddenly started to feel the fatigue of the night for real. Her head was buzzing.

"I guess – well, okay," said Carol Anne.

"Let me suggest something even more troubling," said Vicky. In the darkness, she saw the pale oval of Carol Anne's face turn toward her. "You know about astronaut syndrome?"

"No," said Carol Anne, sounding puzzled.

"People used to go to the moon," said Vicky. "Men did, anyway. I read an article once, where they interviewed guys who walked on the moon. You know something, it was the biggest, most exciting, most important thing that ever happened to them."

"So?" said Carol Anne, apparently not getting the point.

"So they had to come back to earth. So they had to spend the rest of their lives doing things that were incredibly less exciting and important. Politics and selling insurance and writing books were nothing like walking on the moon."

Carol Anne was silent for a while. "So everyone here, I mean, all the women who came in for this gathering thing, they walked on the moon?"

"They all lived," said Vicky. "They survived. Nothing as exciting will ever happen to them again."

"What about you?" said Carol Anne. She clapped her hand over her mouth as if suddenly trying to stop the words.

"I fit the pattern," said Vicky, trying to smile and soften the words. "I've gone through a lot of men, a lot of jobs, a husband, more men, more dead-end jobs. Nothing so powerful has ever happened to me again." She thought, it sounds like a religious experience. *And maybe it is.*

Carol Anne issued something that sounded a little like a sigh, a little bit of a sob.

"Now," said Vicky. "What about you? You're too young for the moon. You know it and I know it. We've been talking about *them*. Now there's just me, and just you. And you've heard about me." Well, most of it, she thought.

Carol Anne reached out blindly and took Vicky's hand. She held it tightly. She seemed to be trying to say something. It wasn't working.

"Calm down," said Vicky. "It's all right. She took the younger woman in her arms. "It's all right," she repeated.

"I never knew him," said Carol Anne, her words muffled against Vicky's shoulder. "Not directly. But I think he killed my mother." She started to cry. Vicky rocked her gently, let her work it out.

"We don't know for sure," Carol Anne said finally. "My dad and I, we just don't know. They never found any remains. I was five back in 1975. My mom was really young when she had me. You know something? My birthday is January 24. And for nineteen years I didn't know what the significance was going to be. In 1989 on my birthday, I only got one present. The execution." She smiled mirthlessly. "Before that. 1975. It was earlier in the winter than when you got away from him. We lived in Vail. We found my mom's car in the public parking lot. It was unlocked and the police said later someone had pulled the coil wire. They said there was no sign of violence. She just vanished. We never saw her again." Carol Anne started again to cry. "She didn't run away, like some people said. He got her. And there are no remains."

After a while, Vicky pulled a clean tissue from her purse. "So why are you here?"

There was a very long silence, after which Carol Anne blew her nose noisily. "I thought maybe something someone might say would give me a clue. About my mother. I've read everything. I've seen all the tapes. Over and over. I just want to know, more than anything else, what happened."

No, thought Vicky, I don't think you do. She knew what would happen when she said it, but she said it anyway. "Your mother's dead, Carol Anne. I'm sorry. I'm very sorry. But you know it."

Carol Anne sobbed for a very long time. She took a fresh tissue from Vicky. "I know it. I know that. I just want to know more. How it happened. Who — "

"It's enough to accept that she's gone," said Vicky. "Maybe someday you'll find out more." She hesitated. "I hope you do."

"I'm 22," said Carol Anne. "My whole life's revolved around this for seventeen years."

"Do you have . . . someone?"

"My father died five years ago. I don't have a boyfriend if that's what you mean." Her voice was mournful. "I guess I don't have much of a life at all."

I'm glad you said it, Vicky thought. "You will," she said aloud. "But you've got to leave all this old baggage. You can't forget it, but you can allow it to fade. Your dues are paid. Believe it." Just say good-bye, she thought. Good night for good, and make it stick. She reached out again for Carol Anne's hand. And then she packed the young woman off to bed. At the door of Carol Anne's room, Vicky said, "I'll see you in the morning. Try to get some sleep."

Carol Anne looked like she was trying to smile bravely. Then she shut the door. Vicky heard the chain lock rattle into place.

Her own room was down a floor and at the opposite end of the wing. The windows overlooked the parking lot. If she craned her neck, Vicky could see the downtown office towers with their cycling crimson aircraft beacons.

She didn't turn on the lights when she entered the room. Vicky lay down on the bed still dressed, the purse and briefcase nestled up against her like kittens. She stared up into the darkness as though she could still see stars. The bright, winking stars of western slope Colorado. The star patterns of 1975. She wondered if she went to the window and looked down, whether she would see moonlight glinting off the shell-like curve of a hunched VW. Bobby's VW? There was something about his name that tickled at the edge of her attention, something she couldn't quite remember.

She found her fingers, as though of their own volition, opening the briefcase and taking out the tightly bound Barbie doll. Vicky couldn't see it, but she could feel the taut loops of monofilament cutting into the vinyl dollflesh. She clutched the talisman and smiled invisibly.

Some men, Vicky thought, would only send flowers.

But then, as the darkness seeped through every pore, every orifice of her body, filling her with night and grief, she thought of Carol Anne and began to cry. Vicky had not cried in all too long. Not in seventeen years, to be exact.

Seventeen years without a life. Seventeen years looking.

At least, she thought, Carol Anne is young. She can go away from this weekend and re-create her life. She doesn't have to be empty.

And what about me? Vicky thought, before clamping down savagely on self-pity.

What, indeed. Seventeen years before. It was perhaps the next-to-biggest event of her life. The most important was still to come. Perhaps. It had been on its way since 1975. And had been derailed in January 1989. No, that's not it either, she thought, feeling the long-time confusion. All I want is to walk on the moon again.

Vicky cried herself to sleep.

She knew she was dreaming, but that did not diminish the effects.

She still lay in her bed, but now it was larger than she could envision and softer than she could hope. She lay bound tightly, so tightly she could not move.

But the thing about helplessness was, she no longer had to take responsibility for anything at all. Almost cocooned in monofilament, she could feel the line cut into her skin, deep into her flesh, thin incisions of pain that burned like lasers.

The pain, she realized, was a mercy compared to the years of numbness. The bindings that restrained her body also retained her heat, and now that heat built and built and suffused her from the core of her flesh to the outer layers of skin.

Blood ran from the corner of her mouth, where the line dug so tight, she could not extend her tongue to lick it away. But some ran back inside anyway. Her blood was warm and slick and salty.

She moaned and moved as best she could inside her bonds. It was almost enough.

Vicky awoke confused, staring in disorientation at the bedside clock. She guessed it was still an hour before dawn. She had not slept for long. But she wanted to stretch, and so she did so. Her body felt alive. More, it felt . . . she searched for an apt word . . . hopeful.

Then she turned her head and recoiled back against the pillow. Bobby Cowell stood at the foot of her bed. His left hand swung back and forth slowly. Something metallic glittered. A pass-key. Vicky tried to speak.

He had been watching her sleep.

He had watched her dream.

"There's just something about you," he said softly. He smiled in the dim light, teeth showing white.

There was no conscious planning. She swung her legs off the bed, hearing the briefcase slide to the carpet, then sat up and took a deep breath or two to counter the sudden vertigo. After a few seconds, she got up and hesitated.

She could lunge for the phone. Or the door. She saw no weapon in evidence other than the key.

"I know who you are," said Bobby. "I know everything you want." He stepped back away from the door. She could flee.

"What do *you* want?" Vicky said.

"To take you for a ride. It's still a beautiful night. We'll go up into the mountains."

It was so much like a dream. She didn't remember to bring a coat, but the late, late night didn't seem to be all that cold, so it didn't matter.

At the bottom of the fire-stairwell, she waited for him. "I figured you'd come," he said softly, taking her arm.

"I will," said Vicky. Was she still sleeping? All in motion only slightly slower than reality.

They exited the stairwell. "I have my car out in the lot," said Bobby.

Vicky nodded and put her free hand over his fingers on her arm. "I figured that," she said. His fingers were warm. The excitement inside her was cold. She looked up and saw the distant, sinking moon.

They passed the mezzanine and turned toward the steps leading down to the parking lot. Vicky, hesitated a split second, stared back over Bobby's shoulder, hesitated a little longer.

At the other end of the platform, Carol Anne stood, leaned away from the city, staring back at them. Her expression altered mercurially. Vicky didn't think Bobby had seen Carol Anne watching them. Maybe she'd see Carol Anne in the morning. Maybe not.

"Come on," said Vicky, turning back to the steps. And at the beginning of the final descent to the outside world, she thought about the last enigmatic expression on Carol Anne's face. Wistful?

She hoped – wished desperately – it was only that.

NICHOLAS ROYLE

Flying into Naples

IT'S BEEN ANOTHER successful year for Nicholas Royle: along with appearances in all three 'Year's Best' horror volumes, his stories have been published in such anthologies as *The Mammoth Book of Werewolves*, *The Mammoth Book of Zombies*, *Dark Voices 5 and 6*, *The Anthology of Fantasy & the Supernatural*, *Little Deaths* and *Shadows Over Innsmouth*, amongst others. His anthologies *Darklands* and *Darklands 2* have been reprinted in the UK by New English Library, and he has sold his first two novels, *Counterparts* and *Saxophone Dreams* to Penguin Books. He also won British Fantasy Awards in 1993 for *Darklands 2* and his story "Night Shift Sister" (which we published in *Best New Horror 4*).

About the following story, the author explains: "I was considering making the trip to Naples by car, in which case it might have been 'Driving into Naples', which would have been a completely different story and, to judge from the standard of driving in the city, I wouldn't have lived to tell the tale.

"The young woman who formed part of the inspiration for the character of Flavia said she hoped I would write more stories based on her. I told her that would require additional research . . ."

F LYING INTO NAPLES the 737 hits some turbulence and gets thrown about a bit. It's dark outside but I can't even see any lights on the ground. I'm a nervous flyer anyway and this doesn't make me feel any better. It's taking off and landing that bother me.

But when we're down and I'm crossing the tarmac to the airport buildings there's a warm humid stillness in the air that makes me wonder about the turbulence. I wander through passport control and customs like someone in a dream. The officials seem covered in a fine layer of dust as if they've been standing there for years just waiting.

No one speaks to me and I get on the bus marked "Centro Napoli." I'm on holiday. All I've got in Naples is a name, a photograph and a wrong number. The name is a woman's – Flavia – and the photograph is of the view from her apartment. The phone number I tried last week to say I was coming turned out to belong to someone else entirely.

I've worked out from the photograph and my map that the apartment is on a hill on the west side of the city. There's not much more to go on. It's too late to go and look for it tonight. Flavia won't be expecting me – beyond occasional vague invitations nothing has been arranged – and she could take a long time to locate.

I knew her years ago when she visited London and stayed in the hotel where I was working the bar. We knew each other briefly – a holiday romance, if you like – but something ensured I would not forget her. Whether it was the sunrise we saw together or the shock of her body in the quiet shadow of my room over the kitchens, or a combination of these and other factors – her smile, my particular vulnerability, her tumbling curls – I don't know, but something fixed her in my mind. So when I found myself with a week's holiday at the end of three difficult months in a new, stressful job. I dug out her letters – two or three only over eight years, including this recent photograph of the view from her apartment – and booked a last-minute flight to Naples.

I'd never been there though I'd heard so much about it – how violent and dangerous it could be for foreigners, yet how beautiful – and I would enjoy the effort required to get along in Italian.

I'm alone on the bus apart from one other man – a local who spends the 20-minute ride talking on a cellphone to his mistress in Rome – and the taciturn driver. I've come before the start of the season, but it's already warm enough not to need my linen jacket.

I'm divorced. I don't know about Flavia. She never mentioned anybody, just as she never revealed her address when she wrote to me. I've been divorced two years and a period of contented bachelorhood has only recently come to a natural end, and with the arrival of spring in London I have found myself watching women once again: following a hemline through the human traffic of Kensington, turning to see the face of a woman in Green Park whose hair looked so striking from behind. It may be spring in Berkeley Square but it feels like midsummer in Naples. The air is still and hot and humid when I leave the bus at the main railway station and begin walking into the centre of the city in search of a cheap hotel. I imagine I'm probably quite conspicuous in what must be one of the most dangerous areas but the hotels in the immediate vicinity – the pavement outside the Europa is clogged with upturned rubbish bins; the tall, dark, narrow Esedra looks as if it's about to topple sideways – look unwelcoming so I press on. It's late, after 10.30pm, and even the bars and restaurants are closed. Youths buzz past on Vespas and Piaggios unhelmeted despite the apparent dedication of the motorists here to the legend "live fast, die young." I hold my bag close and try to look confident but after 15 minutes or so the hotels have disappeared. I reach a large empty square and head deeper into the city. I ask a gun-holstered security guard if there is a pension in the neighbourhood but he shrugs and walks away. I climb a street that has lights burning but they turn out to be a latenight bar and a fruit stand. Two boys call to me from a doorway and as I don't understand I just carry on, but at the top is a barrier and beyond that a private apartment complex, so I have to turn back and the two boys are laughing as I walk past them.

I try in another direction but there are only banks and food stores, all locked up. Soon I realize I'm going to have to go back down to the area round the railway station. I cross the road to avoid the prostitutes on the corner of Via Seggio del Popolo, not because of any spurious moral judgment but just because it seems I should go out of my way to avoid trouble, so easy is it innocently to court disaster in a foreign country. But in crossing the road I walk into a problem. There's a young woman standing in a doorway whom in the darkness I had failed to see. She moves swiftly out of the doorway into my path and I gasp in surprise. The streetlamp throws the dark bruises around her eyes into even deeper perspective. Her eyes are sunken, almost lost in her skull, and under her chin are the dark tough bristles of a juvenile beard. She speaks quickly, demanding something and before I've collected my wits she's produced a glittering blade from her jacket pocket which she thrusts towards me like a torch at an animal. I react too slowly and feel a sudden hot scratch on my bare arm.

My jacket's over my other arm so I'm lucky that I don't drop it and give the woman the chance to strike again. She lunges but I'm away down the street running for my life. When it's clear she's not chasing me I stop for breath. One or two passers-by look at me with mild curiosity. I head back in the direction of the railway station. Down a side street on my right I recognize one of the hotels I saw earlier – the Esedra. Then I hadn't liked the look of it, but now it's my haven from the streets. I approach the glass doors and hesitate when I realize there are several men in the lobby. But the thought of the drugged-up woman makes me go on. So I push open the door and the men look up from their card game. I'm about to ask for a room when one of the men, who's had a good long look at me, says something to the man behind the little counter and this man reaches for a key from room 17's pigeon hole. I realize what's happening – they've mistaken me for someone who's already a guest – and there was a time when I would have been tempted to accept the key in the desire to save money, but these days I'm not short of cash. So, I hesitate only for a moment before saying that I'm looking for a room. The man is momentarily confused but gets me another key – room 19 – from a hook and quotes a price. It's cheap; the hotel is probably a haunt of prostitutes but right now I don't care. I just need a bed for the night.

"It's on the third floor," the man says. I pay him and walk up. There are lightbulbs but they're so heavily shaded the stairs are darker than the street outside. On each landing there are four doors: three bedrooms and one toilet cum shower. I unlock the door to room 19 and close it behind me.

I have a routine with hotel rooms: I lock myself in and switch on all the lights and open all the cupboards and drawers until I feel I know the room as well as I can. And I always check the window.

There are two single beds, some sticks of furniture, a bidet and a washbasin – I open the cold tap and clean up the scratch on my arm. The window is shuttered. I pull on the cord to raise the shutter. I'm overlooking the Corso Uberto I which runs up to the railway station. I step on to the tiny balcony and my hands get covered in dust from the wrought-iron railing. The cars in the street below are filmed with dust also. The winds blow sand here from the deserts of North Africa and it falls with the rain. I pull a chair on to the balcony and sit for a while thinking about Flavia. Somewhere in this city she's sitting watching television or eating in a restaurant and she doesn't know I'm here. Tomorrow I will try to find her.

I watch the road and I'm glad I'm no longer out there looking for shelter. Small knots of young men unravel on street corners and cross streets that don't need crossing. After a while I start to feel an uncomfortable solidity creeping into my limbs, so I take the chair back inside and drop the shutter. I'd prefer to leave it open but the open window might look like an invitation.

I'm lying in bed hoping that sleep will come but there's a scuttling rustling noise keeping me awake. It's coming from the far side of the room near the washbasin and the framed print of the ancient city of Pompeii. It sounds like an insect, probably a cockroach. I'm not alarmed. I've shared hotel rooms with pests before, but I want to go to sleep. There's no use left in this day and I'm eager for the next one to begin.

Something else is bothering me: I want to go and try the door to room 17 and see why the proprietor was about to give me that key. The scratching noise is getting louder and although I can't fall asleep I'm getting more and more tired so that I start to imagine the insect. It's behind the picture where it's scratched out its own little hole and it's lying in wait for me to go and lift the picture aside and it will come at me slow and deadly, like a Lancaster bomber. The noise works deeper into my head. The thing must have huge wings and antennae. Scratch . . . scratch . . . scratch. I can't stand it any more. I get up, pull on my trousers and leave the room.

The stairs are completely dark. I feel my way to the next landing and switch on the light in the WC to allow me to see the numbers on the doors. I push open the door to room 17, feeling a layer of dust beneath my fingertips, and it swings open. The chinks in the shutter admit enough light to paint a faint picture of a man lying on the bed who looks not unlike me. I step into the room and feel grit on the floor under my feet. As I step closer the man on the bed turns to look at me. His lips move slowly.

"I came straight here," he says, "instead of walking into the city to find something better."

I don't know what to say. Pulling up a chair I sit next to him.

"I found her," he continues. "She lives above the city on the west side. You can see Vesuvius from her window."

I grip his cold hand and try to read the expression on his face. But it's blank. The words rustle in his mouth like dry leaves caught between stones.

"She's not interested. Watch out for Vesuvius." he whispers, then falls silent. I sit there for a while watching his grey face for any sign of life but there's nothing. Feeling an unbearable sadness for which I can't reasonably account I return to my room and lie flat on my back on the little bed.

The unknown insect is still busy scratching behind the ruins of Pompeii.

I wake up to heavy traffic under my window, my head still thick with dreams. On my way downstairs I pause on the landing opposite room 17 and feel a tug. But I know the easiest thing is not to think too much about it and just carry on downstairs, hand in the key and leave the hotel for good. Even if I don't manage to locate Flavia I won't come back here. I'll find something better.

I walk across the city, stopping at a little bar for a cappuccino and a croissant. The air smells of coffee, cigarettes and laundry. Strings of clothes are hung out in the narrow passages like bunting. Moped riders duck their heads to avoid vests and socks as they bounce over the cobbles. Cars negotiate alleys barely wide enough to walk down, drivers jabbing at the horn to clear the way. Pedestrians step aside unhurriedly and there are no arguments or remonstrations.

The sun is beating down but there's a haze like sheer nylon stretched above the rooftops – dust in the air. I'm just heading west and climbing through distinct areas. The class differences show up clearly in the homes – the *bassi*, tiny rooms that open directly on to the street, and higher up the huge apartment blocks with their own gate and security – and in the shops and the goods sold in them. Only the dust is spread evenly.

As soon as I'm high enough to see Vesuvius behind me I take

out the photograph and use it to direct my search, heading always west.

It takes a couple of hours to cross the city and locate the right street. I make sure it's the right view before starting to read the names on the bell-pushes. The building has to be on the left-hand side of the road because those on the right aren't high enough to have a view over those on the left. I still don't know if I'm going to find the name or not. Through the gaps between the buildings I can see Vesuvius on the other side of the bay. By looking ahead I'm even able to estimate the exact building, and it turns out I'm right. There's the name – F. Sannia – among a dozen others. I press the bell without thinking about it.

When Flavia comes to open the door I'm surprised. Perhaps it's more her place to be surprised than mine but she stands there with a vacant expression on her face. What a face, though, what extraordinary beauty. She was good looking when we first met, of course, but in the intervening years she has grown into a stunning woman. I fear to lean forward and kiss her cheeks lest she crumbles beneath my touch. But the look is blank. I don't know if she recognizes me. I say her name then my own and I must assume her acquiescence – as she turns back into the hall and hesitates momentarily – to be an invitation. So I follow her. She walks slowly but with the same lightness of step that I remember from before.

As I follow her into the apartment I'm drawn immediately to the far side of the main room where there's a balcony with a spectacular view over the Bay of Naples and, right in the centre at the back, Mount Vesuvius. Unaware of where Flavia has disappeared to, I stand there watching the view for some minutes. Naples is built on hills and one of them rises from the sea to dominate the left middle ground, stepped with huge crumbling apartment buildings and sliced up by tapering streets and alleys that dig deeper the narrower they become. The whole city hums like a hive and cars and scooters buzz about like drones. But the main attraction is Vesuvius. What a place to build a city: in the shadow of a volcano.

It's a while before I realize Flavia has returned and is standing behind me as I admire the view.

"What do you want to do while you are in Naples?" she asks with a level voice. "You'll stay here, of course."

"You're very kind. I meant to give you some notice but I don't think I had the right phone number." I show her the number in my book.

"I changed it," she says as she sits in one of the wicker chairs and indicates for me to do the same. "I've been widowed six times," she says and then falls silent. "It's easier."

I don't know what to say. I think she must have intended to say something else – made a mistake with her English – although she seems so grey and lifeless herself that the statement may well have been true.

We sit on her balcony for half an hour looking out over the city and the volcano on the far side of the bay, during which time I formulate several lines with which to start a fresh conversation but each one remains unspoken. Something in her passivity frightens me. It seems at odds with the élan of the city in which she lives.

But Flavia speaks first. "With this view," she says slowly, "it is impossible not to watch the volcano, to become obsessed by it."

I nod.

"My father was alive when it last erupted," she continues, "in 1944. Now Vesuvius is dormant. Do you want to see Naples?" she asks, turning towards me.

"Yes, very much."

We leave the apartment and Flavia leads the way to a beaten-up old Fiat Uno. Her driving is a revelation: once in the car and negotiating the hairpin, double-parked roads leading downtown Flavia is a completely different woman. Here is the lively, passionate girl I knew in London. She takes on other drivers with the determination and verve she showed in my room overlooking the hotel car park when we took it in turns to sit astride each other. She rode me then as she now drives the Fiat, throwing it into 180-degree corners and touching her foot to the floor on the straights. She's not wearing her seat belt; I unclip mine, wind down my window and put my foot up on the plastic moulding in front of me. At one point – when I draw my elbow into the car quickly to avoid a bus coming up on the other side of the road – Flavia turns her head and smiles at me just as she did eight years earlier before falling asleep.

We skid into a parking place and Flavia attacks the handbrake. Once out of the car she's quiet again, gliding along beside me. "Where are we going?" I ask her. Beyond the city the summit of Vesuvius is draped in thick grey cloud. Out over the sea on our right a heavy wedge of darkest grey thunderheads is making its way landwards trailing skirts of rain. In the space of two minutes the island of Capri is rubbed out as the storm passes over it and into the bay.

"She must want to be alone," Flavia says and, when I look puzzled, continues: "They say that you can see a woman reclining in the outline of the island."

But Capri is lost behind layers of grey veils now and just as Flavia finishes speaking the first drops of rain explode on my bare arms. Within seconds we are soaked by a downpour of big fat sweet-smelling summer rain. My thin shirt is plastered to my back. The rain runs off Flavia's still body in trickles. She seems impervious to the cleansing, refreshing effect that I'm enjoying. Dripping wet with rain bouncing off my forehead, I give her a smile but her expression doesn't change. "Shall we walk?" I suggest, eyeing some trees in the distance that would give us some shelter. She just turns and starts walking without a word so I follow. The trees – which I realize I have seen previously from Flavia's balcony – conceal the city aquarium, housed in the lower ground floor of a heavy stone building. I pay for two tickets and we pass in front of a succession of gloomy windows on to another world. It's so damp down there I feel almost as if we've entered the element of the fishes. My shirt clings to my back, getting no drier under the dim lights. Flavia's white blouse is stuck to her shoulders but there's no tremor of life as far as I can see. She stares unseeing at the fish, the sinister skate and lugubrious octopus which regard us with an expression I feel but can't put a name to. Because I'm beginning to feel quite anxious I hurry past the shrimps and seahorses – which I see only as a blur of commas and question marks – and I'm relieved to get back into the open air.

Flavia takes me to a restaurant she knows and I eat cousins of the creatures we've just seen in the aquarium. Flavia orders mineral water and oysters but then hardly touches them. My teeth grind on tiny particles of grit or shell in my sauce but I don't say anything because it seems to be a city-wide problem. The waiter's black patent leather shoes are matt with a fine layer of dust.

I watch Flavia as I eat and she stares out of the window at the teeming rain. When she moves it's with an incredible slowness that sets up a tension in me. Her stillness makes me want to protect her. She must have suffered so much, like a tree that's been buffeted by so many storms it's been stripped of leaves and twigs, but still stands, proud and defiant. I want to reach across and touch her cheek in the hope she might soften and smile, but such a deliberate act seems reckless. The worst thing would be if she remained indifferent to my advance.

As I continue eating, however, I'm filled with desire for her. I want to take her to bed and hold her and stroke away the years with her thin layers of clothing.

The feeling grows throughout what remains of the day. We go to a couple of basement piano bars and a club where crowds of strikingly beautiful people spill out on to the street. The atmosphere of intoxication and sexual excitement does nothing to spark Flavia into life. She simply trails her fingers through the dust which seems to coat the tables in every bar we go in.

Only in the car does she come alive as we race from one venue to another, bouncing down noisy cobbled escape routes and diving into alleys thin as crevices. The car's headlamps startle cats and in one hidden piazza a huddle of unshaven men emerging from a flyposted door. "This is a dangerous quarter," she says, pointing at streets I remember from my first night. "Camorro. Our Mafia. They kill you here as soon as look at you."

Way past midnight we end up in a park above the city on the same side as Flavia's apartment but further round the bay. "This newspaper," she indicates piles of discarded newsprint lining the side of the road. "People come here in their cars and put the newspaper up to cover the windows. Then they make love."

I look at the vast drifts of newspaper as we drive slowly around the perimeter of the park. "Why?" I ask. "Because they live at home? It's their only chance?"

She shrugs. "They do it in the cars then throw the newspaper out of the window."

"And what a view they have," I say, looking across the bay at the brooding shadow of Vesuvius.

Back home again she retreats inside her shell. The sudden change throws me. I want to touch her, sleep with her, but suddenly it's as if we're complete strangers. She sits on the balcony staring at Vesuvius and I bring her a drink. As I put it down I place my other hand on her arm and give it a brief squeeze. She doesn't react so I pull one of the wicker chairs round to face hers and sit in the darkness just watching her watch the volcano. The moon paints her face with a pale wash. I can see the shape of her breasts under the white blouse and as I concentrate I can see the merest lift as she breathes. Otherwise I might have doubted she was still alive. "Do you want to go to bed?" I ask.

She just looks at me. Inside me the tension is reaching bursting point. When Flavia gets up and walks to her bedroom I follow. She undresses in front of me. The moonlight makes her flesh look grey and very still. I undress and lie beside her. She doesn't push me away but neither does she encourage me in any way.

When I wake in the morning she's gone. The pillow on her side is still indented and warm to the touch. I wish I'd done something the night before but her terrible passivity killed my desire. A night's sleep, however, has returned it to me. If she were here now I'd force her to decide, whether to accept or reject me, either being preferable to indifference.

I get dressed and step out on to the balcony. The top of Vesuvius is covered with cloud. The air over the city is hazy. On the little table there's a note for me from Flavia. She's had to go out for the day and can I entertain myself? I'm to help myself to whatever I want. She suggests I visit Pompeii.

The Circumvesuviana railway trundles out of the east side of Naples and skirts the volcano, calling at St Giorgio and Ercolano, the sun beating down on the crumbling white apartment buildings. I avoid the modern town at Pompeii and head straight for the excavations. German tourists haggle over the entrance fee, I pay and go through, detaching myself from the crowd as soon as I can. They saunter off down the prescribed route armed with guide books from which their self-elected leader will read out loud, peculiarly choosing the English-language section, as they pass by the monuments of particular note. The same man – he's wearing a red shirt which bulges over the waistband of his creamy linen trousers – carries the camcorder and will listen impassively to anyone who suggests they operate it instead. They're a distraction from my surroundings: a city preserved to a far greater degree than anything I had been expecting. I wander off into an area of recent excavations where I'm alone with the buzzing insects and basking lizards that dart away at my approach. The heat is overpowering and after a quarter of an hour threading my way through dug-out paved streets bordered with shoulder-high walls and great swathes of overflowing undergrowth I have to sit down for a rest. I look up at Vesuvius, a huge black shape jiggling from side to side behind the thickening haze.

A bee the size of a fat cockroach lumbers towards me buzzing like a whole canful of blowflies and I have to duck to avoid it. Even when it's gone I can still hear it, as if it hadn't managed to get out of the way quick enough and somehow it got inside my head. The sun, even through the dust in the air, amplifies the noise and cooks my skull so that everything inside it rattles like loose beans. Off down a long straight street to my right I recognize the party of German tourists standing to attention as they listen to the man in the red shirt with the stomach, the camcorder and the guide book. His words are just a low hum to me amid the constant buzz in my ears. My limbs tingle as if electricity is being passed through them, then they go completely numb and the buzzing gets slower and even louder. At the far end of the long straight street the Germans have frozen in position. The man in the red shirt is in the act of raising the camcorder to his eye, a woman in a wraparound top and shorts is caught in the act of leaning backwards – not ungracefully – to correct the fit of her smart training shoe. The air between them and me is thick with shiny dust, glittering in the golden sunshine. The tiny particles are dancing but the figures remain petrified.

Suddenly they're moving but in a group rather than individually. They are shifted silently to one side like a collection of statues on an invisible moving platform. It's as if they're being shunted into another world while I'm left dodging the insects in this one and I want to go with them. Maybe wherever they're going there won't be this terrible grinding noise which is giving the inside of my skull such a relentless battering.

By the time some feeling returns to my arms and legs the German tourists have completely disappeared. I stumble over the huge baking slabs, trying to escape the punishment. Pursuing the merest hint of a decrease in the noise level I turn in through an old stone doorway and begin a desperate chase after silence: over boulders, through tangles of nettles and vines where enormous butterflies make sluggish progress through the haze. As the pain levels out and then begins to abate I know I'm heading in the right direction. A couple more sharp turns past huge grass-covered mounds and collapsed walls where lizards the size of rats gulp at the gritty air; the noise fades right down, the pain ebbs and warm molten peaceful brassy sun flows into my bruised head. I fall to my knees with my hands covering my face and when I take them away I'm looking directly into the empty grey eyesockets of a petrified man. His face is contorted by the pain he felt as the lava flowed over him. I'm screaming because the man looks so much like me it's like looking in a mirror and a lizard suddenly flits out of one of the eyes and slips into the gaping mouth. The pain is back and this time it doesn't go away until I black out.

I'm out for hours because when I come to, rubbing my forehead, the sun casts quite different shadows on the stony face. Dismayingly I have to admit he still looks like me. For several minutes I sit and watch the insects that use his cavities and passages as they would any similar rock formation.

Later I tell Flavia how closely his volcanic features resembled mine.

"It's quite common to hallucinate after an eruption," she says, applying a piece of sticky tape to the newspaper covering the driver's window.

That's all very well, I think, but I'm 2000 years too late. Or did she mean him? But I don't want to dwell on it because the faster the newspaper goes up the sooner I can have her.

It clicked with me that I could make the most of Flavia's carbound vivacity so that her passivity at home would not matter as much.

Through a narrow gap at the top of the windscreen I can see Vesuvius rising and falling as Flavia and I punish the old Fiat's suspension.

In a few hours' time I'll be climbing Vesuvius herself. Flavia's away somewhere – working, she said – so I'm to tackle the volcano alone and although I could have taken a cab to the tourist car park halfway up the mountain I decided to walk all the way from Ercolano which, as Herculaneum, was itself covered by the same lava flows that buried Pompeii. The road folds over on itself as I climb. The routine is soon automatic as I maintain a regular ascent and efficient breathing. My mind is rerunning the night before in Flavia's car. Six times her emotions reached bursting point and boiled over. In the early hours the air in the car was so thick and cloying we had to wind down the window, which meant losing part of our newsprint screen, but the park had emptied hours before.

In her apartment, where I swallowed glass after glass of fresh orange juice, Flavia was once more still and grey. I was thinking about getting her out in the car again but I knew I had to climb the volcano before I left: it had been calling me and this was my last day in the city.

If the air were not so thick with dust, the view from halfway up the mountain would be spectacular. I can just make out a darker shadow which is the centre of Naples and a thin line separating the land from the sea. Only the island of Capri is clear in the distance but its profile is still no more like a woman than the trembling slope beneath my feet. Down here there are trees either side of the road but I can see that higher up the ground is bare. The sun still manages to break through the thickening air and once caught between the ground and the dust the heat cannot escape. I've taken off my shirt and tied it around my neck to soak up some of the sweat. The mountain seems to get no smaller even though I know I'm climbing. The road hugs the side and disappears some way round the back before twisting back on itself to reach the car park and refreshment stand. I have the sense, the higher I get, of the volcano as an egg, its exterior thin and brittle and cracked open at the top. I stop for breath, lean back and stretch. The summit and crater are covered by cloud.

Beyond the empty car park the narrow path zig-zags into the clouds. I climb with the same sense of purpose that took hold of Flavia and me in the car and I sense that the prize is not so far removed from that sweet and fiery memory which even now stirs me. The earth and trees have been left behind and the slate-grey cloud thickens about me like hospital blankets. The mountain is loose cinders and disintegrated volcanic material, a uniform grey-brown, like a dying horse in a burnt field. I'm suddenly engulfed by a wave of sympathy for Flavia and the years of suffering. They have turned her into a brittle shell, but life lingers within her, a dormant energy that last night we fired up. She deserves longer-lasting happiness and yet I know she wouldn't even flicker in some other city; Naples is her only home. Some things are rooted too deeply in the earth to shift.

Never in my life have I felt so alone as I feel now, wrapped in cloud, buffeted by sea winds, following a path to a crater. I can't see more than ten barren yards in any direction.

When I hear the music I think I've died or am still asleep in Flavia's bed and dreaming. Soft notes that gather a little power then fade quickly as the wind blows new ones slightly up or down the scale. I've already called Flavia's name three times before I realize I'm doing it. The name is taken from my lips and wrapped in this soiled cotton wool that surrounds me. Her name rolls on with the cloud over the top of the mountain where the crater must be. It mustn't fall in.

The source of the music comes into view – an abandoned shack supported by an exoskeleton of tubular steel shafts. The wind plays them like panpipes. A sign still attached to the side of the shack advertises the sale of tickets to the crater. I begin to laugh at the absurdity of such an idea and wade on past the chiming tubes and up towards the edge. I know it's up there somewhere although I can't see it and I stumble blindly onwards, scuffing my shoes in coarse, loose material. Then suddenly the ground disappears beneath my feet and I'm clawing at space for a handhold. Somehow I manage to fall back rather than forward and I crouch in the harsh volcanic rubble peering over the edge of the crater. Below me the cloud twists in draughts of warm air. I'm muttering Flavia's name to myself and thinking I should never have gone to look for her. Then I'm thinking maybe I never did go, but stayed in the insect-ridden hotel instead.

As I watch the updraughts of ash and dust I see a recognizable group of shapes take vague form in the clouds. The German tourists – he with the red shirt, the camcorder, the stomach, she of the shorts and smart training shoes, still frozen as an exhibit of statuary – descend through the rising dust as if on a platform. The thicker swirls beneath me envelop them.

They pass into the throat of the giant and are followed by a facsimile of Flavia, falling like a slow bomb. A cast of myself – whether from Pompeii or the hotel, I don't know – is next, slipping in and out of focus behind curtains of clogging ash.

The last thing I remember is the buffeting and turbulence the 737 went through as it passed over Vesuvius on its descent into Naples, and suddenly the whole crazy city with its strange visions and coating of fine dust – from a waiter's shoes to the air rattling in lungs – makes perfect sense.

POPPY Z. BRITE

The Sixth Sentinel

POPPY Z. BRITE has lived all over the American South and has worked as a gourmet candy maker, an artist's model, a cook, a mouse caretaker and an exotic dancer. She currently lives in New Orleans with two cats and two boyfriends.

After publishing a number of acclaimed stories in various small press magazines and anthologies, her debut novel *Lost Souls* appeared in 1992. It became a Book-of-the-Month Club alternate selection and was nominated for a Lambda Award for outstanding gay fiction and a Horror Writers of America Bram Stoker Award for first novel.

Her second novel, *Drawing Blood*, was published in 1993, as was a collection of short stories, *Swamp Foetus*. She has also edited *Love in Vein*, an anthology of erotic vampire stories, and a third novel, *Exquisite Corpse*, is forthcoming.

"Some readers may not be familiar with the famous pirate and privateer Jean Lafitte," explains the author, "who is of course the narrator of this tale. In the mid-nineteenth century, Lafitte ruled the bayou country of south Louisiana. He and his band would rob ships in the Gulf of Mexico, escape into the swamps, then fence the stolen goods in New Orleans. His 'legitimate' cover business, Lafitte's Blacksmith Shop, was located in a ramshackle old building just around the corner from my house. It is now the darkest bar in the French Quarter, and one of the quirkiest."

The writer also adds that she considers the following story as a kind of companion piece to "His Mouth Will Taste of Wormwood", which appeared in *Best New Horror 2*.

I FIRST KNEW Hard Luck Rosalie Smith when she was a thin frayed rope of a child, twenty years old and already well acquainted with the solitude at the bottom of a whiskey bottle. Her hair was brittle from too many dye jobs, bright red last week, black as the grave today, purple and green for Mardi Gras. Her face was fine-boned and faintly feral, the eyes carefully lined in black, the rouged lips stretched tight over the sharp little teeth. If I had been able to touch Rosalie, her skin would have felt silky and faintly dry, her hair would have been like electricity brushing my face in the dark.

But I could not touch Rosalie, not so that she would notice. I could pass my fingers through the meat of her arm, pale as veal and packed like flaky fish flesh between her thin bones. I could wrap my hand around the smooth porcelain ball of her wrist. But as far as she was concerned, my touch went through her like so much dead air. All she could feel of me was a chill like ice crystallizing along her spine.

"Your liver has the texture of hot, wet velvet," I would tell her, reaching through her ribs to caress the tortured organ.

She'd shrug. "Another year in this town and it'll be pickled."

Rosalie came to the city of New Orleans because it was as far south as her money would take her – or so she said. She was escaping from a lover she would shudderingly refer to only as Joe Coffeespoon. The memory of his touch made her feel cold, far colder than my ectoplasmic fingers ever could, and she longed for the wet kiss of tropical nights.

She moved into an apartment in one of the oldest buildings in the French Quarter, above a "shoppe" that sold potions and philtres. At first I wondered whether she would be pleased to find a ghost already residing in her cramped quarters, but as I watched her decorate the walls with shrouds of black lace and photographs of androgynous sunken-cheeked musicians who looked more dead than alive, I began to realize I could show myself safely, without threat of eviction. It is always a nuisance when someone calls in the exorcist. The priest himself is no threat, but the demons that invariably follow him are large as cats and annoying as mosquitoes. It is these, not the intonations and holy water, that drive innocent spirits away.

But Rosalie only gave me a cool appraising look, introduced herself, then asked me for my name and my tale. The name she recognized, having seen it everywhere from the pages of history books to the shingles hanging outside dubious "absinthe" houses in the French Quarter. The tale – well, there were enough tales to entertain her for a thousand nights or more. (I, the Scheherazade of Barataria Bay!) How long had I wanted to tell those tales? I had been without a friend or a lover for more years than I could recall. (The company of other local ghosts did not interest me – they seemed a morbid lot, many of them headless or drenched in gore, manifesting only occasionally to point skeletal fingers at loose fireplace flagstones and then vanish without a word. I had met no personalities of substance, and certainly none with a history as exotic as mine.)

So I was glad for the company of Rosalie. As more old buildings are demolished I must constantly shift about the city, trying to find places where I resided in life, places where a shred of my soul remains to anchor me. There are still overgrown bayou islands and remote Mississippi coves I visit often, but to give up the drunken carnival of New Orleans, to forsake human companionship (witting or otherwise) would be to fully accept my death. Nearly two hundred years, and I still cannot do that.

"Jean," she would say to me as evening fell like a slowly drifting purple scarf over the French Quarter, as the golden flames of the streetlights flickered on, "do you like these panties with the silver bustier, Jean?" (She pronounced my name correctly, in the French manner, like John but with the soft J.) Five nights of the week Rosalie had a job stripping at a nightclub on Bourbon Street. She selected her undress from a vast armoire crammed full of the microscopic wisps of clothing she referred to as "costumes," some of which were only slightly more substantial than my own flesh. When she first told me of the job she thought I would be shocked, but I laughed. "I saw worse things in my day," I assured her, thinking of lovely, shameless octoroon girls I had known, of famous "private shows" involving poisonous serpents sent from Haiti and the oiled stone phalluses of alleged voodoo idols.

I went to see Rosalie dance two or three times. The strip club was in an old row building, the former site of a bordello I remembered well. In my day the place had been decorated entirely in scarlet silk and purple velvet; the effect was of enormous fleshy lips closing in upon you as you entered, drawing you into their dark depths. I quit visiting Rosalie at work when she said it unnerved her to suddenly catch sight of me in the hundreds of mirrors that now lined the club, a hundred spangle-fleshed

Rosalies and a hundred translucent Jeans and a thousand pathetic weasel-eyed men all reflected to a point of swarming infinity far within the walls. I could see how the mirrors might make Rosalie nervous, but I believe she did not like me looking at the other dancers either, though she was the prettiest of a big-hipped, insipid-faced lot.

By day Rosalie wore black: lace and fishnet, leather and silk, the gaudy mourning clothes of the deather-children. I had to ask her to explain them to me, these deathers. They were children seldom older than eighteen who painted their faces stark white, rimmed their eyes with kohl, smudged their mouths black or blood-red. They made love in cemeteries, then plundered the rotting tombs for crucifixes to wear as jewelry. The music they listened to was alternately lush as a wreath of funeral roses and dark as four a.m., composed in suicidal gloom by the androgynes that decorated Rosalie's walls. I might have been able to tell these children a few things about death. Try drifting through a hundred years without a proper body, I might have said, without feet to touch the ground, without a tongue to taste wine or kiss. Then perhaps you will celebrate your life while you have it. But Rosalie would not listen to me when I got on this topic, and she never introduced me to any of her deather friends.

If she had any. I had seen other such children roaming the French Quarter after dark, but never in Rosalie's company. Often as not she would sit in her room and drink whiskey on her nights off, tipping inches of liquid amber fire over crackling ice cubes and polishing it off again, again, again. She never had a lover that I knew of, aside from the dreaded Coffeespoon, who it seemed had been quite wealthy by Rosalie's standards. Her customers at the club offered her ludicrous sums if she would only grant them one night of pleasure more exotic than their toadlike minds could imagine. A few might really have been able to pay such fortunes, but Rosalie ignored their tumescent pleading. She seemed not so much opposed to the idea of sex for money as simply uninterested in sex at all.

When she told me of the propositions she received, I thought of the many things I had buried in the earth during my days upon it. Treasure: hard money and jewels, the riches of the robbery that was my bread and butter, the spoils of the murder that was my wine. There were still caches that no one had found and no one ever would. Any one of them would have been worth ten times the amounts these men offered.

Many times I tried to tell Rosalie where these caches were, but unlike some of her kind, she thought buried things should stay buried. She claimed that the thought of the treasure hidden under mud, stone, or brick, with people walking near it and sometimes right over it each day, amused her more than the thought of digging it up and spending it.

I never believed her. She would not let me see her eyes when she said these things. Her voice trembled when she spoke of the deathers who pursued grave-robbing as a sport. ("They pried up a granite slab that weighed fifty pounds," she told me once, incredulously. "How could they bear to lift it off, in the dark, not knowing what might come out at them?") There was a skeleton in a glass-topped coffin downstairs, in the voodoo shoppe, and Rosalie hardly liked to enter the shoppe because of it – I had seen her glancing out of the corner of her eye, as if the sad little bones simultaneously intrigued and appalled her.

It was some obsessive fear of hers, I realized. Rosalie shied away from all talk of dead things, of things buried, of digging in the ground. When I told her my tales she made me skip over the parts where treasures or bodies were buried; she would not let me describe the fetor of the nighttime swamp, the faint flickering lights of Saint Elmo's fire, the deep sucking sound the mud made when a shovel was thrust into it. She would allow me no descriptions of burials at sea or shallow bayou graves. She covered her ears when I told her of a rascal whose corpse I hung from the knotted black bough of a hundred-year-old oak. It was a remarkable thing, too – when I rode past the remote spot a year later, his perfect skeleton still hung there, woven together by strands of gray Spanish moss. It wound around his long bones and cascaded from the empty sockets of his eyes, it forced his jaws open and dangled from his chin like a long gray beard – but Rosalie did not want to hear about it.

When I confronted her with her own dread, she refused to own up to it. "Whoever said graveyards were romantic?" she demanded. "Whoever said I had to go digging up bones just because I lust after Venal St Claire?" (Venal St Claire was a musician, one of the stick-thin, mourning-shrouded beauties that adorned the walls of Rosalie's room. I saw no evidence that she lusted after him or anyone else.) "I just wear black so that all my clothes will match," she told me solemnly, as if she expected me to believe it. "So I won't have to think about what to put on when I get up in the morning."

"But you *don't* get up in the morning."

"In the evening, then. *You* know what I mean." She tipped her head back and tongued the last drop of whiskey out of her glass. It was the most erotic thing I had ever seen her do. I ran my finger in among the smooth folds of her intestines. A momentary look of discomfort crossed her face, as if she had suffered a gas pain – attributable to the rotgut whiskey, no doubt. But she would not pursue the subject further.

So I watched her drink until she passed out, her brittle hair fanned across her pillow, the corner of her mouth drooling a tiny thread of spit onto her black silk coverlet. Then I went into her head. This was not a thing I liked to do often – on occasion I had noticed her looking askance at me the morning after, as if she remembered seeing me in her dreams and wondered how I had got there. If I could persuade Rosalie to dig up one cache of loot – just one – our troubles would end. She would never have to work again, and I could have her with me all the time. But first I had to find her fear. Until I knew what it was, and could figure out how to charm my way around it, my treasures were going to stay buried in black bayou mud.

So within moments I was sunk deep in the spongy tissue of Rosalie's brain, sifting through her childhood memories as if they were gold coins I had just lifted off a Spanish galleon. I thought I could smell the whiskey that clouded her dreams, a stinging mist.

I found it more quickly than I expected to. I had reminded Rosalie of her fear, and now – because she would not let her conscious mind remember – her unconscious mind was dreaming of it. For an instant I teetered on the edge of wakefulness; I was dimly aware of the room around me, the heavy furniture and flocked black walls. Then it all swam away as I fell headlong into Rosalie's childhood dream.

A South Louisiana village, built at the confluence of a hundred streams and riverlets. Streets of dirt and crushed oyster-shells, houses built on pilings to keep the water from lapping up onto the neat, brightly painted porches. Shrimp nets draped over railings, stiffening with salt, at some houses; crab traps stacked up to the roof at others. Cajun country.

(Hard Luck Rosalie a Cajun girl, she who claimed she had never set foot in Louisiana before! *Mon petit chou*! "Smith" indeed!)

On one porch a young girl dressed in a T-shirt and a home-sewn skirt of fresh calico perches on a case of empty beer bottles. The tender points of her breasts can be seen through the thin fabric of the T-shirt. A medallion gleams at the hollow of her throat, a tiny saint frozen in silver. She is perhaps twelve. It can only be her mama beside her, a large regal-faced woman with a crown of teased and fluffed black hair. The mama is peeling crawfish. She saves the heads in a coffee can and throws the other pickings to some speckled chickens scratching in the part of the dirt yard that is not flooded. The water is as high as Mama has ever seen it.

The young girl has a can of Coca Cola, but she hasn't drunk much of it. She is worried about something: it can be seen in the slump of her shoulders, in the sprawl of her thin legs beneath the calico skirt. Several times her eyes shimmer with tears she is just able to control. When she looks up, it becomes clear that she is older than she appeared at first, thirteen or fourteen. An air of naivete, an awkwardness of limb and gesture, makes her seem younger. She fidgets and at last says, "Mama?"

"What is it, Rosie?" The mother's voice seems a beat too slow; it catches in her throat and drags itself reluctantly out past her lips.

"Mama – is Theophile still under the ground?"

(There is a gap in the dream here, or rather in my awareness of it. I do not know who Theophile is – a childhood friend perhaps. More likely a brother; in a Cajun family there is no such thing as an only child. The question disturbs me, and I feel Rosalie slipping from me momentarily. Then the dream continues, inexorable, and I am pulled back in.)

Mama struggles to remain calm. Her shoulders bow and her heavy breasts sag against her belly. The stoic expression on her face crumbles a little. "No, Rosie," she says at last. "Theophile's grave is empty. He's gone up to Heaven, him."

"Then he wouldn't be there if I looked?"

(All at once I am able to recognize my Rosalie in the face of this blossoming girl. The intelligent dark eyes, the quick mind behind them undulled by whiskey and time.)

Mama is silent, searching for an answer that will both satisfy and comfort. But a bayou storm has been blowing up, and it arrives suddenly, as they will: thunder rolls across the sky, the air is suddenly alive with invisible sparks. Then the rain comes down in a solid torrent. The speckled chickens scramble under the porch, complaining. Within seconds the yard in front of the house is a sea of mud. It has rained like this every day for a month. It is the wettest spring anyone has ever seen in this part of the bayou.

"You ain't goin' anywhere in this flood," Mama says. The relief is evident in her voice. She shoos the girl inside and hurries around the house to take washing off the line, though the faded cotton dresses and patched denim trousers are already soaked through.

Inside the warm little house, Rosalie sits at the kitchen window watching rain hammer down on the bayou, and she wonders.

The storm lasts all night. Lying in her bed, Rosalie hears the rain on the roof; she hears branches creaking and lashing in the wind. But she is used to thunderstorms, and she pays no attention to this one. She is thinking of a shed in the side yard, where her father's old crab traps and tools are kept. She knows there is a shovel in there. She knows where the key is.

The storm ends an hour before dawn, and she is ready.

It is her own death she is worried about, of course, not that of Theophile (whoever he may be). She is at the age where her curiosity about the weakness of the flesh outweighs her fear of it. She thinks of him under the ground and she has to know whether he is really there. Has he ascended to Heaven or is he still in his grave, rotting? Whatever she finds, it cannot be worse than the thing she has imagined.

(So I think at the time.)

Rosalie is not feeling entirely sane as she eases out of the silent house, filches her father's shovel, and creeps through the dark village to the graveyard. She likes to go barefoot, and the soles of her feet are hard enough to walk over the broken edges of the glittering wet oyster-shells, but she knows you have to wear shoes after a heavy rain or worms might eat their way into your feet. So she slogs through the mud in her soaked sneakers, refusing to think about what she is going to do.

It is still too dark to see, but Rosalie knows her way by heart through these village streets. Soon her hand finds the rusty iron gate of the graveyard, and it ratchets open at her touch. She winces at the harsh sound in the predawn silence, but there is no one around to hear.

At least, no one who *can* hear.

The crude silhouettes of headstones stab into the inky sky. Few families in the village can afford a carved marker; they lash two sticks together in the shape of a rough cross, or they hew their own stone out of granite if they can get a piece. Rosalie feels her way through a forest of jagged, irregular memorials to the dead. She knows some of them are only hand-lettered oak boards wedged into the ground. The shadows at the base of each marker are wet, shimmering. Foul mud sucks at her feet. She tells herself the smell is only stagnant water. In places the ground feels slick and lumpy; she cannot see what she is stepping on.

But when she comes near the stone she seeks, she can see it. For it is the finest stone in the graveyard, carved of moon-pale marble that seems to pull all light into its milky depths. His family had it made in New Orleans, spending what was probably their life's savings. The chiseled letters are as concise as razor cuts. Rosalie cannot see them, but she knows their every crevice and shadow. Only his name, stark and cold; no dates, no inscriptions, as if the family's grief was so great that they could not bear to say anything about him. Just inscribe it with his name and leave him there.

The plot of earth at the base of the stone is not visible, but she knows it all too well, a barren, muddy rectangle. There has been no time for grass or weeds to grow upon it; he has only been buried a fortnight, and the few sprouts that tried to come up have been beaten back down by the rain. But can he really be under there, shut up in a box, his lithe body bloating and bursting, his wonderful face and hands beginning to decay?

Rosalie steps forward, hand extended to touch the letters of his name: THEOPHILE THIBODEAUX. As she thinks – or dreams – the name, her fingers poised to trace its marble contours, an image fills her head, a jumble of sensations intense and erotic. A boy older than Rosalie, perhaps seventeen: a sharp pale face, too thin to be called handsome, but surely compelling; a curtain of long sleek black hair half-hiding eyes of fierce, burning azure. Theophile!

(All at once it is as if Rosalie's consciousness has merged completely with mine. My heart twists with a young girl's love and lust for this spitfire Cajun boy. I am dimly aware of Rosalie's drunken twenty-year-old body asleep on her bed, her feminine viscera twitching at the memory of him. O, how he touched her – O, how he tasted her!

She had known it was wrong in the eyes of God. Her mama had raised her to be a good girl. But the evenings she had spent with

Theophile after dances and church socials, sitting on an empty dock with his arm around her shoulders, leaning into the warm hollow of his chest – that could not be wrong. After a week of knowing her he had begun to show her the things he wrote on his ink-blackened relic of an Olympia typewriter, poems and stories, songs of the swamp. And that could not be wrong.

And the night they had sneaked out of their houses to meet, the night in the empty boathouse near Theophile's home – that could not be wrong either. They had begun only kissing, but the kisses grew too hot, too wild – Rosalie felt her insides boiling. Theophile answered her heat with his own. She felt him lifting the hem of her skirt and – carefully, almost reverently – sliding off her cotton panties. Then he was stroking the dark down between her legs, teasing her with the very tips of his fingers, rubbing faster and deeper until she felt like a blossom about to burst with sweet nectar. Then he parted her legs wider and bent to kiss her there as tenderly as he had kissed her mouth. His tongue was soft yet rough, like a soapy washcloth, and Rosalie had thought her young body would die with the pleasure of it. Then, slowly, Theophile was easing himself into her, and yes, she wanted him there, and yes, she was clutching at his back, pulling him farther in, refusing to heed the sharp pain of first entry. He rested inside her, barely moving; he lowered his head to kiss her sore developing nipples, and Rosalie felt the power of all womanhood shudder through her. This could not be wrong.)

With the memories fixed firmly in her mind she takes another step toward his headstone. The ground crumbles away beneath her feet, and she falls headlong into her lover's grave.

The shovel whacks her across the spine. The rotten smell billows around her, heavy and ripe: spoiling meat, rancid fat, a sweetish-sickly odor. The fall stuns her. She struggles in the gritty muck, spits it out of her mouth.

Then the first pale light of dawn breaks across the sky, and Rosalie stares into the ruined face of Theophile.

(Now her memories flooded over me like the tide. Some time after they had started meeting in the boathouse she began to feel sick all the time; the heat made her listless. Her monthly blood, which had been coming for only a year, stopped. Mama took her into the next town to see a doctor, and he confirmed what Rosalie had already dreaded: she was going to have Theophile's baby.

Her papa was not a hard man, nor cruel. But he had been raised in the bosom of the Church, and he had learned to measure his own worth by the honor of his family. Theophile never knew his Rosalie was pregnant. Rosalie's father waited for him in the boathouse one night. He stepped in holding a new sheaf of poems, and Papa's deer shot caught him across the chest and belly, a hundred tiny black eyes weeping red tears.

Papa was locked up in the county jail now and Mama said that soon he would go someplace even worse, someplace where they could never see him again. Mama said it wasn't Rosalie's fault, but Rosalie could see in her eyes that it was.)

It has been the wettest spring anyone can remember, a month of steady rains. The water table in Louisiana bayou country is already so high that a hole will begin to draw water at a depth of two feet or less. All this spring the table has risen steadily, soaking the ground, drowning grass and flowers, making a morass of the sweet swamp earth. Cattails have sprung up near at the edge of the graveyard. But the storm last night pushed the groundwater to saturation point and beyond. The wealthy folk of New Orleans bury their dead in vaults above ground to protect them from this very danger. But no one here can afford a marble vault, or even a brick one.

And the village graveyard has flooded at last.

Some of the things that have floated to the surface are little more than bone. Others are swollen to three or four times their size, gassy mounds of decomposed flesh rising like islands from the mud; some of these have silk flower petals stuck to them like obscene decorations. Flies rise lazily, then descend again in glittering, circling clouds. Here are mired the warped boards of coffins split open by the water's relentless pull. There floats the plaster figurine of a saint, his face and the color of his robes washed away by rain. Yawning eyeless faces thrust out of stagnant pools, seeming to gasp for breath. Rotting hands unfold like blighted tiger lilies. Every drop of water, every inch of earth in the graveyard is foul with the effluvium of the dead.

But Rosalie can only see the face thrust into hers, the body crushed beneath her own. Theophile's eyes have fallen back into their sockets and his mouth is open; his tongue is gone. She sees thin white worms teeming in the passage of his throat. His nostrils are widening black holes beginning to encroach upon the greenish flesh of his cheeks. His sleek hair is almost gone; the few strands left are thin and scummy, nibbled by waterbugs. (Sitting on the dock, Rosalie and Theophile used to spit into the water and watch the shiny black beetles swarm around the white gobs; Theophile had told her they would eat hair and toenails too.) In places she can see the glistening dome of his skull. *The skull behind the dear face; the skull that cradled the thoughts and dreams . . .*

She thinks of the shovel she brought and wonders what she meant to do with it. Did she *want* to see Theophile like this? Or had she really expected to find his grave empty, his fine young body gone fresh and whole to God?

No. She had only wanted to know where he was. Because she had nothing left of him – his family would give her no poems, no lock of hair. And now she had even lost his seed.

(The dogs ran Papa to earth in the swamp where he had hidden and the men dragged him off to jail. As they led him toward the police car, Theophile's mother ran up to him and spat in his face. Papa was handcuffed and could not wipe himself; he only stood there with the sour spit of sorrow running down his cheeks, and his eyes looked confused, as if he was unsure just what he had done.

Mama made Rosalie sleep in bed with her that night. But when Rosalie woke up the next morning Mama was gone; there was only a note saying she would be back before sundown. Sure enough, she straggled in with the afternoon's last light. She had spent the whole day in the swamp. Her face was scratched and sweaty, the cuffs of her jeans caked with mud.

Mama had brought back a basketful of herbs. She didn't fix dinner, but instead spent the evening boiling the plants down to a thin syrup. They exuded a bitter, stinging scent as they cooked. The potion sat cooling until the next night. Then Mama made Rosalie drink it all down.

It was the worst pain she had ever felt. She thought her intestines and her womb and the bones of her pelvis were being wrung in a giant merciless fist. When the bleeding started she thought her very insides were dissolving. There were thick clots and ragged shreds of tissue in the blood.

"It won't damage you," Mama told her, and it will be over by morning."

True to Mama's word, just before dawn Rosalie felt something solid being squeezed out of her. She knew she was losing the last of Theophile. She tried to clamp the walls of her vagina around it, to keep him inside her as long as she could. But the thing was slick

and formless, and it slid easily onto the towel Mama had spread
between her legs. Mama gathered the towel up quickly and would
not let Rosalie see what was inside.

Rosalie heard the toilet flush once, then twice. Her womb and
the muscles of her abdomen felt as if they had gone through
Mama's kitchen grater. But the pain was nothing compared to
the emptiness she felt in her heart.)

The sky is growing lighter, showing her more of the graveyard
around her: the corpses borne on the rising water, the maggot-
ridden mud. Theophile's face yawns into hers. Rosalie struggles
against him and feels his sodden flesh give beneath her weight.
She is beyond recognizing her love now. She is frantic; she fights
him. Her hand strikes his belly and punches in up to the wrist.

Then suddenly Theophile's body opens like a flower made of
carrion, and she sinks into him. Her elbows are trapped in the
brittle cage of his ribs. Her face is pressed into the bitter soup
of his organs. Rosalie whips her head to one side. Her face is a
mask of putrescence. It is in her hair, her nostrils; it films her eyes.
She is drowning in the body that once gave her sustenance. She
opens her mouth to scream and feels things squirming in between
her teeth.

"My cherie Rosalie," she hears the voice of her lover
whispering.

And then the rain pours down again.

Unpleasant.

I tore myself screaming from Rosalie – screaming silently,
unwilling to wake her. In that instant I was afraid of her for
what she had gone through; I dreaded to see her eyes snap open
like a doll's, meeting me full in the face.

But Rosalie was only sleeping a troubled slumber. She muttered
fitful disjointed words; there was a cold sheen of sweat on her
brow; she exuded a flowery, powerful smell of sex. I hovered
at the edge of the bed and studied her ringed hands clenched
into small fists, her darting, jumping eyelids still stained with
yesterday's makeup. I could only imagine the ensuing years and
torments that had brought that little girl to this night, to this room.
That had made her want to wear the false trappings of death, after
having wallowed in the truth of it.

But I *knew* how difficult it would be to talk these memories out
of her. There could be no consolation and no compensation for a

past so cruel. No treasure, no matter how valuable, could matter in the face of such lurid terror.

So I assure you that the thing I did next was done out of pure mercy – *not* a desire for personal gain, or control over Rosalie. I had never done such a thing to her before. She was my friend; I wished to deliver her from the poison of her memories. It was as simple as that.

I gathered up my courage and I went back into Rosalie's head. Back in through her eyes and the whorled tunnels of her ears, back into the spongy electric forest of her brain.

I cannot be more scientific than this: I found the connections that made the memory. I searched out the nerves and subtle acids that composed the dream, the morsels of Rosalie's brain that still held a residue of Theophile, the cells that were blighted by his death.

And I erased it all.

I pitied Theophile. Truly I did. There is no existence more lonely than death, especially a death where no one is left to mourn you.

But Rosalie belonged to me now.

I had her rent a boat.

It was easy for her to learn how to drive it: boating is in the Cajun blood. We made an exploratory jaunt or two down through Barataria – where two tiny hamlets, much like Rosalie's home village, both bore my name – and I regaled a fascinated Rosalie with tales of burials at sea, of shallow bayou graves, of a rascal whose empty eye sockets dripped with Spanish moss.

When I judged her ready, I guided her to a spot I remembered well, a clearing where five enormous oaks grew from one immense, twisted trunk. The five sentinels, we called them in my day. The wind soughed in the upper branches. The swamp around us was hushed, expectant.

After an hour of digging, Rosalie's shiny new shovel unearthed the lid and upper portion of a great iron chest. Her brittle hair was stringy with sweat. Her black lace dress was caked with mud and clay. Her face had gone paler than usual with exertion; in the half-light of the swamp it was almost luminescent. She had never looked so beautiful to me as she did at that moment.

She stared at me. Her tired eyes glittered as if with fever.

"Open it," I urged.

Rosalie swung the shovel at the heart-shaped hasp of the chest and knocked it loose on the first try. Once more and it fell away in a shower of soggy rust. She glanced back at me once more – looking for what, I wonder; seeing what? – and then heaved open the heavy lid.

And the sixth sentinel sat up to greet her.

I always took an extra man along when I went into the swamp to bury treasure. One I didn't trust, or didn't need. He and my reliable henchmen would dig the hole and drag the chest to the edge of it, ready to heave in. Then I would gaze deep into the eyes of each man and ask, in a voice both quiet and compelling, "Who wishes to guard my treasure?" My men knew the routine, and were silent. The extra man – currying favor as the useless and unreliable will do – always volunteered.

Then my top lieutenant would take three steps forward and put a ball in the lowly one's brain. His corpse was laid tenderly in the chest, his blood seeping into the mounds of gold or silver or glittering jewels, and I would tuck in one of my mojo bags, the ones I had specially made in New Orleans. Then the chest was sunk in the mire of the swamp, and my man, now rendered trustworthy, was left to guard my treasure until I should need it.

I was the only one who could open those chests. The combined magic of the mojo bag and the anger of the betrayed man's spirit saw to that.

My sixth sentinel wrapped skeletal arms around Rosalie's neck and drew her down. His jaws yawned wide and I saw teeth, still hungry after two hundred years, clamp down on her throat. A mist of blood hung in the air; from the chest there was a ripping sound, then a noise of quick, choking agony. I hoped he would not make it too painful for her. After all, she was the woman I had chosen to spend eternity with.

I had told Rosalie that she would never again have to wriggle out of flimsy costumes under the eyes of slobbering men, and I had not lied. I had told her that she would never have to worry about money any more, and I had not lied. What I had neglected to tell her was that I did not wish to share my treasures – I only wanted her dead, my Hard Luck Rosalie, free from this world that pained her so, free to wander with me through the unspoiled swamps and bayous, through the ancient buildings of a city mired in time.

Soon Rosalie's spirit left her body and flew to me. It had nowhere else to go. I felt her struggling furiously against my love, but she would give in soon. I had no shortage of time to convince her.

I slipped my arm around Rosalie's neck and planted a kiss on her ectoplasmic lips. Then I clasped her wisp of a hand in mine, and we disappeared together.

RICK CADGER

The Brothers

RICK CADGER is married with three children. He has a full time job in a GM motor car factory, and in his spare time is the editor and publisher of the small press publication *Strange Attractor Magazine*, a guitarist, a juggler, and a magazine and book reviewer. To fill his remaining spare time, he is learning to speak, read and write Hindi and Punjabi!

He admits to no rigid genre tendencies, although the greater part of his published output to date has been horror and dark fantasy in such publications as *Fear*, *Frighteners*, *BBR*, *The Dark Side*, *Chills*, *Dark Horizons*, *Exuberance*, *Works*, *Orion*, *Heliocentric Net*, *Grotesque* and the Barrington Books anthologies *Sugar Sleep* and *The Science of Sadness*. He has also won a number of awards, including the last *Fear* Fiction Award.

It is our pleasure to welcome him to *The Best New Horror* with the nightmarish tale which follows . . .

A S YOU DRIVE over the brow of the hill on the road into Galham, you see the village spread out before you like a patterned rug. Its residential roads and cul-de-sacs, with their two hundred or so houses, stipple a paisley mosaic across the countryside. Neville Maddox has never been here before, and he grunts his approval of your picturesque home. Of course he doesn't see the twin pedestals, one at each end of the village, upon which sit Bokovan and Yusenoi – but then, outsiders never do.

You put the Saab into low gear in readiness for the steep, winding descent; and as the engine begins to protest with the effort of braking the car, Bokovan's head turns toward the source of the sound and he grins at you. Both rostra are squat, cylindrical columns of grey rock some fifty feet tall. Bokovan and Yusenoi seem almost to be extensions of the stone. They are of the same grey hue from the tops of their massive heads to the tips of their pointed serpentine tails. Even sitting, each of them is above fifty feet tall – if they should ever stand erect upon their platforms, their heads would reach nearly a hundred and fifty feet into the air.

Each lays claim to one half of the village population, and of the two, you belong to Bokovan. Despite the distance, his smile warms and caresses you like the summer sunshine.

"You'll do well if you ever decide to sell, Ian," says your brother-in-law. "A lot of people would kill for a house in a place like this."

"I suppose so; but then I've always lived here, so perhaps I don't appreciate it as much as I should."

"Just goes to show that what I've always said is true."

"What's that?"

"That beautiful countryside is wasted on the local yokels. It's the yuppie refugees who pay through the nose that really appreciate it. The indigenous bumpkin is just as happy on an urban council estate. So long as he's got double glazing and satellite telly he thinks he's going up in the world." He bellows with laughter; and in the confined interior of the car the sound is raucous and nerve-shredding. Your ears are still ringing as you turn into your driveway. Neville is out of the car even before you have freed your car keys from the ignition's stubborn grip, and he presses the bell-push beside the front door repeatedly. He is a remarkable man, you decide. You collected him from the station less than half an hour ago, and already he has thoroughly pissed you off.

The breeze murmurs in your ears. There are words there, but you cannot make them out. Vaguely musical, they tease your consciousness offering seductive glimpses of hidden meanings. There is something familiar in the wind-borne incantation and, although you have never heard the sound before, you know its source. You look around to where Bokovan towers above the roof-tops at the end of the village; he smiles serenely, but his gaze is directed elsewhere. Again you turn, this time to face the more distant form of Bokovan's twin. Yusenoi also smiles, but he is looking straight at you – and his is a smile full of malice.

Something in your memory is trying to fight its way to the surface. Something from your childhood; something relevant to this strange and sinister song in the wind.

Alison opens the door. "Hello," she smiles, and kisses you on the cheek. She flashes a grin at Neville, then shows you into the house and through to the lounge. It all seems somehow familiar, but you say nothing.

"How was the journey down?" Alison asks.

"About the same as I thought it would be. How are you, Allie?"

"Great, never better."

You look around the room, still with the feeling that you know it well.

"Anything wrong?" Neville says.

You realise that you are frowning and, with an effort, you wipe the expression from your face, replacing it with a smile. "No, no," you say. "Just a bit of train-lag. I could use a paracetamol though."

"No problem." Neville vanishes for a moment, then returns with a pill and a glass of water.

"Thanks."

"How's Melanie?" Alison asks.

"Okay. Working too hard as usual, but then she's ambitious. Besides, she seems to thrive on hard graft." As you speak a strange disorientation grips you. Your words come readily enough, almost reflexively, in answer to the questions you are asked, but your memory is hazy. You can retrieve little that is coherent from the murk in your head. It seems that details of your identity and your life only present themselves as required and cued by enquiries from your hosts. It is an unsettling feeling, and you wonder briefly if you are ill – a stroke perhaps, or some other failing in the convolutions of your brain; but apart from the clouding of your memory and the slight headache you feel quite well. You decide to say nothing; to wait and see if your head clears when you've rested a while.

"No thought of starting a family yet?" Alison asks.

"Hmm? Not yet, we're both too busy. There'll be plenty of time for that in a couple of years or so. We're still young, there's no rush."

"Fair enough."

"How about you two?" you ask.

"Oh, I dare say we'll produce a couple of kids eventually," says Neville, strolling over to the patio doors and peering out. "We've certainly got the garden for it, and I suppose it's either that or plastic gnomes."

You move to his side to take a look yourself. "Lovely," you nod.

"Are you a gardening man, Ian?"

Are you? "Not really. I think DIY is perhaps more my sort of thing: I'm not a great outdoor activist."

"Well before we get you putting up shelves or building an extension maybe we'd better get you settled in," says Alison.

"Good idea," you say. "It's very good of you to put me up at such short notice. I hope it's not too much of a nuisance."

"No bother at all. Isn't that right Neville?"

"Oh, absolutely. Where exactly did you say this seminar of yours is taking place?"

"At the Royale in Telleridge, from Monday until Thursday."

"Very posh. You'll do okay on the food front then. Always a good spread laid on at that sort of do, eh?"

"So I've heard," you say.

"Anyway, young man." Neville moves to the door and waits, obviously expecting you to follow. "I'll show you where you'll be sleeping, then you can rest up or whatever. After a couple of hours on the train you're probably a bit knackered. Caught the rush hour near the end, did you?"

"Did I ever. I never knew you could fit so many people into such a small space."

"How's the headache?"

"Not so bad, thanks."

The guest room is comfortable and contains everything you

need. Neville neglects to show you which drawers and cupboards are vacant for your use, but you know anyway. Kicking off your shoes and lying on the bed, your eyes instinctively know where to find the smiling face in the cracked ice ceiling tiles.

In your dream time is a malleable thing, a variable that can be defined by your will, and thus you can dip into it as the whim takes you, retrieving images, events and experiences.

Here is your wedding day. Alison radiant in white; you restless in your hired morning suit and ill-fitting hat. There is her brother, Neville; ever the centre of attention, he is pestering the photographer with opinions and suggestions about how the man should arrange his subjects to the best effect. Then he begins to herd the wedding party into their positions for the group photo.

"This geezer is getting on my nerves," mutters your best man. "If I get a few beers inside me later on, he could well be in for a stiff talking-to."

"Be my guest," you murmur. "Just wait until Alison and I are on our way, okay."

"But of course. I wouldn't want to upset the bride."

"There's a good chap."

Neville whistles and waves to get your attention. "Ian, if you and your friend are ready I think we can get the group now. Oh, and get him to straighten his tie, will you."

"Unbelievable," breathes the best man. "I hate to think what your mother-in-law's like."

"I'll introduce you," you grin as you move to stand beside your bride.

"Happy?" she asks.

"Very." You smile through gritted teeth as Neville shoulders past you to take his position in the group.

The next day they take you to Crainham Ridge.

"Visitors always want to see the Ridge," says Neville as he ushers you into the Saab. "An area of outstanding natural beauty and all that."

You really couldn't care less; this excursion was his idea, not yours.

"They say *natural* beauty," grumbles Neville, "but the copse just below the picnic area is far from natural."

"Not artificial trees, surely." Your innocent, wide-eyed expression of amazement disguises the sarcasm in your words. You see Neville glance at your face in his rear view mirror. He looks at you for a moment through narrowed eyes, then returns his attention to the road ahead, apparently deciding that you are some kind of idiot.

"No," he says, "but they were planted there by men, not by nature. They say it's one of the earliest known areas of cultivated forestation in Europe."

What the hell is he talking about?

"Really?"

"Actually," Alison smiles, "every time I go up to the Ridge it reminds me of the downs at Neighwick where we used to do our courting." She giggles and Neville's ears redden.

Conversation dies as the scenery becomes progressively more spectacular. By the time each new and dramatic feature of the terrain is revealed, you already have a detailed picture of it in your mind. The end of the journey brings profound relief, and you climb from the car breathing deeply of the fresh, slightly damp air.

Alison and Neville stand in front of the car, gazing out over the valley; her arm is around his waist, and one of his hands rests upon her buttock. As you look he squeezes her behind and glances over his shoulder to grin at you. You hate him without really knowing why. There is something more than just his overall obnoxiousness, but somehow you just can't –

Alison is chattering away happily. ". . . just like it, the way the whole world seems to be set out before you. We really must come up more often. If anything, the view here is even prettier than at Neighwick."

"Not that we ever spent too much time looking at the sights," Neville leers, nudging her as if the coarse suggestiveness of his remark needs further emphasis.

Alison's embarrassed scolding fades into the background.

Once again there is music in the wind. You are helpless, utterly at the mercy of the wandering zephyr that blows you tumbling across the miles and years.

You are on Neighwick Down, lying on your back in the rippling grass, gazing at the cotton wisps that litter the otherwise immaculate blue of the summer sky. Alison's head is upon your chest, and the vibrations from her voice tickle you when she speaks.

"When are we going to do it?"

"What?"

"The wedding; when are we going to do it?"

You sigh. "As soon as you like."

"Don't sound too enthusiastic."

"Sorry. I just wish it was all over and we were already married. I can't pretend I'm looking forward to all that fuss and carry-on. I would rather it was over so we could be on our own."

Her hand strays mischievously across your thigh. "We are on our own," she giggles. "Or hadn't you noticed?"

"You know what I mean."

"You're just shy, Ian. That's what it is; you're scared of having to stand up in front of all those people to make a speech."

"Next month."

"What? Next month what?"

"The wedding. I've got some vacation due. Give me time to get the honeymoon booked and we'll see whether I'm scared or not."

"Really?" She sits up and faces you with wide eyes. "Are you serious?"

"Come here." You slip a hand under her tee shirt and pull her down on top of you. "And I'll show you how serious I am."

"Ian?"

"Mmm? Oh . . . I beg your pardon."

"Neville said we'd better go. Look . . ." Alison points up at the grey cloud that has crept from behind the hills. You can feel the first hint of rain in the breeze; each tiny droplet makes you flinch as if you had a nervous twitch.

"What a shame, we've only just arrived."

"Well we've had ten minutes, so it could have been worse. At least you got a look at the view before the weather spoiled."

Ten minutes? Surely not. You must have been daydreaming.

Perhaps you should abandon your plans to attend the seminar. The disorientation is worsening, and with it the fear that there might be something seriously wrong with you. You find yourself unable to broach the subject with Alison and her husband: you feel unaccountably embarrassed by the ailment. But it is only the search for an adequate excuse that keeps you from returning home and consulting your own physician. As it is, you plead migraine again, and retire early for the second time.

You wake in darkness, for a moment totally confused as to where you are. The onset of panic is halted by a sound that emerges from the night, giving you something to focus on. Equilibrium and orientation come slowly: you are in your sister's house; you are in bed. Thumbing the backlight button on your watch restores your sense of location in time and space.

The sounds from the night continue. You strain your ears trying to identify the source, and recognise with a shock the sounds of lovemaking from beyond the wall at your head. Vocal and mechanical, the rhythm is unmistakable. Your cheeks burn with shame at this accidental intrusion upon your hosts' privacy. The covers you pull up around your ears do little to obscure the sound. Now you know its origin it is somehow inescapable: it continues to grow in both volume and abandon despite your efforts to block it out with hands and bed linen. The world is filled with the tumultuous noise of fucking.

In an attempt to escape, you go downstairs and into the cool of the garden. You sit on the bench there, resting an elbow on the heavy black iron arm. Light from nearby street lamps and from the curtained windows of neighbourhood insomniacs spills onto the lawn, casting pale shadows on the paler ground. Looking up at the faint blue-grey-black sky, you think you can make out a shape standing out against the heavens. The shape is indistinct in the poor light, but there is something familiar about that huge and vague form. At last all becomes silent, except for the whispering breeze.

The night is cool rather than chill, and it isn't long before your eyelids start to feel heavy. How can you be certain whether it is reality or dream when the wind becomes stronger, and begins to carry snatches of deep, mocking laughter to you.

Your father's face is stern; you know that what he has to say must be important. As the two of you sit in the conservatory, you try hard to keep your attention from straying into the lounge where your brother David sits watching Blue Peter. You push all thoughts of John Noakes's parachute jump from your mind: if your father catches you thinking about television while he's talking you'll get a hiding.

"We have a good life here," he says. "We are well looked after, and we want for little. You must learn to be properly grateful – we all have to learn."

"You mean like saying prayers?"

His smile encourages you; you said the right thing.

"Sort of, Ian, yes. But it's not just God we have to thank for what we have here in Galham." He gazes up at the figure atop the distant rostrum which can be glimpsed between the houses at the end of your garden.

"Bokovan and Yusenoi . . ."

"Yes, son. Or in our case, just Bokovan."

It is no longer an effort to keep your attention on the conversation – your mind hums with activity; it has become an efficient production line, manufacturing questions at the rate of one a second. "I thought we weren't supposed to talk about them," you say.

"Well, no. But the brothers allow a certain amount of discretion in these things." He hesitates; the lull is agonising. You ache with the need to know about Bokovan and Yusenoi.

"Don't worry," he says. "There's really not much to know – not much we're allowed to know. For the things they give us: long life, health, success in the outside world and all the rest, they expect little in return. However, nothing under the sun comes totally free, and the brothers' gifts are no exception."

Can there be something in his tone that, despite the words, suggests resentment?

"People who come here from outside – even the ones who stay – do not see Bokovan and Yusenoi. That's why those of us who do see them must watch our tongues."

"So secrecy is what we have to give in return," you say.

"It's called discretion – but you've got it right. The other part of the price is something that each of us has to go through, but only once in our lifetime."

"What is it?"

"The form it takes is always different. One day something unusual, probably bad, will happen. What you must remember is that if you endure it and still retain your gratitude and faith in Bokovan, all will turn out well in the end. Even if it seems that your world is coming apart, everything will be all right, if you trust him and endure the test."

Despite your questions that spill out, he says little more, just *asks you to repeat what he has told you until he is satisfied that you have taken it in.*

He pauses just long enough to answer a couple more questions.

"Why do they test us like that?"

"I don't know," he says. A slight smile grows around his mouth. "Your grandfather once said he thought the brothers must have a bet going on who will pass and who will crack." He sees your bewildered expression and chuckles. "Don't worry. I'm sure there's a real reason for it." His smile fades, and he murmurs: "There has to be . . ." He gets up and opens the door to the garden.

"Dad."

"Yes?"

"What happens to the people who don't make it?"

"They leave Galham," he says over his shoulder.

Something occurs to him as he steps out into the sunshine, and he turns back to face you; but his words are drowned out by the wind that springs up from nowhere . . .

. . . The wind that wakes you with the same laughter that hounded you into sleep. And then it is gone; faded in the time it took you to sit upright on the bench. It is after dawn, and now you feel the cold.

With the return of consciousness comes realisation, the beginnings of understanding.

The feeling of relief that you feel as you wave goodbye to Neville is almost overwhelming. You stand at the end of your driveway with an arm around your wife's shoulders. The taxi recedes until a bend in the road obliterates both it and your brother-in-law from your life. Alison smiles up at you.

"Nice to have the place to ourselves again, even if he is my brother."

"Absolutely. That's the nice thing about visitors; they bugger off sooner or later."

"Oh, Ian!" She slaps you, but at the same time hugs you with the arm that holds your waist.

As she breaks away from you to go indoors, you pause and look up at the great, towering shape of Bokovan. He is smiling serenely down upon you. There is more than just gratitude and relief in the cocktail of emotions that seethes within you – there is also smugness that you survived your testing.

The day of the dawn that found you shivering on the garden bench saw a return to reality. That bizarre shifting of identities that occurred between you and your brother-in-law was gone as if it had never happened. You went into the house and up the stairs in time to see Neville emerging from the guest bedroom. He was opening the lavatory door when he saw you coming up the stairs.

"Morning," he leered. "I say, Ian. You really should get something done about the walls in this place."

"Pardon?"

"Well, I mean they're paper thin, old thing. I couldn't help hearing you two last night. Hammer and tongs, eh? I almost came in to ask if you wouldn't mind keeping the racket down a bit." He vanished into the bathroom, chuckling to himself. As you went into your bedroom, you could hear him urinating and emitting coarse grunts of relief as the pressure in his bladder was alleviated.

"Where did you go?" Alison was sitting up in bed.

"Just outside. I needed a breath of air." You searched her face and saw that as far as she was concerned all was as it should be. Your memory of the awful chaos that had filled the preceding days was perfectly intact; but it seemed that Alison and Neville had different recollections. As far as they were concerned it had been you who shared the night with your wife.

It is for the best, you decide, now as you walk into the house. Both Alison and her brother were born outside Galham: they know nothing of the two enormous creatures who dominate existence here. How could their sanity have survived intact if they had been forced to remember that perverted and impossible twisting of reality? Alison's ignorance is in itself reason enough for you to feel grateful, despite the burden of your own memory.

She is rearranging the coats on the rack in the hall as you go in, and she turns as you close the front door behind you. "I was thinking, perhaps – " She stops in surprise as you put your arms around her. "What on earth's the matter?"

Your embrace tightens. "Nothing."

How could you have known there would be more to come?
If only there had been some sign, some hint or warning,

perhaps then you might have been prepared. Perhaps then you might not have lost everything. You remember the feeling of smugness you experienced when Neville left, when you thought your ordeal was over, and the memory is a bitter one.

"I'm pregnant," she said a few weeks later. Those were the two simple words that destroyed you.

For the first time in your life you actually touched Bokovan's rostrum. Your trembling hands pressed against the grey stone, as you turned your face upward to scream at the silent monster it supported. If you could have scaled the platform you would have done so, and you would have attacked Bokovan with all your puny human strength. And if your father was still alive you would have turned your wrath upon him also. He lied: he said that if you trusted in your patron everything would be all right. How could this ever be all right? How could anything ever be all right again?

Bokovan did not so much as glance at you. He sat as unmoved as the stone beneath him, gazing serenely out over his domain. As you climbed, shattered and frustrated into your car, you paused and glanced at the far end of the village. Yusenoi's eyes were upon you once more, and his face wore the familiar malicious, and now triumphant, smile.

You drove for hours. The tears and curses subsided after the first few miles, and sanity began to filter back into the world. Your thoughts turned to Alison. Although you had managed to conceal and contain your distress until you were away from the house, she would be worried, so you decided to go home and salvage what you could of your life.

You are still trying to go home. But now after months of trying, the attempt is little more than routine; the urgency has dissipated, and your search is as much habit as anything.

The roads by which you left are still there. The neighbouring villages are still there, and the nearby towns, but Galham is gone. Not just the village, but also the space it should occupy: and the world has shrunk to absorb the void.

In the beginning you asked directions from puzzled-looking locals who apologised most sincerely for never having heard of the place. You bought and searched maps which proved devoid of any mention of your home.

This brief period of idleness upon Neighwick Down brings no feeling of comfort or rest. The grass waves gently in the wind as you gaze out across the valley that looks so much like your home. There is nothing left to try, but you'll go on trying anyway. You have to. Somehow there must be a way back to Galham, to your wife, and to the child – as yet unborn – who you now know with heartbreaking certainty can only be your own.

J. L. COMEAU

The Owen Street Monster

THE FOLLOWING STORY marks Judith Lynn Comeau's third appearance in *The Best New Horror*. She has been writing and publishing stories since 1987, and her skilful short fiction has also appeared in such anthologies as *The Year's Best Horror Stories*, *The Women Who Walk Through Fire*, *Women of the West*, *Borderlands 2 and 3*, *Hottest Blood*, *Noctulpa 8: Eclipse of the Senses*, *Dark Voices 6: The Pan Book of Horror*, *Hot Blood 5* and the collection, *Firebird and Other Stories*, published in Finland.

"This story is one of my particular favourites," reveals the author. "I grew up in one of the locally infamous upper-middle-class Washington DC suburban neighbourhoods where the vast majority of the wives remained at home with their Boomer progeny and tended to pack together in terrifically vicious little cliques. They were a pretty scary bunch, as I recall . . ."

(connect)

"Hi, Addie? It's Janine. I just wanted to call and tell you how sorry I am about your loss and let you know I'm here for you if you need anything. Anything at all. God, it's difficult, I know, but really, Addie, you have to go on for the sake of the other children, and . . . Well . . ."

Sigh. "Yes, Janine. Thank you so much. I saw you at the funeral yesterday, but I just couldn't – "

"Oh, honey, I understand. We all assumed you'd been given a tranquilizer. You hardly seemed to know where you were. God, Addie, it was so terrible for you, I know."

"No one can know what it's like until they've lost one of their own. I – it's unnatural to bury a child. It should have been David burying me, don't you see? He was only a baby. Six years old. Just six."

"Please don't cry, Addie. You still have Sherman, Jr and little Melody. They need you to be strong now. Think of them."

"I know you're right, Janine. Thank heaven school started last week. I don't think I could have held out any longer. Poor little David . . . I, oh . . . God."

"Oh, Addie, Addie. You poor, poor darling. Try to be coura-geous for the others. They need your strength, and you're a very strong woman; we all know you are. And remember, if there's ever anything I or any of the other girls on Owen Street can do to help you through this terrible ordeal, we're here for you. Do you hear me? We-are-here-for-you."

"God bless you, Janine. And thank you for all the food you and the girls brought over to the house. I don't know what I would have done – "

"It was nothing. Absolutely nothing at all. You just take good care of yourself, Addie. We love you. Remember that."

"Oh, Janine . . ."

"Look, honey, I can tell you're a wreck. Go ahead now, get yourself a nice glass of wine and settle down for Oprah. Today she's having on women who've lost their limbs to accidents."

"Arms and legs, you mean?"

"Yes. Can you imagine? Well, look, it's almost four, so I'm going to let you go now."

"Janine?"

"What, hon?"

"Thanks."

"Oh, hush. Bye now."

"Bye bye."

(*disconnect*)

(*connect*)

"Hello, Samantha?"

"Yeah. Janine?"

"Yeah."

"Did you see Oprah today? The one about women who've lost their limbs?"

"Yes. Wasn't that bizarre? What are you making for dinner tonight? I can't come up with a thing."

"Oh, Christ. I guess I'll nuke some chicken and boil up some Rice-a-Roni. Maybe I'll just call out for pizza. Tell you the truth, Janine, this maternity leave is about to kill me. I can't wait to get back to work. The kid screams twenty-four hours a day, Jack's whining for tail all the time, and I – "

"Listen, Sam. I talked to Addie Wilmer this afternoon."

"What?"

"Don't get crazy. I just called her to see how she's getting along."

"What did she say?"

"Well, she's grief-stricken, of course. Who wouldn't be after losing a child?"

"Janine, I think we ought to just leave Addie alone."

"Look, Sam, we all live on Owen Street. We're going to be seeing Addie for a long time. She's our neighbor, after all."

"Maybe if we just cut her off, you know, give her the cold shoulder, she'll move away. We could – "

"No, no. That wouldn't work. We don't want to do that. Addie's a good neighbor, Samantha."

"But that kid. That David."

"David's gone, Samantha. He's not a problem any more."

"Yeah. Okay, I guess you're right, Janine. But I just feel so weird with Addie being right down the block. You know?"

"I know, I know. But listen. That boy is gone, so try to be friendly to Addie and her other kids. Please. It means so much. You're my very closest friend, Samantha. I know you can do it."

"Well . . . All right, Janine. I'll try."

"Promise?"

"Promise."

"So how's your sex life, Sammy? Jack keeping you on your back?"

Laugh. "Naw. I'm keeping him on his."

Laugh. "Good for you. Gotta go."

"Right. See ya."

"Bye."

(*disconnect*)

(*connect*)

"Nicole?"

"Yes?"

"Janine."

"Oh, hi, Janine. I was just thinking about you."

"We do seem to have some sort of mental connection, don't we?"

"Yes, we truly do. It's uncanny, isn't it? Sometimes I know exactly what you're going to say just before you say it."

"It's the most extraordinary thing. I've heard that best friends like us sometimes develop a kind of telepathy."

"Really? Where did you hear that?"

"Donahue or Geraldo, I guess. I can't remember. It's a fact, though."

"Did you see Oprah yesterday? Women without limbs?"

"Yes. Weird, huh? Today she's having on people who mutilate themselves to relieve stress."

"You are kidding."

"Nope. Not to change the subject, Nicole, but I was talking to Samantha yesterday and she's getting a little nuts about this Addie Wilmer thing."

"About the dead kid, you mean."

"Well, not so much that as she's uncomfortable about facing Addie."

"Samantha is such a wimp."

"Really. But we've got to convince her that developing an attitude against Addie at this point would only be counter-productive and possibly detrimental to everyone concerned."

"Samantha is such a dumb bitch."

"Yes, I know, but I'm counting on you to help Sam through this, Nicole. We all have to help her. Remember, we're only as strong as our weakest link."

"Yeah, I guess we're stuck with her now."

"Yes, Nicole. We are."

"Okay, I'll talk to her, but I've got to go now, Janine. The kids

are raising red hell out in the back yard. Christ, I'll be so glad
when they're old enough for school. Oh shit, I think one of them's
bleeding."

"Go ahead, then, Nicole. And remember, be nice to Samantha.
We've all got to help her over the hump."

"I will, I will. Gotta go, Janine. Jason is beating Michelle to
a pulp."

"Okay, go ahead. Bye."

(*disconnect*)

(*connect*)

"Janine?"

"Hilary?"

"Janine, I've got to talk to you."

"What's the matter?"

"What's the matter? Are you kidding?"

"Hilary, you sound terrible."

"I'm scared, Janine. I can't sleep, I can't eat, I – "

"Hilary. Honey. I'm surprised at you. You were the one who
started this whole thing in the first place, remember? You were
the one who convinced us all that we had to do it. And you were
right, Hilary. One hundred percent right. What's going on?"

"Jesus, I don't know. Maybe I was wrong. Maybe I read all the
wrong conclusions into totally innocent behavior. Maybe – "

"Maybe nothing. You were right. You just have a case of the
jitters. It'll pass. I promise. Be strong. Just be strong for a little
while and it'll pass."

"I don't know, Janine. I'm losing it. I'm really losing it."

"That child was a monster, Hilary. David Wilmer was a
monster. Every one of us saw the signs. All the newspapers and
magazines confirmed our suspicions, remember?"

"But those newspapers were tabloids, not the *Washington Post*
or *New York Times*."

"It was in black and white, Hilary: craves attention, unaffected
by punishment, cruelty to animals, setting fires, vivid fantasies.
David displayed all those deviations."

"I don't know, Janine, thinking about it now, I don't think any
of us ever saw David harm an animal."

"He was scared to death of animals; it's the same damn thing.
It's not natural for a little boy. Remember when Nicole's collie
tried to play with David?"

"Lamby knocked David down."

"The dog was just playing, for Christ's sake. Boys are supposed to love dogs. David hated animals, you could tell. He would have hurt one if he'd gotten the chance."

"How about setting fires? We were never entirely sure he caused the Lovett's fire. The firemen said faulty wiring."

"You saw the look on that kid's face as the Lovett house went up. Total fascination. Enchantment. He was a firebug, all right. Funny how he was right there to witness the fire."

"We were all there, Janine."

"Hilary, listen. How would you have felt if six or seven years down the road they found your precious little Sarah dumped out in the woods somewhere, raped and mutilated? Torn to pieces?"

"Oh, God, Janine. Don't say that. Don't breathe it."

"That might have happened, Hilary. We heard what can happen with children like David on all the talk shows. He was a killer in the making. We had to do it."

"Jesus, I can still hear David screaming. I can't get it out of my head."

"Get hold of yourself, Hilary. We're all having a hard time with this. Don't forget, we each took an equal hand in it. Samantha poured the gas, Nicole lured David into the shed, I locked the door, and you threw the lit cigarette in through the window. You started the fire, Hilary. You're the one who actually killed David Wilmer. You. There's a death penalty in this state for murder. You'd be the one to die, Hilary. Just you. The rest of us would probably get off with probation. And think of your family. The publicity would ruin their lives forever. They'd all despise you if they found out."

"Oh, God. What am I going to do?"

"You're going to quit blubbering and pull yourself together, that's what. It's a bit late for tears."

"Janine, I've got to go. I can't talk anymore."

"Please don't do anything stupid, Hilary. For your kids' sake. For Harold. Think about your parents. This would kill them."

"I'm going now, Janine. I can't live with this anymore."

"What are you going to do?"

"I'm going to take a little trip to the stars. I'm going to stop this pain once and for all."

"Hilary, calm down. Take some Valium. Have a Seconal."

"That's just what I intend to do."

(*disconnect*)

(*connect*)
"Nicole? Janine."

"What's the matter?"

"It's Hilary. She's falling apart. Having second thoughts, a guilt attack."

"Oh, no."

"Don't get excited yet. I think she's planning to commit suicide. I just talked to her a minute ago, and I swear I think she's planning to overdose on pills."

"What should we do? Should we call an ambulance?"

Pause. "I don't think so, Nicole. I think we ought to let her go ahead and do it."

"What?"

"Listen to me. Samantha we can handle. She's just a little nervous. She'll be okay. But Hilary . . . I think she'd eventually go to the police."

"Yes. I think we should just bide our time for now. Lay low. Stay cool."

"What if she changes her mind and doesn't take the pills?"

"We'll keep an eye on her house. If either one of us sees her leaving, we'll intercept her. If you see her first, bring her to my house. If I see her first, I'll bring her to yours."

"What then?"

"We'll discuss that when we need to."

Sigh. "Janine, this is getting sticky. I didn't think it would get so complicated."

"Relax, Nicole. Nothing's happened yet. Probably nothing will. Don't worry. Best friends like us, we can handle anything."

"Yeah, you're right. We can handle Samantha and Hilary. We're an invincible duo." Laugh.

"Best friends to the end. And Nicole?"

"What, hon?"

"Keep your eye on that Frazier kid down the street at 510. He seems a little odd."

"Will do. Talk to you later."

"Bye bye."

"Bye."

(*disconnect*)

T.E.D. KLEIN

One Size Eats All

T.E.D. KLEIN is a native New Yorker who has been described as "one of the finest stylists among modern horror writers." After discovering the works of H.P. Lovecraft while studying at Brown University, his acclaimed story "The Events at Poroth Farm" appeared in *The Year's Best Horror Stories: Series II* in 1974.

The story was expanded to novel-length in the American best-seller *The Ceremonies* (winner of the British Fantasy Award), and the author followed it with *Dark Gods* (collecting three novellas, "Petey", "Black Man With a Horn", the World Fantasy Award-winning "Nadelman's God", and the short novel "Children of the Kingdom").

For five years Klein was the editor of the successful *Rod Serling's Twilight Zone Magazine*, he edited the now defunct true-crime monthly *CrimeBeat*, and more recently put together the first edition of *Sci-Fi Entertainment* before resigning. He also scripted Dario Argento's movie *Trauma* (which he describes as "easily the worst film he ever made"), and he is still working on a new novel, entitled *Nighttown*.

It should be pointed out that the following story was originally written for children. The new outdoors magazine *Outside/Kids* (a companion to the popular adult publication *Outside*) asked the author for a "campfire chiller". "One Size Eats All" certainly fits that criterion, no matter what the age of the reader . . .

T HE WORDS HAD been emblazoned on the plastic wrapper of Andy's new sleeping bag, in letters that were fat and pink and somewhat crudely printed. Andy had read them aloud as he unwrapped the bag on Christmas morning.

"'One size eats all.' What's that supposed to mean?"

Jack, his older brother, had laughed. "Maybe it's not really a sleeping bag. Maybe it's a *feed* bag!"

Andy's gaze had darted to the grotesquely large metal zipper that ran along the edge of the bag in rows of gleaming teeth. He'd felt a momentary touch of dread.

"It's obviously a mistake," Andy's father had said. "Or else a bad translation. They must have meant 'One size *fits* all.'"

He was sure that his father was right. Still, the words on the wrapper had left him perplexed and uneasy. He'd slept in plenty of sleeping bags before, but he knew he didn't want to sleep in this one.

And now, as he sat huddled in his tent halfway up Wendigo Mountain, about to slip his feet into the bag, he was even more uneasy. What if it *wasn't* a mistake?

He and Jack had been planning the trip for months; it was the reason they'd ordered the sleeping bags. Jack, who was bigger and more athletic and who'd already started to shave, had picked an expensive Arctic Explorer model from the catalogue. Nothing but the best for Jack. Andy, though, had hoped that if he chose an obscure brand manufactured overseas, and thereby saved his parents money, maybe they'd raise his allowance.

But they hadn't even noticed. The truth was, they'd always been somewhat inattentive where Andy was concerned. They barely seemed to notice how Jack bullied him.

Jack did bully him – in a brotherly way, of course. His bright red hair seemed to go with his fiery temper, and he wasn't slow to use his fists. He seemed to best the younger boy in just about everything, from basketball to campfire-building.

Which was why, just before they'd set out for Wendigo Mountain, Andy had invited his friend Willie along. Willie was small, pale, and even less athletic than Andy. His head seemed much too big for his body. On a strenuous overnight hike like this one, Andy thought, it was nice to have somebody slower and weaker than he was.

* * *

True to form, Willie lagged behind the two brothers as they trudged single-file up the trail, winding their way among the tall trees that covered the base of the mountain, keeping their eyes peeled for the occasional dark green trail-markers painted on the trunks. It was a sunny morning, and the air had begun to lose some of the previous night's chill.

By the time Willie caught up, winded and sweating beneath his down jacket, Andy and Jack had taken off their backpacks and stopped for a rest.

"It's *your* tough luck," Jack was telling him. "You've heard the old saying, 'You made your bed, now lie in it'?"

Andy nodded glumly.

"Well, it's the same thing," said Jack. "You *wanted* the damn bag, so tonight you're just gonna have to lie in it."

All morning, that's exactly what Andy had been worrying about. He eyed the pack at his feet, with the puffy brown shape strapped beneath it, and wished the night would never come. *You made your bed*, he told himself. *Now die in it.*

"Andy, for God's sake, stop obsessing about that bag!" said Willie. "You're letting your fears get the best of you. Honest, it's a perfectly ordinary piece of camping gear."

"Willie's right," said Jack. Hoisting his backpack onto his shoulders, he grinned and added cruelly, "And the people it eats are perfectly ordinary too!"

As they continued up the trail, the trees grew smaller and began to thin; the air grew cooler. Andy could feel the weight of the thing on his back, heavier than a sleeping bag ought to be and pressing against him with, he sensed, a primitive desire – a creature impatient for its dinner.

Ahead of him, Jack turned. "Hey, Willie," he yelled. "Did Andy tell you where his bag is from?"

"No," said Willie, far behind them. "Where?"

Jack laughed delightedly. "Hungary!"

They made camp at a level clearing halfway up the mountain. Andy and Willie would be sharing a tent that night; Jack had one to himself. Late afternoon sunlight gleamed from patches of snow among the surrounding rocks.

The three unrolled their sleeping bags inside the tents. Andy paused before joining the others outside. In the dim light his bag lay brown and bloated, a living coffin waiting for an occupant.

Andy reminded himself that it was, in fact, a fairly normal-looking bag – not very different, in truth, from Jack's new Arctic Explorer. Still, he wished he had a sleeping bag like Willie's, a comfortable old thing that had been in the family for years.

Willie lagged behind again as the brothers left camp and returned to the trail. They waited until he'd caught up. Both younger boys were tired and would have preferred to stay near the tents for the rest of the day, but Jack, impatient, wanted to press on toward the summit while it was still light.

The three took turns carrying a day pack with their compasses, flashlights, emergency food, and a map. The slope was steeper here, strewn with massive boulders, and the exertion made them warm again. Maybe, thought Andy, he wouldn't even need the bag tonight.

The terrain became increasingly difficult as they neared Wendigo's peak, where the trail was blanketed by snow. They were exhausted by the time they reached the top – too exhausted to appreciate the sweeping view, the stunted pines, and the small mounds of stones piled in odd patterns across the rock face.

They raised a feeble shout of triumph, rested briefly, then started down. Andy sensed that they would have to hurry; standing on the summit, he'd been unnerved at how low the sun lay in the sky.

The air was colder now, and shadows were lengthening across the snow. Before they'd gotten very far, the sun had sunk below the other side of the mountain.

They'd been traveling in shadow for what seemed nearly an hour, Jack leading the way, when the older boy paused and asked to see the map. Andy and Willie looked at one another and realized, with horror, that they had left the day pack at the top of the mountain, somewhere among the cairns and twisted trees.

"I thought you had it," said Andy, aghast at the smaller boy's carelessness.

"I thought *you* did," said Willie.

No matter; it was Andy that Jack swore at and smacked on the side of the head. Willie looked pained, as if he, too, had been hit.

Jack glanced up the slope, then turned and angrily continued down the trail. "Let's go!" he snapped over his shoulder. "Too late to go back for it now."

They got lost twice coming down, squeezing between boulders, clambering over jagged rocks, and slipping on patches of ice. But just as night had settled on the mountain, and Andy could no longer make out his brother's red hair or his friend's pale face, they all felt the familiar hard-packed earth of the trail beneath their boots.

They were dog-tired and aching by the time they stumbled into camp. They had no flashlights and were too fatigued to try to build a fire. Poor Willie, weariest of all, felt his way to the tent and crawled inside. Andy hung back. In the darkness he heard Jack yawn and slip into the other tent.

He was alone now, with no light but the stars and a sliver of moon, like a great curved mouth. The night was chilly; he knew he couldn't stay out here. With a sigh, he pushed through the tent flaps, trying not to think about what waited for him inside.

The interior of the tent was pitch black and as cold as outdoors. Willie was already asleep. The air, once crisp, seemed heavy with an alien smell; when he lifted the flap of his sleeping bag, the smell grew stronger. Did all new bags smell like this? He recognized the odors of canvas and rubber, but beneath them lurked a hint of something else; fur, maybe, or the breath of an animal.

No, he was imagining things. The only irrefutable fact was the cold. Feeling his way carefully in the darkness, Andy unlaced his boots, barely noticing that his socks were encrusted with snow. Gingerly he inserted one foot into the mouth of the bag, praying he'd feel nothing unusual.

The walls of the bag felt smooth and, moments later, warm. *Too* warm. Surely, though, it was just the warmth of his own body.

He pushed both legs in further, then slipped his feet all the way to the bottom. Lying in the darkness, listening to the sound of Willie's breathing, he could feel the bag press itself against his ankles and legs, clinging to them with a weight that seemed, for goosedown, a shade too heavy. Yet the feeling was not unpleasant. He willed himself to relax.

It occurred to him, as he waited uneasily for sleep, what a clever disguise a bag like this would make for a creature that fed on human flesh. Like a spider feasting upon flies that had blundered into its web, such a creature might gorge contentedly on human beings stupid enough to disregard its warning: *One size eats all* . . . Imagine, prey that literally pushed itself into the predator's mouth

Human stomach acid, he'd read, was capable of eating through a razor blade; and surely this creature's would be worse. He pictured the thing dissolving bones, draining the very life-blood from its victim, leaving a corpse sucked dry of fluids, like the withered husk a spider leaves behind . . .

Suddenly he froze. He felt something damp – no, *wet* – at the bottom of the bag. Wet like saliva. Or worse.

Kicking his feet, he wriggled free of the bag. Maybe what he'd felt was simply the melted snow from his socks, but in the darkness he was taking no chances. Feeling for his boots, he laced them back on and curled up on top of the bag, shivering beneath his coat.

Willie's voice woke him.

"Andy? Are you okay?"

Andy opened his eyes. It was light out. He had survived the night.

"Why were you sleeping like that?" said Willie. "You must be frozen."

"I was afraid to get back in the bag. It felt . . . weird."

Willie smiled. "It was just your imagination, Andy. That's not even your bag."

"Huh?" Andy peered down at the bag. A label near the top said *Arctic Explorer.* "But how – "

"I switched your bag with Jack's when the two of you were starting for the summit," said Willie. "I meant to tell you, but I fell asleep."

"Jack'll be furious," said Andy. "He'll kill me for this!"

Trembling with cold and fear, he crawled stiffly from the tent. It was early morning; a chilly sun hung in the pale blue sky. He dashed to Jack's tent and yanked back the flaps, already composing an apology.

The tent was empty. The sleeping bag, *his* bag, lay dark and swollen on the floor. There seemed to be no one inside.

Or almost no one; for emerging from the top was what appeared to be a deflated basketball – only this one had red hair and a human face.

DONALD R. BURLESON

Mulligan's Fence

DONALD R. BURLESON's stories have appeared in several anthologies, including *Best New Horror, MetaHorror, The Year's Best Fantasy Stories, Post Mortem, 100 Ghastly Little Ghost Stories* and others, as well as in *Twilight Zone Magazine, The Magazine of Fantasy & Science Fiction, Deathrealm, Grue, 2AM* and many other periodicals. A collection of his short fiction, *Lemon Drops and Other Horrors*, was published by Hobgoblin Press in 1993.

He is also the author of several books of criticism including *Lovecraft: Disturbing the Universe* (University Press of Kentucky) and *Begging to Differ: Deconstructionist Readings* (Hobgoblin).

According to the author, the setting of the following story is "a vague reflection of the site of a creepy apartment building where my wife Mollie tells of having lived as a child in Chicago; the building has long since been torn down, but lives on in nightmare."

IN THE MOONLIGHT the gaunt wooden slats of the fence looked like a long row of lupine teeth, weedy at the gumline, grinning all the way to the corner where 47th Street met Ames Street. She followed the grimy sidewalk down to Ames and turned left to see another wan line of incisors stretching away into the dark. Siamese mouths joined at the corner. She wondered why she was here.

At least when she had been chunky, awkward little Kelly Flynn with her thick glasses and pigtails, she had had a reason for standing around this dismal corner which hadn't been quite so dismal in those days. She had lived here. Now that she was chunky, awkward old widowed Kelly Flynn McNeill with her thicker glasses and only a distant memory of pigtails, her presence here was strange. She had been about nine when her family had moved away, and in the forty-odd intervening years she had seldom even thought of this neighborhood.

Well, she did have an excuse for having come back to the city, though if a librarians' convention had been anything thrilling to stay around the hotel for, she wouldn't have been out walking the streets, even to see where she had spent her early childhood. She usually wasn't the type to reminisce about such things, and hadn't been back to see any of the other places her folks had lived. Looking at this forlorn spot with its tall L-shaped fence guarding a now vacant corner lot, she found it hard to believe that the scene was only seven or eight blocks from the hotel with its multilevel parking garage and keycards and opulent carpets. Here, there was only a deserted fence-lined sidewalk dimly lit at long intervals by half-hearted gooseneck streetlamps, the nearest of which stood at the intersection as if deciding which way to turn. Across the street, brownstone buildings were gradually closing all their paper-lidded yellow eyes and settling into sleep. An occasional distant car horn honked; otherwise all was silence. She drew her coat collar closer to her throat and studied the scene. This corner had changed a great deal over the years.

For one thing, the five-story apartment building that had stood behind this fence no longer existed; the old opening in the fence was now solidly boarded over, and the boards had sprouted staples, with tattered yellow signs that shouted NO TRESPASSING in officious block lettering. She remembered hearing news of the fire, several years ago. The fence, Mulligan's fence – how odd it was to whisper that to herself after all this time – had stayed, probably to keep people out of the charred rubble that must still

lie back there, rubble never really cleaned up, city budgets being
what they were. But the fence itself, heavy planking that had pretty
well withstood the ravages of time and urban humanity, looked
somewhat different from the way she remembered it. It looked
smaller, for one thing; wasn't that the way it was always supposed
to be, though, when you were revisiting childhood haunts? She
wondered what else was different about the fence.

And it all began to come back to her. Good heavens; Mulligan,
Mulligan and his fence.

Sidling along, she peered closely at the wooden surface, which
for one thing now wore a number of coats of cracked and
peeling paint; the uppermost layer was a dreary brown. The
neighborhood kids had evidently had a good time scratching
initials and names and various slogans into the paint, which was
crisscrossed many times over and, in some places, embellished
with the inevitable swaths of spray-paint, atop which in one spot
a squad of scratchy little letters marched in a drunken line to
proclaim: *For a good time call Cindy 884-*, but the rest of the
telephone number had been savagely crossed out, perhaps by an
indignant Cindy. Some things never changed.

Anyway, Kelly knew that these countless markings were merely
a surface phenomenon, feeble and evanescent. Beneath the paint
layers and the scratchings would lie more durable inscriptions,
names and initials of a bygone day, carved deeply into the
wood like the original manuscript state of a medieval pal-
impsest. In those days the fence itself had never known the
paintbrush, and there had been no such thing as a can of
spray-paint, so if you were going to leave your mark, you
wielded a pocket knife. Mostly the boys did it, of course, but
some of the girls, making their way through tomboy phases
toward puberty, had carved on the fence as well. Kelly had.
You were a real outcast if you didn't join in, and even at
that time the wooden slats had been a welter of crude letters,
so much so that the expression "Mulligan's fence" had always
put Kelly in mind of Mulligan's stew; it had indeed been a
stew of its own kind, a graphic concoction redolent of many
contributing chefs.

And that brought back thoughts of Mulligan, who had owned
the fence, not to mention the corner lot and the apartment building
itself, in which he occupied a ground-floor apartment. She had no
particular memory of what kind of landlord he had been, and in

fact couldn't remember his ever being excited about anything but his fence.

You kids mark up my fence, you're going to wish you hadn't. She could hear him now, could see him standing plump, untidy, and sour-faced on the crumbling steps. *You're going to be sorry. You write on my fence, you'll be coming to see me. You just wait.* Somehow the way he delivered this vague threat was frightening, but in the paradoxical way of the childhood world, it only made the kids who lived in the building more perversely determined to leave their initials carved into the boards. Mulligan's fence was sacred ground, and they were strongly inclined to commit sacrilege.

Kelly shivered, and realized that it wasn't the night air that made her do so. Mulligan was – well, maybe she shouldn't be too uncharitable, since after all the man had died in the fire, according to the newspapers. But she remembered things.

Things suddenly so vivid that she leaned closer to the fence and studied its markings. Its lower markings, where a child could have – yes! Yes, there, beneath the more superficial scrawl of a modern age less given to permanence. There – deep in the wood, discernible even under paint, two letters: MC. Mary Connors, the little raven-haired girl upstairs, the one with the lisp.

Kelly traced a finger along the letters. M. Still pretty clear, after all these years. C. A little more worn away, but still –

Suddenly the act of running her finger along these old lineaments brought a stirring of other memories, darker memories that had been trying all evening to surface, and she decided that it was time to get back to the well-lighted hallways and conference rooms of her hotel.

But after another long day of dreary panel discussions on inter-library loans and acquisition techniques and cataloguing, she was back, skipping the convention's evening events again, lingering now on her old corner, where Mulligan's fence grinned its wooden grin at the rising moon. Somehow the fence looked complacent, secure in its swarm of inscriptions.

The front door to the old apartment building had been left of center, and to the left of the now boarded-up gateway in the fence only a short stretch of wooden slats was sufficient to reach the nearest surviving building, an apparently empty brick-faced hulk that extended back from the street and angled right and kept going, forming the side and rear of the vacant lot; over the fence she could see the highest of the dark windows back there, a string of yawning mouths stretching all the way to Ames Street. Here where she stood, there was a narrow gap between the end of Mulligan's fence and the edge of the remaining building, and leaning a little into this gap she could just make out a low tumulus of fallen bricks where the pale wash of moonlight came over the fence to invade the weedy and rubble-strewn lot. She could have squeezed through the opening and inspected the blackened ruins, had she wanted to.

But she chose to edge to the right along the length of the fence, past the barricaded entrance, back to the longer stretch of boards, where a bewilderment of carved and painted legends told their endlessly repeated litany to 47th Street. They, the kids, had always done their carving here on the 47th Street side for some reason, never around the corner on Ames Street, perhaps because it was riskier here; Mulligan might catch you, might notice. The most intrepid carvers of course had done their work nearest the old gate.

Kelly squinted at the deeper carvings, faint but detectable beneath the superficialities of the fence. First came ND and, below that, LD: she remembered, with uncanny clarity now, the blonde, blue-eyed twins Nancy and Lucy Daniels. On a line with them, to the right, was CWYNN: Charlie Wynn, whose father had worked at the drugstore on the corner (gone, she'd noticed; a laundry now). Just below and to the right of Charlie was AB: Alice Baker. Kelly remembered the name but little else. Then, a little higher, were BJ and MR: Billy Jenkins and Mikey Ryan, a pair of neighborhood bullies as she recalled, always together, even here in wooden epitaph. After them came FREDDYS: that would be Freddy Shea (disturbing memories, there); then MC again, little Mary Connors with her raven locks and lisping voice. And just past the halfway point on the way to the corner was GARYW: Gary Williams. At this one she paused, remembering.

Gary had been painfully skinny, with the largest ears she had ever seen, then or since; he was not terribly bad to look at, all in all, but his ears had run nearly the full length of his thin face, like big pink bookends, or like ominous parentheses enclosing his face as an afterthought. He had liked her, had in his childish way made eyes at her and had at one point even tried to kiss her, but she had kept him at a distance, fearing, for one thing, the taunting of the others; most of the kids had made fun of Gary. Absently, she traced out the G with her forefinger, and the A, the R, the Y, the W. Actually, she had thought of him from time to time, wondering what ever became of him; she had visions of him ensconced with a family somewhere, mowing a lawn and tossing a ball with his kids. Where did people go when you lost sight of them?

She passed along to the next inscriptions she could make out: JL and BL, which would be Jerry and Betsy Lloyd, whose mother always had a fresh pie cooling on the windowsill upstairs. Betsy was somewhat older than her brother Jerry, and his leaving his initials on the fence must have emboldened her to add her own. Farther along she found RT: Russell Tully, a boy she only vaguely remembered. Finally, in the least courageous spot, nearest the street corner and far from the apartment entrance, she found the fossil memory of herself: KF. Most of these older letters were rather large and rather deeply gouged into the wood, but it was still surprising that most of them were legible after all this time. She lingered over her own initials, musing.

"Kelly? Is that you?"

Startled, she turned toward the voice. The woman was still a little shorter than she, and some of the shoulder-length raven hair was now streaked with gray; and yes – Kelly had noticed a slight lisp.

She took the woman's proffered hand. "Good heavens. Mary? Mary Connors?"

Mary nodded, smiling, holding the hand a moment longer. "Mary Douglas now. I knew it was you. Somehow you don't seem to have changed that much. And I remembered your place. You're standing by your place on the fence. KF." She laughed, and Kelly did too, but when their eyes met again it was with a certain odd seriousness. Kelly felt compelled to explain her presence there.

"I'm in town for a convention at the Sheraton. I figured while I was back for the weekend I might as well walk over here and have a look. What – what brings you here, Mary?" Even in asking, she half felt that she already knew.

The other woman looked away for a second, then shrugged. "I couldn't say. I live only across town, on the north end, but I never really thought of coming here. Till now. Last night I told Tom – that's my husband – that I had the most peculiar urge – I mean, suddenly I just wanted to come here. Tonight I left straight from work and here I am. Isn't that the strangest thing?"

Kelly studied her face. "Is it?"

All at once Mary looked nervous, as if the conversation were about to take a direction uncomfortable to her. "What do you mean?"

"Well," Kelly said, "do you remember what happened, with Freddy Shea? You can still see his name on the fence, you know, if you look closely." They walked a little away from the corner and Kelly pointed out the name, to the left of MC. "Remember, Mary?"

"I – I'm not sure I do."

"Or not sure you want to?" Kelly asked, trying to let her tone say that she was not being unkind. "I wouldn't blame you. Anyway, I don't know if Freddy ever told you what he told me. Old Mulligan actually caught him carving his name, caught him right in the act, when he was finishing up. Freddy said Mulligan traced his finger along the letters in the fence. Just ran a finger along the letters, staring at Freddy the whole time, and turned and walked away, and went inside. Later Freddy went in and started to walk past Mulligan's door to go upstairs, but couldn't walk past. Just couldn't, for the life of him. Instead, he ended up knocking on Mulligan's door, doing it but not wanting to, and Mulligan opened the door and pulled him inside. Freddy never would tell me what happened in there, but I remember him coming up the stairs later, white as chalk and trembling all over. He never told you any of this?"

Mary shook her head. "No, he never said much of anything to me at all, actually. But I take it you don't know the same sort of thing happened to – what was her name? Alice? And to those twins, you know, Lucy and Nancy. And to the kid whose dad ran the drugstore."

"Charlie?"

"Charlie Wynn, right. Some of those things may have happened after you moved away. Good thing you weren't around. I moved away too, the year after you, or Mulligan might have got around to me next."

Kelly shuddered. "God, what kind of man was he?"

Mary stared at the rough boards for a long time before looking at Kelly again. "No, you know, I think the question is, what kind of thing was his fence?"

By now Kelly felt sure enough to reply: "I would ask what kind of thing *is* his fence."

Mary glared at her. "You mean – the reason I – "

Kelly nodded. "Guess so. It wasn't Mulligan so much. It was – well, yes, I did trace out your initials. Last night. Right here. You know, I think we could get the whole gang back here if we tried."

Mary turned away, and seemed to be mulling this over. When she turned back, it was to ask: "*Did* you call anyone else?"

Kelly hesitated. "I – ah – well. Just Gary."

Mary gaped at her in evident astonishment. "Gary? Gary *Williams*?" Choking back a laugh, she put her hand over her mouth and shook her head slowly, as if in incredulity. "Oh, Kelly, my God, you really are impossible!"

And, trailing a somehow mirthless-sounding laughter, she was around the corner and gone.

Kelly stood on the corner for a while, feeling suddenly very alone. She walked around for a while, and finally headed back to the hotel.

In the lobby, she checked with the clerk at the desk to see if she had any messages; Mrs Fletcher, her neighbor back home, was supposed to call if there were any problems while she was away. There was indeed a message, but when the clerk handed the rumpled note to her and she unfolded it and read it, the message was not from Mrs Fletcher. Instantly Kelly turned around and hurried out the revolving door to the street.

Back on the old corner under the pale lamplight, she asked herself why she had come back here this time. After resisting the idea for some minutes, she admitted to herself that it was to see – to verify that something would *not* happen. Assuredly would not happen. Mary's urge to come back here had to have been a coincidence: a truly remarkable one, but a coincidence nonetheless. Kelly was back here by the fence now to see that nothing *else* was going to happen.

And apparently nothing was. A pair of late-night strollers sauntered by, talking quietly, but otherwise the streets were empty. Across the way, huddled apartments had long since closed their tired eyes and slept. From somewhere far off, vague traffic sounds mingled with the wind that had sprung up, but all else was silence, and she began to feel foolish standing out here unaccountably, pointlessly. What would she say if a policeman came along and asked her why she was here?

She strolled closer to the corner, straining to read the older inscriptions on the fence, those archaeological strata beneath the modern vulgarities. The kids, her old circle of friends – scattered, gone. Where? Anywhere, everywhere, nowhere. Strange, how you never forgot some –

The thought broke off in her mind with the realization that she was listening, had been listening for some time. For what? To what? The wind, her own breath, nothing else.

No – no, there, again. A sort of scraping sound. Faint, vague, distant, but seeming to come closer.

Well, now, this was foolish, letting her imagination go this way. There was nothing to be nervous about. But the sound was closer now, apparently coming from around on Ames Street, approaching the corner, and in the same moment she realized both that it sounded like a shoe scraping along the pavement, and that some undefinable odor now floated on the wind. It took another moment for her to place the odor as damp sod, with some less thinkable smell beneath, but by then the tattered and rail-thin source of these impressions had shambled all the way around the corner. Some feverish region of Kelly's mind chattered: he got here fast, considering how much farther he had to come.

Even mostly eaten away, the ears were still quite large, and she had time only to reflect once more on Mary's note – *Kelly: Gary Williams died a year ago* – before, embracing her, he had pressed what was left of his mouth to hers.

DANIEL FOX

How She Dances

DANIEL FOX is perhaps better known as Chaz Brenchley, the author of four psycho-thrillers, *The Samaritan*, *The Refuge*, *The Garden* and *Mall Time*, as well as three fantasy novels for children. His latest novel, *Paradise*, is described as "an inner city epic of good and evil".

The author lives in Newcastle upon Tyne and has recently completed a year as crimewriter-in-residence at St Peter's Riverside Sculpture Project in Sunderland. He has written around four hundred stories in various genres, and his short horror fiction has appeared in *The Mammoth Book of Frankenstein* and several volumes of *Dark Voices: The Pan Book of Horror*.

S HE PICKED ME up down at the station, on a Saturday night.
    I'd been drinking with friends till the pubs closed, and the
plan was to go on to a nightclub after; but I was in an odd mood,
restless and unsettled, even with people I'd known for years. I
didn't want the evening to end in a fight, but it was heading that
way, I could feel it; and all my own work it'd be, if it happened.
If I let it happen. So I left the others abruptly, with a shrug and
a wave and let them wonder. I didn't know myself what had got
into me that night; but I could sort it out tomorrow. A couple of
phone calls, an apology, they'd laugh it off. They were my friends,
and no problem.

Right now, though, I had nowhere to go but home. And I was
still solvent, thanks to my interrupted evening; and I'd missed the
last bus, and it was a two-mile walk to the flat, and I wasn't so
drunk I wouldn't notice it. So, *what the hell, Mick, treat yourself*.
I went down to the station for a taxi.

There's always a queue that time of night, and it's worse on
Saturdays. I took a look and almost changed my mind; but the
line was moving quickly, a constant stream of taxis picking up.
So I tagged on the end, shuffle-dancing on the spot for warmth,
turning the music up good and loud in my head and wondering
if maybe I should've gone clubbing after all. Dancing always was
therapy, for me. Used to be.

But chances were I'd change my mind again halfway there; and
there were already half a dozen people in line behind me, and
you always feel stupid giving up your place in a queue with no
visible reason. So I stayed, and danced, and looked around, and
saw her.

She would've been hard to miss, in all honesty. A tall, thin woman
wearing a man's raincoat over a long khaki skirt that surely had
to be home-made, there wasn't a shop in the country would sell
a thing like that. And her hair was all tied up in a square of cloth
the same dead colour, and her hands were twisting and shifting
and tangling together, and all in all she just looked mad. I thought
she might be talking to herself too, mutter, mutter, with the odd
shrill curse. Couldn't tell from this distance, she was twenty yards
away or more, but looked the type.

Thing was, though, she was beautiful with it. Not sexy at all, she
was too weird for that, but her face had that modelled perfection

to it that always hits you hard, it's so rare. Like one of those Victorian china dolls – creepy, but flawless. I couldn't guess how old she was. Anywhere from twenty-five to forty: older than me, for sure, but surely too young to be doing this, to be dressing weird and wringing her hands and talking to herself, being noticed by everyone and hurriedly ignored by most.

I didn't ignore her. Not me, not smart Mick Hunter. I was too curious, too interested, head full of questions that eluded any answer. That's an occupational hazard for either a student or a pisshead, and I was both.

So I stood there gawping, and she saw me doing it, and even then I didn't look away; and she thought that was an invitation. And who knows, maybe she was right, maybe it was. *Come on in*, I might have been saying, *even things up, do me a little damage here. I can take it.* Or maybe, *I deserve it.*

Whatever. This is what she did, this is what happened. This is what she did to me.

She came sidling up to me in this odd walk she had, sort of striding but never striding straight, she never did anything straight; she came at me crabwise, and her eyes moved all over, all around my face without ever meeting mine, and she said this, or something like it. Close enough to this.

Said, "I'm sorry, excuse me, I know I shouldn't ask, I shouldn't be asking; only I'm desperate, you see, and my baby, my baby needs me."

Never straight, she never came straight at anything. I just looked at her, dead straight, waiting for the pay-off.

"Are you," she said, "it's silly of me really, I don't suppose you are, you could be going anywhere and you don't know me, but are you, are you going up the West Road at all? In your taxi? Are you waiting for a taxi?"

"Yes," I said, drunk and honest and never mind my sinking heart, "I'm waiting for a taxi; and yes, I'm going west."

I knew what she wanted, and I knew what I'd say. Good middle-class boy, me, ex-Boy Scout, all the right instincts trained in. But I stopped there, I didn't offer. I was going to make her ask, at least.

"Well, could I, do you think I could possibly, would you mind terribly if I shared it? If I came with you? I haven't any money, I can't give you anything towards it, it's stupid of me but I left my purse at home; and I've got to get back, for my baby . . ."

She spoke dead posh, high and hoarse and fluttery, pretty much like you'd expect from the look of her; and her hands moved like her conversation, in gentle jerks and fingerings, reaching to touch my arm and drawing back. And I guessed she'd done this often enough before, but she obviously had a knack for it, unless everyone's as soft a touch as I am. As I was, rather. Back then.

Because I said yes, of course I did. I thought she was glass, I thought I could see through her all the way. I didn't believe the maiden-in-distress act, not for a minute, but I still said yes. She could sit in my taxi, five or ten minutes and there you go. Why not? She'd be safe with me, at least, where she might not be with another man; and it'd make a story for my friends to hear, how I did my knight-errant bit for a crazy lady.

And that's all it would've been if I'd been sharp at all, if I hadn't been muzzy from drinking. That's all it should have been, a seat in my taxi and goodbye, no obligation.

But where she was going, her flat was only one street down from mine, the other side of the cemetery; and the driver took us along the river and up, so we reached hers first. And I wasn't thinking, I got out with her and paid the taxi off, saved myself twenty pence.

Cost myself a whole lot more: a lifetime of paying, maybe. Unless I get lucky. Amnesia or senility, that's what I'm looking for now, that's where my hope is. I just want to get out of my head, I don't like what's in here, can't live with it.

Standing there in the night, in the dark, I still could've saved myself if I'd only simply walked away; but I didn't. Too polite, too well-trained: blame my parents, my culture, blame whoever you like. I just blame myself.

Anyway, I said something, something bland and inane, just making conversation. "My flat's only just round the corner from here, surprised I haven't seen you in the street," it might have been that, or something like it. But whatever it was, it wasn't, "Goodnight."

And she said, "Would you, I don't suppose you would, I expect you want to get off now, don't want to be troubled with me; but would you like to come in? For a coffee?"

And God help me, because no one else can now; but I stood there and looked at her, saw the strangeness and overlooked it, and said yes. Couldn't see any point in the alternative, being home and alone; so I said yes, OK, I'd have a coffee. Thanks, I said.

She had three good locks on her front door, had to find three separate keys in her pockets before she could let us in.

"Dodgy area, isn't it?" I said. "You been burgled yet?"

"No, but I mustn't," she said. "I can't let that happen, I've got to keep my baby safe."

Baby. She'd mentioned the baby half a dozen times by now; but the flat was dark and felt empty, and the door had been so thoroughly, comprehensively locked . . .

"Where's your baby now, then?"

"In her room, of course. She'll be sleeping."

"No babysitter?"

"Oh, no. I couldn't, I couldn't leave her with a stranger."

"You mean you'd rather leave her alone?" I was jolted enough, drunk enough just to say that, straight out.

"It doesn't matter," she said, sounding slightly puzzled. "I always know when she's going to wake up, when she'll want me. I'm always here when she needs me."

That sounded like bullshit from where I stood; but, hell, it was none of my business. Let the social services sort it out, they'd get on to her sooner or later. Probably sooner, if she told other people what she'd just told me.

I followed her up the stairs and into a living room strewn with baby-clothes, cluttered with toys. I didn't know about the clothes, but some of those toys were twenty years old or more, jumble-sale pickings by the look of them, flaking paint and dents and the odd rough edge where something had broken off. Definitely not for babies, I'd have thought, but what did I know?

She made coffee, then left me alone for a couple of minutes. I snooped shamelessly, drawn to the one real oddity in the room, the computer in the corner. There was a sheaf of handwritten pages by the keyboard, a doctoral thesis on anaerobic sewage treatment; and it didn't take a Holmesian intellect to deduce that she took in other people's typing.

She came back with a photograph album, pictures of her baby; and she scrounged a cigarette and gave me an illustrated lecture. The kid's name was Anne-Marie and she was six months old, never a day's illness in her life and the sweetest baby any mother could wish for. And her mother's name was Alice, I learned that too; and yes, Alice typed for a living. And I was a student, was I, yes, of course I was, she could see that, I was an intellectual, it showed in my face; and if I ever needed a dissertation typing up, or any of my student friends, if they did, she was cheaper than the agencies and just as quick . . .

Forty-five minutes of this, and then there were soft wails coming through the wall, and that had to be the baby, bless her; so I used her as an excuse and left, with Alice's business card in my pocket and nothing in my head except to get home, to get away.

But you forget awkwardness and embarrassment, and only remember strangeness; and you get curious, you want to try things twice. Or I do, anyway. I did. And a few months later I did need some typing done, and I really couldn't afford the agencies; so I went back to find Alice.

It took her a while to answer the door, but when she did it felt like I'd been gone only a few minutes, instead of months. The baby was crying – again, obviously, but I almost said *still*, because that's how it felt, as if there'd been no break at all – and Alice was wearing the same strange clothes, and her hands and voice were imitating each other as before, tying words and fingers into soft knots.

"Michael, you came, I didn't expect, I thought, I don't know why you should have bothered. But there, you've got work with you, you haven't come to visit, have you, of course not, you want some typing done. Come in, come up, I'll just, I'll have to settle the baby . . ."

Again she took me to the living room, and left me, and again I snooped among the toys and clothes, fascinated and repelled by both. There were dresses there that would fit a three-year-old, as well as nappies for a newborn; there was an old tin wheeled horse that even a three-year-old would be too small to ride. Alice's buying for the baby looked as obsessive as her conversation, and as ill-planned.

But the baby's crying stopped abruptly, and a minute later Alice came back, privately smiling, practically oozing tender maternity. It ought to have been a performance, she laid it on so thick; but I believed her, I thought she really did feel that deeply towards little Anne-Marie, that deeply attached. Probably she was lonely,

I couldn't see her having many friends (*or any friends*, a more honest echo in the back of my head), and likely a single mother would turn more and more towards her child in a situation like that. I'd never asked, but Alice had to be a single mother.

It couldn't be good for the kid to be so needed, so possessed; but that was no concern of mine. NMP, that was: Not My Problem.

I had to show some interest, though, I had to be polite before we got down to business; and asking about the baby was the easiest way to do that. Safe territory, I thought.

I thought.

"So how is Anne-Marie, then? Crawling all over by now, I imagine, is she?"

"Oh, no," and Alice laughed, high and shrill. "No, she's not crawling yet, not yet. She's only six months old, you know, not time for crawling yet. I can walk her, I can hold her hands and she'll walk, she even dances for me sometimes; but she hasn't started crawling yet, oh no."

And that's when it all turned very bad indeed. That's when I stood there and thought, *get out, Mick, just get out of here, get moving*. And if I'd been moving already it would've been easy, my feet would've done the job for me, no problem, they were itching for it. But I wasn't moving, I was standing still and I couldn't overcome that. I just got stiller, only the tingling in my fingers and my feet to say they were working at all.

So I did the other thing, I lied to myself. I thought, *It's OK, it's a misunderstanding, that's all. Nothing to worry about. No problem.*

Or if there was a problem it wasn't mine, NMP, I thought that too; but even that thought couldn't stop me doing the stupid thing, the thing I did next.

"Only six months?" I said, dragging questions out into the light, where they had to be answered. "But surely, she must be older than that, about eleven months by now, she was six months when I was here before. You showed me photos."

Alice smiled, when I mentioned the photos. I saw how her hands touched an imaginary album, how they smoothed its cover and turned the pages back; and my fingers weren't tingling any more, they were starting to shake.

"That's right," she said, "you've seen the photos, haven't you? You've seen my lovely baby. Six months, one week, three days," she said. "Exactly."

And she smiled another of those sweet smiles, and looked like a living china doll; and I was getting scared now, I was getting thoroughly spooked.

"When," I said, croaking the word out through a tight, tight throat, "when's her birthday, Alice?"

"Oh, we just had her birthday," she said, "you've missed that. Her birthday's in September. The seventeenth."

Which didn't make her six months or eleven either, and oh, I was frightened, and I didn't want to know.

"What year was that, Alice? Seventeenth of September, which year?"

"Year?" She shook her head vaguely. "I forget, it doesn't matter, why would it matter?"

I didn't say anything, for a minute. And then, when I could talk, I said, "Can I see her? Please," I said. "I'd like to see her. Very much."

"She's sleeping."

"I don't think so, Alice. I don't think she is."

"Well, just for a minute, then. Just from the door. She should be sleeping now. She needs her sleep."

Alice led me out onto the landing, and made a great show of tiptoeing down to the furthest door, which stood slightly ajar. She pushed it a little wider and slipped inside, vanished into darkness.

After a moment she reappeared, and beckoned to me. There was barely room for me to put my head in, with the door only half open and her standing there in the gap; and it was so dark in there, I could really see nothing but shadows. But there was a box-like shadow that resolved itself slowly into a cot, I could make out the bars of it and a bundle behind the bars; and the bundle stirred, I saw that. I saw an arm rise and fall, as though the baby were waving; and relief broke through my body like a wave on shingle. Just paranoia and confusion, then, and nothing to get worked up about. Nothing I had to do except be polite, back out of there, talk about typing.

But the baby went on waving, the one arm going up and down, up and down; and the more my eyes adjusted to the dim light, the stranger it looked. And the room smelled strange, too, it smelled musty and unused, almost, surely, unlived-in; and Alice was standing with her back to me, still blocking my way in, and she was sort of chanting baby-talk under her breath in time with that stiff movement, and she sounded utterly mad.

I pressed the light-switch by my shoulder.

Nothing happened, though, except that Alice's head jerked round, and, "No light," she breathed, "you mustn't. I took the bulb away. Mustn't let the light in, baby doesn't like the light, it isn't good for her . . ."

Even then I could just have walked away, and I wish I had. There's always a last chance; that was mine, and I blew it.

It wasn't curiosity driving me now, nothing like it: closer to panic, perhaps, the certainty of horror lurking somewhere in this story, in this room. Waiting for the light. But panic or not, I still needed to resolve it. I still needed to know.

So I pushed past Alice despite her sudden screeching and her clutching hands, I went to the window and I tried to draw the curtain back.

It didn't draw, though, because it wasn't a curtain. It was a blanket, and it was nailed tight across the frame. But I had my own madness now; I stretched up, caught hold of the edge as high as I could reach, dug my fingers in between the nails and yanked hard.

It held for a second, then started to rip. Three good tugs, and the sunlight was flooding into that room where no light had been for far too long.

Now I could see; and now, already, too late already, I wished it all undone.

"The light's not good for baby," Alice said, her voice twisting like her face was twisting, "the light makes baby cry, see? See?"

And her finger stabbed down on a cassette player, and the room filled with the sounds of a baby crying. The sounds I'd heard as I arrived here, a few short minutes ago; the same sounds, the same tape that I'd heard five months back. She must have had it on a time switch then, to start it playing while she was in the other room with me.

"Baby likes dancing," Alice was saying, gasping rather, the words coming in hurried gulps while tears flowed down her porcelain cheeks. "Baby dance for Mama, look, see how she dances . . ."

I could see already, how baby danced. Much the same way as she'd waved, earlier. There were strings, rising from the baby's cot; they ran through loops across the ceiling, and came down the wall by the door, just where Alice was standing. And Alice held the strings in her twitching, fretful hands, and pulled them lovingly; and baby rose from her blankets and danced for me and Mama.

At the inquest, the doctor told us that Anne-Marie had died at around six months, as near as he could tell. *Six months, one week, three days*, I thought, but didn't say. She'd been dead a long time, he told us, he couldn't say how long, with the body so strangely treated; but the birth certificate said she'd been born three years before, and yes, he said, that would fit with what medical evidence, what knowledge he had.

The good news was that she might, she might have died of natural causes. Impossible to be sure, he said, but there were no signs of violence. Not before death, at least. Might have been a cot death, he said, just an inexplicable loss. And that might help to explain the mother, he said, what the mother had done.

That's what I try to remember now, that she might have died sweet and easy, no pain or fear and nothing to do with Alice. That maybe what Alice did after was no worse than a grieving mother trying to hold on to what was gone, no more than a child playing dolls.

That's what I try to remember. Mostly it doesn't work, though. Mostly what I remember is Anne-Marie dancing that day, while her mother pulled the strings.

The tape played, and baby danced to the sounds of her own crying, as if she danced to music. The little crocheted blankets fell away, and I saw a shrivelled brown husk of a thing in a white lace gown, strings sewn to her wrists and elbows, and to the back of her neck.

She hung above her cot and moved in jerks, in a desperate parody. Her blind eyes were sewn shut, *hush, baby's sleeping*, but there were crude blotches of blue painted on the dark dry lids, *look, baby's awake, blue eyes smiling for Mama*. Lipstick was smeared clumsily across her gaping, toothless mouth, *there, baby, don't cry, Mama make you pretty*.

And, of course, Mama made her dance. Her head flopped, forward and back as she jiggled on the strings, and her hands dangled at the end of stick-thin arms; later I learned that Alice had broken every joint in her body, to make her move at the strings' command. That didn't help, but nothing could, much. Nothing can.

Anne-Marie's in the cemetery now, just down the road from my flat. Her mother's in hospital, but I'm not concerned about Alice.

I went to the funeral to see baby buried, to be certain it was done; and I'm trying to save money now, to pay for a headstone. Something good and heavy, to weigh her down.

I wish to God they'd burned her, for surety's sake, but they wouldn't listen to me. Father's wishes, they said, though God knows how they traced the father. Then they sent me to a psychiatrist, but he didn't help either. I still see her dancing, every time I hear a baby cry; and I still get scared, every time I see a baby being taken down the hill to the cemetery. Sometimes I go running after, to be sure the baby's sleeping. *Don't let it wake up,* I tell them, *don't let it cry in that corner. Not in earshot of that corner, where the new graves are . . .*

KARL EDWARD WAGNER

Passages

KARL EDWARD WAGNER is another regular contributor to *The Best New Horror*. Since 1980 he has edited *The Year's Best Horror Stories* series for DAW Books and is currently working on two new novels, *The Fourth Seal* and a book-length version of his disowned DC Comics graphic novel, *Tell Me, Dark*.

He has also recently compiled two new collections of short stories, *Exorcisms and Ecstasies* and *Silver Dagger*, the latter a fourth book of tales featuring his barbarian sorcerer, Kane. Other recent appearances include *Elric: Tales of the White Wolf* (a Kane-meets-Elric crossover), *The Mammoth Book of Frankenstein*, *The Ultimate Witch*, *Touch Wood* and *Phobias*, from which the following story is taken.

As the author explains: "The doctor character is mainly autobiographical. I did have a needle broken in my arm, as described, with subsequent needle phobia etc., as written. I became a psychiatrist rather than a heart surgeon. Think I never lost that light in my eyes (paraphrasing Pink Floyd's 'Poles Apart' on their new album, *The Decision Bell*). I guess."

T HERE WERE THE three of them, seated at one of the corner
tables, somewhat away from the rest of the crowd in the
rented banquet room at the Legion Hall. A paper banner painted
in red and black school colors welcomed back the Pine Hill High
School Class of 1963 to its 25th Class Reunion. A moderately bad
local band was playing a medley of hits from the 1960s, and many
of the middle-aged alumni were attempting to dance. In an eddy
from the amplifiers, it was possible to carry on a conversation.

They were Marcia Meadows (she had taken back her maiden
name after the divorce), Fred Pruitt (once known as Freddie
Pruitt and called so again tonight), and Grant McDade (now
addressed as Dr McDade). The best of friends in high school,
each had gone his separate way, and despite yearbook vows to
remain the very closest of friends forever, they had been out of
touch until this night. Marcia and Grant had been voted Most
Intellectual for the senior class. Freddie and one Beth Markeson
had been voted Most Likely to Succeed. These three were laughing
over their senior photographs in the yearbook. Plastic cups of beer
from the party keg were close at hand. Freddie had already drunk
more than the other two together.

Marcia sighed and shook her head. They all looked so young
back then: pictures of strangers. "So why isn't Beth here tonight?"

"Off somewhere in California, I hear," Freddie said. He was the
only one of the three who had remained in Pine Hill. He owned
the local Porsche-Audi-BMW dealership. "I think she's supposed
to be working in pictures. She always had a good . . ."

". . . body!" Marcia finished for him. The two snorted laughter,
and Grant smiled over his beer.

Freddie shook his head and ran his hand over his shiny scalp;
other than a fringe of wispy hair, he was as bald as a honeydew
melon. A corpulent man – he had once been quite slender – his
double chin overhung his loosened tie, and the expensive suit was
showing strain. "Wonder how she's held up. None of us look the
same as then." Quickly: "Except you, Marcia. Don't you agree,
Grant?"

"As beautiful as the day I last saw her." Grant raised a toast, and
Marcia hoped she hadn't blushed. After twenty-five years Grant
McDade remained in her fantasies. She wished he'd take off those
dark glasses – vintage B&L Ray Bans, just like his vintage white
T-shirt and James Dean red nylon jacket and the tight jeans. His
high school crewcut was now slicked-back blond hair, and there

were lines in his face. Otherwise he was still the boy she'd wanted to have take her to the senior prom. Well, there *was* an indefinable difference. But given the years, and the fact that he was quite famous in his field . . .

"You haven't changed much either, I guess, Grant." Freddie had refilled his beer cup. "I remember that jacket from high school. Guess you heart surgeons know to keep fit."

He flapped a hand across his pink scalp. "But look at me. Bald as that baby's butt. Serves me right for always wanting to have long hair as a kid."

"Weren't you ever a hippie?" Marcia asked.

"Not me. Nam caught up to me first. But I always wanted to have long hair back when I was a kid – back before the Beatles made it OK to let your hair grow. Remember *Hair* and that song? Well, too late for me by then."

Freddie poured more beer down his throat. Marcia hadn't kept count, but she hoped he wouldn't throw up. From his appearance, Freddie could probably hold it.

"When I was a kid," Freddie was becoming maudlin, "I hated to get my hair cut. I don't know why. Maybe it was those Sunday School stories about Samson and Delilah that scared me. Grant – you're a doctor: ask your shrink friends. It was those sharp scissors and buzzing clippers, that chair like the dentist had, and that greasy crap they'd smear in your hair. 'Got your ears lowered!' the kids at school would say."

Freddie belched. "Well, my mother used to tease me about it. Said she'd tie a ribbon in my hair and call me Frederika. I was the youngest – two older sisters – and I was always teased that Mom had hoped I'd be a girl too, to save on buying new clothes, just pass along hand-me-downs. I don't know what I really thought. You remember being a kid in the 1950s: how incredibly naive we all of us were."

"Tell me!" Marcia said. "I was a freshman in college before I ever saw even a *picture* of a hard-on."

"My oldest sister," Freddie went on, "was having a slumber party for some of her sorority sisters one night. Mom and Dad were out to a church dinner; she was to baby sit. I was maybe ten at the time. Innocent as a kitten."

Marcia gave him her beer to finish. She wasn't certain whether Freddie could walk as far as the keg.

Freddie shook his head. "Well, I was just a simple little boy in a house full of girls. Middle of the 1950s. I think one of the sorority girls had smuggled in a bottle of vodka. They were very giggly, I remember.

"So they said they'd initiate me into their sorority. They had those great big lollipops that were the fad then, and I wanted one. But I had to join the sorority.

"So they got out some of my sisters' clothes, and they stripped me down. Hadn't been too long before that that my mother or sister would bathe me, so I hadn't a clue. Well, they dressed me up in a trainer bra with tissue padding, pink panties, a pretty slip, lace petticoats, one of my fourteen-year-old sister's party dresses, a little garter belt, hose and heels. I got the whole works. I was big enough that between my two sisters they could fit me into anything. I thought it was all good fun because they were all laughing – like when I asked why the panties didn't have a Y-front.

"They made up my face and lips and tied a ribbon in my hair, gave me gloves, a handbag, and a little hat. Now I knew why sissy girls took so long to get dressed. When Mom and Dad got home, they presented me to them as little Frederika."

"Did you get a whipping?" Marcia asked.

Freddie finished Marcia's beer. "No. My folks thought it was funny as hell. My mom loved it. Dad couldn't stop laughing and got out his camera. This was 1955. They even called the neighbors over for the show. My family never let me live it down.

"Pretty little Frederika! After that, I demanded to get a crewcut once a week. So now I'm fat, ugly, and bald."

"Times were different then," Marcia suggested.

"Hell, there's nothing wrong with me! I was a Marine in Nam. I got a wife and three sons." Freddie pointed to where his plump wife was dancing with an old flame. "It didn't make me queer!"

"It only made you bald," said Grant. "Overcompensation. Physical response to emotional trauma."

"You should've been a shrink instead of a surgeon." Freddie lurched off for more beers all around. He had either drunk or spilled half of them by the time he returned. He was too drunk to remember to be embarrassed, but would hate his soul-baring in the morning.

Marcia picked up the thread of conversation. "Well, teasing from your siblings won't cause hair loss." She flounced her mass of chestnut curls. "If that were true, then I'd be bald too."

"Girls don't have hair loss," Freddie said, somewhat mopishly.

"Thank you, but I'm a mature forty-one." Marcia regretted the stiffness in her tone immediately. Freddie might be macho, but he was a balding unhappy drunk who had once been her unrequited dream date right behind Grant. Forget it: Freddie was about as much in touch with feminists as she was with BMW fuel injection systems.

Marcia Meadows had aged well, despite a terrible marriage, two maniac teenaged sons, and a demanding career in fashion design. She now had her own modest string of boutiques, had recently exhibited to considerable approval at several important shows, and was correctly confident that a few years would establish her designs on the international scene. She had gained perhaps five pounds since high school and could still wear a miniskirt to flattering effect – as she did tonight with an ensemble of her own creation. She had a marvelous smile, pixie features, and lovely long legs which she kept crossing – hoping to catch the eye of Grant McDade. This weekend's return to Pine Hill was for her something of an adventure. She wondered what might lie beneath the ashes of old fantasies.

"I had – still have – " Marcia corrected herself, "two older brothers. They were brats. Always teasing me." She sipped her fresh beer. "Still do. Should've been drowned at birth."

Her hands fluttered at her hair in reflex. Marcia had an unruly tangle of tight, chestnut-brown curls – totally unmanageable. In the late 1960s it had passed as a fashionable Afro. Marcia had long since given up hope of taming it. After all, miniskirts had come back. Maybe Afros?

"So what did they do?" Freddie prodded.

"Well, they knew I was scared of spiders. I mean, like I *really* am scared of spiders!" Marcia actually shuddered. "I really hate and loathe spiders."

"So. Rubber spiders in the underwear drawer?" Freddie giggled. It was good he had a wife to drive him home.

Marcia ignored him. "We had lots of woods behind our house. I was something of a tomboy. I loved to go romping through the woods. You know how my hair is – has always been."

"Lovely to look at, delightful to hold," said Grant, and behind his dark glasses there may have been a flash of memory.

"But a mess to keep combed," Marcia finished. "Anyway, you know those really gross spiders that build their webs between trees and bushes in the woods? The ones that look like dried-up snot boogers with little legs, and they're always strung out there across the middle of a path?"

"I was a Boy Scout," Freddie remembered.

"Right! So I was always running into those yucky little suckers and getting their webs caught in my hair. Then I'd start screaming and clawing at my face and run back home, and my snotty brothers would laugh like hyenas.

"But here's the worst part." Marcia chugged a long swallow of beer. "You know how you *never* see those goddamn spiders once you've hit their webs? It's like they see you coming, say 'too big to fit into my parlor,' and they bail out just before you plow into their yucky webs. Like, one second they're there, ugly as a pile of pigeon shit with twenty eyes, and then they vanish into thin air.

"So. My dear big brothers convinced me that the spiders were trapped in my hair. Hiding out in this curly mess and waiting to crawl out for revenge. At night they were sure to creep out and crawl into my ears and eat my brain. Make a web across my nose and smother me. Wriggle beneath my eyelids and suck dry my eyeballs. Slip down my mouth and fill my tummy with spider eggs that would hatch out and eat through my skin. My brothers liked to say that they could see them spinning webs between my curls, just hoping to catch a few flies while they waited for the chance to get me."

Marcia smiled and shivered. It still wasn't easy to think about. "So, of course, I violently combed and brushed my hair as soon as I rushed home, shampooed for an hour – once I scrubbed my scalp with Ajax cleanser – just to be safe. So, it's a wonder that I still have my hair."

"And are you still frightened of spiders?" Grant asked.

"Yes. But I wear a hat when I venture into the woods now. Saves wear and tear on the hair."

"A poetess," remarked Freddie. He was approaching the legless stage, and one of his sons fetched him a fresh beer. "So, Grant. So, Dr McDade, excuse me. We have bared our souls and told you of our secret horrors. What now, if anything, has left its emotional scars upon the good doctor? Anything at all?"

Marcia sensed the angry tension beneath Freddie's growing drunkenness. She looked toward Grant. He had always been master of any situation. He could take charge of a class reunion situation. He'd always taken charge.

Grant sighed and rubbed at his forehead. Marcia wished he'd take off those sunglasses, so she could get a better feeling of what went on behind those eyes.

"Needles," said Grant.

"Needles?" Freddie laughed, his momentary belligerence forgotten. "But you're a surgeon!"

Grant grimaced and gripped his beer cup in his powerful, long-fingered hands. Marcia could visualize those hands – rubber-gloved and bloodstained, deftly repairing a dying heart.

"I was very young," he said. "We were still living in our old house, and we moved from there before I was five. My memories of that time go back to just as I was learning to walk. The ice cream man still made his rounds in a horsedrawn cart. This was in the late 1940s.

"Like all children, I hated shots. And trips to the doctor, since all doctors did was give children shots. I would put up quite a fuss, despite promises of ice cream afterward. If you've ever seen – or tried to give a screaming child a shot, you know the difficulty."

Grant drew in his breath, still clutching the beer cup. Marcia hadn't seen him take a sip from it since it had been refilled.

"I don't know why I was getting a shot that day. Kids at that age never understand. Since I did make such a fuss, they tried something different. They'd already swabbed my upper arm with alcohol. Mother was holding me in her lap. The pediatrician was in front of us, talking to me in a soothing tone. The nurse crept up behind me with the hypodermic needle. My mother was supposed to hold me tight. The nurse would make the injection, pull out the needle, quick as a wink, all over and done, and then I could shriek as much as I liked.

"This is, of course, a hell of a way to establish physician-patient trust, but doctors in the 1940s were more pragmatic. If Mother had held my arm tightly, it probably would have worked. However, she didn't have a firm grip. I was a strong child. I jerked my arm away. The needle went all the way through my arm and broke off.

"So I sat in my mother's lap, screaming, a needle protruding from the side of my arm. These were the old days when needles and syringes were sterilized and used over and again. The needle that protruded from my arm seemed to me as large as a ten-penny nail. The nurse stood helplessly. Mother screamed. The doctor moved swiftly and grasped the protruding point with forceps, pulled the needle on through.

"After that, I was given a tetanus shot."

Marcia rubbed goosepimples from her arms. "After that, you must have been a handful."

Grant finally sipped at his beer. "I'd hide under beds. Run away. They kept doctor appointments secret after awhile. I never knew whether a supposed trip to the grocery store might really be a typhoid shot or a polio shot."

"But you got over it when you grew up?" Freddie urged.

"When I was sixteen or so," Grant said, "I cut my foot on a shell at the beach. My folks insisted that I have a tetanus shot. I flew into a panic, bawling, kicking, disgraced myself in front of everyone. But they still made me get the shot. I wonder if my parents ever knew how much I hated them."

"But, surely," said Marcia, "it was for your own good."

"How can someone *else* decide what is *your* own good?"

Grant decided his beer was awful and set it aside. He drank only rarely, but tonight seemed to be a night for confessions. "So," he said. "The old identification with the aggressor story, I suppose. Anyway, I became a physician."

Freddie removed his tie and shoved it into a pocket. He offered them cigarettes, managed to light one for himself. "So, how'd you ever manage to give anybody a shot?"

"Learning to draw blood was very difficult for me. We were supposed to practise on one another one day, but I cut that lab. I went to the beach for a day or two, told them I'd had a family emergency."

Marcia waved away Freddie's cigarette smoke. She remembered Grant as the class clown, his blue eyes always bright with ready laughter. She cringed as he remembered.

Grant continued. "Third-year med students were expected to draw blood from the patients. They could have used experienced staff, but this was part of our initiation ritual. Hazing for us, hell for the patients.

"So, I go in to draw blood. First time. I tie off this woman's arm with a rubber hose, pat the old antecubital fossa looking for a vein, jab away with the needle, still searching, feel the pop as I hit the vein, out comes the bright red into the syringe, I pull out the needle – and blood goes everywhere because I hadn't released the tourniquet. 'Oops!' I say, as the patient in the next bed watches in horror: she's next in line.

"Well, after a few dozen tries at this, I got better at it – but the tasks got worse. There were the private patients as opposed to those on the wards; often VIPs, with spouses and family scowling down at you as you try to pop the vein first try.

"Then there's the wonderful arterial stick, for when you need blood gases. You use this great thick needle, and you feel around the inside of the thigh for a femoral pulse, then you jab the thing in like an icepick. An artery makes a crunch when you strike it, and you just hope you've pierced through and not just gouged along its thick muscular wall. No need for a tourniquet: the artery is under pressure, and the blood pulses straight into the syringe. You run with it to the lab, and your assistant stays there maybe ten minutes forcing pressure against the site so the artery doesn't squirt blood all through the surrounding tissue."

Freddie looked ready to throw up.

"Worst thing, though, were the kids. We had a lot of leukemia patients on the pediatric ward. They'd lie there in bed, emaciated, bald from chemotherapy, waiting to die. By end stage their veins had had a hundred IVs stuck into them, a thousand blood samples taken. Their arms were so thin – nothing but bones and pale skin: you'd think it would be easy to find a vein. But their veins were all used up, just as their lives were. I'd try and try to find a vein, to get a butterfly in so their IVs could run – for whatever good that did. They'd start crying as soon as they saw a white jacket walk into their room. Toward the end, they couldn't cry, just mewed like dying kittens. Two of them died one night when I was on call, and for the last time in my life I sent a prayer of thanks to God."

Grant picked up his beer, scowled at it, set it back down. Marcia was watching him with real concern.

"Hey, drink up," Freddie offered. It was the best thing he could think of to suggest.

Grant took a last swallow. "Well, that was the end of the '60s. I tuned in, turned on, dropped out. Spent a year in Haight-Ashbury doing the hippie trip, trying to get my act together. Did lots of drugs out there, but never any needle work. My friends knew that I was almost a doctor, and some of them would get me to shoot them up when they were too stoned to find a vein. I learned a lot from addicts: How to bring up a vein from a disaster zone. How to use the leading edge of a beveled needle to pierce the skin, then roll it 180 when you've popped the vein. But I never shoved anything myself. I hate needles. Hell, I wouldn't even sell blood when I was stone broke."

"But you went back," Marcia prompted. She reached out for his hand and held it. She remembered that they were staying in the same hotel . . .

"Summer of Love turned into Winter of Junkies. Death on the streets. Went back to finish med school. The time away was therapeutic. I applied myself, as they used to say. So now I do heart transplants."

"A heart surgeon who's scared of needles!" Freddie chuckled. "So, do you close your eyes when the nurses jab 'em in?" He spilled beer down his shirt, then looked confused by the wetness.

"How *did* you manage to conquer your fear of needles?" Marcia asked, holding his hand in both of hers.

"Oh," said Grant. He handed Freddie the rest of his beer. "I learned that in medical school after I went back. It only took time for the lesson to sink in. After that, it was easy to slide a scalpel through living flesh, to crack open a chest. It's the most important part of learning to be a doctor."

Grant McDade removed his dark glasses and gazed earnestly into Marcia's eyes.

"You see, you have to learn that no matter what you're doing to another person, it doesn't hurt *you*."

The blue eyes that once had laughed were dead and dispassionate as a shark's eyes as it begins its tearing roll.

Marcia let go of Grant's hand and excused herself.

She never saw him after that night, but she forever mourned his ghost.

SALLY ROBERTS JONES

Easing the Spring

SALLY ROBERTS JONES cites the reading of her grandmother's copy of *Dracula* as beginning her interest in horror, and she has subsequently passed on the family's addiction to the genre to her three sons.

Born in London, she now lives in Port Talbot, Wales. In 1959 she won first place in the Inter-College Eisteddfod for an essay on science fiction (adjudicated by Kingsley Amis) and her poetry, short stories and local history have been published since the mid-1960s. More recently she has found a long-term interest in genre writing combining with an equally long-term interest in folk lore and Celtic history.

If they're all as good as the atmospheric tale which follows, we look forward to seeing many more stories from this writer whose self-confessed interests include "anything to do with Wales".

A s HE CAME out of the main door of County Hall, Johnson could see his followers dotted across the grass, huddling under their umbrellas in a useless attempt to avoid the persistent drizzle. When they saw him coming, the bedraggled groups of demonstrators slowly moved towards their leader, dragging banners in the damp grass as they went. Johnson waited until they had reached him, then gestured for silence.

"The Council agreed to consider our petition before they decided whether to grant planning permission," he said. "And they'll look at our evidence for the current level of pollution. It's as much as we can hope for at the moment. Now it's up to us to make a strong enough case to convince them that Mynydd Pendar is not the right place for Kleenworld."

"The only case that'd do that is one full of pound notes," called out someone at the back of the group.

There was scattered laughter and a few nods of agreement, then the demonstrators began to wander away towards the car park.

"Don't forget there's a meeting next Wednesday," Johnson called after them. He turned, and saw that two of the younger members were still standing there. "Yes?" he said. "It's David and Owen, isn't it? Can I help you?"

"Mr Edwards brought us over, but he went back early and we haven't got enough money for the bus," explained David.

"We thought maybe you could lend us some," said Owen, hopefully.

"I'll do better than that," said Johnson. "Hop in, and I'll give you a lift home."

There was an accident on the by-pass and they sat impatiently, waiting for the overturned lorry to be removed. To their right, across the glistening grey roofs of the town, a plume of yellowish smoke rose into the air above the chemical works. It went almost straight up for a hundred feet or so, then the prevailing wind seized it and bent it away towards the new housing estate on the mountainside.

"Dad says they're working at the very edge of technology in that place," said Owen. "They don't know themselves what they're making."

"Mam's tights melted on the washing line the other day. There were holes all over them, like acid burns." David stared thoughtfully over the drab back gardens. "The trees are late this year. Almost May and still no leaves. Do you think it's the pollution?"

"Perhaps it's the cold weather," suggested Owen.

"There are no salmon in the river any more, either," David said. "Dad used to go fishing up at Robin's Pool, where the old hut is."

"That writer who came to school told us how Robin's Pool got its name," said Owen. "The men of Pendar and the men of Magor quarrelled about the boundary between the two villages, and people were always getting killed, so they decided to settle it for good. They took this idiot called Robin and let him loose at one end of the boundary, then made him run towards the river, and wherever he ran would be the boundary."

"Did that stop the fighting?" asked Johnson, watching the breakdown crew as they worked on the damaged lorry.

"I suppose so," said Owen. "Only Robin was killed. They'd been throwing things at him to make him run, and someone threw a reaping hook and it killed him – his blood filled the river from side to side!" He savoured the gory details for a moment.

"Not the most constructive way of settling a quarrel," said Johnson wryly. "Look, the traffic's moving at last."

When they reached David's house they had lost an hour over the delay.

"I'd better come in and explain," said Johnson. "Your parents may be worrying and I don't want to lose our prize junior members."

"Our parents have gone to Cardiff for the afternoon," said Owen cheerfully. "And David's gran never minds when he gets in – you should meet her, she knows all about plants and the weather."

"Yes, come in and talk to her," urged David. "Then she can tell my parents it's all right if Dad gets awkward about me going to meetings."

"Well, I don't know," said Johnson, doubtfully. "She might not like the idea of a stranger inviting himself in for tea."

"She likes strangers," the boys assured him, and led him into a small, cluttered living room where an old woman with silver hair and bright dark eyes sat. For a moment, and for no reason that he could grasp, he was almost afraid. But then the fragile old lady gestured to him to sit and whatever it was that he had sensed was gone.

"This is Mr Johnson," said David. "He's with the Friends of Pendar."

"Call me Ian, please. 'Mr Johnson' sounds like a teacher," he said, sitting down.

The table was already laid for four and he wondered how she had known – then remembered the absentees.

"I mustn't eat all your tea. There'll be nothing left for your parents," he said.

"Oh, they won't be back till after supper," David told him. "Gran always knows if we're having visitors."

"So you're David's 'environment man'," said the old lady. "He says you want to save the world."

"Just this little piece of it around Pendar. But if everyone stands up for their *own* little piece, perhaps we *will* save the world."

"And you'd give a lot for that, no doubt." The bright eyes inspected him with cool interest.

"To save the whales and the rain forests? Oh yes, I'd give everything I have to save them if there was a practical way to do it. The world is something abstract, but if I can stop one tree from being cut down needlessly, I've saved a living thing." He felt suddenly uncomfortable at letting his passion show, but the old lady was clearly not embarrassed by his forcefulness. She seemed almost pleased, as though he had passed some test.

"Have a piece of my soul cake," she urged, offering him the plate.

"Soul cake?"

"It's Gran's secret. The best ever," David assured him, and Owen nodded in agreement. "We only have it on special days."

Johnson wondered vaguely why this was a special day, but the cake was already cut. Perhaps it had been someone's birthday. He took a slice, bit into the soft, sticky sweetness, and realised that the boys were right. The cake was definitely something special.

"You're not a teacher, then," said the old woman.

"No. I used to be in the Works but when the cuts came, our department was axed. So now I work up at Pendar House – organising exhibitions, visitor services, that sort of thing."

"That must be very interesting," commented the grandmother. But now her response was only politeness, and he excused himself as soon as he decently could, with a vague apology about another meeting to go to that night.

"You must come again," the old woman told him. "There are some photographs upstairs of Pendar House in the old days. Perhaps they would be useful for your exhibitions."

"I'd like to see them," agreed Johnson.

"Come next Friday. For tea. I'll be expecting you."

He hadn't intended to keep the appointment, but when Friday came, he found himself standing on the doorstep of David's house, being ushered in by David's mother – who, curiously, had an air of serious disapproval about her, though otherwise she was the soul of politeness.

"Here's your visitor, Mother," she announced, opening the door into the middle room. Tea was laid on an immaculate white tablecloth, and David's grandmother presided from her rocking chair at the head of the table. Sitting next to her was a dark-haired young woman whom he recognised as one of the typing pool at the steel works.

"Ceri's grandmother used to work at the House and her grandfather was the head coachman. They're in some of the photographs, so I thought you wouldn't mind if she came too," explained the old woman. "She's often said she'd like to see the pictures."

"No, of course I don't mind," said Johnson, smiling inwardly at what he took to be an attempt at matchmaking.

There was soul cake again and home-brewed wine with an exotic, spicy tang – "My own blend – but don't ask for the recipe, that's a secret. It's come down from mother to daughter since the beginning, berries and herbs – and our own little bit of magic! But my daughter doesn't believe in that sort of thing, so I'll be leaving my secrets to Ceri. A dowry for her, you might say."

After tea they looked at the photographs, all pasted up in a heavy Victorian-style album. Johnson was sharply aware of Ceri's bare arm pressing against him as they bent together over the pages of the book. The perfume she wore was light and flowery, but behind it there was a hint of something more sensuous, and he found it hard to concentrate on the faded sepia views of the great house and its gardens.

"Take Ceri home," commanded the old woman at last. It seemed quite natural then to go with this stranger through the dark streets, under a slender, hallucinatory crescent moon, in at her door and up the stairs into a room that seemed one vast pink feathery bed. Johnson turned to look at her, but Ceri put her palm flat on his chest and pushed. He fell back into immeasurable soft depths, and lay there, unmoving, while her hands busied themselves with buttons and zips, then moved with unbearable delicacy across his skin. She was lying beside him now, her body cool against his, her fingers stroking him into release. High above him the ceiling rose dilated into a pattern of unbelievable beauty . . .

"Mr Johnson! Mr Johnson! It's time to get up!" His landlady was knocking briskly on the door, and in the distance he could hear the eight o'clock milk float purring down the road. Then he remembered.

"Oh my God, if Mrs Thomas finds you here –" he gabbled, rolling over towards Ceri. But there was no one there. He was in his own bed, wearing his own pyjamas; his clothes were neatly laid out on the chair by the window – too neatly.

"Well, if I got so drunk on elderflower wine that I can't remember what happened, it's not likely to happen again," he muttered ruefully, swinging his feet out of bed onto the soft pile of the rug. "I'm coming, Mrs Thomas," he called. "I'll be down in five minutes."

"It's kippers," she announced through the door, and he heard her heavy footsteps going away down the stairs.

He did not expect to hear from Ceri again, but when he got back from taking a group of councillors round the hall the next afternoon, he found a note on his desk asking him to "call this number" when he was free. Somewhat to his surprise, Ceri answered the phone and invited him to a party.

"Nothing special, just a few of us going over to that new club this evening."

"I was going to write up the minutes of the last committee meeting – "

"Hey, come on, live a little," Ceri urged.

"I suppose I *could* leave it," he agreed. "Shall I pick you up?"

"I'll be at the Square at 7.30," she said, and hung up.

As a party, it was a low-key event. Ceri spent most of the evening chatting to her girlfriends; but when he eventually dropped her at her front door, it seemed only natural to follow her in and upstairs. This time things moved at a much steadier pace, and afterwards they lay side by side, in companionable silence.

"I must go," he said at last.

"To write up the minutes of that committee meeting?" There was a note of amusement in her voice.

"Someone has to," said Johnson defensively. "We can't just let the world fall apart."

"There are other ways to save it. All your meetings and protests, they're just part of the problem, more paper, more trees cut down." Ceri rolled over and looked up at him critically as he stood there pulling his trousers on. For a moment he felt like a prize bull being assessed for the butcher's knife, but then she smiled and said, "Pick me up after work tomorrow. I'll take you to Cwm Woods and show you where the badgers have their lair."

"Badgers? Here in Port Ivory?"

"Oh yes. Not everything is recorded in your minutes, you know," she told him gravely. "Now come back to bed. The committee minutes can wait."

There were times in the days that followed when he surfaced enough to wonder seriously if he was under the influence of some mysterious potion administered at the old woman's tea party. But for most of the time all he was aware of was Ceri – her presence, her perfume, her body moving under his. He was drunk with her, obsessed, seeing the world around them with an almost surreal clarity, as though they were living inside a Dali painting. He had phoned in to say that he was unwell; whether Ceri had excused herself he did not ask, he only knew that she was there in the room whenever he turned towards her.

"You need some air," she said one evening. She was standing by the window, her naked body outlined against the pale yellow light of the street-lamps outside.

"I don't think I can stand," he said foolishly.

"Then you do need air. And food. Come here." She helped him into his clothes as though she was dressing a baby – *or an idiot*, he thought wryly, momentarily aware of his condition.

"We'll go to see the badgers," she told him, and led him out of the house and through the streets towards Cwm Woods, high above the town. They went to their usual place, but there were no badgers that night, and after a while it began to rain, a thin misty drizzle.

"We can shelter in the cottage," said Ceri. "They may still come."

The cottage was little more than a ruin, but the front room ceiling was still intact and there was glass in the window. Ceri produced a torch, then pulled some dry sacking from a corner and made a bed for them on the floor.

"Suppose someone comes?" said Johnson, hesitating. The lethargy of the last few days was beginning to wear off in the chill of the hours before dawn and he was conscious of where he was and what they were doing.

"No one will come at this time of night," she said, pulling him down onto the sacking. But the spell had ceased to work. He felt acutely uncomfortable at being there, in such dubious circumstances, with a stranger.

He could see that Ceri sensed his withdrawal, but she made no attempt to urge him further. They sat in silence, listening to the soft drip of water on earth and the occasional squeal of a small animal as its predator found it.

"Nature red in tooth and claw," said Ceri at last. "That's the truth of it, not parades and petitions."

"I didn't know you were so bloodthirsty," muttered Johnson.

"I wasn't named Ceridwen for nothing," she said.

"Ceridwen? Wasn't she the moon goddess? Very appropriate –" But he broke off, seeing her face masklike in the torchlight, and half afraid of what he saw.

"You have enjoyed yourself these last few days, haven't you?" Ceri asked, earnestly. "It's important. That you should be satisfied."

"I have to go," said Johnson abruptly. "My work – I've let things go too far. The committee minutes –" He began to get up, but Ceridwen reached up to him, pulling him down again towards her, her hands twisted in his hair.

"I love you," she said. "You *do* know that?"

"I hadn't thought –" he murmured, staring at her – and never heard the faint rustling behind him, only felt the sudden shock of the blow that sent him toppling into darkness.

At first he thought he was camping out again, the ground was so hard underneath him. His body ached from it. Then he tried to move, to ease the pain and found that his hands and feet were tied, and the dry, flannelly taste in his mouth was just that, some sort of gag. At first he thought he had been blindfolded too, the darkness was so intense. But when he tried again to move, to explore his immediate surroundings, the pain in his head was so great that he flopped back again, whimpering.

How long had he been here? It was still dark – or was the place sealed against the light? When had he and Ceri –? And why –? But nothing fitted. Was Ceri here too? Who would want to do this? His head spun with the effort of trying to make sense of what had happened.

The floor beneath him was cold stone, and gradually he realised that he was naked except for his underpants. Vague stories of kidnappers stripping their victims to humiliate and control them stirred at the back of his mind. *It must be serious then*, he thought. If Ceri was with him, she was not breathing.

He had lost all idea of time, but eventually there was a noise from somewhere in front of him, and the faint squeak of hinges in need of oiling. Light trickled in through the door opening, first the flickering light of a candle and then a flare of brightness as someone switched on a torch. When his eyes adjusted to the light, he saw that he was in the old fisherman's hut that stood by the river, halfway up the valley. Then he saw that the light-bearer was his landlady, Mrs Thomas. There were two other women with her, all of them dressed with total incongruity in flowered overalls.

"He doesn't look too well. I told Ellen not to hit too hard," said one of the women.

"He's still alive. That's the main thing," said Mrs Thomas. "Now, Mr Johnson, we're going to take that gag out of your mouth and untie one hand. Please don't try any tricks, you really won't enjoy what happens if you do."

The woman on her left held up a long, vicious-looking kitchen knife, twisting it as she did so. Johnson stared at it, trying to understand what was happening to him.

Mrs Thomas put the torch on a shelf and knelt down beside him, her fingers pulling at the knots at his wrist. Then she pulled the gag loose, and he winced as the plaster tore free from his skin.

"Give me the water," she ordered, and one of the women handed her a pink earthenware mug. She held it to his lips and he drank gratefully, trying to wash the foul taste of the flannel out of his mouth.

"Why?" he asked, hesitantly, when he could speak again. "What are you going to do?" But Mrs Thomas set her fingers against his lips and hushed him.

"No talking. You'll understand very soon. Now, let's sit you up, you'll be more comfortable." She put her hands under his armpits and hauled him up, propping him against the wall. Then she stood and went over to the other women, who produced a plastic shopping bag. From it they took a bowl and a spoon, and then a thermos flask, pouring something from it into the bowl.

"You'll be hungry, I'm sure," Mrs Thomas told him. She picked up the bowl and brought it over. "Your hand's free, you can feed yourself." She put the food down on the floor beside him and gave him the spoon, then stood back, waiting until he took the first mouthful. It was some kind of porridge, lukewarm, thin and tasteless, but he knew he could not endure the humiliation of being fed.

Once she saw that he was going to eat the gruel, Mrs Thomas turned, picked up the torch and went out of the hut, followed by the others.

"Wait, please," he called after them. "You can't leave me here like this!" But the door shut behind them, and he was left with just the candle-light for company.

At first he tried to free his other hand and his feet, but the ropes had been expertly tied and his struggles only left him with torn fingernails and bloody skin. Finally he gave up and leant back against the rough bricks.

"Logic," he said. "There must be logic to it. Why are they doing this? If I knew that, perhaps I could talk to them . . ."

But the logic refused to come. There was no sense to any of it, no reason except simple lunacy; and, whatever else they were, he was quite sure that Mrs Thomas and her friends were not lunatics.

His head was aching now and the gruel lay heavily on his stomach. Then he heard a low murmur of voices and the door opened again. David's grandmother stood in the doorway, looking at him.

"Oh thank God!" he said painfully. "Please, you must help me. Tell them to let me go –" But as she moved forward he saw her face more clearly, and knew that even this last hope of sanity had failed him.

"Only a little while now and then you'll understand it all," she told him briskly. "It's a great honour, you know. Normally we use our own, but David is too young yet."

"Then it's not – not fatal," he thought. Whatever "it" was, her look of grandmotherly pride surely ruled out serious damage. But he was not convinced. This was not the sweet old lady of tea-parties and home-made wine. Even in the dim light of the candle he sensed an authority in her, a power, and there was a pattern to it all. If only he could remember. If only he could think clearly . . .

She knelt down beside him and untied the rest of the ropes, then stood back while he slowly pulled himself up.

"Come along now, Ceridwen is waiting," she told him. "Just take your pants off and then we can begin."

"My pants?" Johnson stared, and then felt a sudden urge to giggle as he began to realise what the old woman was up to.

"You can't make the offering with your clothes on," she insisted. "No need to feel shy, we've seen it all before." Her fingers tugged at his waist band, and he was too weak to push her away.

"It's for the land," she told him. "You know that?"

"Of course," he nodded, humouring her.

Outside the door, a double row of women led away in a silent avenue towards the river, where Ceridwen waited, a naked silver goddess in the moonlight. David's grandmother stood on his right, and Mrs Thomas fell in on his left; then they began to lead him towards the water's edge.

He went with them unresisting. The silent women gave the procession a ceremonial, even a ritual quality that did away with embarrassment or protest. And Ceridwen – she was standing on a stone in the middle of the water, her hands held out to him. He stepped forward quickly, looking up at her, one foot on the bank, the other on a log that thrust out into the stream. And then the pattern came together, and he knew, and opened his mouth to cry out in terror.

At his side the old woman brought her hand up, the blade of the sickle striking cold fire from the moonlight in the second before she drew it across his throat.

And then he saw nothing but the dark stain of blood, spreading slowly from bank to bank; and heard nothing but the soft patter of rain on the sheltering leaves as the women began to wail.

STEVE RASNIC TEM & MELANIE TEM

Safe at Home

MELANIE TEM has been described by Dan Simmons as "the literary successor to Shirley Jackson and destined to become the new queen of high-quality psychologically disturbing horror fiction." Her work has been published in numerous magazines and anthologies, including *Best New Horror 2*, *Women of Darkness*, *Women of the West*, *Skin of the Soul*, *The Anthology of Fantasy & the Supernatural*, *Dark Voices: The Pan Book of Horror*, *The Mammoth Book of Vampires*, *Isaac Asimov's Science Fiction Magazine*, *Grue*, *Cemetery Dance* and *Snow White Blood Red*.

Her debut novel *Prodigal*, which won the 1992 Bram Stoker Award, was followed by *Blood Moon*, *Wilding*, *Revenant* and *Desmodis*, and with Nancy Holder she is co-writing the multi-volume 'Demon Lover' series, with *Making Love* and *Witch-Light* already completed.

She has recently collaborated with her husband Steve Rasnic Tem (who appears solo elsewhere in this volume) on a number of stories in such anthologies as *Post Mortem*, *Chilled to the Bone*, *The Ultimate Dracula* and *Hottest Blood*, as well as the chapbook *Beautiful Strangers*.

M INDY.
    "Touch me. Here. Like this.
    "You like to touch me, don't you?
    "That's a good girl. Oh, that's right."

Charlie was incredulous. "You want me to take you to another
horror movie? But you hate that stuff."

"The monster in this one has long sticky tentacles that come up
out of a dark pool." Melinda squinted at the newspaper ad and
gave a short, brittle laugh.

"Let me guess: It has a particular affinity for pretty young
women." Charlie's laugh was easier, fuller than hers.

"Don't they all?" she said.

Charlie took her to the movie because she wanted to go,
and also because he knew there was a good possibility of sex
afterward. She didn't begrudge him that. Charlie was a good guy,
and Melinda felt bad about using his baser instincts to get what
she wanted. But it worked. It had always worked.

She didn't love Charlie, not yet. And he didn't love her. She
hoped he didn't love her.

"I love you, Mindy. You're my favorite niece, did you know
that?

    "You want to make your uncle Pat happy, don't you? Let me
show you how to make me happy.

    "Oh, you are such a good girl."

Charlie was a tender, considerate lover. He went slow. He'd never
hurt her. She knew he thought what they did together in bed was
beautiful.

It made her want to throw up.

Monsters made it possible for her to throw up. Monsters
in horror movies especially, with sticky appendages or gaping
maws or formless bodies that oozed from everywhere and never
went away.

At some point during every show she'd get up and hurry to the
ladies' room, hoping there wouldn't be a line. She'd crouch over
a toilet and vomit for a long time. If she'd been able to force
herself to eat any popcorn or candy, it would come out of her
in recognizable chunks, but everything else being expelled from
her body was whitish and viscous, like semen. For a while then –

sometimes minutes, sometimes the rest of the night – she wouldn't be sick to her stomach.

"Oh, no, Mindy, this isn't wrong. We love each other, so how could anything we do together be wrong?

"Show me that you love me, Mindy.

"That's right. That's my girl."

She hated having to chew and swallow in front of people. Sometimes she caught herself imagining that if she opened her mouth too wide a sticky, sinewy monster would slide out and wriggle into the darkness under the house, under the streets, under the world.

She watched Charlie eat. She wanted to see what his teeth did to the food, how his tongue rolled and humped to get the food down. Sometimes in the middle of a meal she'd reach over and very lightly rest her fingertips on the hinge of his jaw, where she could feel the bones and muscles, sinews and tendons, all working together in one building rhythm.

"You're weird," Charlie said the first time she was brave enough to do that. Mouth full of spaghetti, he leaned across the table and kissed her.

Melinda had thought he was going to say he loved her. He'd had that tender, passionate, self-absorbed look on his face that had nothing to do with her. Relieved that he'd said something else, she didn't pull away.

She tried hard not to imagine the spaghetti in his mouth. For some reason it scared her.

Then she gave up and set herself to imagining it as vividly as she could. Whitish sticky tendrils, viscous sauce. Charlie's mouth caressing it, taking everything from it, the inside of a kiss.

"Sweet," Charlie said, still looking at her more intently than she liked. "And very beautiful. But definitely weird."

"Your mommy and daddy didn't mean *me*. I'm your daddy's brother.

"They asked me to babysit this weekend, remember? They asked me to take care of you while they were gone. Don't you think they must trust me a lot to let me take care of their precious little girl?

"So you can trust me, too.

"Come here, Mindy. Come to Uncle Pat."

After the movie they often rode the bus across town to Charlie's house. When she rode the bus alone, Melinda watched all the men waiting for her, in the other seats, at stops, on street corners, on billboards, and on movie posters. During heavy rains there were so many people in doorways that she couldn't tell which ones were waiting for just her, and in the wet shadows she usually couldn't see their hands. There ought to be a law requiring men to keep their hands exposed at all times in the presence of females. Especially girls. Especially little girls.

A man with a narrow face, or maybe with only a penis for a face, stared at her from a narrow passageway when the bus stopped for a light. His long pale tongue slid out of the shadows and down his coat, down one leg and across the sidewalk, leaving a slick, steaming trail. The tongue was wiggling its way toward her when the bus pulled into the intersection. Charlie hugged her and whispered a soft alien language into her ear.

In Charlie's bedroom she took off her clothes, forcing herself to move slowly, holding her breath, hoping the bile in her stomach wouldn't rise into her throat. Charlie watched her adoringly. "You are so beautiful," he kept saying, and Melinda flinched that he would say such a thing out loud. "You are so beautiful."

Melinda could barely let herself hear such nice things about her body, but she liked hearing them, was relieved each time that he didn't say how ugly she was, how pale, how skinny or how fat, how wormlike smooth or how hairy. If she didn't trim her bikini line her pubic hair would just keep growing, would spill out of her crotch and rise above the waistband of her shorts, would wrap itself like monkey tails up and down her limbs.

A woman was never safe. Like all women, Melinda had a wet, hairy hole in the middle of her body. A hole in the middle of her life. Where awful things might enter.

Charlie invited her to stay the night. Melinda said no, she wasn't ready, and Charlie didn't push. He insisted on accompanying her on the bus all the way home. He was so sweet. Gratefully, she kissed him goodbye at her door, although she really didn't want to touch him anymore. She didn't ask him in.

Alone in her apartment, she sat naked in the dark, all the bedclothes pushed well away from her. Cloth would burn her; her bare flesh was already aching with nothing touching it at all.

It hurt her to be exposed like this; it would hurt more to try to cover herself up.

Then she waited until she was too tired to wait anymore. She waited, as she did every night, for something to break her door down or to seep in under it. For something to drag her or coax her into the sticky dark outside.

Safe. Safe at home.

"Mindy, Mindy, you are so beautiful."

That July the annual invasion of miller moths was the worst anybody could remember. They bred somewhere in the South and would go up into the mountains to die, Melinda read, or maybe it was the other way around; when she was afraid of something she tried to find out as much about it as she could, but often she had trouble keeping her facts straight, and that just made her more afraid. It didn't matter anyway; the truth was, they came from everywhere, bred everywhere, and they would never die.

Miller moths were monsters, and she was terrified of them. They swarmed so thickly around the lamp on her bedside stand or the hoodlight on her stove that they looked like clots of curly hair. They got stuck in her food, drowned in her coffee. They flew into her face, into her mouth, into the hole in the middle of her body, leaving everywhere the dust from their wings. The dust from their wings was poisonous. It was also what enabled them to breed.

They were in her bed. When Charlie wasn't there she felt them all night long, flicking against the back of her neck, kissing the insides of her thighs, crawling into her vagina.

Finally, after three virtually sleepless nights, Melinda danced around her bedroom in a frenzy, with a rolled-up newspaper in one hand and a flyswatter in the other. She smashed every moth she saw or thought she saw, until the paper was tattered and the flyswatter was covered with pulpy wing dust and she was faint with exertion and fear. But in the end she was helpless against them. There were miller moths everywhere.

And they would get their revenge. They would pass stories on from one generation to the next about what she'd done to their family, or tried to do, and someday when she thought she was safe at home – in the winter, say, when there weren't supposed to be any moths – one or a dozen or a million of them would lay their eggs inside her.

Monsters were everywhere. Great hairy things with eyes and teeth, miller moths with poisonous wings, squirmy creatures with tentacles that caught and held. All the monsters communicated with all the other monsters – the moths with the beasts, the caterpillars with the men. They spoke a language Melinda frequently understood but could not quite use herself. They talked about her. They watched her every minute of every day and night.

Everything was a monster, monstrous and magical. Everything was family but her. Everything talked.

"If you tell, they won't understand."

"If you tell, they'll be mad at me. And at you."

"If you tell, you'll get us both in big trouble."

"If you tell, you'll tear our family apart."

"If you tell, Mindy, I'll go to jail, and then I won't love you anymore."

Charlie lay back in her arms. He was so sweet, so patient and good to her.

He was watching her. He watched her all the time. Even when they made love he didn't close his eyes; she'd open hers during a long, breathtaking kiss and find him looking at her, his eyes so close they didn't look like eyes anymore but like dark pools out of which anything might rise. Even when she let him spend the night (at her place, at home, never at his, where she wouldn't know where the monsters had bred in the night) and she woke up from her habitually fitful sleep, she knew he was watching her in his dreams. Every minute of every day and night.

"Sometimes you're such a little girl," he observed. "Like when we go to horror shows and you get so scared you have to run to the bathroom and throw up."

Melinda hadn't realized he knew about that. She felt her face and neck go hot.

"And other times," he persisted, "you're like a beautiful, wise old woman. No, not old – ageless. Like you've been alive forever. That's how you seem when we make love."

"Sex is older than we are," Melinda said. "It's older than anybody. It's so old and so powerful it's like a god, or a monster. People will do anything, tell themselves anything, to make what they do all right, just so they can hold onto it for a split second."

She saw Charlie's eyes widen, heard him catch his breath, saw an appendage with a searching eye and clinging membranes slither toward her as he started to say, "Love's like that, too, you know."

She stopped him with a kiss. The tentacle went into her mouth, into her throat. She sucked. The hole in the middle of her body filled up with viscous whitish fluid, and she ran to the bathroom to vomit it away.

"You're growing up now. You're becoming a woman.

"Why do you treat me like this? Why do you hate me?

"I don't understand why you want to hurt me. We've been so close.

"I don't understand.

"I love you."

Charlie sneaked up on her. They were in her bed and she was relaxing in his arms, feeling pleasantly hungry, thinking that even if that furry shadow in the corner of the ceiling was a moth it wouldn't hurt her, that it was as afraid of her as she was of it, when Charlie said before she saw it coming, "I love you."

She was going to throw up. She struggled to get up, to free herself of him, but he wouldn't let her go.

"Melinda, wait. Please don't go. I *love* you."

The miller moth elongated and swelled and inserted itself into her mouth. Its poisonous dust was making her choke. It pushed its way down through her body; she felt it circling her heart, winding among her intestines, nudging the inside of her vagina, but it didn't come out.

"I know you're afraid. I know somebody has hurt you. But I won't hurt you. *I love you.*"

The monster was godlike; the god was monstrous. It had a single wet eye and a bifurcated heart. She would do anything she had to do to keep it away from her, anything to make it forever her own.

But not now. She wasn't ready now.

"Mindy. I love you."

"No no no!" She pulled away from his wet tongue, his hairy hands, his single eye. She sprang from the bed and ran, the monster who loved her stumbling after her.

She ran down the hall, painfully aware of her nakedness, of the hairy, wounded hole in the middle of her body that wanted to be filled, that wanted to be protected from the crawling, slimy vermin that filled the world. Even as she ran she frantically considered what she might use to plug it up.

She ran into the bathroom and slammed the door, locking it. Outside the monster panted, out of breath. "Mindy, Mindy . . . love . . ." And then it fell silent.

She crouched on the cool tile in the corner, her head pressed against cold porcelain. It was too late to vomit. Too late to escape. Under the edge of the door, black hair was spreading toward her.

Melinda tried to pull herself into the hole in the middle of her body, the hole in the middle of her life, the hole she had become. She knew she wouldn't die there, although sometimes that's what she wanted. She hoped she wouldn't have to eat there, that nothing would have to enter her body ever again.

There she knew she could be the monster who never needed to love. She could be the god.

Safe. Safe at home.

CHRISTOPHER FOWLER

Mother of the City

CHRISTOPHER FOWLER lives and works in London, where he runs the Soho film promotion company The Creative Partnership. His first novel, *Roofworld*, became a bestseller and is currently being developed as a movie by Landmark Entertainment in America. His second novel, *Rune*, has also been optioned for filming, and he followed it with *Red Bride* and *Darkest Day*, which together comprise his "London Quartet", set in an alternative city. His latest novel, *Spanky*, has been sold to Universal.

His short fiction is collected in *City Jitters*, *City Jitters Two*, *The Bureau of Lost Souls*, *Sharper Knives*, and *Colder Blood*. He is currently working on *Satyr*, a new novel about Satanists; *Menz Insana*, a series of adult graphic tales illustrated by John Bolton, and *High Tension*, an original screenplay.

About "Mother of the City", the author explains: "I was researching my novel *Spanky*, which is set partly in London's clubland, and I was out with three outrageous women familiar to the club scene. They knew how it worked and how to work it, and showed me the 'inside track' of clubs that you only get on if you're (a) either a gorgeous girl or with one, and (b) familiar with the event organizers.

"By the end of the evening (with one of the girls now handcuffed to a psychotic doorman who had lost the key) I realized that there was part of the city even I was unfamiliar with; a side that was fast, potentially dangerous, and impossible to enter without exactly the right credentials. I used the evening as the core of the story,

191

and perversely had the tale told by someone who hates the city. I believe the essence of the story is true, that your wellbeing is controlled by where you live, and that it is granted to you as a privilege, not a right . . ."

I F MY UNCLE Stanley hadn't passed out pornographic polaroids of his second wife for the amusement of his football mates in the bar of the Skinner's Arms, I might have moved to London. But he did and I didn't, because his wife heard about it and threw him out on the street, and she offered the other half of her house to me.

My parents were in the throes of an ugly divorce and I was desperate to leave home. Aunt Sheila's house was just a few roads away. She wasn't asking much rent and she was good company, so I accepted her offer and never got around to moving further into town, and that's why I'll be dead by the time morning comes.

Fucking London, I hate it.

Here's a depressing thing to do. Grow up in the suburbs, watch your schoolfriends leave one by one for new lives in the city, then bump into them eleven years later in your local pub, on an evening when you're feeling miserable and you're wearing your oldest, most disgusting jumper. Listen to their tales of financial derring-do in the public sector. Admire their smart clothes and the photos of exotic love-partners they keep in their bulging wallets, photos beside which your Uncle Stan's polaroids pale into prudery. Try to make your own life sound interesting when they ask what you've been doing all this time, even though you know that the real answer is nothing.

Don't tell them the truth. Don't say you've been marking time, you're working in the neighbourhood advice bureau, you drive a rusting Fiat Pipsqueak and there's a woman in Safeway's you sometimes sleep with but you've no plans to marry. Because they'll just look around at the pub's dingy flock wallpaper and the drunk kids in tracksuits and say, How can you stay here, Douglas? Don't you know what you've been missing in London all these years?

I know what I've been missing all right. And while I'm thinking about that, my old school chums, my pals-for-life, my mates, my blood-brothers will check their watches and drink up and shake my hand and leave me for the second time, unable to get away fast enough. And once again I stay behind.

You'll have to take my word for it when I say I didn't envy them. I really didn't. I'd been to London plenty of times, and I loathed the place. The streets were crowded and filthy and ripe with menace, the people self-obsessed and unfriendly. People are unfriendly around here as well, only you never see them except on Sunday mornings, when some kind of car-washing decathlon is staged throughout the estate. The rest of the time they're in their houses between the kettle and the TV set, keeping a side-long watch on the street through spotless net curtains. You could have a massive coronary in the middle of the road and the curtains would twitch all around you, but no one would come out. They'll watch but they won't help. They'll say *We thought we shouldn't interfere*.

Fuck, I'm bleeding again.

Seeing as I'm about to die, it's important that you understand; where you live shapes your life. I'm told that the city makes you focus your ambitions. Suburbia drains them off. Move here and you'll soon pack your dreams away, stick them in a box with the Christmas decorations meaning to return to them some day. You don't, of course. And slowly you become invisible, like the neighbours, numb and relaxed. It's a painless process. Eventually you perform all the functions of life without them meaning anything, and it's quite nice, like floating lightly in warm water. At least, that's what I used to think.

Around here the women have become unnaturally attached to the concept of shopping. They spend every weekend with their families scouring vast warehouses full of tat, looking for useless objects to acquire, shell-suited magpies feathering their nests with bright plastic objects. I shouldn't complain. I've always preferred things to people. Gadgets, landscapes, buildings. Especially buildings. As a child, I found my first visit to the British Museum more memorable than anything I'd seen before, not that I'd seen anything. I loved those infinite halls of waxed tiles, each sepulchral room with its own uniformed attendant. Smooth panes of light and dense silence, the exact opposite of my home life. My parents always spoke to me loudly and simultaneously. They complained about everything and fought all the time. I loved them, of course; you do. But they let us down too often, my sister and I, and after a while we didn't trust them any more.

I trusted the British Museum. Some of the exhibits frightened me; the glass box containing the leathery brown body of a cowering Pompeiian, the gilt-encased figures of vigilant guards protecting an Egyptian princess. Within its walls nothing ever changed, and I was safe and secure. I never had that feeling with my parents.

Once my father drove us up from Meadowfields (that's the name of the estate; suitably meaningless, as there isn't a meadow in sight and never was) to the West End, to see some crummy Christmas lights and to visit my mum's hated relatives in Bayswater. When he told the story later, he managed to make it sound as if we had travelled to the steppes of Russia. He and my mother sat opposite my Uncle Ernie and Auntie Doreen on their red leather settee, teacups balanced on locked knees, reliving the high point of our trip, which was a near-collision with a banana lorry bound for Covent Garden. I'd been given a sticky mug of fluorescent orange squash and sent to a corner to be seen and not heard. I was nine years old, and I understood a lot more than they realized. My Uncle Ernie started talking about a woman who was strangled in the next street because she played the wireless too loudly, but my Auntie Doreen gave him a warning look and he quickly shut up.

On the way home, as if to verify his words, we saw two Arab men having a fight at the entrance to Notting Hill tube station. Being impressionable and imaginative, from this moment on I assumed that London was entirely populated by murderers.

A psychiatrist would say that's why I never left Meadowfields. In fact I longed to leave my parents' little house, where each room was filled with swirling floral wallpaper and the sound of Radio One filtered through the kitchen wall all day. All I had to do was get up and go, but I didn't. Inaction was easier. When I moved to Aunt Sheila's I finally saw how far my lead would reach; three roads away. I suppose I was scared of the city, and I felt protected in the suburbs. I've always settled for the safest option.

Look, I've taken a long time getting to the point and you've been very patient, so let me explain what happened last night. I just want you to understand me a little, so you won't think I'm crazy when I explain the insane fix I'm in. It's hard to think clearly. I must put everything in order.

It began with a woman I met two months ago.

Her name is Michelle Davies and she works for an advertising agency in Soho. She's tall and slim, with deep-set brown eyes and masses of glossy dark hair the colour of a freshly creosoted fence. She always wears crimson lipstick, black jeans and a black furry coat. She looks like a page ripped from *Vanity Fair*. She's not like the women around here.

I met her when I was helping with a community project that's tied to a national children's charity, and the charity planned to mention our project in its local press ads, and Michelle was the account executive appointed to help me with the wording.

The first time we met I was nearly an hour late for our appointment because I got lost on the Underground. Michelle was sitting at the end of a conference table, long legs crossed to one side, writing pages of notes, and never once caught my eye when she spoke. The second time, a week later, she seemed to notice me and was much friendlier. At the end of the meeting she caught my arm at the door and asked me to buy her a drink in the bar next to the agency, and utterly astonished, I agreed.

I'll spare you a description of the media types sandwiched between the blue slate walls of the brasserie. The tables were littered with *Time Out*s and transparencies, and everyone was talking loudly about their next production and how they all hated each other.

Listen, I have no illusions about myself. I'm twenty-eight, I don't dress fashionably and I'm already losing my hair. London doesn't suit me. I don't understand it, and I don't fit in. Michelle was seven years younger, and every inch of her matched the life that surrounded us. As we shared a bottle of wine she told me about her father, a successful artist, her mother, a writer of romances, and her ex-boyfriend, some kind of experimental musician. I had no idea why I had been picked to hear these revelations. Her parents were divorced, but still lived near each other in apartments just off the Marylebone Road. She had grown up in a flat in Wigmore Street, and still lived in Praed Street. Her whole family had been raised in the centre of the city, generation upon generation. She was probably one of the last true Londoners. She was rooted right down into the place, and even though I hated being here, I had to admit it made her very urbane and glamorous, sophisticated far beyond her years. As she drained her glass she wondered if I would like to have dinner with her tonight. Did I have to get up early in the morning?

I know what you're thinking – isn't this all a bit sudden? What could she see in me? Would the evening have some kind of humiliating resolution? Did she simply prefer plain men? Well, drinks turned to dinner and dinner turned to bed, and everything turned out to be great. I went back to her apartment and we spent the whole night gently making love, something I hadn't done since I was nineteen, and later she told me that she was attracted to me because I was clearly an honest man. She said all women are looking for honest men.

In the morning, we braved the rain-doused streets to visit a breakfast bar with steamy windows and tall chrome stools, and she ate honey-filled croissants and told me how much she loved the city, how private and protective it was, how she could never live anywhere else and didn't I feel the same way? – and I had to tell her the truth. I said I fucking hated the place.

Yes, that was dumb. But it was honest. She was cooler after that. Not much, but I noticed a definite change in her attitude. I tried to explain but I think I made everything worse. Finally she smiled and finished her coffee and slipped from her stool. She left with barely another word, her broad black coat swinging back and forth as she ran away through the drizzle. Kicking myself, I paid the bill and took the first of three trains home. At the station, a taxi nearly ran me down and a tramp became abusive when I wouldn't give him money.

On my way out of London I tried to understand what she loved so much about the litter-strewn streets, but the city's charms remained elusive. To me the place looked like a half-demolished fairground.

I couldn't get Michelle out of my mind.

Everything about her was attractive and exciting. It wasn't just that she had chosen me when she could have had any man she wanted. I called her at the agency and we talked about work. After the next meeting we went to dinner, and I stayed over again. We saw each other on three more occasions. She was always easygoing, relaxed. I was in knots. Each time she talked about the city she loved so much, I managed to keep my fat mouth shut. Then, on our last meeting, I did something really stupid.

I have a stubborn streak a mile wide and I know it, but knowing your faults doesn't make it any easier to control them. Each time we'd met, I had come up to town and we'd gone somewhere, for dinner, for drinks – it was fine, but Michelle often brought her friends from the agency along, and I would have preferred to see her alone. They sat on either side of her watching me like bodyguards, ready to pounce at the first sign of an improper advance.

On this particular evening we were drinking in a small club in Beak Street with her usual crowd. She began talking about some new bar, and I asked her if she ever got tired of living right here, in the middle of so much noise and violence. In reply, she told me London was the safest place in the world. I pointed out that it was now considered to be the most crime-riddled city in Europe. She just stared at me blankly for a moment and turned to talk to someone else.

Her attitude pissed me off. She was living in a dream-state, ignoring anything bad or even remotely realistic in life. I wouldn't let the subject go and tackled her again. She quoted Samuel Johnson, her friends nodded in agreement, I threw in some crime statistics and moments later we were having a heated, pointless row. What impressed me was the way in which she took everything to heart, as if by insulting London I was causing her personal injury. Finally she called me smug and small-minded and stormed out of the club.

One of her friends, an absurd young man with a pony-tail, pushed me down in my seat as I rose to leave. "You shouldn't have argued with her," he said, shaking his head in admonishment. "She loves this city, and she won't hear anyone criticizing it."

"You can't go on treating her like a child for ever," I complained. "Someone has to tell her the truth."

"That's what her last boyfriend did."

"And what happened to him?"

"He got knocked off his bike by a bus." Pony-Tail shrugged. "He's never going to walk again." He stared out of the window at the teeming night streets. "This city. You're either its friend, or you're an enemy."

After waiting for hours outside her darkened apartment, I returned home to Meadowfields in low spirits. I felt as though I had failed some kind of test. A few days later, Michelle reluctantly agreed to see me for dinner. This time there would be just the two of us. We arranged to meet in Dell'Ugo in Frith Street at nine the next Friday evening.

I didn't get there until ten-thirty.

It wasn't my fault. I allowed plenty of time for my rail connections, but one train wasn't running and the passengers were off-loaded on to buses that took the most circuitous route imagi-nable. By the time I reached the restaurant she had gone. The *maître d'* told me she had waited for forty minutes.

After that Michelle refused to take my calls, either at the agency or at her flat. I must have spoken to her answering machine a hundred times.

A week passed, the worst week of my life. At work, everything went wrong. The money for the charity ads fell through and the campaign was cancelled, so I had no reason to visit the agency again. Then Aunt Sheila asked me to help her sell the house, because she had decided to move to Spain. I would have to find a new place to live. And all the time, Michelle's face was before me. I felt like following her ex-boyfriend under a bus.

It was Friday night, around seven. I was standing in the front garden, breathing cool evening air scented with burning leaves and looking out at the lights of the estate, fifty-eight miles from the city and the woman. That's when it happened. Personal epiphany, collapse of inner belief system, whatever you want to call it. I suddenly saw how cocooned I'd been here in Legoland. I'd never had a chance to understand a woman like Michelle. She unnerved me, so I was backing away from the one thing I really wanted, which was to be with her. Now I could see that she was a lifeline, one final chance for me to escape. OK, it may have been obvious to you but it came as a complete revelation to me.

I ran back into the house, past my Aunt Sheila who was in the kitchen doing something visceral in a pudding basin, and rang Michelle's apartment. And – there was a God – she answered the call. I told her exactly how I felt, begged absolution for my behaviour and explained how desperate I was to see her. For a few moments the line went silent as she thought things through. Once more, my honesty won the day.

"Tomorrow night," she said. "I've already made arrangements with friends, but come along."

"I'll be there," I replied, elated. "When and where?"

She said she would be in a restaurant called the Palais Du Jardin in Long Acre until ten-thirty, then at a new club in Soho. She gave me the addresses. "I warn you, Douglas," she added. "This is absolutely your last chance. If you don't show up, you can throw away my number because I'll never speak to you again."

I swore to myself that nothing would go wrong. Nothing.

*   *   *

Saturday morning.

It feels like a lifetime has passed, but peering at the cracked glass of my watch I realize that it was just twenty hours ago.

I planned everything down to the last detail. I consulted the weather bureau, then rang all three stations and checked that the trains would be running. "Only connect," wrote E.M. Forster, but he obviously hadn't seen a British Rail timetable.

To be safe I left half-hour gaps between each train, so there would be no possibility of missing one of them. I bought a new suit, my first since wide lapels went out. I got a decent hair-cut from a new barber, one without photographs of people who looked like Val Doonican taped to his window. The day dragged past at a snail's pace, each minute lasting an hour. Finally it was time to leave Rosemount Crescent.

I made all my connections. Nothing went wrong until I reached Warren Street, where the Northern Line had been closed because of a bomb scare. It had begun to rain, a fine soaking drizzle. There were no cabs to be seen so I waited for a bus, safe in the knowledge that Michelle would be dining for a while yet. I felt that she had deliberately kept the arrangement casual to help me. She knew I had to make an awkward journey into town.

The first two buses were full, and the driver of the third wouldn't take Scottish pound notes, which for some reason I'd been given at the cashpoint. I was fine on the fourth, until I realized that it veered away from Covent Garden at precisely the moment when I needed it to turn left into the area. I walked back along the Strand with my jacket collar turned up against the rain. I hadn't thought to wear an overcoat. I was late, and it felt as if the city was deliberately keeping me away from her. I imagined Michelle at the restaurant table, lowering her wineglass and laughing with friends as she paused to check her watch. I examined my A to Z and turned up towards Long Acre, just in time for a cab to plough through a trough of kerbside water and soak my legs. Then I discovered that I'd lost the piece of paper bearing the name of the restaurant. It had been in the same pocket as the A to Z, but must have fallen out. I had been so determined to memorize the name of the place, and now it completely eluded me. The harder I searched my mind, the less chance I had of remembering it. I had to explore every single restaurant in the damned street, and there were dozens of them.

I was just another guy on a date (admittedly the most important

date I'd ever had) and it was turning into the quest for the Holy
Grail. It took me over half an hour to cover the whole of Long
Acre, only to find that the Palais Du Jardin was the very last
restaurant in the street, and that I had missed Michelle Davies's
party by five minutes.

At least I remembered the name of the club, and strode on to
it, tense and determined. The bare grey building before me had
an industrial steel door, above which hung a banner reading
"blUeTOPIA". The bricks themselves were bleeding technobeat.
In front of the door stood a large man in a tight black suit, white
shirt, narrow black tie and sunglasses, a Cro-Magnon Blues
Brother.

"Get back behind the rope." He sounded bored. He kept his
arms folded and stared straight ahead.

"How much is it to get in?" I asked.

"Depends which part you're going into."

I tried to peer through the door's porthole, but he blocked my
view. "What's the difference?"

"You're not dressed for downstairs. Downstairs is Rubber?"

"Ah. How much upstairs?" I felt for my wallet. The rain had
begun to fall more heavily, coloured needles passing through
neon.

"Twelve pounds."

"That's a lot."

"Makes no difference. You can't come in."

"Why not?"

"It's full up. Fire regulations."

"But I have to meet someone."

Just then two shaven-headed girls in stacked boots walked
past me, and the bouncer held the door open for them. A wave
of boiling air and scrambled music swept over us. "Why did you
let them in?" I asked as he resealed the door.

"They're members."

"How much is it to be a member?"

"Membership's closed."

"You told me the club was full."

"Only to guests."

"Could I come in if I was with a member?"

The doorman approximated an attitude of deep thought for a
moment. "Not without a Guest Pass."

"What must I give you to get one of those?"

"Twenty-four hours' notice."

"Look." I spoke through gritted teeth. "I can see we have to reach some kind of agreement here, because the rest of my life is dependent on me getting inside this club tonight."

"You could try bribing me." He spoke as if he was telling a child something very obvious. I shuffled some notes from my wallet and held them out. He glanced down briefly, then resumed his Easter Island pose. I added another ten. He palmed the stack without checking it.

"Now can I come in?"

"No."

"You took a bribe. I'll call the police."

"Suit yourself. Who are they going to believe?"

That was a good point. He probably knew all the officers in the area. I was just a hick hustling to gain entry to his club. "I could make trouble for you," I said unconvincingly.

"Oh, that's good." He glanced down at me. "Bouncers love trouble. Every night we pray for a good punch-up. When there's a fight we call each other from all the other clubs," he indicated the doorways along the street, "and have a big bundle."

It was hopeless. My street etiquette was non-existent. I simply didn't know what to do, so I asked him. "This is incredibly important to me," I explained. "Just tell me how I can get in."

I'd already guessed the reply. "You can't."

"Why not?"

"Because you had to ask." He removed his glasses and studied me with tiny deep-set eyes. "You're up from the sticks for your Big Night Out, but it's not in here, not for you. You don't fit."

/ At least he was honest. I knew then that it wasn't just the club. I'd never be able to make the jump, even for a woman like her. Despondent, I walked to the side of the building and pressed my back against the wet brickwork, studying the sky. And I waited. I thought there might be a side exit I could slip through, but there wasn't. Everyone came and went through the front door. Soon my shirt was sticking to my skin and my shoes were filled with water, but I no longer cared. See Suburban Man attempt to leave his natural habitat! Watch as he enters the kingdom of Urbia and battles the mocking resident tribe! Well, this was one Suburban Man who wasn't going down without a fight.

But two hours later I was still there, shivering in the shadowed lea of the building, studying the lengthy queue of clubbers waiting to enter. When the steel door opened and she appeared with Pony-Tail and some black guy on her arm, I stepped forward into the light. One look at her face told me everything. I was sure now that she'd known I wouldn't get in, and was having a laugh at my expense.

I'm not a violent man, but I found myself moving toward her with my arm raised and I think my hand connected, just a glancing blow. Then people from the queue were on me, someone's hand across my face, another pushing me backwards. There was some shouting, and I remember hearing Michelle call my name, something about not hurting me.

I remember being thrown into the alley and hitting the ground hard. In movies they always land on a neat pile of cardboard boxes. No such luck here, just piss-drenched concrete and drains. My face was hurting, and I could taste blood in my mouth. I unscrewed my eyes and saw Pony-Tail standing over me. The black guy was holding Michelle by the arm, talking fast. She looked really sorry and I think she wanted to help, but he wasn't about to allow her near me. I could barely hear what he was saying through the noise in my head.

"I told you this would happen. He got no roots, no family. He don't belong here. You know that." He was talking too fast. I didn't understand. Then Pony-Tail was crouching low beside me.

"Big fucking mistake, man. You can't be near her. Don't you get it?" He was waving his hands at me, frustrated by his efforts to explain. "She's part of this city. Do you see? I mean, really part of it. You hurt her, you hurt – all of this." He raised his arm at the buildings surrounding us.

I tried to talk but my tongue seemed to block my speech. Pony-Tail moved closer. "Listen to me, you're cut but this is nothing. You must get up and run. It watches over her and now it'll fight you. Run back to your own world and you may be able to save yourself. That's all the advice I can give."

Then they were gone, the men on either side protecting her, swiftly bearing her away from harm, slaves guarding their queen. She stole a final glance back at me, regret filling her eyes.

For a few minutes I lay there. No one came forward to help. Eventually I found the strength to pull myself to my feet. It felt as if someone had stuck a penknife into my ribcage. The first time I tried to leave the alley, the indignant crowd pushed me back.

When I eventually managed to break through, the buildings ahead dazzled my eyes and I slipped on the wet kerb, falling heavily on to my shins. I knew that no one would ever come forward to help me now. The city had changed its face. As I stumbled on, blurs of angry people gesticulated and screeched, Hogarthian grotesques marauding across town and time. I milled through them in a maze of streets that turned me back toward the centre where I would be consumed and forgotten, another threat disposed of.

I feel dizzy, but I daren't risk lying down. There's a thick rope of blood running down my left leg, from an artery I think. I'm so vulnerable, just a sack of flesh and bone encircled by concrete and steel and iron railings and brittle panes. A few minutes ago I leaned against a shop window, trying to clear my stinging head, and the glass shattered, vitreous blades shafting deep into my back.

I can't last much longer without her protection.

The first car that hit me drove over my wrist and didn't stop. A fucking Fiat Panda. I think the second one broke a bone in my knee. Something is grinding and mashing when I bend the joint. He didn't stop, either. Perhaps I'm no longer visible. I can't tell if I'm walking in the road, because it keeps shifting beneath my feet. The buildings, too, trundle noisily back and forth, diverting and directing. I feel light-headed. All I know is, I won't survive until daybreak. No chance of reaching safety now. London has shut me out and trapped me in.

It's unfair; I don't think I should have to die. I suppose it's traditional when you screw around with the queen. As the pavement beneath my feet is heading slightly downhill, I think I'm being led toward the Embankment. It will be a short drop to the sluggish river below, and merciful sleep beyond.

I wonder what her real age is, and if she even has a name. Or what would have happened had I learned to love her city, and stay within the custody of her benevolent gaze. Does she look down with a tremor of compassion for those who fail to survive her kingdom, or does she stare in pitiless fascination at the mortals tumbling through her ancient, coiling streets, while far away, suburbia sleeps on?

ELIZABETH HAND

Justice

"JUSTICE" MARKS Elizabeth Hand's third appearance in *The Best New Horror*. Her short fiction has appeared in many magazines and anthologies, and she is the author of the novels *Winterlong*, *Aestival Tide*, *The Eve of Saint Nynex* and *Icarus Descending*.

Her articles and literary criticism have been published in the *Washington Post Book World*, *Detroit Times* and *Penthouse*, and she is a contributing editor to *Reflex* magazine and *Science Fiction Eye*.

The author lives on the coast of Maine with novelist Richard Grant and their children, and she is currently working on a contemporary supernatural novel entitled *Waking the Moon*.

The gods always come. They will come down
from their machines, and some they will save,
others they will lift forcibly, abruptly
by the middle; and when they bring some order
they will retire. And then this one will do one thing,
that one another; and in time the others
will do their things. And we will start over again.

–C.P. Cavafy, "Intervention of the Gods"

I WAS IN A Holiday Inn halfway between Joy and Sulphur,
Oklahoma, when the call came about the mutilations.

"Janet? It's Pete." Peter Green, head of features at *OUR*
magazine back in New York.

"What's the matter?" I said wearily. I'd just left Lyman, my
photographer, back in the motel bar with a tableful of empty
beer bottles and my share of the bill. I was already in bed and
had almost not answered the phone. Now it was too late.

"Moira killed the Bradford story."

I snorted. "The hell she did."

Clink of ice in a glass: it was an hour later back in New York
and two days before the weekly went to press. Pete would be at
home, trying desperately to tie up all the loose ends before Moira
McCain (*OUR* magazine was *her* magazine) started phoning him
with the last-minute changes that had given Pete a heart attack
last year, at the age of thirty-eight. "Too much fallout from the
White's piece."

A month earlier I'd done a story on the mass murderer who'd
rampaged through a White's Cafeteria in Dime Box, singling
out women and children as targets for his AK-47. Turned out
his estranged wife had tried to get a restraining order against
him; she was meeting her mother at the cafeteria for lunch that
day. A few weeks afterward there'd been another shooting spree.
Same town, different restaurant chain, chillingly similar M.O.
– girlfriend dumps guy, guy goes berserk, nine people end up
dead. Now all the tabloids and networks were catching flack for
over-publicizing the killings. Seven families had filed suit against
a tabloid program that had presented the first killer – Jimmie
Mac Lasswell, an overweight teenage boy – as a sensitive loner.

Unbelievably, eight weeks later both killers were still at large.
Not even sighted anywhere, which seemed impossible, given the
scope of the publicity the killings had received. "Legal says put
any kind of killer feature on hold till we find out how many
of those suits are going to trial. That means Bradford. Moira's
already called and canceled your interview."

"*Son of a bitch.*"

I'd been working on this story for six months, contacting all
the principals, writing to Billy Bradford in prison. This was my
third visit to Oklahoma: I was finally going to interview him
face-to-face. The story was slated to run next week.

"I know, Janet. I'm sorry." And he was, too. Pete hated Moira
more than any of us, and he'd helped arrange any number of my
meetings with Bradford's family and attorneys. Billy Bradford
was a forty-two-year-old truckdriver who had sexually abused
his fourteen-year-old stepdaughter. When she'd threatened to go
to her school guidance counselor with the story, he'd killed her.
What made the story gruesomely irresistible, though, was the
fact that Bradford was an amateur taxidermist who had then
stuffed his stepdaughter and hidden her body at his Lake Murray
hunting camp. **PSYCHODADDY**! the *New York Post* had called
him, and everyone got a lot of mileage out of the Norman Bates
connection.

But now the story was dead, and I was furious. "So what the
hell am I supposed to do here in Bumfuck?"

A long pause. More ice rattled on Pete's end of the line. I knew
something bad was coming.

"Actually, there's another story out there Moira wants you to
cover."

"Oh yeah? What?" I spat. "It's too early for the high school
football championships."

"It's, uh – well, it's sort of a ritual thing. A – well, shit, Janet.
It's a cattle mutilation."

"A *cattle mutilation*? Are you crazy?"

"Janet, look, we've got to have something – "

"What is this, I'm being punished? I won six fucking awards
last year, you tell her that! I'm not dicking around with some
UFO bullshit – "

"Janet, listen to me. It's not like that, it's – " He sighed. "Look,
I don't know what it is. Apparently Lyman was talking to her
earlier today – this is *after* she killed the Bradford piece – and

he mentioned hearing something on the radio down there about some cattle mutilations, and since you're both already out there Moira figured maybe you could get a story out of it. Lyman's got the details."

"Lyman's gonna have more than details," I snarled; but that was it. The Bradford story was dead. If Legal was worked up about it, Moira would never override their counsel. I could be in a room with Elvis Presley and the Pope and John Hinckley, and Moira would be whining with her lawyers over lunch at La Bernadine and refuse to run the story.

"Call me tomorrow. Lyman knows where this ranch is – " Lyman was from Oklahoma City, by way of a degree in Classics at Yale and a Hollywood apprenticeship – "hell, he's probably *related* to them – "

"Right. Later."

I clicked off and flopped back into bed.

Cattle mutilations. I should have switched from beer to tequila.

Lyman did know where the ranch was – a few hours outside of Gene Autry, an hour or so from the Texas border and about sixty miles from where we'd been staying.

"I'll meet you there," he said after giving me directions. Already his accent had kicked back in, and he'd resurrected a pair of ancient Tony Lama cowboy boots that he wore beneath his ninety-dollar jeans. "No later than noon, I swear."

He'd made plans to meet some distant cousin for a late breakfast somewhere on the way –

"Great barbecue, Janet, wish you'd join us – "

But I was too pissed to make small talk with Lyman and Don Ray. Instead I told Lyman I'd drop him off, and Don Ray would drive him down to find me in Gene Autry.

But Lyman was still determined that I salvage something from the trip. "Listen here, Janet, if you go about four miles past Sulphur you can get off the Interstate onto old Route 77. It'll take you right where we're going, and it's a real pretty road. I *know* you never got off the Interstate when you were here before. Route 77 goes through the Arbuckle Mountains and Turner Falls. And right before you hit the Interstate again there's a place called Val's Barbecue. Check it out for lunch."

He squeezed my arm and piled out of the rental car, weighted with cameras — he'd prove to the hick cousin that he was a real New York photographer now. And so I drove off, heading south for Gene Autry.

It took a while for Route 77 to get pretty. There was none of that Dustbowl ambiance I'd been expecting when I'd first come out here to meet with Bradford's wife. A lot of Oklahoma looked just like everywhere else now: McDonald's, franchised bars with stupid names, endless lots selling RVs and fancy pickup trucks. But after half an hour or so the landscape changed. The franchises dried up; the tacky ranch houses with over-watered lawns gave way to tiny dogtrot bungalows silvered with age, surrounded by rusting cars and oil wells long since run dry. Behind these stretched what remained of the great prairie — most of it given over to grazing lands now, but oddly empty of cattle or any other signs of cultivation. The sky was pale blue and dizzyingly immense above those endless green-gold plains, though on the southern horizon black clouds stretched as far as I could see, and spikes of lightning played in the distance. I fiddled with the radio till I found George Jones singing "He Stopped Loving Her Today."

"Well shit," I said out loud. Maybe cattle mutilations weren't such a bad thing after all.

After about an hour I saw my first sign for the Arbuckle Mountains. A few miles further and I passed a grimy motel, with a hand-lettered cardboard sign dangling from its neon pilasters. NOW! *AMERICAN* OWNED, it read. Another mile and I saw another sign, this one for the local football team. A crude caricature of an Indian in full headdress, his face scarlet and mouth wide open to show white pointed teeth. In one hand he held a tomahawk, in the other a scalp. The sign proclaimed HOME OF THE SAVAGES. I began to wish I'd waited to come with Lyman.

A few miles out of town, the road started to climb. It narrowed until it was barely wide enough to let two pickups pass, but then I'd only seen three or four cars all morning. To either side white outcroppings of stone appeared, tufted with long brittle grass. Above me the blue sky had been overtaken by the storm front moving up from the south, and spates of rain slashed across the windshield now and again. I glanced down at the map on the seat beside me and decided to get off at the next exit for the Interstate, Turner Falls or not.

Suddenly, without warning the road ahead of me twisted, one hairpin turn after another. The map fell to the floor while I cursed and slowed to a crawl. To either side sheer walls of stone rose, only six or seven feet high but enough to block out any view and much of the yellowish light. Then the last turn ended, seeming to leave me hanging in the air. The radio reception crackled and inexplicably died. I glanced in the rearview mirror to make sure there was no one behind me and eased the car to the side of the road.

I was atop a jagged hill overlooking a vista out of ancient Britain. An expanse of hills that looked as though they had been formed by huge hands crumpling the land together and then gently pulling it apart again. Some of the valleys between these hills formed nearly perfect Vs, their clefts so sharp and steep that no sun seemed to penetrate them. It was like a child's drawing of mountains, although compared to real mountains back east, these were barely tall enough to pass for hills. What made it so creepy were the stones.

There were thousands of them; thousands upon thousands. Pale grey and bleached white, like the tips of shark's teeth protruding from the earth, and arranged in perfect lines, row after row, that dipped and rose as the hills did, until they disappeared upon the horizon. Between them the long prairie grasses grew sparsely, as though sown upon grave mounds. There were no trees, no shrubs, nothing except for the grass and stones. It was impossible to imagine who could have put them there – a task so immense and mindless it seemed beyond human comprehension – but so orderly was the progression it seemed unimaginable that it could be some natural formation.

I pulled my hair back with my bandanna and got out. The wind beat against me, hot and damp, and I could hear the grasses whispering as they bent across the rocks. On another morning, with clear sky overhead and wildflowers nodding between the rows of limestone, it might have been an exhilarating sight. That day I found it nearly unbearable. I hurried back into the car and cranked up the a/c. Ten minutes later I was on the Interstate.

Having circumvented Lyman's directions, it took me a little longer to find the Lauren ranch. The Arbuckle Mountains disappeared as quickly as they had appeared, and soon I was back on the unbroken flatlands, with cottonwood and mesquite along the roadside beneath signs for Stuckey's and Burger King.

Finally I saw signs for Gene Autry, and a few miles later turned down a rutted gravel fire road that ran past tumbledown barns and a single rusting oil well. I was relieved when I saw three pickups pulled over to the side of the road. I checked my face in the mirror, rubbing my damp palms on my jeans and combing my hair back neatly. Too late I wondered if I should have worn a skirt – out here women still dressed like *women*. Not like they did in Texas, where housewives shopping at the H.E.B. all looked like *Dallas* extras; but I'd learned to be careful about how I looked, even for a cattle mutilation.

A hundred yards from the road four men were standing around a dark form sprawled on the ground. I crawled over the barbed wire fence, glad I'd worn my own (new) cowboy boots. Overhead buzzards circled. The heavy wind carried an oppressively sweet smell. The men knotted together, talking with heads downturned beneath their Stetsons and glancing at me sideways. The fourth walked toward me.

"I'm Janet Margolis from *OUR* magazine," I said, holding out my hand. He took it gingerly, nodding. "Thank you for seeing us. My photographer should be here soon."

"Well. I'm Hank Lauren." He cleared his throat uneasily. "This's my land here, some of my men."

I followed him to where the others stood upwind of the first carcass. A few feet behind it was another, and next to that a third. As I approached the men grew silent. One lit a cigarette and tossed the match so that it dropped onto one of the dead animals. Beside me Hank Laurens' feet fell heavily on the stony ground.

I stopped to gaze at the first body, then looked up at him in surprise.

"They're not cows."

He shook his head. "No ma'am. They're wild boars. Least I think they are. Agricultural Extension Office is checking, make sure nobody had some hogs escape the last few days."

"Javelinas," one of the other men explained. When I looked up at him he glanced away, but went on as though talking to the air. "That's a sort of wild pig we got around here. Sometimes they breed with the other kind. These're the biggest ones I ever seen." A shuffle and a murmur of agreement from the others. Hank coughed and waited while I stooped to look more closely.

It was a horrible sight, whatever it had been. An ugly thing to begin with, larger than any pig I'd ever seen, not that I'd seen many. Big enough for a man to ride on, if he could straddle its wide back. It was covered with coarse black hair, rising in a high bristly peak up its spine. Around its neck paler fur, nearly white, formed a collar. I took out my tape recorder and clicked it on.

"What'd you say this animal was called?"

"Javelina," the man answered loudly.

"Peccary," another said, stepping forward to nudge one of its stiff forelegs with his boot. "Collared peccary, that's what the Extension Office calls 'em. Down along the Mexican border they call 'em javelinas."

"Peccary," I repeated into the recorder, adding, "This is one big pig."

From the road echoed the sound of a car rattling along, and I looked back to see a big white Cadillac pull over. After a minute Lyman stumbled out, freighted with gear. He turned to shout thanks as the Cadillac roared away, then picked his way over the fence.

"Take a look at this, Lyman." I waved him over, trying not to grimace as a hot rank wave rose from the carcass at my feet. The men started talking among themselves again as Hank Lauren and Lyman shook hands. "I've never seen an animal this ugly in my life."

"Looks like someone didn't think it was ugly enough." Lyman swung out one of his cameras and started shooting. He squinted up at the sun, pewter-colored through the clouds, then back at the animal's face. "Damn, you all had one sick puppy out here, do that to a damn pig. I'm sorry, Janet," he added in a lower voice. "I shouldn't have made you come out here by yourself."

I frowned, but Lyman only turned back to his shoot. It wasn't until I crouched beside him to examine the thing's head that I saw what he meant. What I had thought to be the peccary's natural, if ugly, visage, was actually the result of some ghoulishly skillful work. The skin had been sliced into roseate petals around the eyes and folded back. Its ears were gone, and flies and gnats crawled in and out of the exposed white tubes that fed into its skull. Its lips were gone, too, so that the tusks and worn yellowed teeth looked enormous and raw, stained with blood and dirt-pocked.

"Jesus," I muttered. I stood, wiping the sweat from my palms, and glanced over at Lauren and his men. They said nothing, fastidiously ignoring me. I walked to the next carcass.

The other bodies were the same. "Mutilation of a ritual, probably sexual nature," I spoke into the recorder. "Damn, this is really sick – " I coughed and detailed some of the more obvious atrocities.

Hank Lauren was near enough to hear what I was saying: out of the corner of my eye I could see him nodding. I looked away, unaccustomedly embarrassed. How often did one use words like *castration*, *sodomy*, *coprophagy* when referring to a pig? Over the last few years I'd learned how to deal with such horrors when associated with women or children – you turned it into righteous outrage, and that turned into money in the pages of *OUR* magazine – but still, I'd never been there to see the bodies uncovered. The sight of those grotesque, pathetic corpses, coupled with the stench of excrement and putrefaction made me feel faint. I switched off my recorder, surreptitiously covered my mouth and took a few deep breaths. I didn't want Lyman to see how this was affecting me. Then I stepped away to join Hank Laurens.

"So this happened last night?"

He shook his head. "Night before. Found them yesterday morning. Vet came out to do an autopsy said it happened that night."

"What do they think it was? Dogs?"

He snorted. "No *dog* could do that. No coyote either. Somebody with a razor – you ever see a dog do *that*?" He pointed at one of the carcasses, its violation grotesquely evident from where we stood.

"So what do they suspect?"

He shrugged but said nothing. One of the other men, the one who'd been smoking, coughed and said, "Something like this happened few weeks ago down in Ladonia. That's Texas, though."

Murmurs. "Last year there was something about it, some place in Colorado," another man put in. "These mutilations. Saw it on *Current Affair*," he added, turning to his boss. "You remember I told you 'bout that?"

I nodded and looked at Hank expectantly, my thumb on the recorder button. He was staring at the buzzards wheeling patiently in the sky. "What do you think, Hank? I mean, anything strange going on around here – cults, stuff like that? Kids listening to weird music?" I didn't usually ask leading questions, but sometimes – with men especially – you had to keep probing before you finally hit a vein.

"Around here we don't go in for that kinder thing." It was one of the other men who answered. He'd been frowning, watching Lyman race through two rolls of film. Now the ground crackled beneath his heavy boots as he walked to join Hank and me with that slightly bowlegged gait. "Church is a big deal out here. Kids don't go in for that satanic music. Ones who do move on out."

The other men nodded. Lyman glanced over at me and winked.

"So nothing that might explain this?" My voice sounded a little desperate. I had visions of the rest of the day blown at the Agricultural Extension Office, trying vainly to come up with some kind of hook for this damn story. "No kind of revenge angle, cattle rustling, anything like that?"

"Don't nobody rustle wild hogs," Hank remarked. The others laughed.

"Well, shit," I muttered, switching off the recorder. The stench from the corpses was starting to overwhelm me. The afternoon air was warm and humid, and clouds of blowflies were erupting from swellings in the pigs' bellies and their raw faces. "Lyman –?"

Lyman had moved out to focus on the four cattlemen, the bloated carcasses in the foreground. The smoker lit another cigarette, cupping cracked hands around a match. He looked up and said, "Hank, what about that business with your sister and Brownen?"

Hank Lauren didn't say anything, but after a moment he nodded. I tried not to look too eager, but fixed him with a quizzical look.

"Your sister?"

Hank Lauren breathed in noisily, raising his head to stare up at the sun raising a gray blister in the clouds. "Don't have a damn thing to do with this," he said.

"I just meant it's been in all the papers, Hank," the first man countered, and Hank sighed. I armed myself with the recorder again.

"Just some problems with her and her ex," he said wearily. "Locked him up on account he beat up on her and my nephew. But they let him out, some kind of restraining order. I testified, I heard that s.o.b. threaten t'kill her and the boy. He's a sorry bastard. Got arrested for dealing drugs, too. Well, they let him out anyway. He started calling her and now he's disappeared. Sue's about ready to leave town, she's so scared he'll come some night'n cut her throat."

"So you think this might be some kind of sick vengeance he's taking on your sister?"

He shrugged, glanced at his watch. His eyes when he raised them again were dull. "Well I sure hope not." He dug his heel into the dirt and tilted his chin toward the pickups leaning at the roadside. "You got to excuse us, but we've got a few things to take care of this afternoon."

We shook hands and Lyman took some more pictures of Lauren and his crew. I got addresses and a few telephone numbers, and promised them the article would be out within the next week or two. Lyman and I watched the trucks leave, firing one after another and spurting off in a haze of dust and gravel.

"Well," I said as we headed to the car. "That was certainly a disgusting waste of time."

Lyman shrugged his equipment from one shoulder to the other. "What was that about his brother-in-law? Sounds like your kind of thing."

I kicked up a cloud of gritty dust, grimacing as we met the barbed-wire fence again. "It's only my kind of thing if he kills his ex-wife and shows up on national news. God, this is a depressing place."

"Well, we're done now. I booked us out tomorrow at eleven. So we can head to Oklahoma City tonight and get a hotel, or wait till morning."

He threw his stuff into the car and leaned against the trunk.

"For god's sake, let's get out of here." I glanced back at the carcasses. A buzzard had landed beside one, hopping about it like an excited kid, finally pouncing on a long ribbon of flesh and tugging at it. "Ugh."

"We-ell – " Lyman eased around to the driver's seat, shading his eyes and looking wistfully into the distance.

"Oh, come on, Lyman!" I yanked my door open, exasperated. "What is it? See Rock City? Best Little Whorehouse in Gene Autry?"

"Nooo . . ." He started the car and we jounced down the road. "Just there's this great place for barbecue up by the Arbuckle Reservoir. Indian territory but not too far from here. Only thing is, it's only open for dinner. But there used to be a pretty good motel – "

I was too dispirited to argue. "Sure, sure. Whatever. You drive, you feed me, whatever you want. Just make sure this time tomorrow I'm home. Okay?"

We found a dusty little motel and checked in. I made a few phone calls about Lauren's brother-in-law. I found his ex in the phone book. She hadn't bothered to change the number, but I'd long since ceased to be surprised by what women wouldn't do to avoid an abusive s.o.b. She was polite enough but didn't want to talk to me; I left the number of the motel in case she changed her mind. Then I called the local constable. According to him, yes, George Brownen had been released; no, there wasn't anything special they could do to protect his ex-wife, and the whole thing was probably being blown way out of proportion.

"Right," I said, dropping the phone in disgust and kicking back onto the bed. These things were always blown out of proportion, the proportions usually made up of some poor woman's face slammed against the wall, or blown to pieces inside a mobile home out by the Piggly Wiggly. But the hell with it. I tried to tell myself it was just a job.

I slept for a while. When I woke I showered, played back my tape and made a few notes, then buzzed Lyman's room. Out: no doubt soaking up more local color, or tracking down another cousin. I changed into jeans and a T-shirt and headed for the motel bar.

The motel sat on a sand-colored hillside, a few miles off Route 77 and with an impressive view of the Arbuckle Mountains rolled out like sepia corduroy to the east. A rusted sign advertising some defunct waterslide clapped loudly in the parking lot. Beneath the westering sun gleamed a tiny swimming pool half-full of overchlorinated water, the chemical smell so strong it made my eyes tear. I glanced vainly around for Lyman, crossed the parking lot, and stopped.

A single other car was parked in the lot, around the corner from our room. Not a car, actually. An RV, a mid-sized late-model leviathan with fake wood trim and darkened windows, identical to a million other RVs holding up traffic from Bar Harbor to Yosemite.

Only I recognized this one. I couldn't figure out how, or from where; but I'd seen it before. I stood staring at it, wiping the sweat from my upper lip and wishing I'd worn my sunglasses. All I had was a vague remembrance of unease, the name and the sight of that van making me distinctly uncomfortable. I walked past it slowly, and as I approached fierce barking broke out from inside. The vehicle shimmied slightly, as a dog – make that dogs – threw themselves against the side; and *that* was familiar, too. A flicker of shadow against one of the windows, then a thump and furious snarling as they leaped against the windows again.

"Huh." I paused, listening as the dogs grew more and more frantic. From the sound of it they were big: no retirees with fluffy cockapoos here. The RV was big enough to house half-a-dozen Dobermans. And whoever owned the van wasn't putting hygiene at a premium – it smelled like the worst kind of puppy mill, with a lingering fecal odor of rotting meat and straw. Still I stood there, until finally I decided this was stupid. I probably *had* seen it before, parked at the motel in Oklahoma City, or even at the Holiday Inn. According to Lyman, the Arbuckle Mountains were supposed to be some big vacation spot. No real mystery.

But I couldn't shake the feeling that the RV was out of context, here; that wherever I'd seen it before, and heard those dogs, it hadn't been on this trip. At last I turned and went inside. The barking didn't cease until the bar door closed behind me.

The bar was one of those places where frigid air conditioning and near-darkness pass for atmosphere. The same Muzak piped into the motel's tiny coffeeshop echoed here, and the paltry clientele seemed to consist of motel employees getting off the three p.m. shift. I found a corner as far from the speakers as possible and sat there nursing a Pearl beer and squinting at the local paper. It was a weekly, nothing there about the animal mutilations yet, but the police blotter said that Susan Brownen, of Pauls Valley, had filed a complaint against her former husband. Seemed he'd tried to set her trailer on fire and, when that didn't work, totalled her car. George Brownen I assumed was still at large. There was also a long feature on someone celebrating her one-hundredth birthday in the Sulphur Rest Home, and a recipe for Frito Pie that used pickled okra. I finished my beer and decided to call Lyman again. Then I saw her.

She was at the bar, that's how I'd missed her before; but now she was turned toward me and smiling as the bartender shoved a mixed drink and a Pearl longneck in front of her. She slipped some money on the counter, took the drinks, and headed for my table.

"Janet Margolis, right?"

I nodded, frowning. "I *knew* I recognized that RV from somewhere. I'm sorry, I don't remember your name – "

She sat down, waving her hand self-deprecatingly as she slid the longneck to me. "Please! How could you? Irene Kirk – "

We shook hands and I thanked her for the beer. She pulled one leg up under her, smoothing the folds of an expensive pleated silk skirt. "We've got to stop meeting like this," she said, her eyes narrowing as she laughed and squeezed a lime into her glass. I nodded, leaning back in my chair as I sipped my beer.

Irene Kirk. I had been covering the trial of Douglas "Buddy" Grogan a year before, the story that had gotten me a Pulitzer nomination – the first ever for *OUR* magazine. It was a horrible experience, because the details of the case were horrible. Another estranged husband, this one granted visitation rights to his three-year-old son. After a year of threatening his ex-wife, then begging her to reconcile with him, one weekend when the little boy was visiting, Buddy Grogan had called her on the telephone and, as she listened and pleaded with him on the other end, shot the child. What made the whole thing almost unbearable, though, was that she had the whole thing on tape – she'd been recording her phone calls since he'd begun threatening her. And it wasn't the sort of thing you got used to hearing, even if you wrote for a tabloid that was trying to tart up its image for a more politically correct decade.

Irene Kirk had been there. She was a lawyer, the kind of feminist the newspapers always described as "ardent" rather than "militant." She lived in Chicago, but traveled all over the country doing *pro bono* work for rape crisis centers and abortion clinics and the like. She was a sort of camp follower of cases of this sort. Since the Grogan trial I'd heard of others running into her, at Congressional hearings, celebrity rape trials, shelters for the abused and homeless. But she wasn't exactly an ambulance chaser. For one thing, she obviously didn't need to work for a living. Small and delicate, with skin like white silk and inky hair pulled into a chignon, even here in the middle of nowhere she wore the kind of clothes you usually only saw on models in the European editions of tony women's magazines. And at the Grogan trial she spent a lot of time talking to women outside the courtroom – friends of Grogan's wife, women from local shelters, women who seemed to have stories not too different from the one I was covering, except they hadn't ended tragically – yet. Every morning she cruised around the courthouse until she found a parking space for her leviathan RV, and I'd wondered what a woman like that – with her sueded silk suits, smelling of Opium and ylang-ylang shampoo – was doing with a van full of snarling dogs. Protection, I finally decided, *I* sure wouldn't want to mess with them.

During the course of the trial we'd spoken several times, mostly to shake our heads over the shameful state of affairs between men and women these days. Eight months later we would have had more to talk about: during a routine transfer to a federal penitentiary, Buddy Grogan somehow had escaped, aided by an unknown woman. He hadn't been heard from since. But that was still a ways off. When the trial ended Irene Kirk gave me her business card, but that was right before I got mugged by a couple of innocent-looking vegan types near Tompkins Square Park and lost my Filofax.

"I was very impressed by the way you handled the White's story," she said. She took a sip of her drink and glanced up at me through slitted black eyes. "It's amazing, isn't it, the way we just keep on going? One thing after another, and still we just can't quit."

I winced, tried to hide my expression behind my beer bottle. I remembered now why I'd been unhappy to see that van outside – Kirk's outspoken but somehow coy insistence that "we" were in this together; that together we formed some heroic bulwark for the victims we exploited, I with my articles, she in some subtler way I couldn't quite get a handle on. "It's my job," I said dryly. "I *can't* quit. Baby needs shoes, you know." I have my reasons for what I do – everybody does – but I'd be damned if I'd share them with Irene Kirk.

"Oh, I didn't mean you and me *individually*." Kirk's cultivated voice was soft, but her eyes glittered in the dimness. "I mean all of us. Women. These terrible things happen but we just keep going on. We just keep fighting."

That last mouthful of beer turned sour in my mouth. I grimaced and looked around the room, as though seeking someone in the empty corners. "Yeah, well."

I thought of the photos I'd seen from the White's massacre:

a mother hunched over the crumpled body of her daughter, a grandmother hugging a tiny limp figure, her face so raw with grief it no longer looked human. *Those* women sure hadn't been fighting. And then unbidden the images from that afternoon rose up in front of me: the bloated blackened carcasses slung out on the gravel, their eyes swollen with larvae and dust. When I looked up again Irene Kirk was still staring at me with those intent black eyes, her expression somewhere between concern and disdain. I suddenly wanted to leave.

"Well, it's all in the capable hands of the State of Oklahoma now." I tried to keep my voice light. "So I guess we just have to keep believing that justice will be done."

"Justice." She laughed, a small hard sound like pebbles clattering in a bowl, and leaned forward to stare into her half-empty glass. "The famous feminist reporter for *OUR* magazine still believes in justice."

The disdain in her voice was my cue to leave. I slid my chair back from the table and rose, giving her a blank smile. "I've got to go meet my photographer. Thanks again for the beer."

"I'll go with you." A slithering sound as the long folds of her skirt slipped down her legs. I shrugged, the smile frozen on my face, and headed for the door.

Outside the sun was dipping below the flattened edge of the prairie. The sawtoothed ridge of the Arbuckle Mountains cut a violet line against the bright sky. When I looked across the lot at Lyman's room I was relieved to see that the curtains had been drawn against the sunset.

"Well," I said again with forced cheerfulness – feeling ungrateful, somehow, and guilty for feeling so. "Nice seeing you again."

"Why are you here?"

The way she said it put an accusatory spin on the question, but when I looked at her she only smiled, her steps slowing as we approached her RV. For some reason I felt like lying. Instead I shrugged and said, "I was covering the Bradford case. But they pulled the story, so we're going back tomorrow."

"Mmm."

I turned to squint at the sun, then glanced back at her. She had an absent, almost dreamy look on her face, as though the name *Bradford* made her think of distant places – white beaches veined with blue water, an empty shoal beneath a midsummer sky. My earlier disgust returned. I whirled around, walking backwards across the empty lot, and called, "Have a good trip — thanks again for the drink — "

She raised a hand to me, her slight figure unnaturally black against the molten sunset. After a moment she turned and headed toward her van. As she approached it I heard again the frantic barking of the dogs inside. Then I was rapping on Lyman's door, falling inside with absurd relief as it swung open and the cool air flowed over my face.

Lyman's Barbecue joint turned out to be small and crowded, run by a small woman named Vera who didn't crack a smile at Lyman's praise and left a handful of mintscented toothpicks beside our plates when she dropped the check. But the barbecue was good, lean and dry and smoky, with a vinegary sauce on the side — Texas-style barbecue, not the sweet soppy mess you get in New York. I asked him about the strange stones I'd seen along the old road.

"Dragon's teeth," he said. He lifted another piece of barbecue on his fork and eyed it dreamily. "That's what they call 'em out here. They're famous, geologically speaking. Arbuckle Mountains are one of the oldest places in the world, after the Black Hills and Olduvai Gorge."

I took a pull of my beer. "Dragon's teeth?"

"Sure. You know — Cadmus sowing dragon's teeth and an army springing up. It's in Aeschylus."

I snorted. "Lyman, you're the only person in this whole damn state ever even heard of Aeschylus."

After we ate he tried to talk me into going to some dive for a beer, but I was exhausted and too aware that the next day I'd be struggling to come up with some kind of story out of a few dead pigs.

"I'll put in for an eight o'clock wakeup call," he said as we stretched and yawned in the darkened parking lot. Overhead the day's clouds had blown on. There was a thin brittle moon and a few brilliant stars that made it seem like the air should be cool and brisk, instead of heavy and smelling of dust.

"Make it seven-thirty. I want to get out of here."

I saluted him and headed for my room, stopped after a few steps to look across the lot. Two other cars were parked beneath the yellow streetlights. I could hear a television shrieking from inside one of the rooms near mine. And Irene Kirk's RV was gone. I walked slowly past where it had been parked earlier and went inside.

It was a while before I could fall asleep. I felt like the whole day had been wasted; like months had been wasted, chasing another grim story and then having to bail out at the last minute. I knew it was absurd, that my coverage of the Bradford case was nothing more than another cheap tabloid hustling to cash in on misery in the Dust Belt. All my pieces were like that, but the process of writing them up and then seeing them in print somehow defused the stories of some of their horror, for me at least. It was like sticking around till the end of some particularly gruesome movie to read every line of the credits, reassuring myself that it was all nothing more than a string of sophisticated special effects and calculated screen writing. Only with Bradford, of course, there were no credits; at least not until the TV movie appeared.

I finally dozed off, the distant grumble of trucks on the Interstate a comforting background roar. I was dreaming about pigs, pork barbecue and beer, when the phone rang for my wakeup call.

"Mrs Margolis?" A woman's twangy voice, like something you'd hear on a Bible call-in show. I groaned, feeling like I'd only been asleep for a few minutes, and rolled over, fumbling on the night table for my alarm clock. "Mrs Margolis, is that you?"

I started to snap that I was *Mrs* Nobody when the woman went on, "This is Sue Brownen. You called me today, n'I, I – "

I sat bolt upright, the clock in my hand. I *had* only been asleep for a few minutes. "Yes!" I said, a little breathlessly. I knocked aside a water glass, looking for my tape recorder, a notebook, anything. "Sue, of course, right. What's going on?"

"George – my husband, George – well, he called me tonight." In the background I could hear a child crying, another woman's comforting voice. "He says I don't meet him at Jojo's he's coming after me."

She stopped, her voice thick. I found a pen, scribbled *Jojo's* on the back of my hand. "You've called the police, right?" I was on my feet now, grabbing my jeans and crumpled T-shirt from the chair where I'd slung them. "And you're not alone, you're not at home, are you? You're not someplace he can find you?"

"No'm, I'm at – " The voice in the background suddenly rang out shrilly, and Sue Brownen choked, "I'm somewhere safe. But

I just thought – well, I been thinking about it, I thought maybe you could write this up, you said maybe you could pay me – "

I got an address, a post office box in Pauls Valley. She wouldn't tell me where she was now, but I made her promise to call me early in the morning, before I checked out. When I hung up I was already dressed.

It was crazy, getting all hyped up over some routine wife-beating case, but I needed some damn angle for that story. It was after eleven. I had no idea what time the bars closed here, but I figured on a weeknight I was probably pushing the limit at midnight. Outside I paused at Lyman's door. His room was dark, the shades still drawn. I thought of waking him up, but then Lyman hated going on any kind of location shoot where he might run into trouble. Although the odds were I'd end up cruising some dead bar with nothing to show for it but an interrupted night's sleep. I stopped at the motel desk, got directions to Jojo's, and left.

Returning from the Lauren Ranch we'd passed several small buildings at the edge of town. One right next to the other, each long and narrow beneath its corrugated tin roof. Names were painted on their fronts – BLACK CAT, ACAPULCO, JOJOS – but only the last was open. A number of pickups were parked in front, more of a clientele than I thought the tiny place could hold. When I drove past I saw men gathered before the crooked screened entry. Not the sort of men I'd want to tangle with alone, not the sort of place most women would go into, with or without an escort. I turned the car around in front of a boarded-up Sinclair station and made another pass, this time pulling into the lot of the shuttered roadhouse next door. I parked in front of the crude drawing of a black cat, shut off the motor and waited.

There wasn't a lot of traffic in and out of Jojo's. The small group remained in front of the door, maybe because there wasn't room inside; but after about ten minutes two uniformed men came out. The rest of the little crowd parted, shuffling and adjusting their gimme caps as they passed, calling out greetings and laughing. The two cops crossed the crowded lot to another pickup, this one silvery blue and with a light on top, and leaned against it for a few more minutes, laughing and smoking cigarettes. Finally they slung their booted feet into the truck and drove off, the men by the door raising chins or hands in muted farewell.

So that was the local justice department. I sat in the car another five minutes, barely resisting the urge to lock myself in. I lived on the Lower East Side, I saw worse than this buying the *New York Times* every morning, but still my heart was pounding. *Stupid, Janet, stupid*, I kept thinking, I should have brought Lyman. But at last I got out and walked over to Jojo's.

No one said a word as I passed. One guy tipped the bill of his cap, and that was it. Inside was dim, lit by red bulbs the color of whorish lipstick. Smoke curled above the floor and a sound system blared a song I hated. It was crowded; I saw two women in booths toward the back, but their appearance didn't reassure me any. Behind the painted plywood bar a tall dark-skinned man yanked beers from a styrofoam cooler and slid them to his customers. The men moved aside as I approached, watching me coldly.

"I'm looking for George Brownen," I said. I pushed a ten dollar bill across the sticky counter. "He been here yet?"

The man looked suspiciously at the bill, finally set a Miller bottle atop it and pulled it toward him. "He's gone," he said shortly. He kept his eye on the bill but still didn't touch it.

"How long ago?"

The bartender turned pointedly to serve another customer. I waited, trying not to lose my temper or my nerve. Still he ignored me, finally crouching to attend to some business behind the plywood counter. A few more minutes passed.

"Sheriff lookin' for him too," a voice announced beside me. I looked up to see a weathered man in a faded Harley T-shirt. He lit a cigarette, holding the pack out to me and then sticking it back in his pocket. He raised his chin to indicate the bartender. "He ain't gonna tell you nothin'."

Another man poked his head over the first's, staring at me appraisingly. "Brownen just left with another gal, young lady. But maybe I can help you."

I smiled tightly, shaking my head, and looked back for the bartender.

"Yessir, he sure did. 'Nother yankee," the first man was saying. "Hey Jo, you bringin' in tourists these days?"

Scattered laughter. The bartender stood and looked at me with dangerous red eyes. I nodded once, turned and fled.

The crowd at the door let me pass again, though this time their voices followed me as I walked back to my car. I did my best not to run; once inside I hit the autolock and sat for a moment trying to compose myself. After a minute or two the faces in front of the roadhouse had all turned away.

Still, I didn't want to sit there, and I sure didn't want anyone to follow me. When I started the car I drove behind the Black Cat, hoping to find a way out, and that was where I saw them.

She had changed her clothes. Now she wore tight jeans and a red blouse, and cowboy boots – surprisingly worn-looking boots, even in the cracked circle of blue light from the single streetlamp I could see how old those boots were, a working man's boots, not some rich urban lawyer's. They were leaning against her RV, arms crossed in front of their chests, talking. Once she threw her head back and laughed, and the man looked at her, confused, before he laughed too. He was tall and good-looking, with dark hair and a neatly trimmed beard. He glanced at my car as I drove by, but Irene Kirk didn't even look up. I knew without a doubt in my mind that he was George Brownen.

Abandoned railroad tracks crisscrossed behind the road-houses. Next to them stood a burned-out warehouse with the rusted logo RED CHIEF flapping from a pole. I shut the engine, killed the lights and sat, watching Kirk and Brownen, trying to imagine what they were saying. Was she doing some kind of research, pretending to be one of her hard-luck clients? Or did she just have a taste for rough trade? The thought made me grimace, and I slid down in my seat so there'd be no way they could see me.

Only a few more minutes passed before she slapped the front of her van and started for the door. Brownen waited, called something and pointed across the lot. I knew he was trying to get her to follow him to his truck. But Irene only laughed, slinging her slight frame up into the driver's seat and leaning over to open the other door. Brownen waited another moment, until she turned on the headlights. Then he walked slowly to the RV and climbed inside. Very faintly I could hear barking, and then that was swallowed by the van's engine and the crunch of flying gravel as the RV pulled away.

I followed them. I knew it was crazy but I felt reckless and pumped up after my visit to Jojo's. Plus there was nothing to worry about, really; there was no way they could recognize me, cruising a safe distance behind them, and back inside my car I felt invulnerable. I don't know what I was thinking –

probably nothing more than some misplaced voyeurism, or maybe a hope that they might stop somewhere and I could see where Brownen lived.

A rusted double-wide trailer on the outskirts of this failing oil town . . .

That would be how I'd write it up but they didn't go to Brownen's place. They headed north, toward the Interstate and the mountains, then turned onto a gravel road that ran parallel to the highway. I slowed until there was a good distance between us; it was easy to keep them in sight. There was no other traffic. After a few minutes we were in open country again.

They drove for a long time. I rolled down the window to catch the night wind, heavy with the smell of wild sage and the ubiquitous taint of petroleum. I didn't turn on the radio, from some faint ridiculous fear that they might somehow hear it.

Overhead the moon was setting, bright as a streetlamp. The stars looked white and surprisingly solid, like salt spilled on a black table. As I drove the land slowly began to rise around me, gentle hills at first, hiding the rolling farmlands and the dull orange glow on the horizon that marked Ardmore to the south. The air streaming through the window was warm and sweet. I was composing my article in my head, thinking how Lyman had enough grisly photos that we wouldn't need much text. Far ahead of me the RV's taillights jounced and swam, twin meteors burning across the darkness.

I don't know when I realized that we were back among the stones. On some unconscious level it must have registered – I'd been climbing steadily for a long time, the prairie somewhere in the soft darkness behind me. But suddenly I jerked upright, as though I had drifted asleep at the wheel.

I hadn't: it was just that it was a shock, to look out the window and suddenly see them like that. In the moonlight they looked more like tombstones than ever. No, not tombstones, really, but something worse, infinitely more ancient and incomprehensible: barrows, menhirs, buried ossuaries. Lyman's comment about dragon's teeth didn't seem so stupid now. I stared out the window at those meticulous rows of bleached sharp spines, and wondered if it was true, if those stones were as ancient as he'd said.

When I looked up again a moment later I thought I'd lost the RV. In front of me the cracked road twisted until it disappeared in the blackness. The van's lights were gone. I had a jolt of panic, then sighted it: it had turned off to the right and parked. It sat on a high ridge overlooking the lines of stones, its rounded bulk silhouetted against the moon on the edge of the world.

Absurdly, I still wanted to follow them. If they'd been watching at all they must have seen the car behind them still, I cut my lights and pulled to the side of the road to park. I was in one of those tiny deep clefts poked into the strata of limestone and scrub. No one could see me, although they might notice that my car had abruptly disappeared. I waited a long time, striving to hear something above the soft hissing of the wind in thorny brush and the staccato cries of a nightjar.

I finally got out of the car. The air felt cooler here. Something scrabbled at my feet and I looked down to see a hairy spider, nearly big as my hand, crouch in a pocket of dust. I turned and began to walk quickly up the rise.

In a few minutes I could hear voices, surprisingly close. As I reached the top of the little hill I crouched down, until I was half walking, half crawling through loose scree and underbrush. When I reached the top I kept my head down, hidden behind a patch of thorns.

I was close enough that I could have thrown a stone and hit the side of the RV. Another sheer drop separated us, a sort of drywash gully. The ridge where they were parked was a little lower than where I crouched. Between us marched three rows of stones, sharp and even as a sawblade. I heard faint music — Irene must have put the radio on — and their voices, soft, rising now and then to laughter.

They were walking around the van. Irene kicked idly at stones. The wind carried the acrid smell of cigarette smoke from where Brownen followed her. I tried to hear what they were saying, caught Irene pronouncing something that sounded like "wife" and then Brownen's laughter. I peered through the brush and saw that she was carrying something in one hand. At first I thought it was a whip, but then I saw it was a stick, something slender and pliable like a forsythia wand. When she slapped it against her thigh it made a whining sound.

That sound and the thought of a whip suddenly reminded me of the dogs. I swore under my breath, squatting back on my heels. And as though the same idea had come to her, Irene headed for the back of her van. She walked slowly, almost unthinkingly but somehow I knew that this was calculated. She'd meant all along to let those dogs out. It was the reason she'd come here; and suddenly I was afraid.

For a moment she stood in front of the door, staring at where Brownen stood with his shoulders hunched, looking at his feet and smoking. Behind her the moon hung like a silver basket. The jagged hills with their lines of stones marched on, seemingly forever, the stones dead-white against the grey earth and somber sky. Still Irene Kirk waited and watched Brownen. She didn't stand there hesitantly. It was more like she was thinking, trying to make up her mind about something. Then, with one sure motion she threw the door open.

I had thought the dogs would bound out, snarling or barking. Instead first their heads and front paws appeared. There were two of them, sniffing and whining and clawing at the air. Big dogs, not as large as mastiffs but with that same clumsy bulk, their heads looking swollen compared to the rest of them. I heard Irene's voice, soothing yet also commanding. Brownen looked up. There was no way for me to tell if he was afraid, but then he dragged on his cigarette and ground it out, shoved his hands in his jeans pockets and looked quickly from Irene to her animals.

The whining grew louder. The dogs still remained at the edge of the van, crouched like puppies afraid to make the little jump to the ground. And then I realized they *were* afraid. When Irene took a step towards them their whining grew louder and they fell over each other, trying to race back into the van; but then she raised that slender wand and called something. Her voice was clear and loud, but I had no idea what she said.

The dogs did, though. At the sound of her voice they stopped. When she repeated the command they turned and leaped from the cab, their great forms flowing to the ground like black syrup poured from a jug. Big as they were they looked starved. Even from where I crouched I could see their ribs, the swollen joints of their legs, and the silvery glint where one still wore a cruel collar around his neck. Sudden panic overcame me: what if they scented me and attacked? But running would only make it worse, so I bellied down against the coarse ground, praying the wind wouldn't turn and bring my scent to them.

And the dogs seemed to want to run. They started to race across the narrow ridge, but once again Irene shouted a command, her switch slashing through the air. As though they'd been shot the dogs dropped, burying their muzzles between their front paws like puppies. Irene turned her back to them and walked towards Brownen.

She walked right up to him, until her hands touched his sides. He drew his arms up to hold her, but I saw how his eyes were on the dogs. Then she thrust her pelvis against his, ran her hands along his thighs and up his arms, until he looked down at her. His head dipped; moonlight sliced a grey furrow across his scalp. I could no longer make out Irene's face beneath his; and that was when she raised her hand.

The slender switch she held hung in the air for a moment. When it dropped I could hear its whistling, so that I thought he'd cry out as it struck his shoulder. But he didn't; only looked up in surprise. He started to draw away from her, puzzled, his mouth opening to say something. He never did.

As smoothly as the dogs had poured from the back of the van, Brownen fell to his knees. For an instant I lost sight of him, thought I was looking at another of the stony cusps stretching across the hills. Then I saw him; saw what he was becoming.

A wail cut across the hillside. I thought it was Brownen at first, but it was one of the dogs. At Irene's feet a dark form writhed, man-size but the wrong shape. In her hand the switch remained, half-raised as though she might strike him again. The shape twisted, as though struggling to get up. I heard a guttural sound, a sort of grunting. My stomach contracted; I thought of running back to my car but that would mean standing, and if I stood there would be no way of pretending that I hadn't seen what had become of Brownen. In another moment it was too late, anyway.

Irene Kirk stepped back. As her shadow fell away the figure at her feet squirmed one last time, tried to rear onto his hind legs and finally rolled onto all fours. It was an animal. A pig: a boar, one of the things I'd seen that afternoon, slaughtered on the Laurens ranch. In the moonlight it looked immense and black, its grizzled collar of fur seeming to cast a sheen upon the ground beneath it. It had tusks, not large but still vicious-looking, and surprisingly dainty feet ending in small pointed hooves. There was no man where Brownen had stood a moment before; nothing but the javelina and Irene Kirk, and crouched a few yards away her two dogs.

My eyes burned. I covered my mouth with one hand, retching, somehow kept from getting sick. I heard a high-pitched sound, something screeching; when I looked up the javelina had darted across the ridge, heading towards the car.

"Jimmie Mac! Buddy!" Irene's voice was clear and loud, almost laughing. She raised her wand, pointed at the boar scrabbling through the brush and yelled something I couldn't make out. I raised myself another inch, in time to see the two dogs burst from their crouch and take off after the javelina.

Within seconds they had it down, within the shadow of the RV. Their snarls and the peccary's screams ripped the still air. I could hear its hooves raining against the metal side of the van, the dogs' snarling giving way to frightened squeals. The sharp odor of shit came to me suddenly, and a musky smell. Then it was quiet, except for low whimpering.

I let my breath out, so loudly I was sure they'd hear me. But the dogs didn't move. They wriggled belly-down against the ground, as though trying to back away from the carcass in front of them. A few feet away Irene watched, her arms lowered now, her stick twitching against her thigh. Then she walked slowly to the animals.

The dogs groaned and whined at her approach, writhing as though chained to the wheels of the van. When she reached them her arm shot up. I thought she would strike them, but instead she brought the switch down upon the javelina's corpse. The moon glinted off the slender wand as though it were a knife; and then it seemed it *was* a knife. Because where she struck the carcass slivers of flesh spun into the air, like a full-blown rose slashed by a child's hand. Ears, lips, nose; gleaming ribbons falling around her feet like leaves. She was laughing, a sweet pure sound, while at her feet the dogs moaned and clawed their muzzles with bloody paws.

I couldn't bear any more. Before I could stop myself I was on my feet and bolting, my feet sliding through the loose scree and dust swirling up all around me. Only a few yards away was my car. I jumped over a pointed tooth of stone, thought almost that I had made it; but then I was screaming, falling beneath some great weight onto the rocky ground.

"Janet."

The weight was gone. Above me something blotted out the sky, and there was warmth and wet all around me. Then I heard kicking, and the dark shape whimpered and fell away. I threw my arm protectively across my face, groaning as I tried to sit up.

"Janet," the voice repeated. I could see her now, arms crossed, a line creasing her forehead where a scratch was drawn as though with red ink. "What are you doing here?" Her tone was disbelieving, but also amused, as though I were a disappointing student who had suddenly seemed to have some faint spark of intelligence.

I said nothing, tried to back away from her. A dog lay at either side of her legs; in between I saw her boots, the worn creased leather now bloodstained and covered with a scruff of dirt. Blinking I looked up again. Her eyes were cold, but she smiled very slightly.

"I have to go now," she said. I flinched as she raised her arms, but she only yawned.

Behind her the sky had faded to the colour of an oyster shell. The moon was gone and now only the stars remained, pale flecks like bits of stone chipped from the ground beneath me. In the ashen light Irene suddenly looked very old: not like an old woman but truly ancient, like a carven image, some cycladic figure risen from among the stones. I thought of Lyman talking about dragon's teeth; of an ancient Greek hero sowing an army from broken stones.

And suddenly I remembered something. An absurd image, thrown back from some movie I'd seen as a child decades before. One of those grim bright Technicolor epics where toga-clad heros fought hydras and one-eyed giants, and sweating men groaned and yelled as they strove against the oars of a trireme. A woman on a white beach, a sea like blue ink spilling behind where she stood smiling at an assembly of shipwrecked men. Then her hands swept up, one of them holding an elaborately carved wand. In front of her the sand whipped up in a shimmering wall. When it subsided the men were gone, and she was surrounded by pink grunting pigs and snarling German shepherds that were stand-ins for wolves. She raised her arms and the wolves turned upon the swine, howling. I could almost remember her name, it was almost familiar . . .

"Good-bye, Janet."

Irene Kirk knelt, bending over one of the dogs; and it came back to me.

Not Kirk. *Circe*.

I struggled to pronounce it, then saw how she held her switch, so tightly her fingers were white.

"Time's up, Buddy," she said softly. Her other hand grasped the dog by its collar, and I saw where something pale fluttered, a piece of tattered cloth wrapped around the leather. There was something printed on it; but before I could focus her hand moved, so swiftly the switch became a shining blur. The dog made a gasping sound, gave a single convulsive shake. When her hands drew back I saw where its throat had been cut, a deep black line across the folds of loose skin where blood quickly pooled over the paler knobs of trachea and bone. Frantically I pushed myself away from it, heedless of the other dog whining beside its mistress.

As quickly as she'd slashed its throat the woman stood. She took a step toward her van, then stopped. She glanced down at me, her eyes black as though hollowed in stone.

"Don't think about it too much," she said, her mouth curving slightly. Then she stooped and with one swift motion flicked the collar from the dead animal's neck. "Or – "

Her smile widened as she finished ironically, "Think of it as *justice*."

She tossed the collar and I shrank back as it landed almost in my lap. There was enough dawn light now that I could see that the scrap of cloth wrapped around the leather had been torn from some kind of uniform. I could make out the faint letters beneath the crust of dirt and blood.

D.I. GROGAN, it read, *US Penitentiary 54779909.*

I watched her walk away. When she called "Jimmie Mac!" the remaining dog stumbled to its feet and followed her, its shadow humping between the lines of stone brightening in the sunrise. Then they stood at the rear of the van, the woman holding the door while the dog whined and groveled at her feet. I stood and staggered to my car, glancing over my shoulder to see if they were watching but neither one looked back at me.

KIM NEWMAN

The Big Fish

KIM NEWMAN'S acclaimed vampire novel, *Anno Dracula*, firmly established him on both sides of the Atlantic, as well as garnering the author a number of awards nominations and interest from various film companies. It joins an impressive line-up of novels (*The Night Mayor*, *Bad Dreams*, *Jago*, *The Quorum*, *The Bloody Red Baron*), non-fiction books and stories. The latter have recently been collected in *The Original Dr Shade & Other Stories* and *Famous Monsters*.

He describes the following story as "a tribute to two great authors, awkward outsiders, who used a despised genre to make genuine contributions to English and American letters. If you write in their genre, you must be influenced by them, and if you're a reader who seeks a way into the genre, you could do no better than start with them: Howard Phillips Lovecraft and Raymond Chandler.

"With 'The Big Fish', I wanted to bring a touch of Lovecraft's Innsmouth to Chandler's Bay City, fusing elements from 'The Shadow Over Innsmouth' and *Farewell My Lovely*."

With a cross-genre narrative typical of the author, we think you'll agree that he has succeeded in his aims admirably . . .

THE BAY CITY cops were rousting enemy aliens. As I drove through the nasty coast town, uniforms hauled an old couple out of a grocery store. The Taraki family's neighbours huddled in thin rain howling asthmatically for bloody revenge. Pearl Harbor had struck a lot of people that way. With the Tarakis on the bus for Manzanar, neighbours descended on the store like bedraggled vultures. Produce vanished instantly, then destruction started. Caught at a sleepy stop light, I got a good look. The Tarakis had lived over the store; now, their furniture was thrown out of the second-storey window. Fine china shattered on the sidewalk, spilling white chips into the gutter like teeth. It was inspirational, the forces of democracy rallying round to protect the United States from vicious oriental grocers, fiendishly intent on selling eggplant to a hapless civilian population.

Meanwhile my appointment was with a gent who kept three pictures on his mantelpiece, grouped in a triangle around a statue of the Virgin Mary. At the apex was his white-haired mama, to the left Charles Luciano, and to the right, Benito Mussolini. The Tarakis, American-born and registered Democrats, were headed to a dustbowl concentration camp for the duration, while Gianni Pastore, Sicilian-born and highly unregistered capo of the Family business, would spend his war in a marble-fronted mansion paid for by nickels and dimes dropped on the numbers game, into slot machines, or exchanged for the favours of nice girls from the old country. I'd seen his mansion before and so far been able to resist the temptation to bean one of his twelve muse statues with a bourbon bottle.

Money can buy you love but can't even put down a deposit on good taste.

The palace was up in the hills, a little way down the boulevard from Tyrone Power. But now, Pastore was hanging his mink-banded fedora in a Bay City beachfront motel complex, which was a real-estate agent's term for a bunch of horrible shacks shoved together for the convenience of people who like sand on their carpets.

I always take a lungful of fresh air before entering a confined space with someone in Pastore's business, so I parked the Chrysler a few blocks from the Sea-view Inn and walked the rest of the way, sucking on a Camel to keep warm in the wet. They say it doesn't rain in Southern California, but they also say the U.S. Navy could never be taken by surprise. This February, three months into a war the rest of the world had been fighting since 1936 or 1939 depending on whether you were Chinese or Polish, it was raining almost constantly, varying between a light fall of misty drizzle in the dreary daytimes to spectacular storms, complete with De Mille lighting effects, in our fear-filled nights. Those trusty Boy Scouts scanning the horizons for Jap subs and Nazi U-boats were filling up influenza wards, and manufacturers of raincoats and umbrellas who'd not yet converted their plants to defence production were making a killing. I didn't mind the rain. At least rainwater is clean, unlike most other things in Bay City.

A small boy with a wooden gun leaped out of a bush and sprayed me with sound effects, interrupting his onomatopoeic chirruping with a shout of "die you slant-eyed Jap!" I clutched my heart, staggered back, and he finished me off with a quick burst. I died for the Emperor and tipped the kid a dime to go away. If this went on long enough, maybe little Johnny would get a chance to march off and do real killing, then maybe come home in a box or with the shakes or a taste for blood. Meanwhile, especially since someone spotted a Jap submarine off Santa Barbara, California was gearing up for the War Effort. Aside from interning grocers, our best brains were writing songs like "To Be Specific, It's Our Pacific," "So Long Momma, I'm Off to Yokahama," "We're Gonna Slap the Jap Right Off the Map" and "When Those Little Yellow Bellies Meet the Cohens and the Kellys." Zanuck had donated his string of Argentine polo ponies to West Point and got himself measured for a comic-opera Colonel's uniform so he could join the Signal Corps and defeat the Axis by posing for publicity photographs.

I'd tried to join up two days after Pearl Harbor but they kicked me back onto the streets. Too many concussions. Apparently, I get hit on the head too often and have a tendency to black out. When they came to mention it, they were right.

The Seaview Inn was shuttered, one of the first casualties of war. It had its own jetty, and by it were a few canvas-covered motor launches shifting with the waves. In late afternoon gloom, I saw the silhouette of the *Montecito*, anchored strategically outside the three-mile limit. That was one good thing about the Japanese; on the downside, they might have sunk most of the U.S. fleet, but on the up, they'd put Laird Brunette's gambling ship out of business. Nobody was enthusiastic about losing their shirt-buttons on a rigged roulette wheel if they imagined they were going to be torpedoed any moment. I'd have thought that would add an extra thrill to the whole gay, delirious business of giving Brunette money, but I'm just a poor, 25-dollars-a-day detective.

The Seaview Inn was supposed to be a stopping-off point on the way to the *Monty* and now its trade was stopped off. The main building was sculpted out of dusty ice cream and looked like a three-storey radiogram with wave-scallop friezes. I pushed through double-doors and entered the lobby. The floor was decorated with a mosaic in which Neptune, looking like an angry Santa Claus in a swimsuit, was sticking it to a sea-nymph who shared a hairdresser with Hedy Lamarr. The nymph was naked except for some strategic shells. It was very artistic.

There was nobody at the desk and thumping the bell didn't improve matters. Water ran down the outside of the green-tinted windows. There were a few steady drips somewhere. I lit up another Camel and went exploring. The office was locked and the desk register didn't have any entries after December 7, 1941. My raincoat dripped and began to dry out, sticking my jacket and shirt to my shoulders. I shrugged, trying to get some air into my clothes. I noticed Neptune's face quivering. A thin layer of water had pooled over the mosaic and various anemone-like fronds attached to the sea god were apparently getting excited. Looking at the nymph, I could understand that. Actually, I realized, only the hair was from Hedy. The face and the body were strictly Janey Wilde.

I go to the movies a lot but I'd missed most of Janey's credits: *She-Strangler of Shanghai*, *Tarzan and the Tiger Girl*, *Perils of Jungle Jillian*. I'd seen her in the newspapers though, often in unnervingly close proximity to Pastore or Brunette. She'd started as an Olympic swimmer, picking up medals in Berlin, then followed Weissmuller and Crabbe to Hollywood. She would never get an Academy Award but her legs were in a lot of cheesecake stills publicizing no particular movie. Air-brushed and made-up like a good-looking corpse, she was a fine commercial for sex. In person she was as bubbly as domestic champagne, though now running to flat. Things were slow in the detecting business, since people were more worried about imminent invasion than missing daughters or misplaced love letters. So when Janey Wilde called on me in my office in the Cahuenga Building and asked me to look up one of her ill-chosen men friends, I checked the pile of old envelopes I use as a desk diary and informed her that I was available to make inquiries into the current whereabouts of a certain big fish.

Wherever Laird Brunette was, he wasn't here. I was beginning to figure Gianni Pastore, the gambler's partner, wasn't here either. Which meant I'd wasted an afternoon. Outside it rained harder, driving against the walls with a drumlike tattoo. Either there were hailstones mixed in with the water or the Jap air force was hurling fistfuls of pebbles at Bay City to demoralize the population. I don't know why they bothered. All Hirohito had to do was slip a thick envelope to the Bay City cops and the city's finest would hand over the whole community to the Japanese Empire with a ribbon around it and a bow on top.

There were more puddles in the lobby, little streams running from one to the other. I was reminded of the episode of *The Perils of Jungle Jillian* I had seen while tailing a child molester to a Saturday matinee. At the end, Janey Wilde had been caught by the Panther Princess and trapped in a room which slowly filled with water. That room had been a lot smaller than the lobby of the Seaview Inn and the water had come in a lot faster.

Behind the desk were framed photographs of pretty people in pretty clothes having a pretty time. Pastore was there, and Brunette, grinning like tiger cats, mingling with showfolk: Xavier Cugat, Janey Wilde, Charles Coburn. Janice Marsh, the pop-eyed beauty rumoured to have replaced Jungle Jillian in Brunette's affections, was well represented in artistic poses.

On the phone, Pastore had promised faithfully to be here. He hadn't wanted to bother with a small-timer like me but Janey Wilde's name opened a door. I had a feeling Papa Pastore was relieved to be shaken down about Brunette, as if he wanted to talk about something. He must be busy, because there were several wars on. The big one overseas and a few little ones at home. Maxie Rothko, bar owner and junior partner in the *Monty*, had been found drifting in the seaweed around the Santa Monica pier without much of a head to speak of. And Phil Isinglass, man-about-town lawyer and Brunette frontman, had turned up in the storm drains, lungs full of sandy mud. Disappearing was the latest craze in Brunette's organization. That didn't sound good for Janey Wilde, though Pastore had talked about the Laird as if he knew Brunette was alive. But now Papa wasn't around. I was getting annoyed with someone it wasn't sensible to be annoyed with.

Pastore wouldn't be in any of the beach shacks but there should be an apartment for his convenience in the main building. I decided to explore further. Jungle Jillian would expect no less. She'd hired me for five days in advance, a good thing since I'm unduly reliant on eating and drinking and other expensive diversions of the monied and idle.

The corridor that led past the office ended in a walk-up staircase. As soon as I put my size nines on the first step, it squelched. I realized something was more than usually wrong. The steps were a quiet little waterfall, seeping rather than cascading. It wasn't just water, there was unpleasant, slimy stuff mixed in. Someone had left the bath running. My first thought was that Pastore had been distracted by a bullet. I was wrong. In the long run, he might have been happier if I'd been right.

I climbed the soggy stairs and found the apartment door unlocked but shut. Bracing myself, I pushed the door in. It encountered resistance but then sliced open, allowing a gush of water to shoot around my ankles, soaking my dark blue socks. Along with water was a three-weeks-dead-in-the-water-with-sewage-and-rotten-fish smell that wrapped around me like a blanket. Holding my breath, I stepped into the room. The waterfall flowed faster now. I heard a faucet running. A radio played, with funny little gurgles mixed in. A crooner was doing his best with "Life is Just a Bowl of Cherries," but he sounded as if he were drowned full fathom five. I followed the music and found the bathroom.

Pastore was face down in the overflowing tub, the song coming from under him. He wore a silk lounging robe that had been pulled away from his back, his wrists tied behind him with the robe's cord. In the end he'd been drowned. But before that hands had been laid on him, either in anger or with cold, professional skill. I'm not a coroner, so I couldn't tell how long the Family Man had been in the water. The radio still playing and the water still running suggested Gianni had met his end recently but the stench felt older than sin.

I have a bad habit of finding bodies in Bay City and the most profit-minded police force in the country have a bad habit of trying to make connections between me and a wide variety of deceased persons. The obvious solution in this case was to make a friendly phone call, absent-mindedly forgetting to mention my name while giving the flatfeet directions to the late

Mr Pastore. Who knows, I might accidentally talk to someone honest.

That is exactly what I would have done if, just then, the man with the gun hadn't come through the door . . .

I had Janey Wilde to blame. She'd arrived without an appointment, having picked me on a recommendation. Oddly, Laird Brunette had once said something not entirely uncomplimentary about me. We'd met. We hadn't seriously tried to kill each other in a while. That was as good a basis for a relationship as any.

Out of her sarong, Jungle Jillian favoured sharp shoulders and a veiled pill-box. The kiddies at the matinee had liked her fine, especially when she was wrestling stuffed snakes, and dutiful Daddies took no exception to her either, especially when she was tied down and her sarong rode up a few inches. Her lips were four red grapes plumped together. When she crossed her legs you saw swimmer's smooth muscle under her hose.

"He's very sweet, really," she explained, meaning Mr Brunette never killed anyone within ten miles of her without apologizing afterwards, "not at all like they say in those dreadful scandal sheets."

The gambler had been strange recently, especially since the war shut him down. Actually the *Montecito* had been out of commission for nearly a year, supposedly for a refit although as far as Janey Wilde knew no workmen had been sent out to the ship. At about the time Brunette suspended his crooked wheels, he came down with a common California complaint, a dose of crackpot religion. He'd been tangentially mixed up a few years ago with a psychic racket run by a bird named Amthor, but had apparently shifted from the mostly harmless bunco cults onto the hard stuff. Spiritualism, orgiastic rites, chanting, incense, the whole deal.

Janey blamed this sudden interest in matters occult on Janice Marsh, who had coincidentally made her name as the Panther Princess in *The Perils of Jungle Jillian*, a role which required her to torture Janey Wilde at least once every chapter. My employer didn't mention that her own career had hardly soared between *Jungle Jillian* and *She-Strangler of Shanghai*, while the erstwhile Panther Princess had gone from Republic to Metro and was being built up as an exotic in the Dietrich-Garbo vein. Say what you like about Janice Marsh's Nefertiti, she still looked like Peter Lorre to me. And according to Janey, the star had more peculiar tastes than a seafood buffet.

Brunette had apparently joined a series of fringe organizations and become quite involved, to the extent of neglecting his business and thereby irking his long-time partner, Gianni Pastore. Perhaps that was why person or persons unknown had decided the Laird wouldn't mind if his associates died one by one. I couldn't figure it out. The cults I'd come across mostly stayed in business by selling sex, drugs, power or reassurance to rich, stupid people. The Laird hardly fell into the category. He was too big a fish for that particular bowl.

The man with the gun was English, with a Ronald Colman accent and a white aviator's scarf. He was not alone. The quiet, truck-sized bruiser I made as a fed went through my wallet while the dapper foreigner kept his automatic pointed casually at my middle.

"Peeper," the fed snarled, showing the photostat of my licence and my supposedly impressive deputy's badge.

"Interesting," said the Britisher, slipping his gun into the pocket of his camel coat. Immaculate, he must have been umbrella-protected between car and building because there wasn't a spot of rain on him. "I'm Winthrop. Edwin Winthrop."

We shook hands. His other companion, the interesting one, was going through the deceased's papers. She looked up, smiled with sharp white teeth, and got back to work.

"This is Mademoiselle Dieudonne."

"Genevieve," she said. She pronounced it "Zhe-ne-vyev," suggesting Paris, France. She was wearing something white with silver in it and had quantities of pale blonde hair.

"And the gentleman from your Federal Bureau of Investigation is Finlay."

The fed grunted. He looked as if he'd been brought to life by Willis H. O'Brien.

"You are interested in a Mr Brunette," Winthrop said. It was not a question, so there was no point in answering him. "So are we."

"Call in a Russian and we could be the Allies," I said. Winthrop laughed. He was sharp. "True. I am here at the request of my government and working with the full co-operation of yours."

One of the small detective-type details I noticed was that no one even suggested informing the police about Gianni Pastore was a good idea.

"Have you ever heard of a place called Innsmouth, Massachusetts?"

It didn't mean anything to me and I said so.

"Count yourself lucky. Special Agent Finlay's associates were called upon to dynamite certain unsafe structures in the sea off Innsmouth back in the '20s. It was a bad business."

Genevieve said something sharp in French that sounded like swearing. She held up a photograph of Brunette dancing cheek to cheek with Janice Marsh.

"Do you know the lady?" Winthrop asked.

"Only in the movies. Some go for her in a big way but I think she looks like Mr Moto."

"Very true. Does the Esoteric Order of Dagon mean anything to you?"

"Sounds like a Church-of-the-Month alternate. Otherwise, no."

"Captain Obed Marsh?"

"Uh-huh."

"The Deep Ones?"

"Are they those coloured singers?"

"What about Cthulhu, Y'ha-nthlei, R'lyeh?"

"Gesundheit."

Winthrop grinned, sharp moustache pointing. "No, not easy to say at all. Hard to fit into human mouths, you know."

"He's just a bedroom creeper," Finlay said, "he don't know nothing."

"His grammar could be better. Doesn't J. Edgar pay for elocution lessons?"

Finlay's big hands opened and closed as if he were rather there were a throat in them.

"Gene?" Winthrop said.

The woman looked up, red tongue absently flicking across her red lips, and thought a moment. She said something in a foreign language that I did understand.

"There's no need to kill him," she said in French. Thank you very much, I thought.

Winthrop shrugged and said "fine by me." Finlay looked disappointed.

"You're free to go," the Britisher told me. "We shall take care of everything. I see no point in your continuing your current line of inquiry. Send in a chit to this address," he handed me a card, "and you'll be reimbursed for your expenses so far. Don't worry. We'll carry on until this is seen through. By the way, you might care not to discuss with anyone what you've seen here or anything I may have said. There's a War on, you know. Loose lips sink ships."

I had a few clever answers but I swallowed them and left. Anyone who thought there was no need to kill me was all right in my book and I wasn't using my razored tongue on them. As I walked to the Chrysler, several ostentatiously unofficial cars cruised past me, headed for the Seaview Inn.

It was getting dark and lightning was striking down out at sea. A flash lit up the *Montecito* and I counted five seconds before the thunder boomed. I had the feeling there was something out there beyond the three-mile limit besides the floating former casino, and that it was angry.

I slipped into the Chrysler and drove away from Bay City, feeling better the further inland I got.

I take *Black Mask*. It's a long time since Hammett and the fellow who wrote the Ted Carmady stories were in it, but you occasionally get a good Cornell Woolrich or Erle Stanley Gardner. Back at my office, I saw the newsboy had been by and dropped off the *Times* and next month's pulp. But there'd been a mix-up. Instead of the *Mask*, there was something inside the folded newspaper called *Weird Tales*. On the cover, a man was being attacked by two green demons and a stereotype vampire with a widow's peak. "'Hell on Earth,' a Novelette of Satan in a Tuxedo by Robert Bloch" was blazed above the title. Also promised were "A new Lovecraft series, 'Herbert West – Re-Animator'" and "'The Rat Master' by Greye la Spina." All for 15 cents, kids. If I were a different type of detective, the brand who said *nom de* something and waxed a moustache whenever he found a mutilated corpse, I might have thought the substitution an omen.

In my office, I've always had five filing cabinets, three empty. I also had two bottles, only one empty. In a few hours, the situation would have changed by one bottle.

I found a glass without too much dust and wiped it with my clean handkerchief. I poured myself a generous slug and hit the back of my throat with it.

The radio didn't work but I could hear Glenn Miller from

somewhere. I found my glass empty and dealt with that. Sitting behind my desk, I looked at the patterns in rain on the window. If I craned I could see traffic on Hollywood Boulevard. People who didn't spend their working days finding bodies in bathtubs were going home not to spend their evenings emptying a bottle.

After a day, I'd had some excitement but I hadn't done much for Janey Wilde. I was no nearer being able to explain the absence of Mr Brunette from his usual haunts than I had been when she left my office, leaving behind a tantalizing whiff of essence de chine.

She'd given me some literature pertaining to Brunette's cult involvement. Now, the third slug warming me up inside, I looked over it, waiting for inspiration to strike. Interesting echoes came up in relation to Winthrop's shopping list of subjects of peculiar interest. I had no luck with the alphabet-soup syllables he'd spat at me, mainly because "Cthulhu" sounds more like a cough than a word. But the Esoteric Order of Dagon was a group Brunette had joined, and Innsmouth, Massachusetts, was the East Coast town where the organization was registered. The Esoteric Order had a temple on the beach front in Venice, and its mumbo-jumbo hand-outs promised "ancient and intriguing rites to probe the mysteries of the Deep." Slipped in with the recruitment bills was a studio biography of Janice Marsh, which helpfully revealed the movie star's place of birth as Innsmouth, Massachusetts, and that she could trace her family back to Captain Obed Marsh, the famous early-19th-century explorer of whom I'd never heard. Obviously Winthrop, Genevieve and the FBI were well ahead of me in making connections. And I didn't really know who the Englishman and the French girl were.

I wondered if I wouldn't have been better off reading *Weird Tales*. I liked the sound of Satan in a Tuxedo. It wasn't Ted Carmady with an automatic and a dame, but it would do. There was a lot more thunder and lightning and I finished the bottle. I suppose I could have gone home to sleep but the chair was no more uncomfortable than my Murphy bed.

The empty bottle rolled and I settled down, tie loose, to forget the cares of the day.

Thanks to the War, Pastore only made page 3 of the *Times*. Apparently the noted gambler-entrepreneur had been shot to death. If that was true, it had happened after I'd left. Then, he'd only been tortured and drowned. Police Chief John Wax dished out his usual "over by Christmas" quote about the investigation. There was no mention of the FBI, or of our allies, John Bull in a tux and Mademoiselle la Guillotine. In prison, you get papers with neat oblongs cut out to remove articles the censor feels provocative. They don't make any difference: all newspapers have invisible oblongs. Pastore's sterling work with underprivileged kids was mentioned but someone forgot to write about the junk he sold them when they grew into underprivileged adults. The obit photograph found him with Janey Wilde and Janice Marsh at the Premiere of a George Raft movie. The phantom Jap sub off Santa Barbara got more column inches. General John L. DeWitt, head of the Western Defence Command, called for more troops to guard the coastline, prophesying "death and destruction are likely to come at any moment." Everyone in California was looking out to sea.

After my regular morning conference with Mr Huggins and Mr Young, I placed a call to Janey Wilde's Malibu residence. Most screen idols are either at the studio or asleep if you telephone before ten o'clock in the morning, but Janey, with weeks to go before shooting started on *Bowery to Bataan*, was at home and awake, having done her 30 lengths. Unlike almost everyone else in the industry, she thought a swimming pool was for swimming in rather than lounging beside.

She remembered instantly who I was and asked for news. I gave her a precis.

"I've been politely asked to refrain from further investigations," I explained. "By some heavy hitters."

"So you're quitting?"

I should have said yes, but "Miss Wilde, only you can require me to quit. I thought you should know how the federal government feels."

There was a pause.

"There's something I didn't tell you," she told me. It was an expression common among my clients. "Something important."

I let dead air hang on the line.

"It's not so much Laird that I'm concerned about. It's that he has Franklin."

"Franklin?"

"The baby," she said. "Our baby. My baby."

"Laird Brunette has disappeared, taking a baby with him?"

"Yes."

"Kidnapping is a crime. You might consider calling the cops."

"A lot of things are crimes. Laird has done many of them and never spent a day in prison."

That was true, which was why this development was strange. Kidnapping, whether personal or for profit, is the riskiest of crimes. As a rule, it's the province only of the stupidest criminals. Laird Brunette was not a stupid criminal.

"I can't afford bad publicity. Not when I'm so near to the roles I need."

Bowery to Bataan was going to put her among the screen immortals.

"Franklin is supposed to be Esther's boy. In a few years, I'll adopt him legally. Esther is my housekeeper. It'll work out. But I must have him back."

"Laird is the father. He will have some rights."

"He said he wasn't interested. He . . . um, moved on . . . to Janice Marsh while I was . . . before Franklin was born."

"He's had a sudden attack of fatherhood and you're not convinced?"

"I'm worried to distraction. It's not Laird, it's her. Janice Marsh wants my baby for something vile. I want you to get Franklin back."

"As I mentioned, kidnapping is a crime."

"If there's a danger to the child, surely . . ."

"Do you have any proof that there is danger?"

"Well, no."

"Have Laird Brunette or Janice Marsh ever given you reason to believe they have ill-will for the baby?"

"Not exactly."

I considered things.

"I'll continue with the job you hired me for, but you understand that's all I can do. If I find Brunette, I'll pass your worries on. Then it's between the two of you."

She thanked me in a flood and I got off the phone feeling I'd taken a couple of strides further into the LaBrea tar pits and could feel sucking stickiness well above my knees.

I should have stayed out of the rain and concentrated on chess problems but I had another four days' worth of Jungle Jillian's retainer in my pocket and an address for the Esoteric Order of Dagon in a clipping from a lunatic scientific journal. So I drove out to Venice, reminding myself all the way that my wipers needed fixing.

Venice, California, is a fascinating idea that didn't work. Someone named Abbot Kinney had the notion of artificially creating a city like Venice, Italy, with canals and architecture. The canals mostly ran dry and the architecture never really caught on in a town where, in the '20s, Gloria Swanson's bathroom was considered an aesthetic triumph. All that was left was the beach and piles of rotting fish. Venice, Italy, is the Plague Capital of Europe, so Venice, California, got one thing right.

The Esoteric Order was up the coast from Muscle Beach, housed in a discreet yacht-club building with its own small marina. From the exterior, I guessed the cult business had seen better days. Seaweed had tracked up the beach, swarmed around the jetty, and was licking the lower edges of the front wall. Everything had gone green: wood, plaster, copper ornaments. And it smelled like Pastore's bathroom, only worse. This kind of place made you wonder why the Japs were so keen on invading.

I looked at myself in the mirror and rolled my eyes. I tried to get that slap-happy, let-me-give-you-all-my-worldly-goods, gimme-some-mysteries-of-the-orient look I imagined typical of a communicant at one of these bughouse congregations. After I'd stopped laughing, I remembered the marks on Pastore and tried to take detecting seriously. Taking in my unshaven, slept-upright-in-his-clothes, two-bottles-a-day lost soul look, I congratulated myself on my foresight in spending 15 years developing the ideal cover for a job like this.

To get in the building, I had to go down to the marina and come at it from the beach-side. There were green pillars of what looked like fungus-eaten cardboard either side of the impressive front door, which held a stained-glass picture in shades of green and blue of a man with the head of a squid in a natty monk's number, waving his eyes for the artist. Dagon, I happened to know, was half-man, half-fish, and God of the Philistines. In this town, I guess a Philistine God blended in well. It's a great country: if you're half-fish, pay most of your taxes, eat babies and aren't Japanese, you have a wonderful future.

I rapped on the squid's head but nothing happened. I looked the squid in several of his eyes and felt squirmy inside. Somehow, up close, cephalopod-face didn't look that silly.

I pushed the door and found myself in a temple's waiting

room. It was what I'd expected: subdued lighting, old but bad
paintings, a few semi-pornographic statuettes, a strong smell of
last night's incense to cover up the fish stink. It had as much
religious atmosphere as a two-dollar bordello.

"Yoo-hoo," I said, "Dagon calling . . ."

My voice sounded less funny echoed back at me.

I prowled, sniffing for clues. I tried saying *nom de* something
and twiddling a non-existent moustache but nothing came to
me. Perhaps I ought to switch to a meerschaum of cocaine and a
deerstalker, or maybe a monocle and an interest in incunabula.

Where you'd expect a portrait of George Washington or Jean
Harlow's Mother, the Order had hung up an impressively ugly
picture of "Our Founder." Capt. Obed Marsh, dressed up like
Admiral Butler, stood on the shore of a Polynesian paradise, his
good ship painted with no sense of perspective on the horizon as
if it were about three feet tall. The Capt., surrounded by adoring
if funny-faced native tomatoes, looked about as unhappy as Errol
Flynn at a Girl Scout meeting. The painter had taken a lot of
trouble with the native nudes. One of the dusky lovelies had
hips that would make Lombard green and a face that put me in
mind of Janice Marsh. She was probably the Panther Princess's
great-great-great grandmother. In the background, just in front
of the ship, was something like a squid emerging from the sea.
Fumble-fingers with a brush had tripped up again. It looked as if
the tentacle-waving creature were about twice the size of Obed's
clipper. The most upsetting detail was a robed and masked figure
standing on the deck with a baby's ankle in each fist. He had
apparently just wrenched the child apart like a wishbone and was
emptying blood into the squid's eyes.

"Excuse me," gargled a voice, "can I help you?"

I turned around and got a noseful of the stooped and ancient
Guardian of the Cult. His robe matched the ones worn by
squid-features on the door and baby-ripper in the portrait. He
kept his face shadowed, his voice sounded about as good as the
radio in Pastore's bath and his breath smelled worse than Pastore
after a week and a half of putrefaction.

"Good morning," I said, letting a bird flutter in the higher
ranges of my voice, "my name is, er . . ."

I put together the first things that came to mind.

"My name is Herbert West Lovecraft. Uh, H.W. Lovecraft the

Third. I'm simply fascinated by matters Ancient and Esoteric, don't ch'know."

"Don't ch'know" I picked up from the fellow with the monocle and the old books.

"You wouldn't happen to have an entry blank, would you? Or any incunabula?"

"Incunabula?" He wheezed.

"Books. Old books. Print books, published before 1500 *anno domini*, old sport." See, I have a dictionary too.

"Books . . ."

The man was a monotonous conversationalist. He also moved like Laughton in *The Hunchback of Notre Dame* and the front of his robe, where the squidhead was embroidered, was wet with what I was disgusted to deduce was drool.

"Old books. Arcane mysteries, don't ch'know. Anything cyclopaean and doom-haunted is just up my old alley."

"The *Necronomicon*?" He pronounced it with great respect, and great difficulty.

"Sounds just the ticket."

Quasimodo shook his head under his hood and it lolled. I glimpsed greenish skin and large, moist eyes.

"I was recommended to come here by an old pal," I said. "Spiffing fellow. Laird Brunette. Ever hear of him?"

I'd pushed the wrong button. Quasi straightened out and grew about two feet. Those moist eyes flashed like razors.

"You'll have to see the Cap'n's Daughter."

I didn't like the sound of that and stepped backwards, towards the door. Quasi laid a hand on my shoulder and held it fast. He was wearing mittens and I felt he had too many fingers inside them. His grip was like a gila monster's jaw.

"That will be fine," I said, dropping the flutter.

As if arranged, curtains parted, and I was shoved through a door. Cracking my head on the low lintel, I could see why Quasi spent most of his time hunched over. I had to bend at the neck and knees to go down the corridor. The exterior might be rotten old wood but the heart of the place was solid stone. The walls were damp, bare and covered in suggestive carvings that gave primitive art a bad name. You'd have thought I'd be getting used to the smell by now, but nothing doing. I nearly gagged.

Quasi pushed me through another door, I was in a meeting room no larger than Union Station, with a stage, rows of comfortable armchairs and lots more squid-person statues. The centrepiece was very like the mosaic at the Seaview Inn, only the nymph had less shells and Neptune more tentacles.

Quasi vanished, slamming the door behind him. I strolled over to the stage and looked at a huge book perched on a straining lectern. The fellow with the monocle would have salivated, because this looked a lot older than 1500. It wasn't a Bible and didn't smell healthy. It was open to an illustration of something with tentacles and slime, facing a page written in several deservedly dead languages.

"The *Necronomicon*," said a throaty female voice, "of the mad Arab, Abdul Al-Hazred."

"Mad, huh?" I turned to the speaker. "Is he not getting his royalties?"

I recognized Janice Marsh straight away. The Panther Princess wore a turban and green silk lounging pyjamas, with a floorlength housecoat that cost more than I make in a year. She had on jade earrings, a pearl cluster pendant and a ruby-eyed silver squid brooch. The lighting made her face look green and her round eyes shone. She still looked like Peter Lorre, but maybe if Lorre put his face on a body like Janice Marsh's, he'd be up for sex-goddess roles too. Her silk thighs purred against each other as she walked down the temple aisle.

"Mr Lovecraft, isn't it?"

"Call me H.W. Everyone does."

"Have I heard of you?"

"I doubt it."

She was close now. A tall girl, she could look me in the eye. I had the feeling the eye-jewel in her turban was looking me in the brain. She let her fingers fall on the tentacle picture for a moment, allowed them to play around like a fun-loving spider, then removed them to my upper arm, delicately tugging me away from the book. I wasn't unhappy about that. Maybe I'm allergic to incunabula or perhaps an undiscovered prejudice against tentacled creatures, but I didn't like being near the *Necronomicon* one bit. Certainly the experience didn't compare with being near Janice Marsh.

"You're the Cap'n's Daughter?" I said.

"It's an honorific title. Obed Marsh was my ancestor. In the Esoteric Order, there is always a Cap'n's Daughter. Right now. I am she."

"What exactly is this Dagon business about?"

She smiled, showing a row of little pearls. "It's an alternative form of worship. It's not a racket, honestly."

"I never said it was."

She shrugged. "Many people get the wrong idea."

Outside, the wind was rising, driving rain against the Temple. The sound effects were weird, like sickening whales calling out in the Bay.

"You were asking about Laird? Did Miss Wilde send you?"

It was my turn to shrug.

"Janey is what they call a sore loser, Mr Lovecraft. It comes from taking all those bronze medals. Never the gold."

"I don't think she wants him back," I said, "just to know where he is. He seems to have disappeared."

"He's often out of town on business. He likes to be mysterious. I'm sure you understand."

My eyes kept going to the squid-face brooch. As Janice Marsh breathed, it rose and fell and rubies winked at me.

"It's Polynesian," she said, tapping the brooch. "The Cap'n brought it back with him to Innsmouth."

"Ah yes, your home town."

"It's just a place by the sea. Like Los Angeles."

I decided to go fishing, and hooked up some of the bait Winthrop had given me. "Were you there when J. Edgar Hoover staged his fireworks display in the '20s?"

"Yes, I was a child. Something to do with rum-runners, I think. That was during Prohibition."

"Good years for the Laird."

"I suppose so. He's legitimate these days."

"Yes. Although if he were as Scotch as he likes to pretend he is, you can be sure he'd have been deported by now."

Janice Marsh's eyes were sea-green. Round or not, they were fascinating. "Let me put your mind at rest, Mr Lovecraft or whatever your name is," she said. "The Esoteric Order of Dagon was never a front for bootlegging. In fact it has never been a front for anything. It is not a racket for duping rich widows out of inheritances. It is not an excuse for motion-picture executives to gain carnal knowledge of teenage drug addicts. It is exactly what it claims to be, a church."

"Father, Son and Holy Squid, eh?"

"I did not say we were a Christian church."

Janice Marsh had been creeping up on me and was close enough to bite. Her active hands went to the back of my neck and angled my head down like an adjustable lamp. She put her lips on mine and squashed her face into me. I tasted lipstick, salt and caviar. Her fingers writhed up into my hair and pushed my hat off. She shut her eyes. After an hour or two of suffering in the line of duty, I put my hands on her hips and detached her body from mine. I had a fish taste in my mouth.

"That was interesting," I said.

"An experiment," she replied. "Your name has such a ring to it. Love . . . craft. It suggests expertise in a certain direction."

"Disappointed?"

She smiled. I wondered if she had several rows of teeth, like a shark.

"Anything but."

"So do I get an invite to the back-row during your next Dagon hoe-down?"

She was businesslike again. "I think you'd better report back to Janey. Tell her I'll have Laird call her when he's in town and put her mind at rest. She should pay you off. What with the War, it's a waste of manpower to have you spend your time looking for someone who isn't missing when you could be defending Lockheed from Fifth Columnists."

"What about Franklin?"

"Franklin the President?"

"Franklin the baby."

Her round eyes tried to widen. She was playing this scene innocent. The Panther Princess had been the same when telling the white hunter that Jungle Jillian had left the Tomb of the Jaguar hours ago.

"Miss Wilde seems to think Laird has borrowed a child of hers that she carelessly left in his care. She'd like Franklin back."

"Janey hasn't got a baby. She can't have babies. It's why she's such a psycho-neurotic case. Her analyst is getting rich on her bewildering fantasies. She can't tell reality from the movies. She once accused me of human sacrifice."

"Sounds like a square rap."

"That was in a film, Mr Lovecraft. Cardboard knives and catsup blood."

Usually at this stage in an investigation, I call my friend Bernie at the District Attorney's office and put out a few fishing lines.

This time, he phoned me. When I got into my office, I had the feeling my telephone had been ringing for a long time.

"Don't make waves," Bernie said.

"Pardon," I snapped back, with my usual lightning-fast wit.

"Just don't. It's too cold to go for a swim this time of year."

"Even in a bathtub."

"Especially in a bathtub."

"Does Mr District Attorney send his regards?"

Bernie laughed. I had been an investigator with the DA's office a few years back, but we'd been forced to part company.

"Forget him. I have some more impressive names on my list."

"Let me guess. Howard Hughes?"

"Close."

"General Stillwell?"

"Getting warmer. Try Mayor Fletcher Bowron, Governor Culbert Olson, and State Attorney General Earl Warren. Oh, and Wax, of course."

I whistled. "All interested in little me. Who'd 'a thunk it?"

"Look, I don't know much about this myself. They just gave me a message to pass on. In the building, they apparently think of me as your keeper."

"Do a British gentleman, a French lady and a fed the size of Mount Rushmore have anything to do with this?"

"I'll take the money I've won so far and you can pass that question on the next sucker."

"Fine, Bernie. Tell me, just how popular am I?"

"Tojo rates worse than you, and maybe Judas Iscariot."

"Feels comfy. Any idea where Laird Brunette is these days?"

I heard a pause and some rumbling. Bernie was making sure his office was empty of all ears. I imagined him bringing the receiver up close and dropping his voice to a whisper.

"No one's seen him in three months. Confidentially, I don't miss him at all. But there are others . . ." Bernie coughed, a door opened, and he started talking normally or louder. ". . . of course, honey, I'll be home in time for Jack Benny."

"See you later, sweetheart," I said, "your dinner is in the sink and I'm off to Tijuana with a professional pool player."

"Love you," he said, and hung up.

I'd picked up a coating of green slime on the soles of my shoes. I tried scraping them off on the edge of the desk and then used yesterday's *Times* to get the stuff off the desk. The gloop looked damned esoteric to me.

I poured myself a shot from the bottle I had picked up across the street and washed the taste of Janice Marsh off my teeth.

I thought of Polynesia in the early 19th century and of those fish-eyed native girls clustering around Capt. Marsh. Somehow, tentacles kept getting in the way of my thoughts. In theory, the Capt. should have been an ideal subject for a Dorothy Lamour movie, perhaps with Janice Marsh in the role of her great-great-great and Jon Hall or Ray Milland as girl-chasing Obed. But I was picking up Bela Lugosi vibrations from the set-up. I couldn't help but think of bisected babies.

So far none of this running around had got me any closer to the Laird and his heir. In my mind, I drew up a list of Brunette's known associates. Then, I mentally crossed off all the ones who were dead. That brought me up short. When people in Brunette's business die, nobody really takes much notice except maybe to join in a few drunken choruses of "Ding-Dong, the Wicked Witch is Dead" before remembering there are plenty of other Wicked Witches in the sea. I'm just like everybody else: I don't keep a score of dead gambler-entrepreneurs. But, thinking of it, there'd been an awful lot recently, up to and including Gianni Pastore. Apart from Rothko and Isinglass, there'd been at least three other closed-casket funerals in the profession. Obviously you couldn't blame that on the Japs. I wondered how many of the casualties had met their ends in bathtubs. The whole thing kept coming back to water. I decided I hated the stuff and swore not to let my bourbon get polluted with it.

Back out in the rain, I started hitting the bars. Brunette had a lot of friends. Maybe someone would know something.

By early evening, I'd propped up a succession of bars and leaned on a succession of losers. The only thing I'd come up with was the blatantly obvious information that everyone in town was scared. Most were wet, but all were scared.

Everyone was scared of two or three things at once. The Japs were high on everyone's list. You'd be surprised to discover the number of shaky citizens who'd turned overnight from chisellers who'd barely recognize the flag into true red, white and blue patriots prepared to shed their last drop of alcoholic blood for their country. Everywhere you went, someone sounded off against Hirohito, Tojo, the Mikado, kabuki and origami. The current rash of accidental deaths in the Pastore-Brunette circle were a much less popular subject for discussion and tended to turn loudmouths into closemouths at the drop of a question.

"Something fishy," everyone said, before changing the subject.

I was beginning to wonder whether Janey Wilde wouldn't have done better spending her money on a radio commercial asking the Laird to give her a call. Then I found Curtis the Croupier in Maxie's. He usually wore the full soup and fish, as if borrowed from Astaire. Now he'd exchanged his carnation, starched shirtfront and pop-up top hat for an outfit in olive drab with bars on the shoulder and a cap under one epaulette.

"Heard the bugle call, Curtis?" I asked, pushing through a crowd of patriotic admirers who had been buying the soldier boy drinks.

Curtis grinned before he recognized me, then produced a supercilious sneer. We'd met before, on the *Montecito*. There was a rumour going around that during Prohibition he'd once got involved in an honest card game, but if pressed he'd energetically refute it.

"Hey cheapie," he said.

I bought myself a drink but didn't offer him one. He had three or four lined up.

"This racket must pay," I said. "How much did the uniform cost? You rent it from Paramount?"

The croupier was offended. "It's real," he said. "I've enlisted. I hope to be sent overseas."

"Yeah, we ought to parachute you into Tokyo to introduce loaded dice and rickety roulette wheels."

"You're cynical, cheapie." He tossed back a drink.

"No, just a realist. How come you quit the *Monty*?"

"Poking around in the Laird's business?"

I raised my shoulders and dropped them again.

"Gambling has fallen off recently, along with leading figures in the industry. The original owner of this place, for instance. I bet paying for wreaths has thinned your bankroll."

Curtis took two more drinks, quickly, and called for more. When I'd come in, there'd been a couple of chippies climbing into his hip pockets. Now he was on his own with me. He didn't appreciate the change of scenery and I can't say I blamed him.

"Look cheapie," he said, his voice suddenly low, "for your own good, just drop it. There are more important things now."

"Like democracy?"

"You can call it that."

"How far overseas do you want to be sent, Curtis?"

He looked at the door as if expecting five guys with tommy guns to come out of the rain for him. Then he gripped the bar to stop his hands shaking.

"As far as I can get, cheapie. The Philippines, Europe, Australia. I don't care."

"Going to war is a hell of a way to escape."

"Isn't it just? But wouldn't Papa Gianni have been safer on Wake Island than in the tub?"

"You heard the bathtime story, then?"

Curtis nodded and took another gulp. The juke box played "Doodly-Acky-Sacky, Want Some Seafood, Mama" and it was scary. Nonsense, but scary.

"They all die in water. That's what I've heard. Sometimes, on the *Monty*, Laird would go up on deck and just look at the sea for hours. He was crazy, since he took up with that Marsh popsicle."

"The Panther Princess?"

"You saw that one? Yeah, Janice Marsh. Pretty girl if you like clams. Laird claimed there was a sunken town in the bay. He used a lot of weird words, darkie bop or something. Jitterbug stuff. Cthul-whatever, Yog-Gimme-a-Break. He said things were going to come out of the water and sweep over the land, and he didn't mean U-boats."

Curtis was uncomfortable in his uniform. There were dark patches where the rain had soaked. He'd been drinking like W.C. Fields on a bender but he wasn't getting tight. Whatever was troubling him was too much even for Jack Daniel's.

I thought of the Laird of the *Monty*. And I thought of the painting of Capt. Marsh's clipper, with that out-of-proportion squid surfacing near it.

"He's on the boat, isn't he?"

Curtis didn't say anything.

"Alone," I thought aloud. "He's out there alone."

I pushed my hat to the back of my head and tried to shake booze out of my mind. It was crazy. Nobody bobs up and down in the water with a sign round their neck saying "Hey Tojo, Torpedo Me!" The *Monty* was a floating target.

"No," Curtis said, grabbing my arm, jarring drink out of my glass.

"He's not out there?"

He shook his head. "No, cheapie. He's not out there alone."

All the water taxis were in dock, securely moored and covered until the storms settled. I'd never find a boatman to take me out to the *Montecito* tonight. Why, everyone knew the waters were infested with Japanese subs. But I knew someone who wouldn't care any more whether or not his boats were being treated properly. He was even past bothering if they were borrowed without his permission.

The Seaview Inn was still deserted, although there were police notices warning people away from the scene of the crime. It was dark, cold and wet, and nobody bothered me as I broke into the boathouse to find a ring of keys.

I took my pick of the taxis moored to the Seaview's jetty and gassed her up for a short voyage. I also got my .38 Colt Super Match out from the glove compartment of the Chrysler and slung it under my armpit. During all this, I got a thorough soaking and picked up the beginnings of influenza. I hoped Jungle Jillian would appreciate the effort.

The sea was swelling under the launch and making a lot of noise. I was grateful for the noise when it came to shooting the padlock off the mooring chain but the swell soon had my stomach sloshing about in my lower abdomen. I am not an especially competent seaman.

The *Monty* was out there on the horizon, still visible whenever the lightning lanced. It was hardly difficult to keep the small boat aimed at the bigger one.

Getting out on the water makes you feel small. Especially when the lights of Bay City are just a scatter in the dark behind you. I got the impression of large things moving just beyond my field of perception. The chill soaked through my clothes. My hat was a felt sponge, dripping down my neck. As the launch cut towards the *Monty*, rain and spray needled my face. I saw my hands white and bath-wrinkled on the wheel and wished I'd brought a bottle. Come to that, I wished I was at home in bed with a mug of cocoa and Claudette Colbert. Some things in life don't turn out the way you plan.

Three miles out, I felt the law change in my stomach. Gambling was legal and I emptied my belly over the side into the water. I stared at the remains of my toasted cheese sandwich as they floated off. I thought I saw the moon reflected greenly in the depths, but there was no moon that night.

I killed the engine and let waves wash the taxi against the side of the *Monty*. The small boat scraped along the hull of the gambling ship and I caught hold of a weed-furred rope ladder as it passed. I tethered the taxi and took a deep breath.

The ship sat low in the water, as if its lower cabins were flooded. Too much seaweed climbed up towards the decks. It'd never reopen for business, even if the War were over tomorrow.

I climbed the ladder, fighting the water-weight in my clothes, and heaved myself up on deck. It was good to have something more solid than a tiny boat under me but the deck pitched like an airplane wing. I grabbed a rail and hoped my internal organs would arrange themselves back into their familiar grouping.

"Brunette," I shouted, my voice lost in the wind.

There was nothing, I'd have to go belowdecks.

A sheet flying flags of all nations had come loose, and was whipped around with the storm. Japan, Italy and Germany were still tactlessly represented, along with several European states that weren't really nations any more. The deck was covered in familiar slime.

I made my way around towards the ballroom doors. They'd blown in and rain splattered against the polished wood floors. I got inside and pulled the .38. It felt better in my hand than digging into my ribs.

Lightning struck nearby and I got a flash image of the abandoned ballroom, orchestra stands at one end painted with the name of a disbanded combo.

The casino was one deck down. It should be dark but I saw a glow under a walkway door. I pushed through and cautiously descended. It wasn't wet here but it was cold. The fish smell was strong.

"Brunette," I shouted again.

I imagined something heavy shuffling nearby and slipped a few steps, banging my hip and arm against a bolted-down table. I kept hold of my gun, but only through superhuman strength.

The ship wasn't deserted. That much was obvious.

I could hear music. It wasn't Cab Calloway or Benny Goodman.

There was a Hawaiian guitar in there but mainly it was a crazy choir of keening voices. I wasn't convinced the performers were human and wondered whether Brunette was working up some kind of act with singing seals. I couldn't make out the words but the familiar hawk-and-spit syllables of "Cthulhu" cropped up a couple of times.

I wanted to get out and go back to nasty Bay City and forget all about this. But Jungle Jillian was counting on me.

I made my way along the passage, working towards the music. A hand fell on my shoulder and my heart banged against the backsides of my eyeballs.

A twisted face stared at me out of the gloom, thickly-bearded, crater-cheeked. Laird Brunette was made up as Ben Gunn, skin shrunk onto his skull, eyes large as hen's eggs.

His hand went over my mouth.

"Do Not Disturb," he said, voice high and cracked.

This wasn't the suave criminal I knew, the man with tartan cummerbunds and patent-leather hair. This was some other Brunette, in the grips of a tough bout with dope or madness.

"The Deep Ones," he said.

He let me go and I backed away.

"It is the time of the Surfacing."

My case was over. I knew where the Laird was. All I had to do was tell Janey Wilde and give her her refund.

"There's very little time."

The music was louder. I heard a great number of bodies shuffling around in the casino. They couldn't have been very agile, because they kept clumping into things and each other.

"They must be stopped. Dynamite, depth charges, torpedoes . . ."

"Who?" I asked. "The Japs?"

"The Deep Ones. The Dwellers in the Sister City."

He had lost me.

A nasty thought occurred to me. As a detective, I can't avoid making deductions. There were obviously a lot of people aboard the *Monty*, but mine was the only small boat in evidence. How had everyone else got out here? Surely they couldn't have swum?

"It's a war." Brunette ranted, "us and them. It's always been a war."

I made a decision. I'd get the Laird off his boat and turn him over to Jungle Jillian. She could sort things out with the Panther Princess and her Esoteric Order. In his current state, Brunette would hand over any baby if you gave him a blanket.

I took Brunette's thin wrist and tugged him towards the staircase. But a hatch clanged down and I knew we were stuck.

A door opened and perfume drifted through the fish stink.

"Mr Lovecraft, wasn't it?" a silk-scaled voice said.

Janice Marsh was wearing pendant squid earrings and a lady-sized gun. And nothing else.

That wasn't quite as nice as it sounds. The Panther Princess had no nipples, no navel and no pubic hair. She was lightly scaled between the legs and her wet skin shone like a shark's. I imagined that if you stroked her, your palm would come away bloody. She was wearing neither the turban she'd affected earlier nor the dark wig of her pictures. Her head was completely bald, skull swelling unnaturally. She didn't even have her eyebrows pencilled in.

"You evidently can't take good advice."

As mermaids go, she was scarier than cute. In the crook of her left arm, she held a bundle from which a white baby face peered with unblinking eyes. Franklin looked more like Janice Marsh than his parents.

"A pity, really," said a tiny ventriloquist voice through Franklin's mouth, "but there are always complications."

Brunette gibbered with fear, chewing his beard and huddling against me.

Janice Marsh set Franklin down and he sat up, an adult struggling with a baby's body.

"The Cap'n has come back," she explained.

"Every generation must have a Cap'n," said the thing in Franklin's mind. Dribble got in the way and he wiped his angel-mouth with a fold of swaddle.

Janice Marsh clucked and pulled Laird away from me, stroking his face.

"Poor dear," she said, flicking his chin with a long tongue. "He got out of his depth."

She put her hands either side of Brunette's head, pressing the butt of her gun into his cheek.

"He was talking about a Sister City," I prompted.

She twisted the gambler's head around and dropped him on the floor. His tongue poked out and his eyes showed only white.

"Of course," the baby said. "The Cap'n founded two settlements. One beyond Devil Reef, off Massachusetts. And one here, under the sands of the Bay."

We both had guns. I'd let her kill Brunette without trying to shoot her. It was the detective's fatal flaw, curiosity. Besides the Laird was dead inside his head long before Janice snapped his neck.

"You can still join us," she said, hips working like a snake in time to the chanting. "There are raptures in the deeps."

"Sister," I said, "you're not my type."

Her nostrils flared in anger and slits opened in her neck, flashing liverish red lines in her white skin.

Her gun was pointed at me, safety off. Her long nails were lacquered green.

I thought I could shoot her before she shot me. But I didn't. Something about a naked woman, no matter how strange, prevents you from killing them. Her whole body was moving with the music. I'd been wrong. Despite everything, she was beautiful.

I put my gun down and waited for her to murder me. It never happened.

I don't really know the order things worked out. But first there was lightning, then, an instant later, thunder.

Light filled the passageway, hurting my eyes. Then, a rumble of noise which grew in a crescendo. The chanting was drowned.

Through the thunder cut a screech. It was a baby's cry. Franklin's eyes were screwed up and he was shrieking. I had a sense of the Cap'n drowning in the baby's mind, his purchase on the purloined body relaxing as the child cried out.

The floor beneath me shook and buckled and I heard a great straining of abused metal. A belch of hot wind surrounded me. A hole appeared. Janice Marsh moved fast and I think she fired her gun, but whether at me on purpose or at random in reflex I couldn't say. Her body sliced towards me and I ducked.

There was another explosion, not of thunder, and thick smoke billowed through a rupture in the floor. I was on the floor, hugging the tilting deck. Franklin slid towards me and bumped, screaming, into my head. A half-ton of water fell on us and I knew the ship was breached. My guess was that the Japs had just saved my life with a torpedo. I was waist deep in saltwater. Janice Marsh darted away in a sinuous fish motion.

Then there were heavy bodies around me, pushing me against a bulkhead. In the darkness, I was scraped by something heavy, cold-skinned and foul-smelling. There were barks and cries, some of which might have come from human throats.

Fires went out and hissed as the water rose. I had Franklin in my hands and tried to hold him above water. I remembered the peril of Jungle Jillian again and found my head floating against the hard ceiling.

The Cap'n cursed in vivid 18th-century language, Franklin's little body squirming in my grasp. A toothless mouth tried to get a biter's grip on my chin but slipped off. My feet slid and I was off-balance pulling the baby briefly underwater. I saw his startled eyes through a wobbling film. When I pulled him out again, the Cap'n was gone and Franklin was screaming on his own. Taking a double gulp of air, I plunged under the water and struggled towards the nearest door, a hand closed over the baby's face to keep water out of his mouth and nose.

The *Montecito* was going down fast enough to suggest there were plenty of holes in it. I had to make it a priority to find one. I jammed my knee at a door and it flew open. I was poured, along with several hundred gallons of water, into a large room full of stored gambling equipment. Red and white chips floated like confetti.

I got my footing and waded towards a ladder. Something large reared out of the water and shambled at me, screeching like a seabird. I didn't get a good look at it. Which was a mercy. Heavy arms lashed me, flopping boneless against my face. With my free hand, I pushed back at the thing, fingers slipping against cold slime. Whatever it was was in a panic and squashed through the door.

There was another explosion and everything shook. Water splashed upwards and I fell over. I got upright and managed to get a one-handed grip on the ladder. Franklin was still struggling and bawling, which I took to be a good sign. Somewhere near, there was a lot of shouting.

I dragged us up rung by rung and slammed my head against a hatch. If it had been battened, I'd have smashed my skull and spilled my brains. It flipped upwards and a push of water from below shoved us through the hole like a ping-pong ball in a fountain.

The *Monty* was on fire and there were things in the water

around it. I heard the drone of airplane engines and glimpsed nearby launches. Gunfire fought with the wind. It was a full-scale attack. I made it to the deck-rail and saw a boat fifty feet away. Men in yellow slickers angled tommy guns down and sprayed the water with bullets.

The gunfire whipped up the sea into a foam. Kicking things died in the water. Someone brought up his gun and fired at me. I pushed myself aside, arching my body over Franklin and bullets spanged against the deck.

My borrowed taxi must have been dragged under by the bulk of the ship.

There were definitely lights in the sea. And the sky. Over the city, in the distance, I saw firecracker bursts. Something exploded a hundred yards away and a tower of water rose, bursting like a puffball. A depth charge.

The deck was angled down and water was creeping up at us. I held on to a rope webbing, wondering whether the gambling ship still had any lifeboats. Franklin spluttered and bawled.

A white body slid by, heading for the water. I instinctively grabbed at it. Hands took hold of me and I was looking into Janice Marsh's face. Her eyes blinked, membranes coming round from the sides, and she kissed me again. Her long tongue probed my mouth like an eel, then withdrew. She stood up, one leg bent so she was still vertical on the sloping deck. She drew air into her lungs – if she had lungs – and expelled it through her gills with a musical cry. She was slim and white in the darkness, water running off her body. Someone fired in her direction and she dived into the waves, knifing through the surface and disappearing towards the submarine lights. Bullets rippled the spot where she'd gone under.

I let go of the ropes and kicked at the deck, pushing myself away from the sinking ship. I held Franklin above the water and splashed with my legs and elbows. The *Monty* was dragging a lot of things under with it, and I fought against the pull so I wouldn't be one of them. My shoulders ached and my clothes got in the way, but I kicked against the current.

The ship went down screaming, a chorus of bending steel and dying creatures. I had to make for a launch and hope not to be shot. I was lucky. Someone got a polehook into my jacket and landed us like fish. I lay on the deck, water running out of my clothes, swallowing as much air as I could breathe.

I heard Franklin yelling. His lungs were still in working order.

Someone big in a voluminous slicker, a sou'wester tied to his head, knelt by me, and slapped me in the face.

"Peeper," he said.

"They're calling it the Great Los Angeles Air Raid," Winthrop told me as he poured a mug of British tea. "Some time last night a panic started, and everyone in Bay City shot at the sky for hours."

"The Japs?" I said, taking a mouthful of welcome hot liquid.

"In theory. Actually, I doubt it. It'll be recorded as a fiasco, a lot of jumpy characters with guns. While it was all going on, we engaged the enemy and emerged victorious."

He was still dressed up for an embassy ball and didn't look as if he'd been on deck all evening. Genevieve Dieudonne wore a fisherman's sweater and fatigue pants, her hair up in a scarf. She was looking at a lot of sounding equipment and noting down readings.

"You're not fighting the Japs, are you?"

Winthrop pursed his lips. "An older war, my friend. We can't be distracted. After last night's action, our Deep Ones won't poke their scaly noses out for a while. Now I can do something to lick Hitler."

"What really happened?"

"There was something dangerous in the sea, under Mr Brunette's boat. We have destroyed it and routed the . . . uh, the hostile forces. They wanted the boat as a surface station. That's why Mr Brunette's associates were eliminated."

Genevieve gave a report in French, so fast that I couldn't follow.

"Total destruction," Winthrop explained, "a dreadful setback for them. It'll put them in their place for years. Forever would be too much to hope for, but a few years will help."

I lay back on the bunk, feeling my wounds. Already choking on phlegm, I would be lucky to escape pneumonia.

"And the little fellow is a decided dividend."

Finlay glumly poked around, suggesting another dose of depth charges. He was cradling a mercifully sleep-struck Franklin, but didn't look terribly maternal.

"He seems quite unaffected by it all."

"His name is Franklin," I told Winthrop. "On the boat, he was . . ."

"Not himself? I'm familiar with the condition. It's a filthy business, you understand."

"He'll be all right," Genevieve put in.

I wasn't sure whether the rest of the slicker crew were feds or servicemen and I wasn't sure whether I wanted to know. I could tell a Clandestine Operation when I landed in the middle of one.

"Who knows about this?" I asked. "Hoover? Roosevelt?"

Winthrop didn't answer.

"Someone must know," I said.

"Yes," the Englishman said, "someone must. But this is a war the public would never believe exists. In the Bureau, Finlay's outfit are known as 'the Unnameables,' never mentioned by the press, never honoured or censured by the government, victories and defeats never recorded in the official history."

The launch shifted with the waves, and I hugged myself, hoping for some warmth to creep over me. Finlay had promised to break out a bottle later but that made me resolve to stick to tea as a point of honour. I hated to fulfil his expectations.

"And America is a young country," Winthrop explained. "In Europe, we've known things a lot longer."

On shore, I'd have to tell Janey Wilde about Brunette and hand over Franklin. Some hack at Metro would be thinking of an excuse for the Panther Princess's disappearance. Everything else – the depth charges, the sea battle, the sinking ship – would be swallowed up by the War.

All that would be left would be tales. Weird tales.

THOMAS TESSIER

In the Desert of Deserts

THOMAS TESSIER apparently never gives interviews and believes that an author's published works say all that needs to be said about him. He was educated at University College, Dublin, and spent several years working as a publisher in London before returning to Connecticut, where he currently lives.

His acclaimed novels of horror and psychological suspense include *The Fates*, *Shockwaves*, *The Nightwalker*, the World Fantasy Award-nominated *Phantom*, *Finishing Touches*, *Rapture*, *Secret Strangers* and *White Gods*.

Along with recent appearances in such anthologies as *Borderlands 3* and *After the Darkness*, his short fiction has been collected in *The Crossing and Other Tales of Panic*, and the story which follows marks his third appearance in *The Best New Horror*.

D RIVE AT NIGHT, somebody told me in Laghouat, and at first I did. But that advice was only good as long as I knew where the road was. The road was quite fair over some stretches, but then it would peter out, fading into the surrounding terrain, becoming invisible until it reappeared a mile or two farther on. That was all right too, if I didn't stray dangerously. A sensitive driver can tell where the road ought to be even when it isn't.

But I found it maddeningly difficult to follow the trail at night. My vision was restricted to the range of the headlights, and I had no useful sense of the landscape. At one point on my first night out I was driving along cautiously when the powerful beams of an oil supply truck lanced the darkness. The truck went by, nearly a mile away from me. *That* was where the road was, I realized unhappily. A trucker could make the desert run at night because he'd done it so many times he knew the way instinctively, but it was impossible for a first-timer to travel like that. I decided to travel the rest of the way by daylight.

Besides, there was more to the challenge than just making it all the way to Niamey. I wanted to experience the Sahara at its most difficult, as well as to enjoy it at its beautiful best. It would be a shame to drive through the desert mostly at night, and come away like some empty-handed thief.

I spent much of the second day in Ghardaia, where I topped up the water and petrol tanks. I gave the Range Rover a careful examination, and was satisfied. I checked the spare parts list, but I already had everything on it. I had done these same things the day before, at Laghouat, only a hundred miles away. But this was my last chance to correct any problems or pick up something I might need. Ghardaia has supplies, equipment, skilled mechanics and even cold soda. The oil pipeline runs nearby. It's a fairly busy town, considering the fact that it's located out on the edge of the edge.

I don't distrust people but I slept with one eye on my Rover and its load of supplies. I was up before dawn, feeling as eager as I was nervous, and I left Ghardaia when the first infiltration of grey light began to erode the blackness. Now the crossing was truly underway.

I was travelling south through the Great Western Erg, and my next stop was In Salah, more than three hundred miles away. This would be the easy part of my journey, I reckoned. The desert was immediately fierce and formidable, but I knew there was an oasis at El Golea and some kind of a military outpost at Fort Miribel, both of which were on my route.

South of In Salah the terrain would become much rougher, the climate even more hellish, and although in theory there were more villages in that part of the country I knew that they would prove to be fly-speck settlements that offered little. I had been told that in the Sahara what you think you see on a map is usually not what you find on the ground. I had no fear of dying of thirst or starvation, nor even of heat, but I did worry about a mechanical breakdown that could strand me indefinitely in some heatblasted cluster of huts on the far side of nowhere.

At first I made relatively good time, but by midday the road deteriorated predictably and I had to drive more slowly. After a break for lunch I proceeded, and soon got stuck. The sand in the Sahara can be deceptive and treacherous. One moment it may be as firm and hard-packed as an old gravel road, and then it will turn into something like dry water, all but impossible to stand in or move through. My right rear tire slid into just such a hole, and it took me nearly two hours to extricate myself with the help of aluminum tracks.

Even so, I felt reasonably pleased by the time I decided to stop for the night because I had experienced no major trouble and nothing unexpected had come up. I picked a place where the road was clearly visible, then pulled off about a quarter of a mile to set up camp.

That last night of peace I fancy I absorbed something of the remorseless clarity of the Sahara. This is a world composed of a few simple elements – sand, air, the disappearing sky, then the blue, red, yellow and white stars – but each one of them is huge in its singularity. They are so vivid and immediate that after a while they begin to seem unreal to the human observer, like stage props for a drama that never happens and involves no one. In the Sahara, it is said, God talks to himself. I had not come to the desert looking for any mystical fix or tourist inspiration, but I did find something like joy in the loneliness and insignificance it constantly threw in my face.

I ate, cleaned up, drank a single neat scotch and then slept well. It was chilly, but I had of course expected that and was warmly wrapped, and if there was any night wind it didn't disturb me at all.

Before dawn, as I prepared to leave, I found the footprints. I knew at once that they were not mine.

I almost laughed. I felt a little bit like Robinson Crusoe, shocked, amused, fascinated. After the initial wave of reaction passed, I began to feel uncomfortable. Crusoe had a pretty good idea of what he was up against, but the footprints I'd discovered made no apparent sense. For one thing, they shouldn't have been there at all.

They formed a counter-clockwise trail, roughly in the shape of a circle, around my little camp. They looked like the tracks of a solitary adult male wearing ordinary shoes and walking at an ordinary pace. The footprints stopped twice, overlapping tightly before continuing, as if at those two points the unknown visitor had paused to stare and think for a moment. It was disturbing to know that he could only have been looking at me as I slept just a few yards away, inside the circle.

I calmed down after a few minutes. The headlights of an oil company truck passing by on the road must have caught part of the Rover in the darkness, and the driver stopped to investigate. It was so obvious, I felt silly. The fact that I could see no trail to or from the circle was strange, but a breeze could have hidden them or perhaps the driver had walked a particularly hardpacked stretch of ground that would show no footprints.

Once I was on the road again I thought no more about it. My progress was slow because the wind started up and the road became more difficult to follow. It was a long day, hot and demanding, but late in the afternoon the conditions changed abruptly, as so often happens in the Sahara. The wind died away and at the same time I hit a good section of the road. I covered more ground in the last four hours than I had in the previous eight.

This time I camped a little farther from the road, beyond a ridge, where no headlights could spot me. I didn't like the idea of anyone sneaking up on me in the middle of the night, out there in the depths of the desert. My vehicle and equipment were worth a small fortune, and the next person might not think twice about bashing my head in and hiding them. He could always return later with a partner to collect the goods. The chances of anybody else finding my remains would be virtually nonexistent.

I felt so secure that I was not at all prepared to come upon anything unusual the next morning, but I did. The same unmarked heels and soles, coming from nowhere, going nowhere, but circling my ground, stopping once or twice.

I was shaken. I didn't want to be there anymore, and yet I sat down. It was as if I could not bring myself to leave. I had to reason my way out of this threatening situation. Whoever had left those tracks couldn't have followed me on foot because I had come too many miles yesterday. He could have followed me by car, or truck, or even on a camel, but surely I would have seen him at some point, and if he stayed too far back he couldn't be certain of finding the point where I left the road for the night.

Besides, why would anyone bother to shadow me like this? To approach me in the darkness, but then do nothing? If he intended to attack me he could have done so twice by now. The whole thing made no sense at all. It was precisely the fact that nothing had happened that worried me most. It seemed somehow more menacing, as if I were being monitored.

Could it be a Bedouin, a nomadic Arab? It seemed unlikely. I'd been told that they travel in clans and that they seldom come through this part of North Africa. There's nothing for them here and it isn't on any of their usual routes. Besides, I doubt that the Bedouins wear ordinary Western-style shoes.

I put my hand to the ground and touched one footprint. Yes, it was real. I was not hallucinating. I traced the indentation in the sand. He had big feet, like me. I placed my right foot next to one of the footprints. Nearly a perfect match. However, my high-top camping shoes had corrugated soles, and no heels.

It was theoretically possible that I had made the footprints in the middle of the night, because I did have a pair of ordinary shoes packed away in the Rover, but I simply couldn't believe it. I had absolutely no recollection of taking them out, putting them on, walking the circles, obscuring my tracks back to the van, and then packing the shoes away again. Not the slightest glimmer of any such memory. If it was my doing, asleep or awake, I was well on the way to losing my mind.

But isn't that what the desert is supposed to do to a person who wanders through it alone? Madness creeping in, like the sand in your socks. I told myself it wasn't possible, at least not in the first three days out of Laghouat. All that desert mythology was nothing more than a load of romantic rubbish.

Nonetheless, I decided to push on all the way until I got to

In Salah. I stopped only to eat and drink, and to let the engine cool down a little. I got stuck a couple of times but never lost the road, and made pretty good time. The changes in the Sahara were largely lost on me, however. When my eyes weren't fixed on the road ahead they were glancing up at the rearview mirror. But I never saw another vehicle or person.

When I reached In Salah I was so exhausted that I slept for eleven hours. I spent another day working on the Rover, stocking up on supplies, and enjoying the break in my journey. I even had a stroll around the town, what there is of it.

And I decided to change my plans. Instead of heading south, through the moderately populated mountains of the Ahaggar, as I'd originally intended, I would now turn west to Zaouiet Reggane and then drive south through the Tanezrouft all the way to Mali, and from Bourem I would follow the course of the Niger River on into Niamey. The net effect would be to shorten my journey and make it less scenic but also perhaps more challenging. The Tanezrouft is vast, empty and closer to sea level, therefore hotter than the Ahaggar. The oil trucks don't run in that part of Algeria. Some people believe that the Tanezrouft is the worst part of the whole Sahara Desert.

So why do it? I don't know. I must have been thinking that no one would dare follow me across the Tanezrouft. Before I left In Salah I bought a gun, an ugly Czech pistol. I don't know if I was indulging my own crazy delusions, or pursuing them.

These actions and decisions of mine had an irrelevance that I could not completely ignore. It was as if I sensed that I was merely distracting myself with them, and that they didn't really matter. If the man was real, he'd be there. And if he was other than real, well, he might be there anyway.

One hundred miles south of Zaouiet Reggane, I awoke. I went out about fifty feet, looking for the footprints. Nothing. So I went a little farther, but again found nothing, no sign, no mark, that didn't belong to that place. I broke into a trot, circling my camp site, scouring the ground as I went. Still nothing of an unusual nature.

I ran right past it, then stopped sharply, one foot skidding out from under me as I turned back. Even then I didn't see it, I smelled it. And, as the saying goes, I thought I saw a ghost. A pencil-line of blue fluttering in the air. It was smoke. In the sand were two footprints, just two, not my own. The same shoes. The heel marks were so close they almost touched each other, but the toes were apart, forming a V on the ground. It was as if the man had squatted on his haunches there, staring at me while I was sleeping. Nearby, a discarded cigarette. It was still burning, almost to the filter now, and it had an inch-long trail of intact ash. I don't smoke.

I touched the smoldering tip just to convince myself that it was real, and it was. I jumped up and looked around, but there was no one in sight for half a mile in any direction. I'd chosen a natural basin, so there was nowhere to hide and even if someone was lying flat and trying to insinuate himself into the sand he'd still be easily seen. There was no one. No tracks. Just me and those two footprints, and the cigarette.

I picked it up and examined it carefully. Any trademark had already burned away, but there was enough left for me to see that the cigarette had the slightly flattened, oval shape that is more common to the Middle East than Europe or America. But that told me nothing. I wish it had lipstick on it.

I say that, but I drove scared, and the farther I went the more frightened I became. There was nowhere on the entire planet I could feel safe, because I could drive until I passed out and I would still be in the middle of the Sahara. When I reached Bidon 5, a desperate little waterhole, I sat off by myself and let the engine cool for three hours. They thought I was another of those wandering Englishmen who go to the most awful places in the world and then write articles about it for *The Sunday Times*.

I considered driving on, but common sense finally prevailed and I stayed the night. I must have been even more tired than I thought, for I slept late into the morning and no one bothered to wake me. Early starts are like a matter of religion to me, but I felt so much better, refreshed, that I wasn't annoyed. Besides, I had plenty of time. The change of route gave me an extra three or four days.

I was also encouraged by the fact that I was approaching the southern limits of the Sahara. Another three hundred miles, and I would be rolling through the grassy plains of Mali. When I got to Bourem I might even take a side trip and visit the fabled city of Timbuktu, a center of Islamic teaching in the 15th century. I have heard that Timbuktu is just a dull and decayed backwater of a place nowadays, but I was tempted to take a look. How could I come to within a hundred miles or so of what was once regarded as the remotest spot on earth, and pass it by?

But I still had the last of the Sahara to deal with, and the road soon disappeared. My progress was slow, I got stuck and had to dig my way out several times, and the heat was devastating. I pushed on, regarding the desert now as nothing but an obstacle to be overcome as quickly as possible. Mileage is deceptive because the road, when you haven't strayed from it, meanders this way and that in its endless pursuit of firm ground, and one hundred miles on the map is usually a hundred and twenty-five or thirty on the clock. I think I reached the border, or even crossed it, when I had to stop for the night. Another day, a day and a half, two at most, and I would leave the Sahara behind me.

This time I parked only a few yards off the road. There was no traffic at all this far south so I had nothing to fear in that respect, and the sand was too treacherous to risk venturing into any farther than necessary. I checked the air pressure in all of the tires, checked my gun, had a glass of scotch, and got into my sleeping bag.

It was still quite dark when I awoke. Just like in a film, my eyes opened but the rest of my body didn't move. I was lying on my side, and I knew immediately that I was not alone. My mind wasn't working yet, I was still in a fog, and at first I thought I saw a single red eye staring at me from some distance away. It was the glowing tip of a cigarette, I realized dimly. I couldn't make out anything of the person who held it. I was overcome by a wave of choking fear that seemed to be strangling me from within. A dozen hungry lions circling closer wouldn't have frightened me as much as that burning cigarette did.

I had the gun in my hand, my elbow dug into the sand. I was still lying there in my sleeping bag, and I forced my drowsy eyes to focus on the tiny red speck of fire. A moment later it traced a gentle arc, came to a stop, and then brightened sharply. As he inhaled, I squeezed the trigger. The explosion seemed distant, a curiously muffled noise that might have come from another part of the desert. I shut my eyes, having no idea what had taken place, and I fell back into sleep.

The brightness woke me later. I didn't believe anything had actually happened during the night because my memory was blurred, dream-like, unreal. The gun was where I had put it when I got in the sleeping bag last night, between carefully folded layers of a towel on the ground nearby. If I had fired it at some point in the night, surely I wouldn't have put it back so neatly.

But when I sat up and looked around, I saw the body. I felt calm, yet desolate. He was about twenty yards away. I got to my feet and walked slowly toward him. My shot had been true, like a sniper in one of the old European wars. The slug had smashed his face into a bowl of bloody mush.

His hair was black and curly, his skin olive-colored, and he wore a plain white short-sleeved shirt, faded khaki slacks, and a pair of ordinary shoes. A man so dressed, on foot, wouldn't last more than a few hours in the desert. His presence there was such a vast affront to sanity and nature that I felt a flash of anger. It gave way, a moment later, to cold helplessness.

I found a few loose cigarettes and a box of matches in his shirt pocket, but he carried nothing else on his person. I don't smoke, but I took them. I checked inside the shirt collar but it had no label or markings.

It seemed to me that I would never know who this man was, or how he came to be in the desert with me, what he wanted, or why I had been compelled to kill him, so I got my shovel and buried him on the spot. Dead bodies are supposed to be heavy and cumbersome but he felt as light as a bundle of sticks.

Somewhere along the way in Mali I gave up thinking about it. There was nothing to do, there were no answers to be discerned in the lingering confusion of fact and fear. Guilt? No. I've seen enough of the world to know how superfluous human life really is. I drove, losing myself once again to the rigors and pleasures of simple movement.

Bourem offered little, Timbuktu less. I looked at the dust, the mud, the crumbling and overgrown buildings that seemed to be receding into prehistory before my eyes, and I left. In Niamey I relaxed, celebrated and got laid. I made my way eventually down to the beaches at Accra. I ate with Swedish and German tourists who fretted about the unofficial fact that ninety percent of West African whores are HIV-positive.

That didn't bother me. I drank bottled French water with my scotch, but I also busied myself with the women. Day after day, night after night. There's not much else to do, except drink and lie about. Besides, there are moments in your life when you just know you're meant to live.

"Why?"

Ulf was a well-meaning, earnest and somewhat obsessive Swede who had developed a spurious concern for my reckless behavior. I shrugged absently at his question. He wanted an answer but I did not care to mislead him.

"Regardless."

Ulf had money and nothing to do, nowhere to go, like me, and so we drove to Abidjan, then Freetown, finally Banjul. I enjoyed his company, but by the time we were in the Gambia the charm wore thin and I was eager to be alone again. Still, I agreed that Ulf could tag along as far as Dakar. He was still with me days after that, as I approached Tindouf far to the north.

"I'm heading east," I told him.

"But it's just a short run to Marrakesh now." Ulf was quite disturbed. He consulted the map. "There's nothing to the east, only the Sahara. No road. Nothing."

"There's always a road".

Ulf hired someone to drive him to Marrakesh. I stayed on in Tindouf for a couple of days, working on the Rover and restocking my supplies. I was serious about driving east. True, there was no road, but I believed I could make it anyway. I had it in mind to reach Zaouiet Reggane, four hundred miles away, and then take the road south until I found my campsite near the border. It was the last arc in a big circle.

Why indeed? At times I was crazy with disbelief. I thought I had to return to the spot and dig up the dead man, just to make sure that he was real. The missing bullet in my gun was not good enough, nor were the stale cigarettes I still carried with me. I had to see the body again. In some strange and unfathomable way, the rest of my life seemed to depend on it.

But there were moments of clarity too. I was caught up in a senseless odyssey. I could ramble around Africa until I died, of old age or stupidity. I argued with myself, dawdled, hung on for days in the soporific dullness of Tindouf. I dreamed of the dead man's hands reaching up out of the sand to strangle me, like some corny turn in a horror movie. I dreamed that the grave was still there, and I found it, but it was empty. Most of all, I imagined that I would never locate the place again, that I would just burn and blister myself to a blackish lump as I dug pointless holes in the desert.

I did, after all, drive east. A few miles from the village, the ground became tricky. I pushed on, often swerving one way or another on an immediate impulse. Progress was slow. Late in the afternoon, I had a sense that I would never make it anywhere near Zaouiet Reggane. Then all four tires sank into a trough of very fine sand. I got out. The Rover was in it up to the axles, with no chance at all that I could extricate it by myself. I reckoned I was between twenty and twenty-five miles east of Tindouf, which was a long one-day walk. I prepared to spend the night there. I would set off early and reach the village by nightfall. I would return the day after, with helpers, and we would haul my vehicle onto solid ground. They would laugh, I would pay, and later I'd drive to Marrakesh, perhaps catch up with Ulf, and that would be the end of it.

I woke up in the middle of the night. Unable to get back to sleep, I pulled on my jacket and walked into the chilly darkness. I didn't go far. When the dim outline of the Rover began to fade in my vision I stopped. This is what he saw, I realized.

I was still fogged with sleepiness. I sat on my haunches, with my heels together and toes apart. It's often rather bright in the Sahara at night, when the stars form a brilliant skyscape, but some high thin clouds now cast everything in shades of black. The Rover was an inky lump against the charcoal expanse of sand. This is what he saw.

Without thinking, I took one of his crumpled cigarettes from my jacket and lit it. I didn't inhale, but puffed at it, and the glowing red tip only seemed to emphasize the blackness around me. I imagined a shape stirring out there, mysterious and unknowable, secure in the anonymity of the night. I imagined it noticing me behind my tiny pinpoint of fire, fixing on me. As if I were the only stain on all that emptiness. And then I thought that maybe I had been wrong from the beginning.

It was like looking deeply into your own eyes, and finding nothing there.

TERRY LAMSLEY

Two Returns

TERRY LAMSLEY was born in the South of England but has "cheerfully misspent" most of his life in the North. He admits to falling in love with supernatural fiction at the age of six, "when my young mind was corrupted by reading American horror comics." He has been writing, on and off, all his life, but has only recently concentrated on his fiction seriously.

He published his first collection of supernatural tales, *Under the Crust*, in 1993. The book is set in his home town of Buxton, Derbyshire, and the surrounding Peak District, as is about half his fiction output to date. He is preparing another book of local stories, *High Peaks of Fear*, and a collection of "true" Buxton spook sightings and other odd occurrences. His Jamesian ghost stories have also appeared in *Ghosts and Scholars* 17 and *The Year's Best Horror Stories XXII* edited by Karl Edward Wagner.

The author explains that the story which follows ". . . was inspired by standing on desperately gloomy, empty little local stations alone at night, and pub conversations with two friends who were writing a biography of the Victorian architect who designed many of Buxton's best buildings. Their man, unlike mine, was an all-round good guy, however, and – as far as I know – never took to haunting."

AFTER CAREFULLY LOWERING his bags of Christmas shopping on to the platform Mr Rudge shook his wrist out of his overcoat to reveal his watch. Noting that he had a wait of nine minutes before his train was due to arrive, he looked about him for a seat. He had had an exhausting day, and the half mile walk just completed had left him limp and sweating under his thick winter clothes. When he had set out in the morning it had been a cold, bright day promising snow, and he had dressed for that. Later, misty rain had brought an evening of muggy warmth that seemed to draw the energy out of him. He longed for the short rest the train journey home would provide.

He spotted a single bench at the end of the platform, lugged his bags over to it, and sat down.

The position offered no protection from the weather, but the seat was wide and comfortable. He drew his head down into his coat collar, regretting that he had not brought a hat, and tried to lull himself into a cosy frame of mind. The persistent, almost invisible rain blowing into his face made this state impossible to achieve however, and he presently found himself gazing at the bricked-up windows, graffitied-over walls, and snaggle-tiled roof of the redundant ticket office and waiting room on the platform opposite him across the line.

The whole station was lit by a few crude lamps of unbreakable glass set in tight metal cages about ten feet up the walls. These gave merely adequate illumination, and the quality of the light was garish and alarming, splashing the wet platforms with puddles and streams of orange, like sticky juice. There were no shadows, only intensities and absences of this golden glow, and drifting veils of drizzle, shining and fading, increased the illusion of insubstantiality adopted for the evening by the stolid, utilitarian railway buildings.

Mr Rudge tried to remember the station as it had been years ago, before it had been all but closed down, but the details that had made it individual had been stripped away, leaving it as featureless as a child's drawing of a barn.

"The *genius loci* has deserted this place," he mused, depressed by the dereliction and air of used-up emptiness.

He was not surprised that there were no other people waiting with him for the train. The little town the station served had almost forgotten the existence of its rail link with Manchester, and few of the population would care to risk the long, dark, crumbling Station Approach Road on a winter evening. It would have been pleasant if there had been others with him to give the place a human presence, as long as they were the right sort of people, of course. Company was not always companionship.

The last time he had been waiting on a lonely station at night he had been stranded with a couple who seemed to be holding each other up against a wall. He had turned his back on what he assumed was lovemaking, and dismissed them from his mind so successfully that, wandering up and down a few minutes later, he suddenly found himself face to face with them. They were both men, looked drunk or drugged, and were watching him with an intensity of greed that had scared him. They had made him feel his age, his vulnerability, and, foolishly, with his hand, the place above his heart where his wallet was buttoned into the inside pocket of his obviously expensive suit. Luckily his train had arrived seconds later, and saved him from the mugging he had been sure he was about to get.

He looked at his watch again and was sorry to see that only four minutes had passed since he had last referred to it. He yawned. His neck was stiff, so he waggled it from side to side.

As he did so, he caught a movement at the far end of the platform at the down-line end. A dark, rectangular shape opened out of a wall against the liquid light. It wavered, and faded away at once. He assumed a door had been swiftly opened and shut; or had it? Perhaps it had been opened all the way, flat against the wall. He squirmed round in his seat, took off his rain-misted glasses to wipe them, and screwed up his eyes to see as best he could.

For some moments there was no further movement, and he was just replacing his spectacles onto his nose and settling back again, when he caught a glimpse of something, a single motion, down where he thought the door had opened. He could see more clearly now, and thought he must have been right about the door, as a shape like the top half of a human torso, the outline of a head, one shoulder, and part of the second, now protruded out of the wall, some three feet from the ground.

The form was silhouetted against the light from a lamp situated immediately behind and above it. Because of the position of this light it was not possible to determine any features on the face of the individual, but he was sure that it was turned towards him, as he felt himself stared at.

Or even glared at, he corrected himself uncomfortably, as he sensed that he was subject to a most intense scrutiny.

"Why doesn't the beggar move?" he thought, "and why is he standing like that, as though he were peering round from behind a tree?"

He found himself staring back with his chin jutting out and his mouth gaping childishly open. He turned to look behind him to check that some other person had not silently joined him on the platform, and could therefore be the object of his distant observer's attention, but the end of the platform was as empty as it had been when he had stepped onto it. It stretched away, quite desolate, into the murky dark.

"Well, you'll know me when you see me again," he thought, aware that his own face was lit by a light some five feet ahead of him.

Then, for what seemed a long time, but was probably less than a minute, the two of them watched each other.

Mr Rudge was beginning to think that he had been mistaken, and that what he had taken for a head and shoulders was in fact some broken thing, part of a door that had blown open in the wind and become stuck, when the figure moved.

It stepped out.

It took one stride, quick and purposeful, giving him a glimpse of a pale face and shining black hair, then turned towards him and stood quite motionless again.

Mr Rudge was convinced that he had been – identified.

The figure was that of a tall man, above six foot. He stood with his legs apart, and seemed to have his arms folded across his chest. He wore, as far as Mr Rudge was able to make out, some kind of cape slung over his shoulders.

Mr Rudge began to recall that the building from which the door had opened, and from which the figure had emerged, was the old, original part of the station. That section had long ago been vandalized and declared unsafe. It had been due for demolition, but enough local people and lovers of railway history had objected to this to save the basic structure. As a compromise, to preserve what was left, all the doors and windows had been bricked up. The building was sealed tight.

Mr Rudge stood up and walked a little way down the platform towards the figure. He wanted to say something, if only to hear the sound of his own voice.

When he did speak, he was surprised to hear himself say, in a high, almost pleading voice, "Is everything all right? Can I help you at all?"

He stood and waited for some response. None came.

The two of them stared at each other in static silence until a distant clanking rumble announced that the train Mr Rudge was waiting for was about to arrive. Behind the dark figure, the lights of the driver's cabin swung round a curve in the line, and the little, toylike train began to slow down as it approached the platform.

"Now I shall get a look at you," muttered Mr Rudge, whose gaze had momentarily been diverted by the train.

But the man, whoever he was, moved again.

He stepped back against the wall and, as he did so, his arms and legs appeared to fold into him, like blades returning to the handle of a knife. Mr Rudge blinked, and the figure was gone. A shadow remained against the wall, fading in the light from the windows of the train.

Mr Rudge snatched up his shopping bags and ran down the length of the station. When he got to the place where the figure had disappeared, something of the shadow still hung upon the wall. Sure enough, it suggested, in vague outline, the figure he had seen; but nothing stood near to cast such a shadow.

He reached out to touch the darkness against the wall as, behind him, the doors of the train slid open, and a tiny quantity of passengers disembarked.

The wall felt just as a wall should.

Confused, Mr Rudge took a few steps backward. Close to him a peevish child complained to its parents, saying it was tired, and begging to be carried. Its father growled a "No."

Hardly able to take his eyes off the dark place on the wall, Mr Rudge backed towards the carriage closest to him, sidled through one of the doors, and tumbled into a seat.

There was plenty of room on the train. He sank back, clutching his bags on his lap, and pressed his face against the grimy window to look out.

He saw the back of someone – a late arrival, perhaps? – dashing for the carriage in front of his.

He wondered if the doors had closed in time to shut whoever it was out.

He hoped they had; but feared they had not.

* * *

Mr Rudge used the time the train took to haul itself up the long, steep incline towards Buxton to try to reconnect with normalcy, or was it reality?

His bags of shopping had received a bashing as he had stumbled into the train. To occupy his mind, he checked the contents of each. The fact that one of the sparsely populated yet costly boxes of chocolates that he had purchased for his family was badly dented was no catastrophe, and he was much relieved to see that the two bottles of Laphroaig Malt, one of which was his present to himself, were undamaged. However, the plastic bag containing these items had begun to split. He stood up and began transferring its contents to the pockets of his overcoat. Not everything would fit, so he had to juggle some of the gifts from bag to bag.

Doing this in his highly nervous state was perplexing. He put one bag in the aisle for a moment, satisfied that it was as full as he could get it, and at once kicked it over. Bending down to retrieve it, he became aware of eyes upon him. Not surprising, considering all the fuss he was making, but whose eyes were they?

He turned his attention to the other occupants of the carriage.

A few seats away a bloated, pink-faced man with wild cork-screws of yellow hair blinked slowly back at him from under drink-weighted lids. Beyond him sneered a small tribe of adolescents in outfits of cake-icing pinks and greens. One of them, hairless as a baby rat, made a gesture at him with his finger that the others at once copied. Its significance escaped Mr Rudge, who looked away at a figure close to them.

All he could see of this passenger was his dark hair above the back of his seat. He was lolling against the window, and something about him, perhaps only the fact that he was obviously a tall man, made Mr Rudge uneasy. He tried to manoeuvre himself into a position from which he could get sight of the man's reflection in the window, and must have made himself look absurd in doing so, as the teenagers began to laugh aloud at him. This caused the tall man to turn to see what the noise was about.

The pasty, gaunt face that twisted towards him made Mr Rudge's heart skip once, before he recognized it to be that of a man who he had seen about on the streets of Buxton for years. He nodded in embarrassed recognition, and hastily sat down again, satisfied that, if his fellow passengers were not the most attractive examples of humanity, they were at least that; human.

With that thought, his mind returned to the consideration of what he had seen, or thought he had seen, back at the station. Somewhere inside him was an urge to walk into the next carriage, perhaps under the pretext of searching for the toilet, just to reassure himself about who might be travelling there, but it was an urge he found he was easily able to resist. Instead, he turned his attention to what he would do when he got to Buxton, assuming that whoever it was who may have got on with him happened to be heading for the same destination.

Being a methodical man, Mr Rudge began to devise a stratagem, in case such a situation should arise.

He decided he would be first off the train at Buxton Station. To put his mind at rest he would wait on the platform until all the other passengers had disembarked, and he was satisfied that the train was empty. Then, although it was less than a ten minute walk to his flat, he would ring for a taxi to take him home.

When the train was half a mile from Buxton Mr Rudge rose up, with his bags and his bulging pockets, and placed himself at the centre of the sliding doors. He was somewhat shamefaced about his fears by now, but determined to proceed with his plan. Nevertheless, as the train drew to a halt, he was nervous; his teeth were dry, and his tongue tasted of iron.

He pressed through the doors the instant they opened.

As his feet touched the platform, out of the corner of his eye, he noticed that the doors of the carriage in front of him were still moving apart. He planned to stand by the station's only exit, and made towards it as, behind him, other passengers tumbled out into the damp night air.

When he had almost reached the exit a long shape strode past him very quickly. Like a shadow in the lights of a moving car, it rose and fell in one smooth, swift motion, and passed out of sight through the exit door.

Baffled at that moment, Mr Rudge forgot his plan. He hurried after the figure.

He passed into the waiting room where a guard lurked, intending to collect tickets. The man was staring out into the car-park at the front of the station, looking uneasy, dismayed.

Mr Rudge knew that he could have passed through without showing his ticket, and was tempted to do so, but a lifetime of orderly conduct could not be denied. This transaction took precious seconds. As he left the station he saw a figure moving away beyond the road outside, on the far side of the pedestrian crossing.

The crossing light was red. He waited while cars slid by on the slick velvet tarmac, and jabbed at the button to get the green man walking.

He noticed that it was raining harder. His glasses were mottled with large drops, warping his vision.

To his right, squatting on its hill, the vast citadel that was the Palace Hotel hunched its padded shoulders against the wind and blinked down at the town through dozens of lighted windows. Ahead of him and to his left, a lumination which had no single source hung low over Spring Gardens, the main shopping centre, open late that night for the pre-Christmas rush. Hundreds of spots of light from the outer residential districts encircled him on the hills that surround the town. Previously he had found this sight a comfort; it had pleased him to be part of a small community that could be taken in with one circular gaze; but tonight he felt somehow engulfed by it all. He felt that he had walked into something inexplicable, and that he had no alternative but to go in deeper.

He crossed the road and hurried down the slope towards the town.

It was almost nine o'clock and the shops were beginning to close. Few people remained to brave the weather. By the taxi rank and phone booths a large Christmas tree, scantily decorated with cheerless lights, drooped its arms under the weight of rain. Next to it a crib stood empty and unblessed due to the depredations of hooligans who had run off with the statues of the Holy Family and their guests. The ululation of seasonal pop music nagged away out in the darkness.

His way home led him past The Crescent, Buxton's major claim to architectural distinction, and he took advantage of the sheltered promenade at the front of the building to get out of the rain. The many small arches, dimly lit, the boarded-up windows along the first floor of the empty, decaying building, made Mr Rudge, who had once been taken to an exhibition of Di Chirico's work, feel that he had walked into one of that painter's sinister, vacant, echoing canvases.

Twice, through the arches curving to the left ahead of him, he thought, no – he was sure – he saw the dark figure hurrying along. The fact that he, Mr Rudge, now found himself trailing behind whoever it was that he had first feared had been following him, was particularly distasteful to him. The figure could almost have been leading him back to his own home!

He was reluctant to consider the implications of this; indeed, he felt a general dullness throughout his system, a numbness blanketing a core feeling of dread that had come to occupy the base of his consciousness.

As he was passing the "Old Hall Hotel", his favourite local eating and drinking place, he had what was almost his last glimpse of the figure that he had first seen less than forty minutes earlier, on the otherwise empty station. He had just come in sight of the front of his flat, on the first floor of a block that overlooked the parklands of the Pavilion Gardens, when he clearly saw the tall, caped form, now almost familiar, crossing the road ahead of him.

It was running.

It took the road that forked behind the buildings along the Broadwalk, the pedestrianized lane that fronted Mr Rudge's flat. That was the road that he would have to take, as the only entrance to the flat was from the rear.

Feeling in his pocket for his key, Mr Rudge went in pursuit.

The door of his flat was safely locked when he reached it. He had feared that it would not be. He had a vision of it hanging open wide; perhaps smashed off its hinges.

Inside all was quiet.

He cautiously ventured through into his kitchen and switched on his electric kettle. He took off his soaked overcoat, took the gifts out of its pockets, and draped it over the back of a chair. He pulled a clean towel out of a drawer and set about drying his face and what little remained of his hair. He put his bags in a corner, intending to deal with them later, and made a pot of tea. His hands were shaking so he made his drink in a mug with a big handle.

He discovered he had a headache and took two paracetamol.

After half an hour he felt better, but very tired. Despite the fact that his mind was full of the events of the evening, he decided he would go to bed and try to sleep. He picked up his overcoat, and went into the hallway to hang it on its customary peg.

Someone had beaten him to it.

In the place where he always hung his coat was a dark cape that did not belong to him. It looked old. Its surface shone with damp. It had a drawstring of faded yellow cord around the neck.

It was some time before Mr Rudge could bring himself to go near it. He watched it intently, as though he expected it to move, to jump down, or run off. It did none of these things. When at last he did come close to it, he noticed at once its smell. It stank of soot, hot coal, and steam. And age; it smelled of old sweat and decay.

It was somehow both disgusting and deeply intimidating.

Close up, he could see the collar of the cape was frayed with use. Otherwise, it was undamaged except for a number of sharp tears, or cuts, a few inches long, on the left front.

Mr Rudge, who had fought in a war, had never felt panic charge up inside him with such force before. Panic and loathing!

He absent-mindedly touched his lips with a finger that had touched the cape, in a gesture of bewilderment, and there was a flavour like acid on his tongue. He spat grossly, and scrubbed his mouth with his sleeve, to be rid of the taste.

Angry now, he stepped over to a large brass pot where he kept his collection of walking sticks and a few umbrellas. He selected his biggest stick and swiped out at the cape as though he was being assailed by it. He hit it again and again. The cape swung to and fro until at last it fell off the peg. Mr Rudge gave a grunt of satisfaction, kicked it into a ball, then kicked the ball away down the hall towards the door. He leaned against the wall, gasping from the violence he had done, and watched the cape, waiting for something to happen.

He waited a long time, and nothing did happen. Satisfied, he hung his coat on the peg, and went back into the kitchen. Thirsty, he made more tea. He drank two cups slowly, washed his mug, and went back through the hallway towards his bedroom.

In the hall, the cape was back on the peg and his coat, torn to shreds where it had been pulled down, lay on the floor.

Mr Rudge snatched the cape and ran with it into the kitchen. Holding it firmly under his arms, he found a roll of plastic sacks and tore one off. He thrust the cape inside the sack with the vigour of a man trying to drown a large animal. He tied a tight knot at the top of the bag and flung it to the ground. He went out of the kitchen and into his study, closing the door behind him. He waited there for almost an hour, then went back into the kitchen.

To his surprise, the bag was just as he had left it.

He looked out into the hallway. He coat also lay where he had left it, and the peg was empty.

Feeling almost cheerful, Mr Rudge returned to the kitchen and prodded the bin bag with his foot. He could feel the cape inside it. For some reason he felt the need to put a weight on the bag. He found a wooden box, placed it on the bag, and filled it with the heaviest items he could find.

Then he went to bed and tried to sleep with the light on.

Next morning, tired and timorous after his nightmarish night, Mr Rudge stepped gingerly into his kitchen at just after nine o'clock.

The box had not been moved and the plastic sack remained under it. He knew the cape was still inside the bag because the shape of its surface had not changed.

There were tears in his eyes as he made his breakfast. He was scared that he was going mad or senile.

He forced fried food into himself, in spite of a total lack of appetite, then imagined that he felt much better. He left the bin bag under the box and kept himself busy all day with various non-urgent tasks about the flat. At nine in the evening he sat down in front of the TV and drank two inches of whisky from a bottle of Bells; not his favourite, but cheaper than broaching the Laphroaig.

Then, when his dander was well and truly up, as he would have phrased it, he went into the kitchen and hauled the box off the black plastic bag. He lifted the bag, feeling with satisfaction the weight of the cape inside, and slung it into a cupboard under the stairs that led to the flat above his.

Then he went to bed and slept for twelve hours.

During the next couple of days Mr Rudge found it difficult to settle to anything but, on the third morning, he woke up feeling more like his old, calm, clear and capable self.

With a shock he realized that it was less than a week to Christmas.

He spent the morning wrapping presents and signing and addressing cards. After a trip to the Post Office to send them off, he returned to the flat with the determination to dig out his box of Christmas decorations. It was time to brighten things up a bit.

Though he never did much about Christmas, he had discovered that it was better, since his wife had died and he had been living alone, to make some concessions to the festive season, rather than try to turn his back and ignore it. It was his habit on Christmas Day to eat a turkey dinner at the Old Hall Hotel then, if the weather permitted, to take a turn or two round the Pavilion Gardens. He would then return to his flat and, sitting under strips and chains of coloured paper and, with a bottle of malt by his side, he would read or watch television until his eyes drooped shut. It was the only sensible way to deal with Christmas.

On Boxing Day he would visit his daughter in Derby, staying overnight and returning next day. He never lingered longer. His daughter's toleration of him only lasted twenty-four hours at most.

The Christmas decorations he kept on a shelf at the back of the cupboard under the stairs.

He opened the door and paused for some seconds before switching on the light.

The air smelt stale in there.

"No," he thought, poking his head inside, "it smells downright unpleasant; it stinks!"

He had noticed a smell in the flat for a few days now.

He flicked the switch on. The low-powered bulb lit with a pallid light tidy piles of bags and boxes and orderly shelves stacked with household equipment and cleaning materials. The only object in there that had not been placed with neat precision was the plastic bag containing the cape. It sprawled at an angle up against a wall. Mr Rudge, who had not visited the cupboard since he had flung it there, noticed that it had become fuller. The bag now looked as though it had something in it other than, or as well as, the cape, because it was bulging where it had once been flat.

Mr Rudge decided to throw it out.

He reached down, grabbed the knotted part, and gave a tug. It was surprisingly heavy; very heavy, in fact. He felt the plastic stretch as he pulled it.

"God, don't let it burst!", he thought, and let go of it.

He stood considering the situation for some moments. He thought of untying the knot to look inside the bag but dismissed the idea because he was sure the smell was coming from inside there, and he thought it would be best to leave it undisturbed. He bent down closer and gave it a prod with the tip of a tin of wax spray polish. It was only a gentle prod, but something hard inside fell away, or did it move away? It almost looked as though something had – retreated.

He stood up and, as he did so, whatever he had moved swiftly slid back in place. There was a soft sound in the cupboard, the kind of noise an old, sick dog might make when it was dreaming. It could only have come from inside the sack.

Mr Rudge flicked off the light and slammed the door shut with a speed remarkable for a man his age.

It was hours before he remembered why he had gone to the cupboard. Then he decided he would do without Christmas decorations for once that year.

The incident in the cupboard brought back thoughts about his homeward journey three days previously, which he was just beginning to hope he had put at the back of his mind for ever. Now, he had to confront them.

He sat in the classic posture of a deeply troubled man, with his elbows on his knees and his head in his hands, and went over and over the events that had occurred while he had been waiting on the station and, after that, when he had returned home.

Particularly he had in mind the image of the figure he had seen then, of the man in the cape. Memories began to stir, fugitive, fragmentary, and trivial, of something he had seen or done, perhaps years ago, that had some connection with the figure. He remembered how quickly the shape of it had become almost familiar to him that night, and he began to think that somewhere, somehow, he had seen the figure before. Then, for no apparent reason, his mind filled with reminiscences of his working life.

He had been a junior school teacher until he had retired at sixty, nine years before. Out of a haze of general impressions of that time, he began to recall some of the work he had so enthusiastically done. He had been a very good teacher, and it had been a pleasure for him to organise extracurricular activities and projects for the children in his classes, because he had the knack of stirring their interest, and because they responded so well, and produced sometimes quite remarkable work for him. Some of the projects had unearthed facts and information of such high quality he had thought them worth preserving and even, in some cases, publishing, if only in a very small, limited way. He had never actually got round to this, but he still kept a lot of work from those years, meaning to take a look at it again someday. He had piles of such stuff in his little study.

Then he remembered a particular project; one he had set the older children in the top form.

It had been called, not very excitingly, "The Story of my Home".

He had asked his pupils to research back as far as they could go to discover what they could about the places where they lived. Some of them, with the aid of their mothers and fathers, aunts and uncles, came up with some astonishing facts, amounting almost to family histories. To set an example of what he hoped to achieve from the project, he had compiled a history of his own home; the flat he now occupied, but had then been living in for little more than a year.

Suddenly, disturbed by some foreboding, Mr Rudge jumped up. He went into his study and began sifting through boxes of files. It took some finding, but at last he had it; a dingy green folder, faded across the top by sunlight, and stuffed full to bursting.

The photographs he wanted were close to the top, in the opening section of the project. They were both of the same man; Mr Rudge remembered his name as he lifted them out; George Nathan-Dyson, Architect and Engineer. A "Great Man" of the Victorian period. He had designed and built a huge range of buildings in his brief life, but he was in Mr Rudge's file because he had built the house where he, Mr Rudge, now lived. Nathan-Dyson had put the place up with his own money and had lived in the very same apartment that Mr Rudge had moved into over one hundred years later. He had lived there until the time of his death.

The first photograph had been taken at an extensive building site, at the early, excavational stage of the work. Men with shovels toiled in deep mud in the background while, in the left foreground, others hauled cumbersome equipment into place. A little right of centre of the picture, also in the foreground, a tall, imperious, youngish looking man was watching the work in progress. He stood with his legs apart, with one hand on his hip while the other, clenched into a fist, hung by his side. The photographer had got the focus slightly wrong, bringing out more detail in the middle distance than in the foreground so the central figure's features were indistinct, but there was no mistaking his body language; his posture was quite unambiguous. Here was an arrogant, egotistical, merciless man who would have his own way, no matter what. Here was George Nathan-Dyson.

Mr Rudge studied the picture for a long time. He noted that Nathan-Dyson wore the tight, tapered trousers of the period and that he wore a cape over his shoulders. Also, the picture was not so blurred that Mr Rudge could not, with the aid of a magnifying glass, make out the loops of a pale cord tied under the man's chin to hold the cape in place.

The other picture was a formal portrait of Nathan-Dyson taken at home in his study. This was not the small room that Mr Rudge called his study, but the larger one next to it.

At first glance, the picture was of little interest. Nathan-Dyson, his pose as wooden as the chair he sat in, stared at the photographer and, down the years, at Mr Rudge, with an expression of tight-lipped, self-satisfied contempt.

He was surrounded by tables almost invisible under masses of bric-a-brac. Glass-fronted cases, full of more of the same, stood in the background. To Mr Rudge it looked as though anyone who took two steps in any direction would send dozens of ornaments and artefacts tumbling. *He* certainly would have done. It was hard to imagine a man the size of Nathan-Dyson moving amongst them without accident, but the ability to do so was plainly one of his many skills and talents.

Mr Rudge was interested in the details of the room. It was fascinating to compare the way it had looked then to the way it was now. His eyes wandered from window to fireplace, from fireplace to door, and he noticed the door behind Nathan-Dyson was open. He could see out into the hall. A beam of light shone, as it still did on sunny days, through the window above the main door, making every detail of the hall's interior astonishingly clear.

"Some of those Victorian photographers produced remarkable results with what must have been quite primitive equipment," mused Mr Rudge, as he explored details revealed in the hall with his magnifying glass.

It was then he saw the cape, hanging on its peg.

It was clearly to be seen, even without the aid of the glass, hanging where he had found it a few days earlier, in the place where he had used to hang his own coat in recent years. The cape in the photograph was the one that he had stuffed into the plastic sack and hidden under the stairs; he knew it, and dark clouds, present at the back of his mind for days, began to roll forward.

He threw the photograph down and pushed the file away from him.

Facts he had forgotten about Nathan-Dyson, products of his researches into the life of the man, returned to Mr Rudge out of nowhere. Facts so unpleasant he had decided not to include them in a project that children would read.

Nathan-Dyson had a reputation for cruelty. His wife had left him after only two months of marriage and there had been a national scandal when she had revealed details of his treatment of her in court. Prostitutes had come forward to support her allegations against him, and to add their own. Mrs Nathan-Dyson got her divorce, and the man escaped prison by a hair's breadth.

Nathan-Dyson used and abused the people who worked for him without scruple. That had finally caused his downfall. The wife of a man who had died in an accident caused by Nathan-Dyson's negligence stabbed him in the heart. The woman had waited on a station for him to arrive by train. There was a story that he had pulled the knife out of his heart and stabbed the woman in the face and arms in the moments before he died.

The murder had taken place on the platform where Mr Rudge had been waiting a few nights earlier.

The clouds in Mr Rudge's mind stormed forwards thick and fast.

They became a tempest.

Two days later Mr Rudge visited the library to do some research.

He was dressed in a bizarre collection of sweaters, jackets, and scarves topped by an overcoat that hung in shreds about his shoulders. He had not shaved, his eyes were vivid red, and there was a ghastly smell about him.

He tottered as he walked, and he tumbled over a chair in the Local History section.

An almost empty bottle of expensive malt whisky slid from his pocket and smashed on the floor as he tried to get up.

To the librarian's question concerning any assistance she could provide, he gave no reply. He talked to himself, however. As he pulled rare and valuable volumes from the shelves and, after glancing at them, tossed them aside, he was heard to mutter the name Nathan-Dyson again and again. It was a name that the knowledgeable librarian recognised at once.

"We do have books on that subject," she said, "but not on the open shelves. If you'd like to take a chair and wait, I can get them for you." She had no intention of doing this. She was going to call the police.

"Get what out?" stormed Mr Rudge. "You won't get me out! That's what he wants to do, but he won't. He wants his old place back, that's what he's after, the bastard. And he's been dead all that time; all those years!"

A couple who knew Mr Rudge slightly, and were aghast at the state he was in, and who happened to be browsing in the library, stepped in to help. They took him by the arms and led him out to their car.

Surprisingly, he offered no resistance.

They drove him home.

They tried to get a social worker to look in on Mr Rudge. They described the conditions he was living in, the chaotic state of his flat, and how foul it smelt in there, but were told nobody would be available to visit him until after Christmas.

On the afternoon of Christmas Eve Mr Rudge, dressed in most of his clothing as he had been for his visit to the library (he kept all his windows open all the time now because of the smell, and it was well below freezing outside), drank the last drop of whisky he had in the house, lurched up out of his chair, and stumbled towards the cupboard under the stairs.

Because his fingers were very cold he had trouble with the catch on the door. When it did lift, and the door flew open, he flicked on the light switch with a jab of the side of his hand, and peered inside through watery eyes.

The big plastic bag was full now.

He had thought once that the cape might have been rotting away in there, and producing a gas. That would account for the swelling and the smell, but gasses cause things to swell like balloons. The bag was full of lumps and bumps and angles. Parts of it moved from time to time.

No, it wasn't gas.

Mr Rudge looked very sad as he reached out to untie the top of the sack. He sighed as his stiff fingers refused to do their business again, and the job was made even harder because pressure inside the bag had forced the knot tighter.

But, at last, it unravelled, and the top of the bag gaped open.

"Right," said Mr Rudge, leaning forward to see inside. "Let's have a look at you."

And he did get one brief glimpse of a familiar face as the contents of the sack unfolded and extended around him, silently and swiftly.

He seemed to go a very long way in a very short time. When he got to the end of his journey, there was nothing there.

Nothing at all.

When her father did not turn up as expected on Boxing Day, and did not phone her with an excuse, Mr Rudge's daughter, who worried guiltily about him sometimes, called the Buxton police and asked them to check his flat.

The constable who was sent on the job noticed the open windows and went for a ladder.

He climbed through the window into the stinking rooms. After looking round, he reported his findings back to base.

"It's a bad one," he said, in a shocked voice. "There's a corpse, I think, in a jumbo bin bag. Been dead a while from the stench. Get a team round. As soon as you can. It's very nasty."

When the police untied the knot at the top of the plastic sack they discovered Mr Rudge inside. He had been strangled by a yellow cord that was still around his neck. The police believed the cord had been taken from a cape that was discovered hanging on a peg in the hallway; an antique item.

The cape was taken away for use as evidence, but did not prove to be at all helpful in the hunt for the murderer.

The cape's owner was not much disturbed by his loss. He had no further use for it because, as the unfortunate couple who moved into the flat to replace Mr Rudge some weeks later were to discover, this time he was home to stay.

CHET WILLIAMSON

The Moment the Face Falls

CHET WILLIAMSON'S first story was published in 1981, since when his fiction has appeared in *The New Yorker*, *Playboy*, *The Magazine of Fantasy & Science Fiction*, *Twilight Zone*, *Alfred Hitchcock Magazine* and many other periodicals and anthologies.

His debut novel, *Soulstorm*, appeared in 1986, and was followed by *Dreamthorp*, the Bram Stoker Award-nominated *Ash Wednesday*, *Lowland Rider*, *McKain's Dilemma* and *Reign*.

Recent projects include an *Aliens* graphic novel sequence, *Music of the Spears*, for Dark Horse Comics; *Ravenloft*: *Mordenheim*, a gothic horror novel from TSR, and another new novel, *Second Chance*, from CD Publications.

About "The Moment the Face Falls", the author explains: "When Robert Bloch asked me to do a story for *Monsters in Our Midst*, I knew I didn't want to do a serial killer or anything of that ilk – I guess I thought it would seem presumptuous to try and outpsycho the author of the same! So I decided to make my 'monster' one of the quieter types, who gets his jollies off the emotional misery of others.

"I suppose I used a Hollywood setting since Bob's had so much experience there, and also because it seemed like the perfect place to damage egos, since the ones there are so much *larger* than in the rest of the world, and are so much more likely to be bruised . . ."

REBIRTH, PAUL KENYON thought. Re-frigging-birth. One call on the phone that hadn't rung casually in days, warmly in weeks, importantly in years, and suddenly Kenyon's apartment didn't look at all like a four-hundred-dollar-a-month rat hole, but like the home of a man the industry still wanted.

"Yes," he said as he looked at the framed clippings, yellow with age, that hung over his desk.

"Yes," he said louder as his gaze fell on the poster for *Trail Dust*, Jimmy Stewart tight-lipped behind his six-shooter, Dan Duryea in the background, clutching a rifle with wicked intent, Jeanne Crain with one hand-tinted glove on Jimmy's narrow shoulder, and those magic words in small print at the bottom, "Written by Dennis Collins and Paul Kenyon."

And "*Yes*," he said for the third time as he looked at the cover of the June 1954 *Screen Stars*, from which he and Clare DuPont, his first wife, waved gaily at fans and photographers, two nominees running the gauntlet to where those priceless, golden statuettes would be doled out.

Kenyon stood up and walked across the small room that held everything he owned. He looked at the pulp magazines, the digests, the paperbacks that began in the late fifties and ended just last year. The earliest had his name on the spines, but the later ones, the ones that all looked and read the same, had "Brent Stock" in letters much smaller than the word, *Gunman*, the appellation of a series hero with a name as simple as his motivations.

Paul Kenyon had been Brent Stock for books number 21 through 47, and number 48, *Bloody Gun*, was in the typewriter now. Four books a year at four grand each was a living, though not much of one. Enough for rent and food and booze, enough to see some movies to keep up with what was hot, thinking that one day his agent would place a script again, and writing, always writing.

But, he thought as he looked at the piles of pulp, no more of this shit. One call had changed all that.

The caller's name was Richard Dunne, and he was an independent producer funded by Paramount. He sounded sharp and savvy, and best of all he wanted Kenyon, actually *wanted* him.

"It's an unpublished novel," he had said on the phone. "Simon and Schuster's gonna do it, contemporary western, *The Big Chill* married to *Lonesome Dove*, got that scope, got the characters. It's the greatest thing I've ever read."

"But . . . why did you call me?"

"Because ever since I was a kid and saw that movie you wrote for Jimmy Stewart — the one Anthony Mann directed — hell, it just knocked me out. The script, well Christ, it's incredible, but I didn't realize until I was grown up the script made that movie. You were nominated for it, right?"

"Yes, I — "

"Shoulda won. Shoulda won hands-down. What won that year anyway?"

"*From Here to Eternity*."

"Shit. That screenplay was all *over* the place. Never focused, too many characters. *That* Oscar rode in on the others' coattails. Goddam sweeps. Anyway, you're the guy I want. It's a done deal, Costner and Julia Roberts are a go, and Jim Cameron's just about locked to direct. Now don't tell me to call your agent, I'll do that, we don't have to talk money, money's the least of the worries, but I want to *meet* you first, meet the guy who's given me so damn much pleasure over the years. Okay?"

"Well . . . well, *sure*."

"Great. Lunch at Nicky Blair's. Today. One. Meet you right at the door."

"Uh . . . sure. Okay. One. At the door."

When he hung up, Kenyon thought it might be a dream, but he was awake. Then he thought maybe he was drunk and had imagined it all, but his hangover told him otherwise. Finally he thought it might be a joke one of his ex-wives was playing, but since he hadn't had any contact with the three Norns for six years, he dismissed that as well.

No, it was for real. Somebody remembered. The good work he did nearly forty years before was finally paying off, and what a long, strange trip it had been.

Western movies had started dying when they got big on TV. He had tried to make the transition, but the weekly pressures had been too much for him. And now that he had finally learned to write to deadline, TV westerns were deader than Duke Wayne. His whole career had been a study in frustration. Until now.

Jesus, Costner and Julia Roberts and James Cameron, things were cooking, dammit, cooking. He could pay off his bills, even get back on top again. He thought about calling his agent, but he knew that even if he got through it would be the old *Sorry, babe, money's on the other line, I'll call you right back*, and he never did.

Well, maybe he wouldn't cut Lou in on this one. Maybe he'd find another agent to handle this deal and just let Lou fuck himself. Maybe he'd do that. But now he had to dress. Had to look good. Had to look like a successful writer that only a wonderful film opportunity could lure out of the ivory towers of fiction. He chose a dark blue suit with broad shoulders, an offwhite shirt, and a bold patterned tie. Looking at himself in the chipped mirror on the closet door, he thought the illusion was satisfactory. He didn't look like a drunk, and toothpaste and mouthwash assured that he didn't smell like one.

He knew who Dunne was right away. He wore a standard producer's uniform – small, round tortoiseshell glasses, a gray Italian-cut jacket, brown campaign shirt, pants so loose they resembled garment bags, and a belt whose array of studs and mesh even Gene Autry in his heyday would have found ostentatious.

Kenyon figured he must have been as easily recognizable, for a smile creased Dunne's clean-shaven face, and he came up to Kenyon, said, "Paul, right?" and pumped the older man's hand. The man was younger than Kenyon had thought he would be, probably in his early thirties. His hair was blond and cut short, and he ran his hand through it once, then gestured to the door. "Let's go."

Inside, Dunne gave his name, and they were shown to a table near the back. "I like privacy, you know?" Dunne said by way of explanation. "I'm past that 'gotta be seen' crap. Besides, I want to talk to you without anybody interrupting us."

They sat, and Dunne set the box he was carrying on the floor. Kenyon guessed that it contained the manuscript of the novel. Dunne ordered a Saratoga water, then said to Kenyon, "Have something stronger if you want," but Kenyon just smiled tightly and asked for coffee.

When they were alone, Dunne leaned forward. "Damn, it's a pleasure to meet you, Paul. You're really one hell of a screenwriter. What you been doing with yourself?"

Kenyon shrugged. He had known the question would come up. "Semi-retirement. I've done a few recent films, but nothing big. Not many westerns anymore."

"Shame to waste your talent in retirement."

"*Semi*," Kenyon repeated, smiling. "I do the occasional novel."

"Really? I haven't seen anything by you."

"Oh, pseudonymously. I keep Paul Kenyon for film work."

Dunne grinned, then winked. "Say no more. So. I'm really excited about working with you, my friend. Now, I'm a hands-on guy, so I hope that won't bother you. I'm good with story, like to see a nice tight arc, and this novel moves around a little too much."

"*From Here to Eternity*," Kenyon said.

Dunne laughed. "Yeah! Yeah, that's how it goes all right, from here to eternity. I wanta bring it back *here*, to earth, concentrate on the main characters, zero in, you know?" He reached down and picked up the box, then passed it to Kenyon. "This is it. Guy's first book, long mother, thousand pages in manuscript. High six-figure advance, you read about it?" Kenyon shook his head. "Guaranteed bestseller. My best D-girl nailed it. She suggested Bob Towne, but when I read it I said fuck him, I know who this is right for if I can find him. So I got your name out of that *Films of Jimmy Stewart* book, and you're still in the Guild, so here we are."

With his thumb Kenyon started to slit the tape that held on the box cover, but Dunne held up a hand. "Ah, read it later. You're gonna skim a thousand pages before lunch?"

The waiter brought the drinks, and Dunne raised his glass of Saratoga. "Here's to a profitable relationship, huh?"

"Here's to it," Kenyon said, feeling foolish, but lifting his coffee cup anyway, clinking it against the glass.

After they both sipped, Dunne shook his head. "I can't believe I got you here. That movie of yours just stayed with me, you know? When I was a kid, I used to play that I was Jimmy Stewart, and the bad guy had me and that old prospector pinned down from the cliff? And one of my friends would climb a tree and be Robert Ryan, and I'd sneak up on the other side, and . . ."

Dunne rattled on, but Kenyon didn't hear it. All he heard was a rushing sound, as if all the blood in his body had suddenly surged into his ears. He didn't feel the smooth ceramic of the cup in his fingers. All he felt was a terrible mixture of cold and heat that clamped a fist around his chest and squeezed.

The world had fallen out from under him. Old prospector? Robert Ryan? They weren't in *Trail Dust*.

But Kenyon knew what film they *were* in.

"Greatness," Dunne was saying. "Absolute joy. They don't tell *stories* like that anymore." He shook his head, still looking at Kenyon, smiling at him, and took another drink of water.

"The . . ." Kenyon began, but his throat was too dry, and he cleared it, then sipped his coffee, wishing it was bourbon. "I think you . . . uh . . ." He stopped and started again, slowly. "The movie. The movie of mine. What, uh, what was the movie?"

Dunne pressed his eyebrows together and grinned, as though Kenyon was putting him on. "Whatta you talking about? *Your* movie, Paul – Jimmy Stewart, Anthony Mann, Oscar nomination, hell, you know what movie."

The words didn't want to come, but Kenyon forced them out. "*The Naked Spur.*"

Dunne shrugged and laughed. "Well, yeah, *sure, The Naked Spur.*"

Kenyon looked down at the surface of the coffee. The dark liquid caught the light and reflected red, like blood. When he spoke again, the words were very quiet and controlled. "I . . . didn't write *The Naked Spur.* I did *Trail Dust.* With Mann and Stewart. They were both with Mann and Stewart."

He looked up at Dunne, whose smile was still there, but mixed with puzzlement. "*Trail Dust?*" Dunne said, and Kenyon nodded. "*Trail Dust.* Ah. Ah." It sounded as if Dunne was cooing to a baby. "Who, uh, else was in that?"

"Dan Duryea. Jeanne Crain." Nobodies now. Long forgottens. Has-beens, like me, Kenyon thought.

Dunne frowned. Then a tongue came out and licked his lower lip, and he shook his head again. It was probably, Kenyon thought, as mortified as Dunne ever allowed himself to look.

"Jesus," Dunne breathed, his eyes never leaving Kenyon's face. "Jesus, I feel like *such* an asshole."

"It's okay," Kenyon said, trying to smile, thinking that maybe, just maybe this didn't have to be a wash. "Did you ever see *Trail Dust?*"

"Don't think so. Seen most of Mann's stuff, but not that one. On video?" Kenyon nodded. "I'll have to check it out."

"If you liked *The Naked Spur*, you'd like *Trail Dust.*"

"Yeah. Probably would."

The waiter came to the table and asked if they were ready to order. Dunne smiled and said, "Might as well eat, since we're here," then deferred to Kenyon, who, having no appetite, asked for a salad. Dunne ordered lemon chicken.

When the waiter left, Dunne chuckled and waved a hand in the air. "Well, this has to be one of the most awkward moments I've ever had. My apologies, Paul."

"Oh, that's . . . all right. It's easy to confuse two films so much alike."

"Uh-huh. Oh, could I have the . . . uh . . ." Kenyon handed over the manuscript box, and Dunne smiled. "Thanks. Wouldn't want to forget it."

Neither spoke until the food came, but halfway through his chicken, Dunne asked, very casually, "By the way, do you know if the screenwriter for that *Naked Spur* thing is still around?"

Kenyon didn't.

After the meal was over, Dunne paid and offered to drive Kenyon home. Kenyon accepted with a nod, and they climbed into a dark blue Testarossa. When they got near Kenyon's apartment, Kenyon asked Dunne to pull over and let him off at the corner. Dunne apologized again, and added, "Listen, I'm gonna get this *Trail Dust* and if anything comes up I think you'd be right for, I'll definitely be in touch. Hey, it's just a matter of time. But good meeting you, Paul. Take care."

"Thanks," Kenyon said, and began to shuffle away.

Dunne sat and watched him go. He thought he understood why Kenyon had wanted off at that corner. There was a bar up the street.

When he saw Kenyon enter its doors, Dunne pulled the Testarossa out into traffic, and drove over to West Hollywood, where he dropped the car off at a rental agency, paid the fee, and got into his own 1986 Ford Escort. He drove a few blocks to the small apartment he shared with an actress, parked the car, climbed the stairs. The door was unlocked, which meant that she was home.

"Where were you?" she asked, not looking up from a script she was studying. "Bob called."

Bob was Dunne's agent. "Yeah?"

"The studio turned down your script."

"I know." He tossed the manuscript box full of empty sheets of paper on the couch.

"You *know*?" She looked up now, saw how he was dressed.

"I ran into one of their D-girls jogging this morning."

"Oh Christ . . ."

"What?"

"Christ, you did it again, didn't you?"

"Come on, Greta – "

"We can't *afford* it, Rick! A goddam Jag again? Or a Mercedes this time? And where'd you go for lunch? Morton's? La Dome?"

"Nicky Blair's."

"Nicky . . . Christ, you're a sick fucker sometimes, you know that?"

"I need this, Greta."

"Need it? Need to fuck people that way?"

"How I stay sane, baby. We all have ways to deal with disappointment. No matter how bad things get, I know that there are people worse off than me."

"And that makes it okay."

"Yeah, that makes it so I can keep going. So I can crank out another flying-glass script and maybe someday Schwarzenegger or Bruce Willis will drive their cars through the windows *I* made up. I *need* this. I need to know that at least I'm not at the bottom."

She looked at him for a long time, enraged, and he wondered again why she didn't leave him. But she didn't, and that was enough. Finally she turned away angrily, concentrated on her script again.

"You ought to see it," he said softly.

She didn't say a word.

"When I start filling in details, when it starts to dawn on them that hey, that's not *me* you're talking about, and finally when they're sure, when they know, when their face falls so far you swear you can hear their jaw hit the table like in a Tex Avery cartoon."

She kept reading her script, turned a page with a sharp snap of paper.

"It's not as good as selling a script," he said, "but it's better than a lot of things. It's better than coming."

He didn't wait to watch her cry. Instead he went into the bedroom, walked to the desk, sat down, turned on his computer, and brought up the word processing program from the hard disk. He retrieved the file named COMEBACK, and the list came up on the monitor, white letters on a blue background.

The list was long. There were hundreds of names of writers,

performers, directors, all of whom had seen little work since the first time the gods had blessed them, then left them behind for fresher faces, newer talents. Paul Kenyon's name was at the top, along with the words, "TRAIL DUST/1953/J. Stewart/A. Mann/AAN." He blocked the line and moved it down to the bottom of the list, thinking that by the time he came to him again, Kenyon would be ready once more. Hope springs eternal in the town of dreams, Dunne thought, and so does despair and humiliation.

Then he closed COMEBACK, and opened the file of a spec screenplay he had nearly finished. He felt like working now. The disappointment was gone. He was whole again, ready to write.

A little while later he thought of the two names Kenyon had mentioned, Dan Duryea and Jeanne Crain. He hadn't heard about either of them in a very long time, and wondered if they were still alive. He would have to check. If they were, they just might be interested in a comeback.

S.P. SOMTOW

Darker Angels

S.P. SOMTOW (aka Somtow Sucharitkul) was born in Bangkok and educated at Eton and St Catherine's College, Cambridge. His grandfather, whose two sisters were both married to King Rama VI of Siam, was the proud possessor of a small harem, and the author currently commutes between his homes in Bangkok and Los Angeles.

An avant-garde composer, screenwriter/director (*The Laughing Dead* and *Ill Met By Moonlight*) and the author of around thirty genre novels (*Vampire Junction*, *Valentine*, *Moon Dance* etc.), his most recent book is *Jasmine Nights*, a mainstream novel set in mid-1960s Thailand, published in the UK by Hamish Hamilton.

ONE DAY there'll be historians who can name all the battles and number the dead. They'll study the tactics of the generals and they'll see it all clear as crystal, like they was watching with the eyes of the angels.

But it warn't like that for me. I can't for the life of me put a name to one blame battle we fought. I had no time to number the dead nor could I see them clearly through the haze of red that swam before my eyes. And when the gore-drenched mist settled into dew, when the dead became visible in their stinking, wormy multitudes, I still could not tell one from another: it was a very sea of torsos, heads, and twisted limbs; the dead was wrapped around one another so close and intimate they was like lovers; didn't matter no more iffen they was ours or theirs.

I do not recollect what made me stay behind. Could be it was losing my last shinplaster on the cockroach races. Could have been the coffee which warn't real coffee at all but parched acorns roasted with bacon fat and ground up with a touch of chicory. Could be it was that my shoes was so wore out from marching that every step I took was like walking acrosst a field of brimstone.

More likely it was just because I was a running away kind of a boy. Running was in my blood. My pa and me, we done our share of running, and I reckon that even after I done run away from *him* and gone to war, the running fever was still inside of me and couldn't be let go.

And then, after I lagged behind, I knowed that if I went back they'd shoot me dead, and if they shot me, why then I'd go straight on to the everlasting fire, because we was fighting to protect the laws of God. I just warn't ready for Hell yet, not after a mere fourteen years on this mortal earth.

That's why I was tarrying amongst the dead, and that's how I come to meet the old darkie that used to work down at the Anderson place.

The sun was about setting and the place was right rank, because the carrion had had the whole day to bloat up and rot and to call out for the birds and the worms and the flies. But it felt good to walk on dead people because they was softer on my wounded feet. The bodies stretched acrosst a shallow creek and all the way up to the edge of a wood. I didn't know where I was nor where I was going. There warn't much light remaining and I wanted to get somewhere, anywhere, before nightfall. It was getting cold. I took a jacket off of one dead man and a pair of new boots from another, but I couldn't get the boots on past them open sores.

You might think it a sin to steal from the dead, but the dead don't have no use for gold and silver. There was scant daylight left for me to rifle through their pockets looking for coins. Warn't much in the way of money on that battlefield. It's usually only us poor folks which gets killed in battle.

It was slippery work wading through the corpses, keeping an eye for something shiny amongst the ripped-up torsos and the sightless heads and the coiling guts. I was near choking to death from the reek of it, and the coat I stole warn't much proof against the cold. I was hungry and I had no notion of where to find provender. And the mist was coming back, and I thought to myself, I'll just take myself a few more coppers and then I'll cross over into the wood and build me a shelter and mayhap a fire. Won't nobody see me, thin as a sapling, quiet as a shadow.

So I started to wade over the creek, which warn't no trouble because there was plenty of bodies to use as stepping stones. I was halfway acrosst when I spotted the old nigger under a cotton-wood tree, in a circle which was clear of carrion. He had a little fire going and something a-roasting over it. I could hear the crackling above the buzz of the flies, and I could smell the cooking fat somewhere behind the stench of putrefying men.

I moved nearer to where he sat. I was blame near fainting by then and ready to kill a body for my supper. He was squatting with his arms around his knees and he was a-rocking back and forth and I thought I could hear him crooning some song to himself, like a lullaby, in a language more kin to French than nigger-talk. Odd thing was, I had heard the song before. Mayhap my momma done sung it to me onc't, for she was born out Louisiana way. The more I listened, the less I was fixing to kill the old man.

He was old, all right. As I crept closer, I seen he warn't no threat to me. I still couldn't see his face, because he was turned away from me and looking straight into the setting sun. But I could see he was withered and white-haired and black as the coming night, and seemed like he couldn't even hear me approaching, for he never pricked up his ears though I stood nary a yard or two behind his back, in the shadow of the cottonwood.

That was when he said to me, never looking back, "Why, *bonjour*, Marse Jimmy Lee; I never did think I'd look upon you face again."

And then he turned, and I knew him by the black patch over his right eye.

Lord, it was strange to see him there, in the middle of the valley of the dead. It had been ten years since my pa and me gone up to the Anderson place. Warn't never any call to go back, since it burned to the ground a week after, and old man Anderson died, and his slaves was all sold.

"How did you know it was me?" I asked him. "I was but four years old last time you laid eyes on me."

"Your daddy still a itinerant preacher, Marse Jimmy Lee?" he says.

"I reckon," said I, for I warn't about ready to tell him the truth yet. "I ain't with my pa no more."

"You was always a running away sort of a boy," he said, and offered me a piece of what he was roasting.

"What is it?"

"I don't reckon I ought to tell you."

"I've had possum before. I've had field rat. I'm no stranger to strange flesh." I took a bite of the meat and it was right tasty. But I hadn't had solid food for two days, and soon I was a heaving all over the nearest corpse.

He went back to his crooning song, and I remembered then that I had heard it last from his own lips, that day Pa shot Momma in the back because she wanted to go with the Choctaw farmer. I can't say I blamed her, because leastways the man was a landowner and had four slaves besides. Pa let her pack her bags and walk halfway acrosst the bridge afore he blew her to kingdom come. Then he took my hand and set me up on his horse and took me to the Anderson place, and when I started to squall, he slapped me in the face until it were purple and black, saying, between his blows, "She don't deserve your tears. She is a woman taken in adultery; such a woman should be stoned to death, according to the scriptures; a bullet were too good for her. I have exercised my rights according to the law, and iffen I hear one more sob out of you, I shall take a hickory to you, for he who spareth the rod loveth not his child." And he drained a flask of bug juice and burped, I did not hear the name of Mary Cox from his lips again for ten long years.

Pa was not a ordained minister, but plantation folks reckoned him book-learned enough to preach to their darkies, which is what he done every Sunday, a different estate each week, then luncheon with the master and mistress of the house or sometimes, if they was particular about eating with white trash, then in the kitchen amongst the house niggers. The niggers called him the Reverend Cox, but to the white folks he was just Cox, or Bug Juice Cox, or Blame-Fuckster Cox, or wretched, pitiable Cox so low that his wife done left him for a Injun.

At the Anderson place he preached in a barn, and he took for his subject adultery; and as there was no one to notice, I stole away to a field and sat me down in a thicket of sugar cane and hollered and carried on like the end of the world was nigh, and me just four years old.

Then it was that I heard the selfsame song I was hearing now, and I looked up and saw this ancient nigger with a patch over one eye, and he says to me, "Oh, honey, it be a terrible thing to be without a mother." I remember the smell of him, a pungent smell like fresh crushed herbs. "I still remembers the day my *mamman* was took from me. Oh, do not grieve alone, white child."

"How'd you come to lose that eye?"

"It the price of knowledge, honey," he said softly.

Choking back my sobs, a mite embarrassed because someone had seen me in my loneliness, I said to him, "You shouldn't be here. You should be in that barn listening to my father's preaching, lessen you want to get yourself a whupping."

He smiled sadly and said, "They done given up on whupping old Joseph."

I said, "Is your momma dead too, Joseph?"

"Yes. She be dead, oh, nigh on sixty year now. She died in the revolution."

"Oh, come," I said, "even I know that the revolution was almost a hundred years ago, and I know you ain't that old, because a white man's time is threescore years and ten, and a nigger's time is shorter still." Now I wasn't comprehending anything I was saying; this was all things I heard my pa say, over and over again, in his sermons.

"Oh," said old Joseph, "I ain't talking about the white man's revolution, but the colored folks' revolt which happened on a island name of Haiti. The French, they tortured my *mamman*, but she wouldn't betray her friends, so they killed her and sold me to a slaver, and the ship set sail one day before independence; so sixty years after my kinfolk was set free, I's still in bondage in a foreign country."

I knew that niggers was always full of stories about magic and distant countries, and they couldn't always see truth from fantasy; my daddy told me that truth is a hard, solid thing to us white folks, as easy to grasp as a stone or a horseshoe, but to them it was slippery, it was like a phantom. That was why I didn't take exception to the old man's lies. I just sat there quietly, listening to the music of his voice, and it soothed me and seemed like it helped to salve the pain I was feeling, for pretty soon when I thought of Momma lying on the bridge choking on her own blood, I felt I could remember the things I loved about her too, like the way she called my name, the way her nipples tasted on my lips, for she had lost my newborn sister and she was bursting with milk and she would sometimes let me suckle, for all that I was four years old.

And then I was crying again, but this time they was healing tears.

Then old Joseph, he said, "You listen to me, Marse Jimmy Lee. I ain't always gone be with you when you needs to open up your heart." Now this surprised me, because I didn't recollect telling him none of what was going through my mind. "I's gone give you a gift," he said, and he pulls out a bottle from his sleeve, a vial, only a inch high, and in that bottle was a doll that was woven out of cornstalks. It were cunningly wrought, for the head of the doll was bigger than the neck of the bottle, and it must have taken somebody many hours to make, and somebody with keen eyesight at that. "Now this be a problem doll. It can listen to you when no man will listen. It a powerful magic from the island where I was born."

He held it out to me and it made me smile, for I had oftentimes been told that darkies are simple people and believe in all kinds of magic. I clutched it in my hands, but mayhap he saw the disbelief in my face, for he said to me with the utmost gravity, "Do not mock this magic, white child. Among the colored people which still fears the old gods, they calls me a *boungan*, a man of power."

"The old gods?" I said.

"Shangó," he said, and he done a curious sort of a genuflecting hop when he said the name. "Obatala; Ogun; Babalu Ayé. . . ."

The names churned round and round in my head as I stared into his good eye. I don't recollect what followed next or how my pa found me. But everything else I remembered just as though the ten years that followed, the years of wandering, Pa's worsening cruelty and drunkenness, hadn't never even happened.

It was as though I had circled back to that same place and time. Only instead of the burning sunlight of that summer's day there was the gathering cold and the night. Instead of the tall cane sticky with syrup, we was keeping company with the slain. And I warn't a child no more, although I warn't a man yet, neither.

"The *poupée* I give you," old Joseph said as I sat myself down beside him, "does you still got it?"

"My pa found it the next day. He said he didn't want no hoodoo devil dolls in his house. He done smashed it and throwed it in the fire, and then he done wore me out with his hickory."

"And you a soldier now."

"I run away."

"Lordy, honey, you a sight to see. Old Joseph don't got no more dolls for you now. Old Joseph got no time for he be making dolls. There be a monstrous magic abroad now in this universe. This magic it the onliest reason old Joseph still living in this world. Old Joseph hears the magic summoning him. Old Joseph be stay behind to hear what the magic it have to tell him."

Like a fool, I thought him simple when I heard him speak of magic. It made me smile. It was the first time I had smiled in many months. I smiled to keep from crying, for weeping ill becomes a man of fourteen years who has carried his rifle into battle to defend his country.

"You poor lost child," said Joseph, "you should be awaking up mornings to the song of the larks, not the whistle of miniés nor the thunder of cannon. You at the end of the road now, ain't nowhere left for you to go; that's why us has been called here to this valley of the shadow of death. It was written from the moment we met, Marse Jimmy Lee. Ten years I wandered alone in the wilderness. Now the darker angels has sent you to me."

"I don't know what you mean."

"Be not afraid," he said, "for I bring you glad tidings of great joy." I marveled that he knew the words of the evangelist, for this was the man who would not go hear my father's preaching.

He nibbled at the charred meat. For a moment I entertained the suspicion that it were human flesh. But it smelled good. I ate my fill and drank from the bloody stream and fell asleep beside the fire to the lilt of the old man's lullaby.

I had not told old Joseph all the truth. It warn't only the need to run that forced me from my father's house. Pa was a hard man and a drinking man and a man which had visions, and in those visions he saw other worlds. He was unmerciful to me, and oftentimes he would set to whipping the demons out of me, but everything he did to me was in keeping with holy scripture, which tells a father that love ain't always a sweet thing but can also come with bitterness and blows.

I had visions too, but they warn't heavenly the way his was. I would not wear my shoes. I played with the nigger children of the town, shaming him. I ran wild and I never went to no school. But I could read some, for that my pa set me to studying the scriptures whenever he could tie me down.

This is how I come to join the regiment:

We was living in a shack in back of the Jackson place, right next to the nigger burial plot. Young Master Jackson had all his darkies assembled in the graveyard to hear a special sermon from my pa, because the rumors of the 'mancipation proclamation was rife amongst the slaves. There was maybe thirty or forty of them, and a scattering of pickaninnies underfoot, sitting on the grass, leaning against the wooden markers.

I was sitting in the shack, minding a kettle of stew. Through the open window I could hear my pa preaching. "Now don't you darkies pay this emancipation proclamation no mind," came his voice, ringing and resonant. "It is an evil trickery. They are trying to fool you innocent souls into running away and joining up with those butchers who come down to rape and pillage our land, and they hold out freedom as a reward for treachery. But the true reward is death, for if a nigger is captured in the uniform of a Yankee it has been decreed by our government that he shall be shot without trial. No, this is no road to freedom! There is only one way there for those born into bondage, and that is through the blood of our savior Jesus Christ, and your freedom is not for this world, but for the next, for is it not written, 'In my father's house there are many mansions'? There is a mansion for you, and you, and you, and you, iffen you will obey your master in this life and accept the yoke of lowliness and the lash of repentance; for is it not written, 'By his stripes we are healed' and 'Blessed are the meek'? It's not for the colored people, freedom in this world. But the wicked, compassionless Yankees would prey on your simplicity. They would let you mistake the kingdom of heaven for a rebellious kingdom on earth. 'To everything there is a season.' Yes, there will be mansions for you all. Mansions with white stone columns and porticoes sheltered from the sun. The place of healing is beyond the valley of the shadow of death. . . ."

My pa could talk mighty proper when he had a mind to, and he had a chapter and verse for everything. I didn't pay no heed to his words, though, because there is different chapters and verses for niggers, and when they are quoted for white folks they do not always mean the same thing. No, I was busy stirring the stew and hiding the whisky, for Pa had always had a powerful thirst after he was done preaching, and with the quenching of thirst came violence.

After the preaching, the darkies all starts singing with a passion. They done sung "All God's Chillun Got Wings" and "Swing Low, Sweet Chariot." Pa didn't stay for the singing but come into the shack calling for his food. It warn't ready, so he throwed a few pots and pans around, with me scurrying out of the way to avoid being knocked about, and then he finally found where I had hidden the bottle and he lumbered into the inner room to drink.

Presently the stew bubbled up, and I ladled out some in a tin cup and took it to the room. This was the room me and him slept in, on a straw pallet on the floor; a bare room with nothing but a chest of drawers, a chair with one leg missing, and a hunting rifle. He kept his hickories there too, for to chastise me with.

I should have knocked, because Pa warn't expecting me.

He was sitting in the chair with his britches about his ankles. He didn't see me. In one hand, he was holding a locket which had a picture of Momma. In the other hand, he was holding his bony cocker, and he was strenuously indulging in the vice of Onan.

I was right horrified when I saw this. I was full of shame to see my father unclothed, for was that not the shame of the sons of Noah? And I was angered, because in my mind's eye I seen my momma go down on that bridge, fold up and topple over, something I hadn't thought on for nigh on ten years. I stood there blushing scarlet and full of fury and grieving for my dead mother, and then I heard him a-murmuring, "Oh, sweet Jehovah, Oh, sweet Lord, I see you, I see the company of the heavenly host, I see you, my sweet Mary, standing on a cloud with your arms stretched out to me, naked as Eve in the Garden of Eden. Oh, oh, oh, I'm a-looking on the face of the Almighty and a-listening to the song of the angels."

Something broke inside me all at once when I heard him talk that way about Momma. Warn't it enough that she was dead withouten him blasphemously lusting after her departed soul? I dropped the tin of stew, and he saw me and I could see the rage burning in his eyes, and I tried to force myself to obey the fifth commandment, but words just came pouring out of me. "Shame on you, Pa, pounding your cocker for a woman you done gunned down in cold blood. Don't you think I don't remember the way you kilt her, shot her in the back whilst she were crossing that bridge, and the Choctaw watching on t'other side in his top hat and morning dress, with his four slaves behind him, waiting to take her home?"

My pa was silent for a few moments, and the room was filled with the caterwauling of the niggers from the graveyard. We stood there staring each other down. Then he grabbed me by the scruff of the neck and dragged me over to the chair, lurching and stumbling because he hadn't even bothered to pull his britches back up, and I could smell the liquor on him; and he murmured, "You are right, I have sinned; I have sinned, but it is for the son to take on the sins of the world; the paschal lamb; you, Jimmy Lee; oh, God, but you do resemble her, you do remind me of her; oh, it is a heavy burden for you, my son, to take on the sins of the world, but I know that you do it for love," and suchlike, and he reached for the hickory and stripped the shirt off of my back and began to lay to with a will, all the while crying out, "Oh, Mary, oh, my Mary, I am so sorry that you left me . . . oh, my son, you shall bear thirty-nine stripes on your back in memory of our savior . . . oh, you shall redeem me . . ." And the hickory sang and I cried out, not so much from the pain, for that my back was become like leather from long abuse and warn't much feeling left in it. I gritted my teeth and try to bear it like I borne it so many times before, but this time it was not to be borne, and when the thirty-ninth stripe was inflicted, I tore myself loose from the chair and I screamed, "You ain't hurting me no more, because I ain't no paschal lamb and your sins is *your* sins, not mine," and I pushed him aside with all my strength.

"God, God," he says in a whisper, "I see God." And he rolls his eyes heavenward, excepting that heaven were a leaky roof made from a few planks leftover from the slaves' quarters.

Then I took the rifle from the wall and pounded him in the head with the stock, three, four, five, six times until he done slumped onto the straw.

Oh, I was raging and afeared, and I run away right then and

there, without even making sure iffen he was kilt or not. I run right through them darkies, who was a-singing and a-carrying on to wake the very dead; they did not see a scrawny boy, small for his age, slip through them and out toward the woods.

I run and run with three dimes in my pocket and a sheaf of shinplasters that I stole from the chest of drawers; I run and I don't even recollect iffen I put out the fire on the stove.

And that was how I come to be with the regiment, tramping through blood and mud and shitting my bowels away with the flux each day; and that was how I come to be sleeping next to old Joseph, the hoodoo doctor, who become another father to me.

I did not confess to old Joseph or even to myself that I had done my father in. Mayhap he was still alive. I tried not to think on him. My old life was dead. Surely I could not go back to the Jackson place, nor the army, nor any other place from which I run. There was just me and the old nigger now, scavengers, carrion birds, eaters of the dead.

Yes, and sure it was human flesh old Joseph fed me that night, and again that morning. He showed me the manner of taking it, for there was certain corpses that cried out to be let be, whilst others craved to be consumed. We followed the army a safe distance, and when they moved on we took possession of the slain. He could always sniff out where a battle was going to be. He never carried nothing with him excepting a human skull, painted black, that was full of herbs – the same herbs that he always smelled of.

Oh, it was God's country we done passed through – hills, forests, meadows, creeks – and all this beauty marred by the handiwork of men. Old Joseph showed me not to drink from the bloodied streams but to lick the dew from flower petals and cupped leaves of a morning. As his trust of me grew, he became more bold. We went into encampments and sat amongst the soldiers, and they never seen us, not once.

"We is invisible," old Joseph told me.

And then it struck me, for we stood in broad daylight beside a willow tree, and on the other side of the brook was mayhap fifty tents and behind them a dense wood. The air was moist and thick. I could see members of my old company, with their skull faces too small for their gray coats, barely able to lift their bayonets off the ground, and they was sitting there huddled together waiting for gruel, but there I was, nourished by the dead, my flesh starting to fill out and the redness back in my cheek. It struck me that they couldn't see me even though I was a-jumping up and down on the other side of the stream, and I said to old Joseph, "I don't think we are invisible. I think . . . oh, old Joseph, I think we have been dead ever since the day we met."

Old Joseph laughed – it were a dry laugh, like the wind stirring the leaves in autumn – and he said, "You ain't dead yet, honey; feel the flesh on them bones. No, your *beau-père* he nurturing you back to life."

"Then why don't they see us? Even when we walk amongst them?"

"Because I has cast a cloak of darkness about us. We be wearing the face of a dark god over our own."

"I don't trust God. Whenever my pa seen God, he hurt me."

Smiling, he said, "You daddy warn't a true preacher, honey; he just a *boungan macoute*, a man which *use* the name of God to adorn hisself."

And taking my hand, he led me across that branch and we was right amongst the soldiers, and still they did not see me. We helped ourselves to hardtack and coffee right out of the kettle. In the distance I heard the screams of a man whose leg they was fixing to hack off. Around us men lay moaning. There is a sick-sweet body smell that starving men give off when they are burning up their last shreds of flesh to fuel their final days. That's how I knew they was near death. They was shivering with cold, even though it were broad daylight. Lord, many of them was just children, and some still younger than myself. I knew that the war was lost, or soon would be. I had no country, and no father save for a darkie witch doctor from Haiti.

There come a bugle call and a few men looked up, though most of them just goes on laying in their misery. Old Joseph and I saw soldiers come into the camp. They had a passel of niggers with them, niggers in blue uniforms, all chained up in a long row behind a wagon that was piled high with confiscated arms. They was as starved and miserable as our own men. They stared ahead as they trudged out of the wood and into the clearing. There was one or two white men with them two: officers, I reckoned.

A pause, and the bugle sounded again. Then a captain come out of a tent and addressed the captives. He said in a lugubrious voice, as though he were weary of making this announcement:

"According to the orders given me by the congress of the Confederate States of America, all Negroes apprehended while in the uniform of the North are not to be considered prisoners of war, but shall be returned instantly to a condition of slavery or shot. Any white officer arrested while in command of such Negroes shall be considered to be inciting rebellion and also shot." He turned and went back into his tent, and the convoy moved onward, past the camp, upstream, toward another part of the woods.

"*Oba kosó!*" the old man whispered. "They gone kill them."

"Let's go away," I said.

"No," said old Joseph, "I feels the wind of the gods blowing down upon me. I feels the breath of the loa. I is standing on the coils of Koulèv, the earth-serpent. Oh, no, Marse Jimmy Lee. I don't be going nowhere, but you free to come and go as you pleases of course, being white."

"You know that ain't so," I said. "I'm less free than you. And I know if I leave you I will leave the shelter of your invisibility spell." I gazed right into the eyes of the prisoners, and tasted their rancid breath, and smelled the pus of their wounds, and seen no sign of recognition. There was something to his magic, though I was sure it come of the dark places, and not of God.

So I followed him alongside the creek as the captives were led into the wood, followed them uphill aways until we reached the edge of a shallow gully, and there was already niggers there digging to make it deeper, and I seen what was going to happen and I didn't want to look, because this warn't a battle, this were butchery pure and simple.

Our soldiers didn't mock the prisoners and didn't call them no names. They were too tired and too hungry. The blacks and the whites, they didn't show no passion in their faces. They just wanted it to end. Our men done lined the niggers and then officers up all along the edge of the ditch and searched through their pockets for any coins or crumbs, and they turned them so they faced the gully and they done shot them in the back, one by one, until the pit was filled. Then the Southerners turned and filed back to the camp. Oh, God! As the first shots rung out, it put me in mind of my mother Mary, halfway across the bridge, with her old life behind her and her new life ahead of her, dead on her face, and the bloodstain spreading from her back onto the lace and calico.

And old Joseph said, "Honey, I seen what I must do. And it a dark journey that I must take, and maybe you don't be strong enough to come with me. But I hates to journey alone. Old Joseph afraid too, betimes, spite of his 'leventy-leven years upon this earth. I calls the powers to witness, *ni ayé àti ni òrun*."

"What does that mean, old Joseph?"

"*In heaven as it is in earth*."

I saw the way his eye glowed and I was powerful afraid. He had become more than a shrunken old man. Seemed like he drew the sun's light into his face and shone brighter than the summer sky. He set his cauldron-skull down on the ground and said, again and again, "*Koulèv, Koulèv-O! Damballah Wedo, Papa! Koulèv, Koulèv-O! Damballah Wedo, Papa!*"

And then he says, in a raspy voice, "Watch out, Marse Jimmy Lee, the god gone come down and mount my body now . . . stand clear less you wants to be swept away by the breath of the serpent!" And he mutters to hisself, "Oh, *dieux puissants*, why you axing me to make biggest magic, me a old magician without no *poudre* and no herbs? Oh, take this cup from me, take, take this bitter poison from he lips, for old Joseph he don't study life and death no more."

And his old body started to shake, and he ripped off his patch and threw it onto the mud, and I looked into the empty eye socket and saw an inner eye, blood-red and shiny as a ruby. And he sank down on his knees in front of the pit of dead men and he went on a-mumbling and a-rocking, back and forth, back and forth, and seemed like he was a-speaking in tongues. And his good eye rolled right up into its socket.

"Why, old Joseph," I says to him, "what are you fixing to do?"

But he paid me no mind. He just went on a-shimmying and a-shaking, and presently he rose up from where he was and started to dance a curious hopping sort of dance, and with every hop he cried, "*Shangó! Shangó!*" in a voice that was steadily losing its human qualities. And soon his voice was rolling like thunder, and presently it *was* the thunder, for the sky was lowering and lightning was lancing the cloud peaks.

Oh, the sky became dark. The cauldron seethed and glowed, though he hadn't even touched it. I knew he were sure possessed. The dark angels he done told me of, they was speaking to him out of the mouth of hell.

I reckoned I was not long for this world, for the old man was a-hollering at the top of his lungs and we warn't far from the encampment, but no one came looking for us. Mayhap they was huddled in their tents hiding from the thunder. Presently it began to rain; it pelted us and soaked us, that rain. It were a hot rain, scalding to my skin. And when the lightning flashed, I looked into the pit and I thought I saw something moving. Mayhap it were just the rushing waters, throwing the corpses one against t'other. I crept closer to the edge of the gully. I didn't heed old Joseph's warning. I peered over the edge, and in the next flash of lightning I saw them a-writhing and a-shaking their arms and legs, and their necks a-craning this way and that, and I thought to myself, old Joseph he is raising the dead.

Old Joseph just went on screaming out those African words and leaping up and waving his arms. The rain battered my body and I was near fainting from it, for the water flooded my nostrils and drenched my lungs, and when I gasped for air I swallowed more and more water. I don't know how the old man kept on dancing; in the lightning flashes I saw him, dark and lithe, and the sluicing rain made him glisten and made his chest and arms to look like the scales of a great black serpent. I looked on him and breathed in the burning water, and the pit of dead niggers quooked as iffen the very earth were opening up, and there come a blue light from the mass grave, so blinding that I could see no more; and so, at last, I passed out from the terror of it.

When I done opened my eyes, the rain was just a memory: the sun was rising; the forest was silent and shrouded in mist. And I thought to myself, I have been dreaming, and I am still beside the creek where the dead bodies lay, and I never did see no old Joseph out of my past; but then I saw him frying up a bit of salt pork he done salvaged from the camp. Warn't no morning bugle calls, and I reckon the company done up and gone in the middle of the night, soon as the storm subsided.

Old Joseph, the patch over his eye again, was singing to hisself, that song I heard as a child. And when he saw me stir, he said, "Marse Jimmy Lee, you awake now."

"What is that song?" I asked him.

"It called 'Au Claire de la Lune,' honey: 'by the light of the moon.'"

I sat up. "Joseph?"

"What, Marse Jimmy Lee?"

"Last night I had the strangest dream . . . more like a vision. I dreamed you were possessed, and you pranced about and waved your arms and sang songs in a African language, and you raised up nigger soldiers from the grave."

"Life is a dream, honey," he says, "we calls them *les zombis*. It from a Kikongo word, 'nzambi,' that mean a dead man that walk the earth."

The fog began to clear a little and I saw their feet. Black feet, still shackled, still covered with chafing sores. We was surrounded by them. And as the sunlight began to dissipate the mist. I could see their faces; it was them which had been kilt and buried in the pit – I knew some of their faces. For though they stirred, they moved, they looked about them, there were no fire in their eyes, and didn't have no breath in their nostrils. Mayhap they wasn't dead, but they wasn't alive, neither.

They stood there, looming over us. Each one with a wound clean through him. Each one smelling of old Joseph's herbs.

"The magic still in me," old Joseph said, "even without the *coup poudre*."

I reckon I have never been more scared than I was then. My skin was crawling and my blood was racing.

"I never thought that old magic still in me," said Joseph again. There was wonderment in his voice. No fear. The dead men surrounded us, waiting; seemed like they had no mind of their own.

"Oh, Joseph, what are we going to do?"

"Don't know, white child. I's still in the dark. The vision don't come as clear to me no more; old Joseph he old, he old."

He fed me and gave me genuine coffee to drink, for the slain Yankees had carried some with them. I rose and went over to the pit, and it were sure enough empty save for the two white officers. "Why didn't you raise them too?" I said.

"Warn't no sense in it, Marse Jimmy Lee. For white folks there is a heaven and a hell; there ain't no middle ground. Best to forget them."

So we threw dirt over them and we marched on, and the column of undead darkies followed us. I could not name the places that we passed, but old Joseph knew where he was going. It was toward the rising sun, so I guessed it was southeast.

At nightfall we rested. We found a farmhouse. There warn't

no people and the animals was all took away, but I found a ham
a-hanging in the larder, and I feasted. In the night I slept in a
real bed. Old Joseph sat out on the porch. The *zombis* did not
sleep. They stood in a ring outside the house and swayed softly
to the sound of Joseph's singing. As I looked out of the smashed
window I could see them in the moonlight; there was still no fire
in their eyes, and I recollected that they hadn't partaken of no
victuals. What was it like to be a *zombi?* Iffen that the eyes are
the windows of the soul, then surely there warn't no souls inside
those fleshy shells.

We found plenty of gold in the abandoned house; they done
hid it in a well, which was surrounded by dead Yankees. I reckon
they done poisoned it so that the Northerners wouldn't be able
to drink their water. But poison means naught to the dead.

And we walked on, and the passel of walking dead became
a company, for wherever we went we found niggers that had
been kilt, not just the ones in Yankee uniform but sometimes a
woman lying dead in a ditch, or a young buck chained to a tree
that was just abandoned and let starve to death when his masters
fled from the enemy, and one time we found seven high-yaller
children dead in a cage, with gunshot wounds to their heads; for
they was frenzied times, and men were driven to acts not thought
upon in times of peace. It was amongst the dead children that I
found another cornstalk *poupée* like the one old Joseph gave me
ten years before, a-sitting in a vial in the clenched fist of a dead
little girl. After we done wakened them, she held it out to me, and
I thought there were a glimmer in her eye, but mayhap it were only
my imagination.

"Get up and walk," old Joseph said. And they walked.

And I said over and over to him, "Old Joseph, where are we
going?"

And he said, "Towards freedom."

"But freedom is in the north, ain't it?"

"Freedom in the heart, honey."

We marched. For many days we didn't see no white folks at
all. We saw burned hulks of farms and stray dogs hunting in
packs. We passed other great battlefields, and them that was
worth reviving, that still had enough flesh on them to be able
to march, old Joseph raised up. He was growing in power. It got
so he would just wave his hands and say one or two words, and
the dead man would climb right out of the ground. And I took

to repeating the words to myself, soundlessly at first, just moving my lips; then softly, then – for when he were a-concentrating on his magic, he couldn't see nothing of the world – I would shout out those words along with him, I would wrap my tongue around them twisted and barbarian sounds, and I would tell myself, 'twas I which raised them, I which reached into the abyss and drawed them out.

Still we encountered no sign of human life. The summer sun streamed down on us by day, and seemed like I sweat blood. It warn't at all certain to me that we was still alive and on this earth, for the land was a wasteland, spite of the verdant meadows and the mountains blanketed with purple flowers, spite of the rich-smelling earth and the warm rain. Sometimes I think that the country we was wandering in was an illusion, a false Eden. Or that we was somehow half-in, half-out of the world.

Though I didn't know where the road was leading, yet I was happy. I trusted old Joseph, and I didn't have no one else left in the world. The only times I become sad was thinking on my pa and momma's death, and wondering iffen my pa was with God now, for he said he done seen the face of God before I smashed his head. Sometimes I dreamed about coming home to see him well again. But they was only dreams. I knew that I had kilt him.

On the seventh day, we come onc't more into the sight of living men.

The road become wider and we was coming into the vicinity of a town. I knew this was a port, maybe Charleston. There warn't no signs to tell us, but Pa and I had been booted out of Charleston once; I remembered the way the wind smelt, wet and tangy. A few miles outside town, our road joined up with a wider road that come in a straight line from due north. On the other road, straggling down to meet us, we saw a company of graycoats.

Not many of them, maybe three dozen. They warn't exactly marching. Some was leaning on each other, some hobbling, and one, a slip of a boy, tapped on the side of a skinless drum. Their clothes was in tatters and most of them didn't have no rifles. They was just old men and boys, for the able-bodied had long since fallen.

They seen us, and one of them cried out, "Nigger soldiers!" They fell into a pathetic semblance of a formation, and them which had rifles aimed them, and them which had crutches brandished them at us.

I shouted out, "Let us pass . . . we don't have no quarrel with you." For they were wretched creatures, these remnants of the Southern army, and I was sure that the war was already lost and they was coming back to what was left of their homes.

But one boy, mayhap their leader, screamed at me, "Nigger lover! Traitor!" I looked in his eyes and saw we were just alike, poor trash fighting a rich man's war, him and me; and I pitied the deluded soul. Because I knew now that there warn't no justice in this war, and that neither side had foughten for God, but only for hisself.

"It's no use!" I shouted at the boy who was so like myself. "These darkies ain't even alive; they're shadows marching to the sea; they ain't got souls to kill."

And old Joseph said, "March on, my children."

They commenced to fire on us.

This was the terriblest thing which I did witness on that journey. For the nigger soldiers marched and marched, and not a bullet could stop them. The miniés flew and the white boys shrieked out a ghostly echo of a rebel yell, and *les zombis* kept right on coming and coming, and me and old Joseph with them, untouched by the bullets, for his magic still shielded our mortal flesh. The niggers marched. Their faces was ripped asunder and still they marched. Their brains came oozing from their skulls, their guts came writhing from their bellies, and still they marched. They marched until they were too close for bullets. Then the white boys flung themselves at us, and they was ripped to pieces. They was tore limb from limb by dead men which stared with glazed and vacant eyes. It took but a few minutes, this final skirmish of the war. Their yells died in their throats. The *zombis* broke their necks and flung them to the ground. Their strength warn't a human kind of strength. They'd shove their hands into an old man's belly and snap his spine and pull out the intestines like a coil of rope. They'd take a rifle and break the barrel in two.

There was no anger in what the *zombis* done. And they didn't make no noise whilst they was killing. They done it the way you might darn a sock or feed the chickens; it were just something which had to be done.

And we marched onward, leaving the bodies to rot; it was getting on toward sunset now.

Oh, I was angry. The boys we kilt warn't no strangers from the North; they could have been my brothers. Oh, I screamed in rage at old Joseph. I didn't trust him no more; the happiness had left me.

"Did you hear what he called me?" I shouted. "A traitor to my people. A nigger lover. And it's God's plain truth. If you wanted freedom, why didn't you go north into the arms of the Yankees? You spoke to me of a big magic, and of the coils of the serpent Koulèv, and the wind of the gods, and the voices of darker angels . . . to what end? It were Satan's magic, magic to give the dead an illusion of life, so you could kill more of my people!"

"Be still," he said to me, as the church spires of the port town rose up in the distance. "Your war don't be my war. You think the Yankees got theyselfs kilt to set old Joseph free? You think the 'mancipation proclamation was wrote to give the nigger back he soul? I say to you, white child, that a piece of paper don't make men free. The black man in this land he ain't gone be free tomorrow nor in a hundred years nor in a thousand. I didn't bring men back from the outer darkness so they could shine you shoes and wipe you butts. The army I lead, he kingdom don't be of this earth."

"You are mad, old Joseph," I said, and I wept, for he was no longer a father to me.

We marched into the town. Children peered from behind empty beer kegs with solemn eyes. Horses reared up and whinnied. Women stared sullenly at us. The Yankees had already took the town; half the houses was smoldering, and we didn't see no grown men. The stars and stripes flew over the ruint courthouse. I reckon folks thought we was just another company of the conquering army.

We reached the harbor. There was one or two sailing ships docked there: rickety ships with tattered sails. The army of dead men stood at attention and old Joseph said to me: "Now I understands why you come with me so far. There a higher purpose to everything, *ni ayé àti ni òrun.*"

I didn't want to stay with him anymore. When I seen the way *les zombis* plowed down my countrymen, I had been moved to a powerful rage, and the rage would not die away. "What higher purpose?" I said. And the salt wind chafed my lips.

"You think," said old Joseph, "that old Joseph done tricked

you, he done magicked you with mirrors and smoke; but I never told you we was fighting on the same side. But we come far together, and I wants you to do me one last favor afore we parts for all eternity."

"And what sort of favor would that be, old sorcerer? I thought you could do anything."

"Anything. But not this thing. You see, old Joseph a nigger. Nigger he can't go into no portside bar to offer gold for to buy him a ship."

"You want a ship now? Where are you fixing to go? Back to Haiti, where the white man rules no more?"

Old Joseph said, "Mayhap it a kind of Haiti where we go." He laughed. "Haiti, yes, Haiti! And I gone see my dear *mamman*, though she be cold in her grave sixty year past. Or mayhap it mother Africa herself we go to. *Oba kosó!*"

And I remembered that he had told me: *My kingdom is not of this earth.* He had used the words of our savior and our Lord. Oh, the ocean wind were warm, and it howled, and the torn sails clattered against the masts. The air fair dripped with moisture. And the niggers stood like statues, all-unseeing.

"I'll do as you ask," I said, and I took the sack of gold we had gathered from the poisoned well, and I walked along the harbor until I found a bar and ship's captain for hire, which was not hard, for the embargo had starved their business. And presently I come back and told old Joseph everything was ready. And the niggers lined up, ready to embark. Night was falling.

But as they prepared themselves to board that ship, I could hold my tongue no more. "Old Joseph," I said, "your kingdom is founded on a lie. You have waked these bodies from the earth, but where are their souls? You may dream of leading these creatures to a mystic land acrosst the sea, and you may dream of freeing them forever from the bonds of servitude, but how can you free what can't be freed? How can you free a rock, a tree, a piece of earth? Dust they were and dust they ever shall be, world without end."

And the *zombi* warriors stood, unmoving and unblinking, and not a breath passed their lips, though that the wind was rising and whipping at our faces.

And old Joseph looked at me long and hard, and I knew that I had said the thing that must be said. He whispered, "Out of the mouths of babes and sucklings hast thou ordained strength, O Lord." He fell down on his knees before me and said, "And all this time I thought that *I* the wise one and you the student! Oh, Marse Jimmy Lee, you done spoke right. There be no life in *les zombis* because I daresn't pay the final price. But now I's *gone* make that sacrifice. Onc't I done gave my eye in exchange for knowledge. But there be *two* trees in Eden, Marse Jimmy Lee; there be the tree of knowledge, and there be the tree of life."

So saying he covered his face with his hands. He plunged his thumb into the socket of his good eye and he plucked it out, screaming to almighty God with the pain of it. His agony was real. His shrieking curdled my blood. It brought back my pa's chastisements and my momma's dying and the tramping of my bare feet on sharp stones and the sight of all my comrades, pierced through by bayonets, cloven by cannon, their limbs ripped off, their bellies torn asunder, their lives gushing hot and young and crimson into the stream. Oh, but II craved to carry his pain, but he were the one that were chosen to bear it, and I was the one which brung him to the understanding of it.

And now his eye were in his hand, a round, white, glistening pearl, and he cries out in a thunderous voice, "If thine eye offend thee, pluck it out!" and he takes blind aim and hurls the eye with all his might into the mighty sea.

I clenched the *poupée* in my hand.

Then came lightning, for old Joseph had summoned the power of the serpent Koulèv, whose coils were entwined about the earth. Then did he unleash the rain. Then did he turn to me, with the gore gushing from the yawning socket, and cry to me, a good-for-nothing white trash boy which kilt his own father and stole from the dead, "Thou hast redeemed me."

Then, and only then, did I see the *zombis* smile. Then, as the rain softened, as the sky did glow with a cold blue light that didn't come from no sun nor moon, then did I hear the laughter of the dead, and the fire of life begin to flicker in their eyes. But they was already trooping up the gangplank, and presently there was only the old man, purblind now and like to die. I thought.

"Farewell," he says to me.

And I said, "No, old Joseph. You are blind now. You need a boy to hold your hand and guide you, to be your eyes against the wild blue sea."

"Not blind," he said. "I *chooses* not to see. I gone evermore be looking inward, at the glory and the majesty of eternal light."

"But what have I? Where can I go, excepting that I go with you?"

"Honey, you has lived but fourteen of your threescore and ten. It don't be written that you's to follow a old man acrosst the sea to a land that maybe don't even *be* a land save in that old man's dream. Go now. But first you gone kiss your *beau-père* goodbye, for I loves you."

My tears were brine and his were blood. As I kissed his cheek, the salt did run together with the crimson. I saw him no more; I did not see the ship sail from the port, for my eyes was blinded with weeping.

So I walked and walked until I come back to the Jackson place. The mansion were a cinder, and even the fields was all burnt up, and the animals was dead. The place was looted good and thorough; warn't one thing of value in the vicinity, not a gold piece nor a silver spoon nor even the rugs that the Jacksons done bought from a French merchant.

I walked up the low knoll to where the nigger graveyard was and where our shack onc't stood. The wooden markers was all charred, and here and there was a shred of homespun clinging to them. I thought to myself, mayhap the Yankees come down to the Jackson place not an hour after I done run away, whilst the slaves was still a-singing their spirituals. That cloth was surely torn off some of the slave women, for the Yankees loved to have their way with darkies. And I thought, mayhap my pa is still laying inside that shack, in the inner room, beside the locket with Mamma's picture, with his hickory in his fist, with his britches down about his ankles.

And so it was I found him.

He warn't rank no more. It had been many months since I run off. Warn't much left of his face that the worms hadn't ate. At his naked loins, the bone poked through the papery hide, and there was a swarm of ants. It was a miracle there was this much left of him, for there was wild dogs roaming the fields.

I set down the *poupée* on the chair and got to wondering what I should do. What I wanted most in life were a new beginning. I spoke to that doll, for I knew that old Joseph's spirit was in it somehow, and I said, "I don't know where you come from, and I don't know where you are. But oh, give me the strength to begin onc't more. Oh, carry me back from the land of the dead."

Without thinking, I started to murmur the words of power, the African words I done mimicked when I watched him raise the dead. I knelt down beside the corpse of my pa and waited for the breath of the serpent. I whispered them words over and over until my mind emptied itself and was filled with the souls of darker angels.

I reckon I knelt all night long, or mayhap many nights. But when I opened my eyes again, there was flesh on my father's bones, and he was beginning to rouse himself; and his eyes had the fire of life, for that old Joseph had sacrificed his second eye.

"You sure have growed, son," he says softly. "You ain't a sapling no more; you're a mighty tree."

"Yes, Pa," says I.

"Oh, son, you have carried me back from a terrible dream. In that dream I abandoned you, and I practiced all manner of cruelty upon you, and a dark angel came to you and became your new pa; and you followed him to the edge of the river that divides the quick from the dead."

"Yes, Pa. But I stopped at the riverbank and watched him sail away. And I come back to you."

"Oh, Jimmy Lee, my son. I have seen hell. I have been down into the fire of damnation, and I've felt the loneliness of perdition. And the cruelest torture was being cut off from you, my flesh and blood. Oh, sweet Jesus, Jimmy Lee, it were only that you made me think on her so much – she which I killed, she which I never loved more even as I sent the bullet flying into her back."

And this was strange, for in the old days my pa had only spoke of heaven, and of seeing the face of God, and when he done seen God he would wear me out, calling on His holy name to witness his infamy and my sacrifice. But now he had seen hell and he was full of gentleness.

And then he said to me, "My son, I craves your forgiveness."

"Ain't nothing to forgive."

"Then give me your love," says he, "for you are tall and strong, and I have become old. And it is now for you to be the father , and I the child."

It were time to cross the bridge. It were time to heal the hurting.

"My love you have always had, Pa."

So saying, I embraced him; and thus it was our war came to an end.

KATHE KOJA &
BARRY N. MALZBERG

The Timbrel Sound
of Darkness

BARRY N. MALZBERG was one of the most controversial science fiction writers and critics of the 1970s and he is the author of more than three hundred short stories and over ninety novels. A winner of the John W. Campbell Memorial Award, he has also been a finalist for both the Hugo and Nebula Awards.

The author's many books include *Beyond Apollo*, *The Falling Astronauts*, *Revelations*, *The Remaking of Sigmund Freud*, *The Destruction of the Temple*, the movie novelization *Phase IV*, and a volume of critical essays, *The Engines of the Night*. His short fiction has recently been included in *Alien Pregnant by Elvis*, *Journeys to the Twilight Zone*, and Dennis Etchison's anthologies *MetaHorror* and *Masters of Darkness II*, while his collaborations with Kathe Koja have appeared in *Christmas Ghosts*, *Temporary Walls* and *Dark Voices 6*.

O N NOVEMBER 15, 1900, one week before his death, Sir Arthur Sullivan is visited for the second and last time by the specter who had made these last years so lively for him in retrospect. The first visit came just after *Ivanhoe* had opened in 1893 and the news had been astonishingly grim. "Your grand opera will fail," the specter had said, through a smile which was in no way seemly. "Your grand opera will run two hundred performances and bankrupt Rupert D'Oyly Carte and will never be performed again in this country in this century. It will fail as well in Berlin. It will not be taken up in America. It will be heard of no more. Your fate is to be remembered as the composer of the operettas. Your name and Gilbert's will be linked through all of the decades; you will be famous and your tunes subject for laughter while your cantatas and oratorios and symphony collapse into the dust. This is the true and ageless verdict of history and of all forthcoming prophecy." How distressed Sullivan had been! This cruel and ungiving news, delivered by a shapeless creature who claimed to be the ghost of the killer in Whitechapel, the notorious Mystery Jack himself, had driven Sullivan into a stupor of rage and futility which had not abated in these intervening years even though (or perhaps because) the prediction of the specter more and more seemed to have some basis in fact. The *Golden Legend* sunk, *The Martyr of Antioch* exhumed for the Leeds Festival only because Sullivan had insisted upon conducting it. The disaster of *Ivanhoe* in Berlin. Even the last two operettas with the wretched Gilbert toward which he had been driven only for the cold pounds, and make no mistake of it, had been failures, *Utopia Limited* lasting for only half a year and emptying out at the end (like a slopjar, like a dregged glass), *The Grand Duke* a disastrous one hundred twenty-three performances for the most venomous responses of his career, worse than anything even for the ill-fated *Ivanhoe*. Oh, he was glad to have been out of it then, but the words of the specter had stayed with him for all these years and there was – despite the momentary reassurances, the false gilt of his own devisings – no release, no release. Now in his rooms in London, arched numb against the bedclothes, feeling the true seediness and devastation of his fifty-eight years and welded to the conviction that his health had collapsed, Sullivan stared at the specter with loathing and attention, the fine features of the ghost hazy and uncertain in the weary off-light of the dawn. He had given up disbelief a long time ago. The night was filled with portents and now all of his friends were dying. Like Sir Ruthven Murgatroyd, descended from the painting on the wall in the second act of *Ruddigore*, the specter seemed very sure of himself, raised a hand in graceful and indolent greeting.

"And is it as I predicted?" the ghost asked, with the smile of one who is sure of his answer. "Have you any reason now to doubt what I have said?"

Sullivan looked at the anima, then away, toward the streaks of light. In Whitechapel, prostitutes had been found with their features grazed, then eviscerated; in a dingy room for copulation a prostitute, once as dingy, had been found dismembered in ways so intricate and horrifying that the police would release no details. But nothing done, no violence, no ravages perpetrated on those prostitutes could have been as thorough as what this specter had done to Sullivan's psyche. "Why?" he said, feeling like the hapless Murgatroyd descendant, "why do you haunt me so?"

"Nothing else to be done," the specter said. "Fills in the time, you have no idea whatsoever – but you will, you will – of how eternal eternity can be and I was, I am a man of action after all. Your reputation," and what a twist to the word, must the ghost utilize that particular tone, "is quite secure, you know you will last through the next century, your works will be played everywhere but will be particularly popular in England and America. Your works with Gilbert, that is to say. The rest of them – well, there's no need to review that depressing business again, is there?"

"William Shwenk Gilbert is a swine," Sullivan said with what be felt to be a pure dispassion. He pulled the bedclothes toward him, feeling their warmth, their sheer corporeality; surely he was not dreaming this. "He is a cheap hack and a synonym for dishonor. He would have turned me into an accompanist, an organ grinder for his monkey rhymes, had I not forced him to be otherwise. And what would you have of that?"

"Very little," the specter said. "Oh, *The Lost Chord* will survive and *Onward Christian Soldiers* . . . but they will survive to be mocked, as examples of art gone bad. The *Overture di Ballo* will be played now and then as well. But that's pretty much the certainty of it, Arthur. I wish I could give you better news, I know how ambitious and serious you are, but there's no way I can manipulate the truth. You have advanced kidney failure and your heart – surely you can feel it – is in perilous condition; the extreme hydration has put terrible untoward pressure on the organ. I understand these things, you see, it is part of my insight. All part of the job." The light through his features paler than gaslight, was it light he carried or only the treacherous dawn? "It won't be much longer for you, I am sorry to say, but I won't tell you the exact date or time of your death. That would be, I think – and I think you agree? – much too cruel."

Sullivan feels the arch of his mortality, a cold descending triad, then feels the hammer of that betraying heart as if it were the dead march in *Yeoman of the Guard*. "Oh, it is too cruel," he says, "too, too cruel for you to come and berate me so, to confront me with omens of my impermanence and folly. You, too, are a man, were a man, are you not? I would not do the same to you if our positions were reversed." Killer of prostitutes, he thinks, torturer of women, creature of apostasy and terror in the night, in a hundred nights and a thousand, man of legend free to create his own. What, is this my penance for deferring to Carte's demands, Gilbert's slimy mockery, my own helpless lust for a good tune, and the easy response of fools? I could not have done it so, he thinks. "Begone," Sullivan says, as had Murgatroyd in the second act of *Ruddigore*. "Begone, specter, I will speak with you no more." The hoots of Jack's amusement fill Sullivan's hot and crowded bedroom and he feels a thin and desperate clutching in his throat, some prescience or prestidigitation of doom as the light shifts within the room and he falls back against the sheets, stunned and exhausted, astonished by the force of his grief. He could not have thought of himself as such a simple and vulnerable man.

But there are vulnerabilities and vulnerabilities, simplicities masquerading as cunning complexities as Jack, Mystery Jack, Springheeled Jack himself must masquerade: through dark and light: as toff, as workingman, as doctor, as empty-eyed and smiling drunk: simple as a couplet of Gilbert's base doggerel, come with his hands out to the prostitute herself as simple and base, smiling in the soot and blackness of the alleyways, smiling as he palped and fingered the breast, the belly, her hot and dirty dress rucked up and bare beneath and mumbling about the money first, sir all the gentlemen must pay first, but for what he seeks no payment is sufficient, no coin can be tendered or accepted; it is a gift, after all, freely given: it is legend in the making; it is art. Imagining him now – as Sullivan lies sleepless in the fretful and unforgiving light imagining his glide through streets made empty by the rumor of his passing, the surety and elegance of that passing, the shocking shape of the kidney in the box, *kidne*, he had spelled it, a deliberate joke, anything for a laugh. Give the people what they ask for: who in fact, is subsidizing this performance? The police? The newspapers, panting yellow journalists chasing his exploits with ignorant fervor, keeping score with the dead bodies of women? To whom does he answer, Jack with his mystery and his smiling knife, to whom must he account? *Has he no partner, no collaborator?* No? – in the huffing dawn, light upon light and the thin wheeze of Sullivan's lungs like the sound of failure itself, no, there is only Jack to come before him, Sullivan in his tormented bed, to bring the news of defeats and disasters and to smile like a gentleman as he does.

Lying with Fanny Ronalds in the rut of the night, attempting to express himself to her as he never has, even in silhouette, been able to open to the common herd, Sullivan in 1884 has a vivid intimation of what Gilbert's death will be like: seventy-five years old in 1911, he will be lying indolently by the lake on his estate, the cries of a woman visitor, some inconsequential friend of Nancy McIntosh in from London will take herself to be in trouble in the water and Gilbert, always a fool and helpless to the distressed sounds of women, will toss aside the newspaper, rush bumbling to the lake and attempt to rescue the young woman, a large and resolute bulk who floundered like a freighter atop the waters, protesting. At that moment Gilbert's heart would give out, Gilbert would feel the empty and suddenly unmotivated coursing of the blood and then Gilbert's ears would fill with the dull and doglike sounds of a man in real distress: that man himself. Terrified all his life by drowning, seized by images and intimations of drowning, Gilbert at last would come to pay to fate what he had so maliciously and gleefully extracted over the decades.

Fanny in his arms, crushed against him in her own swim and pallor, Sullivan refracts the panting and desperate noises of Gilbert's breath with a roaring and coursing of his own, the sound must be so distressing in this isolate bedroom at an inn in Shepperton that Fanny clutches him and cries, "Arthur, Arthur, are you all right?" He does not know if he is all right. Truly, he can make no sense of it. *I have a song to sing-o*. The waters rush in and out of his brain, he is *sunk*, excavated, drowning, and as he clutches Fanny in the desperate baggage of his own grip he hears the Executioner's lament in *Mikado*, someday a victim must be found and that villain is Shwenk. No, it is Seymour, Arthur Seymour Sullivan. He chokes, trying to drag himself to the surface through the force of his grasp of Fanny. She groans with pain and as Sullivan rises Gilbert sinks into the stinking lake, his emergent, flatulent corpse as helpless and desolate as any Whitechapel victim, riven with bubbles and dust, sea-creatures and foam, and try as he may in that flickering recession of vision, Arthur Sullivan cannot see himself amongst the mourners.

Sullivan conducts *The Martyr of Antioch* in London. The chorus tosses him flowers, Sterndale Bennet pays him compliments, after the performance Parry and Stanford, their virginal faces dolorous with envy pay their abashed regards. Surely his music is of consequence, such triumphs cannot have been contrived — as was perhaps *The Tempest* or *In Memoriam* — upon youth and access, the oratorio is one which Mendelssohn himself would have signed. Over and again Sullivan is assured of this in the haze and glow of the performance and yet somehow he cannot bring himself to sufficient conviction; in the night wind, howling, he hears not benediction but hysterical, harsh laughter. D'Oyly Carte tells him that he is behind on his commitment; what will fill the theatre if *Patience* does not come in? At the reception which should have made his brilliance heat and light for the night wind within, Sullivan finds himself unable to take any comfort whatsoever. Gilbert sends him a polite note the next day congratulating him upon the triumph yet reminding him, like the tolling of a mourning bell made of lead, that rehearsals soon enough must begin. Sullivan stares at the note for a long time, the sound of his brother Fred's voice in *Cox and Box* resonating through the room. Poor Fred, more than a decade passed and never, never to come again. Rataplan, rataplan.

"You see," the specter from Whitechapel says to Sullivan most reasonably, "trying to replicate or relive your life will, in fact, change nothing. All of the choices have been made, they are as irreversible and remorseless as that skein of rope with which I dragged poor Dolly over the edge to her doom. Besides," the specter continues, "it is not a bad fate. It is not nearly the worst fate you could have," with the silent laugh of one to whom fate is a commodity to be delivered, not an appointment to be kept. "Your work will, after all, be remembered after a fashion and who is to contend with the judgment of history? Certainly not those abominable women of the night with whom no man of decency would ever consort, am I right?" Sullivan nods solemnly. The wretchedness from his kidneys and bowels, that new wretchedness which seems to foreshadow his eventual oblivion has coursed through him with the speed of utter conviction. Now and at the end of this, his eyes are fully open to his awful situation. "I mistreated no one," Sullivan says, "I wrote honestly. I missed no effective deadline, not even with *The Grand Duke*. I always produced. Did I want too much? Were my ambitions so unreasonable?"

"You mistreated Fanny," the specter says, as sternly as befits a man who has known and plumbed the secrets of women, who has flexed and griped like a raptor through darkness to ultimate light. "You led her along and gave her only what she needed to continue to bed with you. You lied to other women of affections you could not feel; you never completed your Second Symphony or another major orchestral work; you throttled the Leeds festival when you felt threatened by younger and better composers. Your sins were not great, no," in the musing judgment of a true sinner, a liar, a killer, a spreader of chaos and blood and truly in the face of such disorder, Sullivan thought, his own sins were as nought, depressing as it might be to have them listed this way, "not great but they were recognizable. Gilbert will live only through your music; your music will live only through Gilbert's doggerel. Could one conceive a more fitting fate for either of you, gentlemen of such persuasion and fixity? Come now," the ghost says, "consider the alternatives. You could be one of those women, boxed gizzard, floating intestines, perfect and sacrificial teeth glinting at the horrified constable. Instead, you are going to die in your own bed and make a good job of it, too. You should have no real objection to your fate."

Sullivan does not know what to say to this. Truly, there is nothing to say, he has indeed, as the ghost, as Fanny, as D'Oyly Carte, as Sterndale Bennet had told him, made of his fate what it should be. Victoria had predicted major work from him, had persuaded him to attempt *Ivanhoe*, then had not even had the kindness to attend any of the performances of the opera. There was more to this certainly than simple sloth and indolence. "No more," he says, "I know my health is not good; I can feel that decline within me. I must rest, I must rest. I tried in life to give no hurt, if I failed it was not from an excess of passion but its deficit, that is all."

Silent in light the ghost regards him; in silence he regards the ghost, smelling in the heat and disorder of the bedroom another smell unpresent, a smell hotter still and not of death; but only the moment that precedes it. And in that moment, itself composed of light, it is again as if he rides in the spectator's seat, with helplessly opened eyes to see the Whitechapel streets, the rowdy shine of the taverns emptying into the larger darknesses: the sallow defeated drunkenness of the prostitute, in her ears one of the tavern songs, on her lips the base quartet of its refrain and: his hand, her breast: his smile, her stare: his motion, her transfixion – like the stare that greets the true emergence of art, the eyes that see clearly, the ears spoiled now and forever for the cheap grind of tavern songs, popular tunes no longer able to enter these ears now ringing to the muffled song of screams: and ripped skirts and spooling guts and that faint whicker of breath as the busy hands stay busy and the night becomes one music in this last and greatest collaboration: she is music and its consummation, it is her song which will live forever: and he her conductor, her accompanist, her instrument as well: and Sullivan behind those eyes sees everything, everything, with the immediacy with which he viewed the death of Gilbert but none of the attending bitterness or satisfaction.

Watching the specter emerge from its portrait, Sullivan had had a sudden, flickering apprehension of his father, the bandmaster, and the professors at the Leipzig Institute, a solemn and portentous bunch like his father, all of them clustered toward him, filled with ideas of what should be done, of what constituted form. He had given them a symphony, then the music for *The Tempest* in response to their urgings and what had he gotten in return? An easy success which went nowhere, then after the travels with Grove, the triumph of the recovered Schubert manuscripts, they had gotten him *Cox and Box* and later *Trial by Jury* and the rest and the – well, then what? What had he become, what had Gilbert been? Dealers in magic and spells and blessings and curses and all kinds of verses, they had lived so that Gilbert – Sullivan had seen with such perfect clarity – would drown and he now would be taunted by the perceived ghost of a madman in Whitechapel who had carved out the bowels of prostitutes in the effort, the solemn and serious effort to produce the light of the world. No less than Sullivan himself, Jack had sought the Light of the World.

Sullivan lay back on the bed, sensing with a sudden and terrible apprehension, the full circularity of his life. So be it then, he said though not aloud. Worthless lover, despoiler of women (but never their eviscerator!), sacker and pillager of his own talent, he lay on the bed, facing the taunting mask of the specter, and said in reply nothing at all, passing at last into some apprehension of a future which neither included nor excluded but simply accommodated him: as Jack was accommodated: as the women in their bloody silence and defeat were accommodated, and preserved.

A week later, Jack, the ghost of past and future as well, came with enormous and clever hands in the early dawn. "Not my kidneys, not that now but my heart!" Sullivan screamed desperately and banged the bell beside him with the heel of his hand, banged and banged the bell, but when his nephew came he could see it was already too late; the dead face of the composer arched against the escaping hands of the assassin seeking the Light of the World, trying to find the Lost Chord while the dusty, unheard choirs urged him indolently to his destiny.

THOMAS LIGOTTI

The Tsalal

THOMAS LIGOTTI has been described as "the most startling and unexpected discovery since Clive Barker", and his distinctive fiction has appeared in such anthologies as *The Best Horror from Fantasy Tales, Prime Evil, Fine Frights, A Whisper of Blood, The Dedalus Book of Femmes Fatales, The Year's Best Fantasy and Horror* and each of the previous volumes of *The Best New Horror.*

His stories have been collected in *Songs of a Dead Dreamer, Grimscribe: His Lives and Works* and, more recently, *Noctuary* from Robinson/Carroll & Graf, and *The Agonizing Resurrection of Victor Frankenstein and Others* published by Silver Salamander Press.

" 'The Tsalal' is just another instance demonstrating my fondness for really crummy small towns," reveals the author. "I'd love to see a photography book devoted to these wonderfully dispirited places that run the length of the United States."

We doubt that any photographer could capture the bizarre nature of Moxton and its strange inhabitants as well as Ligotti does with the following novella . . .

1 Moxton's leavetaking

None of them could say how it was they had returned to the skeleton town. Some had reached the central cross streets, where a single traffic light, long dead, hung down like a dark lantern. There they paused and stood dumbstruck, scarecrows standing out of place, their clothes lying loose and worn about scrawny bodies. Others slowly joined them, drifting in from the outskirts or disembarking from vehicles weighted down with transportable possessions. Then all of them gathered silently together on that vast, gray afternoon.

They seemed too exhausted to speak and for some time appeared not to recognize their location among the surrounding forms and spaces. Their eyes were fixed with an insomniac's stare, the stigma of both monumental fatigue and painful attentiveness to everything in sight. Their faces were narrow and ashen, a few specks mingling with the dusty surface of that day and seeking to hide themselves within its pale hours. Opposing them was the place they had abandoned and to which they had somehow returned. Only one had not gone with them. He had stayed in the skeleton town, and now they had come back to it, though none of them could say how or why this had happened.

A tall, bearded man who wore a flat-brimmed hat looked up at the sky. Within the clouds was a great seeping darkness, the overflow of the coming night and of a blackness no one had ever seen. After a moment the man said, "It will be dark soon." His words were almost whispered and the effort of speaking appeared to take the last of his strength. But it was not simply a depleted vigor that kept him and the others from turning about and making a second exodus from the town.

No one could say how far they had gone before they reversed their course and turned back toward the place which they believed themselves to have abandoned forever. They could not remember what juncture or dead end they had reached that aborted the evacuation. Part of that day was lost to them, certain images and experiences hidden away. They could feel these things closeted somewhere in their minds, even if they could not call them to memory. They were sure they had seen something they should not remember. And so no one suggested that they set out again on the road that would take them from the town. Yet they could not accept staying in that place.

A paralysis had seized them, that state of soul known to those who dwell on the highest plane of madness, aristocrats of insanity whose nightmares confront them on either side of sleep. Soon enough the wrenching effect of this psychic immobility became far less tolerable than the prospect of simply giving up and staying in the town. Such was the case with at least one of these cataleptic puppets, a sticklike woman who said, "We have no choice. He has stayed in *his* house." Then another voice among them shouted, "He has stayed too long."

A sudden wind moved through the streets, flapping the garments of the weary homecomers and swinging the traffic light that hung over their heads. For a moment all the signals lit up in every direction, disturbing the deep gray twilight. The colors drenched the bricks of buildings and reflected in windows with a strange intensity. Then the traffic light was dark once more, its fit of transformation done.

The man wearing a flat-brimmed hat spoke again, straining his whispery voice. "We must meet together after we have rested."

As the crowd of thin bodies sluggishly dispersed there was almost nothing spoken among them. An old woman shuffling along the sidewalk did not address anyone in particular when she said, "Blessed is the seed that is planted forever in darkness."

Someone who had heard these words looked at the old woman and asked, "Missus, what did you say?" But the old woman appeared genuinely confused to learn she had said anything at all.

2 The one who stayed behind

In the house where a man named Ray Starns and a succession of others before him once resided, Andrew Maness ascended the stairway leading to the uppermost floor, and there entered a small room that he had converted to a study and a chamber of meditation. The window in this room looked out over the rooftops in the neighborhood to offer a fair view of Moxton's main street. He watched as everyone abandoned the town, and he watched them when they returned. Now far into the night, he was still watching after they had all retreated to their homes. And every one of these homes was brightly illuminated throughout the night, while Main Street was in darkness. Even the traffic light was extinguished.

He looked away from the window and fixed his eyes on a large book that lay open on his desk a few steps across the room. The pages of the book were brown and brittle as fallen leaves. "Your wild words were true," he said to the book. "My friends did not go far before they were sent trudging back. You know what made them come home, but I can only guess. So many things you have devoutly embellished, yet you offer nothing on this point. As you say, 'The last vision dies with him who beholds it. Blessed is the seed that is planted forever in darkness.' But the seed that has been planted still grows."

Andrew Maness closed the book. Written in dark ink upon its cover was the word TSALAL.

3 The power of a place

Before long everyone in Moxton had shut themselves in their houses, and the streets at the center of town were deserted. A few streetlights shone on the dull facades of buildings: small shops, a modest restaurant, a church of indefinite denomination, and even a movie theater, which no one had patronized for some weeks. Surrounding this area were clusters of houses that in the usual manner collect about the periphery of skeleton towns. These were structures of serene desolation that had settled into the orbit of a dead star. They were simple pinewood coffins, full of stillness, leaning upright against a silent sky. Yet it was this silence that allowed sounds from a fantastic distance to be carried into it. And the stillness of these houses and their narrow streets led the eye to places astonishingly remote. There were even moments when the entire veil of desolate serenity began to tremble with the tumbling colors of chaos.

Everything seems so unusual in the plainness of these neighborhoods that clutter the margins of a skeleton town. Often no mention is made of the peculiar virtues of such places by their residents. Even so, there may be a house that does not stand *along* one of those narrow streets but at its *end*. This house may even be somewhat different from the others in the neighborhood. Possibly it is taller than the other houses or displays a weathervane that spins in the wind of storms. Perhaps its sole distinguishing quality is that it has been long unoccupied, making it available as an empty vessel in which much of that magical desolation of narrow streets and coffin-shaped houses comes to settle and distill like an essence of the old alchemists. It seems part of a design – some great inevitability – that this house should exist among the other houses that clutch at the edges of a skeleton town. And the sense of this vast, all-encompassing design in fact arises within the spindly residents of the area when one day, unexpectedly, there arrives a red-headed man with the key to this particular house.

4 Memories of a Moxton childhood

Andrew Maness closed the book named TSALAL. His eyes then looked around the room, which had not seemed so small to him in the days when he and his father occupied the house, days too long ago for anyone else to recall with clarity. He alone was able to review those times with a sure memory, and he summoned the image of a small bed in the far corner of the room.

As a child he would lie awake deep into the night, his eyes wandering about the moonlit room that seemed so great to his doll-like self. How the shadows enlarged that room, opening certain sections of it to the black abyss beyond the house and beyond the blackness of night, reaching into a blackness no one had ever seen. During these moments things seemed to be changing all around him, and it felt as if he had something to do with this changing. The shadows on the pale walls began to curl about like smoke, creating a swirling murkiness that at times approached sensible shapes – the imperfect zoology of cloud-forms – but soon drifted into hazy nonsense. Smoky shadows gathered everywhere in the room.

It appeared to him that he could see what was making these shadows which moved so slowly and smoothly. He could see that simple objects around him were changing their shapes and making strange shadows. In the moonlight he could see the candle in its tarnished holder resting on the bedstand. The candle had burned quite low when he blew out its flame hours before. Now it was shooting upwards like a flower growing too fast, and it sprouted outward with tallowy vines and blossoms, waxy wings and limbs, pale hands with wriggling fingers and other parts he could not name. When he looked across the room he saw that something was moving back and forth upon the windowsill with a staggered motion. This was a wooden soldier which suddenly stretched out the claws of a crab and began clicking them against the windowpanes. Other things that he could barely see were also changing in the room; he saw shadows twisting about in strange ways. Everything was changing, and he knew that he was doing something to make things change. But this time he could not stop the changes. It seemed the end of everything, the infernal apocalypse . . .

Only when he felt his father shaking him did he become aware that he had been screaming. Soon he grew quiet. The candle on his bedstand now burned brightly and was not as it had been a few moments before. He quickly surveyed the room to verify that nothing else remained changed. The wooden soldier was lying on the floor, and its two arms were fixed by its sides.

He looked at his father, who was sitting on the bed and still had on the same dark clothes he had worn when he held church services earlier that day. Sometimes he would see his father asleep in one of the chairs in the parlor or nodding at his desk where he was working on his next sermon. But he had never known his father to sleep during the night.

The Reverend Maness spoke his son's name, and the younger Andrew Maness focused on his father's narrow face, recognizing the crown of white hair, which yet retained a hint of red, and the oval-shaped spectacles reflecting the candle flame. The old man whispered to the boy, as if they were not alone in the house or were engaged in some conspiracy.

"Has it happened again, Andrew?" he asked.

"I did not want to make it happen," Andrew protested. "I was not by myself."

The Reverend Maness held up an open hand of silence and understanding. The glare of the candlelight on his spectacles concealed his eyes, which now turned toward the window beside his sons's bed. "The mystery of lawlessness doth already work," he said.

"The Epistles," Andrew swiftly responded, as if the quote had been a question.

"Can you finish the passage?"

"Yes, I think I can," answered Andrew, who then assumed a solemn voice and recited: "Now there is one that restraineth, until he be taken out of the way; and then shall be revealed the lawless one, whom the Lord will slay and bring to nought."

"You know it well, that book."

"The Holy Bible," said Andrew, for it sounded strange to him not to name the book in the proper way.

"Yes, the Holy Bible. You should know its words better than you know anything else on earth. You should always have its words in mind like a magical formula."

"I do, Father. You have always told me that I should."

The Reverend Maness suddenly stood up from the bed and towering over his son shouted: "Liar! You did not have the words in your mind on this night. You could not have. You allowed the lawless one to do its work. *You* are the lawless one, but you must not be. You must become the other one, the *katechon*, the one who restrains."

"I'm sorry, Father," Andrew cried out. "Please don't be angry with me."

The Reverend Maness recovered his temper and again held up his open hand, the fingers of which interlocked and separated several times in what appeared to be a deliberate sequence of subtle gesticulations. He turned away from his son and slowly walked the length of the room. When he reached the window on the opposite side he stared out at the blackness that covered the town of Moxton, where he and his son had first arrived some years before. On the main street of the town the reverend had built a church; nearby, he had built a house. The silhouette of the church bell-tower was outlined against moonlit clouds. From across the room the Reverend Maness said to his son, "I built the church in town so that it would be seen. I made the church of brick so that it would endure."

Now he paced the floor in an attitude of meditation while his son looked on in silence. After some time he stood at the foot of his son's bed, glaring down as though he stood at the pulpit of his church. "In the Bible there is a beast," he said. "You know this, Andrew. But did you know that the beast is also within you? It lives in a place that can never see light. Yes, it is housed here, inside the skull, the habitation of the Great Beast. It is a thing so wonderful in form that its existence might be attributed to the fantastic conjurings of a sorcerer or to a visitation from a far, dark place which no one has ever seen. It is a nightmare that would stop our hearts should we ever behold it gleaming in some shadowy corner of our home, or should we ever — by terrible mischance — lay our hands upon the slime of its flesh. This must never happen, the beast must be kept within its lair. But the beast is a great power that reaches out into the world, a great maker of worlds that are as nothing we can know. And it may work changes on this world. Darkness and light, shape and color, the heavens and the earth – all may be changed by the beast, the great reviser of things seen and unseen, known and unknown. For all that we see and know are but empty vessels in which the beast shall pour a new tincture, therewith changing the aspect of the land, altering the shadows themselves, giving a strange color to our days and our nights, making the day *into* night, so that we dream while awake and can never sleep again. There is nothing more awful and nothing more sinful than such changes in things. Nothing is more grotesque than these changes. All changes in things are grotesque. The very possibility of changes in things is grotesque. And the beast is the author of all changes. You must never again consort with the beast!"

"Don't say that, Father!" Andrew screamed, the palms of his hands pressed to his ears in order to obstruct further words of judgment. Yet he heard them all the same.

"You are repentant, but still you do not read the book."

"I do read the book."

"But you do not have the words of the book always in your mind, because you are always reading other books that are forbidden to you. I have seen you looking at my books, and I know that you take them from my shelves like a thief. Those are books that should not be read."

"Then why do you keep them?" Andrew shouted back, knowing that it was evil to question his father and feeling a great joy in having done so. The Reverend Maness stepped around to the side of the bed, his spectacles flashing in the candlelight.

"I keep them," he said, "so that you may learn by your own will to renounce what is forbidden in whatever shape it may appear."

But how wonderful he found those books that were forbidden to him. He remembered seeing them for the first time cloistered on high shelves in his father's library, that small and windowless room at the very heart of the house the Reverend Maness had built. Andrew knew these books on sight, not only by the titles which had such words in them as Mystery, Haunted, Secret, and Shadow, but also by the characters that formed these words – a jagged script closely resembling the letters of his own Bible – and by the shades of their cloth bindings, the faded vestments of autumn twilights. He somehow knew these books were forbidden to him, even before the reverend had made this fact explicit to his son and caused the boy to feel ashamed of his desire to hold these books and to know their matter. He became bound to the worlds he imagined were revealed in the books, obsessed with what he conceived to be cosmology of nightmares. And after he had wrongfully admitted himself to his father's library, he began to plot in detail the map of a mysterious universe – a place where the sun had passed from view, where towns were cold and dark, where mountains trembled with the monstrosities they concealed, woods rattled with secret winds, and all the seas were horribly calm. In his dreams of this universe, which far surpassed the darkest visions of any of the books he had read, a neverending night had fallen upon every imaginable landscape.

In sleep he might thus find himself standing at the rim of a great gorge filled with pointed evergreens, and in the distance were the peaks of hills appearing in black silhouette under a sky chaotic with stars. Sublime scenery of this type often recurred in those books forbidden to him, sometimes providing the subject for one of the engraved illustrations accompanying a narrative. But he had never read in any book what his dream showed him in the sky above the gorge and above the hills. For each of the bright, bristling stars would begin to loosen in the places where the blackness held them. They wobbled at first, and then they rolled over in their bed of night. Now it was the other side of the stars that he saw, which was unlike anything ever displayed to the eyes of the earth. What he could see resembled not stars but something more like the underside of large stones one might overturn deep in damp woods. They had changed in the strangest way, changed because everything in the universe was changing and could no longer be protected from the changes being worked upon them by something that had been awakened in the blackness, something that desired to remold everything it could see . . . and had the power to see all things. Now the faces of the stars were crawling with things that made them gleam in a way that stars had never gleamed before. And then these things he saw in his dream began to drip from the stars toward the earth, streaking the night with their gleaming trails.

In those nights of dreaming, all things were subject to forces that knew nothing of law or reason, and nothing possessed its own nature or essence but was only a mask upon the face of absolute darkness, a blackness no one had ever seen.

Even as a child he realized that his dreams did not follow the

creation taught to him by his father and by *that book*. It was
another creation he pursued, a counter-creation, and the books
on the shelves of his father's library could not reveal to him what
he desired to know of this other genesis. While denying it to his
father, and often to himself, he dreamed of reading the book that
was truly forbidden, the scripture of a deadly creation, one that
would tell the tale of the universe in its purest sense.

But where could he find such a book? On what shelf of what
library would it appear before his eyes? Would he recognize it
when fortune allowed it to fall into his hands? Over time he
became certain he would know the book, so often did he dream of
it. For in the most unlikely visions he found himself in possession
of the book, as though it belonged to him as a legacy. But while he
held the book in dreams, and even saw its words with miraculous
clarity, he could not comprehend the substance of a script whose
meaning seemed to dissolve into nonsense. Never was he granted
in these dreams an understanding of what the book had to tell
him. Only as the most obscure and strangest sensations did it
communicate with his mind, only as a kind of presence that
invaded and possessed his sleep. On waking, all that remained
was a euphoric terror. And it was then that objects around him
would begin their transformations, for his soul had been made
lawless by dreams and his mind was filled with the words of the
wrong book.

5 The author of the book

"You knew it was hopeless," said Andrew Maness as he stood
over the book that lay on the desk, glaring at the pages of old
handwriting in black ink. "You told me to always read the right
words and to always have them in my mind, but you knew I would
read the wrong words. You knew what I was. You knew that such
a being existed only to read the wrong words and to want to see
those words written across the sky in a black script. Because you
yourself were the author of the book. And you brought your son
to the place where he would read your words. This town was the
wrong place, and you knew it was the wrong place. But you told
yourself it was the only place where what you had done . . . might
be undone. Because you became afraid of what you and those
others had done. For years you were intrigued by the greatest madness, the most atrocious secrets and schemes, and then you became

afraid. What did you discover that could make you so afraid, you and the others who were always intrigued by the monstrous things you told of, that you sang of, in the book? You preached to me that all change is grotesque, that the very possibility of change is evil. Yet in the book you declare 'transformation as the only truth' – the only truth of the Tsalal, that one who is without law or reason. 'There is no nature to things,' you wrote in the book. 'There are no faces except masks held tight against the pitching chaos behind them.' You wrote that there is not true growth or evolution in the life of this world but only transformations of appearance, an incessant melting and molding of surfaces without underlying essence. Above all you pronounced that there is no salvation of any being because no beings exist as such, nothing exists to be saved – everything, everyone exists only to be drawn into the slow and endless swirling of mutations that we may see every second of our lives if we simply gaze through the eyes of the Tsalal.

"Yet these truths of yours that you kept writing in your book cannot be the reason you became afraid, for even while your voice is somber or trembling to speak of these things, your phrases are burdened with fascination and you are always marvelling at the grand mockery of the universal masquerade, the 'hallucination of lies that obscures the vision of all but the elect of the Tsalal.' It is something of which you will not speak or cannot speak that caused you to become afraid. What did you discover that you could not face without renouncing what you and those others had done, without running to this town to hide yourself in the doctrines of a church that you did not truly uphold? Did this knowledge, this discovery remain within you, at once alive and annihilated to your memory? Was it this that allowed you to prophesy that the people of Moxton would return to their town, yet prevented you from telling what phenomenon could be more terrible than the nightmare they had fled, those grotesque changes which had overtaken the streets and houses of this place?

"You knew this was the wrong place when you brought me here as a child. And I knew that this was the wrong place when I came home to this town and stayed here until everyone knew that I had stayed too long in this place."

6 The white-haired woman

Not long after Andrew Maness moved back to the town of

Moxton, an old woman came up to him late one afternoon on the street. He was staring into the window of a repair shop that closed early. Corroded pieces of machinery were strewn before him, as if on display: the guts and bones of a defunct motor of some kind. His reverie was disturbed when the old woman said, "I've seen you before."

"That is possible, ma'am," he replied. "I moved into a house on Oakman a few weeks ago."

"No, I mean that I've seen you before that."

He smiled very slightly at the old woman and said, "I lived here for a time, but I didn't think anyone would remember."

"I remember the hair. It's red but kind of greenish too, yellow maybe."

"Discolored through the years," he explained.

"I remember it the way it was. And it's not much different now. My hair's white as salt."

"Yes, ma'am," he said.

"I told those damn fools I remembered. No one listens to me. What's your name?"

"My name, Mrs . . ."

"Spikes," she snapped.

"My name, Mrs Spikes, is Andrew Maness."

"Maness, Maness," she chanted to herself. "No, I don't think I know Maness. You're in the Starns house."

"It was in fact purchased from one of Mr Starns' family who inherited the house after he died."

"Used to be the Waterses lived there. Before them the Wellses. And before them the McQuisters. But that's getting to be before my time. Before the McQuisters is just too damn long to remember. Too damn long." She was repeating these words as she charged off down the street. Andrew Maness watched her thin form and salt-white hair recede and lose all color in the drab surroundings of the skeleton town.

7 Revelations of a unique being

For Andrew Maness, the world had always been divided into two separate realms defined by what he could only describe as a *prejudice of soul*. Accordingly he was provided with a dual set of responses that he would have to a given locale, so that he would know if it was a place that was right for him, or one that was wrong. In places of the former type there was a separation between his self and the world around him, an enveloping absence. These were the great empty spaces which comprised nearly the whole of the world. There was no threat presented by such places. But there were other places where it seemed a presence of some dreadful kind was allowed to enter, a force that did not belong to these places yet moved freely within them . . . and within him. It was precisely such places as this, and the presence within them, which came to preside over his life and determine its course. He had no choice, for this was the scheme of the *elect persons* who had generated him, and he was compelled to fall in with their design. He was in fact the very substance of their design.

His father knew that there were certain places in the world to which he must respond, even in his childhood, and which would cause him to undergo a second birth under the sign of the Tsalal. The Reverend Maness knew that the town of Moxton was among such places – outposts on the desolate borderlands of the real. He said that he had brought his son to this town so that the boy would learn to resist the presence he would feel here and elsewhere in the world. He said that he had brought his son to the right place, but he had in fact brought him to a place that was entirely wrong for the being that he was. And he said that his son should always fill his mind with the words of that book. But these words were easily silenced and usurped by those other words in those other books. His father seemed to entice him into reading the very books he should not have read. Soon these books provoked in Andrew Maness the sense of that power and that presence which may manifest itself in a place such as the town of Moxton. And there were other places where he felt that same presence. Following intuitions that grew stronger as he grew older, Andrew Maness would find such places by hazard or design.

Perhaps he would come upon an abandoned house standing shattered and bent in an isolated landscape – a raw skeleton in a boneyard. But this dilapidated structure would seem to him a temple, a wayside shrine to that dark presence with which he sought union, and also a doorway to the dark world in which it dwelled. Nothing can convey those sensations, the countless nuances of trembling excitement, as he approached such a decomposed edifice whose skewed and ragged outline suggested another order of existence, the truest order of existence, as though such places as this house were only wavering shadows cast down to earth by a distant, unseen realm of entity. There he would experience the touch of something outside himself, something whose will was confused with his own, as in a dream wherein one feels possessed of a fantastic power to determine what events will transpire and yet also feels helpless to control that power, which, *through* oneself, may produce the chaos of nightmare. This mingling of mastery and helplessness overwhelmed him with a black intoxication and suggested his life's goal: to work the great wheel that turns in darkness, and to be broken upon it.

Yet Andrew Maness had always known that his ambition was an echo of that conceived by his father many years before, and that the pursuit of this ambition had been consummated in his own birth.

8 Not much more than a century ago

"As a young man," the Reverend Maness explained to his son, who was now a young man himself, "I thought myself an adept in the magic of the old gods, a communicant of entities both demonic and divine. I did not comprehend for years that I was merely a curator in the museum where the old gods were on display, their replicas and corpses set up in the countless galleries of the *invisible* . . . and now the *extinct*. I knew that in past millennia these beings had always replaced one another as each of them passed away along with the worlds that worshipped them. This mirror-like succession of supreme monarchs may still seem eternal to those who have not sensed the great shadow which has always been positioned behind every deity or pantheon. Yet I was able to sense this shadow and see that it had eclipsed the old gods without in any way being one of their kind. For it was even older than they, the dark background against which they had forever carried on their escapades as best they could. But its emergence into the foreground of things was something new, an advent occurring not much more than a century ago. Perhaps this great blackness, this shadow, has always prevailed on worlds other than our own, places that have never known the gods of *order*, the gods of *design*. Even this world had long prepared for it, creating certain places where the illusion of a reality was worn quite thin and where the gods of order and design could barely breathe. Such places as this town of

Moxton became fertile ground for this blackness no one had ever seen.

"Yes, it was not much more than a century ago that the people of this world betrayed their awareness of a new god that was not a god. Such an awareness may never be complete, never reach a true agony of illumination, except among an elect. I myself was slow in coming to it. The authenticity of my enlightenment may seem questionable and arbitrary, considering its source. Nonetheless, there is a tradition of revelation, an ancient protocol, by which knowledge of the unseen is delivered to us through inspired texts. And it is by means of these scriptures dictated from beyond that we of this world may discover what we have not and cannot experience in a direct confrontation. So it was with the Tsalal. But the book that I have written, and which I have named *Tsalal*, is not the revealed codex of which I am speaking. It is only a reflection, or rather a distillation, of those other writings in which I first detected the existence, the emergence, of the Tsalal itself.

"Of course, there have always been writings of a certain kind, a primeval lore which provided allusions to the darkness of creation and to monstrosities of every type, human and inhuman, as if there were a difference. Something profoundly dark and grotesque has always had a life in every language of this world, appearing at intervals and throwing its shadow for a moment upon stories that try to make sense of things, often confounding the most happy tale. And this shadow is never banished in any of these stories, however we may pretend otherwise. The darkness of the grotesque is an immortal enigma: in all the legends of the dead, in all the tales of creatures of the night, in all the mythologies of mad gods and lucid demons, there remains a kind of mocking nonsense to the end, a thick and resonant voice which calls out from the heart of these stories and declares: 'Still I am here'. And the idiot laughter of that voice – how it sounds through the ages! This laughter often reaches our ears through certain stories wherein this grotesque spirit itself has had a hand. However we have tried to ignore the laughter of this voice, however we have tried to overwhelm its words and protect ourselves by always keeping other words in our minds, it still sounds throughout the world.

"But it was not much more than a century ago that this laughter began to rise to a pitch. You have heard it yourself, Andrew, as you furtively made incursions into my library during your younger days, revelling in a Gothic feast of the grotesque. These books do not hold an arcane knowledge intended for the select few but were written for a world which had begun to slight the gods of order and design, to question their very existence and to exalt in the disorders of the grotesque. Both of us have now studied the books in which the Tsalal was being gradually revealed as the very nucleus of our universe, even if their authors remained innocent of the revelations they were perpetrating. It was from one of the most enlightened of this sect of Gothic storytellers that I took the name of that one. You recall, Andrew, the adventures of an Arthur Pym in a fantastic land where everything, people and landscape alike, is of a *perfect blackness* – the Antarctic country of Tsalal. This was among the finest evocations I had discovered of that blackness no one had ever seen, a literary unveiling of being without soul or substance, without meaning or necessity – not a universe of design and order but one whose sole principle was that of senseless transmutation. A universe of the grotesque. And from that moment it became my ambition to invoke what I now called the Tsalal, and ultimately to effect a worldly incarnation of the thing itself.

"Through the years I found there were others who had become entranced with an ambition so near to my own that we formed a league ... the elect of the Tsalal. They too had been adepts of the old gods who had been made impotent or extinct by the emergence of that one, an inevitable advent which we were avid to hasten and lose ourselves in. For we had recognized the mask of our identities, and our only consolation for what we had lost, a perverse salvation, was to embrace the fatality of the Tsalal. Vital to this end was a woman upon whom was performed a ceremony of conception. And it was during these rites that we first came into the most intimate communion with that one, which moved within us all and worked the most wonderful changes upon so many things.

"None of us suspected how it would be when we gathered that last night. This all happened in another country, an older country. But it was nevertheless a place like this town of Moxton, a place where the appearances of this world seem to waver at times, hovering before one's eyes as a mere fog. This place was known among our circle as the Street of Lamps, which was the very heart of a district under the sign of the Tsalal. In recollection, the lamps seem only a quirk of scene, an accident of atmosphere, but at the time they were to us the eyes of the Tsalal itself. These sidewalk fixtures of radiant glass upheld by dark metal stems formed a dreamlike procession up and down the street, a spectacle of infinite pathos and mystery. One poet of the era called them 'iron lilies,' and another compared their jewel-like illumination to the yellow topaz. In a different language, and a different city, these devices – *les réverbères, les becs de gaz* – were also celebrated, an enigmatic sign of a century, a world, that was guttering out.

"It was in this street that we prepared a room for your birth and your nurturing under the sign of the Tsalal. There were few other residents in this ramshackle area, and they abandoned it some time before you were born, frightened off by changes that all of us could see taking place in the Street of Lamps. At first the changes were slight: spiders had begun laying webs upon the stones of the street and thin strands of smoke spun out from chimney stacks, tangling together in the sky. When the night of your birth arrived the changes became more intense. They were focused on the room in which we gathered to chant the invocation to the Tsalal. We incanted throughout the night, standing in a circle around the woman who had been the object of the ceremony of conception. Did I mention that she was not one of us? No, she was a gaunt denizen of the Street of Lamps whose body we appropriated some months before, an honorary member of our sect whom we treated very well during her term of captivity. As the moment of your birth drew closer she lay upon the floor of the ceremonial room and began screaming in many different voices. We did not expect her to survive the ordeal. Neither did we expect the immediate consequences of the incarnation we attempted to effect, the consummation of a bond between this woman and the Tsalal.

"We were inviting chaos into the world, we knew this. We had been intoxicated by the prospect of an absolute disorder. With a sense of grim exaltation we greeted the *intimations* of a universal nightmare – the ultimate point of things. But on that night, even as we invoked the Tsalal within that room, we came to experience a realm of the unreal hitherto unknown to us. And we discovered that it had never been our desire to lose ourselves in the unreal, not in the manner which threatened us in the Street of Lamps. For as you, Andrew, began to enter the world through this woman, so was the Tsalal also entering the world through this woman. She was now the *seed* of that one, her flesh radiant and swelling in the fertile ground of the unreal which was the

Street of Lamps. We looked beyond the windows of that room, already contemplating our escape. But then we saw that there was no longer any street, nor any buildings along that street. All that remained were the streetlamps with their harsh yellow glow like rotten stars, endless rows of streetlamps that ascended into the all-encompassing blackness. Can you imagine: endless rows of streetlamps ascending into the blackness. Everything that sustained the reality of the world around us had been drained away. We noticed how our own bodies had become suddenly drawn and meager, while the body of that woman, the seed of the coming apocalypse, was becoming ever more swollen with the power and magic of the Tsalal. And we knew at that moment what needed to be done if we were ever to escape the unreality that had been sown in that place called the Street of Lamps."

9 A skeleton town

Even in the time of the McQuisters, which almost no one could remember very well, Moxton was a skeleton town. No building there had ever seemed new. Every crudded brick or faded board, every crusted shingle or frayed awning appeared to be handed down from the demise of another structure in another town, cast-offs of a thriving center that had no use for worn out materials. The front windows of stores were cloudy with a confusion of reflected images from someplace else. Entire establishments might have been dumped off in Moxton, where buildings stood along the street like odd objects forgotten on a cellar shelf.

It was less a real town than the semblance of a town, a pasteboard backdrop to an old stage show, its outlines crudely stroked with an antique paintbrush unconcerned with the details of character and identity, lettering the names of streets and shops with senseless scribbles no one was ever meant to read. Everything that might have been real about the town had somehow become thwarted. Nothing flourished there, nothing made a difference by its presence or absence.

No business could do more than anonymously survive in Moxton. Even larger enterprises such as a dimestore or a comfortable hotel could not assert themselves but were forced to assume the same air of unreality possessed by lesser establishments: the shoe store whose tiny front window displayed merchandise long out of style, the clothes store where dust collected in the folds of garments worn by headless mannikins, the repair shop at which a good number of the items brought in were left unclaimed and lay corroding in every cranny of the place.

Many years ago a movie theater opened on the prominent corner of Webster and Main, decades before a traffic light had been hung over the intersection of these streets. A large neon sign with letters stacked in a vertical file spelled out the word RIVIERA. For a moment this word appeared in searing magenta against the Moxton twilight, calling up and down the street to everyone in the town. But by nightfall the glowing letters had been subdued, their glamor suffocating in a rarefied atmosphere where sights and sounds were drained of reality. The new movie theater now burned no more brightly than McQuister's Pharmacy across the street. Both of them were allotted a steady and modest patronage in a skeleton town that was no more enchanted with the one than the other.

Thus was the extent of Moxton's compromise with any manifestation of the real. For there are certain places that exist on the wayside of the real: a house, a street, even entire towns which have claims upon them by virtue of some nameless affinity with the most remote orders of being. They are, these places, fertile ground for the unreal and retain the minimum of immunity against exotic disorders and aberrations. Their concessions to a given fashion of reality are only placating gestures, a way of stifling it through limited acceptance. It was unnecessary, even perverse, to resist construction of the movie theater or the new church (founded in 1893 by the Rev. Andrew Maness). Such an action might imbue these things with an unwarranted measure of substance or power, and in a skeleton town there is little substance, while all power resides only in the unreal. The citizens of such a place are custodians of a rare property, a precious estate whose true owners are momentarily absent. All that remains before full proprietorship of the land may be assumed is the planting of a single seed and its nurturing over a sufficient period of time, an interval that has nothing to do with the hours and days of the world.

10 A plea in the past

As Andrew Maness grew older in the town of Moxton he watched his father submit to the despair and the wonder that he could not unmake the thing that he and those others had *incarnated*. On several occasions the reverend entered his son's room as the boy slept. With knife and ax and long-handled scythe he attempted to break the growing bond between his son and the Tsalal. In the morning young Andrew's bedroom would reek like a slaughterhouse. But his limbs and organs were again made whole and a new blood flowed within them, proving the reality of what had been brought into the world by his father and those other enthusiasts of that one.

There were times when the Reverend Maness, in a state of awe and desperation, awoke his son from dreams and made his appeal to the boy, informing him that he was reaching a perilous juncture in his development and begging him to submit to a peculiar ritual that would be consummated by Andrew's ruin.

"What ritual is this?" Andrew asked with a novitiate's excitation. But the reverend's powers of speech became paralyzed at this question and many nights would pass before he again broached the subject.

At last the Reverend Maness came into his son's room carrying a book. He opened the book to its final pages and began to read. And the words he read laid out a scheme for his son's destruction. These words were his own, the ultimate chapter in a great work he had composed documenting a wealth of revelations concerning the force or entity called the Tsalal.

Andrew could not take his eyes off the book and strained to hear every resonance of his father's reading from it, even if the ritual the old man spelled out dictated the atrocious manner of Andrew's death – the obliteration of the seed of the apocalypse which was called the Tsalal.

"Your formula for cancelling my existence calls for the participation of others," Andrew observed. "The elect of . . . that one."

"Tsalal," the Reverend Maness intoned, still captivated by an occult nomenclature.

"Tsalal," Andrew echoed. "My protector, my guardian of the black void."

"You are not yet wholly the creature of that one. I have tried to change what I could not. But you have stayed too long in this place, which was the wrong place for a being such as you. You are undergoing a second birth under the sign of the Tsalal. But there is still enough time if you will submit yourself to the ritual."

"I must ask you, Father: who will carry it out? Will there be a convocation of strangers in this town?"

After a painfully reflective pause, the reverend said: "There are none remaining who will come. They would be required to relive the events following your birth, the first time you were born."

"And my mother?" Andrew asked.

"She did not survive."

"But how did she die?"

"By the ritual," the Reverend Maness confessed. "At the ritual of your birth it became necessary to perform the ritual of death."

"Her death."

"As I told you before. This ritual had never been performed, or even conceived, prior to that night on which you were born. We did not know what to expect. But after a certain point, after seeing certain things, we acted in the correct manner, as if we had always known what needed to be done."

"And what needed to be done, Father?"

"It is all in this book."

"You have the book, but you're still lacking for those others. A congregation, so to speak."

"I have my congregation in this very town. They will do what needs to be done. To this you must submit yourself. To the end of your existence you must consent."

"And if I don't?"

"Soon," the Reverend Maness began, "the bond will be sealed between you and the other, that one which is all nightmare of grotesque metamorphoses behind the dream of earthly forms, that one which is the center of so-called entity and so-called essence. To the living illusions of the world of light will come a blackness no one has ever seen, a dawn of darkness. What you yourself have known of these things is only a passing glimpse, a flickering candleflame besides the conflagration which is to come. You have found yourself fascinated by those moments after you have been asleep, and awake to see how the things around you are affected in their form. You look on as they change in every freakish manner, feeling the power that changes them to be connected to your own being, conveying to you its magic through a delicate cord. Then the cord grows too thin to hold, your mind returns to you, and the little performance you were watching comes to an end. But you have already stayed long enough in this place to have begun a second birth under the sign of the Tsalal. The cord between you and that one is strong. Wherever you go, you will be found. Wherever you stay, there the changes will begin. *For you are the seed of that one*. You are just as the *luz*, the bone-seed of rabbinic prophecy: that sliver of every mortal self from which the whole body may be reconstructed and stand for judgement at the end of time. Wherever you stay, there the resurrection will begin. You are a fragment of the one that is without law or reason. The body that will grow out of you is the true body of all things. The changes themselves are the body of the Tsalal. The changes are the truth of all bodies, which we believe have a face and a substance only because we cannot see that they are always changing, that they are only fragile forms which are forever being shattered in the violent whirlpool of truth.

"This is how it will be for all your days: you will be drawn to a place that reveals the sign of the Tsalal – an aspect of the unreal, a forlorn glamor in things – and with your coming the changes will begin. These may go unnoticed for a time, affecting only very small things or greater things in subtle ways, a disruption of forms that you very well know. But other people will sense that something is wrong in that place, which may be a certain house or street or even an entire town. They will go about with uneasy eyes and become emaciated in their flesh, their very bones growing thin with worry, becoming worn down and warped just as the world around them is slowly stripped of whatever seemed real, leaving them famished for the sustenance of old illusions. Rumors will begin to pass among them about unpleasant things they believe they have seen or felt and yet cannot explain – a confusion among the lower creatures, perhaps, or a stone that seems to throb with a faint life. For these are the modest beginnings of the chaos that will ultimately consume the stars themselves, which may be left to crawl within that great blackness no one has ever seen. And by their proximity to your being they will know that you are the source of these changes, that *through your being* these changes radiate into the world. The longer you stay in a place, the worse it will become. If you leave such a place in time, then the changes can have no lasting power – the ultimate point will not have been reached, and it will be as the little performances of grotesquerie you have witnessed in your own room."

"And if I do stay in such a place?" asked Andrew.

"Then the changes will proceed toward the ultimate point. So long as you can bear to watch the appearances of things become degraded and confused, so long as you can bear to watch the people in that place wither in their bodies and minds, the changes will proceed toward their ultimate point – the disintegration of all apparent order, the birth of the Tsalal. Before that happens you must submit to the ritual of the ultimate point."

But Andrew Maness only laughed at his father's scheme, and the sound of this laughter almost shattered the reverend entirely. In a deliberately serious voice, Andrew said: "Do you really believe you will gain the participation of others?"

"The people of this town will do the work of the ritual," his father replied. "When they have seen certain things, they will do what must be done. Their hunger to preserve the illusions of their world will surpass their horror at what must be done to save it. But it will be your decision whether or not you will submit to the ritual which will determine the course of so many things in this world."

11 A meeting in Moxton

Everyone in the town gathered in the church that the Reverend Maness had built so many years ago. No others had succeeded the reverend, and no services had been held since the time of his pastorate. The structure had never been outfitted with electricity, but the illumination of numerous candles and oil lamps the congregation had brought supplemented the light of a grayish afternoon that penetrated the two rows of plain, peaked windows along either side of the church. In the corner of one of those windows a spider fumbled about in its web, struggling awkwardly with appendages that resembled less the nimble legs of the arachnid than they did an octet of limp tentacles. After several thrusts the creature reached the surface of a window pane and passed into the glass itself, where it began to move about freely in its new element.

The people of Moxton had tried to rest themselves before this meeting, but their haggard look spoke of a failure to do so. The entire population of the town barely filled a half dozen pews at the front of the church, although some were collapsed upon the floor and others shuffled restlessly along the center aisle. All of them appeared even more emaciated than the day before, when they had attempted to escape the town and unaccountably found themselves driven back to it.

"Everything has gotten worse since we returned," said one man, as if to initiate the meeting which had no obvious hope or purpose beyond collecting in a single place the nightmares of the people of Moxton. A murmur of voices rose up and echoed throughout the church. Several people spoke of what they had witnessed the night before, reciting a litany of grotesque phenomena that had prohibited sleep.

There was a bedroom wall which changed colors, turning from its normal rosy tint that was calm and pale in the moonlight to a quivering and luminescent green that rippled like the flesh of a great reptile. There was a little doll whose neck began to elongate until it was writhing through the air like a serpent, while its tiny doll's head whispered words that had no sense in them yet conveyed a profoundly hideous meaning. There were things no one had seen that made noises of a deeply troubling nature in the darkness of cellars or behind the doors of closets and cupboards. And then there was something that people saw when they looked through the windows of their houses toward the house where a man named Andrew Maness now lived. But when anyone began to describe what it was they saw in the vicinity of that house, which they called the McQuister house, their words became confused. They did see something and yet they saw nothing.

"I also saw what you speak of," whispered the tall, bearded man who wore a flat-brimmed hat. "It was a blackness, but it was not the blackness of the night or of shadows. It was hovering over the old McQuister place, or around it. This was something I had not seen in Moxton even since the changes."

"No, not in Moxton, not *in the town*. But you *have* seen it before. We have all seen it," said a man's voice that sounded as if it came from elsewhere in the church.

"Yes," answered the tall man, as if confessing a thing that had formerly been denied. "But we are not seeing it the way it might be seen, the way we had seen it when we were outside the town, when we tried to leave and could not."

"That was not blackness we saw then," said one of the younger women who seemed to be wresting an image from her memory. "It was something . . . something that wasn't blackness at all."

"There were different things," shouted an old man who suddenly stood up from one of the pews, his eyes fixed in a gaze of revelation. A moment later this vision appeared to dissolve, and he sat down again. But the eyes of others followed this vision, surveying the empty spaces of the church and watching the flickering lights of the many lamps and candles.

"There *were* different things," someone started to say, and then someone else completed the thought: "But they were all spinning and confused, all swirling together."

"Until all we could see was a great blackness," said the tall man, gaining his voice again.

A silence now overcame the congregation, and the words they had spoken seemed to be disappearing into this silence, once more drawing the people of Moxton back to the refuge of their former amnesia. But before their minds lost all clarity of recollection a woman named Mrs Spikes rose to her feet and from the last row of the church, where she sat alone, cried out, "Everything started with him, the one in the McQuister house."

"How long has it been?" one voice asked.

"Too long," answered Mrs Spikes. "I remember him. He's older than I am, but he doesn't look older. His hair is a strange color."

"Reddish like pale blood," said one.

"Green like mold," said another. "Or yellow and orange like a candleflame."

"He lived in that house, that same house, a long time ago," continued Mrs Spikes. "Before the McQuisters. He lived with his father. But I can only remember the stories. I didn't see anything myself. Something happened one night. Something happened to the whole town. Their name was Maness."

"That is the name of the man who built this church," said the tall man. "He was the first clergyman this town had seen. And there were no others after him. What happened, Mrs Spikes?"

"It was too long ago for anyone to remember. I only know the stories. The reverend said things about his son, said the boy was going to do something and how people had to keep it from happening."

"What happened, Mrs Spikes? Try to remember."

"I'm trying. It was only yesterday that I started to remember. It was when we got back to town. I remembered something that the reverend said in the stories about that night."

"I heard you," said another woman. "You said, 'Blessed is the seed that is planted forever in darkness.'"

Mrs Spikes stared straight ahead and lightly pounded the top of the pew with her right hand, as though she were calling up memories in this manner. Then she said: "That's what he was supposed to have been saying that night, 'Blessed is the seed that is planted forever in darkness.' And he said that people had to do something, but the stories I heard when I was growing up don't say what he wanted people to do. It was about his son. It was something queer, something no one understood. But no one did anything that he wanted them to do. When they took him home, his son wasn't there, and no one saw that young man again. The stories say that the ones who brought the reverend to his house saw things there, but no one could explain what they saw. What everyone did remember was that late the same night the bells started ringing up in the tower of this church. That's where they found the reverend. He'd hung himself. It wasn't until the McQuisters moved into town that anyone would go near the reverend's house. Then it seemed no one could remember anything about the place."

"Just as we could not remember what happened only yesterday," said the tall man. "Why we came back to this place when it was the last place we wanted to be. The blackness we saw that was a blackness no one had ever seen. That blackness which was not a blackness but was all the colors and shapes of things darkening the sky."

"A vision!" said one old man who for many years had been the proprietor of McQuister's Pharmacy.

"Perhaps only that," replied the tall man.

"No," said Mrs Spikes. "It was something *he* did. It was like everything else that's been happening since he came here and stayed so long. All the little changes in things that kept getting worse. It's something that's been moving in like a storm. People have seen that it's in the town now, hanging over that house of his. And the changes in things are worse than ever. Pretty soon it's us that'll be changing."

Then there arose a chorus of voices among the congregation, all of them composing a conflict between "we must do something" and "what can be done?"

While the people of Moxton murmured and fretted in the light of lamps and candles, there was a gradual darkening outside the windows of the church. An unnatural blackness was overtaking the gray afternoon. And the words of these people also began to change, just as so many things had changed in that town. Within the same voices there mingled both keening outcries of fear and a low, muttering invocation. Soon the higher pitched notes in these voices diminished and then wholly disappeared as the deeper tones of incantation prevailed. Now they were all chanting a single word in hypnotic harmony: *Tsalal, Tsalal, Tsalal*. And standing at the pulpit was the one who was leading the chant, the man whose strangely shaded hair shone in the light of candles and oil lamps. At last he had come from his house where he had stayed too long. The bell in the tower began to ring, sounding in shattered echoes. The resonant cacophony of voices swelled within the church. For these were the voices of people who had lived so long in the wrong place. These were people of a skeleton town.

The figure at the pulpit lifted up his hands before his congregation, and they grew quiet. When he focused his eyes on an old woman sitting alone in the last row, she rose from her seat and walked to the double doors at the rear of the church. The man at the pulpit spread his arms wider, and the old woman pushed back each of the doors.

Through the open doorway was the main street of Moxton, but it was not as it had been. An encompassing blackness had descended and only the lights of the town could be seen. But these lights were now as endless as the blackness itself. The rows of yellowish streetlamps extended to infinity along an avenue of the abyss. Fragments of neon signs were visible, the vibrant magenta letters of the movie theater recurring again and again, as though reflected in a multitude of black mirrors. In the midst of the other lights hovered an endless succession of traffic signals that filled the blackness like multi-colored stars. All these bright remnants of the town, its broken pieces in transformation, were becoming increasingly dim and distorted, bleeding their radiance into the blackness that was consuming them, even as it freakishly multiplied the shattered images of the world, collecting them within its kaleidoscope of colors so dense and so varied that they lost themselves within a black unity.

The man who had built the church in which the people of Moxton were gathered had spoken of the ultimate point. This was now imminent. And as the moment approached, the gathering within the church moved toward the figure at the pulpit, who descended to meet them. They were far beyond their old fears, these skeleton people. They had attained the stripped bone of being, the last layer of an existence without name or description, without nature or essence: the nothingness of the blackness no

one had ever seen . . . or would ever see. For no one had ever
lived except as a shadow of the blackness of the Tsalal.

And their eyes looked to the one who was the incarnation of the
blackness, and who had come to them to seal his bond with that
other one. They looked to him for some word or gesture in order
to bring to fulfilment that day which had turned into night. They
looked to him for the thing that would bind them to the blackness
and join them within the apocalypse of the unreal.

Finally, as if guided by some whim of the moment, he told them
how to do what must be done.

12 What is remembered

The story that circulated in later years among the people of
Moxton told how everyone had gathered in the church one
afternoon during a big storm that lasted into the night. Unused for
decades before this event, the church was strongly constructed and
proved a suitable shelter. There were some who recalled that for
weeks prior to this cataclysm a variety of uncommon effects had
resulted from what they described as a season of strange weather
in the vicinity of the town.

The details of this period remain unclear, as do memories of
a man who briefly occupied the old McQuister place around
the time of the storm. No one had ever spoken with him except
Mrs Spikes, who barely recollected their conversation and who
died of cancer not long after the biggest storm of the year. The
house in which the man had lived was previously owned by
relatives of Ray Starns, but the Starns people were no longer
residents of Moxton. In any case, the old McQuister place was
not the only untenanted house in the skeleton town and there
was no reason for people to concern themselves with it. Nor
did anyone in Moxton give serious thought to the church once
the storm had passed. The doors were once again secured against
intruders, but no one ever tested these old locks which had been
first put in place after the Reverend Maness hung himself in the
church tower.

Had the people of the town of Moxton ventured beyond the
doors of the church they might have found what they left behind
following the abatement of the storm. Lying twisted at the foot of
the pulpit was the skeleton of a man whose name no one would
have been able to remember. The bones were clean. No bit of their

flesh could be discovered either in the church or anywhere else in the town. Because the flesh was that of one who had stayed in a certain place too long. It was the seed, and now it had been planted in a dark place where it would not grow. They had buried his flesh deep in the barren ground of their meager bodies. Only a few strands of hair of an unusual color lay scattered upon the floor, mingling with the dust of the church.

CHARLES GRANT

In the Still, Small Hours

CHARLES GRANT has been described as "one of the premier horror writers" (Stephen King) and "one of the authors who have given us a new golden age of horror fiction" (*Publishers Weekly*).

The undisputed master of "quiet" horror, as the following story proves, he made his fiction debut in 1968 with "The House of Evil" in *The Magazine of Fantasy & Science Fiction*. Since then he has presented his own unique brand of dark fantasy in such novels as *The Hour of the Oxrun Dead*, *The Nestling*, *The Tea Party*, *The Pet*, *In a Dark Dream*, *Stunts*, *Something Stirs*, *Raven* and many others.

His short fiction has been collected in *Tales from the Nightside*, *A Glow of Candles* and *Nightmare Seasons*, and he has edited the acclaimed *Shadows*, *Midnight* and *Greystone Bay* anthology series. The author also writes adventure fiction, fantasy spoofs and horror for young adults under a number of pseudonyms.

A SLOW STRONG wind took to the sky after midnight, dragging litter from the corners of every corner of the airport, dancing with the debris, mostly tattered paper, until it tired; and when it tired, it moved on, dragging grit across the windows like the clatter of muted hail, stinging the cheeks and closing the eyes of those who wandered outside because the inside was too quiet; snapping a flag on the pole near the terminal's main entrance, the ropes slapping and whipping against the pitted metal shaft to ring a tuneless hollow bell; gusting now and then across the nearly empty parking lots, across the deserted entrance road, across the runways and grass between, startling pilots, wobbling planes, and moving on without a sound.

It should have been cold, the wind that scoured the night-stained tarmac, and it should have had a voice – at the very least, a thunderstorm.

The best it did, however, was a monotone hum as it slid across the panes of the observation deck, a sound so low and constant Lucas barely even heard it.

But it was enough.

It could have been a moan.

And he shivered, only once, and blamed the faulty air-conditioning that, like everything else, was scarcely working these days. The only place he could find a small measure of peace was in this place, tucked away in the Dry Plains terminal that served the smaller, local flights.

He lit a cigarette.

The room was little more than a fairly wide corridor two-and-a-half stories above the ground, blank plaster wall on one side, an inward canted wall of glass on the other, and at their junction above his head a spotty row of fluorescent bulbs. The floor was carpeted, the carpeting worn, and at the north end, a heavy metal door with a small window, no handle or bar on either side, just a strong push to get it open. Although a waist-high metal rail ran the room's length, no one had thought to install chairs or benches. To watch the landings, to watch the take-offs, as he did most every week, he had to stand.

A chilly place.

Unfriendly.

Deliberately so, he gathered, because there was no money to be made here, no concessions, no machines, no poster advertise-ments, not even a water fountain.

He didn't care.

He seldom stayed for very long, just long enough to watch the lonely three o'clock flight from Dallas make its landing. When it had taxied to its destination – a long extension from the main building off to his left, rounded at the end to accommodate a dozen gates – and the jetway umbilical made its connection, he would watch the handful of passengers ghost along the glass-wall corridor back toward the exits.

He would watch, but he'd never see her.

Tonight would be no different, yet there was a difference anyway.

He was no expert, neither an engineer nor a former pilot, just a man who rented floor space in brand-new empty buildings, but he could tell that the aircraft coming in this summer night were having more than a little trouble. They landed more like stones than gliding birds to a welcome pond. They'd drop onto the runway hard, tires smoking at frantic brakes, and once, not an hour ago, a 727 fishtailed and he'd held his breath, hoping it would make it.

It had.

But only barely.

The wind slapped the pane, shimmered it, and he blinked.

A glance at his watch; he had an hour to go.

Though the lighting wasn't bright, barely bright enough to see the floor since only every other narrow bulb was lit, he squinted as he tried to make some sense of the still-black morning sky. There were stars, the moon long gone, but he couldn't see a single cloud, or a blank spot up there that would tell him a cloud was passing. Nothing, as far as he could figure, that would signal unsafe weather.

Nothing but the wind.

Then he saw himself in the glass and gave himself a nod and smile.

In all the months he'd been coming here, no one had ever stopped him, no one ever asked why an ordinary-looking man in a decent suit, a decent tie, would make his way so late to this place just to watch the planes. And precious few of them there were these days, he thought as he crushed the cigarette beneath his heel. From midnight to one, an even dozen; from one to two there were only eight; and from two to dawn he'd be lucky to count them on the fingers of one hand.

One night there hadn't been any.

A week ago, one had crashed on take-off, thankfully out of his sight.

He leaned lightly against the railing, looking westward toward the main terminal. Lights and dim shadows and the glint of steel and polished plastic. It made him nervous; especially now. When he had arrived tonight, just after twelve-thirty, there hadn't been a single soul inside. The ticket counters had been deserted, the shops closed and locked, not even a man with a broom working over the mirrored floor.

Nothing.

No one.

He hadn't heard a sound.

As he hurried toward the covered walkway that led to the smaller building and the observation deck, his footsteps had followed him, echoing faintly, faintly mocking, until he'd found himself virtually on his toes, so as not to break the silence.

And once he had arrived, he had almost stumbled and fallen, not realizing until he touched the cold railing for balance that he'd been holding his breath most of the way.

He had shaken his head then, and he shook his head now, frowning, wondering what the hell was going on. If Joan had been here, she would have poked him in the side, teased him about omens, portents, the stuff that she claimed to believe, although she had never tried to force him to share her beliefs.

"Either you believe or you don't," she had said that last time, the last night they had been together, waiting in the reception area for the call to her outbound flight. "But sooner or later, you're going to have to admit that there are coincidences, and then there are coincidences that only look like coincidences." Then she'd kissed him good-bye, a sisterly brush on his cheek, and he had hurried over here to watch her leave for Dallas, and points west.

He did believe in one thing – that she would be back five days later, briefcase filled with papers that would make her richer than she already was.

He also believed he still had a chance, had to have a chance, to somehow win her back.

He believed it implicitly until the moment he saw the ball of flame the following week, an amateur video filling the TV screen with dying color as the reporter on the scene tried to explain what had happened fifty miles west of its Texas destination. It had something to do with an engine valve and a fuel leak; the reporter wasn't very good.

It really didn't matter.

That night he stayed home, flicking aimlessly from channel to channel, waiting for the awful error to be admitted, the flight number to be corrected. He watched, he didn't weep, not until dawn and the call from her mother, weeping herself, begging him to help her put Joan to rest.

He had.

What was left of her.

None of them ever knew; the coffin had been closed.

And one night, no night in particular a handful of weeks later, he found himself dressed and in his car, heading for Dry Plains, found himself looking out the airport window, waiting for her plane.

He never asked why, never asked anyone if maybe he was going crazy.

He just did it.

But now, tonight, he thought he knew.

It didn't make him happy.

In fact, it made him feel . . . almost nothing.

A sigh, a silent scolding for being so damn melodramatic, and he watched a small, private jet slip swiftly out of the stars, out of the dark to his right, and aim for the runway. Its noise was muffled, but he knew instantly something was wrong with this one, too. The engines sputtered, and the aircraft, so unbearably tiny and pale, began to slip from side to side. He put a palm against the glass and leaned closer, feeling the rail press into his stomach.

Side to side.

Moving so slowly as it drew even with his position that he couldn't imagine what held it up. It couldn't have been more than twenty or thirty feet above the tarmac. Side to side. Abruptly dropping like a stone just before the gate arm blocked it from view.

He held his breath, waiting for the explosion, the scream of the emergency vehicles, the race of workers from their caves beneath the building.

There was nothing.

Thank God, there was nothing.

He sighed loudly, closed his eyes for a moment, and let the relief ease him back from the rail until he heard a noise in the hallway, as if something large had fallen onto something not quite soft. He turned, head cocked, listening for a curse or a call for help.

There was nothing.

Just the door.

He stared at the door's small window, but all he could see through it from where he stood was a square piece of the cinder block wall, painted a faded green. He supposed the color, when it had been originally applied, was supposed to be restful, but it only reminded him of a hospital.

A quiet noise, then, deep in his throat.

All right, he told himself, all right. Not just any hospital; the hospital where Joan's mother had been, recovering from a mild heart attack. In the hall, the pale green hall, outside the woman's room, Joan had suggested in a whisper that when she returned from her next trip, perhaps they ought to consider not seeing each other for a while.

"We don't seem to be getting anywhere, Lucas," she had said, expression regretful, voice calm and laced with reason. "It's almost a cliché, isn't it – it doesn't seem like either one of us is ready to commit to anything else but more of the same."

He probably should have argued, if only for the sake of his ego. He probably should have done a lot of things. But as always, he didn't.

She was right.

She was, when he thought about it, always right. Just as she always made the decisions, the big ones, the small ones, the ones he never found the energy to care about and so deferred to her with a quip and grin.

A puzzled frown then, when yet another plane, this one much larger, maybe a DC-10, wallowed over the far end of the runway. Though he couldn't make out much of its body the swinging lights on its wings told the story, and once again he held his breath until it had touched down safely, and much easier than the small jet that had vanished a while ago.

Weird, he thought; they were coming in as if it were the middle of the day.

The door opened.

He didn't turn right away, but he was surprised to realize he was annoyed. This deck was his place this late at night – or this early in the morning – and he resented someone disturbing him.

A foolish notion, perhaps, but he had been alone here for so long, nearly six months to the day, that he supposed the reaction was fairly natural.

"Well, damn."

He looked toward the voice, and wasn't sure how to react.

The man stumbling through the doorway was tall, easily a head taller than he, and large. Almost huge. A soft grey blazer with something gold pinned to the lapel, black slacks, black shoes; a white shirt with tiny specks, and a tie that matched the jacket. What was left of his hair was dark and slicked straight back, not quite reaching the blazer collar. Thin mustache. Thick eyebrows. His jawline was fleshy, not many years to go before they began to sport some jowls.

"Damn."

The man shook his hand vigorously to one side as he crossed the floor, blowing on the palm now and then, his puffed face alternately folding up, smoothing out as he pulled his lips away from his teeth and muttered, "Damn," a third time.

"Trouble?" Lucas asked.

The newcomer stopped, obviously surprised to see Lucas there, grimaced again and came over. "Damn stairs," he complained. A mound of fat pressed against his shirt, pushing the buttons to their limit, and his tie was twisted and skewed to one side. "Not watching where I'm going, you know what I mean? Can't even see my goddamn feet, they hook a step, I fall like a kid that can't handle his stupid beer." He stomped his foot once. "You'd think they'd put some carpet down out there, you'd think that. Cheap bastards."

He shook his hand again, and Lucas realized the specks on his shirt were droplets of blood. Startled, he checked his own clothes, and saw a drop on his breast pocket. He wiped it off with a quick grimace as the man held out his hand for inspection, skin harshly abraded and nastily red.

"Here," Lucas said, reached into his hip pocket and pulled out a handkerchief.

"Grateful," the man said, shook his hand one more time, blew on it one more time, and wrapped the cloth gingerly around his palm. "Tell you, buddy, this place is turning into one goddamn obstacle course, you know what I mean? Jesus." He shook his head, took a breath, and propped a hip against the railing. "You waiting on someone?"

Lucas nodded before he thought.

"Daryl," the man said, jabbing a thumb at his own chest. "Daryl Rayman."

"Lucas Nelson."

They shook hands; Rayman's was soft, hot, moist, and strong.

"Hell of a name, ain't it, Luke," Rayman said, easing back a few steps, gazing out at the runway. "Hippo like me with a name like Daryl. 'Course, my momma didn't plan on having a hippo. Think she was hoping more along the lines of something like a basketball player." He snorted a laugh, stared at his bandaged hand. "Didn't plan on tearing myself up either, come to that."

"Maybe you ought to get it looked at."

Rayman shook his head. "Here? You're kidding. This place's going to hell on the express, buddy, and I wouldn't trust a hangnail to those idiots down the First Aid Center, swear to God." He shifted until his stomach rested on, folded over the railing. "My last night tonight," he said, voice lower but without regret. "Thought I'd take a last look around, you know what I mean? Over ten years, but I ain't gonna miss it, not anymore."

He flicked a finger against the gold pin, which Lucas realized now was the stylized shape of a soaring airliner — it was a Dry Plains Courtesy Crew badge. He had seen it several times, usually on women, and assumed that the company representatives spent their shifts wandering around the terminal, answering questions, directing lost passengers, handling complaints, spreading cheer, and softening tempers. But he had a hard time imagining this one walking all day; he looked as if he had barely made it here without passing out. His face had the sheen of a man preparing to explode in sweat, and he wheezed softly breathing through a slightly open mouth.

Movement outside caught his attention, and another plane swooped in, this time without trouble, and turned almost immediately to the gate arm on the left.

"Amazing, ain't it?" Rayman nodded toward the airliner maneuvering along the blue-lighted runway sidepaths. "Ten years, I ain't seen so many come wandering in this late." He glanced at Lucas. "Kind of like they want to get it over with, you know what I mean?" He shook his head, smacked his lips. "Hardly anyone showed up tonight, you know." He gestured vaguely toward the main building. "It's kinda like New Year's Eve, after twelve – nobody flying in or out, you have the whole place practically to yourself."

"I guess."

Lucas followed the plane to its gate, squinted, but could see no one inside.

"Ain't no guess about it, buddy. This place is dying."

The lights went out.

It happened so abruptly, no flickering or buzzing, that he gripped the railing tightly as the glass wall vanished and the outside lunged toward him, clearer now, details no longer blurred by reflections or ghostly smears. He swallowed heavily against a rise of vertigo, looked up at the ceiling, and made a face. It wouldn't have been so bad had he been alone, he supposed, just a little startling, but the shadowed hulk of Rayman only a few feet away made him inexplicably uneasy.

The outside glow gave the man's face a sickly yellow tinge.

"What'd I tell you? Place is going to hell."

So leave, Lucas thought sourly. You don't like it here so bad, leave, and leave me alone.

Figures in coveralls scurried around the parked aircraft, unloading luggage, blocking the wheels, fussing here and there with open hatches on wings and undercarriage that he didn't understand. A check of the corridor that led to the terminal showed him nothing; it was empty.

If there's luggage, he thought, where are all the people?

From someplace in the warrens beneath them, another worker appeared, this one pushing a long and low empty handcart across the runway toward the plane.

"Feels like them pictures you see in school," Rayman said quietly as he followed the handcart's progress. "You know. The gods on that mountain?"

"Olympus," Lucas said automatically.

"Yeah, that's right. You always see them looking down, dropping some lightning on some poor guy's head once in a while, butting in when they're bored, or just watching, doing nothing. Wearing sheets or robes or whatever." He chuckled, and plucked at a lapel. "I don't think this sorry outfit's gonna make it, do you?"

Lucas couldn't help it; he grinned.

One by one the little men finished their jobs and deserted the plane, hand signals directing them to one place or another, vans and electric carts speeding away into the dark.

Lucas lifted his wrist and peered at his watch — close to two-thirty.

Joan's plane will be in soon.

His eyes closed, and he felt a faint sting there, not as bad as those first nights, but far from leaving him forever.

That's when he decided this would be the last time. It had to be. Whatever therapy he supposed he had thrown himself into either wasn't working, or it had worked and he hadn't known what it would do. Either way, this was stupid. He had an office to run, a life to get on with, and there were still those photographs in his desk at home. He wondered if it would have been worse had they been married.

He didn't think so.

"Son of a bitch," Rayman said. "Look at that fool."

"What?" Lucas scanned the shadowed area below the window, around the parked airplane, not seeing anyone who didn't seem to belong.

Then he spotted the man with the handcart.

He was pushing it straight for the runway.

"Damn fool." Rayman leaned farther over the railing, his forehead nearly touching the glass. "That boy's just walking there, Luke. He's just walking there."

Lucas snapped his gaze to the right, not really wanting to see if there was another plane on the way in, and was relieved when he saw nothing but stars out there.

Until two of them moved.

"Jesus," he whispered.

"Boy's got trouble."

Lucas looked around the room. "We have to tell someone, find a phone." He took a step toward the door, looked out, and changed his mind.

It was too late.

The worker had already reached the runway.

The airliner, another DC-10, had already touched down.

There was no sound but the whine and roar of engines, muted only slightly by the thickness of the panes.

Lucas couldn't watch the plane, and he couldn't stop watching the man and his empty cart.

Oh my God, he thought when the plane was less than a hundred feet away; he whirled and stared at the blank wall, swallowing hard, fast, one hand pressed to his stomach, one clawing at his shirt. Sweat curled down his left cheek from his temple. For some reason, he expected to hear the squeal of brakes, the crunch of metal against metal, as if it were an automobile accident he could witness from his porch.

The roar rose swiftly, peaked, and instantly faded.

Rayman said nothing.

Wheezing filled the silence.

Lucas ordered himself not to look, just turn and go for the door. He didn't need to stay. Joan's plane would land or it wouldn't, and she wouldn't be on it, and this kind of grief he didn't need tonight.

He did turn.

He did start for the door.

But curiosity made him look, and astonishment made him stop.

The worker was alive, pushing his handcart on the runway's far side, and Lucas watched him shrink, fade, vanish into the far dark, not a shadow left behind. He clung to the railing while his legs decided if they were going to work or not. He wanted to laugh, giggle a little, maybe scream once just to be rid of the pressure that had expanded to fill every cell in his chest; he wanted to throw up; he wanted to grab the fat man's arm and demand an explanation.

Instead he simply stared.

"Know her, you know," Rayman said, still looking out at the deserted tarmac.

Lucas paid him no attention. As the shock wore off and his heart stopped its heavy thumping, he figured he would take the day off, stay in bed until his back ached, take himself out to dinner, and maybe do a little downtown cruising. It had been a while. Over a year, as a matter of fact. A couple of bars, a couple of beers, and if he didn't get lucky it wouldn't really make any difference. What mattered was the effort. He didn't believe there'd be a miracle, like the guy there with the handcart, but maybe just a glimpse of a pretty lady, maybe a pleasant smile in his direction, would be another step, maybe the last, toward whatever they called it when mourning came to an end.

"Hey, Luke?"

The first step had come on the drive out here tonight, when he finally admitted to himself that, heartless as it may seem, Joan's dying had spared him the trouble of agreeing with her decision. The moment he had seen the fire, heard the reporter, heard the sirens, some part of him knew that he wouldn't have to tell her that she was, as always, right. What they had left from their year together wasn't really love. It might have been, once, but if so, it had withered, or faded, or whatever love does when it doesn't feed properly and isn't properly fed.

They had both been cowards, each waiting for the other to take the first step, both knowing it would be her because that's the way it was.

That realization, harsh and horrid, had made him sick enough to pull over and wait until he was sure he wasn't going to throw up.

The coward saved by an act of God in the form of a faulty valve and a fuel leak.

Jesus.

"I know her."

Lucas passed a hand over his face, drove away the demon. "Excuse me?"

Rayman still wasn't looking at him. "I know her. Joan Becker, that right? Some kind of commodities broker, something like that?"

He couldn't find the words.

The fat man gestured outside with a lazy crooked finger. "Them boys out there, they're gonna strike soon, you know. Heard them grousing about it the other day. Stuff going on around here you wouldn't believe, buddy, and they're getting a little riled. Bet if you came back in a couple of days, this place'd be shut down."

Noises in the hall, people laughing, someone talking.

Lucas looked to the door, looked back at Rayman. "You knew Joan? But . . . how?"

Rayman turned his head slowly, one side of his face yellowed, the other blanked in shadow.

One eye.

He could only see one dark eye.

Another plane landed, engines screaming, tires blasting smoke into the slow night wind.

The door squealed as it opened.

"This time of night," Rayman said, "it's kind of special, you know what I mean?" He sighed contentedly. "Peaceful. Real peaceful."

Lucas couldn't see his lips move.

He could only see the one dark eye.

Suddenly the fat man straightened, taller, his face all in shadow despite the reach of the outside glow.

Lucas took a step away, and though it was yards behind him he could still feel the doorless wall at his back, no escape.

Then a voice, a woman's voice, as someone stepped into the room: "Daryl? Daryl honey?"

Rayman turned quickly, slapped a joyful hand against his thigh as he laughed heartily, and hurried over to the small figure hesitating on the threshold. "Momma!" He wrapped his arms around the tiny woman, gave her a smothering long hug, then turned them both around. "Momma, this boy here, he's Luke Nelson. He's waiting on someone, just like I was waiting on you."

Lucas smiled politely, and took a few steps forward, not sure if he should extend his hand, or simply nod.

"Who's he waiting for, Daryl?"

Before Lucas could explain, Rayman said, "Joan. Joan Becker. She was on your plane, remember? Cute little thing, blonde hair, big blue eyes?"

"Oh . . . yes. Yes."

The lights flickered, bright and dark.

Lucas averted his eyes and squinted, as if the room had been touched by lightning.

"Momma, look, we got to go. It's a long drive, you know that, and I don't want to speed. You know how you hate when I have to speed."

The woman nodded. "He's just terrible, you know, Mr Nelson," she said gaily as Rayman steered her gently toward the door. "Eats me out of house and home, speeds like a demon, you don't know what a chore it is just to make him behave. He's terrible!"

The fat man laughed.

A dark hand fluttered in the air. "But you know, I don't think he can live without me, poor soul" A laugh of her own, hoarse and woman-soft. "Not that he'd admit it to the Devil, the big oaf."

The lights flickered again just as Rayman, laughing harder, pushed the door open.

Bright and dark.

"Hey . . . uh . . . Daryl?"

"Nice to meet you, Mr Nelson," Mrs Rayman called. "You get home safe now, y'hear? Find yourself a nice girl, a boy like you shouldn't ought to be left alone, the time of night like this."

Lucas felt his temper spark, but he didn't move, couldn't move when Rayman waved good-bye, and his mother glanced over her shoulder to give him a wave as well.

In the corridor light, just before the door closed, he saw her clearly for the first time.

Her clothes were shreded and black; there was nothing left of her face but charred bone.

The door closed.

Slammed.

Another plane landed, and he checked automatically, just in time to see it veer off the runway onto the grass, swing around violently and hit the runway again. Somehow it managed to straighten out before skidding off the other side, and when it rumbled past the gate, Lucas sprinted for the door and slammed it open with his shoulder.

The corridor was empty.

Sixty yards of it in four sections marked by steps, and no doors except the one he propped open with his foot.

The Raymans were gone.

He put a hand to the side of his neck and rubbed the skin there until it burned.

They were gone.

They couldn't be.

"Daryl!"

No place to hide.

"Mrs Rayman?"

The other voices, the other people.

Nothing left but the light, and dark hand-smudges along the wall.

He stumbled back inside and took hold of the rail, lowered his head and waited until he could think again, until he could stand alone. It was the lighting, of course, and probably not a small amount of guilt at not feeling worse for Joan's dying. All this time he had been kidding himself – the tears, the glum expressions, the solemn nodding when his friends passed condolences and sympathy his way . . . some of it was real, most of it was sham. And Mrs Rayman there, clearly loving her son as her son clearly loved her, had only underscored the acting he'd been doing all along.

In a way, the admission, like the admission in the car, was a relief.

He still felt like a monster, like something less than human, but it was still a relief.

Burdens lifted, he thought, and all that psychobabble crap.

So when Joan's plane landed smoothly at precisely three o'clock and taxied to its gate, he blew it a kiss and wished it well, smiling as he watched the unloading proceed without a hitch.

Rayman was right.

The silence here was peaceful. Restful.

These still, small hours of a day yet unborn were indeed something special; wasting them here would be a sin.

"Okay, you heard the lady," he said to his reflection in the glass. "Get your sorry ass home."

He grinned.

He pushed the door open and saw Joan waiting at the corridor's far end.

Suit black and shredded.

"I've changed my mind," she called, smiling broadly as she waved.

Face more bone than flesh.

"She's right, Lucas, darlin'. You shouldn't have to be alone."

STEVE RASNIC TEM

Ice House Pond

STEVE RASNIC TEM is one of the most prolific and successful short fiction writers currently working in the field. Although he has only published one novel (*Excavation*), he has written around two hundred stories, and among the recent anthologies he has contributed to are *MetaHorror, Borderlands 3, In the Fog, Snow White Blood Red, The Ultimate Witch, The Anthology of Fantasy & the Supernatural, In Dreams, The Mammoth Book of Vampires, The Year's Best Horror Stories*, and each volume of *The Best New Horror* to date.

In 1993, Necronomicon Press published his three-story collection *Decoded Mirrors: 3 Tales After Lovecraft*, and other chapbooks include *Fairytales, Celestial Inventory* and *Absences: Charlie Goode's Ghosts*.

The author lives in a supposedly haunted Victorian house in Denver, Colorado, with his wife, the writer Melanie Tem.

I

"That pond is much bigger than it is," Rudy had said to the realtor the last time, the first time, he'd seen Ice House Pond. He would never be sure exactly where the perception came from: something about the way the great stretch of level ice – pewter-colored that late in the afternoon, highlighted with occasional painful stabs of silver – disappeared into blinding snow that rose in clouds he would have thought more typical of high altitudes, snow that expanded and exploded as if with an angry energy. It had been a silly thing to say, really, and he had felt a little embarrassed around this proper New Englander. But it had also been the perfect thing to say, and now, on his return trip to take over ownership of the pond and everything attached to it, Rudy was pleased to see that his original perception still held true. The pond *was* much bigger than it was.

And Rudy was in desperate need of just such a place. In the real world, in his old world, things surprised you: They seemed so pitifully small after you'd lived with them for a while.

"I can't honestly say that this is the perfect deal, you understand," the realtor had said that first time. His name was Lorcaster, which, the fellow at the gas station where Rudy'd asked for directions was quick to point out, was one of the oldest names in the Bay. "Unless, of course, it's *exactly* what you're looking for." He didn't look like the scion of a great family. He had the belly, certainly, but none of the air. His clothes were a mismatch of pale greens and dark blues. And here he was, actively discouraging the sale and they hadn't even gotten to the place yet.

A small, wooded hill, more like a bump really, still obscured the property. The dirt road to the pond was so iced over they'd had to park on the narrow secondary that had brought them out of town, then walk a "short" jog crosscountry. Lorcaster had supplied an extra coat and snowshoes. Although there was very little wind, it seemed much colder out here than in town. "It'll require some fixing up, no doubt about that. But if you're handy with tools –"

"I'm not," Rudy interrupted. "But I have a little money set aside." More than a little. The deaths of two families in ten years and the resulting insurance payoffs had seen to that. His father had believed in insurance, had insisted on it for himself and for

Rudy's families, but Rudy would always wonder if he hadn't, literally, bought himself trouble. And now he was about to buy himself a new life with the death money, the pain money.

Lorcaster said nothing more about money for the rest of their walk. In fact, he seemed a bit uncomfortable that Rudy had brought up the subject in the first place.

"Just a few feet more," Lorcaster had puffed, trudging up the wooded rise, grabbing on to occasional nude trunks for support. "Watch your step, real slippery through here. You know, I'd hoped to be selling this place in the summertime. Beautiful out here in the summer." He paused at the top of the small hill, holding fast to a thick branch, and looked back down at Rudy, who still struggled. "You'll need to be getting a snowmobile, or a Cat."

Rudy stopped and looked around. The snow here was wet and heavy, not the fluff he was used to. And for the most part the snow surfaces were rough and icy. It was like a hardened white sludge that stuck to everything. The trees, instead of looking decorated with lace, seemed assaulted by the snow, encased in it as it froze. Not exactly pretty, but he would hardly call it ugly, either. Perhaps *uncompromising* was the word he wanted. "I don't know." Rudy grimaced from the cold. The temperature appeared to drop noticably each foot closer to the place. Rudy had never experienced such cold, but he was reluctant to tell Lorcaster that. "Maybe I'll want to stay put all winter."

Lorcaster stared at him appraisingly, as if at some questionable piece of property. "Maybe you will at that," he said after a while. "Anyplace you go, there's always some that stay to themselves, and don't mingle in town. Old Finney, the one that built the house and the ice house as well, they say he was like that. Well . . . speaking of . . . looks like we're there."

Rudy forced himself up the few remaining feet, chagrined that this fat old man was actually in better shape than he was.

He couldn't believe the increase in cold.

"Heating system's in good shape, or so they tell me. You'll *need* it."

The property was in an enormous saucer of land, edged by the small rise, with its trees, around two-thirds the circumference, and a short arc of hand-fitted stones along the remaining third. Beyond that wall were the far edges of the forest, and beyond that, farmland, although Lorcaster had made it clear that the closest farm was still some miles away. He could see the bright white, two-story house with the odd angles that so often characterized owner-built homes – unassuming but interesting – and connected to that was another large white building with a walkway around it, but with no windows, which Rudy assumed to be the ice house itself. The truly dramatic feature of the landscape was the pond, which extended in all directions beyond the buildings: Ice House Pond. From this angle, it seemed more like a lake than a pond, and it seemed to have its own movements, its own weather.

The air moving above the pond was whiter than the air surrounding it, and more active, with eddies and sudden swirls, transient movements of white and silver which disappeared as soon as Rudy thought he had found some pattern. Now he knew where the intense cold lay: The pond obviously trapped cold, but he had no idea how. It appeared to be snowing just over the pond, but nowhere else.

"The old-timers, the ones who knew about it before Old Finney bought the property, called it Bear Paw Pond," Lorcaster said. "I suppose because of those four little projections along the north shore. They kept calling it that even after Finney had renamed it and posted that sign – Ice House Pond." Lorcaster paused. "Well, there *was* a sign. Looks like somebody's torn the blamed thing down. Anyway, even before that some of the old maps have it named as 'The Hand,' but it doesn't look like any hand to me." Rudy could detect five long shadows growing out of that north end, four of them being extensions of the four small projections; during high water periods, or maybe times of flooding, they might indeed make the pond look like a hand. But he didn't argue. "Don't know where the water comes from. No sign of a spring, or any kind of exit. There may be some sort of tunnel under the surface, I suppose, that would lead up into an underground body of water. Folks around here will give you more explanations of exactly how the pond came to be than you'll ever need. Or maybe you'll just want to make up your own."

Every now and then the snowy air above the pond would clear a space, and Rudy could then see all the way to the surface of the ice. It was grey and silver, like frozen fog. Rudy thought he could detect streaks, dark branching cracks – shadowed areas like smudges, mounds, or many small things, or one large thing, floating or swimming just beneath the surface of the ice.

That was when he said the thing that would later embarrass

him: "That pond is much bigger than it is." He hadn't meant to say something so provocative, or poetic as that. His mouth had just acted on its own, giving voice to a silly thought he'd been unable to shake from his consciousness.

He had been uncomfortably aware of Lorcaster staring at him. But he couldn't bring himself to turn and look at the man. "Do tell," Lorcaster finally said. "Then I suppose you'd be getting more for your money that way."

The deal had gone swiftly after that. After a cursory examination of the property (although that first glimpse had told him everything he needed to know), Rudy told Lorcaster he wanted the place and flew home to settle his affairs, which mostly consisted of calling up the relatives of his two dead wives and letting them know that they could have whatever they wanted from the house. The remainder of the dealings with Lorcaster were handled by mail and over the phone with his secretary, a Miss Pater. Rudy eventually came to believe that Lorcaster found discussions of contracts and money ill suited to his old-money background. The man probably believed that such dealings left the founders of the first families of Greystone Bay rolling in their graves. Except he did pass on one note directly, and in his own hand rather than Miss Pater's errorless typing, suggesting perhaps that Rudy might prefer moving in during the spring. Lorcaster even offered to supply a short-term caretaker "with my compliments." But Rudy wouldn't hear of it. Although he couldn't have put his reasons into words, more than anything he wanted to reside at Ice House Pond before winter was out, when there was still plenty of rough snow and hard ice on those grounds.

But even when he got back to Greystone Bay he had to live a few days at the SeaHarp Hotel – the locals seemed oddly reluctant to rent him a truck capable of negotiating the road, and the small moving van bearing the few household furnishings he hadn't given away to in-laws refused to take them out there in those conditions. Fortunately, a cooperative manager at the hotel agreed to store the items for a small fee until Rudy was able to get to a neighbouring town, buy his own pickup truck, and return. By the time he got out to the pond with his belongings, it was near dark on the fifth day.

And the pond *was* much bigger than it was, even bigger than in the dreams he'd had of it every night since that first visit.

Rudy had a little trouble with slippage getting the new truck up over the shallow rim of hills, but the snow-packed road leading down into the saucer itself was in much better shape than what had preceded it, as if getting around on the property itself had long been a higher priority than getting back into town. The surrounding trees had already blended into one large, irregular shadow, but the difference in the air suspended over the pond was even more pronounced than before. Floating ice crystals caught the light and magnified it, like dancing, low-hanging stars. Rudy pulled his topcoat more tightly around him, hoping he had brought enough warm clothes. An extensive shopping trip before he left the city had readied him at least for an arctic expedition, but already he was having his doubts. The reality of such hard, inexplicable cold as that generated by the pond was a bit difficult to accept.

An intense storm again was blowing the width of the pond, lifting the snow off the ice into towering clouds of mist, white as powdered sugar. Then the mist began to tear apart into arms and fingers, and, like any schoolchild watching clouds some late summer, Rudy imagined dancers and boxers, fleeing men and drowning women in the separating mist. Just as the truck was leaving the rise for the flat drive to the house, the mist was blown away completely and Rudy got a clear view of the entire pond. And there was the broad palm scarred with life and death and fortune lines, the slight knobs to the north elongated, by drifting ice and snow and moon-silvered shadow, into long white fingers, as ready to stroke a sad cheek as tear out a heart with their razor-sharp nails.

The truck bumped its way into the front drive and slid sideways to a halt. Rudy leaned over the wheel, trying to cough out the slivers of ice that he'd suddenly sucked into his lungs.

Rudy brought in only what he knew he'd need that first night, along with anything that might be damaged by freezing. The rest of the truck could wait until tomorrow. He'd need more furniture from town, but he had plenty of time – years – to get it.

The house was even emptier than he remembered it, but then that wasn't what had concerned him most during his first visit. Of the few furnishings which remained, a good number were in such bad repair they were unusable. Rudy collected such debris from three of the front rooms into one large room, to give him a little bit of living space for now.

The empty rooms reminded him of life back before he was married, when he either couldn't afford the furniture or didn't think he needed it, or because his life hadn't yet been full enough to leave him with bits and pieces to haul around from one place to the next.

After Eva, his first wife, and their daughter Julie had died in the car accident, he'd held on to every furnishing from that life he possibly could, including most of Julie's toys. He thought it protected him from the empty rooms. Not until a few days prior to his marriage to Marsha had he thrown those items away. With Marsha had come still more things to fill his life. A fire at a downtown theater took her from him, and the unnamed baby she'd been carrying, and again he discovered he could not let go of her things. He had surrounded himself with them, even put them out on display.

His father used to tell him that in the concentration camps the "veterans" encouraged the newcomers to let go of their personal possessions as soon as possible. Sooner or later, they had to learn that their past, their lives, their status meant nothing now – they had only their naked bodies to depend on. The major reason his father had changed the name from Greensburg to Green when he came to America wasn't because of anticipated anti-Semitism, but because he didn't want to rely on his old name for comfort. If he had had a choice, he claimed, he would have preferred to go by no name at all. Names meant nothing in such a world.

So his first night at Ice House Pond, Rudy Green would sleep naked, in an empty room. At least he had heat. Within a few hours of turning on the furnace the place was like an oven. If anything, the heating plant worked too well. He would have to bring someone out to check the thermostat.

He took a flashlight and made a quick tour of the remaining rooms. The house certainly wasn't in as bad a shape as Lorcaster had suggested; the walls in what he supposed had been the living room would require a complete replastering, and the wooden baseboards had been removed in a parlour-sized room. Two of the upstairs bedrooms were in fine shape, complete with essentially usable beds, bookcases, and dressers (although he'd certainly want to replace the rotted mattresses). The other two bedrooms – one upstairs, one down – needed some new furniture and a few patches on the walls, but that was about it. The kitchen was old-fashioned, needed new linoleum, but was workable. The only true disaster area in the house was an ancient nursery at the back of the second floor, which for some reason Rudy hadn't seen during his first visit here. He couldn't have forgotten it.

He suspected that the nursery had been out of use much longer than other parts of the house – the crib and bassinet were rotting antiques, and the walls so severely water-damaged that great areas of plaster had melted away, revealing the wooden lathe which itself was rotting and falling. Much of the ceiling had come down, exposing beams just below the roofline and blackened, crumbling electrical cable. Here and there charred areas of the exposed wood revealed intermittent fire damage. At first Rudy was angry, but then decided that that kind of deception didn't fit the realtor's character; Lorcaster must not have known about the damage.

He and Marsha had been about to build a nursery when he'd lost them both. And now, with a sick feeling, he realized he was liking the idea of having a nursery here in this house, whatever its shape. Solitary people didn't have nurseries in their houses, nor did lonely young bachelors, nor did people with no more hope left for the future. Whatever changes he would make to this house, he knew that in some form this nursery would stay. There was something not quite right about that, he knew, but he didn't care. After his first family had died, the thought of having children had terrified him, although he'd still had the desire. He'd never told Marsha about any of these feelings; he'd acted as excited and happy as she was.

More life meant more death – that's what it finally came down to. The awful fecundity of the world, the terrifyingly long reach of life and its death accompaniment seemed to him a perversion. Every birth seemed to take place within a flowering of rot. What had nearly driven his father insane in the camps was having to live in ultimate exposure to so many people, their naked bodies, their bad habits, their stares, their breakdowns, their piss and shit violating his own flesh. And yet with such an overwhelming sense of massed living, breathing, sweating humanity, they still lived in a *cemetery*. There was no escaping it. More life meant more death, and what did it matter that your child died as long as you yourself survived? Rudy's father used to say that his own papa would have pushed him into the ovens before him if he'd had the chance and if it would have helped him save himself. But Rudy's father had lived and his grandfather perished. Who could figure it? Friends, families meant nothing. So much death in life, so much terror of both – the mathematics were unacceptable, yet inescapable.

What little wallpaper remained in the ancient nursery had yellowed to the point of brownness, so murky that its pattern was indecipherable. Rudy came as close to the wall as he dared, for the very walls stank of ancient damp and sewer smell. After a while he determined that the figures painted beneath the brown were cartoonish images of cute tiger cubs and lamb babies playing together, but the browning and other damage had so distorted their features they looked almost depraved, soiled and chewed upon. *Just the thing for a nursery in a mausoleum*, he mused, and felt disgust with himself for this errant thought.

He went to the side of the bassinet and rested his hand there. A miniature baby's pillow of pink silk lay on a greying, dusty blanket. The pillow was creased in such a way that Rudy could almost see the wrinkles where new eyes squeezed shut, where a new nose had just shown itself, where thin lips pursed into an upside-down W. The surface of the face began to crinkle and collapse, rotted cloth giving way, dark insect heads flooding out of pores and blisters and cavities to swarm across the blanket, eating and laying and multiplying even as they filled the bottom of the bassinet with a thick, writhing soup. Rudy stepped back as the tide lapped over the edge of the bassinet, long chains of the insects hanging out like the waving, reaching fingers of a dark hand.

But then he knew that wasn't what he was seeing at all. A *few* insects, no more, stains and shadows imitating the rest. With the little self-control Rudy had remaining, he left the room slowly, pulling the door tightly shut behind him.

Downstairs by the stairwell was the one door in the house he hadn't yet tried. It was cold to the touch, despite the severe heat in the other rooms – so cold his fingertips adhered painfully to the metal knob. He hadn't gone through this door his first visit – Lorcaster had said it led to the ice house. He'd planned to leave any examination of the ice house until he actually moved in. He hadn't been sure if it was usable, if he even wanted to use it, or if he'd have it torn down.

He found himself wrapping his fingers around the cold metal of the knob again and again as if trying to warm it. But the knob would not warm, and each time, he came dangerously close to losing some skin. And yet still his hand seemed to need to caress the painfully cold knob. Finally he brought his hand away bleeding, the fingers extended and spread, unable to touch each other. Rudy waved the hand around in the air to help ease the pain. It fluttered like a wounded, bleeding bird. It fluttered as if seeking something to hold, another hand, or maybe something sharp that would take the skin off.

An exploration of the ice house itself would wait until tomorrow. Rudy went back into the empty living room, skinned out of his clothes, and put his bare body down on the clean white sheet he'd used to cover the floor. A slight trickle of blood from his hand painted the sheet as he tossed and turned, searching for sleep in the worn patterns of the floor-boards.

This was all he had left, but it didn't matter. He had plenty of money – death money, pain money, blood money – to buy himself an entire new world of possessions.

II

Rudy woke up cold again. Sometime during the night the furnace had shut off.

His belly, arms, thighs were smeared with cold dried blood. The cold gobbets of blood around the wounds on his hand looked like cherry Jell-O. *Jesus, what have I done to myself?* He thought about the previous night and knew he had had some trouble with a door, but couldn't remember anything more than that. *Jesus . . .* He wadded up the bloodied sheet and tossed it into the corner. *The shock of changing heat and cold must have gotten to me . . . hallucinations . . .* He staggered into the kitchen and pushed hard on the tap with his good hand. He was pleased to see that the pipes weren't frozen, but he would always wonder why not. He shoved his bloody hand under the tap and grimaced. The water wasn't exactly freezing, but cold enough. After a few minutes it began to warm; thin threads of blood and bits of torn skin swirled dizzily down the drain. *Jesus . . .*

He looked out the kitchen window. The sun was high and bright, probably close to ten o'clock. Ice-melt flowing over the window distorted the view, but the bright snow and sun against yellow-and-orange trees actually made the outside world look halfway inviting. He tied his hand up in a towel and padded off to his pile of gear in one corner of the living room to find some warm clothes.

In the morning glare the house appeared even less friendly than it had the afternoon before. The rooms seemed concentrated with dust – transfusing the air, dusting the walls, powdering the rough wooden floorboards – as if the intense cold had sealed the atmosphere inside, permitting nothing to escape. The house needed a good airing out, but Rudy was more than reluctant to open up the windows. As a compromise he cracked one window in the living room and one upstairs. After a few minutes a ribbon of icy cold wound its way past him and up the stairs, dust motes crystallized and shining as they rode along its back.

The walls looked even worse than they had the day before. He began to wonder if any of them were salvageable. He imagined stripping the house down to its skeleton and rebuilding its walls with blocks of ice – thin, hard sheets of it for windows, curtained with lacy frost. His fantasies made him colder; he pulled on long underwear, two pairs of socks, the warmest pants and shirt he could find, shiny virgin boots thick as elephant hide. He felt swollen and uneasy in his new down-filled jacket, but he knew activity would lessen that discomfort.

The front door stuck when he tried to open it. A few hard pushes and it broke free with a snap. Tiny bits of ice stung his scalp, forehead, cheekbones.

Outside, the sun was like a huge white eye with a burning stare. If he looked into it long enough, Rudy knew he'd be able to see the deadly dark pupil hiding within. He pulled on his hood to protect himself – not from moisture, but from that fearsome sun.

During the night, light snow had pushed up on both sides of the door and was frozen in place. Now small holes were melting through the delicate membranes of ice – a woman's dazzling white lingerie dripping on the line. He almost expected her to come walking out of the snowbank that filled half of the yard, naked, pale, and cold. Rudy walked around the side of the house and could see the pond and the distant trees beyond. Snow still capped the branches, but enough had melted so he could now see the distant darkness inside the trees.

From here he could see how badly the exterior of his house had weathered the years. Below one of the upstairs windows the wood had cracked and a brown stain spread from there down to a window on the first floor. Always a bad sign –

there was a good possibility of structural damage underneath. But the rest of the structure was promising: A lot of scraping, a little puttying, replacement of a few shingles, and a good paint job would probably take care of it all.

As he continued down the slope to the ice-house portion of the structure, he couldn't help watching the pond, looking for some of the shadows he'd seen the day before. An oval near the center had melted – he could see rough waters rise here and there above the ice as if attempting escape. *That water's too rough for a landlocked pond*, he thought. He could sense the sun's heat battling the cold trapped over the pond. He found this perceived invisible activity unsettling, and looked away, gazing at his feet as they stalled and slipped their way down the slope by the ice house.

The ice house looked to be as sturdy a wooden building as Rudy had ever seen. It had two whitewashed levels: the ice house itself – level with the main house and with its own wraparound porch – and directly below it, a stone-walled cellar of some sort, or maybe it was an old-fashioned cooling chamber. Dead vines clung to the outside of the stone – he wondered if he would see it green up come spring. A rotting top hat had been nailed directly to the stone, a hole cut into the top. He stepped closer; an ancient bird's nest rested inside. The outside door to this lower level was only a few yards from the pond. Several shade trees planted close together made a protective shield for the southern exposure. A little canal three feet across led from the pond to a small hatch to the right of the door – for transporting the cut ice blocks, apparently. The roof of the ice house had a sharper pitch than that of the house, and its eaves were unusually wide, wide enough to shade the walls of the ice house even when the sun was low in the sky. The wraparound porch was similarly wide, so that thick posts had had to be used to support it. This would leave the outer stone walls of that lower level in shadow virtually all the time.

Of course there were no windows in the ice house, and Rudy could detect no doors off that upstairs porch, just a connecting walkway to the side of the main house and an outside staircase leading down to the pond. Other than the untouchable door inside the house he'd tried the night before, the only other entrance into the structure appeared to be the outside door to the lower level. If he was to find any more he'd have to go through that door.

This wasn't to be easily accomplished. Although the door had no lock, Rudy couldn't budge it. It was a thick door, heavy wood, and swollen from all the moisture. Rudy didn't think the damage had been caused by snow – the overhanging porch kept the area in front of the door relatively clear, and a small stone wall served as a windbreak for snow blowing off the frozen pond. Rather, it looked to have been underwater for a long period, as if at some time the pond had overflowed its banks. Something else Lorcaster had failed to mention, or perhaps hadn't known about. In any case, if Rudy used the ice house the door would have to be replaced.

Rudy retrieved the heavy-duty crossbar and a large flashlight from the new truck. He rammed the sharp end of the bar into the doorjamb and started prying. Dark wood splintered with a dull, damp sound. He had to pry away chunks all up and down the edge of the door before it finally creaked partway open; the edge looked gnawed by giant teeth. He wedged his heavy boot into the opening and used hands and knees to open it the rest of the way.

Bright, ice-reflected light flooded the stone chamber. The stark shadows of the support posts and Rudy's own upright form alternated with the bright gleamings of ice and metal. He fumbled for the light switch, and was pleased to see that the bulb was still good. The room became evenly brown. He breathed a heavy earth smell. The thick stone walls had troughs on each side, probably for keeping milk, meat, cheeses, vegetables cool during the summer. And, he suddenly recalled from some forgotten novel, for keeping the dead until the undertaker could get there. Tar had been used to seal the joints where walls met ceiling and floor. Antique ice pikes, picks, knives, and saws hung from pegs in the support beams overhead. The floor was sloped for drainage, as was the ceiling overhead, giving it a dangerous, caved-in look. From the lowest point of the ceiling a small pipe protruded above the drain in the floor, several foot-long icicles hanging from its open end. Above him were the press and cold of several tons of ice.

As he walked toward the back, his boot crunched through something brittle. He glanced down. The toe of his boot was wrapped in a tiny rib cage of greying bone threaded with dried flesh. He shook his leg and the bones separated and fell. The skull of the thing peered out at him from the side of one of the support beams.

A staircase rose in the center of the back wall. Rudy began climbing the dark well of it, intent on viewing the ice. With much effort, he was able to push aside the cellar-style doors in the ceiling. Old, dark sawdust rained heavily onto his head and shoulders. He was suddenly afraid of insects in his hair and down his collar, but he didn't really think any could live in such cold. Finally the air overhead was still. With no breeze to distribute it, the cold had the presence and intensity of stone. He turned on the flashlight and directed it overhead.

Tall columns of sawdust-caked ice rose up into the darkness of the roofline where Rudy's flashlight beam could not reach. An ice cathedral. An ice tomb. Rudy moved the beam around. He could see little detail under the grimy sawdust: a collage of shadows, light-absorbing grit, and isolated, jeweled ice reflections.

His back was damp with sweat inside the multiple layers of clothing. He could feel it turning to sleet as the chamber air drifted over him, as he thought about this dark, cold interior, this temporary storage place for the dead.

As a child he'd seen an old black-and-white movie late one night on television, a night like so many others in which he'd tried fruitlessly to sleep. He couldn't remember the name, but it was a science-fiction thing in which a scientist had frozen the bodies of Nazis in order to bring them back later, into a world less cautious, perhaps less aware of the evil. The interior of Rudy's ice house reminded him somewhat of the stark blacks and whites of the mad scientist's freezing chamber.

At the time he'd become obsessed with the image of that freezing place, where sleeping Nazis waited. Strangely enough, he found himself thinking of that freezing place as a kind of analogue for the gas chambers and ovens his father had survived. He felt compelled to reimagine his father's time in the camps as if they had been places of freezing, where the naked bodies had been stacked into great freezers instead of gas chambers, ovens, and mass graves, their postures of agony preserved for all time, until some future scientist devised a way of safely thawing them, and they were able to wander naked among their descendants, minds perhaps damaged by the intense cold so that they shuffled and stared, but still able to bear witness to their terrible ordeal.

Rudy's father had signed himself into a nursing home before the cancer finally took him.

"This is the *worst* place you could have chosen!" Rudy had screamed at him.

His father had smiled sadly. "I know."

"I don't *understand*. You have the money for a good place." The halls bore the constant stench of shit and piss. Half-naked residents shambled through the halls.

His father had looked around dreamily, calling to the residents he had never met before, using the old Jewish names from the distant past. Then Rudy had known: This was his father's own way of reimagining the camps.

Rudy closed the doors to the ice chamber and backed down the steps. He sat on the edge of a stone trough waiting for his eyes to adjust, then he went back out into blinding light and ice, closing the broken door behind him as best he could.

"So, you plannin' to sell some of that ice?"

Rudy spun around so fast his feet slid out from under him He recovered by throwing his knees together, but not without considerable embarrassment. He felt ridiculous; he was sure he looked even worse. The man staring at him from the other side of an ancient green snowmobile was tall but sickly-looking – lids and eyes so dark it was like looking into two holes. He wore a dirty green-checkered jacket and flop-eared cap – standard New England farmer issue. "Can I help you?" Rudy managed, trying not to betray the aching pain in his ankles.

"Didn't mean . . . to startle you," the man said. Rudy took the comment more as an assertion of position than as an apology.

"No problem," Rudy said. "And you wanted . . .?" These New Englanders could beat around the bush all they wanted to, but Rudy wasn't about to play that game.

"I asked if you were puttin' the place back into business again. Sellin' the ice. Talk has it you're gonna harvest this year. First time in twenty, I reckon."

"Well, sir . . . I guess I didn't catch your name. Mine's Rudy. Rudy Green."

"Netherwood." He stuck out his hand and Rudy latched onto it with an odd sense of desperation. For such a sickly-looking fellow, Netherwood's hand was enormous, and strong. "B.B. is what folks call me."

"Well, Mr Netherwood, I don't know where that talk came from, but I've made no such plans. I haven't made any decisions in that area at all, as a matter of fact."

"Folks 'round Greystone love to talk, Mr Green. That's about all there is to do around here – don't matter if it's true or not. But I take it you haven't decided *not* to open her up then, have you?"

"No, I can't say that I've ruled it out completely. But I don't think it's likely either. I don't know a thing about the ice business. That's not the reason I bought this place. So you're in the market for ice, are you?"

Netherwood shook his head. "Got all I need. Just figured you might be needing some help around here. I work cheap."

"Well, I'll keep that in mind . . ."

"*Real* cheap. I *love* this old place." Netherwood looked almost ridiculous in his sudden enthusiasm. "And I love the ice business. You won't do better than calling on me."

Rudy stared at this man who seemed to have grown healthier even as they talked. He tried to gauge his age, but between the years in his face and the strength in his hands Rudy found he could not. "I'll seriously consider that, Mr Netherwood," he said. "I certainly will."

That night Rudy spent a few hours hauling debris out of the rooms and piling it onto a snowbank on the north side of the front yard. He figured he could live with the mess in his yard until spring, when he could hire a truck to take it away. He knew he'd be sleeping in the living room temporarily and so swept its floor clean and attacked the windows with ammonia, then caulk and heavy curtains to keep out the cold. This would be the last night he could stand it without a real bed, however. One of the next day's projects was going to consist of moving a bed down from upstairs and fixing it up with some sort of mattress substitute. He couldn't imagine lying down on any of the mattresses that had been left behind.

Rudy was putting the broom back into a narrow closet by the stairwell when one of his stockinged feet slipped into a pool of cold water. He looked down. He didn't know why he'd thought it water – it was viscous, like syrup or oil, and when he lifted his foot thin strands of it tugged at his sock.

He jerked his foot and the strands let go. They curled back into the clear pool and then the center of the pool turned milky, then appeared to solidify, looking something like a clump of torn whitefish meat or waterlogged tissue.

Rudy turned on the light hanging by the stairwell. A yellow

glow seeped from the bulb. In slow motion, he thought, as if the air were impossibly thick here, or full of dust, but he could neither see nor feel anything unusual in the air.

At least the yellow light allowed him to see the extent of the leak – he was already thinking of it as a leak even though he had no idea what it might be leaking from. It had gathered into a spot approximately two feet across in the center of this section of grey flooring, with a narrow tail that wriggled its way underneath the door to the ice house.

Rudy had a sudden terror of the entire ice house turning to slush and pushing its way through the walls of his home, mashing the place into soggy kindling. He suddenly felt in touch with the terrible *potential* of all that ice.

A thawing was impossible. It was just too damn *cold*.

He grabbed a mop out of the closet and pushed it gingerly into the area of the leak. The mop rapidly filled with the damp and became so heavy Rudy could barely lift it from the floor. After a few seconds the mop head appeared to bleach. Rudy bent closer and discovered the bleached effect was in fact ice. The leak had frozen again, and the mop had frozen to the floor.

Rudy went back into the living room for his boots, picked up his tire bar off the floor, and worked it back and forth between the door and the metal jamb where thin layers of melting and refreezing ice had glued the two pieces together. His breath made tortured clouds of white mist in the air. Now and then he shoved so hard against the bar he wasn't sure if the resulting cracking noise was the ice or his own bones giving way.

Finally he felt the door beginning to ease open. Tiny fragments of ice showered the floor. A sudden explosion of cold air tightened the skin of his face and forced his eyes closed. As he heard more ice cracking the weight of the door took it out of his hands. His eyes still closed, he heard the door bang against the wall as if from a great distance. He imagined a delicate balance of atmospheres between the space of his house and the space of the ice house. He imagined the ice house melting all at once: boards and timbers melting down to the foundation stones. And as an alternative vision he imagined his house frosting through from the inside, all the walls and floors rimed to a slick, glasslike finish.

But nothing so dramatic occurred when he opened his eyes. The passage into the ice house was dark, and smelled of old, cold air, but the switch just inside the door still made a bank of bulbs recessed into frosted cages overhead burn orange-under-white. Overhead the light disappeared into the dark recesses of the quarter-pitch roof. He could hear the faint whirring of the ventilator up there removing any collected vapor. Ahead of him a series of boards had been slid behind two upright timbers to hide the passage to the ice beyond. Bundles of long straw had been packed tightly around these as insulation. Intense cold had blackened the boards and straw and, as in his fantasy, had turned portions of these to black ice that bled darkly from the heat pushing in from the warm house. Here on the other side of these black boards was the oldest ice, the ice he hadn't been able to see from the cooling chamber below.

Rudy went back for his tire bar and used it to loosen the ice that cemented the boards together. Then, by wiggling each board back and forth, he was able to free them from the hidden ice blocks. It took him two hours to remove the top five boards, exposing a window of antique ice three feet square.

The array of ice blocks was grey, like frozen fog, with occasional shiny specks buried deep inside which vaguely reflected the light from the caged overheads.

Rudy stepped closer, shielding his eyes for the best view, careful not to actually touch the ice for fear his skin would adhere to it.

Faint shadows melted across the ice. He twisted around, feeling as if someone had stepped behind his shoulder and momentarily blocked the light. But nothing was there.

He came back around, and stared into shadowed sockets, and beneath those a dark gaping mouth frozen in the act of swallowing ice.

Rudy shouted, and the face in the ice before him fogged over. And all his wiping and scraping on the dim ice would not bring it back.

When he finally shut the door behind him he discovered that the mop had become unstuck, fallen over, and the leak was drying. Only a small, pulpy, white residue was left, and that turned to frost, then pale fog even as he watched.

III

The second visitor to Rudy's new home was Mrs Lorcaster, the realtor's wife.

He'd awakened late. The furnace definitely seemed to have a

mind of its own, and his sleep had been disturbed several times during the night because of alternating intense heat and intense cold. He was bound to come down with something serious if he didn't get it taken care of quickly. He'd been dressed only a short time when he heard the knocking at his door.

From what he could see, the woman standing on the other side of the icy door-panes seemed to be warmly but elegantly dressed: a dark suit and white blouse draped with a tailored, muted red cape of brushed wool. She tapped lightly, directly on the ice-covered frame. Ice broke and fell beneath the steady rap of her dark-gloved knuckles.

She was obviously nonplussed to be suddenly viewing his early-morning face distorted on the other side of the icy glass. But she recovered with a practiced smile. Rudy made a feeble attempt to smile back. He pulled as hard as he could on the door. It stuck, then let go all at once, showering her with a blizzard in miniature. Embarrassed, Rudy reached out to dust off her cape, but reconsidered when she reacted with a step backwards into the snow. "I'm sorry," he said quickly. "Can I help you?"

"Quite all right." She stepped past his arm and into the house. "I'm Emily Lorcaster. I believe you know my husband?"

Apparently not as well as I thought. He couldn't match up this elegant creature with Lorcaster. He stared at a silver lock of her hair trapped within a fold in her hood. A snowflake hung within the curl like a jewel, refusing to melt. "Yes. He sold me . . ." Rudy made a nervous, sweeping gesture. "All this." He stopped, not knowing what else to say. "I feel very lucky," he added awkwardly.

"Yes. Of course." She tried to look past him into the rooms beyond. He found himself shifting his stance, purposely blocking her view. He didn't know why — having just moved in he obviously wasn't responsible — but he was embarrassed by the condition of the place. She gave up and looked at him directly. "I used to live here. In fact, I grew up in this house." She looked at him in anticipation, but he had no idea what she expected from him.

"That's very interesting," he said, feeling increasingly inferior to this creature. He wondered if Lorcaster felt the same way. Perhaps that was why the man dressed the way he did.

"I've heard you may start up the ice operation again. My

grandfather designed and built the ice house, as well as the living quarters here. My maiden name was Finney, you see."

Rudy quickly tried to remember what Lorcaster had said about "Old Finney." He couldn't remember the specifics, just that it had had a negative tone to it. The previous owner hadn't been a Finney, though – some investor in New York by the name of Carter. So it had passed out of the family. Now Rudy could make some rough guesses concerning Lorcaster's reluctant style of salesmanship. "Just a rumor, I'm afraid," Rudy said. "I don't know how it started. Actually, I hadn't really decided. You know, just yesterday a man named Netherwood came by – "

"*Netherwood*," she interrupted. "I see. Still about, is he?"

Rudy didn't think she really wanted the question answered. "I have to admit this interest in the ice has me curious," he said. "I might have to look into it."

"Oh, by all *means!* My grandfather, and my father after him had quite a lucrative business. And you'll still find those very interested in the ice from this particular pond."

"Magic ice, eh? Something special?" Rudy tried to chuckle, but it caught in his throat.

She eyed him coldly. "Perhaps. I wouldn't know. But I know there is a market."

"I'm surprised. Surely with modern refrigerators and freezers . . ."

"Tradition, Mr Green. The people of Greystone value it most seriously. And some would cherish just the novelty of that sort of ice, I'm sure. And then there's the ice palace. We had wonderful ice palaces! Many here still remember them."

"Ice palaces?"

"Winters, for years, the whole town would come out to the pond and help Grandfather cut and haul the ice. Blocks two feet wide and almost three in length. They'd lay the blocks out on a pattern staked out in the snow on the other side of the stone wall; the forest wall made a beautiful backdrop. There they'd build up ice walls, and ramparts, and Grandfather would chisel turrets into the huge towers. People would come from towns many miles away to see the palace and spend their money. It was a great boon to the town."

"I take it the custom eventually stopped?"

"They *used* my grandfather." She looked almost, but not quite angry. "Or at least he thought so. He said they only cared about money, or whatever they had in hand. He said they had changed, all of them. He said they sat around in their houses doing nothing, breathing in the fog off the Bay, letting it fill up their lungs. He said there were just too many of them for comfort. Too many eyes to stare at him in their pain. Too many mouths to feed. Too many bodies old and dying. Finally, too many to bury. He said they didn't even behave like human beings anymore."

"That's pretty strong, isn't it?"

She smiled faintly. "I suppose my grandfather wasn't very well at the time. He worked very hard, you see. Other than the construction of the palace each winter, he would permit no one to help him, except for occasional odd jobs he would offer my father when he was young. He would hire no one, and my grandmother was not allowed near the ice. He discouraged visitors; he no longer had any friends in the town. He suffered the customers for his ice simply as a necessary evil. 'My own personal poison,' he would say, and laugh – the only time I ever heard him laugh. He'd cut the ice himself and guide it down the trough from the pond to the cooling room. He wore the pike handles down until they snapped from his using them, his hands moving constantly around and around their shafts in that nervous way he had when he worked the ice.

"Back when there were ice palaces he used to let me play inside. I was the *princess*, you see. He said the ice palace was my castle, and I could do what I wanted. Once he stopped building the palaces he had very little to say to me. He'd simply haul the ice that would have gone into the palace up into the ice house, and once the ice house was full he'd still cut the blocks and lay them out on the bank, leaving them there for spring melt. Fewer and fewer customers came, so there was always a large surplus left on the bank."

"So why did he bother cutting up the ice? Just to have something to do?"

"My grandfather never did *anything* 'just to have something to do.' Everything was done with a purpose. I used to think that at his age he believed he needed to repeat the habitual gestures of his job again and again or else his muscles would lose their edge and forget what was required of them. Eventually it became clear that he viewed it as he would view the milking of a cow: It was necessary."

"If you don't milk them they become swollen and in pain.

Eventually they go dry," he said. She looked at him quizzically. He smiled. "My father kept a cow in his garage in the city, until enough of his neighbors complained. He had liked that cow more than people, and trusted it far more. He had said that the cow was infinitely more reliable. Forgive me for saying so . . . but I imagine the town found that to be very strange behavior."

"Certainly. They did. But things happened when he failed to harvest the ice. I know. I saw them." She paused, as if waiting for him to guess. *Get on with it*, he thought, but said nothing. And still she waited.

"What happened?" he finally asked, angered by this petty use of power.

"At first the ice turned very grey. Greyer than any fog. If you put your tongue on it it would taste sour. Some got very sick doing that – a few even died. And you could see all kinds of shadows trapped inside, or worse still, vaguely moving if you had the right angle on it. Sometimes you thought you saw faces there, as if someone were looking up at you through a foggy window, but you could never be sure. If you put your hand on the ice too long the ice hurt the skin. It burned, or ached for days. And a few times the ice went completely black, coal black, surely unlike any ice that ever was. Grandfather said harvesting the ice was the only way to keep the pond pure, to put things right again. He said that it was dangerous if left too long."

"You saw this?" he asked.

"I did. And tasted it. And felt it."

Rudy turned and looked out a side window. He could see one corner of the pond where the ice had melted and dead leaves floated, swirling in a small circle. White chunks of ice bobbed to the surface like drowned hunks of flesh. In the yard, snow and ice encrusted the old furniture he'd tossed there, making it resemble brilliant white formations of coral. "How long has it been since the ice was last harvested here?" he asked.

"Too long, Mr Green." She almost smiled. "Better a dazzling clean ice palace, don't you think, than that great stretch of frozen grey fog?"

The wind picked up after lunch, keeping Rudy inside. He spent several hours staring out of an upstairs window at the pond and the distant trees. By late afternoon white snow-mist was blowing off the frozen water – a solid expanse of it, no breaks now –

turning to grey fog once it got a few yards over the land. The brilliant white eye in the sky had shut its lid. Ice trees bent and broke into glistening shards as the wind picked up. The skin of the pond grew greyer still. It seemed to turn to night in the pond before it turned to night in the sky.

The visitors had soured Rudy. He'd come here for escape, and now they wanted him to revive a business – to build ice palaces, no less. Despite his fascination with the ice house and its history, the thought of all the other visitors that that might bring, all the customers, appalled him. He just wanted to be alone. With his thoughts, his memories, his imagined relationships with dead families. He could live with the invisible presence of Old Finney, even his father – that seemed to fit, that seemed inevitable. But no one else.

That night Rudy set up one of the old beds in his living room, tightening all the rusted wood-screws and hammering in a few large nails for additional support, and constructing a mattress out of sewn-together sheets with rags and odd bits of clothing stuffed inside. He shut the furnace off completely, thinking that he'd sleep better in his clothes, with several heavy blankets laid on top.

But after only a short time he was awake again, the sweat pouring off him, the distant sound of the furnace a hot static in his ears. He stared up at the ceiling. He thought he could see the waves of heat flowing there, gesturing to him with their long curves and heated mouths. Sweat popped up out of his flesh and immediately went cold, so that he could track the progress of every drip across his painfully warm skin.

The furnace was working overtime to protect him from the deadly cold. As if it had its own intelligence. The cold was tricky: It hid in the corners, under the bed, around the windows. It could seep through an unprotected electrical outlet or along a pipe coming through the wall. It prowled the floorboards in search of ill-protected feet.

But more than that, a mass of it hid just on the other side of the badly insulated wall. The oldest cold Rudy had ever known, heavy and full of memory.

He'd always insisted that couples who had separate beds – or, worse still, separate bedrooms – could not really call themselves married at all. It was the body heat that was important, that they needed to share, the heat that signified their living, their working and doing. And of course at no time was that plainer than on a cold night, when the skin sent out the messages of *I live, I need*, and *I love*. He wouldn't even allow himself to buy an electric blanket. Now his memories of his wives and children were cool ones – they lacked the heat of life, the heat of love. In memory there was only numbing, deadly cold.

He did not know how long he'd been hearing the dripping before he recognized it for what it was. He slipped his boots on and went out to the stairwell, but there was no leak or stain on the floorboards. And yet he could smell the damp; he could smell the cold. He looked at the door to the ice house, and there the stain of head-shaped damp, the torso, a slow ooze of water through the pores of the cracked and peeling wood making the bare beginnings of the legs.

Rudy walked slowly to the door to examine it. As his warm breath – life breath, love breath – hit the stain, it vanished.

He opened the door without much difficulty; he'd pretty much destroyed the jamb the night before. Only a small amount of the light from the stairwell lamp slipped into the chamber, but tonight he was reluctant to switch on the overhead bulbs inside the ice house. The square of ice ahead of him seemed to glow with its own inner, grey light. From this distance fog appeared to swirl just beneath the hard surface.

In the camps, his father had told him, you eventually had nothing but your naked body to protect you from the cold. Any clothing you might have meant very little. As did wealth or status. Then his father had told him the cancer felt like an invasion of ice into his body. Cold, numbing memory that froze his cells one at a time, not at all like the consuming fire he'd always imagined cancer to be. Rudy approached the square window of grey ice. Staring into it was like staring into a cross section of the frozen pond itself. Shadows flickered across the grey surface. He twisted his head, looking for moths against the light, but there were none. He stared again at the ice, and knew then that the shadows were just beneath the surface, and not on its top. He stretched his hands out, fingers spread, and set them gingerly against the ice, careful to keep the contact on the subtle side, afraid his fingertips might adhere and then he'd lose them, substituting wounds for them. The ice grew dark where he touched it; the shadows of his hands in the ice appeared to grasp the hands themselves. Then the shadows of his hands in the ice floated away from his hands and grasped the sides of his shadow head, his skull head with gaping eye holes and absent mouth screaming and screaming as it stared at him. Rudy backed away but his shadow self in the ice did not move. Rudy backed away and saw the naked form floating in the ice, emaciated and cold, consumed by hatred, accusing him with its stare. And Rudy thought of Auschwitz, and Treblinka, and that last picture of his father's cancer-ridden body, and some poor soul drowned so long ago in Ice House Pond, harvested and preserved in Old Finney's secret ice palace.

The body disappeared, and the ice was a murky grey again.

IV

The last thing Rudy wanted to do that next morning was negotiate the road into Greystone Bay, but he had little choice now.

Lately, mornings had been warm enough to cause considerable snowmelt each day, but that actually made the roads even more treacherous. The pickup veered dangerously as it topped the slight hill that marked the edge of his property. Rudy fought the wheel and then let the car slide down most of the remainder of the decline.

Greystone Bay's biggest bookstore was the Harbor Bookshop, which had a large selection of local histories, most of them of the privately-printed kind. There were also several volumes of facsimile newspapers, compilations of historically significant police reports, and other document collections of historical interest. A small selection of contemporary paperback novels were displayed on wire racks at the front of the store; they appeared to be largely ignored. During the two hours Rudy spent in the store he saw only one customer examine them: a fat man in a fuzzy red coat who eventually bought one of the dark-covered horror novels whose cover displayed a man's decaying head, worms encircling the fixed iris of the left eye. The man asked for directions to the nearest hotel and the elderly clerk told him how to get to the SeaHarp.

The rest of the stock was about a twenty/eighty per cent mix of new and used hardcovers, university and scientific presses, local and small presses, handmade volumes, fine editions, charts and prints, and occasional unclassifiable dusty paperbacks. All in no particular order. In the few instances where shelves had actually been labeled, the labels were nonsensical (Books We Wished We Had Read, Imaginary Countries, Working Titles, Character Assassinations), or useless (the three shelves carefully labeled Classics were empty). But the good grey clerk appeared to know where every book contained within the shop's shadowed walls was located, however obscure. Each of Rudy's inquiries brought a flood of title names and locations. Eventually, he had gathered all the sources he thought he might need. The clerk guided him to an overstuffed chair, almost showing its springs, and left him.

Rudy found what he wanted in *The Greystone Papers: A Century of Headlines, Major Stories, and Oddities*, in the chapters concerning a twenty-year stretch of the Bay's history. Old Finney's stretch.

BAKER CHILD STILL MISSING

Constable Biggs still reports no leads in the case of John Baker, age six, still missing after twelve days. The boy was last seen in a field near The Hand where his father, Philip Baker, was gathering firewood . . .

PRESUMED ELOPEMENT

Mary Buchanan, mother of Ellen Buchanan, wishes to announce the elopement of her daughter with William Colbert of Hinkley. Earlier reports of foul play, Mrs Buchanan informs us, are certainly the products of perverse and overactive imaginations . . .

HUNTERS LOST

County deputies and rescue workers are still searching the North Forest for Joseph Netherwood and his son Paul, who were separated from their hunting party Friday afternoon at approximately three P.M. when their dog Willy . . .

Dozens of other stories described similar events. Rudy gladly paid the exorbitant ransom the clerk wanted for the book.

The Harbor Bookshop sported an old-fashioned pay phonebooth. There were six Netherwoods in the phone book, but only one B.B.

Before leaving the store, Rudy made two more purchases: yellowed handbooks concerning the construction, maintenance, and day-to-day use of ice houses.

* * *

He ran into Mrs Lorcaster coming out of the bookstore. She was bowed from the weight of packages, heading for an old station wagon. He grasped her elbow gently as she walked past, not recognizing him. "You didn't tell me about all the missing people," he said quietly.

She staggered slightly, and part of her load began to tilt. Rudy reached out to steady it. He caught a small bag in mid-fall and nestled it inside one of the larger ones. One of her lovely eyes peeked out at him from between the two largest bags. She didn't seem so self-assured, so powerful now. She seemed more like what he'd have expected Lorcaster's wife to be. "I . . . don't understand," she said.

"*Emily.*" He shook his head. "All those people a number of years back who ended up missing? *Rural* people, for the most part? People your grandfather would have known?"

"You've been talking to Mr Netherwood. He's a bitter, *disturbed* man," she said.

"I've been talking to him, yes. But not about his missing relatives. I figure he'll tell me all about them in his own good time. But I've seen some things at the ice house, Em . . . Mrs Lorcaster. In ice that must date back to your grandfather's time."

She put her bags down on the hood of the station wagon, letting them tumble. She was a sad lady, suddenly looking old. Now Rudy was feeling insensitive. "He was my grandfather and I loved him very much," she said. "And he . . . he *hated* people around here. He'd come to that, all right. But I cannot believe he would actually *do* anything to anyone. I never knew that to be a part of his nature."

"That house. That pond." Rudy hesitated, searching for the right word. "They aren't *right*."

"Then *do* something, Mr Green. At one time my grandfather built palaces."

"And then?"

"And then my aunt died. She was three years old when she lost herself in the fog, and drowned in the pond. My grandmother, who'd always been so quiet, stewing in her silence, became quite mad. And something happened to my grandfather. He grew frightened of people, the way the mass of them intruded, the way life created death. He said that the Bay had its own will and its own way of populating itself out of the fog. He came to see the townspeople as not simply other, but *other*. They were no

longer human, as far as he was concerned. But I cannot believe
he would have killed. My grandfather built *palaces*, Mr Green.
Those hints of murder . . . that is simply Mr Netherwood's brand
of gossip."

"I'll be hiring Mr Netherwood, Emily. I think you should
know that."

"Whatever for?"

"For the ice business. And maybe I'll be building palaces
as well."

V

Two days later, B.B. Netherwood met Rudy by Ice House Pond
at six in the morning, as arranged. Netherwood was already there
by the time Rudy had gotten out of bed and dressed and made
his way through the thick snow around the side of the building.
Snow had fallen again all evening, as it had several evenings in a
row. And although the sun was out and there were no clouds in
the sky, this was the coldest morning Rudy had yet experienced
at the pond. It seemed as if his newfound determination to take
charge of things had brought out a renewed stubbornness in the
weather. The cold seemed to have leeched much of the color
out of the trees and sky, even his own clothes. The landscape
he saw was like a faded picture in some grandparent's photo
album.

The distant trees looked stiff and dead. There was no breeze.
The thick snow swallowed his footprints.

He found B.B. Netherwood standing by a large pile of gear,
apparently unloaded from the battered green snowmobile and
its attached sled. Netherwood gazed out over the frozen pond,
fixed and motionless, as if frozen himself.

Rudy purposely made as much noise as he could thrashing
through the snow. Netherwood turned and went over to the
bottom of the slope to wait for him.

"You have a personal interest in the pond, I believe," Rudy
said.

Netherwood scratched at his chin. "You must have figured
that out from something you read in town, am I correct? An
old newspaper or something?"

"According to the papers two Netherwoods were missing, I
assumed, of course, they were relatives."

"My daddy and my older brother Paul. Helluva kid, and a helluva dad, if truth be told. Although I was pretty mad at them for going hunting without me that day. But then I was only eight; I could hardly hold up the rifle." Netherwood shuffled his feet, his hands buried in his baggy pants pockets as if that would keep him warmer.

Anxiety makes you cold, especially out here, Rudy thought. And then: *This is crazy*. "And you've thought about it all this time. Considered where, and how."

"You don't stop thinking about it, Mr Green. The folks around here talk about things – I hear you have a lot on your mind, too. The fact that I was just a kid at the time doesn't make much difference in the thinking about it, the dreaming about it, except maybe I've had a longer time for doing it."

Rudy took a deep breath. The cold air seized his lungs, squeezing until they began to burn. "But why this place? What makes you think you'll find out something about them *here*?"

"The same reason you called me, Rudy. I really didn't see you for somebody who'd go into the ice business, despite my coming to visit you the other day. Same thing that told me I'd find out something about what happened to Daddy and Brother right here on the pond, I suspect." He looked directly into Rudy's eyes. "Seen anything since you been here? Anything you're afraid to tell 'cause folks might think you're crazy?"

Rudy told him about the alternating freezing and melting leak, and the shadowy form in the ice trying to grasp his hand.

B.B. just nodded. "I've seen the worst storms you can imagine, bad as any tornado or hurricane, right over this pond and nowhere else. When they move away from the ice they don't go anywhere – they just disappear. I've seen shadows big as a house floating under the ice. I've seen smaller ones, too, man-size and smaller. And sometimes they do a little dance, a little ballet. And there are days in summer, I swear the water gets all rusty and stinks like a slaughter-house."

"Something strange here, B.B., something very odd," Rudy said.

"Something cold," B.B. Netherwood replied.

Netherwood had brought his own tools: a carpenter's toolbox and some good door stock, a push broom, some weatherproof paint, and various tools for cutting and handling the ice, although the tools hanging up in the cooling room were still in remarkable shape, greased, with the metal parts wrapped in oilcloth. Rudy told B.B. that frankly he knew nothing himself, except for what he'd read quickly in the two old handbooks he'd purchased, and so B.B. shouldn't hesitate to give the orders. B.B. told Rudy to "get to sweeping, then," while B.B. worked on the splintered door and jamb. "Looks like something *et* it," B.B. said. Rudy told him what he'd had to do to get in and B.B. just shook his head.

The dust, seemingly harder to push in such cold, created a stench when it was disturbed, so bad that Rudy had to tie a handkerchief over his mouth and nose while he worked. He didn't even want to think about what caused that smell. He used a shovel to remove the animal skeleton he'd found the other day.

He was impatient to get to what needed to be done, and find some answers. But he also wanted to do things right, and he knew this man Netherwood knew how to do things right. But still the practical and ultimately meaningless chore of putting the ice house back into working order reminded Rudy of nursing homes and concentration camps.

"You think you'll do the ice palace?" B.B. asked.

"If that's what it takes," Rudy replied.

"Hmmmm . . ." was all B.B. said, working his plane up and down the edge of the door.

Rudy swept until he could see clean stone flooring to all four corners. B.B. was still working on the door, trying to make it fit the opening, muttering about old houses, how there "wasn't a single parallelogram in the whole damn lot of 'em," so Rudy got ammonia and brushes and started scrubbing down the stone troughs. Even under the sharp bite of the ammonia he thought he could smell spoiled milk and vegetables, meat left too long in the season, even its blood starting to grey.

After another hour Rudy's patience was wearing thin. The weight of the ice overhead oppressed him, and he imagined he could feel the pressure of the tons of frozen ice in the pond behind him, pressing its weight against the embankments, pressing against the world, freezing its way slowly to the muddy bottom, pushing its argument toward China, if it could. And turning greyer by the hour. Rudy expected an explosion at any moment would rip off the back of his skull.

"Done," B.B. called from the doorway, his form a silhouette against the brilliant light that filled the doorway. "Give me a few minutes to shovel out the raceway and chip the ice off the gate, then we can start. I brought along a few sandwiches we can munch on while we're working, providing you got a clean jacket pocket."

The raceway and gate took more than a little shoveling and chipping, but B.B. eventually got it done. The ice was like concrete; B.B. was scarlet-cheeked and drenched by the time he finally broke through. The dark, cold water rushed down the raceway to the front of the ice house. "It's full of silt . . . or pollution . . . something . . ." Staring down at the water filling the raceway, Rudy could not see the bottom, even though it was only a couple of feet deep. The water was black, and dangerous-looking. Steam escaped where the water made contact with the warmer metal of the raceway.

"Yeah . . . something . . ." B.B. said, going for two sets of tools. "I just wouldn't put my hand in it if I were you. I wouldn't even *look* at it too long. Come on . . . we got ice to cut."

B.B. brought out two each of two different styles of saw, as well as two "choppers" – something like thin-bladed hatchets. The chopper felt especially good in Rudy's hand – as well-balanced and perfectly formed as a surgeon's instrument.

"Don't waste the ice," B.B. said. He chopped off a little from the edge where he'd begun removing the ice, making a remarkably clean horizontal line by the open, dark water. Then he used the chopper to make his lines. "Two by three feet is a good size," he said. "The size Old Finney designed this setup for anyway. Ice should be about a foot, foot and a half thick here. If we're lucky it won't get much thicker or thinner than that anyplace else in the pond. But I don't suppose we can hope for luck in these particular waters." He chopped deeper through the lines, then used his saws to cut the rest of the way. The block looked remarkably perfect, like a giant ice cube, crisp corners, and grey as woodsmoke.

"I've never been good at estimating measurements," Rudy told him, trying to keep his mind off the grey of the ice, or the even darker shadows that seemed to change position as B.B. used the pike to move the block down through the raceway. Or the vague unpleasant smell when a minuscule portion of the ice block melted, condensing on its upper surfaces.

"Don't worry. The more of these you cut, the closer you'll be getting to a perfect two-by-three. You won't be able to help yourself. Once we cut a certain number of blocks, we move them down the raceway like this, then we'll use a block and tackle to drag them up the ramp into the ice house upstairs. Usually another team works on that end of it, but the two of us'll just have to work it double."

B.B. proceeded to cut out enough of the ice to provide Rudy with a horizontal edge to start his own row. Or, rather, double row: Both men started using five cuts to carve out two huge blocks at a time.

Rudy thought about Old Finney performing the same task so many years ago. He thought he even had Old Finney's saw and chopper – they were far more worn than B.B.'s set. After a time he was able to lose himself in the work, chopping and sawing, aware only of the proscribed movements of his muscles, and the endless grey.

At times the rhythmic chopping made Rudy think of hundreds of pairs of hard boots marching across polished wood floors, across fitted stones, across ice. The wind picked up and blew snow across his knuckles, freezing and burning them, finally numbing them. Now and then he would look up at the sky – he could see no approaching storms, but he could feel them. His joints ached. He looked over at B.B., who stared at the grey ice as he worked, who stared into the dark cold water, into nothing.

"Do you always think about them?" Rudy asked, as he began to saw.

B.B. said nothing for a few moments, letting his saw make the only noise, scratching and tearing through the ice, the sound rising when it reached the really hard sections, sounding like a cat caught on a hook. "Not always," he finally said. "But every day, sometime. Paul was already a pretty good man, the way I remember it. Just like Daddy. I'll never know if I'm as good a man. I was too young when it happened – not much judgment yet. What about you? You thinking about them now?" B.B. asked without looking up, his gaze drawn along with the maddening saw.

Rudy slowed down his own saw so he could hear himself think. "They're there, somewhere, even when I don't have their precise image in front of me. My second wife – this sounds terrible – I think I married her when I did partly so I could start putting an end to the grieving for my first wife."

"But you loved her, too, right?"

"Very much."

"I figured. But you still knew what you did, why you did it, and you felt guilty as hell about it. I know about guilt."

They widened a highway of dark water toward the center of the pond. By lunchtime the dark water was looking grey and beginning to freeze again. They had to go back down the expanse, breaking up any new connections frozen in between the floating blocks. The tiny specks of snow in the bright air were growing slightly larger.

Walking down either side of the carved-out waterway, they used their pikes to herd the blocks to the raceway. A huge hook at the end of the block and tackle allowed them to pull several blocks up the ramp at a time, although sometimes they had to use B.B.'s ancient snowmobile for additional pulling power. Once up in the ice house, they used portable ramps and levers to stack the blocks.

Rudy kept looking for angular, naked shadows in the stacks of older ice, but he really hadn't the time to do a thorough search. The new ice blocks, even greyer than the old ones, seemed to trap and absorb the light. The overhead caged bulbs in the ice house made little headway.

Once surrounded by the towers of ice, Rudy found it difficult to breathe.

During a rest break, Rudy lay on the frozen pond, a strip of ragged canvas underneath to protect him from the cold, and to keep his skin from adhering to that sticky grey exterior.

He used the edge of the chopper to scrape away a little of the silver rime. His lips looked blue in the reflection, his eyes dark coals, his snowy skin shifting loosely on the bones.

In late afternoon the fog rolled in, thicker than before. Although nothing was said, they both increased the pace of their work, despite their weariness. Rudy's arms grew steadily colder, despite the energy he tried to will into them, the pace at which he pushed them. They looked translucent in the fog-filtered light. Translucent ice skin.

The fog was turning to cold, to ice and snow. Rudy looked up:

He seemed to be standing on the bottom of an ice white sea. He waited for the slow drift of generations of small animal skeletons to reach the bottom of his sea and cover him over. If he opened his mouth he could taste their deaths on his tongue.

"I think the pressure's lifting," he heard B.B. say, although he couldn't see him for all the fog and snow.

Rudy looked down at the pond. The grey ice had turned whiter, cleaner. The open expanse of water was clearing.

The huge white eye in the sky was obscured by eddies and winding sheets of hard-driven snow. Whatever remained of the late-afternoon sunlight had diffused, spread itself out so that each of these tiny ice crystals might grab a piece and carry it to the ground. So the world became a darker and colder place as the snow continued to fall.

Rudy had lost track of B.B. some time ago, although every now and then he thought he could hear the sound of metal hitting ice, the steady pace of the chopper, followed a few minutes later by the sound of the cat being torn apart, its screams muffled from the heavy snow filling its mouth. Rudy had lost his ice saws somewhere on the frozen pond – he had no idea where. He hoped he hadn't dropped them into the water.

He wondered how Old Finney had stood it out there. And what kind of wife he must have had, to live with a man who could stand such a thing. He could not imagine a more desolate place to live.

He stopped himself, not quite believing what he had been thinking. He, too, had chosen to live in this place, and despite all that had happened, perhaps *because* of all that had happened, he was still convinced that this was the right place for him. Maybe he was as crazy as Old Finney.

The light was fading rapidly. He could see nothing beyond the few feet of snowy air surrounding him. His feet had gone numb, despite his heavy boots; they felt as if the ice were rising through them, penetrating the skin and infecting the bone. B.B. must have gone back to the shore, he thought. Surely no one could work under such conditions. Rudy turned round and round until he was dizzy, trying to determine in which direction lay his ice house and his home – but the foreground of blowing snow was uniform, and the distant backgrounds of trees or buildings were invisible. He could not find where he had last cut into the ice. He could find nothing.

Sin otra luz y guía, sino la que en el corazón ardía. It was a Spanish poem he had read many times. St John of the Cross, about the Dark Night: *No other light to mark the way but fire pounding my heart.* He would just have to choose a direction and go with it. There was a slight movement in the snow falling ahead of him, a slight turning. He started in that direction.

A pale skirt, twirling. A vague drift of white-blonde hair. *That flaming guided me more firmly than the noonday sun.* A tiny child's face, leeched of color by the cold, her iced hair floating up around her cheeks and blue crystal eyes.

Rudy saw the little girl burning up in the snow, the snow becoming flames. She twirled and twirled, dancing, dressed in the flames. His sweet sweet baby, Julie. His daughter Julie burning up in the car with his wife. Was this reimagining of her death any better? Was ice any easier to take than fire?

That flaming guided me more firmly than the noonday sun. He watched the child stumbling, first snow and then fire attacking her pale form, and he cried out, but did not run to her. He seldom thought of Julie; he couldn't let himself think of Julie. The images of her death were poisonous; he shut them out of his thoughts. He could think of Eva and he could think of Marsha, even of the unborn child Marsha had carried. But he had not been able to think of Julie for a very long time. He wondered if she would hate him for that betrayal.

The girl stumbled and fell to the ice and lay there. Unable to stay away, Rudy stepped slowly through the snow that continued to accumulate on the surface of the pond. He looked down at the small form.

The child was too thin. Her arms too white, too short. This was not his daughter. Then he remembered that Emily Lorcaster had lost an aunt, a little girl, Old Finney's daughter. Who had drowned in the pond.

The blonde head turned and looked up at him. The lips had swollen to fifty times or more their normal size. The child's head was all mouth. It opened, showing its huge hungry tongue. The small white arms lifted to give him a hug.

Rudy screamed and stepped back, slipping on the ice, then crawled away from the monstrous child who wanted to hold him, who wanted to hug him, who more than anything else wanted him to remember her. Children were hungry mouths — that's mostly what they were, "hungry mouths to feed." They would eat you if they could – not out of malice – that's just what they were. Healthy, maturing, growing mouths. People fed off each other; it was the only way they could live. *O tender night that tied lover and the loved one, loved one and the lover fused as one*! But Rudy had gotten far enough away. The child's body diminished, hair disappearing, skin receding to the bone, until finally it was a corpse on a hard slab. It slowly sank into the ice and disappeared. *In darkness I escaped, my house at last was calm and safe*.

Rudy got to his feet. Of the surrounding curtain of snow, one portion appeared lighter than the rest. He went in that direction.

"You cannot know what life is until you have been forced to live with those events which cannot, with any justice, be survived." His father hadn't said it like that, not all in one breath like that. He'd coughed and spat and started over again and again and failed in his search for the right words. Finally he'd demanded a piece of paper and a pencil and Rudy had had to help him get the words down with numerous erasures, strikeouts, substitutions. He'd been drunk when he finally delivered to Rudy this final message of his life, two weeks before he'd signed himself into the nursing home. The cancer had left him bald and ravaged his body. He had broken all the mirrors in the house, unable to look at himself anymore. It was because the concentration camp had finally caught up with him; he now looked too much like those who had failed to survive.

There was much that could not be lived with. His father had been sickened and appalled that he still breathed and walked around, consuming, evacuating his bowels, dribbling his piss like any animal.

"Rudy . . ." his father whispered. Rudy came to him and his father clutched his shoulder with a skeletal hand, pulling him up close to his face. "God made a poor choice in me." The sentence stank of his father's failing organs. "So many died. So *many*."

Rudy could not bear to think of Julie. Thoughts of Julie were razor-sharp and tore down his throat and through the layers of his belly so that he could not eat, could not sleep. She was too much to survive. God had made a terrible choice.

After his daughter's death Rudy had had fantasies of murdering other children in the neighborhood. He'd imagined that he would sneak up to their bedrooms at night and smother them in their sleep. At least he would not let them suffer as Julie had suffered – their deaths would be quick and relatively painless. They probably would have no idea what was happening to them.

He often wondered how their parents would grieve, what form it would take. He wondered if any would grieve the way he did and whether it would show in their faces. He was not sure he would ever know the full extent of what he felt until he saw its terrible landmarks in the landscape of another's face.

But these were fantasies, and they passed. Now when he heard of the death of another's child he locked himself in his house and railed. And yet even in his screaming he would not let himself think of Julie.

During those flights of fantasy he had been no better than Old Finney, if indeed Old Finney was guilty of the crimes Rudy and B.B. were accusing him of. Rudy would have brought the world to death if he could, guided by the dark light of his heart.

He imagined he could see the distant white eye up in the sky again, behind the snow, drawn to the cold ice of the pond. As it began to sink, the eye turned red, the falling snow like frozen flakes of blood.

Rudy heard a murmur from the pond as the ice around his feet began to break.

Once the hard ice began to crack, it went rapidly. Rudy opened his mouth to shout as the cold arms of the pond reached up over his body to pull him under, but only cold air came out, the ice of the pond already in him and working its way up to his brain. He pushed frantically with his arms against loose pieces of floating ice, trying to force himself out of the water, but they slipped from his grasp and crashed back into him, forcing him under once again.

His vision went to grey. Cold infected his thoughts. Cold pushed him farther and farther down into the depths of the pond, the ice skin on the pond growing thicker, expanding downward, chasing him and forcing him into the pond's dark heart. Where all he'd ever known or imagined dead swam out to greet him, their narrow arms poised for an embrace, their eyes staring wide in their attempts to see all that he was, their mouths gaping in their hunger for their lost lives, their bellies empty and rotted away, the cold of Ice House Pond filling them through every opening. By the hundreds they crowded and jostled him, begging him, forcing him, pressing the issue of the intolerableness of their deaths.

Rudy twisted away from them, thrashing toward the surface. Old Finney had put them here, not he. These weren't people he had known, but death made all people the same.

Julie's voice was calling him, asking him to come to her room and tell her a story, give her a good-night kiss. But he ignored her, as he had so many times before.

Rudy gasped as he broke the surface, his eyes wide to the darkness. Even before he caught his first breath, it occurred to him that it had stopped snowing – the storm was gone, the night clear and full of stars.

He choked on his first icy gulps. The sudden exposure to cold air numbed him. He could barely see an edge of ice a few yards in front of him. He tried to swim, but his frozen clothes made him stiff.

Suddenly he felt a sharp point at his back. He tried to turn around, but whatever had snagged him was dragging him rapidly with it. He braced himself to be dragged back beneath the surface.

"Don't fight it!" B.B. shouted behind him. "It's just the pike! Have you out in just a second!"

Rudy could barely feel it when his back bumped up against the edge of the ice. Now that he had been exposed to the dark air, the cold in his limbs had gone to work rapidly, spreading and numbing him clean through to the bone. He barely heard B.B. grunt as he grabbed Rudy under the arms and began dragging him backwards up onto the ice. The big man's strong embrace barely registered.

"It's my fault!" B.B. said breathlessly. "I should've been watching you, you being new at this. But I got too busy harvesting the ice, watching the ice, looking at all the shadows under it and trying to figure out what all might be down there."

"It's . . . not . . ."

"Save it. I almost let you drown down there. And one thing this pond sure don't need is another ghost."

Two hours of blankets, hot coffee, and his overactive furnace, and Rudy was beginning to feel a little like a human being again. B.B. hovered over him like a nervous aunt, running back and forth, second-guessing his every need. Rudy felt a little guilty about it, but didn't make an effort to stop him.

B.B. collapsed on the floor beside him. "You could use a little more furniture, you know," B.B. said.

"I've had other things on my mind of late," Rudy replied. "You could have my chair. I'm feeling much better, you know ... Thanks."

B.B. made a gesture of dismissal. "I cut a lot of ice. Most of it's still floating out there, so I'll need to break it up a little in the morning — some of the blocks will bond together overnight. But that isn't a big job. If you're feeling up to it we can finish filling the ice house, and stack the rest out on the shore. Then you can do with it what you like."

"You sound disappointed."

B.B. studied his hands. Rudy could see how raw they were, from repeated frostbite and ice abrasion. B.B. finally looked up at him. "I'm no closer now to figuring out exactly what happened here than I was before. It's true we got some of that old grey ice out of there, and things have calmed down a bit — the pressure is off. But what about my father and brother? So you saw things deep down in the pond; I don't even know what they mean."

"It means, B.B., that we'll have to do considerably more to lure out some of the pond's secrets; it means that this year Greystone Bay is going to get its ice palace," Rudy said.

VI

B.B. informed Rudy that once they had all the pieces cut, with generous help from the townspeople the castle would require about a day to assemble. A cold day, of course, would be best. Rudy left it up to B.B. to predict the coldest day for the event.

On the chosen day, the townspeople started gathering by the pond in late afternoon. Some had seen the flyers posted around town; others claimed to have heard the news from friends. Rudy was distressed to see that most of the volunteers were elderly, those who had first-hand memories of the pond. Most of the young people appeared to be relatives they'd dragged along with them, no doubt with promises of great fun. The ones who didn't stand around with looks of interminable boredom immediately occupied themselves with snowball fights or sledding on the ice. Groups of old men and women followed Rudy around wherever he went, telling him stories about Ice House Pond, The Hand, Old Finney, and how the ice was handled back in the old days.

"Once me and a few pals helped a fellow over to Maryville – put away five hundred blocks in his ice house in one day!" one old-timer said, his tobacco-stained teeth a mere inch or so away from Rudy's face. The old fellow waved his hands in excitement. "I worked for four of the five ice companies here in Greystone, even worked on one of these here castles. But not for Old Finney. Hell, he didn't want no help, but I'd be damned if I'd a gone to work for him anyway. Cantankerous sonuvabitch!"

Rudy nodded and smiled, looking over the old man's head for B.B. He finally spotted him supervising a motley crew of old men and women and young kids as they attempted to erect a corner of the palace. "So you gonna hire me, Mr Boss-man?" Rudy looked down at the man. The man winked up at him. Behind the old man a couple of his elderly friends nodded and smiled. Everywhere he looked Rudy saw eager old faces, their bright red lips and cheeks blowing out great clouds of steam.

"I'm afraid there's no pay," Rudy said. "You could just call this a historical ice harvest and castle construction, I guess."

"Oh, I *know* there's no pay," the old man said eagerly. "Couldn't make much of a go at an ice house these days, anyway, what with all the Frigidaires and Whirlpools. I just like working with the ice! Hell, I'd pay *you*!"

"Then Mr B.B. can show you where you can help out the best."

"B.B.? Oh, B.B. knows me. B.B. knows I'm experienced!"

"I know, sir – you'll be a great help. Mr B.B. will put you where you'll be the most useful." Rudy glanced over the man's head at his silent, smiling friends. "*All* of you should report to Mr B.B. for your assignments."

The old man trotted off happily, his elderly contingent struggling to follow with the same energy. It occurred to Rudy then that the one thing he and B.B. had never discussed was liability insurance. Rudy watched as B.B. and his helpers finished erecting the first of four corners for the castle. Then the helpers went on to the next corner while B.B. walked back to Rudy. Rudy was amused to see that the old man he had just talked to now seemed to be in charge of the "corners crew."

"Are you sure these old people can handle all this construction?" Rudy asked. "Those blocks are heavy."

"Two hundred pounds, easy," B.B. replied. "And you got some learning to do about just how much an old person can do." B.B. chuckled. "Don't worry. This is just about the age group I wanted – they'd be the ones that would have the skills and any understanding about what we're trying to do here." His voice went soft. "They won't say anything to you, but most of them have somebody they know that's been lost. They know something's been wrong here a long time." He crouched down in the snow and scratched lightly at its surface. Rudy watched with an odd sort of anxiety. "I laid out a bottom row for a foundation, and once all the corners are up they shouldn't have any trouble filling in the walls. I'll plumb the walls ever' now and then to check the angles, but we got old-time carpenters out there – they know what they're doing. And a few of the young'uns'll help out where they need a little more strength on the job."

"And the openings?"

"I've got a couple of fellows picked out to help me on those. It should look pretty much the way Old Finney had it, I guess. I'll do a little sculpting on the towers, and once the sun's down it should be cold enough to use a sprayer for freezing up some interesting effects. So that should do it, right?"

Rudy watched the second corner go up. B.B. was right: The old man seemed to know exactly what he was doing. "B.B., you said these old people have an understanding about what we're trying to do here."

"Yeah."

"What *is* it that we're trying to do here?"

B.B. continued to scratch at the snow. Rudy was beginning to find it irritating. "Hell . . . I don't know, Rudy. We're harvesting the ice out of the pond, getting out way more than we need – I've got a fellow and some kids out there now cutting even more – because that's the way Old Finney did it. We're building that castle, too, because that's what Old Finney did. We're doing everything he did, and we'll see what happens. Maybe nothing – I don't know. But what else do we do?"

Rudy looked out over the pond, which today, with so much of its ice removed, looked very much like any other pond. The water was perfectly calm, reflecting the deep blue of the sky. The morning's clouds had blown away so that the afternoon grew steadily colder, but no colder than might be expected in this climate. He tried to trace the steps that had led him to this ice-harvesting party he was throwing, this ice-castle-raising by his pond, but he could not — it was as if he had been on automatic pilot since his arrival here. It had started with some shadows he had seen in the ice, and which had both surprised and appalled him — he knew that much — and it also had something to do with what he had been thinking about survival, and guilt, and terrible grief and what other people meant to you. When they surrounded you so tightly you could not breathe, what did they mean? Were they the essence of life, or the threat of your imminent death? "I don't know," he said out loud.

"Then let's just continue this and see what happens," B.B. said.

After B.B. went back to the construction site, Rudy watched for several hours as the blocks of ice rose rapidly out of the cold, forming walls and entranceways, gates and towers. Every now and then he would go over and lend a hand, raise a block or use a chisel, but most of the time he was obviously just in the way. The blazing white eye overhead gradually went away.

Twilight came and soon God could no longer see what humankind was up to. *That pond is much bigger than it is*, he thought, as the castle expanded, using up more and more ice, far more ice than Rudy thought the pond could possibly contain. He watched as B.B. climbed on top of the towers and created ice domes with tall spires growing from their centers. He watched as B.B. used a hose attachment to throw misted curtains of water over parts of the structure, where they froze into lacy contours and intricate ornamentations. He watched as minarets and turrets were added, ceilings with long icy stalactites, stalagmite pillars, ramparts and slides and secret pockets in the ice.

The castle followed a plan B.B. had drawn up based on a few old photographs and the recollections of a few of the old-timers around town. It was an elaborate structure — Rudy was beginning to see why it would have been a tourist attraction — and it went up far more quickly than Rudy could have imagined, as if the ice came directly out of the pond prefitted, and each block helped its carrier find the perfect spot for its placement. Despite the often uneven surface of the ice, Rudy could barely make out the seams as the blocks were assembled into walls.

"It's beautiful!" a woman's voice said behind him. "It's just like I remember it!"

Rudy turned to face Emily Lorcaster, who gazed at the castle with tears in her eyes. Rudy thought to caution her against crying, to warn her that her tears might freeze, but talked himself out of the silly notion.

"Where's your husband?" he asked.

"Oh, he won't come *here*. He doesn't approve" – she gestured vaguely at the ice castle – "of all *this*." Again, she seemed transfixed by her glimpse of the ice castle.

"And why's that?"

"He thinks I live too much in the past as it is. He thinks we all do, and that it isn't healthy. Besides, he never much cared for my grandfather."

No one did besides you, Emily, he thought.

"But from here . . . it's *so* magnificent!" she exclaimed.

"You can take a closer look," he said. Much to his surprise she grabbed his hand and pulled him along with her to the castle. She suddenly seemed like a young girl, and he began to wonder what it was she wanted from him.

She forced him to move too fast for the snow and icy slush that fronted the castle. Each stumble threatened to send them both face-first into the frozen ground. As they moved awkwardly around the shore of the pond he found he was amazed by its clarity. If the sky weren't so dark now he might be able to see all the way to its bottom. Gone were the shadows, the sense of something lurking just beneath the surface. The ice blocks of the castle varied in color from frothy white to near-transparent. *All the shades of purity*, he thought. Apparently, the ice harvest had done something to the essential quality of the ice.

"It's gorgeous!" she cried, leading him through the huge ice archway that formed the main entrance. Townspeople pushed past them laughing and singing, some of them even dancing, their hands stretched out, reaching, striving to form a massive daisy chain with everyone they passed. Even in their heavy winter garb, they moved with no awkwardness, no stiffness, as if they wore nothing at all.

He looked overhead as they entered the first big room. Icicles hung down in clusters like a series of elaborate chandeliers, the illusion made more perfect when they caught the last rays of the dying sun coming through the entranceway. The room was almost a perfect circle. Several ice tunnels led off to other parts of the castle.

"This is *incredible*!" he said. "It *is* a palace!" In fact, it reminded him more of the make-believe castles in fairy stories, or the way he'd imagined Spanish cities must be when he was a child: exquisite in their appearance and unfailingly comfortable. And it was the heaven his father had believed in as a child, but had been denied in the years after his release from the camps.

They wandered through a series of ice caves and larger chambers, passing more and more of the townspeople, some of whom laughed their way through, others shambling in silent awe. In some rooms were ice benches and chairs where people sat. If they remained there too long, would they be able to get up, or would their clothes be frozen to the ice? Now and then he thought he heard B.B.'s voice winding its way from some other part of the castle, but he never did see him.

Some of the townspeople stood in darkened corners of the structure, as if waiting for something. It bothered him. Everyone was watching him.

The castle was much bigger than it had first appeared from the outside. *They hadn't had enough time to build all this*. Again, he looked around nervously for B.B., to explain things to him. Fog swirled in some of the entrances and under some of the doors – condensation and sudden changes of temperature, he thought. Old men and women came in and out of the fog, but none said anything to him. When they came close he moved, afraid to have them touch him.

He came to see the townspeople as not simply other, but *other*. Their faces were grey and shadowed. *They were no longer human* ... Sometimes in distant halls he could hear a small girl's laughter.

Near the back of the castle they arrived at a short staircase of ice blocks. "This way," Emily whispered. "We can get away from all these people." Then she pushed him up the stairs.

The ice walls here were imperfectly formed, their surfaces streaked and cracked. In fact, a crevasse had formed on one wall, so large that Rudy feared for the safety of the entire structure. "I think we'd better warn ..." he said, turning around, but Emily Lorcaster wasn't there.

The castle suddenly seemed very quiet. He turned back around and looked at the damaged walls. The outer layers of ice were shaving off and dropping onto the floor. Dark stains flowed down the walls as the ice began to melt. Black rivulets crisscrossed the ice floor.

Rotted chunks of ice fell from the castle roof, shattering into bone-shaped fragments at his feet.

In one corner of the room was a crib sculpted out of ice. He walked over to it. Black holes had melted into the bottom of the crib. He bent closer to peer inside: The holes seemed endless. Their edges melted together, widened, the dripping ice around those edges half-frozen into icicle teeth. Rudy stepped back. They looked like a nest of hungry mouths.

He turned away and stared at the slight shadows of countless children trapped within the crumbling ice walls. Their faces came closer to the surface. He could see that all their mouths were open. Their shadow hands came up to the surface of the ice, fingers outstretched, and then their emaciated arms and skeleton fingers thrust completely through the ice, begging, desperate to touch. Their porous skin hung like pale, damp tissue from their bones, as if they had been underwater for a very long time.

The ice walls began to split. They leaned precariously. In the distance he could hear other parts of the structure rumbling. Rudy could feel the closeness of a terrible cold.

In me, he thought. *The terrible cold in my heart and in Old Finney's heart is responsible for all this ice.*

The floor split open as the ice blocks beneath him slipped and faulted. Rudy fell past long curls of ice, broken white cornices, shattered pinnacles many feet tall, curtains of icicles and fragile accumulations of rime. *The pond is much bigger than it is.* Countless frozen hands tried to grab him, whether to hurt or help him he had no idea. *We all live in a cemetery, all of us — there's no escaping it.* He thought of concentration camps where the dead were stacked into huge freezers, then shipped into the German mountains by the thousands in order to cool the Führer's summer home. His arms and legs grew numb, his chest almost too cold to move the air through his lungs.

He could barely feel. *But isn't that what I've wanted?*

The sudden halt in his descent left him dizzy and unable to breathe. He was inside a huge bubble of ice it seemed, the only entrance or exit being the hole he'd torn through the ceiling during his descent. *I'm down inside the frozen pond. The pond has a basement.*

Around him lay hundreds of small hummocks of ice. Mounds of snow. The air was so cold that the warmth of his body, carried in his breath, created great stretches of white cloud across the chamber. Scattered about were larger pieces of ice, almost small bergs, with hollows and soft places, the ravaged ice skulls of a tribe of giants.

The coldness in my heart created this cemetery. He thought about Eva, sweet Julie, Marsha and their unborn child, his father dead of cancer ("I caught it in the camps. It sounds crazy but I swear – I know it's true."). His life had become a tombstone. His heart was a headstone of ice.

Thin hands with broken fingernails broke through the surface of the icy hummock beside him. The sounds of cracking and shifting ice filled the chamber, echoing back and forth from wall to wall until it overlapped his own thoughts and it was his thoughts cracking, his nerves splitting and thawing his emotions.

Across the chamber, hands and knees and feet and heads emerged from the ice, flesh tearing on the ragged edges of ice, bones breaking audibly. But there were no outcries. No blood. Pale faces tight against the bone. Slow shuffling gaits. Eyes straight ahead, uninterested in what lay around them. Mouths gaping, moving, hungry for something but not knowing what. All those Old Finney had murdered over the years and dumped into Ice House Pond rose up and began to walk.

The forces of memory set in motion, ready to devour the living. The pond was much much bigger. Once he'd set them in motion, Rudy could not avoid the moving walls of ice. The walls of ice crushed everything in their path.

The moving figures were multiplying with a perverse fecundity. The bodies – so many of them – pressed up against him, touching, rubbing, pushing him hard against the ice. Now and then one would reach out to hold him, and he'd feel guilty when he evaded its grasp.

Rudy was appalled to discover that there was more than one layer of bodies below the icy hummocks. After the first wave had passed and gone to the icy sides of the bubble where it futilely attempted to scale the walls, more pale hands and feet and heads appeared from the ragged holes. The dead staggered forth, their hands outstretched, clutching one another in a great, obscene daisy chain. Flesh rubbed against flesh until they began to meld.

And after these another wave, and then still another. All the Greystone dead rising up through the pond, through the doorway Old Finney's coldness had created and Rudy's own coldness had allowed to continue. They rubbed and joined until all these pasts were the same, all flesh the same, and Rudy was able to crawl his way out of the hole in the ceiling on top of this great mound of death.

Back on the shore, the ice castle was collapsing. He joined Emily and B.B. to watch the end. He thought about his family, his families, now long gone. *When they died, the world should have died. If the world doesn't die on its own, sometimes you have to murder it.* Obviously he hadn't been the first to feel that way. Old Finney knew. But now Rudy felt the freest he had in years. His families were gone forever. But he was still alive.

After a few days Rudy gave serious thought to what he would have to do to get back to the city and start his life over again. He thought it likely that Mr Lorcaster would be eager to buy the place back from him, especially if Rudy had Mrs Lorcaster on his side. Ice House Pond belonged to Greystone Bay – it was too dangerous to permit some outsider to live there. B.B. would help straighten up things around the place, board up the windows, shut off the furnace for good. And seal up all entrances to the ice house. B.B. had claimed to have achieved some peace after what he'd seen in the ice castle, although he never would tell Rudy exactly what he had seen.

But Rudy knew such plans were useless. He knew he wouldn't be leaving. Not anytime soon at least. When the next cold weather arrived in the Bay, pushing the fog into great pools that filled every depression, he was aware of the invisible hands on his body, seeking comfort and release.

Rudy's father used to read him a story from one of the big fairy-tale books in his study, an adaptation of one of the Norse myths, having to do with the end of the world. Rudy had read the story to Julie hundreds of times, from the time she was four years old. She had loved it very much. When she had curled up against his chest during those readings, his stronger breath seeming to support and drive hers, he had thought he was protecting her from all harm. He had believed he was insuring her a long and happy life. As far as he had been concerned, Julie was going to live forever.

When the end of the world finally came – and certainly few were surprised that it came, having seen it in their dreams for years, having seen it even in the faces of their newborn children – the seas, lakes, and rivers were all frozen solid. The fish were all fixed in their places, their final sea-thoughts preserved for all time, so that looking through the ice the fisherman believed these fish had simply been painted on the underside of the ice, and they went home without their daily catch, waiting for death with their families.

When the gods died they began to dream, and those dreams took the form of snowfall. And the dead gods dreamed for a very long time. ("I guess they had nothing else better to do," his father had always remarked.) The snow piled up unendingly.

The winds screamed. There was no heat in the sun, which had become old and white, a blind eye.

The great wolf Skoll, who had pursued the sun through the heavens for millennia, finally caught up with it, leapt upon it, and devoured it. ("You can't escape the past," Rudy had told her, hugging her close against the cold, hoping she would remember this someday. "You just learn to live with its ghosts.")

The moon died in the night. The stars flickered and went out, leaving a darkness greater than any before.

DENNIS ETCHISON

The Dog Park

DENNIS ETCHISON has been called "America's premier writer of horror stories" (*Fantasy Newsletter*), "The finest writer of psychological horror this genre has produced" (Karl Edward Wagner) and "The most original living horror writer in America" (*The Penguin Encyclopedia of Horror and the Supernatural*).

A multiple winner of both the World Fantasy Award and the British Fantasy Award, his short fiction has appeared in many of the major genre magazines and anthologies and is collected in *The Dark Country*, *Red Dreams* and *The Blood Kiss*.

He is also the editor of the landmark anthologies *MetaHorror*, *Cutting Edge* and three volumes of *Masters of Darkness*. Besides novelizations of *The Fog*, *Halloween II and III*, and *Videodrome*, his novels include *Darkside*, *Shadowman*, *California Gothic* and *The Channel*.

The author lives in Los Angeles, and he draws on the Southern California milieu he knows so well in the disturbing story which follows, which was nominated for the Horror Writers Association Bram Stoker Award . . .

MADDING HEARD THE dogs before he saw them.

They were snarling at each other through the hurricane fence, gums wet and incisors bared, as if about to snap the chain links that held them apart. A barrel-chested boxer reared and slobbered, driving a much smaller Australian kelpie away from the outside of the gate. Spittle flew and the links vibrated and rang.

A few seconds later their owners came running, barking commands and waving leashes like whips.

"Easy, boy," Madding said, reaching one hand out to the seat next to him. Then he remembered that he no longer had a dog of his own. There was nothing to worry about.

He set the brake, rolled the window up all the way, locked the car and walked across the lot to the park.

The boxer was far down the slope by now, pulled along by a man in a flowered shirt and pleated trousers. The Australian sheepdog still trembled by the fence. Its owner, a young woman, jerked a choke chain.

"Greta, sit!"

As Madding neared the gate, the dog growled and tried to stand.

She yanked the chain harder and slapped its hindquarters back into position.

"Hello, Greta," said Madding, lifting the steel latch. He smiled at the young woman. "You've got a brave little dog there."

"I don't know why she's acting this way," she said, embarrassed.

"Is this her first time?"

"Pardon?"

"At the Dog Park."

"Yes . . ."

"It takes some getting used to," he told her. "All the freedom. They're not sure how to behave."

"Did you have the same trouble?"

"Of course." He savoured the memory, and at the same time wanted to put it out of his mind. "Everybody does. It's normal."

"I named her after Garbo — you know, the actress? I don't think she like crowds." She looked around. "Where's your dog?"

"Down there, I hope." Madding opened the gate and let himself in, then held it wide for her.

She was squinting at him. "Excuse me," she said, "but you work at Tri-Mark, don't you?"

Madding shook his head. "I'm afraid not."

The kelpie dragged her down the slope with such force that she had to dig her feet into the grass to stop. The boxer was nowhere in sight.

"Greta, heel!"

"You can let her go," Madding said as he came down behind her. "The leash law is only till three o'clock."

"What time is it now?"

He checked his watch. "Almost five."

She bent over and unfastened the leash from the ring on the dog's collar. She was wearing white cotton shorts and a plain, loose-fitting top.

"Did I meet you in Joel Silver's office?" she said.

"I don't think so." He smiled again. "Well, you and Greta have fun."

He wandered off, tilting his face back and breathing deeply. The air was moving, scrubbed clean by the trees, rustling the shiny leaves as it circulated above the city, exchanging pollutants for fresh oxygen. It was easier to be on his own, but without a dog to pick the direction he was at loose ends. He felt the loss tugging at him like a cord that had not yet been broken.

The park was only a couple of acres, nestled between the high, winding turns of a mountain road on one side and a densely overgrown canyon on the other. This was the only park where dogs were allowed to run free, at least during certain hours, and in a few short months it had become an unofficial meeting place for people in the entertainment industry. Where once pitches had been delivered in detox clinics and the gourmet aisles of Westside supermarkets, now ambitious hustlers frequented the Dog Park to sharpen their networking skills. Here starlets connected with recently divorced producers, agents jockeyed for favour with young executives on the come, and actors and screenwriters exchanged tips about veterinarians, casting calls and pilots set to go to series in the fall. All it took was a dog, begged, borrowed or stolen, and the kind of desperate gregariousness that causes one to press business cards into the hands of absolute strangers.

He saw dozens of dogs, expensive breeds mingling shamelessly with common mutts, a microcosm of democracy at work. An English setter sniffed an unshorn French poodle, then gave up and joined the pack gathered around a honey-coloured cocker spaniel. A pair of black Great Dane puppies tumbled over each other golliwog-style, coming to rest at the feet of a tall, humourless German shepherd. An Afghan chased a Russian wolfhound. And there were the masters, posed against tree trunks, lounging at picnic tables, nervously cleaning up after their pets with long-handled scoopers while they waited to see who would enter the park next.

Madding played a game, trying to match up the animals with their owners. A man with a crewcut tossed a Frisbee, banking it against the setting sun like a translucent UFO before a bull terrier snatched it out of the air. Two fluffed Pekingese waddled across the path in front of Madding, trailing colourful leashes; when they neared the gorge at the edge of the park he started after them reflexively, then stopped as a short, piercing sound turned them and brought them back this way. A bodybuilder in a formfitting T-shirt glowered nearby, a silver whistle showing under his trimmed moustache.

Ahead, a Labrador, a chow and a schnauzer had a silkie cornered by a trash bin. Three people seated on a wooden bench glanced up, laughed, and returned to the curled script they were reading. Madding could not see the title, only that the cover was a bilious yellow-green.

"I know," said the young woman, drawing even with him, as her dog dashed off in an ever-widening circle. "It was at New Line. That was you, wasn't it?"

"I've never been to New Line," said Madding.

"Are you sure? The office on Robertson?"

"I'm sure."

"Oh." She was embarrassed once again, and tried to cover it with a self-conscious cheerfulness, the mark of a private person forced into playing the extrovert in order to survive. "You're not an actor, then?"

"Only a writer," said Madding.

She brightened. "I knew it!"

"Isn't everyone in this town?" he said. "The butcher, the baker, the kid who parks your car . . . My drycleaner says he's writing a script for Tim Burton."

"Really?" she said, quite seriously. "I'm writing a spec script."

Oh no, he thought. He wanted to sink down into the grass and disappear, among the ants and beetles, but the ground was damp from the sprinklers and her dog was circling, hemming him in.

"Sorry," he said.

"That's OK. I have a real job, too. I'm on staff at Fox Network."

"What show?" he asked, to be polite.

"*C.H.U.M.P.* The first episode is on next week. They've already ordered nine more, in case *Don't Worry, Be Happy* gets cancelled."

"I've heard of it," he said.

"Have you? What have you heard?"

He racked his brain. "It's a cop series, right?"

"Canine-Human Unit, Metropolitan Police. You know, dogs that ride around in police cars, and the men and women they sacrifice themselves for? It has a lot of human interest, like *L.A. Law*, only it's told through the dogs' eyes."

"*Look Who's Barking*," he said.

"Sort of." She tilted her head to one side and thought for a moment. "I'm sorry," she said. "That was a joke, wasn't it?"

"Sort of."

"I get it." She went on. "But what I really want to write is Movies-of-the-Week. My agent says she'll put my script on Paul Nagle's desk, as soon as I have a first draft."

"What's it about?"

"It's called *A Little-Known Side of Elvis*. That's the working title. My agent says anything about Elvis will sell."

"Which side of Elvis is this one?"

"Well, for example, did you know about his relationships with dogs? Most people don't. *Hound Dog* wasn't just a song."

Her kelpie began to bark. A man with inflatable tennis shoes and a baseball cap worn backwards approached them, a clipboard in his hand.

"Hi!" he said, all teeth. "Would you take a minute to sign our petition?"

"No problem," said the young woman. "What's it for?"

"They're trying to close the park to outsiders, except on weekends."

She took his ballpoint pen and balanced the clipboard on her tanned forearm. "How come?"

"It's the residents. They say we take up too many parking

places on Mulholland. They want to keep the canyon for themselves."

"Well," she said, "they better watch out, or we might just start leaving our dogs here. Then they'll multiply and take over!"

She grinned, her capped front teeth shining in the sunlight like two chips of paint from a pearly-white Lexus.

"What residents?" asked Madding.

"The homeowners," said the man in the baseball cap, hooking a thumb over his shoulder.

Madding's eyes followed a line to the cliffs overlooking the park, where the cantilevered back-ends of several designer houses hung suspended above the gorge. The undersides of the decks, weathered and faded, were almost camouflaged by the weeds and chaparral.

"How about you?" The man took back the clipboard and held it out to Madding. "We need all the help we can get."

"I'm not a registered voter," said Madding.

"You're not?"

"I don't live here," he said. "I mean, I did, but I don't now. Not any more."

"Are you registered?" the man asked her.

"Yes."

"In the business?"

"I work at Fox," she said.

"Oh, yeah? How's the new regime? I hear Lili put all the old-timers out to pasture."

"Not the studio," she said. "The network."

"Really? Do you know Kathryn Baker, by any chance?"

"I've seen her parking space. Why?"

"I used to be her dentist." The man took out his wallet. "Here, let me give you my card."

"That's all right," she said. "I already have someone."

"Well, hold on to it anyway. You never know. Do you have a card?"

She reached into a Velcro pouch at her waist and handed him a card with a quill pen embossed on one corner.

The man read it. "*C.H.U.M.P.* – that's great! Do you have a dental adviser yet?"

"I don't think so."

"Could you find out?"

"I suppose."

He turned to Madding. "Are you an actor?"

"Writer," said Madding. "But not the kind you mean."

The man was puzzled. The young woman looked at him blankly. Madding felt the need to explain himself.

"I had a novel published, and somebody bought an option. I moved down here to write the screenplay."

"Title?" said the man.

"You've probably never heard of it," said Madding. "It was called *And Soon the Night*."

"That's it!" she said. "I just finished reading it – I saw your picture on the back of the book!" She furrowed her brow, a slight dimple appearing on the perfectly smooth skin between her eyes, as she struggled to remember. "Don't tell me. Your name is . . ."

"David Madding," he said, holding out his hand.

"Hi!" she said. "I'm Stacey Chernak."

"Hi, yourself."

"Do you have a card?" the man said to him.

"I'm all out," said Madding. It wasn't exactly a lie. He had never bothered to have any printed.

"What's the start date?"

"There isn't one," said Madding. "They didn't renew the option."

"I see," said the man in the baseball cap, losing interest.

A daisy chain of small dogs ran by, a miniature collie chasing a longhaired dachshund chasing a shivering chihuahua. The collie blurred as it went past, its long coat streaking like a flame.

"Well, I gotta get some more signatures before dark. Don't forget to call me," the man said to her. "I can advise on orthodontics, accident reconstruction, anything they want."

"How about animal dentistry?" she said.

"Hey, why not?"

"I'll give them your name."

"Great," he said to her. "Thanks!"

"Do you think that's his collie?" she said when he had gone.

Madding considered. "More likely the Irish setter."

They saw the man lean down to hook his fingers under the collar of a golden retriever. From the back, his baseball cap revealed the emblem of the New York Yankees. Not from around here, Madding thought. But then, who is?

"Close," she said, and laughed.

The man led his dog past a dirt mound, where there was a drinking fountain, and a spigot that ran water into a trough for the animals.

"Water," she said. "That's a good idea. Greta!"

The kelpie came bounding over, eager to escape the attentions of a randy pit bull. They led her to the mound. As Greta drank, Madding read the sign over the spigot:

CAUTION!
Watch Out For Mountain Lions

"What do you think that means?" she said. "It isn't true, is it?"

Madding felt a tightness in his chest. "It could be. This is still wild country."

"Greta, stay with me . . ."

"Don't worry. They only come out at night, probably."

"Where's your dog?" she said.

"I wish I knew."

She tilted her head, uncertain whether or not he was making another joke.

"He ran away," Madding told her.

"When?"

"Last month. I used to bring him here all the time. One day he didn't come when I called. It got dark, and they closed the park, but he never came back."

"Oh, I'm so sorry!"

"Yeah, me too."

"What was his name?"

"He didn't have one. I couldn't make up my mind, and then it was too late."

They walked on between the trees. She kept a close eye on Greta. Somewhere music was playing. The honey coloured cocker spaniel led the German shepherd, the Irish setter and a dalmatian to a redwood table. There the cocker's owner, a woman with brassy hair and a sagging green halter, poured white wine into plastic cups for several men.

"I didn't know," said Stacey.

"I missed him at first, but now I figure he's better off. Someplace where he can run free, all the time."

"I'm sorry about your dog," she said. "That's so sad. But what I meant was, I didn't know you were famous."

It was hard to believe that she knew the book. The odds against it were staggering, particularly considering the paltry royalties. He decided not to ask what she thought of it. That would be pressing his luck.

"Who's famous? I sold a novel. Big deal."

"Well, at least you're a real writer. I envy you."

"Why?"

"You have it made."

Sure I do, thought Madding. One decent review in the *Village Voice Literary Supplement*, and some reader at a production company makes an inquiry, and the next thing I know my agent makes a deal with all the money in the world at the top of the ladder. Only the ladder doesn't go far enough. And now I'm back to square one, the option money used up, with a screenplay written on spec that's not worth what it cost me to Xerox it, and I'm six months behind on the next novel. But I've got it made. Just ask the IRS.

The music grew louder as they walked. It seemed to be coming from somewhere overhead. Madding gazed up into the trees, where the late-afternoon rays sparkled through the leaves, gold coins edged in blackness. He thought he heard voices, too, and the clink of glasses. Was there a party? The entire expanse of the park was visible from here, but he could see no evidence of a large group anywhere. The sounds were diffused and unlocalized, as if played back through widely spaced, out-of-phase speakers.

"Where do you live?" she asked.

"What?"

"You said you don't live here any more."

"In Calistoga."

"Where's that?"

"Up north."

"Oh."

He began to relax. He was glad to be finished with this town.

"I closed out my lease today," he told her. "Everything's packed. As soon as I hit the road, I'm out of here."

"Why did you come back to the park?"

A good question, he thought. He hadn't planned to stop by. It was a last-minute impulse.

"I'm not sure," he said. No, that wasn't true. He might as well admit it. "It sounds crazy, but I guess I wanted to look for my dog. I thought I'd give it one more chance. It doesn't feel right, leaving him."

"Do you think he's still here?"

He felt a tingling in the pit of his stomach. It was not a good feeling. I shouldn't have come, he thought. Then I wouldn't have had to face it. It's dangerous here, too dangerous for there to be much hope.

"At least I'll know," he said.

He heard a sudden intake of breath and turned to her. There were tears in her eyes, as clear as diamonds.

"It's like the end of your book," she said. "When the little girl is alone, and doesn't know what's going to happen next . . ."

My God, he thought, she did read it. He felt flattered, but kept his ego in check. She's not so tough. She has a heart, after all, under all the bravado. That's worth something – it's worth a lot. I hope she makes it, the Elvis script, whatever she really wants. She deserves it.

She composed herself and looked around, blinking. "What is that?"

"What's what?"

"Don't you hear it?" She raised her chin and moved her head from side to side, eyes closed.

She meant the music, the glasses, the sound of the party that wasn't there.

"I don't know."

Now there was the scraping of steel somewhere behind them, like a rough blade drawn through metal. He stopped and turned around quickly.

A couple of hundred yards away, at the top of the slope, a man in a uniform opened the gate to the park. Beyond the fence, a second man climbed out of an idling car with a red, white and blue shield on the door. He had a heavy chain in one hand.

"Come on," said Madding. "It's time to go."

"It can't be."

"The security guards are here. They close the park at six."

"Already?"

Madding was surprised, too. He wondered how long they had been walking. He saw the man with the crewcut searching for his Frisbee in the grass, the bull terrier at his side. The group on the bench and the woman in the halter were collecting their things. The bodybuilder marched his two ribboned Pekingese to the slope. The Beverly Hills dentist whistled and stood waiting for his dog to come to him. Madding snapped to, as if waking up. It really was time.

The sun had dropped behind the hills and the grass under his feet was darkening. The car in the parking lot above continued to idle; the rumbling of the engine reverberated in the natural bowl of the park, as though close enough to bulldoze them out of the way. He heard a rhythm in the throbbing, and realized that it was music, after all.

They had wandered close to the edge, where the park ended and the gorge began. Over the gorge, the deck of one of the cantilevered houses beat like a drum.

"Where's Greta?" she said.

He saw the stark expression, the tendons outlined through the smooth skin of her throat.

"Here, girl! Over here . . .!"

She called out, expecting to see her dog. Then she clapped her hands together. The sound bounced back like the echo of a gunshot from the depths of the canyon. The dog did not come.

In the parking lot, the second security guard let a Dobermann out of the car. It was a sleek, black streak next to him as he carried the heavy chain to his partner, who was waiting for the park to empty before padlocking the gate.

Madding took her arm. Her skin was covered with gooseflesh. She drew away.

"I can't go," she said. "I have to find Greta."

He scanned the grassy slopes with her, avoiding the gorge until there was nowhere left to look. It was blacker than he remembered. Misshapen bushes and stunted shrubs filled the canyon below, extending all the way down to the formal boundaries of the city. He remembered standing here only a few weeks ago, in exactly the same position. He had told himself then that his dog could not have gone over the edge, but now he saw that there was nowhere else to go.

The breeze became a wind in the canyon and the black liquid eye of a swimming pool winked at him from far down the hillside. Above, the sound of the music stopped abruptly.

"You don't think she went down there, do you?" said Stacey. There was a catch in her voice. "The mountain lions . . ."

"They only come out at night."

"But it *is* night!"

They heard a high, broken keening.

"Listen!" she said. "That's Greta!"

"No, it's not. Dogs don't make that sound. It's –" He stopped himself.

"*What*?"

"Coyotes."

He regretted saying it.

Now, without the music, the shuffling of footsteps on the boards was clear and unmistakable. He glanced up. Shadows appeared over the edge of the deck as a line of heads gathered to look down. Ice cubes rattled and someone laughed. Then someone else made a shushing sound and the silhouetted heads bobbed silently, listening and watching.

Can they see us? he wondered.

Madding felt the presence of the Dobermann behind him, at the top of the slope. How long would it take to close the distance, once the guards set it loose to clear the park? Surely they would call out a warning first. He waited for the voice, as the seconds ticked by on his watch.

"I have to go get her," she said, starting for the gorge.

"No . . ."

"I can't just leave her."

"It's not safe," he said.

"But she's down there, I know it! Greta!"

There was a giggling from the deck.

They can hear us, too, he thought. Every sound, every word magnified, like a Greek amphitheatre. Or a Roman one.

Rover, Spot, Towser? No, Cubby. That's what I was going to call you, if there had been time. I always like the name. *Cubby*.

He made a decision.

"Stay here," he said, pushing her aside.

"What are you doing?"

"I'm going over."

You don't have to. It's my dog . . ."

"Mine, too."

Maybe they're both down there, he thought.

"I'll go with you," she said.

"No."

He stood there, thinking, It all comes down to this. There's no way to avoid it. There never was.

"But you don't know what's there . . .!"

"Go," he said to her, without turning around. "Get out of here while you can. There's still time."

Go home, he thought, wherever that is. You have a life ahead of you. It's not too late, if you go right now, without looking back.

"Wait . . .!"

He disappeared over the edge.

A moment later there was a new sound, something more than the breaking of branches and the thrashing. It was powerful and deep, followed immediately by a high, mournful yipping. Then there was only silence, and the night.

From above the gorge, a series of quick, hard claps fell like rain.

It was the people on the deck.

They were applauding.

GAHAN WILSON

The Marble Boy

GAHAN WILSON is still best known as one of America's most popular cartoonists, his macabre work appearing regularly in *The New Yorker*, *Playboy*, *The Magazine of Fantasy & Science Fiction*, *National Lampoon*, *Punch* and *Paris Match*.

His short fiction has been published in a number of magazines and anthologies, including *Best New Horror 2*, and his own books include *Gahan Wilson's Graveside Manner*, *"And Then We'll Get Him"*, *Is Nothing Sacred?*, *I Paint What I See*, *Nuts*, *Eddy Deco's Last Caper*, *Still Weird*, *Everybody's Favorite Duck* and the children's series *Harry, The Fat Bear Spy*. In 1992 the Horror Writers of America presented him with their Life Achievement Award.

He recently contributed more than thirty full-page illustrations to Roger Zelazny's comic horror novel, *A Night in the Lonesome October*, and painted the jacket artwork for Robert M. Price's *Tales of the Lovecraft Mythos* and the paperback edition of Neil Gaiman and Stephen Jones's *Now We Are Sick*.

About the following story, he says: "Like all of the Lakeside Stories, this story is vaguely autobiographical, although this one is more autobiographical than most because there was a graveyard just like the one described. And it was part of a kid's tradition where I grew up to sneak into it and wander around. There actually was a marble boy – a little statue like that; it was a particularly spooky graveyard. But it was a great place in my childhood and I loved it."

IT WAS LIKE A huge hole cut into our ordinary world; a great, aching gap sawed right out of the middle of everything that made us and our world seem to make sense, a fatal hollow dug into the very center of the simple, optimistic philosophies our parents were trying to make us live by.

I did by no means realize at the time that I thought of it in those terms, but I know now that is what all of us, all the children, knew the Lakeside Cemetery to be. It wasn't just a weird place isolated permanently from the day to day pretend reality of the grownups, it was an accessible and explorable proof to us, to their young, that even our adults – so huge and powerful, so full of rights and wrongs from the newspapers – were just as fragile and afraid as we were, after all.

The graveyard spread itself out northward from just this side of the city border for five blocks where it ran into the alley in back of Mulberry Street and living people in houses and was temporarily stopped. To the east, it crowded all the way up to the beach drive so that its grey fence and ominous, high gates could remind us of the eventual certainty of our mortality just when we had bobbed up wet and blinking into the summer air after momentarily convincing ourselves otherwise by holding our breath for a full minute underwater. To the west it was bordered firmly by the train tracks which were the extension of the city's elevated line, now turned suburban and ground bound. If you were up there on the track in order to put pennies on them so that the copper would be squished flat and spread bigger than a half dollar by the wheels of passing trains, you had a fine, panoramic view of the graveyard spread out beneath you like a verdigris carpet splotched with fuzzy brown stains and sprinkled with a multitude of tiny little stones and statues and tombs.

It was, and is, a fine graveyard, thanks to the prosperity and grief of many Lakesidians from the far and near past, and it boasts as excellent and varied a collection of midwestern funerary art as you could hope to come across. There are any number of elaborate and diverting memorials; rows and rows of mausoleums vie with one another in sustained contests of marble pomposity, and the number of flamboyantly sculptured mourning angels is past counting.

Of course we, like kids of any generation, were perpetually fascinated with death, and of course we had long since learned that grownups were useless in any consultations on the subject since they seriously disliked talking about even the possibility of dying with their children, and, astonishingly, they never seemed to bring the subject up even among themselves unless one or another of them had recently expired, so we had to satisfy ourselves by quizzing one another on the subject in alleys and other dark places where adults wouldn't hear and disapprove and stop us.

Why, we earnestly asked one another, do pets expire even when we love them so much? How come the universe permits birds to be flattened into gory, smelly messes by cars, one wing still pointing prettily skyward like a sail? Is it fair that a friend as young as ourselves can sicken and die because he or she caught a bug drinking from a public fountain, or from inhaling the wrong stranger's breath in a movie theater? Does everybody rot the same, or do we all do it differently, and are we in the body when it happens or have we already left it when the eyes melt and fall into the hollow space where the brain was before it shriveled down to the size of a nut? *Why* does death happen? How *can* it happen? *Must* it happen?

So, if we were in the mood for a particularly adventurous and daring sort of day, a visit to the graveyard was always likely to be suggested, if only to widen everybody's eyes a little, and now and then we actually went ahead and did it.

Naturally, any expedition to the cemetery was always very heavily draped in secrecy, unannounced and unrecounted to any parent, and we made a great business of carefully avoiding the men who gardened its grounds and dug its graves and patched up its tombs because we had a highly detailed, horrifying body of superstition about what these men would do to us if they caught us, most of them involving, one way or another, fiendish misuse of formaldehyde.

When we made our plans we never even considered going in either one of the two huge, lacy iron gates because they each had an attached gatehouse with dark little windows for watchmen smelling of embalming fluid to hide behind and peer out of. Our preferred means of entry was a certain part of the graveyard's heavy, chain-link fence which faced the alley to its north and was satisfactorily lined with the backs of grimy garages and intriguingly decorated with tilting garbage cans full of spoiled, smelly things.

At some time in the ancient past, no one knew when or by what means, this section of the fence had become detached at its base so that it could be lifted up and crawled under and then carefully replaced so that no patrolling gardener or digger or patcher would ever know a child had snuck into their domain and was available for formaldehyde experiments.

This secret and ancient means of entrance was the one chosen by Andy Hoyle and George Dulane one mild November day when they decided the time had come for another tour of the graveyard with all its tests.

Andy and George were friends of long standing, and they had visited the graveyard once before that year in a group of five and enjoyed it very much. Today was Andy's twelfth birthday – George had been twelve for three months – and the two of them, after a long and serious discussion, had come to the conclusion that since George had used up sneaking into the school building at night without the superintendent knowing, a graveyard exploration would be a properly scary and solemn way for Andy to mark the occasion.

They looked carefully up and down the alley and when they were sure that the only living thing in sight was a small dog who was totally preoccupied in trying to tug an interesting bone covered with dried blood out of a box, they pulled firmly at the chain links. Of course the fence held firmly for a moment, as it always held, and Andy and George went through the usual, breath-holding moment before it let go and the two of them knew for certain that the fence's bottom still remained unattached.

They scuttled under it, pressing their fronts against the cold, leafy ground and, once inside, followed the time-honored tradition of pushing its base back down and burying it under the leaves so that no one would know. Then they scuttled a yard or two into the cemetery and paused by the gnarled, mossy side of a concrete log molded into the corner of a sooty rustic tomb.

They brushed chilled, damp bits of sod from the knees of their pants, pretended their hearts were not pounding in their chests, and looked at each other and the tall, bare trees and the endless ranks and files of stones and statues and tombs with an almost convincing casualness, and once they'd managed to get their breathing under control they savored the oldness and moldiness in the air and the way the menace of death all around them ran through their veins and arteries.

Afar off to the east they heard the metal dither of a lawn mower of the old timey, non-powered variety, and began wandering, taking paths which veered from the sound.

Old friends loomed before them as they walked: the tomb with the stone clock fixed forever at three thirty over its door, which prompted them once again to speculate whether this signified the exact hour of the occupant's death; the eight foot high angel with one missing ear and carved tears running down its pitted, grey cheeks; and, one of their particular favorites, the oddly cheerful skull whose jolly grin still beamed out from under the tilting urn pressed against the back of its cranium.

The sound of the mower faded and stopped and they angled back to the east, taking the path pointed toward one of the goals especially selected for this day: a particularly sinister looking mausoleum which you knew contained dead members of a family named Baker because they had carved that name boldly and deeply across its ornate pediment. The Bakers, or at least the Baker who had commissioned the tomb, had been deeply enamored of rococo ornamentation and the little house of death was so heavily burdened with scrollings and floral fantasies that it looked like an ossified wedding cake or the rump of a Spanish galleon turned to stone.

But it wasn't the gorgeous architectural detail of the Bakers' tomb which drew Andy and George to it, it was the delicious almost-openness of its heavy, rusting, iron door. Thick chains and a huge padlock insured that the door would go no more than ajar, but ajar it was, and you could peer through the opening at the cobwebby dimness beyond and, even better, you could whisper hoarsely into the tomb and hear the sibilant echoes which your voice had raised.

They glanced at each other and then, because he was the bravest, Andy pressed his body against the door, enjoyed a quick shiver when it gave ever so slightly, and hissed softly into the spooky dark.

"Hello?" he whispered. "Bakers?"

George, standing just behind, felt goosebumps popping out all over his arms.

"Bakers?" Andy persisted relentlessly. "Are there any Bakers lying in there?"

After a fair pause, Andy turned to George and whispered: "I guess there aren't any Bakers."

To which George replied on cue: "Or, if there *are* any Bakers . . ."

Then together, in a ghastly wail: ". . . then they must be *dead*!"

And that, as usual, was their signal to turn as one and run off at a full gallop as if pursued by generations of moldering Bakers and not to stop running until they were both satisfactorily winded.

That had been the high point in their last adventure in the graveyard and, in their planning, they had assumed it would be the high point in this one as well, but it turned out not to be so because, thanks to an odd break in the clouds and the sudden appearance of a bold shaft of sunlight, both boys simultaneously spotted a bright glinting among the stones off to their left. Something, they had no idea what, was shining like a huge diamond.

Without saying a word the two began walking together toward the spot of brilliance. The closer they got to it, the less it became pure radiance and the more it took on solid shape until they saw it was a case of glass mounted on a raised marble casket, and as they came even closer they could make out, through the shining of the glass, a small, standing figure.

There was a pale marble boy carved full size in the glass case. He had only been eight, you could figure that out by subtracting the dates, and he had been alive a long time ago. His marble clothes were very old-fashioned with many marble buttons on the jacket and knickers, and a fluffy marble bow was tied at his throat.

The case was sealed with some black substance at the joinings of the glass, but the closure was now far from perfect, the passing of all those years had made the black stuff shrivel, and there were many tiny droplets of water shining on the inside of all its panes.

The boy's marble hair was curly, and his carved marble eyes stared out with colorless irises and pupils and gave the odd illusion of seeming to be looking directly at the viewer no matter where he stood.

Andy and George remained silent for a good, long while, staring at the marble boy, wondering about him and speculating, each one secretly to himself, about his own mortality.

At length Andy stirred and pointed to the small sarcophagus the statue and its case stood upon. The case, like the statue, was carved from pale, unveined stone, and was waxy smooth.

"Do you suppose he's in that thing or buried underground?" Andy asked.

George stared and pursed his lips in thought.

"I think he's in there," he said at last. "It's just about the right size, isn't it?"

Andy nodded and then he stiffened and pointed.

"Look at that!" he said.

There was a crack running wavelike through the lid of the sarcophagus from one side to the other of its middle. It was clearly not only a surface crack. The lid was split.

"I'll bet you could open that if you wanted to," said Andy.

He crouched down and bent close to the crack in the lid. He reached out his right hand and traced the crack with his forefinger.

"Hey!" said George. "What're you *doing*?"

Andy looked up at him thoughtfully, then back at the crack, then he placed both hands, timidly at first, palms down on the lower half of the lid.

"Hey!" said George again.

"Shut up," said Andy, softly, and he pressed down on the lid and felt it wobble.

"It's loose," he said, still in the same soft tone.

"Come on, now, Andy," said George, "Stop that! You aren't supposed to do things like that!"

Andy ignored him, pushing the lid carefully in the direction of the foot of the little marble coffin. The cement which had held the lid in place had crumbled from more than a hundred years of rain and frost and rot and, with a grating sound which sent chills up both their backs, Andy got the lid moving until the crack was a little over two inches wide. Then Andy withdrew his hands and the two boys stared quietly at the opening.

"I can't see anything," George said in a muffled voice. "Can you see anything?"

Andy bent down until his nose poked just through the crack and squinted.

"No," he said.

He cupped his hands around his eyes to block out sidewise rays of sunlight and continued to peer until George could hardly stand it any more and then he finally spoke.

"It's just dark," he said.

George could not figure out whether he was relieved or disappointed when his eyes widened in horror as he saw Andy lean back on his knees and begin pulling back the right sleeve of his jacket until he had bared his whole forearm.

"Oh, *no*, Andy!" said George.

"I'm going to do it," Andy said, and, slowly but steadily, he put his hand through the crack and reached in and down, and further down, and only when his arm was in the little marble casket all the way to the elbow did he stop. He looked up at George with a thoughtful expression.

"I'm touching something," he said.

"Oh, gee!" said George. "Oh, gee, Andy, whyn't you stop this? Whyn't you just *stop* it?"

"It's him," said Andy, and suddenly there were little drops of perspiration all over his forehead. "I'm touching him."

He looked up, staring blankly ahead, and began searching with his unseen hand in the darkness of the marble box. He paused, took a deep breath, and made a decisive movement.

"I've got something," he said, pulling his hand out into the light and staring wide-eyed at something small and green held between his thumb and forefinger.

George backed up and almost tripped over a gravestone.

"Put it back!" he cried. "For Pete's sake, Andy!"

But Andy stood, still holding his prize. He looked over at George with mixed triumph and confusion.

"I never thought I could ever do anything like this," he said, in an exultant whisper. "Jeez, I really didn't think I could *do* it!"

George opened his mouth to speak but stopped with an abrupt, startled jerk of his whole body at a sudden rustling coming, unmistakably, absolutely unmistakably, from the interior of the little marble casket.

"What's *that*?" he hissed.

Then they both ran, this time really ran, hard as they could, banging their feet onto the graveyard earth. Andy fell once, heavily, with a loud thud, but he scrambled up almost as quickly as a ball bounces.

Somehow or other, with no idea at all how they did it or any memory whatsoever of doing it, they made their way to the fence and through it, and only when they were clear of the alley and more than half a block up Mercer Avenue to the east did they become aware of what they were doing or where they were.

Still moving, they shot quick glances to their rear and began reviewing what had happened.

First it was only gabble, but then, with a little more distance between them and the graveyard and that small, marble box, they began to make a little sense. Eventually they were only walking very rapidly.

"Was it him?" George gasped, staring sidewise at his friend. "Was it the marble boy made that noise is there?"

But they had to walk on another full half block before Andy got his answer ready.

"Yes," he said. "'Cause he was rotting. The air got at him and he fell apart."

He looked over at George and George looked back at him and they went on a little more in silence.

"I think he was just kind of caving in," Andy continued. "It wasn't that he was really moving."

"It wasn't?" George asked.

"No."

By the time they had reached Maple Street and Main Street they were walking at a reasonable pace. This was the corner where Andy would turn east and George continue on north. George reached out and touched Andy's arm.

"Let me see," he said.

They both looked around, making sure no one was near, and then Andy opened his hand.

The green thing rested on Andy's palm as the two of them studied it in awe. It was a tiny, withered business, like a broken off stick.

"What's that?" George asked, pointing at a sort of curved flake growing out of one end of the thing.

"I don't know," said Andy, frowning and squinting his eyes. "I can't figure it out."

"Oh," said George in a hushed voice, after a pause, "I think I know what it is."

"What?"

"Can't you see?" asked George, reaching out to touch the edge of the flake, but then shying away from it. "It's his fingernail!"

"Wow!" said Andy, his eyes shining brighter and brighter. "Wow!"

That evening, at dinner, Andy's parents asked him a few carefully casual questions as it was obvious that something more or less serious was preoccupying their child, but when all they learned was that he had been nowhere in particular where nothing much had happened, they gave up on it, as they usually did, on the theory that whatever it was would eventually come out if it was really important enough to *have* to come out.

After dinner Andy unconvincingly pretended to do his homework, then he bid his mother and father good night a good full half hour before the usual time, and quietly made his way to his room.

In bed, with his pajamas on, after listening carefully to make sure no one was in the hall outside, he leaned over and carefully slid the drawer of his bedside table open, noticing for the first time in his life that it moved with a slightly sinister *shushing* noise.

He licked his lips, for they had become suddenly very dry, and bent to look inside the drawer, doing it slowly so as not to rush the moment. It was still there, just where he had placed it, in the exact center of the bottom of the drawer. The two top joints of the left index finger of the marble boy. He knew exactly which finger it was because he had felt the rest of the marble boy's dry, tiny hand in the darkness in that casket when he had pulled the finger loose.

Andy stared at it with a kind of solemn joy and shook his head in wonder. He had never had such a thing. He had never heard of any other kid having had such a thing.

Wait until Chris Tyler had a look at it! Or Johnny Marsh! Or, *yes*, Elton Weaver! Andy could hardly wait to see the sick, envious expression on Elton Weaver's usually smug face when he got a look at it!

He smiled at the finger affectionately, then gently closed the drawer, *shush*, then turned off the lamp and settled into his bed with a sigh of deep contentment. He pulled the covers up until they were just under his chin and, with a clear, shining vision of Elton Weaver's tortured face floating before him, he drifted contentedly off to sleep.

When he awoke, some hours later, he had no idea why. He stirred, blinked, and then looked up with a growing sense of wrongness to observe that the bedroom door was open. He could see the pale paint of its outer surface gleaming faintly in the dim light coming from the bathroom down the hall.

He sat up, puzzled. He was sure that the door had been closed. He *knew* that it had been closed. He had been particularly careful that evening about closing it because of the finger. Had his father or mother peeked in and then gone off and left the door open by mistake? It didn't seem like them.

But then he realized that something was happening to the door even as he looked at it. It was changing shape, growing narrower. He couldn't understand how that could possibly be happening until he realized, with a sharp, hurtful pang in his chest, that he was watching the door being slowly and deliberately closed.

He had just cowered back to the headboard in a kind of half sitting position when he heard the faint, crisp click of the latch announce that the door's shutting was complete. He peered into the gloom at the foot of his bed but he could see nothing. Absolutely nothing.

He swallowed and opened his mouth in order to speak, but found he couldn't. He swallowed again and this time managed to whisper: "*Who's there?*"

Had he heard a noise? Had there been a brittle grating? An odd, grotesquely unsuccessful effort to reply from somewhere in the darkness over there?

He tried again: "Who's *there?*"

This time he knew he'd heard a noise, a different sort of noise than the last one, but definitely a noise. What had it been? A sort of dry rustle, that was it. There'd been a faint sort of rustle at the foot of his bed in the darkness over there. He pulled more of himself nearer to the headboard until he was crouching against it as far away as possible from the bed's foot. He gathered the sheets and blankets, bunching them in front of him like a soft, cloth wall. He strained his eyes, peering into the darkness as hard as he could.

Was there something there in the dark? It almost seemed so. It almost seemed he could barely make out a small something only barely higher than the top of the bed. Something moving.

Andy squeezed his knees against his chest and lifted the edge of the sheets and blankets so that only his eyes looked over the top edge. He was sure, now, absolutely certain that he was seeing something in the dark, even though he could only make it out as a faint silhouette.

It was working its way along the side of the bed. Very slowly. Very, very carefully. Awkwardly. Now Andy was able to see just a little something of the shape of the silhouette. It was round at the top.

Then he realized that he was breathing so hard that it was impossible to listen to anything else, particularly to the sort of soft sounds he'd heard before when he'd seen the bedroom door close, so he held his breath completely and, sure enough! he could hear the rustling which he'd heard before. And it was much closer.

Andy let himself breathe again because he realized he didn't want to hear the rustling after all, because he'd heard it before, and not just tonight but earlier that day! He'd told himself and George a lie about the rustling, saying it was probably only the falling in of old bones and rotting fabric, but he'd known better. He'd known it hadn't been any such thing at all. He'd known, deep down inside of him, standing by the cracked casket back there in the graveyard, that he and George were listening to the stirrings of the marble boy!

There was something else in the bedroom which he remembered from the graveyard: the sour, bitter smell which had oozed out of the casket when he'd opened up its lid, only this time it came from next to his bedside table where the silhouette now stood.

But, being this close to Andy, it was no longer just a silhouette. There was a lace collar, the sunken shoulders of the jacket were moldering velvet, and the brass buttons had all turned to lumps of verdigris. There was quite a bit of straight blond hair left on the skull and though someone had long ago carefully parted it in the middle, it stood up at all sorts of horrible angles. He could make out nothing of its face.

"Your finger's in the drawer!" Andy whispered with a great effort and hardly any breath at all to do it with. "I'm sorry I took it! Honest I am!"

It wavered and half turned to the bedside table. It even reached out to it, and a black little spider of a hand hooked its fingers over the knob, but then it slowly rotated its head on its thin little log of a neck until it was staring directly at Andy and he could just make out the stirring of leathery wrinklings deep inside its sockets. It made a small forward lurch and reached out spastically toward the bed with both of its shriveled, stumpy arms. A great gust of foul air puffed out from it.

"I'm sorry," said Andy in a voice so weak and faint he could barely hear himself. "I'm sorry!"

It clutched the blanket and pulled itself up onto the bed and as it dragged its stiff little body over the covers, closer and closer to Andy, he could see its rigid smile widen terribly.

He opened his mouth to plead again and had just discovered that he lacked the breath to even whimper when it suddenly grabbed both his wrists with an unyielding, merciless grip and bent its round, sour head over his left hand and bit the edges of its sharp little teeth deeper and deeper into the skin of Andy's forefinger.

It wasn't going to settle for what was in the drawer.

HARLAN ELLISON

Mefisto in Onyx

WHAT CAN ANYONE say about Harlan Ellison that has not already been said? The *Washington Post* called him "one of the great living American short story writers," and the *Los Angeles Times* said, "It's long past time for Harlan Ellison to be awarded the title: 20th century Lewis Carroll."

In a career spanning nearly forty years, he has won more awards than any other fantasist for the sixty-plus books he has written and edited, the more than 1700 stories, essays, articles and newspaper columns, two dozen teleplays and a dozen motion pictures he has created.

The author is currently working as the Conceptual Consultant for the television series *Babylon 5*, and his most recent books include *Dreams With Sharp Teeth* and *Mind Fields*, the latter with Polish artist Jacek Yerka. His 1992 novelette, "The Man Who Rowed Christopher Columbus Ashore" was selected from among more than 6,000 short stories published in America for inclusion in the 1993 edition of *The Best American Short Stories*, and he was awarded the Life Achievement Award at the 1993 World Fantasy Convention.

The powerful novella which follows (which the author refers to as a "toad-strangler") is one of Ellison's longest pieces of fiction for some years. The version which appears here was originally published as a handsome hardcover by Mark V. Ziesing Books, and the story has been optioned for filming by MGM.

O NCE. I only went to bed with her once. Friends for eleven years – before and since – but it was just one of those things, just one of those crazy flings: the two of us alone on a New Year's Eve, watching rented Marx Brothers videos so we wouldn't have to go out with a bunch of idiots and make noise and pretend we were having a good time when all we'd be doing was getting drunk, whooping like morons, vomiting on slow-moving strangers, and spending more money than we had to waste. And we drank a little too much cheap champagne; and we fell off the sofa laughing at Harpo a few times too many; and we wound up on the floor at the same time; and next thing we knew we had our faces plastered together, and my hand up her skirt, and her hand down in my pants . . .

But it was just the *once*, fer chrissakes! Talk about imposing on a cheap sexual liaison! She *knew* I went mixing in other peoples' minds only when I absolutely had no other way to make a buck. Or I forgot myself and did it in a moment of human weakness.

It was always foul.

Slip into the thoughts of the best person who ever lived, even Saint Thomas Aquinas, for instance, just to pick an absolutely terrific person you'd think had a mind so clean you could eat off it (to paraphrase my mother), and when you come out – take my word for it – you'd want to take a long, intense shower in Lysol.

Trust me on this: I go into somebody's landscape when there's *nothing else* I can do, no other possible solution . . . or I forget and do it in a moment of human weakness. Such as, say, the IRS holds my feet to the fire; or I'm about to get myself mugged and robbed and maybe murdered; or I need to find out if some specific she that I'm dating has been using somebody else's dirty needle or has been sleeping around without she's taking some extra-heavy-duty AIDS precautions; or a co-worker's got it in his head to set me up so I make a mistake and look bad to the boss and I find myself in the unemployment line again; or . . .

I'm a wreck for weeks after.

Go jaunting through a landscape trying to pick up a little insider arbitrage bric-a-brac, and come away no better heeled, but all muddy with the guy's infidelities, and I can't look a decent woman in the eye for days. Get told by a motel desk clerk that they're all full up and he's sorry as hell but I'll just have to drive on for about another thirty miles to find the next vacancy, jaunt into his landscape and find him lit up with neon signs that got a lot of the word *nigger* in them, and I wind up hitting the sonofabitch so hard his grandmother has a bloody nose, and usually have to hide out for three or four weeks after. Just about to miss a bus, jaunt into the head of the driver to find his name so I can yell for him to hold it a minute Tom or George or Willie, and I get smacked in the mind with all the garlic he's been eating for the past month because his doctor told him it was good for his system, and I start to dry-heave, and I wrench out of the landscape, and not only have I missed the bus, but I'm so sick to my stomach I have to sit down on the filthy curb to get my gorge submerged. Jaunt into a potential employer, to see if he's trying to lowball me, and I learn he's part of a massive cover-up of industrial malfeasance that's caused hundreds of people to die when this or that cheaply-made grommet or tappet or gimbal mounting underperforms and fails, sending the poor souls falling thousands of feet to shrieking destruction. Then just *try* to accept the job, even if you haven't paid your rent in a month. No way.

Absolutely: I listen in on the landscape *only* when my feet are being fried; when the shadow stalking me turns down alley after alley tracking me relentlessly; when the drywall guy I've hired to repair the damage done by my leaky shower presents me with a dopey smile and a bill three hundred and sixty bucks higher than the estimate. Or in a moment of human weakness.

But I'm a wreck for weeks after. For weeks.

Because you can't, you simply can't, you absolutely *cannot* know what people are truly and really like till you jaunt their landscape. If Aquinas had had my ability, he'd have very quickly gone off to be a hermit, only occasionally visiting the mind of a sheep or a hedgehog. In a moment of human weakness.

That's why in my whole life – and, as best I can remember back, I've been doing it since I was five or six years old, maybe even younger – there have only been eleven, maybe twelve people, of all those who know that I can "read minds," that I've permitted myself to get close to. Three of them never used it against me, or tried to exploit me, or tried to kill me when I wasn't looking. Two of those three were my mother and father, a pair of sweet old black folks who'd adopted me, a late-in-life baby, and were now dead (but probably still worried about me, even on the Other Side), and whom I missed very very much, particularly in moments like this. The other eight, nine were either so turned off by the knowledge that they made sure I never came within a mile of them – one moved to another entire country just to be on the safe side, although her thoughts were a helluva lot more boring and innocent than she thought they were – or they tried to brain me with something heavy when I was distracted – I still have a shoulder separation that kills me for two days before it rains – or they tried to use me to make a buck for them. Not having the common sense to figure it out, that if I was *capable* of using the ability to make vast sums of money, why the hell was I living hand-to-mouth like some overaged grad student who was afraid to desert the university and go become an adult?

Now *they* was some dumb-ass muthuhfugguhs.

Of the three who never used it against me, my mom and dad, the last was Allison Roche. Who sat on the stool next to me, in the middle of May, in the middle of a Wednesday afternoon, in the middle of Clanton, Alabama, squeezing ketchup onto her All-American Burger, imposing on the memory of that one damned New Year's Eve sexual interlude, with Harpo and his sibs; the two of us all alone except for the fry-cook; and she waited for my reply.

"I'd sooner have a skunk spray my pants leg," I replied.

She pulled a napkin from the chrome dispenser and swabbed up the red that had overshot the sesame-seed bun and redecorated the Formica countertop. She looked at me from under thick, lustrous eyelashes; a look of impatience and violet eyes that must have been a killer when she unbottled it at some truculent witness for the defense. Allison Roche was a Chief Deputy District Attorney in and for Jefferson County, with her office in Birmingham. Alabama. Where near we sat, in Clanton, having a secret meeting, having All-American Burgers; three years after having had quite a bit of champagne, 1930s black-and-white video rental comedy, and black-and-white sex. One extremely stupid New Year's Eve.

Friends for eleven years. And once, just once; as a prime example of what happens in a moment of human weakness. Which is not to say that it wasn't terrific, because it was; absolutely terrific; but we never did it again; and we never brought it up again after the next morning when we opened our eyes and looked at each other the way you look at an exploding can of sardines, and both of us said *Oh Jeeezus* at the same time.

Never brought it up again until this memorable afternoon at the greasy spoon where I'd joined Ally, driving up from Montgomery to meet her halfway, after her peculiar telephone invitation.

Can't say the fry-cook, Mr. All-American, was particularly happy at the pigmentation arrangement at his counter. But I stayed out of his head and let him think what he wanted. Times change on the outside, but the inner landscape remains polluted.

"All I'm asking you to do is go have a chat with him," she said. She gave me that look. I have a hard time with that look. It isn't entirely honest, neither is it entirely disingenuous. It plays on my remembrance of that one night we spent in bed. And is just *dis*honest enough to play on the part of that night we spent on the floor, on the sofa, on the coffee counter between the dining room and the kitchenette, in the bathtub, and about nineteen minutes crammed among her endless pairs of shoes in a walk-in clothes closet that smelled strongly of cedar and virginity. She gave me that look, and wasted no part of the memory.

"I don't *want* to go have a chat with him. Apart from he's a piece of human shit, and I have better things to do with my time than to go on down to Atmore and take a jaunt through this crazy sonofabitch's diseased mind, may I remind you that of the hundred and sixty, seventy men who have died in that electric chair, including the original 'Yellow Mama' they scrapped in 1990, about a hundred and thirty of them were gentlemen of color, and I do not mean you to picture any color of a shade much lighter than that cuppa coffee you got sittin' by your left hand right this minute, which is to say that I, being an inordinately well-educated African-American who values the full measure of living negritude in his body, am not crazy enough to want to visit a racist '*co*-rectional center' like Holman Prison, thank you very much."

"Are you finished?" she asked, wiping her mouth.

"Yeah. I'm finished. Case closed. Find somebody else."

She didn't like that. "There *isn't* anybody else."

"There has to be. Somewhere. Go check the research files at Duke University. Call the Fortean Society. Mensa. *Jeopardy*. Some 900 number astrology psychic hotline. Ain't there some semi-senile Senator with a full-time paid assistant who's been trying to get legislation through one of the statehouses for the last five years to fund this kind of bullshit research? What about the Russians . . . now that the Evil Empire's fallen, you ought to be able to get some word about their success with Kirlian auras or whatever those assholes were working at. Or you could – "

She screamed at the top of her lungs. *"Stop it, Rudy!"*

The fry-cook dropped the spatula he'd been using to scrape off the grill. He picked it up, looking at us, and his face (I didn't read his mind) said *If that white bitch makes one more noise I'm callin' the cops.*

I gave him a look he didn't want, and he went back to his chores, getting ready for the after-work crowd. But the stretch of his back and angle of his head told me he wasn't going to let this pass.

I leaned in toward her, got as serious as I could, and just this quietly, just this softly, I said, "Ally, good pal, listen to me. You've been one of the few friends I could count on, for a long time now. We have history between us, and you've *never*, not once, made me feel like a freak. So okay, I trust you. I trust you with something about me that causes immeasurable goddam pain. A thing about me that could get me killed. You've never betrayed me, and you've never tried to use me.

"Till now. This is the first time. And you've got to admit that it's not even as rational as you maybe saying to me that you've gambled away every cent you've got and you owe the mob a million bucks and would I mind taking a trip to Vegas or Atlantic City and taking a jaunt into the minds of some high-pocket poker players so I could win you enough to keep the goons from shooting you. Even *that*, as creepy as it would be if you said it to me, even *that* would be easier to understand than *this*!"

She looked forlorn. "There isn't anybody else, Rudy. *Please*."

"What the hell is this all about? Come on, tell me. You're hiding something, or holding something back, or lying about – "

"I'm not lying!" For the second time she was suddenly, totally, extremely pissed at me. Her voice spattered off the white tile walls. The fry-cook spun around at the sound, took a step toward us, and I jaunted into his landscape, smoothed down the rippled Astro-Turf, drained away the storm clouds, and suggested in there that he go take a cigarette break out back. Fortunately, there were no other patrons at the elegant All-American Burger that late in the afternoon, and he went.

"Calm fer chrissakes down, will you?" I said.

She had squeezed the paper napkin into a ball.

She was lying, hiding, holding something back. Didn't have to be a telepath to figure *that* out. I waited, looking at her with a slow, careful distrust, and finally she sighed, and I thought, *Here it comes.*

"Are you reading my mind?" she asked.

"Don't insult me. We know each other too long."

She looked chagrined. The violet of her eyes deepened. "Sorry."

But she didn't go on. I wasn't going to be outflanked. I waited.

After a while she said, softly, very softly, "I think I'm in love with him. I *know* I believe him when he says he's innocent."

I never expected that. I couldn't even reply.

It was unbelievable. Unfuckingbelievable. She was the Chief Deputy D.A. who had prosecuted Henry Lake Spanning for murder. Not just one murder, one random slaying, a heat of the moment Saturday night killing regretted deeply on Sunday morning but punishable by electrocution in the Sovereign State of Alabama nonetheless, but a string of the vilest, most sickening serial slaughters in Alabama history, in the history of the Glorious South, in the history of the United States. Maybe even in the history of the entire wretched human universe that went wading hip-deep in the wasted spilled blood of innocent men, women and children.

Henry Lake Spanning was a monster, an ambulatory disease, a killing machine without conscience or any discernible resemblance to a thing we might call decently human. Henry Lake Spanning had butchered his way across a half-dozen states; and they had caught up to him in Huntsville, in a garbage dumpster behind a supermarket, doing something so vile and inhuman to what was left of a sixty-five-year-old cleaning woman that not even the tabloids would get more explicit than *unspeakable*; and somehow he got away from the cops; and somehow he evaded their dragnet; and somehow he found out where the police lieutenant in charge of the manhunt lived; and somehow he slipped into that neighborhood when the lieutenant was out creating roadblocks – and he gutted the man's wife and two kids. Also the family cat. And then he killed a couple of more times in Birmingham and Decatur, and by then had gone so completely out of his mind that they got him again, and the second time they hung onto him, and they brought him to trial. And Ally had prosecuted this bottom-feeding monstrosity.

And oh, what a circus it had been. Though he'd been *caught*, the second time, and this time for keeps, in Jefferson County, scene of three of his most sickening jobs, he'd murdered (with such a disgustingly similar m.o. that it was obvious he was the perp) in twenty-two of the sixty-seven counties; and every last one of them wanted him to stand trial in that venue. Then there were the other five states in which he had butchered, to a total body-count of fifty-six. Each of *them* wanted him extradited.

So, here's how smart and quick and smooth an attorney Ally is: she somehow managed to coze up to the Attorney General, and somehow managed to unleash those violet eyes on him, and somehow managed to get and keep his ear long enough to con him into setting a legal precedent. Attorney General of the state of Alabama allowed Allison Roche to consolidate, to secure a multiple bill of indictment that forced Spanning to stand trial on all twenty-nine Alabama murder counts at once. She meticulously documented to the state's highest courts that Henry Lake Spanning presented such a clear and present danger to society that the prosecution was willing to take a chance (big chance!) of trying in a winner-take-all consolidation of venues. Then she managed to smooth the feathers of all those other vote-hungry prosecuters in those twenty-one other counties, and she put on a case that dazzled everyone, including Spanning's defense attorney, who had screamed about the legality of the multiple bill from the moment she'd suggested it.

And she won a fast jury verdict on all twenty-nine counts. Then she got *really* fancy in the penalty phase after the jury verdict, and proved up the *other* twenty-seven murders with their flagrantly identical trademarks, from those other five states, and there was nothing left but to sentence Spanning – essentially for all fifty-six – to the replacement for the "Yellow Mama."

Even as pols and power brokers throughout the state were murmuring Ally's name for higher office, Spanning was slated to sit in that new electric chair in Holman Prison, built by the Fred A. Leuchter Associates of Boston, Massachusetts, that delivers 2,640 volts of pure sparklin' death in 1/240th of a second, six times faster than the 1/40th of a second that it takes for the brain to sense it, which is – if you ask me – much too humane an exit line, more than three times the 700 volt jolt lethal dose that destroys a brain, for a pus-bag like Henry Lake Spanning.

But if we were lucky – and the scheduled day of departure was very nearly upon us – if we were lucky, if there was a God and Justice and Natural Order and all that good stuff, then Henry Lake Spanning, this foulness, this corruption, this thing that lived only to ruin ... would end up as a pile of fucking ashes somebody might use to sprinkle over a flower garden, thereby providing this ghoul with his single opportunity to be of some use to the human race.

That was the guy that my pal Allison Roche wanted me to go and "chat" with, down to Holman Prison, in Atmore, Alabama. There, sitting on Death Row, waiting to get his demented head tonsured, his pants leg slit, his tongue fried black as the inside of a sheep's belly ... down there at Holman my pal Allison wanted me to go "chat" with one of the most awful creatures made for killing this side of a hammerhead shark, which creature had an infinitely greater measure of human decency than Henry Lake Spanning had ever demonstrated. Go chit-chat, and enter his landscape, and read his mind, Mr. Telepath, and use the marvelous mythic power of extra-sensory perception: this nifty swell ability that has made me a bum all my life, well, not *exactly* a bum: I do have a decent apartment, and I do earn a decent, if sporadic, living; and I try to follow Nelson Algren's warning never to get involved with a woman whose troubles are bigger than my own; and sometimes I even have a car of my own, even though at that moment such was not the case, the Camaro having been repo'd, and not by Harry Dean Stanton or Emilio Estevez, lemme tell you; but a bum in the sense of – how does Ally put it? – oh yeah – I don't "realize my full and forceful potential" – a bum in the sense that I can't hold a job, and I get rotten breaks, and all of this despite a Rhodes scholarly education so far above what a poor nigrah-lad such as myself could expect that even Rhodes hisownself would've been chest-out proud as hell of me. A bum, mostly, despite an *outstanding* Rhodes scholar education and a pair of kind, smart, loving parents – even for foster-parents – shit, *especially* for being foster-parents – who died knowing the certain sadness that their only child would spend his life as a wandering freak unable to make a comfortable living or consummate a normal marriage or raise children without the fear of passing on this special personal horror . . . this astonishing ability fabled in song and story that I possess . . . that no one else seems to possess, though I know there must have been others, somewhere, sometime, somehow! Go, Mr. Wonder of Wonders, shining black Cagliostro of the modern world, go with this super nifty swell ability that gullible idiots and flying saucer assholes have been trying to prove exists for at least fifty years, that no one has been able to isolate the way I, me, the only one has been isolated, let me tell you about *isolation*, my brothers; and here I was, here was I, Rudy Pairis . . . just a guy, making a buck every now and then with nifty swell impossible ESP, resident of thirteen states and twice that many cities so far in his mere thirty years of landscape-jaunting life, here was I, Rudy Pairis, Mr. I-Can-Read-Your-Mind, being asked to go and walk through the mind of a killer who scared half the people in the world. Being asked by the only living person, probably, to whom I could not say no. And, oh, take me at my word here: I *wanted* to say no. *Was*, in fact, saying no at every breath. What's that? Will I do it? Sure, yeah sure, I'll go on down to Holman and jaunt through this sick bastard's mind landscape. Sure I will. You got two chances: slim, and none.

All of this was going on in the space of one greasy double cheeseburger and two cups of coffee.

The worst part of it was that Ally had somehow gotten involved with him. *Ally!* Not some bimbo bitch . . . but *Ally*. I couldn't believe it.

Not that it was unusual for women to become mixed up with guys in the joint, to fall under their "magic spell," and to start corresponding with them, visiting them, taking them candy and cigarettes, having conjugal visits, playing mule for them and smuggling in dope where the tampon never shine, writing them letters that got steadily more exotic, steadily more intimate, steamier and increasingly dependant emotionally. It wasn't that big a deal; there exist entire psychiatric treatises on the phenomenon; right alongside the papers about women who go stud-crazy for cops. No big deal indeed: hundreds of women every year find themselves writing to these guys, visiting these guys, building dream castles with these guys, fucking these guys, pretending that even the worst of these guys, rapists and woman-beaters and child molesters, repeat pedophiles of the lowest pustule sort, and murderers and stick-up punks who crush old ladies' skulls for food stamps, and terrorists and bunco barons . . . that one sunny might-be, gonna-happen pink cloud day these demented creeps will emerge from behind the walls, get back in the wind, become upstanding nine-to-five Brooks Bros. Galahads. Every year hundreds of women marry these guys, finding themselves in a hot second snookered by the wily, duplicitous, motherfuckin' lying greaseball addictive behavior of guys who had spent their sporadic years, their intermittent freedom on the outside, doing *just that*: roping people in, ripping people off, bleeding people dry, conning them into being tools, taking them for their every last cent, their happy home, their sanity, their ability to trust or love ever again.

But this wasn't some poor illiterate naive woman-child. This was *Ally*. She had damned near pulled off a legal impossibility, come *that* close to Bizarro Jurisprudence by putting the Attorneys General of five other states in a maybe frame of mind where she'd have been able to consolidate a multiple bill of indictment *across state lines*! Never been done; and now, probably, never ever would be. But she could have possibly pulled off such a thing. Unless you're a stone court-bird, you can't know what a mountaintop that is!

So, now, here's Ally, saying this shit to me. Ally, my best pal, stood up for me a hundred times; not some dip, but the steely-eyed Sheriff of Suicide Gulch, the over-forty, past the age of innocence, no-nonsense woman who had seen it all and come away tough but not cynical, hard but not mean.

"I think I'm in love with him." She had said.

"I *know* I believe him when he says he's innocent." She had said.

I looked at her. No time had passed. It was still the moment the universe decided to lie down and die. And I said, "So if you're certain this paragon of the virtues *isn't* responsible for fifty-six murders – that we *know* about – and who the hell knows how many more we *don't* know about, since he's apparently been at it since he was twelve years old – remember the couple of nights we sat up and you told me all this shit about him, and you said it with your skin crawling, *remember*? – then if you're so damned positive the guy you spent eleven weeks in court sending to the chair is innocent of butchering half the population of the planet – then why do you need me to go to Holman, drive all the way to Atmore, just to take a jaunt in this sweet peach of a guy?

"Doesn't your 'woman's intuition' tell you he's squeaky clean?

Don't 'true love' walk yo' sweet young ass down the primrose path with sufficient surefootedness?"

"Don't be a smartass!" she said.

"Say again?" I replied, with disfuckingbelief.

"I said: don't be such a high-verbal goddamned smart aleck!"

Now *I* was steamed. "No, I shouldn't be a smartass: I should be your pony, your show dog, your little trick bag mind-reader freak! Take a drive over to Holman, Pairis; go right on into Rednecks from Hell; sit your ass down on Death Row with the rest of the niggers and have a chat with the one white boy who's been in a cell up there for the past three years or so; sit down nicely with the king of the fucking vampires, and slide inside his garbage dump of a brain — and what a joy *that's* gonna be, I can't believe you'd ask me to do this — and read whatever piece of boiled shit in there he calls a brain, and see if he's jerking you around. *That's* what I ought to do, am I correct? Instead of being a smartass. Have I got it right? Do I properly pierce your meaning, pal?"

She stood up. She didn't even say *Screw you, Pairis!*

She just slapped me as hard as she could.

She hit me a good one straight across the mouth.

I felt my upper teeth bite my lower lip. I tasted the blood. My head rang like a church bell. I thought I'd fall off the goddam stool.

When I could focus, she was just standing there, looking ashamed of herself, and disappointed, and mad as hell, and worried that she'd brained me. All of that, all at the same time. Plus, she looked as if I'd broken her choo-choo train.

"Okay," I said wearily, and ended the word with a sigh that reached all the way back into my hip pocket. "Okay, calm down. I'll see him. I'll do it. Take it easy."

She didn't sit down. "Did I hurt you?"

"No, of course not," I said, unable to form the smile I was trying to put on my face. "How could you possibly hurt someone by knocking his brains into his lap?"

She stood over me as I clung precariously to the counter, turned halfway around on the stool by the blow. Stood over me, the balled-up paper napkin in her fist, a look on her face that said she was nobody's fool, that we'd known each other a long time, that she hadn't asked this kind of favor before, that if we were buddies and I loved her, that I would see she was in deep pain, that she was conflicted, that she needed to know, *really* needed to know without a doubt, and in the name of God – in which she believed, though I didn't, but either way what the hell – that I do this thing for her, that I just *do it* and not give her any more crap about it.

So I shrugged, and spread my hands like a man with no place to go, and I said, "How'd you get into this?"

She told me the first fifteen minutes of her tragic, heart-warming, never-to-be-ridiculed story still standing. After fifteen minutes I said, "Fer chrissakes, Ally, at least *sit down*! You look like a damned fool standing there with a greasy napkin in your mitt."

A couple of teen-agers had come in. The four-star chef had finished his cigarette out back and was reassuringly in place, walking the duckboards and dishing up All-American arterial cloggage.

She picked up her elegant attaché case and without a word, with only a nod that said let's get as far from them as we can, she and I moved to a double against the window to resume our discussion of the varieties of social suicide available to an unwary and foolhardy gentleman of the colored persuasion if he allowed himself to be swayed by a cagey and cogent, clever and concupiscent female of another color entirely.

See, what it is, is this:

Look at that attaché case. You want to know what kind of an Ally this Allison Roche is? Pay heed, now.

In New York, when some wannabe junior ad exec has smooched enough butt to get tossed a bone account, and he wants to walk his colors, has a need to signify, has got to demonstrate to everyone that he's got the juice, first thing he does, he hies his ass downtown to Barney's, West 17th and Seventh, buys hisself a Burberry, loops the belt casually *behind*, leaving the coat open to suh-*wing*, and he circumnavigates the office.

In Dallas, when the wife of the CEO has those six or eight upper-management husbands and wives over for an *intime*, *faux*-casual dinner, sans placecards, sans *entrée* fork, *sans cérémonie*, and we're talking the kind of woman who flies Virgin Air instead of the Concorde, she's so in charge she don't got to use the Orrefors, she can put out the Kosta Boda and say *give a fuck*.

What it is, kind of person so in charge, so easy with they own self, they don't *have* to laugh at your poor dumb struttin' Armani suit, or your bedroom done in Laura Ashley, or that you got a gig writing articles for *TV Guide*. You see what I'm sayin' here? The sort of person Ally Roche is, you take a look at that attaché case, and it'll tell you everything you need to know about how strong she is, because it's an Atlas. Not a Hartmann. Understand: she could *afford* a Hartmann, that gorgeous imported Canadian belting leather, top of the line, somewhere around nine hundred and fifty bucks maybe, equivalent of Orrefors, a Burberry, breast of guinea hen and Mouton Rothschild 1492 or 1066 or whatever year is the most expensive, drive a Rolls instead of a Bentley and the only difference is the grille . . . but she doesn't *need* to signify, doesn't *need* to *suh-wing*, so she gets herself this Atlas. Not some dumb chickenshit Louis Vuitton or Mark Cross all the divorcee real estate ladies carry, but an Atlas. Irish hand leather. Custom tanned cowhide. Hand tanned in Ireland by out of work IRA bombers. Very classy. Just a state understated. See that attaché case? That tell you why I said I'd do it?

She picked it up from where she'd stashed it, right up against the counter wall by her feet, and we went to the double over by the window, away from the chef and the teen-agers, and she stared at me till she was sure I was in a right frame of mind, and she picked up where she'd left off.

The next twenty-three minutes by the big greasy clock on the wall she related from a sitting position. Actually, a series of sitting positions. She kept shifting in her chair like someone who didn't appreciate the view of the world from that window, someone hoping for a sweeter horizon. The story started with a gang-rape at the age of thirteen, and moved right along: two broken foster-home families, a little casual fondling by surrogate poppas, intense studying for perfect school grades as a substitute for happiness, working her way through John Jay College of Law, a truncated attempt at wedded bliss in her late twenties, and the long miserable road of legal success that had brought her to Alabama. There could have been worse places.

I'd known Ally for a long time, and we'd spent totals of weeks and months in each other's company. Not to mention the New Year's Eve of the Marx Brothers. But I hadn't heard much of this. Not much at all.

Funny how that goes. Eleven years. You'd think I'd've guessed or suspected or *some*thing. What the hell makes us think we're friends with *any*body, when we don't know the first thing about them, not really?

What are we, walking around in a dream? That is to say: what the fuck are we *thinking*!?!

And there might never have been a reason to hear *any* of it, all this Ally that was the real Ally, but now she was asking me to go somewhere I didn't want to go, to do something that scared the shit out of me; and she wanted me to be as fully informed as possible.

It dawned on me that those same eleven years between us hadn't really given her a full, laser-clean insight into the why and wherefore of Rudy Pairis, either. I hated myself for it. The concealing, the holding-back, the giving up only fragments, the evil misuse of charm when honesty would have hurt. I was facile, and a very quick study; and I had buried all the equivalents to Ally's pains and travails. I could've matched her, in spades; or blacks, or just plain nigras. But I remained frightened of losing her friendship. I've never been able to believe in the myth of unqualified friendship. Too much like standing hiphigh in a fast-running, freezing river. Standing on slippery stones.

Her story came forward to the point at which she had prosecuted Spanning; had amassed and winnowed and categorized the evidence so thoroughly, so deliberately, so flawlessly; had orchestrated the case so brilliantly; that the jury had come in with guilty on all twenty-nine, soon – in the penalty phase – fifty-six. Murder in the first. Premeditated murder in the first. Premeditated murder with special ugly circumstances in the first. On each and every of the twenty-nine. Less than an hour it took them. There wasn't even time for a lunch break. Fifty-one minutes it took them to come back with the verdict guilty on all charges. Less than a minute per killing. Ally had done that.

His attorney had argued that no direct link had been established between the fifty-sixth killing (actually, only his 29th in Alabama) and Henry Lake Spanning. No, they had not caught him down on his knees eviscerating the shredded body of his final victim – ten-year-old Gunilla Ascher, a parochial school girl who had missed her bus and been picked up by Spanning just about a mile from her home in Decatur – no, not down on his knees with the can opener still in his sticky red hands, but the m.o. was the same, and he was there in Decatur, on the run from what he had done in Huntsville, what they had *caught* him doing in Huntsville, in that dumpster, to that old woman. So they *couldn't* place him with his smooth, slim hands inside dead Gunilla Ascher's still-steaming body. So what? They could not have been surer he was the serial killer, the monster, the ravaging nightmare whose methods were so vile the newspapers hadn't even *tried* to cobble up some smart-aleck name for him like The Strangler or The Backyard Butcher. The jury had come back in fifty-one minutes, looking sick, looking as if they'd try and try to get everything they'd seen and heard out of their minds, but knew they never would, and wishing to God they could've managed to get out of their civic duty on this one.

They came shuffling back in and told the numbed court: hey, put this slimy excuse for a maggot in the chair and cook his ass till he's fit only to be served for breakfast on cinnamon toast. This was the guy my friend Ally told me she had fallen in love with. The guy she now believed to be innocent.

This was seriously crazy stuff.

"So how did you get, er, uh, how did you . . .?"

"How did I fall in love with him?"

"Yeah. That."

She closed her eyes for a moment, and pursed her lips as if she had lost a flock of wayward words and didn't know where to find them. I'd always known she was a private person, kept the really important history to herself – hell, until now I'd never known about the rape, the ice mountain between her mother and father, the specifics of the seven-month marriage – I'd known there'd been a husband briefly; but not what had happened; and I'd known about the foster homes; but again, not how lousy it had been for her – even so, getting *this* slice of steaming craziness out of her was like using your teeth to pry the spikes out of Jesus's wrists.

Finally, she said, "I took over the case when Charlie Whilborg had his stroke . . ."

"I remember."

"He was the best litigator in the office, and if he hadn't gone down two days before they caught . . ." she paused, had trouble with the name, went on, ". . . before they caught Spanning in Decatur, and if Morgan County hadn't been so worried about a case this size, and bound Spanning over to us in Birmingham . . . all of it so fast nobody really had a chance to talk to him . . .

I was the first one even got *near* him, everyone was so damned scared of him, of what they *thought* he was . . ."

"Hallucinating, were they?" I said, being a smartass.

"Shut up.

"The office did most of the donkeywork after that first interview I had with him. It was a big break for me in the office; and I got obsessed by it. So after the first interview, I never spent much actual time with Spanky, never got too close, to see what kind of a man he *really* . . ."

I said: "Spanky? Who the hell's 'Spanky'?"

She blushed. It started from the sides of her nostrils and went out both ways toward her ears, then climbed to the hairline. I'd seen that happen only a couple of times in eleven years, and one of those times had been when she'd farted at the opera. *Lucia di Lammermoor.*

I said it again: "Spanky? You're putting me on, right? You call him *Spanky*?" The blush deepened. "Like the fat kid in *The Little Rascals* . . . c'mon, I don't fuckin' *believe* this!"

She just glared at me.

I felt the laughter coming.

My face started twitching.

She stood up again. "Forget it. Just forget it, okay?" She took two steps away from the table, toward the street exit. I grabbed her hand and pulled her back, trying not to fall apart with laughter, and I said, "Okay okay okay . . . I'm *sorry* . . . I'm really and truly, honest to goodness, may I be struck by a falling space lab no kidding 100 per cent absolutely sorry . . . but you gotta admit . . . catching me unawares like that . . . I mean, come *on*, Ally . . . *Spanky*!?! You call this guy who murdered at least fifty-six people Spanky? Why not Mickey, or Froggy, or Alfalfa . . .? I can understand not calling him Buckwheat, you can save that one for me, but *Spanky*???"

And in a moment *her* face started to twitch; and in another moment she was starting to smile, fighting it every micron of the way; and in another moment she was laughing and swatting at me with her free hand; and then she pulled her hand loose and stood there falling apart with laughter; and in about a minute she was sitting down again. She threw the balled-up napkin at me.

"It's from when he was a kid," she said. "He was a fat kid, and they made fun of him. You know the way kids are . . . they corrupted Spanning into 'Spanky' because *The Little Rascals* were on television and . . . oh, shut up, Rudy!"

I finally quieted down, and made conciliatory gestures.

She watched me with an exasperated wariness till she was sure I wasn't going to run any more dumb gags on her, and then she resumed. "After Judge Fay sentenced him, I handled Spa . . . *Henry's* case from our office, all the way up to the appeals stage. I was the one who did the pleading against clemency when Henry's lawyers took their appeal to the Eleventh Circuit in Atlanta.

"When he was denied a stay by the appellate, three-to-nothing, I helped prepare the brief when Henry's counsel went to the Alabama Supreme Court; then when the Supreme Court refused to hear his appeal, I thought it was all over. I knew they'd run out of moves for him, except maybe the Governor; but that wasn't ever going to happen. So I thought: *that's that.*

"When the Supreme Court wouldn't hear it three weeks ago, I got a letter from him. He'd been set for execution next Saturday, and I couldn't figure out why he wanted to see *me.*"

I asked, "The letter . . . it got to you how?"

"One of his attorneys."

"I thought they'd given up on him."

"So did I. The evidence was so overwhelming; half a dozen counselors found ways to get themselves excused; it wasn't the kind of case that would bring any litigator good publicity. Just the number of eyewitnesses in the parking lot of that Winn-Dixie in Huntsville . . . must have been fifty of them, Rudy. And they all saw the same thing, and they all identified Henry in lineup after lineup, twenty, thirty, could have been fifty of them if we'd needed that long a parade. And all the rest of it . . ."

I held up a hand. *I know*, the flat hand against the air said. She had told me all of this. Every grisly detail, till I wanted to puke. It was as if I'd done it all myself, she was so vivid in her telling. Made my jaunting nausea pleasurable by comparison. Made me so sick I couldn't even think about it. Not even in a moment of human weakness.

"So the letter comes to you from the attorney . . ."

"I think you know this lawyer. Larry Borlan; used to be with the ACLU; before that he was senior counsel for the Alabama Legislature down to Montgomery; stood up, what was it, twice, three times, before the Supreme Court? Excellent guy. And not easily fooled."

"And what's *he* think about all this?"

"He thinks Henry's absolutely innocent."

"Of all of it?"

"Of everything."

"But there were fifty disinterested random eyewitnesses at one of those slaughters. Fifty, you just said it. Fifty, you could've had a parade. All of them nailed him cold, without a doubt. Same kind of kill as all the other fifty-five, including that schoolkid in Decatur when they finally got him. And Larry Borlan thinks he's not the guy, right?"

She nodded. Made one of those sort of comic pursings of the lips, shrugged, and nodded. "Not the guy."

"So the killer's still out there?"

"That's what Borlan thinks."

"And what do *you* think?"

"I agree with him."

"Oh, jeezus, Ally, my aching boots and saddle! You got to be workin' some kind of off-time! The killer is still out here in the mix, but there hasn't been a killing like Spannings' for the three years that he's been in the joint. Now *what* do that say to you?"

"It says whoever the guy *is*, the one who killed all those people, he's days smarter than all the rest of us, and he set up the perfect freefloater to take the fall for him, and he's either long far gone in some other state, working his way, or he's sitting quietly right here in Alabama, waiting and watching. And smiling." Her face seemed to sag with misery. She started to tear up, and said, "In four days he can stop smiling."

Saturday night.

"Okay, take it easy. Go on, tell me the rest of it. Borlan comes to you, and he begs you to read Spanning's letter and . . .?"

"He didn't beg. He just gave me the letter, told me he had no idea what Henry had written, but he said he'd known me a long time, that he thought I was a decent, fair-minded person, and he'd appreciate it in the name of our friendship if I'd read it."

"So you read it."

"I read it."

"Friendship. Sounds like you an' him was *good* friends. Like maybe you and I were good friends?"

She looked at me with astonishment.

I think *I* looked at me with astonishment.

"Where the hell did *that* come from?" I said.

"Yeah, really," she said, right back at me, "where the hell *did* that come from?" My ears were hot, and I almost started to say something about how if it was okay for *her* to use our Marx Brothers indiscretion for a lever, why wasn't it okay for me to get cranky about it? But I kept my mouth shut; and for once knew enough to move along. "Must've been *some* letter," I said.

There was a long moment of silence during which she weighed the degree of shit she'd put me through for my stupid remark, after all this was settled; and having struck a balance in her head, she told me about the letter.

It was perfect. It was the only sort of come-on that could lure the avenger who'd put you in the chair to pay attention. The letter had said that fifty-six was not the magic number of death. That there were many, *many* more unsolved cases, in many, *many* different states; lost children, runaways, unexplained disappearances, old people, college students hitchhiking to Sarasota for Spring Break, shopkeepers who'd carried their day's take to the night deposit drawer and never gone home for dinner, hookers left in pieces in Hefty bags all over town, and death death death unnumbered and unnamed. Fifty-six, the letter had said, was just the start. And if she, her, no one else, Allison Roche, my pal Ally, would come on down to Holman, and talk to him, Henry Lake Spanning would help her close all those open files. National rep. Avenger of the unsolved. Big time mysteries revealed. "So you read the letter, and you went . . ."

"Not at first. Not immediately. I was sure he was guilty, and I was pretty certain at that moment, three years and more, dealing with the case, I was pretty sure if he said he could fill in all the blank spaces, that he could do it. But I just didn't like the idea. In court, I was always twitchy when I got near him at the defense table. His eyes, he never took them off me. They're blue, Rudy, did I tell you that . . .?"

"Maybe. I don't remember. Go on."

"Bluest blue you've ever seen . . . well, to tell the truth, he just plain *scared* me. I wanted to win that case so badly, Rudy, you can never know . . . not just for me or the career or for the idea of justice or to avenge all those people he'd killed, but just the thought of him out there on the street, with those blue eyes, so blue, never stopped looking at me from the moment the trial began ... the *thought* of him on the loose drove me to whip that case like a howling dog. I *had* to put him away!"

"But you overcame your fear."

She didn't like the edge of ridicule on the blade of that remark. "That's right. I finally 'overcame my fear' and I agreed to go see him."

"And you saw him."

"Yes."

"And he didn't know shit about no other killings, right?"

"Yes."

"But he talked a good talk. And his eyes was blue, so blue."

"Yes, you asshole."

I chuckled. Everybody is somebody's fool.

"Now let me ask you this – very carefully – so you don't hit me again: the moment you discovered he'd been shuckin' you, lyin', that he *didn't* have this long, unsolved crime roster to tick off, why didn't you get up, load your attaché case, and hit the bricks?"

Her answer was simple. "He begged me to stay a while."

"That's it? He *begged* you?"

"Rudy, he has no one. He's *never* had anyone." She looked at me as if I were made of stone, some basalt thing, an onyx statue, a figure carved out of melanite, soot and ashes fused into a monolith. She feared she could not, in no way, no matter how piteously or bravely she phrased it, penetrate my rocky surface.

Then she said a thing that I never wanted to hear.

"Rudy ..."

Then she said a thing I could never have imagined she'd say. Never in a million years.

"Rudy ..."

Then she said the most awful thing she could say to me, even more awful than that she was in love with a serial killer.

"Rudy ... go inside ... read my mind ... I need you to know, I need you to understand ... Rudy ..."

The look on her face killed my heart.

I tried to say no, oh god no, not that, please, no, not that, don't ask me to do that, please *please* I don't want to go inside, we mean so much to each other, I don't *want* to know your landscape. Don't make me feel filthy, I'm no peeping-tom, I've *never* spied on you, never stolen a look when you were coming

out of the shower, or undressing, or when you were being sexy
. . . I never invaded your privacy, I wouldn't *do* a thing like that
. . . we're friends, I don't need to know it all, I don't *want* to go
in there. I can go inside anyone, and it's always awful . . . please
don't make me see things in there I might not like, you're my·
friend, please don't steal that from me . . .

"Rudy, *please*. Do it."

Oh jeezusjeezusjeezus, again, she said it again!

We sat there. And we sat there. And we sat there longer. I
said, hoarsely, in fear, "Can't you just . . . just *tell* me?"

Her eyes looked at stone. A man of stone. And she tempted
me to do what I could do casually, tempted me the way
Faust was tempted by Mefisto, Mephistopheles, Mefistofele,
Mephostopilis. Black rock Dr. Faustus, possessor of magical
mind-reading powers, tempted by thick, lustrous eyelashes and
violet eyes and a break in the voice and an imploring movement
of hand to face and a tilt of the head that was pitiable and the
begging word *please* and all the guilt that lay between us that
was mine alone. The seven chief demons. Of whom Mefisto was
the one "not loving the light."

I knew it was the end of our friendship. But she left me nowhere
to run. Mefisto in onyx.

So I jaunted into her landscape.

I stayed in there less than ten seconds. I didn't want to know
everything I could know; and I definitely wanted to know
nothing about how she really thought of me. I couldn't have
borne seeing a caricature of a bug-eyed, shuffling, thick-lipped
darkie in there. Mandingo man. Steppin Porchmonkey Rudy
Pair . . .

Oh god, what was I thinking!

Nothing in there like that. Nothing! Ally wouldn't *have*
anything like that in there. I was going nuts, going absolutely
fucking crazy, in there, back out in less than ten seconds. I want
to block it, kill it, void it, waste it, empty it, reject it, squeeze
it, darken it, obscure it, wipe it, do away with it like it never
happened. Like the moment you walk in on your momma and
poppa and catch them fucking, and you want never to have
known that.

But at least I understood.

In there, in Allison Roche's landscape, I saw how her heart

had responded to this man she called Spanky, not Henry Lake Spanning. She did not call him, in there, by the name of a monster; she called him a honey's name. I didn't know if he was innocent or not, but *she* knew he was innocent. At first she had responded to just talking with him, about being brought up in an orphanage, and she was able to relate to his stories of being used and treated like chattel, and how they had stripped him of his dignity, and made him afraid all the time. She knew what that was like. And how he'd always been on his own. The running-away. The being captured like a wild thing, and put in this home or that lockup or the orphanage "for his own good." Washing stone steps with a tin bucket full of gray water, with a horsehair brush and a bar of lye soap, till the tender folds of skin between the fingers were furiously red and hurt so much you couldn't make a fist.

She tried to tell me how her heart had responded, with a language that has never been invented to do the job. I saw as much as I needed, there in that secret landscape, to know that Spanning had led a miserable life, but that somehow he'd managed to become a decent human being. And it showed through enough when she was face to face with him, talking to him without the witness box between them, without the adversarial thing, without the tension of the courtroom and the gallery and those parasite creeps from the tabloids sneaking around taking pictures of him, that she identified with his pain. Hers had been not the same, but similar; of a kind, if not of identical intensity.

She came to know him a little.

And came back to see him again. Human compassion. In a moment of human weakness.

Until, finally, she began examining everything she had worked up as evidence, trying to see it from *his* point of view, using *his* explanations of circumstantiality. And there were inconsistencies. Now she saw them. Now she did not turn her prosecuting attorney's mind from them, recasting them in a way that would railroad Spanning; now she gave him just the barest possibility of truth. And the case did not seem as incontestable.

By that time, she had to admit to herself, she had fallen in love with him. The gentle quality could not be faked; she'd known fraudulent kindness in her time.

I left her mind gratefully. But at least I understood.

"Now?" she asked.

Yes, now. Now I understood. And the fractured glass in her voice told me. Her face told me. The way she parted her lips in expectation, waiting for me to reveal what my magic journey had conveyed by way of truth. Her palm against her cheek. All that told me. And I said, "Yes."

Then, silence, between us.

After a while she said, "I didn't feel anything."

I shrugged. "Nothing to feel. I was in for a few seconds, that's all."

"You didn't see everything?"

"No."

"Because you didn't want to?"

"Because . . ."

She smiled. "I understand, Rudy."

Oh, do you? Do you really? That's just fine. And I heard me say, "You made it with him yet?"

I could have torn off her arm; it would've hurt less.

"That's the second time today you've asked me that kind of question. I didn't like it much the first time, and I like it less *this* time."

"You're the one wanted me to go into your head. I didn't buy no ticket for the trip."

"Well, you were in there. Didn't you look around enough to find out?"

"I didn't look for that."

"What a chickenshit, wheedling, lousy and *cowardly* . . ."

"I haven't heard an answer, Counselor. Kindly restrict your answers to a simple yes or no."

"Don't be ridiculous! He's on Death Row!"

"There are ways."

"How would *you* know?"

"I had a friend. Up at San Rafael. What they call Tamal. Across the bridge from Richmond, a little north of San Francisco."

"That's San Quentin."

"That's what it is, all right."

"I thought that *friend* of yours was at Pelican Bay?"

"Different friend."

"You seem to have a lot of old chums in the joint in California."

"It's a racist nation."

"I've heard that."

"But Q ain't Pelican Bay. Two different states of being. As hard time as they pull at Tamal, it's worse up to Crescent City. In the Shoe."

"You never mentioned 'a friend' at San Quentin."

"I never mentioned a lotta shit. That don't mean I don't know it. I am large, I contain multitudes."

We sat silently, the three of us: me, her, and Walt Whitman. *We're fighting*, I thought. Not make-believe, dissin' some movie we'd seen and disagreed about; this was nasty. Bone nasty and memorable. No one ever forgets this kind of fight. Can turn dirty in a second, say some trash you can never take back, never forgive, put a canker on the rose of friendship for all time, never be the same look again.

I waited. She didn't say anything more; and I got no straight answer; but I was pretty sure Henry Lake Spanning had gone all the way with her. I felt a twinge of emotion I didn't even want to look at, much less analyze, dissect, and name. *Let it be*, I thought. Eleven years. Once, just once. *Let it just lie there and get old and withered and die a proper death like all ugly thoughts.*

"Okay. So I go on down to Atmore," I said. "I suppose you mean in the very near future, since he's supposed to bake in four days. Sometime very soon: like today."

She nodded.

I said, "And how do I get in? Law student? Reporter? Tag along as Larry Borlan's new law clerk? Or do I go in with you? What am I, friend of the family, representative of the Alabama State Department of Corrections; maybe you could set me up as an inmate's rep from 'Project Hope.'"

"I can do better than that," she said. The smile. "Much."

"Yeah, I'll just bet you can. Why does that worry me?"

Still with the smile, she hoisted the Atlas onto her lap. She unlocked it, took out a small manila envelope, unsealed but clasped, and slid it across the table to me. I pried open the clasp and shook out the contents.

Clever. Very clever. And already made up, with my photo where necessary, admission dates stamped for tomorrow morning, Thursday, absolutely authentic and foolproof.

"Let me guess," I said, "Thursday mornings, the inmates of Death Row have access to their attorneys?"

"On Death Row, family visitation Monday and Friday. Henry

has no family. Attorney visitations Wednesdays and Thursdays, but I couldn't count on today. It took me a couple of days to get through to you . . ."

"I've been busy."

". . . but inmates consult with their counsel on Wednesday and Thursday mornings."

I tapped the papers and plastic cards. "This is very sharp. I notice my name and my handsome visage already here, already sealed in plastic. How long have you had these ready?"

"Couple of days."

"What if I'd continued to say no?"

She didn't answer. She just got that look again.

"One last thing," I said. And I leaned in very close, so she would make no mistake that I was dead serious. "Time grows short. Today's Wednesday. Tomorrow's Thursday. They throw those computer-controlled twin switches Saturday night midnight. What if I jaunt into him and find out you're right, that he's absolutely innocent? What then? They going to listen to me? Fiercely high-verbal black boy with the magic mind-read power?"

"I don't think so. Then what happens, Ally?"

"Leave that to me." Her face was hard. "As you said: there are ways. There are roads and routes and even lightning bolts, if you know where to shop. The power of the judiciary. An election year coming up. Favors to be called in."

I said, "And secrets to be wafted under sensitive noses?"

"You just come back and tell me Spanky's telling the truth," and she smiled as I started to laugh, "and I'll worry about the world one minute after midnight Sunday morning."

I got up and slid the papers back into the envelope, and put the envelope under my arm. I looked down at her and I smiled as gently as I could, and I said, "Assure me that you haven't stacked the deck by telling Spanning I can read minds."

"I wouldn't do that."

"Tell me."

"I haven't told him you can read minds."

"You're lying."

"Did you . . .?"

"Didn't have to. I can see it in your face, Ally."

"Would it matter if he knew?"

"Not a bit. I can read the sonofabitch cold or hot, with or

without. Three seconds inside and I'll know if he did it all, if he did part of it, if he did none of it."

"I think I love him, Rudy."

"You told me that."

"But I wouldn't set you up. I need to know . . . that's why I'm asking you to do it."

I didn't answer. I just smiled at her. She'd told him. He'd know I was coming. But that was terrific. If she hadn't alerted him, I'd have asked her to call and let him know. The more aware he'd be, the easier to scorch his landscape.

I'm a fast study, king of the quick learners: vulgate Latin in a week; standard apothecary's pharmacopoeia in three days; Fender bass on a weekend; Atlanta Falcon's play book in an hour; and, in a moment of human weakness, what it feels like to have a very crampy, heavy-flow menstrual period, two minutes flat.

So fast, in fact, that the more somebody tries to hide the boiling pits of guilt and the crucified bodies of shame, the faster I adapt to their landscape. Like a man taking a polygraph test gets nervous, starts to sweat, ups the galvanic skin response, tries to duck and dodge, gets himself hinky and more hinky and hinkyer till his upper lip could water a truck garden, the more he tries to hide from me . . . the more he reveals . . . the deeper inside I can go.

There is an African saying: *Death comes without the thumping of drums.*

I have no idea why that one came back to me just then.

Last thing you expect from a prison administration is a fine sense of humor. But they got one at the Holman facility.

They had the bloody monster dressed like a virgin.

White duck pants, white short sleeve shirt buttoned up to the neck, white socks. Pair of brown ankle-high brogans with crepe soles, probably neoprene, but they didn't clash with the pale, virginal apparition that came through the security door with a large, black brother in Alabama Prison Authority uniform holding onto his right elbow.

Didn't clash, those work shoes, and didn't make much of a tap on the white tile floor. It was as if he floated. Oh yes, I said to myself, oh yes indeed: I could see how this messianic figure could wow even as tough a cookie as Ally. *Oh my, yes.*

Fortunately, it was raining outside.

Otherwise, sunlight streaming through the glass, he'd no doubt have a halo. I'd have lost it. Right there, a laughing jag would *not* have ceased. Fortunately, it was raining like a sonofabitch.

Which hadn't made the drive down from Clanton a possible entry on any deathbed list of Greatest Terrific Moments in My Life. Sheets of aluminum water, thick as misery, like a neverending shower curtain that I could drive through for an eternity and never really penetrate. I went into the ditch off the I-65 half a dozen times. Why I never plowed down and buried myself up to the axles in the sucking goo running those furrows, never be something I'll understand.

But each time I skidded off the Interstate, even the twice I did a complete three-sixty and nearly rolled the old Fairlane I'd borrowed from John the C Hepworth, even then I just kept digging, slewed like an epileptic seizure, went sideways and climbed right up the slippery grass and weeds and running, sucking red Alabama goo, right back onto that long black anvil pounded by rain as hard as roofing nails. I took it then, as I take it now, to be a sign that Destiny was determined the mere heavens and earth would not be permitted to fuck me around. I had a date to keep, and Destiny was on top of things.

Even so, even living charmed, which was clear to me, even so: when I got about five miles north of Atmore, I took the 57 exit off the I-65 and a left onto 21, and pulled in at the Best Western. It wasn't my intention to stay overnight that far south – though I knew a young woman with excellent teeth down in Mobile – but the rain was just hammering and all I wanted was to get this thing done and go fall asleep. A drive that long, humping something as lame as that Fairlane, hunched forward to scope the rain ... with Spanning in front of me ... all I desired was surcease. A touch of the old oblivion.

I checked in, stood under the shower for half an hour, changed into the three-piece suit I'd brought along, and phoned the front desk for directions to the Holman facility.

Driving there, a sweet moment happened for me. It was the last sweet moment for a long time thereafter, and I remember it now as if it were still happening. I cling to it.

In May, and on into early June, the Yellow Lady's Slipper blossoms. In the forests and the woodland bogs, and often on some otherwise undistinguished slope or hillside, the yellow and purple orchids suddenly appear.

I was driving. There was a brief stop in the rain. Like the eye of the hurricane. One moment sheets of water, and the next, absolute silence before the crickets and frogs and birds started complaining; and darkness on all sides, just the idiot staring beams of my headlights poking into nothingness; and cool as a well between the drops of rain; and I was driving. And suddenly, the window rolled down so I wouldn't fall asleep, so I could stick my head out when my eyes started to close, suddenly I smelled the delicate perfume of the sweet May-blossoming Lady's Slipper. Off to my left, off in the dark somewhere on a patch of hilly ground, or deep in a stand of invisible trees, *Cypripedium calceolus* was making the night world beautiful with its fragrance.

I neither slowed, nor tried to hold back the tears.

I just drove, feeling sorry for myself; for no good reason I could name.

Way, way down – almost to the corner of the Florida Panhandle, about three hours south of the last truly imperial barbeque in that part of the world, in Birmingham – I made my way to Holman. If you've never been inside the joint, what I'm about to say will resonate about as clearly as Chaucer to one of the gentle Tasaday.

The stones call out.

That institution for the betterment of the human race, the Organized Church, has a name for it. From the fine folks at Catholicism, Lutheranism, Baptism, Judaism, Islamism, Druidism ... Ismism ... the ones who brought you Torquemada, several spicy varieties of Inquisition, original sin, holy war, sectarian violence, and something called "pro-lifers" who bomb and maim and kill ... comes the catchy phrase Damned Places.

Rolls off the tongue like *God's On Our Side*, don't it?

Damned Places.

As we say in Latin, the *situs* of malevolent shit. The *venue* of evil happenings. Locations forever existing under a black cloud, like residing in a rooming house run by Jesse Helms or Strom Thurmond. The big slams are like that. Joliet, Dannemora, Attica, Rahway State in Jersey, that hellhole down in Louisiana called Angola, old Folsom – not the new one, the old Folsom –

Q, and Ossining. Only people who read about it call it "Sing Sing." Inside, the cons call it Ossining. The Ohio State pen in Columbus. Leavenworth, Kansas. The ones they talk about among themselves when they talk about doing hard time. The Shoe at Pelican Bay State Prison. In there, in those ancient structures mortared with guilt and depravity and no respect for human life and just plain meanness on both sides, cons and screws, in there where the walls and floors have absorbed all the pain and loneliness of a million men and women for decades . . . in there, the stones call out.

Damned places. You can feel it when you walk through the gates and go through the metal detectors and empty your pockets on counters and open your briefcase so that thick fingers can rumple the papers. You feel it. The moaning and thrashing, and men biting holes in their own wrists so they'll bleed to death.

And I felt it worse than anyone else.

I blocked out as much as I could. I tried to hold on to the memory of the scent of orchids in the night. The last thing I wanted was to jaunt into somebody's landscape at random. Go inside and find out what he had done, what had *really* put him here, not just what they'd got him for. And I'm not talking about Spanning; I'm talking about every one of them. Every guy who had kicked to death his girl friend because she brought him Bratwurst instead of spicy Cajun sausage. Every pale, wormy Bible-reciting psycho who had stolen, buttfucked, and sliced up an altar boy in the name of secret voices that "tole him to g'wan *do* it!" Every amoral druggie who'd shot a pensioner for her food stamps. If I let down for a second, if I didn't keep that shield up, I'd be tempted to send out a scintilla and touch one of them. In a moment of human weakness.

So I followed the trusty to the Warden's office, where his secretary checked my papers, and the little plastic cards with my face encased in them, and she kept looking down at the face, and up at my face, and down at my face, and up at the face in front of her, and when she couldn't restrain herself a second longer she said, "We've been expecting you, Mr. Pairis. Uh. Do you *really* work for the President of the United States?"

I smiled at her. "We go bowling together."

She took that highly, and offered to walk me to the conference room where I'd meet Henry Lake Spanning. I thanked her the way a well-mannered gentleman of color thanks a Civil Servant who can make life easier or more difficult, and I followed her along corridors and in and out of guarded steel-riveted doorways, through Administration and the segregation room and the main hall to the brown-paneled, stained walnut, white tile over cement floored, roll-out security windowed, white draperied, drop ceiling with 2″ acoustical Celotex squared conference room, where a Security Officer met us. She bid me fond adieu, not yet fully satisfied that such a one as I had come, that morning, on Air Force One, straight from a 7–10 split with the President of the United States.

It was a big room.

I sat down at the conference table; about twelve feet long and four feet wide; highly polished walnut, maybe oak. Straight back chairs: metal tubing with a light yellow upholstered cushion. Everything quiet, except for the sound of matrimonial rice being dumped on a connubial tin roof. The rain had not slacked off. Out there on the I-65 some luck-lost bastard was being sucked down into red death.

"He'll be here," the Security Officer said.

"That's good," I replied. I had no idea why he'd tell me that, seeing as how it was the reason I was there in the first place. I imagined him to be the kind of guy you dread sitting in front of, at the movies, because he always explains everything to his date. Like a *bracero* laborer with a valid green card interpreting a Woody Allen movie line-by-line to his illegal-alien cousin Humberto, three weeks under the wire from Matamoros. Like one of a pair of Beltone-wearing octogenarians on the loose from a rest home for a wild Saturday afternoon at the mall, plonked down in the third level multiplex, one of them describing whose ass Clint Eastwood is about to kick, and why. All at the top of her voice.

"Seen any good movies lately?" I asked him.

He didn't get a chance to answer, and I didn't jaunt inside to find out, because at that moment the steel door at the far end of the conference room opened, and another Security Officer poked his head in, and called across to Officer Let-Me-State-the-Obvious, "Dead man walking!"

Officer Self-Evident nodded to him, the other head poked back out, the door slammed, and my companion said, "When we bring one down from Death Row, he's gotta walk through the

Ad Building and Segregation and the Main Hall. So everything's locked down. Every man's inside. It takes some time, y'know."

I thanked him.

"Is it true you work for the President, yeah?" He asked it so politely, I decided to give him a straight answer; and to hell with all the phony credentials Ally had worked up. "Yeah," I said, "we're on the same *bocce* ball team."

"Izzat so?" he said, fascinated by sports stats.

I was on the verge of explaining that the President was, in actuality, of Italian descent, when I heard the sound of the key turning in the security door, and it opened outward, and in came this messianic apparition in white, being led by a guard who was seven feet in any direction.

Henry Lake Spanning, sans halo, hands and feet shackled, with the chains cold-welded into a wide anodized steel belt, shuffled toward me; and his neoprene soles made no disturbing cacophony on the white tiles.

I watched him come the long way across the room, and he watched me right back. I thought to myself, *Yeah, she told him I can read minds. Well, let's see which method you use to try and keep me out of the landscape.* But I couldn't tell from the outside of him, not just by the way he shuffled and looked, if he had fucked Ally. But I knew it had to've been. Somehow. Even in the big lockup. Even here.

He stopped right across from me, with his hands on the back of the chair, and he didn't say a word, just gave me the nicest smile I'd ever gotten from anyone, even my momma. *Oh, yes,* I thought, *oh my goodness, yes.* Henry Lake Spanning was either the most masterfully charismatic person I'd ever met, or so good at the charm con that he could sell a slashed throat to a stranger.

"You can leave him," I said to the great black behemoth brother.

"Can't do that, sir."

"I'll take full responsibility."

"Sorry, sir; I was told someone had to be right here in the room with you and him, all the time."

I looked at the one who had waited with me. "That mean you, too?"

He shook his head. "Just one of us, I guess."

I frowned. "I need absolute privacy. What would happen if I

were this man's attorney of record? Wouldn't you have to leave us alone? Privileged communication, right?"

They looked at each other, this pair of Security Officers, and they looked back at me, and they said nothing. All of a sudden Mr Plain-as-the-Nose-on-Your-Face had nothing valuable to offer; and the sequoia with biceps "had his orders."

"They tell you who I work for? They tell you who it was sent me here to talk to this man?" Recourse to authority often works. They mumbled yessir yessir a couple of times each, but their faces stayed right on the mark of *sorry, sir, but we're not supposed to leave anybody alone with this man.* It wouldn't have mattered if they'd believed I'd flown in on Jehovah One.

So I said to myself *fuckit* I said to myself, and I slipped into their thoughts, and it didn't take much rearranging to get the phone wires restrung and the underground cables rerouted and the pressure on their bladders something fierce.

"On the other hand . . ." the first one said.

"I suppose we could . . ." the giant said.

And in a matter of maybe a minute and a half one of them was entirely gone, and the great one was standing outside the steel door, his back filling the double-pane chickenwire-imbedded security window. He effectively sealed off the one entrance or exit to or from the conference room; like the three hundred Spartans facing the tens of thousands of Xerxes's army at the Hot Gates.

Henry Lake Spanning stood silently watching me.

"Sit down," I said. "Make yourself comfortable."

He pulled out the chair, came around, and sat down.

"Pull it closer to the table," I said.

He had some difficulty, hands shackled that way, but he grabbed the leading edge of the seat and scraped forward till his stomach was touching the table.

He was a handsome guy, even for a white man. Nice nose, strong cheekbones, eyes the color of that water in your toilet when you toss in a tablet of 2000 Flushes. Very nice looking man. He gave me the creeps.

If Dracula had looked like Shirley Temple, no one would've driven a stake through his heart. If Harry Truman had looked like Freddy Krueger, he would never have beaten Tom Dewey at the polls. Joe Stalin and Saddam Hussein looked like sweet, avuncular friends of the family, really nice looking, kindly guys

— who just incidentally happened to slaughter millions of men, women, and children. Abe Lincoln looked like an axe murderer, but he had a heart as big as Guatemala.

Henry Lake Spanning had the sort of face you'd trust immediately if you saw it in a tv commercial. Men would like to go fishing with him, women would like to squeeze his buns. Grannies would hug him on sight, kids would follow him straight into the mouth of an open oven. If he could play the piccolo, rats would gavotte around his shoes.

What saps we are. Beauty is only skin deep. You can't judge a book by its cover. Cleanliness is next to godliness. Dress for success. What saps we are.

So what did that make my pal, Allison Roche?

And why the hell didn't I just slip into his thoughts and check out the landscape? Why was I stalling?

Because I was scared of him.

This was fifty-six verified, gruesome, disgusting murders sitting forty-eight inches away from me, looking straight at me with blue eyes and soft, gently blond hair. Neither Harry nor Dewey would've had a prayer.

So why was I scared of him? Because; that's why.

This was damned foolishness. I had all the weaponry, he was shackled, and I didn't for a second believe he was what Ally *thought* he was: innocent. Hell, they'd caught him, literally, redhanded. Bloody to the armpits, fer chrissakes. Innocent, my ass! *Okay, Rudy,* I thought, *get in there and take a look around.* But I didn't. I waited for him to say something.

He smiled tentatively, a gentle and nervous little smile, and he said, "Ally asked me to see you. Thank you for coming."

I looked *at* him, but not *into* him.

He seemed upset that he'd inconvenienced me. "But I don't think you can do me any good, not in just three days."

"You scared, Spanning?"

His lips trembled. "Yes I am, Mr. Pairis. I'm about as scared as a man can be." His eyes were moist.

"Probably gives you some insight into how your victims felt, whaddaya think?"

He didn't answer. His eyes were moist.

After a moment just looking at me, he scraped back his chair and stood up. "Thank you for coming, sir. I'm sorry Ally imposed on your time." He turned and started to walk away. I jaunted into his landscape.

Oh my god, I thought. He was innocent.

Never done any of it. None of it. Absolutely no doubt, not a shadow of a doubt. Ally had been right. I saw every bit of that landscape in there, every fold and crease; every bolt hole and rat run; every gully and arroyo; all of his past, back and back and back to his birth in Lewistown, Montana, near Great Falls, thirty-six years ago; every day of his life right up to the minute they arrested him leaning over that disemboweled cleaning woman the real killer had tossed into the dumpster.

I saw every second of his landscape; and I saw him coming out of the Winn-Dixie in Huntsville; pushing a cart filled with grocery bags of food for the weekend. And I saw him wheeling it around the parking lot toward the dumpster area overflowing with broken-down cardboard boxes and fruit crates. And I heard the cry for help from one of those dumpsters; and I saw Henry Lake Spanning stop and look around, not sure he'd heard anything at all. Then I saw him start to go to his car, parked right there at the edge of the lot beside the wall because it was a Friday evening and everyone was stocking up for the weekend, and there weren't any spaces out front; and the cry for help, weaker this time, as pathetic as a crippled kitten; and Henry Lake Spanning stopped cold, and he looked around; and we *both* saw the bloody hand raise itself above the level of the open dumpster's filthy green steel side. And I saw him desert his groceries without a thought to their cost, or that someone might run off with them if he left them unattended, or that he only had eleven dollars left in his checking account, so if those groceries were snagged by someone he wouldn't be eating for the next few days . . . and I watched him rush to the dumpster and look into the crap filling it . . . and I felt his nausea at the sight of that poor old woman, what was left of her . . . and I was with him as he crawled up onto the dumpster and dropped inside to do what he could for that mass of shredded and pulped flesh.

And I cried with him as she gasped, with a bubble of blood that burst in the open ruin of her throat, and she died. But though *I* heard the scream of someone coming around the corner, Spanning did not; and so he was still there, holding the poor mass of stripped skin and black bloody clothing, when the cops screeched into the parking lot. And only *then*, innocent of anything but decency and rare human compassion, did Henry Lake Spanning begin to understand what it must look like to middle-aged *hausfraus*, sneaking around dumpsters to pilfer cardboard boxes, who see what they think is a man murdering an old woman.

I was with him, there in that landscape within his mind, as he ran and ran and dodged and dodged. Until they caught him in Decatur, seven miles from the body of Gunilla Ascher. But they had him, and they had positive identification, from the dumpster in Huntsville; and all the rest of it was circumstantial, gussied up by bedridden, recovering Charlie Whilborg and the staff in Ally's office. It looked good on paper – so good that Ally had brought him down on twenty-nine-*cum*-fifty-six counts of murder in the vilest extreme.

But it was all bullshit.

The killer was still out there.

Henry Lake Spanning, who looked like a nice, decent guy, was exactly that. A nice, decent, goodhearted, but most of all *innocent* guy.

You could fool juries and polygraphs and judges and social workers and psychiatrists and your mommy and your daddy, but you could *not* fool Rudy Pairis, who travels regularly to the place of dark where you can go but not return.

They were going to burn an innocent man in three days.

I had to do something about it.

Not just for Ally, though that was reason enough; but for this man who thought he was doomed, and was frightened, but didn't have to take no shit from a wiseguy like me.

"Mr. Spanning," I called after him.

He didn't stop.

"Please," I said. He stopped shuffling, the chains making their little charm bracelet sounds, but he didn't turn around.

"I believe Ally is right, sir," I said. "I believe they caught the wrong man; and I believe all the time you've served is wrong; and I believe you ought not die."

Then he turned slowly, and stared at me with the look of a dog that has been taunted with a bone. His voice was barely a whisper. "And why is that, Mr. Pairis? Why is it that you believe me when nobody else but Ally and my attorney believed me?"

I didn't say what I was thinking. What I was thinking was that I'd been *in* there, and I *knew* he was innocent. And more than that, I knew that he truly loved my pal Allison Roche.

And there wasn't much I wouldn't do for Ally.

So what I said was: "I know you're innocent, because I know who's guilty."

His lips parted. It wasn't one of those big moves where someone's mouth flops open in astonishment; it was just a parting of the lips. But he was startled; I knew that as I knew the poor sonofabitch had suffered too long already.

He came shuffling back to me, and sat down.

"Don't make fun, Mr. Pairis. Please. I'm what you said, I'm scared. I don't want to die, and I surely don't want to die with the world thinking I did those . . . those things."

"Makin' no fun, captain. I know who ought to burn for all those murders. Not six states, but eleven. Not fifty-six dead, but an even seventy. Three of them little girls in a day nursery, and the woman watching them, too."

He stared at me. There was horror on his face. I know that look real good. I've seen it at least seventy times.

"I know you're innocent, cap'n, because *I'm* the man they want. *I'm* the guy who put your ass in here."

In a moment of human weakness. I saw it all. What I had packed off to live in that place of dark where you can go but not return. The wall-safe in my drawing-room. The four-foot-thick walled crypt encased in concrete and sunk a mile deep into solid granite. The vault whose composite laminate walls of judiciously sloped extremely thick blends of steel and plastic, the equivalent of six hundred to seven hundred mm of homogenous depth protection approached the maximum toughness and hardness of crystaliron, that iron grown with perfect crystal structure and carefully controlled quantities of impurities that in a modern combat tank can shrug off a hollow charge warhead like a spaniel shaking himself dry. The Chinese puzzle box. The hidden chamber. The labyrinth. The maze of the mind where I'd sent all seventy to die, over and over and over, so I wouldn't hear their screams, or see the ropes of bloody tendon, or stare into the pulped sockets where their pleading eyes had been.

When I had walked into that prison, I'd been buttoned up totally. I was safe and secure, I knew nothing, remembered nothing, suspected nothing.

But when I walked into Henry Lake Spanning's landscape, and I could not lie to myself that he was the one, I felt the earth crack. I felt the tremors and the upheavals, and the fissures started at my feet and ran to the horizon; and the lava boiled up and began to flow. And the steel walls melted, and the concrete turned to dust, and the barriers dissolved; and I looked at the face of the monster.

No wonder I had such nausea when Ally had told me about this or that slaughter ostensibly perpetrated by Henry Lake Spanning, the man she was prosecuting on twenty-nine counts of murders I had committed. No wonder I could picture all the details when she would talk to me about the barest description of the murder site. No wonder I fought so hard against coming to Holman.

In there, in his mind, his landscape open to me, I saw the love he had for Allison Roche, for my pal and buddy with whom I had once, just once . . .

Don't try tellin' me that the Power of Love can open the fissures. I don't want to hear that shit. I'm telling *you* that it was a combination, a buncha things that split me open, and possibly maybe one of those things was what I saw between them.

I don't know that much. I'm a quick study, but this was in an instant. A crack of fate. A moment of human weakness. That's what I told myself in the part of me that ventured to the place of dark: that I'd done what I'd done in moments of human weakness.

And it was those moments, not my "gift," and not my blackness, that had made me the loser, the monster, the liar that I am.

In the first moment of realization, I couldn't believe it. Not me, not good old Rudy. Not likeable Rudy Pairis never done no one but hisself wrong his whole life.

In the next second I went wild with anger, furious at the disgusting thing that lived on one side of my split brain. Wanted to tear a hole through my face and yank the killing thing out, wet and putrescent, and squeeze it into pulp.

In the next second I was nauseated, actually wanted to fall down and puke, seeing every moment of what I had done, unshaded, unhidden, naked to this Rudy Pairis who was decent and reasonable and law-abiding, even if such a Rudy was little better than a well-educated fuckup. But not a killer . . . I wanted to puke.

Then, finally, I accepted what I could not deny.

For me, never again, would I slide through the night with the scent of the blossoming Yellow Lady's Slipper. I recognized that perfume now.

It was the odor that rises from a human body cut wide open, like a mouth making a big, dark yawn.

The other Rudy Pairis had come home at last.

They didn't have half a minute's worry. I sat down at a little wooden writing table in an interrogation room in the Jefferson County D.A.'s offices, and I made up a graph with the names and dates and locations. Names of as many of the seventy as I actually knew. (A lot of them had just been on the road, or in a men's toilet, or taking a bath, or lounging in the back row of a movie, or getting some cash from an ATM, or just sitting around doing nothing but waiting for me to come along and open them up, and maybe have a drink off them, or maybe just something to snack on . . . down the road.) Dates were easy, because I've got a good memory for dates. And the places where they'd find the ones they didn't know about, the fourteen with exactly the same m.o. as the other fifty-six, not to mention the old-style rip-and-pull can opener I'd used on that little Catholic bead-counter Gunilla Whatsername, who did Hail Mary this and Sweet Blessed Jesus that all the time I was opening her up, even at the last, when I held up parts of her insides for her to look at, and tried to get her to lick them, but she died first. Not half a minute's worry for the State of Alabama. All in one swell foop they corrected a tragic miscarriage of justice, knobbled a maniac killer, solved fourteen more murders than they'd counted on (in five additional states, which made the police departments of those five additional states extremely pleased with the law enforcement agencies of the Sovereign State of Alabama), and made first spot on the evening news on all three major networks, not to mention CNN, for the better part of a week. Knocked the Middle East right out of the box. Neither Harry Truman nor Tom Dewey would've had a prayer.

Ally went into seclusion, of course. Took off and went somewhere down on the Florida coast, I heard. But after the trial, and the verdict, and Spanning being released, and me going inside, and all like that, well, oo-poppa-dow as they used to say, it was all reordered properly. *Sat cito si sat bene*, in Latin: "It is done quickly enough if it is done well." A favorite saying of Cato. The Elder Cato.

And all I asked, all I begged for, was that Ally and Henry Lake Spanning, who loved each other and deserved each other, and whom I had almost fucked up royally, that the two of them would be there when they jammed my weary black butt into that new electric chair at Holman.

Please come, I begged them.

Don't let me die alone. Not even a shit like me. Don't make me cross over into that place of dark, where you can go, but not return – without the face of a friend. Even a former friend. And as for you, captain, well, hell didn't I save your life so you could enjoy the company of the woman you love? Least you can do. Come on now; be there or be square!

I don't know if Spanning talked her into accepting the invite, or if it was the other way around; but one day about a week prior to the event of cooking up a mess of fried Rudy Pairis, the warden stopped by my commodious accommodations on Death Row and gave me to understand that it would be SRO for the barbeque, which meant Ally my pal, and her boy friend, the former resident of the Row where now I dwelt in durance vile.

The things a guy'll do for love.

Yeah, that was the key. Why would a very smart operator who had gotten away with it, all the way free and clear, why would such a smart operator suddenly pull one of those hokey courtroom "I did it, I did it!" routines, and as good as strap himself into the electric chair?

Once. I only went to bed with her once.

The things a guy'll do for love.

When they brought me into the death chamber from the holding cell where I'd spent the night before and all that day, where I'd had my last meal (which had been a hot roast beef sandwich, double meat, on white toast, with very crisp french fries, and hot brown country gravy poured over the whole thing, apple sauce, and a bowl of Concord grapes), where a representative of the Holy Roman Empire had tried to make amends for destroying most of the gods, beliefs, and cultures of my black forebears, they held me between Security Officers, neither one of whom had been in attendance when I'd visited Henry Lake Spanning at this very same correctional facility slightly more than a year before.

It hadn't been a bad year. Lots of rest; caught up on my reading, finally got around to Proust and Langston Hughes, I'm ashamed to admit, so late in the game; lost some weight; worked out regularly; gave up cheese and dropped my cholesterol count. Ain't nothin' to it, just to do it.

Even took a jaunt or two or ten, every now and awhile. It didn't matter none. I wasn't going anywhere, neither were they. I'd done worse than the worst of them; hadn't I confessed to it? So there wasn't a lot that could ice me, after I'd copped to it and released all seventy of them out of my unconscious, where they'd been rotting in shallow graves for years. No big thang, Cuz.

Brought me in, strapped me in, plugged me in.

I looked through the glass at the witnesses.

There sat Ally and Spanning, front row center. Best seats in the house. All eyes and crying, watching, not believing everything had come to this, trying to figure out when and how and in what way it had all gone down without her knowing anything at all about it. And Henry Lake Spanning sitting close beside her, their hands locked in her lap. True love.

I locked eyes with Spanning.

I jaunted into his landscape.

No, I *didn't*.

I *tried* to, and couldn't squirm through. Thirty years, or less, since I was five or six, I'd been doing it; without hindrance, all alone in the world the only person who could do this listen in on the landscape trick; and for the first time I was stopped. Absolutely no fuckin' entrance. I went wild! I tried running at it full-tilt, and hit something khaki-colored, like beach sand, and only slightly giving, not hard, but resilient. Exactly like being inside a ten-foot-high, fifty-foot-diameter paper bag, like a big shopping bag from a supermarket, that stiff butcher's paper kind of bag, and that color, like being inside a bag that size, running straight at it, thinking you're going to bust through . . . and being thrown back. Not hard, not like bouncing on a trampoline, just shunted aside like the fuzz from a dandelion hitting a glass door. Unimportant. Khaki-colored and not particularly bothered.

I tried hitting it with a bolt of pure blue lightning mental power, like someone out of a Marvel comic, but that wasn't how mixing in other people's minds works. You don't think yourself in with a psychic battering-ram. That's the kind of arrant foolishness you hear spouted by unattractive people on public access cable channels, talking about The Power of Love and The Power of the Mind and the ever-popular toe-tapping Power of a Positive Thought. Bullshit; I don't be home to *that* folly!

I tried picturing myself in there, but that didn't work, either. I tried blanking my mind and drifting across, but it was pointless. And at that moment it occurred to me that I didn't really know *how* I jaunted. I just . . . did it. One moment I was snug in the privacy of my own head, and the next I was over there in someone else's landscape. It was instantaneous, like teleportation, which also is an impossibility, like telepathy.

But now, strapped into the chair, and them getting ready to put the leather mask over my face so the witnesses wouldn't have to see the smoke coming out of my eye-sockets and the little sparks as my nose hairs burned, when it was urgent that I get into the thoughts and landscape of Henry Lake Spanning, I was shut out completely. And right *then*, that moment, I was scared!

Presto, without my even opening up to him, there he was: inside my head.

He had jaunted into *my* landscape.

"You had a nice roast beef sandwich, I see."

His voice was a lot stronger than it had been when I'd come down to see him a year ago. A *lot* stronger inside my mind.

"Yes, Rudy, I'm what you knew probably existed somewhere. Another one. A shrike." He paused. "I see you call it 'jaunting in the landscape.' I just called myself a shrike. A butcherbird. One name's as good as another. Strange, isn't it; all these years; and we never met anyone else? There *must* be others, but I think – now I can't prove this, I have no real data, it's just a wild idea I've had for years and years – I think they don't know they can do it."

He stared at me across the landscape, those wonderful blue eyes of his, the ones Ally had fallen in love with, hardly blinking.

"Why didn't you let me know before this?"

He smiled sadly. "Ah, Rudy. Rudy, Rudy, Rudy; you poor benighted pickaninny."

"Because I needed to suck you in, kid. I needed to put out a bear trap, and let it snap closed on your scrawny leg, and send you over. Here, let me clear the atmosphere in here . . ." And he wiped away all the manipulation he had worked on me, way back a year ago, when he had so easily covered his own true thoughts, his past, his life, the real panorama of what went on inside his landscape – like bypassing a surveillance camera with a looped tape that continues to show a placid scene while the joint is being actively burgled – and when he convinced me not only that he was innocent, but that the real killer was someone who had blocked the hideous slaughters from his conscious mind and had lived an otherwise exemplary life. He wandered around my landscape – and all of this in a second or two, because time has no duration in the landscape, like the hours you can spend in a dream that are just thirty seconds long in the real world, just before you wake up – and he swept away all the false memories and suggestions, the logical structure of sequential events that he had planted that would dovetail with my actual existence, my true memories, altered and warped and rearranged so I would believe that I had done all seventy of those ghastly murders . . . so that I'd believe, in a moment of horrible realization, that I was the demented psychopath who had ranged state to state to state, leaving piles of ripped flesh at every stop. Blocked it all, submerged it all, sublimated it all, me. Good old Rudy Pairis, who never killed anybody. I'd been the patsy he was waiting for.

"There, now, kiddo. See what it's really like?

"You didn't do a thing.

"Pure as the driven snow, nigger. That's the truth. And what a find you were. Never even suspected there was another like me, till Ally came to interview me after Decatur. But there you were, big and black as a Great White Hope, right there in her mind. Isn't she fine, Pairis? Isn't she something to take a knife to? Something to split open like a nice piece of fruit warmed in a summer sunshine field, let all the steam rise off her . . . maybe have a picnic . . ."

He stopped.

"I wanted her right from the first moment I saw her.

"Now, you know, I could've done it sloppy, just been a shrike to Ally, that first time she came to the holding cell to interview me; just jump into her, that was my plan. But what a noise that Spanning in the cell would've made, yelling it wasn't a man, it was a woman, not Spanning, but Deputy D.A. Allison Roche . . . too much noise, too many complications. But I *could* have done it, jumped into her. Or a guard, and then slice her at my leisure, stalk her, find her, let her steam . . .

"You look distressed, Mr. Rudy Pairis. Why's that? Because you're going to die in my place? Because I could have taken you over at any time, and didn't? Because after all this time of your miserable, wasted, lousy life you finally find someone like you, and we don't even have the convenience of a chat? Well, that's sad, that's really sad, kiddo. But you didn't have a chance."

"You're stronger than me, you kept me out," I said.

He chuckled.

"Stronger? Is that all you think it is? Stronger? You still don't get it, do you?" His face, then, grew terrible. "You don't even understand now, right now that I've cleaned it all away and you can *see* what I did to you, do you?

"Do you think I stayed in a jail cell, and went through that trial, all of that, because I couldn't do anything about it? You poor jig slob. I could have jumped like a shrike any time I wanted to. But the first time I met your Ally I saw *you*."

I cringed. "And you waited . . .? For me, you spent all that time in prison, just to get to me . . .?"

"At the moment when you couldn't do anything about it, at the moment you couldn't shout 'I've been taken over by someone else, I'm Rudy Pairis here inside this Henry Lake Spanning body, help me, help me!' Why stir up noise when all I had to do was bide my time, wait a bit, wait for Ally, and let Ally go for you."

I felt like a drowning turkey, standing idiotically in the rain, head tilted up, mouth open, water pouring in. "You can . . . leave the mind . . . leave the body . . . go out . . . jaunt, jump permanently . . .?"

Spanning sniggered like a schoolyard bully.

"You stayed in jail three years just to get *me*?"

He smirked. Smarter than thou.

"Three years? You think that's some big deal to me? You don't think I could have someone like you running around, do you? Someone who can 'jaunt' as I do? The only other shrike I've ever encountered. You think I wouldn't sit in here and wait for you to come to me?"

"But three *years* . . ."

"You're what, Rudy . . . thirty-one, is it? Yes, I can see that. Thirty-one. You've never jumped like a shrike. You've just entered, jaunted, gone into the landscapes, and never understood that it's more than reading minds. You can change domiciles, black boy. You can move out of a house in a bad neighborhood – such as strapped into the electric chair – and take up residence in a brand, spanking, new housing complex of million-and-a-half-buck condos, like Ally."

"But you have to have a place for the other one to go, don't you?" I said it just flat, no tone, no color to it at all. I didn't even think of the place of dark, where you can go . . .

"Who do you think I am, Rudy? Just who the hell do you think I was when I started, when I learned to shrike, how to jaunt, what I'm telling you now about changing residences? You wouldn't know my first address. I go a long way back.

"But I can give you a few of my more famous addresses. Gilles de Rais, France, 1440; Vlad Tepes, Romania, 1462; Elizabeth Bathory, Hungary, 1611; Catherine DeShayes, France, 1680; Jack the Ripper, London, 1888; Henri Désiré Landru, France, 1915; Albert Fish, New York City, 1934; Ed Gein, Plainfield, Wisconsin, 1954; Myra Hindley, Manchester, 1963; Albert DeSalvo, Boston, 1964; Charles Manson, Los Angeles, 1969; John Wayne Gacy, Norwood Park Township, Illinois, 1977.

"Oh, but how I do go on. And on. And on and on and on, Rudy, my little porch monkey. That's what I do. I go on. And on and on. Shrike will nest where it chooses. If not in your beloved Allison Roche, then in the cheesy fucked-up black boy, Rudy Pairis. But don't you think that's a waste, kiddo? Spending however much time I might have to spend in your socially unacceptable body, when Henry Lake Spanning is such a handsome devil? Why should I have just switched with you when Ally lured you to me, because all it would've done is get you screeching and howling that you weren't Spanning, you were this nigger son who'd had his head stolen . . . and then you might have manipulated some guards or the Warden . . .

"Well, you see what I mean, don't you?

"But now that the mask is securely in place, and now that the electrodes are attached to your head and your left leg, and now that the Warden has his hand on the switch, well, you'd better get ready to do a lot of drooling."

And he turned around to jaunt back out of me, and I closed the perimeter. He tried to jaunt, tried to leap back to his own mind, but I had him in a fist. Just that easy. Materialized a fist, and turned him to face me.

"Fuck you, Jack the Ripper. And fuck you twice, Bluebeard. And on and on and on fuck you Manson and Boston Strangler and any other dipshit warped piece of sick crap you been in your years. You sure got some muddy-shoes credentials there, boy.

"What I care about all those names, Spanky my brother? You really think I don't know those names? I'm an educated fellah, Mistuh Rippuh, Mistuh Mad Bomber. You missed a few. Were you also, did you inhabit, hath thou possessed Winnie Ruth Judd and Charlie Starkweather and Mad Dog Coll and Richard Speck and Sirhan Sirhan and Jeffrey Dahmer? You the boogieman responsible for *every* bad number the human race ever played? You ruin Sodom and Gomorrah, burned the Great Library of Alexandria, orchestrated the Reign of Terror *dans Paree*, set up the Inquisition, stoned and drowned the Salem witches, slaughtered unarmed women and kids at Wounded Knee, bumped off John Kennedy?

"I don't think so.

"I don't even think you got so close as to share a pint with Jack the Ripper. And even if you did, even if you *were* all those maniacs, you were small potatoes, Spanky. The least of us human beings outdoes you, three times a day. How many lynch ropes you pulled tight, M'sieur Landru?

"What colossal egotism you got, makes you blind, makes you think you're the only one, even when you find out there's someone else, you can't get past it. What makes you think I didn't know what you can do? What makes you think I didn't let you do it, and sit here waiting for you like you sat there waiting for me, till this moment when you can't do shit about it?

"You so goddam stuck on yourself, Spankyhead, you never give it the barest that someone else is a faster draw than you.

"Know what your trouble is, Captain? You're old, you're *real* old, maybe hundreds of years who gives a damn old. That don't count for shit, old man. You're old, but you never got smart. You're just mediocre at what you do.

"You moved from address to address. You didn't have to be Son of Sam or Cain slayin' Abel, or whoever the fuck you been . . . you could've been Moses or Galileo or George Washington Carver or Harriet Tubman or Sojourner Truth or Mark Twain or Joe Louis. You could've been Alexander Hamilton and helped found the Manumission Society in New York. You could've discovered radium, carved Mount Rushmore, carried a baby out of a burning building. But you got old real fast, and you never got any smarter. You didn't need to, did you, Spanky? You had it all to yourself, all this 'shrike' shit, just jaunt here and jaunt there, and bite off someone's hand or face like the old, tired, boring, repetitious, no-imagination stupid shit that you are.

"Yeah, you got me good when I came here to see your landscape. You got Ally wired up good. And she suckered me in, probably not even knowing she was doing it . . . you must've looked in her head and found just the right technique to get her to make me come within reach. Good, m'man; you were excellent. But I had a year to torture myself. A year to sit here and think about it. About how many people I'd killed, and how sick it made me, and little by little I found my way through it.

"Because . . . and here's the big difference 'tween us, dummy:

"I unraveled what was going on . . . it took time, but I learned. Understand, asshole? *I* learn! *You* don't.

"There's an old Japanese saying – I got lots of these, Henry m'man – I read a whole lot – and what it says is, 'Do not fall into the error of the artisan who boasts of twenty years experience in his craft while in fact he has had only one year of experience – twenty times.'" Then I grinned back at him.

"Fuck you, sucker," I said, just as the Warden threw the switch and I jaunted out of there and into the landscape and mind of Henry Lake Spanning.

I sat there getting oriented for a second; it was the first time I'd done more than a jaunt . . . this was . . . *shrike*; but then Ally beside me gave a little sob for her old pal, Rudy Pairis, who was baking like a Maine lobster, smoke coming out from under the black cloth that covered my, his, face; and I heard the vestigial scream of what had been Henry Lake Spanning and thousands of other monsters, all of them burning, out there on the far horizon of my new landscape; and I put my arm around her, and drew her close, and put my face into her shoulder and hugged her to me; and I heard the scream go on and on for the longest time, I think it was a long time, and finally it was just wind . . . and then gone . . . and I came up from Ally's shoulder, and I could barely speak.

"Shhh, honey, it's okay," I murmured. "He's gone where he can make right for his mistakes. No pain. Quiet, a real quiet place; and all alone forever. And cool there. And dark."

I was ready to stop failing at everything, and blaming everything. Having fessed up to love, having decided it was time to grow up and be an adult – not just a very quick study who learned fast, extremely fast, a lot faster than anybody could imagine an orphan like me could learn, than *anybody* could imagine – I hugged her with the intention that Henry Lake Spanning would love Allison Roche more powerfully, more responsibly, than anyone had ever loved anyone in the history of the world. I was ready to stop failing at everything.

And it would be just a whole lot easier as a white boy with great big blue eyes.

Because – get on this now – all my wasted years didn't have as much to do with blackness or racism or being overqualified or being unlucky or being high-verbal or even the curse of my "gift" of jaunting, as they did with one single truth I learned waiting in there, inside my own landscape, waiting for Spanning to come and gloat:

I have always been one of those miserable guys who *couldn't get out of his own way.*

Which meant I could, at last, stop feeling sorry for that poor nigger, Rudy Pairis. Except, maybe, in a moment of human weakness.

STEPHEN JONES &
KIM NEWMAN

Necrology: 1993

1993 ONCE AGAIN PROVED to be a depressing year in which we lost a number of major writers, artists, performers and technicians who significantly shaped the horror, science fiction and fantasy genres in fiction and film . . .

AUTHORS/ARTISTS

Collector, publisher, journalist and dealer **Gerry** (aka Gerreaux) **de la Ree** died of cancer of the kidney and lymph glands on January 2nd, aged 68. At one time he had one of the three biggest science fiction collections in the world. He entered semi-professional publishing in 1954 and produced many books, chapbooks and portfolios devoted to the work of such artists as Virgil Finlay, Hannes Bok and Stephen E. Fabian.

Dark fantasy/horror writer **T. (Terry) L. (Lee) Parkinson** died on January 7th of complications resulting from AIDS.

Gordon W. Fawcett who, with his three brothers built the Fawcett publishing empire, died of heart failure on January 16th, aged 81. In 1977, Fawcett Publications was sold to CBS for $50 million.

Science fiction author (John) **Keith Laumer** died from a stroke on January 22nd. He was aged 67. A prolific writer, he is best remembered for his "Worlds of the Imperium" series and novelizations for *The Avengers* and *The Invaders* TV series. His novel *The Monitors* was filmed in 1969.

Screenwriter and novelist **Aben Kandel**, aged 96, died on January 28th. His 1936 novel *City for Conquest* was filmed starring James Cagney, and his scripts for Hollywood include *I Was a Teenage Werewolf*, *How to Make a Monster*, *Horrors of the Black Museum*, *Black Zoo*, *Konga*, and *Trog*.

Gustav Hasford, author of *The Short-Timers* (which was filmed as *Full Metal Jacket*), died from untreated diabetic complications in Greece on January 29th. He was 45. In 1988, the year he was nominated for an Oscar for co-scripting *Full Metal Jacket*, he was investigated concerning the theft of nearly 800 books from 62 libraries around the world.

Scott Meredith, owner of the Scott Meredith Literary Agency and one of the most successful literary agents of all time, died of cancer on February 11th. He was 69. His many clients included Arthur C. Clarke, Marion Zimmer Bradley, P.G. Wodehouse, Norman Mailer, Carl Sagan and Roseanne Arnold, amongst others.

One of the comics greats, **Harvey Kurtzman**, died of liver cancer on February 21st, aged 68. His first cartoon was published when he was 14, and in the early 1950s he began working for William M. Gaines and EC Comics, creating *Mad* magazine in 1952 and its mascot Alfred E. Neuman. In later years he illustrated the "Little Annie Fanny" strip for *Playboy*.

Author **Fletcher Knebel** committed suicide with sleeping pills on February 26th, aged 81. He was suffering from lung cancer and heart ailments. With Charles W. Bailey III he co-wrote *Seven Days in May*, about a military plot to take over of the USA, which was successfully filmed in 1963. His other novels include *Night of Camp David*, *The Zin Zin Road*, *Dark Horse*, *Vanished* and a study of the Hiroshima bombing, *No High Ground*.

TV writer/producer **Ed Jurist** died on March 12th, aged 76. He was a principal writer on *Bewitched* from 1964–68 and produced *The Flying Nun* from 1968–70.

Bookseller, reviewer and author **Baird Searles** died of lymphatic throat cancer in Canada on March 22nd, aged 58. With his partner of 43 years, Martin Last, he owned and operated The Science Fiction Shop in New York City's West Village from 1973–86. A regular reviewer for *Isaac Asimov's Science Fiction Magazine* for thirteen years, he was a consulting editor for Warner Books and his non-fiction volumes include *A Reader's Guide to Science Fiction* (with Last), *A Reader's Guide* to *Fantasy*, *The Science Fiction Quiz Book*, *Films of Science Fiction and Fantasy*, and *Epic! History of the Big Screen*. He co-edited the 1991 anthology *Halflings, Hobbits, Warrows, & Weefolk*.

Acclaimed children's author **Robert** (Atkinson) **Westall** died from respiratory failure caused by pneumonia on April 15th, aged 63. His numerous books, usually involving the supernatural, include his first novel *The Machine Gunners* (winner of the prestigious Carnegie Medal in 1975), *The Watch House*, *The Devil on the Road*, *Scarecrows* (winner of the 1982 Carnegie Medal), *The Haunting of Chas McGill and Other Stories* and the adult collection *Antique Dust*, from which "The Last Day of Miss Dorinda Molyneaux" was reprinted in the first volume of *Best New Horror*.

Mystery writer **Leslie Charteris** (aka Leslie Charles Bowyer Yin), the creator of fictional hero The Saint, died the same day, aged 85. The first Saint novel, *Enter the Tiger*, was published in 1928 and led to movies and two TV series featuring the character. Charteris also wrote scripts for Hollywood, including the plots for the Basil Rathbone *Sherlock Holmes* movies and *Tarzan and the Huntress*.

Coin expert, SF fan and one-time husband of Marion Zimmer Bradley (she divorced him in 1991), **Walter** (Henry) **Breen** died April 30th from colon cancer while confined to prison on charges of child molestation. He was 64.

Author and editor **Avram Davidson** died suddenly of a heart attack on May 8th. He was 70. His first professional sale was to *Orthodox Jewish Life Magazine* in 1946. His science fiction and fantasy novels include *Rogue Dragon*, *Masters of the Maze*, *The Island Under the Earth* and *The Phoenix and the Mirror*, and he wrote two mysteries under the "Ellery Queen" byline. The best of his highly distinctive short stories are collected in *Or All the Seas with Oysters*, *Strange Seas and Shores* and the recent *The Adventures of Doctor Esterhazy*. He edited *The Magazine of Fantasy & Science Fiction* from 1962–64.

Author, editor and critic **Lester del Rey** died May 10th from a heart attack, aged 77. Ramon Felipe San Juan Mario Silvio Enrico Smith Heathcourt-Brace Sierra y Alvarez-del Rey y de los Verdes was born in Minnesota in 1915. He sold his first short story, "The Faithful" to *Astounding* in 1938, and by the 1950s was editor or associate editor of such magazines as *Space*

Science Fiction, Fantasy Magazine, Science Fiction Adventures and *Rocket Stories*. He also contributed features to *Galaxy* and *If*. He married his fourth wife, Judy-Lynn Benjamin in 1971 (she died in 1986) and together they built up the SF and fantasy lines at Ballantine Books. As editor of the Del Rey fantasy imprint, he discovered Stephen Donaldson, Terry Brooks, David Eddings and Barbara Hambly, amongst others. He wrote a number of adult and juvenile novels, and his short fiction is collected in *And Some Were Human*, *Robots and Changelings*, and *Early Del Rey*.

Screenwriter **Roger MacDougall**, who scripted *The Man in the White Suit* and *The Mouse That Roared*, died on May 27th, aged 82.

Florence Hanley, who ran the specialist Hanley's Book Shop in Chicago for twenty-five years, died on June 4th after a short illness.

Cartoonist **Vincent Hamlin**, who created caveman *Alley Oop* in the early 1930s, died on June 14th, aged 93.

Bruce C. Herbert, the son of *Dune* author Frank Herbert, died of AIDS-related pneumonia on June 15th.

Sir William Golding died from a heart attack on June 19th, aged 81. The author of *Lord of the Flies*, which has been filmed twice, his other books include *Pincher Martin*, *The Spire*, *Darkness Visible*, *Fire Down Below*, and the SF novel, *The Inheritors*. He won the Nobel Prize for literature in 1983 and was knighted in 1988.

Thomas D. (Dean) **Clareson**, founder of the Science Fiction Research Association and *Extrapolation: A Journal of Science Fiction and Fantasy*, died July 6th from lung cancer after a long illness. He was 66. He also compiled a number of reference books.

Film, radio and mystery expert **Chris Steinbrunner** died from a heart attack on July 7th, aged 59. He was co-editor, with Otto Penzler, of *The Encyclopedia of Mystery and Detection*, which won the Mystery Writers of America Edgar Award. His other books include *Detectionary*, *The Films of Sherlock Holmes* and *Cinema of the Fantastic*.

Screenwriter **John Beaird**, whose credits include the psycho-thrillers *My Bloody Valentine* and *Happy Birthday to Me*, died on July 9th, aged 40.

Anthropologist and science fiction author **Chad Oliver** (aka

Symmes Chadwick Oliver), died after a long battle with cancer on August 9th, aged 65. His first SF sale was to *Super Science Stories* in 1950. His novels included *Mists of Dawn*, *Shadows in the Sun*, *Winds of Time*, *Unearthly Neighbors*, *The Shores of Another Sea* and *The Cannibal Owl*, while his short fiction is collected in *Another Kind*.

Screenwriter **Ken Englund** died on August 10th, aged 79. Among his credits is *The Secret Life of Walter Mitty* starring Boris Karloff.

Scriptwriter **Ellis St Joseph** died on August 21st, aged 82. Best known for his contributions to such TV shows as *The Outer Limits* and *Logan's Run*, he also co-scripted the 1943 anthology movie *Flesh and Fantasy*.

Cartoon and comedy writer **Cal Howard** died on September 10th after a long illness. He was 82, and his many credits include the Fleischer Studio's animated *Gulliver's Travels* and *Mr Bug Goes to Town* (aka *Hoppity Goes to Town*).

Songwriter **Harold Rome**, who wrote "Horror Boys of Hollywood", sung by The Ritz Brothers in *One in a Million*, died in late October. He was 85.

Anthony Burgess (aka John Anthony Burgess Wilson) died of cancer on November 25th, aged 76. His first novel, *Time for a Tiger*, was published in 1956, but he is best remembered for *A Clockwork Orange*, which Stanley Kubrick turned into a controversial film in 1971. His other novels include *The Wanting Seed*, *The End of the World News* and *A Dead Man in Deptford*.

Lyricist **Mack David** died December 30th, aged 81. Among his credits are the songs "A Dream is a Wish Your Heart Makes" and "Bibbidi-Bobbidi-Boo" from Disney's *Cinderella* (1949), *Scared Stiff*, *Hush . . . Hush, Sweet Charlotte*, and the themes for such 1960s TV shows as *77 Sunset Strip* and *Hawaiian Eye*.

ACTORS/ACTRESSES

American actor **Glenn Corbett** died of lung cancer on January 16th, aged 59. His credits include William Castle's *Homicidal* and Hammer's *Pirates of Blood River*.

Oscar-winning, Belgium-born actress **Audrey Hepburn** (aka Edda van Heemstra Hepburn-Ruston) died of colon cancer on January 20th in Switzerland, aged 63. Her film credits include

Breakfast at Tiffany's, *Paris When It Sizzles*, *Wait Until Dark*, *Robin and Marian* and Steven Spielberg's fantasy *Always*.

7-foot, 4-inch professional wrestler and actor **André the Giant** (aka André René Roussimoff) died of an apparent heart attack on January 27th, aged 46. He appeared in *The Princess Bride* as the gentle giant Fezzick.

Stuntman **Tim "Tip" Tipping** was killed when his parachute failed to open during a TV stunt on February 5th. He was aged 34 and had appeared in the Indiana Jones and James Bond series.

British actress **Jacqueline Hill** died from cancer on February 18th. She was 63 and starred as Barbara Wright in the BBC's *Doctor Who* series from 1963–66.

American-born actor **Eddie Constantine** died at his home in Germany on February 25th. He was 75. Among his many film roles, he will be remembered as futuristic FBI agent Lemmy Caution in Jean-Luc Godard's *Alphaville* and a series of lesser films.

Muppeteer **Eren Ozker** died of cancer the same day. Aged 44, she joined *The Muppet Show* in 1976.

American silent star **Lillian Gish** (aka Lillian de Guiche) died in her sleep on February 27th, aged 99. A discovery of D.W. Griffith, she made her debut in *Birth of a Nation* (1914) and went on to appear in *Portrait of Jennie*, *Night of the Hunter*, *The Whales of August* with Vincent Price, and a 1969 TV version of *Arsenic and Old Lace* co-starring Helen Hayes and Fred Gwynne.

British actress **Joyce Carey** died on February 28th, aged 94. She appeared in the 1945 movie adaptation of Noel Coward's *Blithe Spirit* and TV's *The Avengers*.

Supporting actor **Terry Frost** died of heart failure on March 1st, aged 86. His credits include *Dick Tracy vs. Crime Inc.*, *Captain America* (1943), *The Monster Maker*, *The Flying Serpent*, *Atom Man vs. Superman*, *Mysterious Island* (1951) and many others.

Bandleader **Bob Crosby**, the brother of Bing who appeared in *Road to Bali*, died of cancer on March 9th, aged 80.

The First Lady of American Theatre, **Helen Hayes** (Brown), died on March 17th, aged 92. The winner of two Tony Awards, two Oscars and an Emmy, she appeared on Broadway in 1935 with Vincent Price in *Victoria Regina* and during the early 1970s she co-starred with Mildred Natwick in *The Snoop Sisters* series of TV movies (1973–74). Her film credits include Disney's *Herbie Rides Again* and *One of Our Dinosaurs is Missing*. In tribute, the lights on Broadway were dimmed for one minute at 8 p.m. on the day she died.

Actress **Kate Reid** died of cancer on March 27th, aged 62. She starred in *The Andromeda Strain* and *Death Ship*.

Brandon Lee, the son of martial arts expert Bruce, was killed in a bizarre shooting accident on the set of *The Crow* on March 31st. He was 28.

Mexican comic bullfighter, circus clown, prize-fighter and actor Mario Moreno Reyes, better known as **Cantinflas**, died of lung cancer on April 20th, aged 81. In *Around the World in 80 Days* (1956) he played Passepartout, Phineas Fogg's faithful valet.

Lon Ralph Chaney, son of Lon Chaney Jr and the grandson of Lon Chaney Sr, died on May 5th from injuries sustained in a car crash. He was 64.

British actress **Ann Todd** died of a stroke on May 6th, aged 82. She played Mary Gordon in the 1936 SF classic *Things to Come*, and her other film credits include *The Ghost Train* (1931), *The Seventh Veil*, *The Sound Barrier* (aka *Breaking the Sound Barrier*) for then-husband David Lean, Hammer's *Taste of Fear* (aka *Scream of Fear*) with Christopher Lee, and *The Fiend* (aka *Beware! The Brethren*).

Silent star **Mary Philbin** died on May 7th, aged 89. As Christine she revealed Lon Chaney Sr's horrific face to the world in *The Phantom of the Opera* (1925), and co-starred with Conrad Veidt in *The Man Who Laughs* and *The Last Performance*. Her career ended with the advent of talkies.

Character actor **Dan Seymour**, who appeared in *Abbott and Costello Meet the Mummy*, *Return of the Fly*, and *Escape to Witch Mountain*, died from a stroke on May 25th, aged 78.

Evelyn Karloff, the widow of Boris Karloff, died of cancer on June 1st.

Leading lady **Alexis Smith** (aka Gladys Smith) died of cancer on June 9th, aged 72. Her many films include *The Smiling Ghost*, *The Horn Blows at Midnight*, *The Woman in White* and *The Little Girl Who Lives Down the Lane*. She was married to actor Craig Stevens.

Richard Webb, who portrayed TV's titular *Captain Midnight* (aka *Jet Jackson, Flying Commando*) from 1954–58 shot himself to death on June 10th. He was 77 and had been suffering from a debilitating respiratory illness. He also appeared in such movies as *The Night Has a Thousand Eyes*, *Among the Living*, *The Invisible Monster*, *Hillbillys in a Haunted House* and *Beware! The Blob* (aka *Son of Blob*). A later interest in the supernatural led to him writing *Great Ghosts of the West*, *Voices from Another World* and *These Came Back*.

Character actor **Bernard Bresslaw** died on June 11th, aged 59. Best known for his appearances in the *Carry On* films (including *Carry On Screaming*), his many other credits include Hammer's *The Ugly Duckling* and *Moon Zero Two*, *Blood of the Vampire*, *Vampira* (aka *Old Dracula*), *Jabberwocky*, *Hawk the Slayer* and *Krull*.

George "Spanky" McFarland, the chubby child star of the *Our Gang* and *Little Rascals* series, died on June 30th, aged 64.

Fred Gwynne, who will always be remembered for his role as the Frankenstein Monster-like Herman in the TV series *The Munsters* (1964–66), died of pancreatic cancer on July 2nd. He was 66. He recreated the role of Herman Munster in the feature film *Munster, Go Home!* and the TV movie *The Munsters' Revenge*, as well as appearing in the Stephen King adaptation *Pet Sematary*.

Curly Joe DeRita, the last surviving member of the Three Stooges, died of pneumonia on July 3rd, aged 83. He joined the comedy team in the late 1950s, replacing Joe Besser, for such films as *Have Rocket Will Travel*, *The Three Stooges Meet Hercules* and *Snow White and the Three Stooges*.

Actress **Nan Grey** (aka Eschal Miller) died of heart failure on July 25th, her 75th birthday. She appeared in *Dracula's Daughter*, and co-starred with Vincent Price in *Tower of London* (1939), *The Invisible Man Returns* and *The House of the Seven Gables*. She was married to singer Frankie Laine.

British actor **James Donald**, who starred as Dr Roney in Hammer's *Quatermass and the Pit* (aka *Five Million Years to Earth*) died after a long illness on August 3rd. He was 76.

British-born leading man **Stewart Granger** (aka James Lablanche Stewart) died of cancer on August 16th, aged 80. The swashbuckling star's many films included *Gaslight*, *King Solomon's Mines* (1950), *Moonfleet*, *Footsteps in the Fog* and the TV movies *The Hound of the Baskervilles* (1972, as Sherlock Holmes) and *Chameleons*.

Actor and stage director **Richard Jordan**, who appeared in such films as *Logan's Run*, *Dune*, *Solarbabies* and *The Hunt for Red October*, died of a brain tumour on August 31st. He was aged 56.

Actress and author **Rene Ray** (aka Irene Creese) died on Jersey on August 28th, aged 81. Her film credits include *High Treason*, *The Passing of the Third Floor Back*, *Once In a New Moon* and *The Return of the Frog*. Her novel *The Strange World of Planet X* was the basis of a BBC-TV series and the 1957 film *The Strange World* (aka *Cosmic Monsters*).

Hervé Villechaize, who played the diminutive Tatoo in TV's *Fantasy Island* series, died of a self-inflicted gunshot wound on September 4th, aged 50. In a note he said he was despondent over longtime health problems. The 3-foot 11-inch, French-born actor also appeared in such movies as *Seizure*, *The Man With the Golden Gun* and *Forbidden Zone*.

Canadian actor **Raymond** (William Stacy) **Burr** died on September 12th from metastatic cancer of the liver, aged 76. Although most famous for his TV roles in *Perry Mason* and *Ironside*, he also appeared (often playing the heavy) in such films as *Black Magic*, *Gorilla at Large*, *Tarzan and the She-Devil*, *Rear Window*, *Bride of the Gorilla*, *Casanova's Big Night*, *The Whip Hand*, *Godzilla King of the Monsters*, *Godzilla 1985*, *Delirious* and the TV movie *The Curse of King Tutankhamun's Tomb*.

Zita Johann, who starred opposite Boris Karloff in *The Mummy* (1932) died of pneumonia on September 24th, aged 89. Her other film credits include *Raiders of the Living Dead*.

Irish actor **Cyril Cusack** died of motor neuron disease in London on October 7th, aged 82. His many film credits include *Fahrenheit 451* and *Nineteen Eighty-Four* (1984).

Veteran actor **Leon Ames** (aka Leon Wycoff), the last surviving founder of the Screen Actors Guild, died following a stroke on October 12th. He was 91. His first film role was as the hero in *Murders in the Rue Morgue* (1932) opposite Bela Lugosi, and he also appeared in *Thirteen Women*, *Mysterious Mr Moto*, *The Absent-Minded Professor*, *On a Clear Day You Can See Forever*, *Hammersmith Is Out*, *Jake Speed* and *Peggy Sue Got Married*. He was a regular on the TV series *Mr Ed*.

Horror great **Vincent Price** died on October 25th after a five-year battle against lung cancer. He was 82. His credits include more than 100 films and 75 stage plays. He appeared in *Tower* of London, *The Invisible Man Returns*, *The House of the Seven Gables*, *Shock* and *Dragonwyck*, before the 1953 3-D movie *House of Wax* turned him into a horror film star. For the next four decades he was typecast in such classics as William Castle's *House on Haunted Hill* and *The Tingler*; Roger Corman's Edgar Allan Poe series: *The Fall of the House of Usher*, *The Pit and the Pendulum*, *The Raven*, *The Masque of the Red Death*, etc., and Robert Fuest's two Dr Phibes movies. Amongst his best films are *The Fly* (1958), *The Tomb of Ligeia*, *Witchfinder General* (aka *The Conquerer Worm*) and *Theatre of Blood*. In 1982 he teamed up with Christopher Lee, Peter Cushing and John Carradine for *House of the Long Shadows*, and in 1990 he played the kindly inventor in Tim Burton's *Edward Scissorhands*.

Twenty-three-year-old **River Phoenix** collapsed and died from a drug cocktail in Hollywood on Hallowe'en. He made his debut at the age of 15 in *Explorers*, and went on to star in *Stand By Me* and play the young Indy in *Indiana Jones and The Last Crusade*. At the time of his death he was working on a horror film, *Dark Blood*, and was set to have appeared as the reporter in *Interview With a Vampire*.

Character actor **Charles Aidman** died of cancer in November 7th aged 68. He was the narrator on the new *Twilight Zone* TV series from 1985–87. His many film credits include *Twilight's Last Gleaming*, *Cult of the Damned*, *House of the Dead* and the TV movie *The Picture of Dorian Gray* (1973).

Actress **Evelyn Venable** died of cancer on November 16th, aged 80. The first model for Columbia Pictures' Statue of Liberty logo, she starred opposite Frederic March in *Death Takes a Holiday* (1933) and was the voice of the sexy Blue Fairy in Disney's *Pinocchio*. She retired in 1943.

Veteran character actor **Fritz Feld** died on November 18th, aged 93. He made his film debut in the 1917 production *Der Golem und die Tanzerin*, and after moving to Hollywood in 1923, his many film credits include *Bringing Up Baby*, *The Phantom of the Opera* (1943), *Passport to Destiny*, *The Catman of Paris*, *The Secret Life of Walter Mitty* and *Herbie Goes Bananas*. On TV he appeared as intergalactic department store manager Zumdish in three episodes of *Lost in Space*.

Actor/director **Bill Bixby** died on November 21st after a year-long battle with cancer. He was 59. On TV he starred with Ray Walston in the SF sitcom *My Favorite Martian* (1963–66) and as scientist David Banner in *The Incredible Hulk* (1978–82). In the late 1980s he revived the character for a number of *Incredible Hulk* TV movies.

Kenneth Connor, best remembered for his roles in the *Carry On* series, died of cancer on November 28th. He was 77. His other credits include the comedy/horror thriller *What a Carve Up!* (aka *No Place Like Homicide*), based on Frank King's novel *The Ghoul*, and *Captain Nemo and the Underwater City*. He was awarded the MBE in 1991.

Hollywood leading man **Don Ameche** (aka Dominic Felix Amici) died of prostate cancer on December 6th, aged 85. After starring in many films during the 1930s and '40s, including the fantasy *Heaven Can Wait*, his career was revitalised in 1985 when he won the Academy Award for Best Supporting Actor for *Cocoon*. He went on to appear in *Cocoon The Return* and *Harry and the Hendersons* (aka *Bigfoot and the Hendersons*).

Hollywood leading actress **Myrna Loy** (aka Myrna Williams) died in New York City on December 14th, aged 88. She starred opposite Boris Karloff in *The Mask of Fu Manchu*, and co-starred with William Powell in the popular *Thin Man* series of the 1930s and '40s. Her other credits include *The Cave Man* (1926), *Noah's Ark*, *Midnight Lace* (1960), and the TV movies *Death Takes a Holiday* (1970), and *Ants* (aka *It Happened at Lake Wood Manor/Panic at Lake Wood Manor*).

Actor **Jeff Morrow** died on December 26th after a long illness, aged 86. He starred as Exeter, the Metalunan scientist in the 1955 SF classic *This Island Earth*, and his other credits include *The Creature Walks Among Us*, *Kronos*, *The Giant Claw*, *Octaman* and *Legacy of Blood*.

FILM/TV TECHNICIANS

Writer, director and producer **Joseph L. Mankiewicz** died of heart failure on February 5th. He was aged 83. In 1929 he scripted *The Mysterious Dr Fu Manchu*, made his writing/directing debut with *Dragonwyck* starring Vincent Price, and was also responsible for the 1947 fantasy *The Ghost and Mrs Muir*.

Film and TV director **Douglas Heyes** died of congestive heart failure on February 8th, aged 73. He scripted *The Groundstar Conspiracy* and directed various episodes of *The Twilight Zone*, *Thriller* and *Night Gallery*.

Sharon Disney Lund, the daughter of Walt and an executive with the Walt Disney Co., died of cancer on February 16th, aged 56.

British director (and father of critic Barry) **Leslie Norman** died of heart failure on February 18th, aged 81. His credits include *The Night My Number Came Up*, Hammer's *X the Unknown*, and TV's *The Avengers*. He was replaced by Michael Carreras on Hammer's *The Lost Continent* (1968).

Japanese director **Inoshiro** (aka Ishiro) **Honda**, best known for his series of *Godzilla* (aka *Gojira*) movies dating back to 1954, died on February 28th in Tokyo. He was 81, and his many other films include *Rodan*, *The Mysterians*, *The H-Man*, *Atragon*, *Mothra*, *Frankenstein Conquers the World*, *King Kong Escapes* etc.

Harper Goff, who designed the Nautilus for Disney's *2000 Leagues Under the Sea* (1954) died on March 3rd, aged 81. His other credits include *Casablanca*, *Fantastic Voyage* and *Willy Wonka and the Chocolate Factory*.

Robert Becker, who directed two episodes of TV's *Star Trek the Next Generation*, was killed in a car accident on May 6th. He was 47.

Producer **Paul Malvern** died on May 29th at the age of 91. He started his film career as a stunt man, but went on to produce many movies for Monogram and Universal Studios during the 1940s, including *Doomed to Die*, *Phantom of Chinatown*, *The Mad Doctor of Market Street*, *The Mystery of Marie Roget*, *House of Frankenstein* and *House of Dracula*.

James Bridges, who scripted *Colossus The Forbin Project* and wrote and directed *The China Syndrome*, died of intestinal cancer on June 6th, aged 57.

TV producer **Sam Rolfe** died of a heart attack while playing tennis on July 10th, aged 69. Among his many credits, he created and produced the sci-spy series *The Man from U.N.C.L.E.* (1964–68) and *The Girl from U.N.C.L.E.* (1966–67).

John Beck, who produced the fantasies *Harvey* (1950) and *One Touch of Venus*, died on July 18th, aged 83.

Robert Glass, who won an Oscar for his sound work on *E.T. The Extra-Terrestrial*, was found stabbed to death in his Los Angeles home on July 21st, apparently the victim of a robbery. He was 53.

Jazz pianist **Roy Budd** died from a brain haemorrhage, aged

46. His final work was a symphonic score for the silent *The Phantom of the Opera* (1925).

Cinematographer **Claude Renoir**, the nephew of film director Jean Renoir, died on September 5th in France, aged 79. His credits include *The Witches of Salem* (aka *The Crucible*), *Blood and Roses*, *Barbarella* and *The Spy Who Loved Me*.

Charles Lamont, who directed such comedies as *That's the Spirit*, . . . *Meet the Invisible Man*, *Abbott and Costello Meet Dr Jekyll and Mr Hyde*, *Abbott and Costello Meet the Mummy*, *Abbott and Costello Go to Mars* and *Francis in the Haunted House*, died of pneumonia on September 12th, aged 98.

Film editor **Christian Nyby**, who is credited as directing Howard Hawks' *The Thing from Another World* (1951), died on September 17th, aged 80. He also directed several episodes of the original *Twilight Zone* TV series.

TV writer/producer **Richard Landau** died on September 18th of complications following surgery. He was 79 and his many credits include *The Wild Wild West*, *Space: 1999*, *The Six Million Dollar Man* and *Beyond Westworld*.

Director **Gordon Douglas** died on September 29th, aged 85. His many movie credits include thirty *Our Gang* shorts, *Zombies on Broadway*, *Gildersleeve's Ghost*, *Them!*, *The Fiend Who Walked West*, *In Like Flint* and *Skullduggery*.

Writer and animator **Leo Salkin**, who inspired the character of Mr Magoo, died of congestive heart failure on October 13th, aged 80. His credits include Disney's *Lady and the Tramp*, *2000 Year Old Man* starring Mel Brooks, and the TV cartoon *The Addams Family*.

Italian writer/director **Federico Fellini** died on October 31st, aged 73. He was in a coma for two weeks after suffering a heart attack caused by choking on a piece of mozzarella cheese. The five-time Oscar winner made around thirty films, including *La Strada*, *Nights of Cabiria*, *8¹/2*, *Juliet of the Spirits*, *Spirits of the Dead*, *Fellini's Satyricon*, *The Clowns* and *Amarcord*.

British director and screenwriter **Duncan Gibbins**, whose credits include *Eve of Destruction*, died on November 3rd from burns he suffered in the series of Malibu wildfires when he went back into his blazing home to rescue a cat. He was aged 41 and his other films include *Fire With Fire* and *Third Degree Burn*.

Italian producer **Mario Cecchi Gori** died of a heart attack in

Rome on November 5th, aged 73. His many credits include *Toto in the Moon*, *The Church* and *The Devil's Daughter* (aka *The Sect*).

Gerald Thomas, director of the *Carry On* series (including *Carry On Spying* and *Carry On Screaming*) died on November 9th, aged 72.

Disney art director **Ken Anderson**, aged 84, died on December 13th after suffering a stroke. He worked on *Snow White and the Seven Dwarfs*, *Pinocchio*, *Fantasia*, *Sleeping Beauty* and *Pete's Dragon*, and was the principal designer of the original Disneyland.

Actor and director **Sam Wanamaker** died on December 18th after a five year battle against cancer. He was 74 and received a CBE in July in recognition of his campaign to build a replica of Shakespeare's Elizabethan Globe theatre next to London's River Thames. In 1977 he directed *Sinbad and the Eye of the Tiger*.

Alexander Mackendrick, who directed the SF comedy *The Man in the White Suit*, died of pneumonia in Los Angeles on December 22nd. Aged 81, his other credits included *The Ladykillers*, *Whisky Galore* (aka *Tight Little Island*) and *A High Wind in Jamaica*.

Hollywood agent **Irving "Swifty" Lazar** died of kidney failure on December 30th, aged 86. His clients included Humphrey Bogart, Ernest Hemingway, Noel Coward, Truman Capote, Richard Nixon, Cole Porter, Franco Zeffirelli and Faye Dunaway.